John William Griffith, Arthur Henfrey

Micrographic dictionary

A guide to the examination and investigation of the structure and nature of

microscopic objects

John William Griffith, Arthur Henfrey

Micrographic dictionary
A guide to the examination and investigation of the structure and nature of microscopic objects

ISBN/EAN: 9783742828118

Manufactured in Europe, USA, Canada, Australia, Japa

Cover: Foto ©Andreas Hilbeck / pixelio.de

Manufactured and distributed by brebook publishing software (www.brebook.com)

John William Griffith, Arthur Henfrey

Micrographic dictionary

cotyledons. These are the VASA PROPRIA, and are described under that head.

The importance of liber as a material for textile fabrics has been spoken of under FI-BROUS STRUCTURES, and examples cited; figures of various kinds of liber-fibre are given in Plate 21. A few particulars relating to the structure and arrangement of liber-cells may be given here.

In Dicotyledonous stems they are usually placed in large bundles opposite to the fibro-vascular bundles of the wood, as in *Urtica, Viscum, Clematis, Quercus,* &c.; sometimes in small irregular groups, as in *Vinca* and *Linum*; in other cases they stand in single rows, alternating with parenchyma or *vasa propria* (*Cupressineæ* and *Taxineæ*), while in many plants they are irregularly scattered, as in *Rhizophora, Cinchona, Nerium,* &c. Isolated liber-cells occur in the pith of young shoots, and may be readily seen in the elder and *Rhizophora*; in the long woody radicles developed from the seeds of the Rhizophoreæ (Pl. 39. fig. 31), and in the bark and pericarp of *Gnetum,* isolated branched liber-fibres occur scattered throughout the whole mass.

In many Dicotyledons the thick-walled liber-cells are formed only in the first year, the subsequent formation in this region consisting of new layers of *vasa propria* and parenchymatous cells (*Betula alba* and *Fagus sylvatica*). In *Viburnum Lantana* the thick-walled liber is entirely wanting.

In the Monocotyledons they occur associated with short wood-cells in the fibro-vascular bundles; but they form alone the *fibrous bundles* often intermixed with and prolonged from the ends of these, occurring especially in the outer part of the stem of herbaceous Monocotyledons, such as Lilies and Grasses, and in the fleshy cortical layer of rhizomes, as in *Sparganium,* &c.

In both families they occur with the spiral vessels and wood-cells in the ribs or veins of leaves (as in *Phormium tenax*), bracts, spathes of Palms, &c.

Liber-cells are generally drawn out very gradually to a point at each end; sometimes they are very long; Schleiden states he has seen them 5″ or 6′. Sometimes they exhibit expansions at particular points, as in the Apocynaceæ commonly. The branched forms in Rhizophoreæ, *Gnetum,* &c. are usually much shorter than the simple fibres, and their form is often very irregular (Pl. 39. fig. 31). The diameter varies a great deal in some plants, and we should scarcely ven-

ture to say that the microscopic appearance of a liber-fibre would suffice for the determination of the material of any (vegetable) textile fabric, beyond the distinction of *cotton* (or vegetable *hair*) from *linen* or other *liber*; but reagents affect them differently. The appearance presented by many kinds of fibre under the microscope, in the state in which they occur in commerce and after treatment with acids, is shown in Pl. 21. figs. 2–7, 25 & 26. The figures are taken from very characteristic examples; but many modifications occur in subordinate quantity. Flax (*Linum usitatissimum*) (fig. 2) has the walls much thickened, with distinct pores; it exhibits a very oblique close striation after boiling with nitric acid. Jute, the liber of *Corchorus capsularis,* has thinner walls, with constrictions at intervals and blunter ends (fig. 3); no spiral streaks come out here on boiling with nitric acid. The fibre from the Cocoa-nut husk occurs in bundles (fig. 4); when isolated or boiled with acid, the walls are found thin, with wide, open, spiral streaks (slits in the secondary layers); the ends are blunt (fig. 5 *a, b*). The fibre of hemp (*Cannabis sativa*) somewhat resembles flax, but is coarser and becomes swollen up and brittle, readily breaking across, when boiled with nitric acid (fig. 6); no spiral streaks. The liber-fibres from the bundles of *Musa textilis* (fig. 7) are fine and tough, and not much altered by boiling. Those of *Bœhmeria nivea* (fig. 25) are coarse, rough on the outside, swell up much and exhibit marked spiral slits when boiled with acid, also very distinct lamination of the thick wall (fig. 25 c). *Bœhmeria Puya* (fig. 26) closely resembles the former; but the spiral striation is not very evident, and the wall splits readily in the longitudinal direction (fig. 26 c). The spiral striation is well seen in fig. 30 of Pl. 39, which represents the end of a liber-fibre from *Vinca minor* after boiling with nitric acid.

The *liber-bundles* of bark are sometimes set free as loose stringy fibres by the decay of the outer parts of the bark, as in the vine, *Clematis,* &c. In some plants they take a wavy course, anastomosing laterally so as to form connected reticulated sheets over the cambium: in the lime these sheets, formed year after year, may be detached by maceration, and form *bast,* the material used for matting, &c. In the THYMELÆACEÆ (lace-bark trees) the annual layers of liber can be detached from each other, and form sheets of fibrous tissue, sometimes firm and tough, sometimes almost as delicate as muslin.

2 E

BIBL. Mohl, *Vegetable Cell, Botanische Zeitung*, xiii. p. 873; Schacht, *Die Pflanzenzelle*, p. 208; *Ann. des Sc. Nat.* 4 sér. viii. p. 164.

See also under LATICIFEROUS TISSUE.

LIBERTELLA, Desmaz. See NEMASPORA.

LICEA, Schrad.—A genus of Myxogastres (Gasteromycetous Fungi), growing on damp rotten wood, in garden frames, &c., with the peridia of elongate form, grouped together, of only one layer, and containing few or no filaments among the spores. Four species are described as British, of which *L. fragiformis*, Nees, is not uncommon on wet very rotten wood, moss, &c.; the groups of peridia just before maturity somewhat resembling a strawberry; afterwards brownish.

BIBL. Berk. *Brit. Fl.* ii. pt. 2. p. 321; *Ann. Nat. Hist.* 2 ser. v. p. 367; Greville, *Sc. Crypt. Fl.* pl. 308; Fries, *Syst. Mycol.* iii. p. 195; *Summa Veg.* p. 458.

LICHENS.—A class of Thallophytes or cellular plants standing between the Algæ and the Fungi, exhibiting in the various genera relations sometimes approaching very closely to the one, sometimes to the other of these two classes. Some authors abolish the independent existence of a class of Lichens, regarding them as inseparable from the Fungi; while, on the other hand, Schleiden increases the Lichens by adding to them all the thecasporous Fungi. De Bary has recently given his adhesion to this on other grounds. Here we shall consider the Lichens under their ordinary limitation, as constituting a class of Thallophytes distinguished from the Algæ in almost every case by the structure of the thallus, the characters of the reproductive organs, and the aërial habit; and from the Fungi in most cases by the character of the thallus, above all by the presence of globular gonidia with green cell-contents, and in most cases by the dry crustaceous habit, as opposed to the fleshy consistence of the majority of Fungi. The parasitic Lichens, such as ABROTHALLUS, being, however, destitute of a free thallus and of green gonidia, are undistinguishable from Fungi by any definite character.

The Lichens are almost universally either dry encrusting bodies, growing upon bark of trees, stones, earth, &c., as a pulverulent, or rough and horny, or laminated and mostly wrinkled and curled crust; or as horny or leathery, foliaceous or shrubby, ragged or bristling patches, seldom rising much from the surface which they overgrow; of grey, greyish green, brown, yellowish, or even reddish colour, and with a dead, pulverulent, and opake surface. Some, however, are para-

Fig. 395.

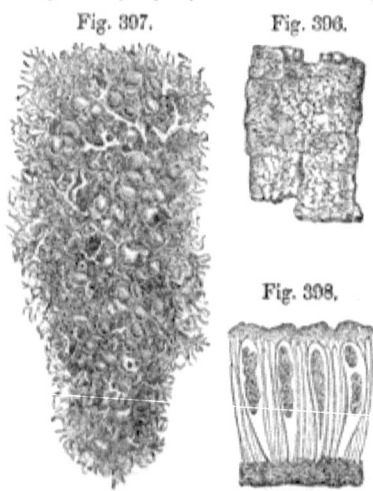

Sphærophoron coralloides.
Thallus with apothecia.
Nat. size.

sitic on other Lichens (*Abrothallus*), or upon living leaves (*Strigula*). The fructifications,

Fig. 397.   Fig. 396.

Fig. 398.

Fig. 396. Opegrapha atra. Thallus with lirellæ. Nat. size.

Fig. 397. Borrera ciliaris. Thallus with apothecia. Nat. size.

Fig. 398. Section of thalamium. Magn. 150 diams.

in which the spores are produced, are either

little nodules (fig. 395), often with a minute pore at the summit, or raised lines (fig. 396), or round, shield-shaped or cup-shaped bodies (fig. 397) scattered over the surface of their fronds, or borne at the summits of the branches of the shrubby kinds. In some species the 'fruits' are the only parts visible to the naked eye, the thallus being composed of very small collections of microscopic elements, more or less concealed in the matrix on which the plants grow.

In the simplest kind of Lichens, the frond or thallus consists of microscopic branched filaments penetrating among the superficial layers of the cells of the bark or epidermis upon which the plants grow. These filaments usually present globular cells here and there growing out from them, filled with green matter, which globular cells are capable of reproducing the plant when detached; they are called *gonidia*, and are regarded as analogous to the *buds* of the Flowering plants and the cellular *gemmæ* of the higher Cryptogams. In the simple forms here alluded to, the gonidia are not sufficiently numerous to give a coloured tinge to the structure as seen by the naked eye; in some even the filaments make no show, while in others they form whitish patches (*Opegrapha, Verrucaria*). In the forms rather more developed we find a layer of globular epidermal cells, with whitish contents, closely coherent together, constituting a 'cortical layer' covering the upper surface, to which the filamentous structure (or *hypothallus*) then forms the 'medullary layer.' The crustaceous kinds overgrowing stones have this filamentous medullary layer very solid; and in some of them its lowest filaments are seen growing out all round the borders, in the direction in which the plant is extending, the upper filaments with the gonidia and the cortical layer by degrees overgrowing these lowest filaments, which in the meantime have extended further out. Some of the crustaceous Lichens grow out in more or less regular lobes at their borders, and thence lead to the pseudo-foliaceous forms, of which the common *Parmelia parietina*, the yellow Lichen so abundant on walls, and *Borrera ciliaris*, common on branches of trees (fig. 397), may serve as examples. The thin paper-like thallus of the former exhibits *four* distinct regions (Pl. 29. fig. 2) : —1. on the upper face a layer of thick cells, firmly connected together, coloured yellow at the surface (*upper cortical* or *epidermal layer*); 2. a layer like the preceding, but

white, forming the inferior surface of the thallus (*lower cortical* or *epidermal layer*); 3. beneath the upper cortical layer lie the *gonidia*; and 4. under these lie the *medullary* filaments forming the central substance, at the upper part of which lie the gonidia arising from these filaments, which are interlaced and imprison air between them. From the lower face arise laminæ or fibrous processes, like roots, serving as cramps by which the plant attaches itself to the surface on which it grows. In *Peltigera canina* there is no inferior epidermal or cortical layer, the filamentous medullary structure forming the irregular veined surface, prolonged here and there into pseudo-radical processes. In *Endocarpon* and other fronds of solid texture, the medullary layer is formed of slender linear cells, closely packed, with few air-passages. The species of *Cladonia* exhibit a structure of the thallus intermediate between that of the foliaceous kind just referred to and the shrubby sort. In the foliaceous expansion resting on the ground, of *C. pyxidata*, for example, we detect the upper epidermis, next the gonidial layer, which again rests on the closely-felted filamentous medullary substance. In the branches of *C. rangiferina*, as in a great number of its congeners, there is no well-defined epidermis. The branches are tubes, vacant in the centre, formed of a cartilaginous structure, in which only two zones can be distinguished, the inner and more solid of which is composed of almost simple, parallel, solid filaments intimately glued together by mucous substance; the outer zone is formed of a felted mass of filaments, likewise solid, but branched and divaricated. The solidity of these filaments arises from the obliteration of the cell-cavity by secondary layers on its walls, giving the filaments a horny texture. In the outer loose layer are found scattered groups of gonidia. In *Stereocaulon denudatum* the branches are solid and formed exclusively of parallel filaments, as is the case also with those of *Ramalina scopulorum*. In *Evernia vulpina* there is a solid axis formed of parallel filaments enclosed in a layer of interlaced fibres, between which and the horny coat, which is either solid or very obscurely cellular, gonidia are here and there to be observed.

In many Lichens, when exposed to excess of moisture, the proper fructification is not developed, and the gonidial structure is produced so abundantly as to burst through the superficial cortical layer and become naked, giving a mealy appearance to the thallus. Lichens reproduced by gonidia commonly grow at first into a pulverulent stratum by the multiplication of the cells, giving rise to the forms which were at one time thought distinct genera, such as LE-PRARIA.

The fronds of *Collema* are remarkable for their gelatinous texture, and differ greatly in organization from the foregoing, approaching the simplicity of the Nostochaceæ (Algæ). The thallus of *C. cheileum* consists of branched and colourless filaments or tubes, imbedded in an abundance of mucilage ; in *C. jacobeæfolium*, there exist in addition very numerous green granules, almost all arranged in long beaded lines (Pl. 29. fig. 13), some being larger than others, the whole mixed with the continuous filaments and imbedded in mucus. Both species have long, whitish, branched, filamentous pseudo-radical processes.

Putting aside the *gonidia* or gemmule-cells of the thallus, the reproductive organs of the Lichens are of three kinds:—1. the *apothecia*, which, according to their forms, receive different names, and are all characterized by producing the sacs (*thecæ*) containing spores; 2. the *spermogonia*, which some regard as antheridia, and which produce extremely minute cylindrical bodies (*spermatia*) growing at the ends of short pedicels, from which they are ultimately detached, like the spores of many Fungi; and 3, *pycnidia*, in which are developed *stylospores* like those of Fungi.

The commonest form of the *apothecia* is that of sessile or stalked disks or cushions, flat, convex, or hollowed into a cup (fig. 397); in other cases they are linear: these open forms characterize the division called Gymnocarpous Lichens, while in the Angiocarpous genera the apothecia are closed globular receptacles or conceptacles, analogous to those of the *Sphæriæ* among the Fungi, opening finally at the summit to discharge the spores (fig. 395). The *apothecium* may be composed of two parts, the *thalamium* and the *excipulum*; the latter, which is not always present, may be in the Gymnocarpi a cup-like envelope derived from the thallus, and of the same colour (*thalline*), or may differ in colour and texture, in which case it is termed a *proper* excipulum. In the Angiocarpous forms it may entirely or only partly surround the thalamium and thecæ, and then forms the

perithecium. The *thalamium* is represented by the body of the apothecium, open or closed; and the layer of its cells immediately lining the bottom of the cup, shield, or conceptacle is sometimes called the *hypothecium*, which bears the *thecæ* and the *paraphyses* (fig. 398); the latter are filiform or clavate cells (Pl. 29. figs. 6 & 12), probably abortive thecæ, among which they are intermingled; both these and the thecæ stand perpendicularly upon the hypothecium. The *thecæ* (Pl. 29. figs. 6 & 12) are usually ovoid or elongated cells with thick walls, containing the spores; the thecæ are shorter than the paraphyses surrounding them, and the whole are usually glued firmly together by their contiguous lateral surfaces.

The *spores* present many points of difference in different genera and species. In *Verrucaria muralis* they are ellipsoid, colourless, perfectly smooth and semi-transparent, containing granular matter; while in *V. epidermidis* and *atomaria* they are bilocular bodies, representing a pair of obovoid cells adherent by their thick ends. In their earlier stages of development they appear solid; subsequently four nuclei or oily globules are seen in them, each occupying a spherical cavity. The membrane of the spore then becomes thinner, and finally its two cavities coalesce into one. When ripe, these spores are about 1-1500″ in length and about 1-4000″ broad. There are eight in each theca, and they are separately enveloped in a mucilaginous coat. The spores are largest in the Angiocarpous genus *Pertusaria*. Those of *P. communis* are visible to the naked eye, and observed in water soon after emission from the thecæ, they are not less than 7-1000″ to 8-1000″ long by 5-2000″ broad. Their simple cavity is filled with granular semi-transparent matter, usually with oil-globules of various sizes. The epispore is very broad, transparent, and formed of several lamellæ; these also are coated with mucus. The genus *Parmelia* offers both simple and bilocular spores. Of the former, *P. parietina* gives an example, though in some cases a transverse partition is formed, and this is the normal state in *P. stellaris* (Pl. 29. figs. 6 & 7). In *Peltigera* (Pl. 29. fig. 11) the spores are elongated. In *Collema* and other genera, the spores are divided into four chambers by three transverse septa.

In several species of *Lecanora*, *Lecidea*, *Urceolaria*, and a great number of Angiocarpous Lichens, a more complex form of spore exists, longitudinal together with transverse septa dividing the cavity into several series of chambers. Those of *Urceolaria* (Pl. 29. fig. 17) have eight or ten compartments; those of *Lecanactis urceolata, Thelotrema lepadina, Umbilicaria pustulata* (Pl. 29. fig. 18), and other Lichens (called muriform spores), have a much larger number of little cavities, each containing a distinct *nucleus*.

The emission of the ripe spores takes place in the same way as in the *Pezizæ, Helvellæ, Sphærjæ,* and many other Fungi of the same kind. If a portion of the thallus, moistened, is placed in a common phial, with the apothecia turned toward one side, in about eight or ten hours the surface of the glass opposite each apothecium will be found covered with patches of spores, easily perceptible by their colour, these having been projected from the apothecia with force. If placed on a moist surface, and a slip of glass laid over them, the latter will become covered with them in the same way; and Tulasne states that they are projected to a distance of more than half an inch from the theciferous layer, the spores being emitted continuously for a long time. The experiment may be tried either in winter or summer, and has been made with success on several common species of *Parmelia, Lecanora, Peltigera, Collema, Borrera ciliaris, Verrucaria muralis, Endocarpon hepaticum, Pertusaria, Urceolaria, Opegrapha,* &c.

Tulasne explains the elastic discharge of the spores in the following way:—If a thin vertical section is cut from the middle of the apothecium, and divided so as to separate the *hypothecium* (or layer supporting the thecæ) from the subjacent tissues, and the parts thus dissected are placed in water, the hypothecium becomes greatly curved, presenting its external surface outwards and convex, while the other part, representing the body or *excipulum* of the apothecium, is curved with equal force, but its upper extremities are directed inwards to meet one another. Thus it seems that both the hypothecial layer and the outer wall of the apothecium eagerly absorb water, much more than the tissues separating them. Consequently when an entire apothecium is wetted, the borders tend to approach one another, curving inwards, while the layer bearing the thecæ becomes bulged out above, whence arises a pressure on the thecæ,

ultimately bursting them at the summit, and causing the expulsion of their contents. The expulsion of the spores of the Lichens takes place slowly, while that of some Ascomycetous Fungi is sudden, which may be accounted for by the different consistence of the surrounding structures.

Eight is generally set down as the normal number of spores in each theca, but this is not universal here any more than in the Ascomycetous Fungi; some species of *Endocarpon, Parmelia,* &c., have polysporous thecæ containing a considerable number, while there are often less than eight.

Spermogonia. In addition to the preceding, the Lichens exhibit another form of reproductive organs, which are liable to be confounded with *Sphæronemei* and other Fungi growing on the Lichens, or with parasitical Lichens in similar positions. They appear as black or brown points, usually near the margins of the thallus (Pl. 29. fig. 1), and have been found in *Borrera, Parmelia, Sticta, Cladonia, Collema, Opegrapha, Sphærophoron, Lichina, Endocarpon,* &c., and seem to be universal.

The spermogonia are hollow pustules, resembling more or less the conceptacles of the *Melanconei* among the Coniomycetous Fungi. In most cases they are immersed in the substance of the thallus (Pl. 29. figs. 2 & 13), and are perceptible externally only by a little projection, if at all; in rare cases they are free and borne above the thallus (some *Cladoniæ, Cetrariæ, Gyalectæ,* &c.). The ordinary form is globular, ellipsoidal or irregularly oblong, and sometimes with a sinuous outline. The spermogonia have either a simple undivided cavity (Pl. 29. figs. 13, 16), or are multilocular, divided in different ways into a variable number either of separate chambers or narrow cavities, all communicating with a common orifice, which is the *ostiole* or *pore* of the apparatus. This structure bears a close relation to that usual in the related Fungi (Coniomycetous forms, *Cytispora, Septoria,* &c.), and bears testimony to the close connexion between the Lichens and Fungi. The form and dimensions of the *spermatophores,* or peduncles of the *spermatia,* vary much. The simplest are short slender stalks, simple or branched, or they are articulated branches composed of a great number of cylindroid or globular cells (Pl. 29. figs. 3 & 14), or the branches are reduced to two or three elongated cells. The *spermatia* are terminal on the spermatophores, and consist of exceedingly minute bodies, ordinarily linear, very thin, short or longish, straight or curved (Pl. 29. figs. 3, 10, 15, 16), without appendages and motionless, and lie in a mucilage of extreme transparency. The *spermatophores* and their *spermatia* usually fill up the cavity of the spermogonia when just mature; afterwards, when the development is complete and the spermatia discharged, the spermogonia are found empty and discoloured.

The minute bodies, called *spermatia*, are regarded by most of those who have observed them as analogues of the spermatozoids produced in the antheridia of the higher Cryptogams. Itzigsohn imagined that he saw a spontaneous motion of them when lying in water beneath the microscope; but this appears to have been an error, and the only movement really existing has been regarded, probably most correctly, as merely molecular—that universal in extremely minute bodies, living or dead, lying in a fluid.

Stylospores. This name is given to certain very rare organs discovered by Tulasne in *Abrothallus* and *Scutula*, consisting of isolated spores borne upon shortish simple stalks. They are produced in conceptacles, to which is applied the name of *pycnidia*. They are closely analogous to the structures of the same name found in some Fungi (see STYLOSPORES).

Mr. Berkeley has described another structure in *Lecidea sabuletorum*, namely a kind of *basidium*, or enlarged cell supporting spores, developed from some of the paraphyses. Tulasne questions the correctness of the observation.

The Lichens are ordinarily divided into two orders, according to the structure of their apothecia, which are either closed at first, bursting subsequently by a pore or an irregular orifice, containing the *thecæ* in a *nucleus* in the interior; or they are open from an early period, and bear the *thecæ* on the upper, mostly concave surface (*disk*).

GYMNOCARPI is the title of the order of Lichens characterized by bearing open apothecia, in the form of shields (*scutellæ*), cups (*scyphi*), rings (*annuli*), or irregular cracks or lines (*lirellæ*), with raised borders, &c. These apothecia are either sessile on a flat spreading thallus, or raised on more or less developed stalk-like processes of the branched and shrubby forms. The upper, open, often concave surface of the apothecia,

called the *disk*, is clothed with thecæ and paraphyses.

ANGIOCARPI, the second of the orders into which Lichens are divided, are characterized by the closed apothecia, where the thecæ and paraphyses are collected into a *nucleus* enclosed in a case called the *perithecium*, bursting at the summit by a pore or an irregular opening to discharge the spores. The apothecium is more or less globular, and either imbedded in the thallus or distinct and raised above it. The perithecium either entirely encloses the nucleus or is hemispherical (*dimidiate*), clothing the upper, projecting portion.

Synopsis of the Families.

A. **Gymnocarpi.** Apothecia open, thalamium expanded.

* *Thallus crustaceous or foliaceous.*

1. Apothecia sessile, shield-shaped, or rarely peltate. Disk somewhat waxy, with a border formed by the thallus .... PARMELIEÆ.

2. Apothecia free, circular, soon convex, with an indistinct margin. Disk always open, in a special excipulum........ LECIDINEÆ.

3. Thallus sparing or almost absent, mostly parasitic. Disk expanded, orbicular, arising immediately from the medullary layer, without an excipulum .... COCCOCARPEÆ.

4. Apothecia with a circular disk, excipulum distinct from the horizontal foliaceous thallus (mostly fixed by the centre), at first closed, superficial .... PYXINEÆ.

5. Apothecium oblong, linear or waved, channeled. Disk at first connivent or with a veil .. GRAPHIDEÆ.

6. Apothecia at first in the medullary substance of the crust then expanded and surrounded by the thallus, which is pustular. Excipulum absent or spurious . ... GLYPHIDEÆ.

7. Apothecia circular or globose, always open. Disk pulverulent. CALYCIEÆ.

** *Thallus gelatinous when fresh.*

8. Apothecia circular; thallus composed of cylindrical and moniliform filaments . . . . COLLEMEÆ.

B. **Angiocarpi.** Apothecia closed, opening by a terminal pore and bursting irregularly, thalamium subglobose, included.

* *Thallus crustaceous.*

9. Thallus shrubby; apothecia at the ends of the branches . . . . SPHÆROPHOREÆ.
10. Thallus horizontal, leaf-like or encrusting; apothecia immersed . . . . ENDOCARPEÆ.
11. Thallus encrusting; apothecia rounded, projecting from the thallus . . . . VERRUCARIEÆ.
12. Thallus encrusting, covered with pustules, consisting of a heterogeneous stroma surrounded by a cortical excipulum, with one or more immersed ostiolate apothecia . . . . TRYPETHELIEÆ.
13. Thallus encrusting; apothecia rounded, with a carbonaceous hypothecium, apothecia bursting in various ways, nucleus mostly waxy, hard. . LIMBORIEÆ.

** *Thallus gelatinous or soft-cartilaginous.*

14. Apothecia terminal, on lobes of the thallus . . . . LICHINEÆ.

BIBL. L. R. Tulasne, *Mémoire pour servir à l'histoire organographique et physiologique des Lichens, Ann. des Sc. Nat.* 3 sér. xvii. 1, 153 *et seq.*; *On the Reproduction of Lichens and Fungi, Ann. Nat. Hist.* 2nd ser. vol. viii. p. 114 (translated from *Comptes Rendus,* March 1851); Körber, *Grundriss der Kryptogamenkunde,* Breslau, 1848, *Systema Lichenum,* 1854-8; Fries, *Lichenographia europœa reformata,* Lund, 1831; Schærer, *Enumeratio critica Lichenum europœorum,* Bern, 1850; Hedwig, *Theoria generationis, &c.*; Acharius, *Lichenographia universalis*; Wallroth, *Naturgeschichte der Flechten,* Frankfurt-a.-M. 1825; Meyer,

*Die Entwickl. &c. der Flechten (Nebenstunden meiner Beschäftigungen,&c.),*1828; Montagne. *Aperçu morphologique de la famille des Lichens, Dict. univ. d'hist. nat.* Paris, 1846; Bayrhoffer, *Einig. üb. Lichen.,* Berne, 1851; Itzigsohn, *Botan. Zeit.* viii. 393, 913, ix. 153; Flotow, numerous papers in the *Flora* and *Botanische Zeitung*; Leighton, *British Angiocarpous Lichens*; Ray publications, 1851; Lindsay, *Popular History of Lichens*; Speerschneider, *Bot. Zeit.* xiii. 345.

LICHINA, Ag.—A genus of Lichineæ (Lichens), allied to COLLEMA and EPHEBE in many respects, formerly included among the Algæ on account of their growing on the sea-shore (near high-water mark); but having the thallus of a lichen, and bearing true *apothecia* and *spermogonia.* The apothecia occur at the ends of the branches of the thallus; in *L. pygmœa* the spermogonia occur underneath the apothecia, in *L. confinis* at the apices of the branches and often on the apothecia. The spores appear generally to adhere to the walls of the thecæ, which break up.

BIBL. Harvey, *Brit. Alg.* 1 ed. p. 22; Hook. *Brit. Fl.* ii. pt. 1. p. 274; Tulasne, *Ann. des Sc. Nat.* 2 sér. pp. 81 & 188, pls. 9, 10; Greville, *Alg. Brit.* pl. 6.

LICHINEÆ.—A family of Angiocarpous Lichens, of remarkable habit, the species of which were formerly regarded in their perfect and imperfect states as Algæ. The branched thallus is of gelatinous texture, very soft when wet, cartilaginous when dry, growing on wet rocks, *Lichina* being marine. The fructification consists of closed *apothecia* and *spermogonia* formed in the substance or at the ends of the branches.

British Genera.

1. *Lichina.* Frond cartilaginous, smooth, dichotomous, bearing the apothecia at the ends of the branches.

2. *Ephebe.* Frond cartilaginous, hairy, much branched, bearing the apothecia excavated in the swollen branches (not terminal).

LICMOPHORA, Ag.—A genus of Diatomaceæ.

Char. Frustules in front view cuneate, elongate, radiating in a fan-shaped manner from a branched stipes; side view (valves) convex, inflected at the larger end and furnished with transverse striæ (rows of dots). Marine.

L. radians, K. (*L. flabellata,* S.) (Pl. 13. fig. 3).

The species (one other British, Sm., five

in all, Kütz.) are too doubtfully distinct to deserve description.

BIBL. Smith, *Brit. Diat.* i. 85; Kützing, *Bacill.* 123, and *Sp. Alg.* 113.

LIEBERKUHN. INTROD., p. xviii.

LIGAMENTS and TENDONS.—With the

Fig. 399.

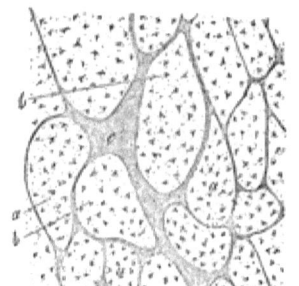

Magnified 60 diameters.

Transverse section of the tendon of the tibialis posticus; numan: *a*, secondary bundles; *b*, larger nuclear fibres; *c*, interstitial areolar tissue.

Fig. 400.

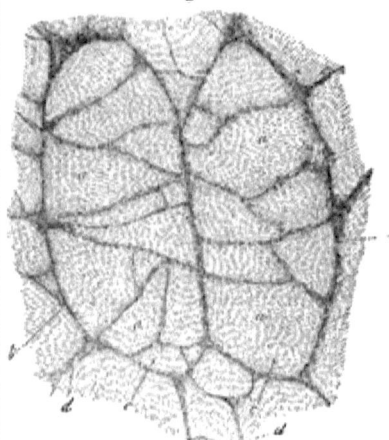

Magnified 20 diameters.

Transverse section of a tendon of a calf: *a*, secondary, *b*, tertiary bundles; *c*, nuclear fibres, obliquely divided; *d*, interstitial areolar tissue.

Fig. 401.

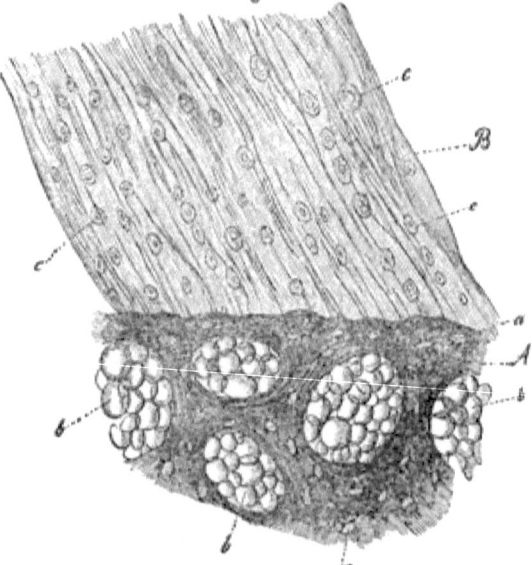

Magnified 300 diameters.

Portion of the tendo Achillis attached to the os calcis; human: *A*, bone with lacunæ *a*, medullary and fat-cells *b*; *B*, tendon with fibrillæ and cartilage-cells *c*.

exception of the elastic ligaments, which are noticed under that head, the structure of ligaments and tendons is essentially the same. They consist of areolar tissue, with a small quantity of elastic tissue. The fibres or fibrillæ of the areolar tissue are very minute, longitudinal, parallel, closely connected, and pursue a straight or undulatory course. Their union into bundles is sometimes very indistinct, and only to be shown by drying transverse sections, and afterwards treating them with alkalies. In other instances the bundles are easily recognizable, of a polygonal, rounded or elongated form (fig. 400), and connected by loose interstitial areolar tissue.

The elastic tissue of tendons exists as slender nuclear fibres, sometimes forming rows of narrow spindle-shaped cells connected by slender processes, at others uniform fibres, or isolated spindle-shaped cells. These are placed at regular distances apart, between the bundles of areolar tissue.

When tendons are in contact with bones, they frequently contain cartilage-cells, either isolated or arranged in rows (fig. 401 c); these sometimes undergo ossification.

The aponeuroses, fasciæ, and tendinous sheaths consist of the same elements, but in various proportions and differently arranged according to their functions,—sometimes the areolar fibres being predominant, the structure agreeing with that of tendon, whilst at others the elastic tissue is greatly developed (fig. 402). Some of these tissues also contain cartilage-cells.

Fig. 403.

Magnified 350 diameters.

Cartilage-cells from the membranous ligament surrounding the popliteus muscle: a, cell with one nucleus; b, cell with two nuclei; c, cell containing one, d, two secondary cells, the contents of both of which are more consistent.

The intervertebral ligaments consist fibro-cartilage, surrounded by osseous tissue; the centre is soft and containing concentric cartilage corpuscles (fig. 101, p. 119).

BIBL. Kölliker, *Mikroskop. Anatomie,* i.; Henle, *Allgem. Anat.*; Donders, *Mulder's Physiol. Chem.*

Fig. 402.

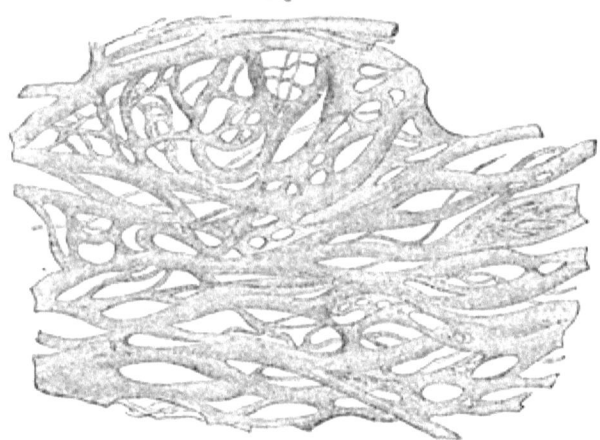

Magnified 450 diameters.

Elastic fibres from the inner part of the fascia lata, human; densely interwoven and forming an elastic membrane.

LIGNINE. — A modified condition of cellulose is obtained from old wood-cells, and called by this name. It differs in its reactions from pure cellulose, being coloured yellow by sulphuric acid and iodine; but after boiling in nitric acid and washing, tincture of iodine and water give it a blue colour. See SECONDARY DEPOSITS.

LIMBORIEÆ.—A family of Angiocarpous or closed-fruited Lichens characterized by rounded apothecia closed in by a carbonaceous special perithecium, finally bursting in various ways, containing a somewhat waxy nucleus, which grows hard.

British Genera.

1. *Pyrenothea.* Thallus crustaceous. Apothecia round, carbonaceous, perforated by a simple opening, protruding a globular nucleus, which at length falls to pieces, ultimately dehiscent, spread out, evacuated.

2. *Strigula.* Parasitic on coriaceous perennial leaves. Thallus mostly produced beneath the cuticle. Perithecium subglo-

bose, collapsing at length, opening by an irregular fissure or minute pore. Nucleus at first gelatinous, at length hard, becoming black and cracking when exposed.

LIME, SALTS OF.

Carbonate of lime. This substance is well known as forming chalk, marble, &c., and as occurring in hard animal structures, as bone, shell, &c. It is not unfrequently met with in the form of granules as a component of various animal secretions, as the urine, &c. In this liquid, it sometimes, but rarely, also occurs in little spheres or disks, consisting of groups of radiating needles. This we first found to be the case in human urine (Pl. 9. fig. 8); but it was subsequently detected in that of herbivorous animals, as the cow and the horse (Pl. 9. fig. 7), in which its occurrence is common. It is also a component of otolithes, in which it exists either as granules or minute prisms, often with six sides and trilateral summits. From river- and spring-water it is usually deposited in irregular and imperfect forms (Pl. 9. fig. 6), all of which consist of grouped needles. Sometimes it assumes the rhombohedral form, as in the shell of the oyster (Pl. 37. fig. 10), and frequently in chemical solutions. When treated with a dilute acid, after having been thoroughly washed in a watch-glass, it is dissolved with effervescence from the escape of carbonic acid gas. During the solution it first becomes more transparent, exhibiting the internal crystalline structure, and frequently a concentric or nuclear appearance, which finally disappears. When derived from animal secretions, it leaves undissolved an organic cast of the original, provided the acid be not too strong, or its action too long continued. If the number and size of the minute bodies be relatively very small in proportion to the amount of water, on adding the acid, effervescence will not occur, the water holding in solution the carbonic acid evolved. The presence of the lime may be tested in the ordinary way, by the addition of oxalate of ammonia, when the precipitate is insoluble in acetic acid, or by adding dilute sulphuric acid, when crystalline needles of the sulphate of lime (Pl. 6. fig. 16) are formed.

The spheres or disks naturally occurring in the urine, are closely imitated by those formed in urine to which chloride of calcium has been added, and which has been subsequently kept for some time.

Lactate of lime may be obtained by acting upon carbonate of lime with lactic acid. It is soluble in water and alcohol. The microscopic crystals consist of tufts of delicate radiating needles (Pl. 7. fig. 19).

Oxalate of lime. This salt exists in solution in the contents of many vegetable cells combined with a proteine-compound; it is also probably a normal constituent of the human blood in small quantity, combined and dissolved as in vegetables.

In the cells of plants it is very frequently deposited in a crystalline form, constituting RAPHIDES. From human blood it has been obtained in crystals by treating the alcoholic extract with acetic acid. It is very commonly met with in the crystalline form in various secretions of animals, as the urine, the mucus of the gall-bladder, that of the surface of the pregnant uterus, the liquid of the allantois, the contents of the Malpighian vessels, and the so-called true renal vessels of insects, cysts, &c.

Its most characteristic form is the square flattened octohedron (Pl. 9. fig. 9); but it also occurs in the form of the square prism terminated by quadrilateral pyramids, of fine needles, and in that of a flattened body with an ellipsoidal outline, frequently constricted so as to resemble a dumb-bell, or variously excavated at parts of the surface (Pl. 9. figs. 11 & 12). It may be obtained artificially in most of these forms (Pl. 9. fig. 13), by dissolving artificial oxalate of lime in dilute nitric acid and evaporating; some of the forms thus obtained resemble those of carbonate of lime. When obtained by mixing oxalate of ammonia with soluble salts of lime, as chloride of calcium, &c., the crystals are generally peculiar (Pl. 9. fig. 14), although sometimes the regular octohedra are obtained.

It is insoluble in hot and cold water, acetic acid and ammonia, but is soluble in dilute mineral acids without effervescence.

Phosphate of lime. This salt is most frequently deposited from animal liquids in an amorphous or granular state. It may be obtained in the crystalline form by mixing a solution of phosphate of soda with chloride of calcium. The crystals are mostly thin rhombic plates (Pl. 6. fig. 17).

They are soluble in acetic and dilute mineral acids without effervescence, but not in potash or water. Some of the compound crystals resemble those of the ammonio-phosphate of magnesia, from which they may be distinguished by the addition of dilute sulphuric acid, which causes the formation of needles of sulphate of lime.

Sulphate of lime. Well known as forming gypsum, alabaster, selenite, &c. It rarely or never occurs in the crystalline form in animal or vegetable products. When rapidly formed in chemical testing, the crystals consist of minute needles or prisms (Pl. 6. fig. 16); when more slowly formed, these are larger and mixed with rhombic plates.

The crystals are but little soluble in water, and not in acetic or the dilute mineral acids. They are sometimes found in bottles containing spirit in which marine animals have been preserved.

Medicinal precipitated sulphur is very commonly adulterated with sulphate of lime. The microscope at once enables the crystals of the salt to be recognized.

Urate of lime. See URATES.

See RAPHIDES and URINARY DEPOSITS.

BIBL. That of CHEMISTRY, ANIMAL.

LIMNIAS, Schrank.—A genus of Rotatoria, of the family Floscularinæa.

Char. Eyes (when young) two, red; urceoli or sheaths single; rotatory organ with two lobes. Teeth forming a row in each jaw.

L. ceratophylli (Pl. 34. fig. 45). Urceolus at first whitish, subsequently becoming brown or blackish, smooth, or in consequence of its viscidity covered with foreign bodies. Aquatic; length 1-24 to 1-18″.

BIBL. Ehrenberg, *Infus.* p. 401.

LIMNOCHARES, Latr.—A genus of Arachnida, of the order Acarina and family Hydrachnea.

Char. Palpi small and short, with the fifth joint small and forming a claw; mandibles with the last joint subulate; rostrum cylindrical, elongate; eyes four, approximate; coxæ concealed beneath the skin, the anterior larger than the posterior; legs ambulatory.

L. aquatica (*holosericea*) (Pl. 2. fig. 27). The only species. It differs from all other water-spiders by its walking instead of swimming.

Body very soft and often spontaneously variable in form; epidermis covered with little conical granules (?); no hairs upon the body, and but few upon the legs; eyes attached to a lanceolate scaly piece (*d*), and surrounded by hairs; rostrum partly concealed beneath the skin, the anterior exserted half (*b*) cylindrical and accompanied by the palps, the last joint of which is very slender and obtuse; by pressure the broader base of the rostrum is made to protrude (*f*); tarsi (*c*) thickened at the end, with large claws; coxæ of four posterior pairs of legs longer than the others, which is contrary to what occurs in *Hydrachna, Atax,* &c.; coxæ of the anterior two pairs of legs closely approximate, as are also those of the two posterior pairs (*e*), but the two groups are widely separated.

The larvæ have six legs, a large head-like rostrum, with two large palps and two black latero-anterior eyes, and fix themselves upon or near the head of *Gerris lacustris*; they subsequently detach themselves from this insect, fall into the water, and pass their nymph-stage under submersed stones, the perfect animal making its appearance at the end of fifteen days.

BIBL. Dugès, *Ann. des Sc. Nat.* 2 sér. i. p. 159; Gervais, *Walckenaer's Arachn.* p. 208; Koch, *Deutschlands Crustac., &c.*

LIMNOCHILIDÆ, Kütz. See APHANIZOMENON.

LIMNORIA, Leach.—A genus of marine Crustacea, of the order Isopoda, and family Asellota.

L. terebrans (Pl. 44. fig. 27) is of interest on account of the great ravages which it commits in submerged timber, as the piles of piers, flood-gates, docks, &c., which it perforates in every direction. Head large, rounded; antennæ four, of nearly equal length; eyes two, lateral, black, composed of about seven ocelli; body elongato-subcylindrical, thorax with seven joints, legs seven pairs, formed for walking; abdomen six-jointed, the last joint large, suborbicular, and with two styles; length about 1-6″. It contracts into a ball when disturbed.

BIBL. Leach, *Linn. Trans.* xi. 370; Coldstream, *Edin. New Phil. Journ.* 1834; Hope, *Entom. Trans.* i.; Dalyell, *Wonders of Creation,* i.

LINDIA, Duj.—A genus of Rotatoria, of the family Hydatinæa, E. (Furcularina, Duj.).

Char. Body oblong, almost vermiform, with transverse folds, rounded in front, but no rotatory organ, cilia or eye; tail-like foot with two conical and short segments or toes; jaws very complicated (and imperfectly described).

L. torulosa (Pl. 34. fig. 40). Aquatic; length 1-75″.

Cohn describes two wedge-shaped retractile rotatory organs, wheel-shaped at the ends; a single dorsal eye-speck, red in young, black in adult animals; behind this, a sac containing highly refractive granules.

BIBL. Dujardin, *Infus.* p. 653; Cohn. *Siebold & Kölliker's Zeitsch.* 1858. p. 286.

LINDSÆA, Dryander.—A genus of Davallieæ (Polypodioid Ferns). Exotic (fig. 404).

Fig. 404.

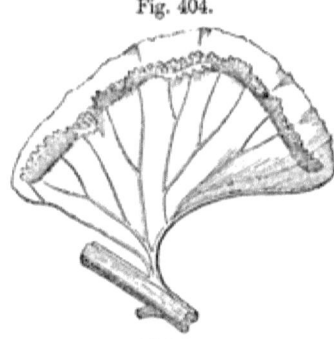

Lindsæa.

A pinnule.　Magn. 10 diams.

LINGULINA, D'Orb.—A genus of Foraminifera, of the order Stichostegia, and family Æquilateralidæ.

Char. Shell equilateral, vitreous, oval-oblong or elongate, straight; chambers compressed, partly embracing; the last very convex, but not prolonged; orifice terminal, median, forming a transverse fissure on the upper convexity of the last chamber.

L. carinata. Shell compressed, peripheral margin entire; chambers about seven; length 1-90″. British; recent; very rare.

Some unnamed British fossil species have been found in the Gravesend chalk.

BIBL. That of the order.

LINUM, L. See FLAX.

LIOTHEUM, Nitzsch.—A genus of Insects, of the order Anoplura, and family Liotheidæ.

Char. Antennæ clavate or capitate; maxillary palpi conspicuous; mouth with strong mandibles; tarsi with two claws.

Antennæ four-jointed; mandibles with two teeth; maxillary palpi long, filiform, four-jointed; labial palpi very short, two-jointed.

The genus has been subdivided into seven subgenera. The species are very numerous, and are parasitic upon birds.

L. (Menopon) pallidum (Pl. 28. fig. 7). Elongate, of a pale straw colour, shining and smooth; head slightly sinuate on each side, with a dark pitchy spot before each eye. Length 1-24 to 1-16″. Common upon the domestic fowl.

BIBL. Denny, *Anoplur. Monographia,* p. 204.

LITHIC ACID. See URIC ACID.

LITHOCYSTIS, Allm.—A genus of Corallinaceæ (Florideous Algæ), consisting of a single species, *L. Allmanni,* Hass., which has been found as an epiphyte, forming minute white dots upon *Chrysimenia clavellosa.* The minute dots consist of one or more fan-shaped fronds composed of square cells. The plant is colourless, brittle, and effervesces in acid. The fan-shaped frond somewhat resembles in structure imperfect or segmental fronds of COLEOCHÆTE.

BIBL. Hass. *Brit. Mar. Alg.* p. 111, pl. 14 B; *Phyc. Brit.* pl. 166.

LITHODESMIUM, Ehr.—A genus of Diatomaceæ.

Char. Frustules in side view triangular, united so as to form a prismatic filament. Marine.

L. undulatum (Pl. 13. fig. 4 *a,* front view; 4 *b,* side view). Surface without markings, very pellucid, two of the sides undulate, the third plane and with two marginal notches; angles obtuse; length of joints 1-480″.

This organism requires further examination; its Diatomaceous structure is very obscure.

BIBL. Ehrenberg, *Abhandl. d. Berl. Akad.* 1840; Kützing, *Bacill.* p. 135, and *Sp. Alg.* p. 133.

LITHOFELLINIC ACID.—This substance is a component of certain concretions called bezoars, and found in the alimentary canal of various kinds of goat in the East, as in Persia, &c.

It is crystalline, insoluble in water, readily so in hot alcohol, but little in æther.

The perfect crystals form six-sided prisms with truncated ends; but when somewhat rapidly deposited from an alcoholic solution, they are modified as represented in Pl. 7. fig. 14.

BIBL. See CHEMISTRY.

LITHONEMA, Hass. See AINACTIS.

LITOBROCHIA, Presl.—A genus of Adianteæ (Polypodioid Ferns). Exotic.

LITOSIPHON, Harv.—A genus of Punctariaceæ (Fucoid Algæ), with fronds composed of cartilaginous filiform unbranched filaments, at first solid, afterwards tubular, composed of several rows of cells; epiphytic on *Chorda filum* (*L. pusillus*) and *Alaria* (*L. Laminariæ*), the former 2 to 6″ long, the latter 1-4 to 1-2″. The sporanges occur either solitary or aggregated, scattered on the surface of the filaments, which in *L. pusillus* are clothed with pellucid hairs, in *L. Laminariæ* smooth.

BIBL. Harv. *Brit. Mar. Alg.* p. 43, pl. 8 D; Thuret, *Ann. des Sc. Nat.* 4 sér. iii. p. 14.

LITUOLA, Lam.—A genus of Foraminifera, of the order Helicostegia, and family Nautiloidæ.

Char. Shell nautiloid when young, the subsequent chambers rectilinear; composed of internal cavities, filled with irregular partitions; orifices very numerous, on the last chambers.

The species are fossil, in chalk; *L. nautiloidea* is British.

BIBL. That of the order.

LIVER.—It need scarcely be said that the liver is the glandular organ which secretes the bile.

On examining the surface of the liver or a transverse section of that organ with the naked eye, it usually presents a mottled appearance, numerous spots of a dark or light red colour being surrounded by a

Fig. 405.

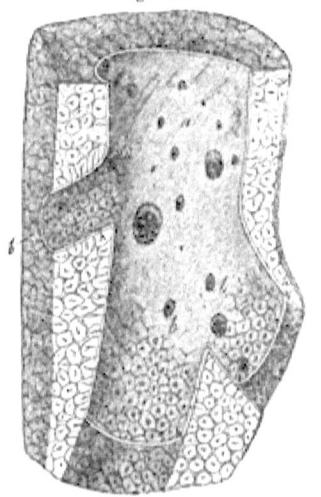

Magnified about 3 diameters.

Portion of the liver of a pig, with divided branches of the vena cava; the lobules are visible upon the divided surfaces: *a*, large vein, no orifices of the intralobular veins being visible; *b*, branches of the same, with distinct orifices of the intralobular veins, and the bases of the lobules seen through their walls.

margin of a paler or darker colour. These spots correspond to the lobules of the liver.

The lobules are rounded or polygonal, and about 1-2 to 1''' in diameter (fig. 405).

Between the lobules run branches of the vena portæ, forming the interlobular veins (coloured red in Pl. 31. fig. 33); these throughout their course send off numerous smaller branches into the substance of the lobules, which terminate in the capillary plexus of the lobules.

Fig. 406.

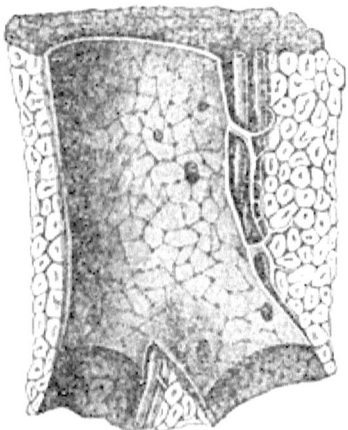

Magnified about 4 diameters.

Section of the liver of a pig through a branch of the vena portæ, with accompanying branches of the hepatic artery and duct. On the right are seen two branches of the vena portæ giving off the interlobular veins.

The branches of the vena portæ are accompanied by branches of the hepatic duct and ramifications of the hepatic artery, the whole being surrounded by areolar tissue prolonged from Glisson's capsule. Hence in a section of the uninjected liver, those branches of the vena portæ and of the vena cava which are visible to the naked eye are readily distinguishable from each other, by the orifices of the former collapsing, whilst those of the latter are kept open by their close contact with the lobules.

In the centre of each lobule arises a branch of the vena cava, by the union of numerous smaller branches (coloured yellow in Pl. 31. fig. 33), which take their origin in the capillary plexus of the lobule; these central branches form the intralobular veins.

The capillaries of the lobules form a close

and elegant plexus between the branches of the inter- and intralobular veins, the rest of the lobules being filled up with the secreting epithelium (fig. 408).

Fig. 407.

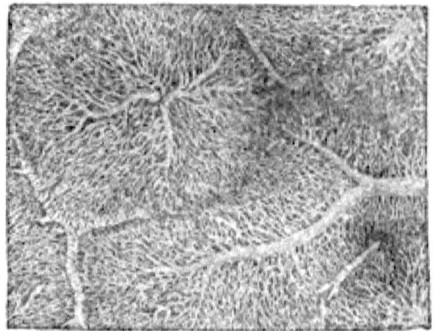

Magnified 35 diameters.

Section of a portion of the liver of a rabbit, showing the entire course of one of the intralobular veins, the roots only of the others.

Fig. 408.

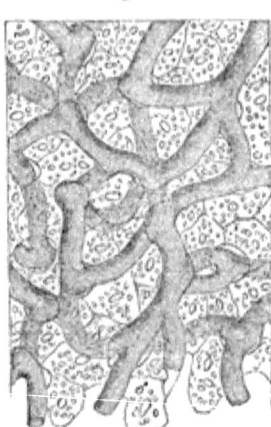

Magnified 350 diameters.

Secreting cells and capillaries of the liver of a pig. [The spaces between the capillaries and the cells have been left through error of the draughtsman.]

The branches of the biliary ducts accompany those of the vena portæ as far as the interlobular spaces, where they do not enter the lobules, but terminate in cœcal extremities. The biliary ducts consist of an

outer coat of areolar tissue, the bundles of fibres of which are difficultly separable, and an internal epithelial layer. The areolar coat is most distinct in the larger branches, being almost absent in the terminal interlobular ducts; it contains numerous nuclei and nuclear fibres. The epithelium of the larger ducts is cylindrical, that of the smaller of the pavement kind. In the hepatic duct, the outer coat contains scattered muscular fibre-cells. The ducts also contain small mucus-glands. The secreting cells of the lobules fill up the interspaces between the blood-vessels, forming a network with radiating meshes. They are very transparent, of a rounded or polygonal form, about 1-1000" in diameter, containing a nucleus or not unfrequently two nuclei, with a number of granules, and a few small globules of fat (fig. 160, page 208).

Fig. 409.

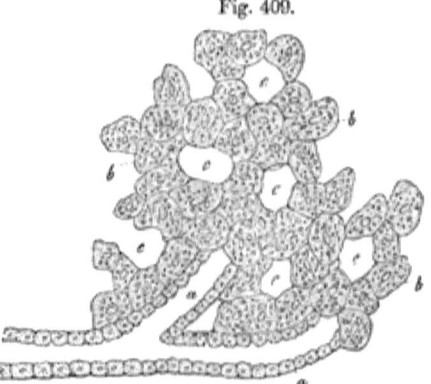

Magnified 350 diameters.

Secreting cells and terminal interlobular ducts; human. a, ducts; b, cells; c, spaces occupied by blood-vessels.

The division of the substance of the liver into lobules is rather apparent than real, being effected by the peculiar arrangement of the vessels, the lobules having no true coat or envelope. The areolar tissue which accompanies the vena portæ and its branches becomes less and less in quantity as the branches become smaller, and is lost in the interlobular spaces. It is much more abundant in animals, as the pig, than in man, rendering the lobular arrangement much more distinct.

The branches of the hepatic artery are distributed to the portal vessels, the hepatic ducts, Glisson's capsule with its prolongations, and the peritoneal coat. They are often elegantly tortuous.

Among the more common morbid states of the liver may be mentioned that called cirrhosis, in which the areolar tissue is excessively developed and mixed with a large number of fibro-plastic corpuscles, producing an atrophied state of the epithelial structure ; an increase in the amount of fatty matter in the cells (fig. 160, page 208) ; and the presence in these also of granules of the pigment of the bile, rarely with crystals of cholesterine and bilifulvine.

The examination of the arrangement of the blood-vessels is best made in a liver which has been injected with two kinds of injection, as yellow (chromate of lead) and red (vermilion), or red and white (carbonate of lead) ; the yellow or white being injected into the hepatic vein. As the injection is being proceeded with, the surface of the liver should be examined with a lens to ascertain whether the intralobular veins are well filled, and the injection has reached the capillaries ; the red injection should then be thrown into the portal vein until it is filled. The general vascular arrangement is best observed in an injection in which the capillaries themselves are not filled, but only the smaller portal and hepatic branches.

To examine the ducts as to their course and termination, the portal vein should previously be injected. If this be not done, the injection easily bursts through the walls of the terminal ducts, and escapes into the intralobular plexus ; and thus the appearance of a plexus of vessels prolonged from the terminal ducts is produced.

The structure of the hepatic cells is easily seen on scraping the surface of a section of the liver, and placing the portion thus obtained between two pieces of glass as usual.

The general arrangement of the secreting cells is observed in sections made with Valentin's knife.

In many animals, as fishes, the loading of the cells of the liver with fat, which in man represents the morbid state of fatty degeneration, is normal, and renders it a matter of some difficulty to distinguish clearly the outlines of the cells, which are also very delicate.

BIBL. Kölliker, *Mikroskop. Anat.* ii. ; Kiernan, *Phil. Trans.* 1833 ; H. Jones, *Phil. Trans.* 1846 and 1849 ; Guillot, *Ann. des Sc. Nat.* 3 sér. 1848 ; Leidy, *Silliman's Journ.* 1848 ; Beale, *On the Liver.*

LOASACEÆ.—A family of Dicotyledonous Flowering plants, with stinging hairs upon the epidermis. *Loaza, Bartonia* and *Blumenbachia* are often to be obtained in gardens.

LOMARIA, Willd.—A genus of Adianteæ (Polypodioid Ferns), of which the native species is sometimes called BLECHNUM or *Pteris Spicant* ; it has distinct barren and fertile leaves.

LONCHITIS, Presl.—A genus of Adi-

Fig. 410.

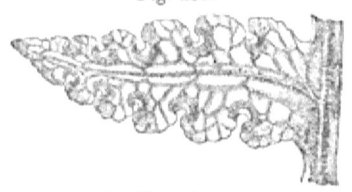

Lonchites pubescens.
A pinnule with sori.
Magnified 10 diameters.

anteæ (Polypodioid Ferns). Exotic (fig. 410).

LOPHIUM, Fr.—A genus of Phacidiacei (Ascomycetous Fungi), remarkably distinguished by the form of the *perithecia* resembling a bivalve shell with the valves *in situ* (figs. 411 & 412). The nucleus contained

Fig. 411. Fig. 412. Fig. 413.

Lophium mytilinum.
Fig. 411. A perithecium, seen sidewise.
Fig. 412. The same, seen endwise.
Fig. 413. A perithecium cut open.
Magn. 25 diams.

within the carbonaceous perithecium consists of erect asci mixed with paraphyses, containing minute spores, and soon falling away into a powder. *L. mytilinum,* Pers. (figs. 411–3) occurs on the bark or naked wood of fir-trees. *L. elatum,* Carm. also occurs on fir-wood. These plants are known from allied genera by the remarkable form of the perithecia.

BIBL. Berk. *Brit. Flor.* ii. pt. 2. p. 280; Fries, *Syst. Myc.* ii. p. 533; *Summa Veg.* p. 401; Greville, *Sc. Crypt. Flor.* pl. 177.

LOPHOCOLEA, Nees. — A genus of Jungermannieæ (Hepaticæ), including the *J. bidentata*, L. and *J. heterophylla*, Schrad., growing in moist situations, at the roots of trees, &c.

BIBL. Hook. *Brit. Jungerm.* pls. 30, 31; *Brit. Flor.* ii. pt. 1. p. 122.

LOPHOPUS, Dumortier.—A genus of freshwater Polyzoa, of the order Hippocrepia, and family Plumatellidæ.

Char. Polypidom sacciform, hyaline, gelatinous, with a disk serving for attachment; orifices scattered; ova elliptical, with a ring, but no spines.

L. crystallinus, the only species, is found in ponds and ditches, attached to the submerged parts of *Lemna* and various other aquatic plants.

This polyzoon is comparatively large and transparent, and well calculated to display the structure of the class.

BIBL. Allman, *Freshwater Polyzoa (Ray Soc.)*, 83; Johnston, *Brit. Zooph.* 391.

LORICA. See CARAPACE.

LOUSE. See PEDICULUS and ANOPLURA.

LOXODES, Ehr.—A genus of Infusoria, of the family Trachelina.

Char. Body covered with rows of cilia; no teeth; anterior and upper portion of the body (lip) obliquely truncate, or bent towards one side (hatchet-shaped, E.), and with a row of large cilia. Ehrenberg describes four species.

1. *L. bursaria*, E. (*Paramecium bursaria*, Focke) (Pl. 24. fig. 41). Oblong, green, anterior end depressed and obliquely truncate, posterior end rounded and turgid; aquatic; length 1-288″.

The rotation of the contents of the body takes place in this infusorium. Reproduction by the formation of swarm-germs, according to the process 2 b (p. 374), has also been observed.

2. *L. rostrum*, E. (*Pelecida rostrum*, D.) (Pl. 24. fig. 39). White, lanceolate, anterior portion bent on one side; aquatic; length 1-144 to 1-60″.

Dujardin's genus *Loxodes* does not agree with that of Ehrenberg; but, according to Stein, the observations upon which the differences are founded depend upon faulty observation.

Thus *L. cucullulus*, D., and *L. dentatus*, D. (Pl. 24. fig. 40) are young states of *Chilodon cucullulus*, E.; and *L. reticulatus*, D. is the same infusorium distended with alimentary matters.

BIBL. Ehrenberg, *Infus.* p. 323; Dujardin, *Infus.* p. 449; Stein, *Infus.* p. 238, &c. and the *Bibl.*

LOXOPHYLLUM, Duj.— A genus of Infusoria, of the family Paramecia.

The species belong to the genera *Amphileptus*, E. and *Trachelius*, E. See PARAMECIA.

BIBL. Dujardin, *Infus.* p. 487.

LOXSOMA, R. Brown.—A genus of Hymenophyllaceous Ferns, distinguished by the projecting column bearing the sporangia (figs. 415, 416).

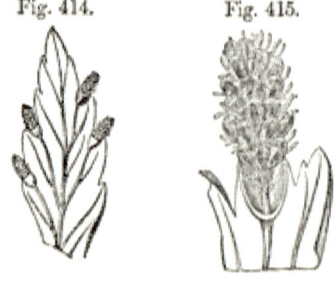

Fig. 414.   Fig. 415.

Fig. 416.

Loxsoma Cunninghamii.

Fig. 414. A pinnule with marginal sori. Magn. 5 diams.
Fig. 415. A sorus opened. Magn. 25 diams.
Fig. 416. Columella with sporanges. Magn. 50 diams.

LUNGS.—The internal respiratory sacs of animals.

Under this head we shall notice also the larynx, trachea, and bronchi.

Larynx.—The cartilages of the larynx do not all possess the same minute structure. The thyroid, cricoid, and arytenoid cartilages consist of true cartilage, the basis being homogeneous, and containing disseminated cartilage-corpuscles. The walls of the corpuscles are usually thick. The basis often becomes fibrous, and both corpuscles and basis encrusted with calcareous salts, or completely ossified. Their perichondrium is firm, and is composed of areolar tissue, with fine elastic fibres, vessels, and nerves.

The epiglottis (Pl. 40. fig. 40) and the appendices of the arytenoid consist of fibro-cartilage; and the corpuscles are frequently more or less filled up by secondary deposit.

The mucous membrane, as also the submucous tissue of the larynx, consists of areolar tissue with networks of fine elastic fibres; at the surface it becomes more homogeneous, but does not form a separable basement layer or membrane. It contains a number of small racemose glands, the vesicles of which are lined with pavement-, the ducts with cylindrical epithelium. Its surface is covered with ciliated epithelium, agreeing in structure with that of the trachea.

Trachea and larger bronchi.—The incomplete cartilaginous rings of these tubes are surrounded and connected together by a firm, elastic, fibrous membrane, forming their perichondrium, which also covers the posterior part of the tubes as a somewhat thinner layer. The cartilage is of the true kind. At the posterior part of the tubes is a layer of unstriated muscular fibres, most

Fig. 417.

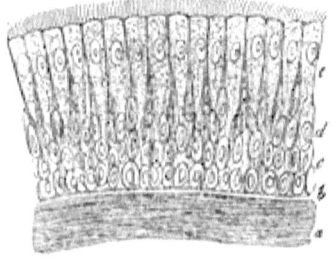

Epithelial cells of the trachea *in situ*; human. *a*, longitudinal elastic fibres; *b*, homogeneous outer (basement) layer of the mucous membrane; *c*, deep layers of round cells; *d*, intermediate layers; *e*, outer ciliated cells.

Magnified 350 diameters.

of which form transverse, but a few longitudinal bundles. The elastic tissue of the mucous membrane is greatly developed,

forming a distinct internal layer of principally longitudinal anastomosing fibres.

The epithelium is ciliated, and consists of several layers.

The deepest layers consist of roundish cells with distinct rounded nuclei, those succeeding being elongated, whilst those next the surface are still longer, greatly narrowed at the base, and with oval nuclei; these forms are most distinct in the detached cells.

Those of the last row are covered with vibratile cilia.

Fig. 418.

The *smaller bronchi* differ somewhat in structure from the larger. Thus the cartilage forms angular plates distributed throughout their circumference, while the elastic and areolar coats become thinner, and the transverse muscular fibres smaller and less closely placed; the latter probably extend as far as the air-cells. The ciliated epithelium extends to the termination of the bronchi, forming, however, a single layer only of cells in the smaller ones.

Isolated epithelial cells from the surface of the trachea; human.

Magnified 350 diameters.

The walls of the pulmonary air-cells consist of two layers, a fibrous and an epithelial layer. The former is composed of a basis of homogeneous areolar tissue, with numerous elastic fibres, vessels, and nerves (fig. 419).

The elastic fibres surround the air-cells in the form of elegant wavy bundles and separate fibres which anastomose and constitute a dense network, most obvious at those parts where several cells are in contact with each other; whilst in other parts the areolar element supporting the numerous capillaries predominates, and the elastic elements are more sparing and slender. The epithelium is of the pavement kind, not ciliated, consisting of rounded or polygonal nucleated cells, about 1-2000″ in diameter.

Each terminal bronchus does not end in a separate air-cell, as was formerly supposed, but in a group of them, in which the cells are partially fused together, forming a common cavity (fig. 420). These groups of air-cells form the lobules of the lungs, and are separated from each other by areolar tissue mixed with nuclear fibres,

Fig. 419.

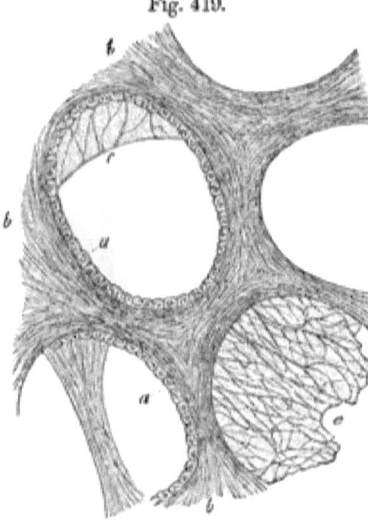

Air-cells of a human lung. a, epithelium ; b, fibrous portion, where the walls of several air-cells are confluent ; c, thinner walls of air-cells.

Magnified 350 diams.

Fig. 420.

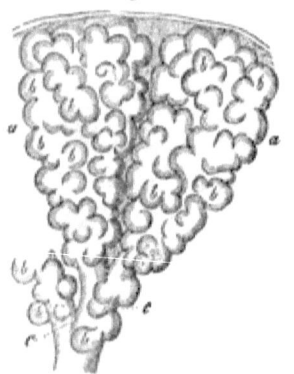

Two pulmonary lobules a a, with the air-cells b b, and the terminations of the bronchi c c ; from an infant newly born.

Magnified 25 diameters.

containing in adult animals (fig. 421) black pigment in the form of distinct or

isolated granules, sometimes also crystals. The lobules are best seen in the lungs of young animals.

Fig. 421.

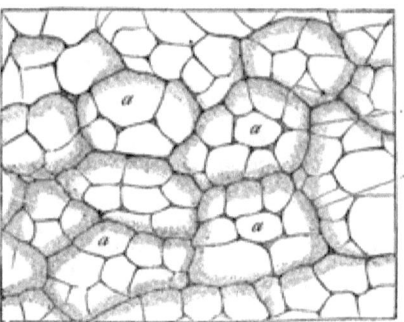

Outer surface of the lung of a cow, the air-cells of which were injected with wax : a, a, a, air-cells ; b, b, boundaries of the (primary) lobules.

Magnified 30 diameters.

These smaller or primary lobules are aggregated to form larger secondary lobules—the lobules of descriptive anatomists, and the outlines of which in adults are principally mapped out by lines of pigment.

The lobular structure of the lungs is best shown in the lungs of fœtal animals injected from the trachea or bronchi.

Fig. 422.

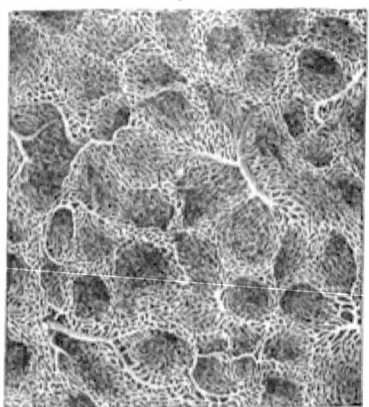

Capillaries of the human lung.
Magnified 60 diameters.

The capillaries of the lungs are extremely

minute and very difficult to inject fully; and the finest injection is required for the purpose.

In the lower vertebrate animals, the structure of the lungs is much simpler than in the higher. Thus in the *Triton* each forms a simple tubular sac, whilst in the frog and toad (Pl. 31. fig. 34) each lung may be compared to a single lobule of a lung of the Mammalia, having a cavity in the centre, with which comparatively few large cells extending into the periphery communicate. The capillaries are also much larger, especially in the two animals last mentioned.

The capillaries may often be well seen in thin sections of the inflated and dried organs. The altered structure of emphysematous lungs may also be best shown by this method.

BIBL. Kölliker, *Mikrosk. Anat.* ii.; Rainey, *Med. Chi. Trans.* xxviii. & xxxi.; Stannius, *Vergl. Anat.*

LUNULARIA, Michel. — A genus of Marchantieæ, growing on the ground in shady places, having the perigones spreading like rays from the top of the receptacle (figs. 329–331, p. 348), which is a mere peduncle, so that an approach is made to the character of Jungermannieæ.

BIBL. Bischoff, *Ueb. Lebermoose, Nova Acta*, xvii. p. 1008; Berkeley, *Crypt. Botany*, p. 442.

LYCOGALA, Mich. — A genus of Myxogastres (Gasteromycetous Fungi), consisting of somewhat globular bodies, verrucose on the outside, composed of a double papery peridium, containing capillitium and spores, growing on rotten wood, &c. *L. epidendrum* varies from the size of a pea to that of a nut, is globular when solitary, deformed when growing in groups, and of a red colour. *L. parietinum* is bluish black, and the peridia do not exceed 1·20″ in diameter.

BIBL. Berk. *Brit. Flor.* ii. pt. 2. p. 307; *Ann. Nat. Hist.* 2 ser. v. p. 365; Grev. *Sc. Crypt. Fl.* pl. 38; Fries, *Syst. Mycol.* iii. 79; *Summ. Veg.* p. 448.

LYCOPODIACEÆ. — This order of Cormophytous Flowerless Plants, which derives its name from the *Lycopodia* or Club-mosses, is difficult to characterize in general terms. The bifurcating branched stem, rooting at each fork by a slender thread-like adventitious root, and the ordinarily small overlapping leaves, distinguish most of the species of *Lycopodium*; but there is considerable variation from this

habit in the *Psiloteæ*, especially in *Isoëtes*, and the nature of the fructification is the only mark generally applicable. The Lycopodiaceæ bear spores which are found in

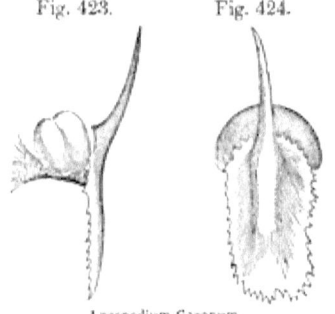

Fig. 423.　　Fig. 424.

Lycopodium Gayanum.

Fig. 423. Scale of spike with axillary sporange; side view.

Fig. 424. The same seen from the outside.

Magnified 20 diameters.

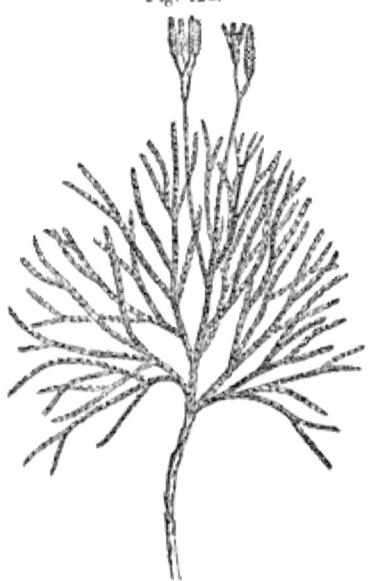

Fig. 425.

Lycopodium complanatum.
One-third the natural size.

small dehiscent cases at the bases of the leaves (figs. 423, 426 & 427), on the upper face or imbedded in it; and these fertile leaves are either scattered all along the

Fig. 426.   Fig. 427.

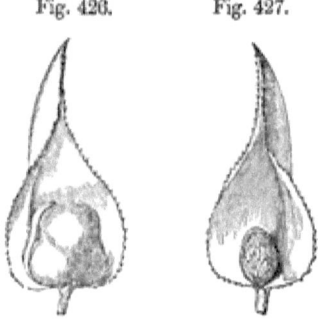

Selaginella apoda.

Fig. 426. Scale with oosporange. Magn. 20 diams.
Fig. 427. Scale with pollen-sporange. Magn. 20 diams.

Fig. 430.

Selaginella cernua.   Half natural size.

stem, or collected into spikes resembling, on a small scale, elongated Pine-cones (figs. 425, 435). The plants of the genus *Lycopodium* proper exhibit both these conditions; but in all these the spores are small and numerous. In *Selaginella*, to which belong the elegant creeping Club-mosses, with flattened leafy stems (often with a metallic lustre), now so much grown in Wardian

cases (fig. 430), the capsular leaves are in spikes, which are found forming one arm of a bifurcation of the stem, while the other continues the vegetative growth; and in these spikes we find the capsules on the lowest scales (*oosporanges*) producing only

Fig. 428.   Fig. 429.

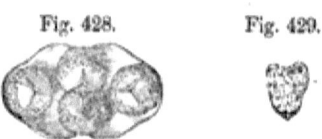

Fig. 428. Oosporange with four large spores. Magn. 20 diams.
Fig. 429. Pollen-sporange burst, containing small spores. Magn. 20 diams.

four spores (figs. 426, 428), of much larger size than those contained in large number in the other spore-cases (*pollen-sporanges*) (figs. 427, 429). In *Lycopodium* and *Selaginella* the sporanges have but one cavity; in *Tmesipteris* the sporanges are two-celled, and in *Psilotum* three-celled. In *Isoëtes* (fig. 376), where all the leaves are seated on a tuberous stem, and most of them fertile, the sporanges containing spores of each kind are many-celled, and immersed in the substance of the bases of the leaves.

The anatomical structure of the stem of the Lycopodieæ is not very complex. There is an outer thickish rind, composed of cellular tissue, and, on cutting across a stem, the ends of isolated fibro-vascular bundles are sometimes seen traversing this; these isolated bundles are merely a portion of those forming a kind of cord running up the centre of the stem, whence they have been sent off to supply the leaves. The fibro-vascular bundles are composed of spiral-fibrous ducts surrounded by elongated cellular tissue (see TISSUES, VEGETABLE), which in large woody stems become lignified by secondary deposits. The roots have also a central fibro-vascular cord, connected with the central cord of the stem. The structure of the little-developed tuberous stem of *Isoëtes* is very different, and exhibits a remarkable mode of growth, forming annual layers of woody structure (see ISOËTES).

The leaves are of very simple structure; but their arrangement exhibits many curious peculiarities. In PSILOTUM, one of the simplest forms, where they are mere minute scales on a widely bifurcated stem, they are alternate; in some *Lycopodia* they are opposite, in others whorled. When the leaves are in whorls, they vary in number, not only in different species, but often in the same species in different localities, or even in the same plant: thus, the arrangement is often different on the main stem and on the branches.

Fig. 432.　　Fig. 431.　　Fig. 433.

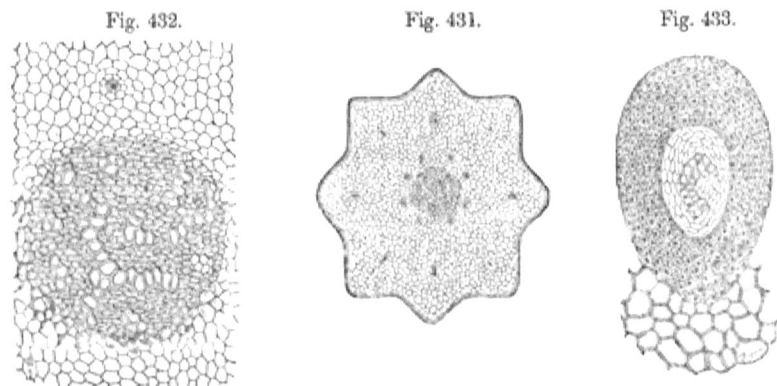

Lycopodium phlegmaria.

Fig. 431. Section of the stem. Magnified 20 diameters.
Fig. 432. The centre of ditto. Magnified 100 diameters.
Fig. 433. One of the isolated bundles of ditto. Magnified 200 diameters.

Fig. 434.　　Fig. 435.　　Fig. 436.

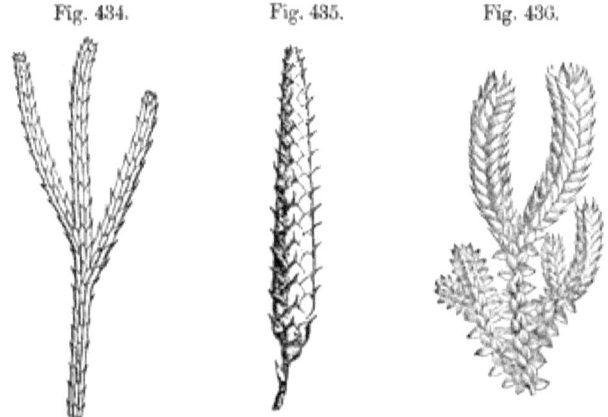

Fig. 434. Lycopodium complanatum. Young shoot.
Fig. 435. Lycopodium lucidulum. Spike of fruit. Magnified 3 diameters.
Fig. 436. Selaginella apoda. Young shoot. Magnified 2 diameters.

When the leaves are opposite, those forming the pairs sometimes differ both in dimensions and form ; in *Lycopodium complanatum* (fig. 434), the pairs of opposite leaves cross alternately at right angles so as to form four rows up the stem ; in two (opposite) rows the leaves are alike and flattened laterally ; of the other two rows, one consists of leaves like the two just described, but flattened against the stem ; and the fourth row (opposite the third) of minute scale-like bodies. In other cases, in *Selaginella apoda* for example (fig. 436), the corresponding leaves of the pairs are unequal, and are so arranged that the smaller lie in two contiguous vertical rows, on the front of the stem, very much resembling the amphigastria of *Hypopterygium* and some of the *Jungermannieæ*. In most of the Lycopodiaceæ the leaves are simple and almost sessile ; but in *Tmesipteris* they have a blade developed into two lobes, and borne on a long stalk, and in *Psilotum* the short scale-like leaf is also divided into two lobes and supported on a petiole. The leaves of *Isoëtes* are again different, consisting of long, quill-like bodies of a delicate structure, composed of large cells; these are aquatic plants with very peculiar habits and characters (see ISOËTES).

The reproduction of the Lycopodiaceæ, upon which much light has recently been thrown, is very curious; it is only accurately understood as yet, however, in the genera *Selaginella* and *Isoëtes*, in which, as above stated, two kinds of spores are known to exist. It is found that when both kinds of spore are sown, the results of their germination are totally distinct. The small dust-like spores burst their outer coat after a time; and the delicate inner membrane, which is protruded, likewise bursts subsequently and discharges extremely minute cellules, in each of which is developed an actively moving spiral filament (spermatozoid) like those of the FERNS. This breaks out and swims about rapidly in the water when seen beneath the microscope.

The large spore exhibits no external change for a period varying from a few weeks to a few months ; but a section shows that a process of cell-formation has commenced in its interior, which results in the production of a kind of disk of cellular tissue in the upper part, beneath that portion of the outer spore-coat which exhibits the three converging ridges produced by the pressure of the four spores in the parent-sac

during their development. At this period the spore appears to have three coats—an outer tough, coloured coat, a second coat lining this, and a third which lines the second over the great cavity of the spore, but at the upper part invests the inside of the newly-formed disk of cellular tissue, which thus lies between the second and third coats. This disk of tissue is a *prothallium*, analogous to the green body developed from the free spores of the FERNS and EQUISETACEÆ. On its upper surface are developed a number of *archegonia* of very simple structure. A cell of the substance of the *prothallium*, taking on the function of an *embryo-sac*, developes a free cell (*embryo-cell*) in its interior ; and the cells between this and the surface become modified and part, so as to leave an intercellular canal between the contiguous angles of four adjoining cells, leading down to the embryo-cell,—the four cells growing up from the surface so as to form a kind of perforated cellular papilla, something like that of the archegone of the Ferns. At a certain stage of this development, the outer coat of the spore bursts at the converging ridges, and the angular flaps resulting turn back and expose the prothallium on the upper surface. One (sometimes two, but as an irregularity) of the embryo-cells is then fertilized by the spiral filaments produced by the small spores (*pollinic spores*), if these exist at the right stage of the development in the vicinity. After this, the embryonal cell undergoes multiplication, first growing down as a cellular filament which breaks through into the great cavity of the spore ; the lower end lying there then increases until it acquires the form of a cellular nodule, which breaks out above and exhibits on its free portion the first adventitious root and the first pair of leaves ; the rootlet makes its way downwards into the soil, and the leaves are gradually elevated on a thread-like stalk, and separate, displaying two terminal buds between them, whence the first bifurcation of the stem proceeds.

This mode of reproduction allies the family very closely to the double-spored Marsileaceæ, and separates them from the Ferns and Equisetaceæ, in which the prothallium is formed outside the spores, after the germination of the single and only kind of spore which these plants possess. But a difficulty still exists with regard to those species of Lycopodiæœ in which only the smaller kind of spore has been met with, such as our common *Lycopodium clavatum*, *inundatum*, &c. No one has yet been able to raise these from the spores, although De Bary has lately observed their earliest stages of germination, in which they form a little cellular nodule. The ultimate fate of this, whether it becomes a prothallium and bears both archegonia and antheridia, as in the Ferns, or forms a solitary archegonium to be fertilized by spermatozoa furnished by an antheridial spore, remains to be determined.

The order Lycopodiaceæ is divided into two families, in accordance with the structure of the sporanges.

Families.

I. LYCOPODIEÆ. Sporanges simple, one-celled.

II. PSILOTEÆ. Sporanges compound, many-celled.

BIBL. Spring, *Monograph. des Lycopodiacées, Mém. Acad. Bruxell.* xv.; Müller, *Entw. der Lycopodiaceen, Bot. Zeit.* iv. 1846 (*Ann. Nat. Hist.* xix. p. 27, &c.); Bischoff, *Krypt. Gew.* Nürnberg, 1828. p. 97; Hofmeister, *Vergleich. Untersuch.* Leipsic, 1851. p. 111, &c.; Mettenius, *Beitr. zur Botanik,* Heidelb. 1850; De Bary, *Ann. des Sc. Nat.* 4 sér. ix. p. 30, *Ann. Nat. Hist.* 3 ser. iii. p. 189. See also ISOËTES.

LYCOPODIEÆ.—A family of Lycopodiaceous plants, distinguished by their simple one-celled sporanges. The existing kinds are all herbs, mostly creeping over the ground; but some of the fossil kinds, met with especially in the Coal-measures, were large trees.

Genera.

1. *Lycopodium*, Linn. Sporanges all of one kind, containing numerous small spores resembling pollen-grains.

2. *Selaginella*, P. de Beauv. Sporanges of two kinds, the greater part resembling those of *Lycopodium*; one, situated at the base of the spikes, larger, often four-lobed, and containing only four large spores.

LYCOPODIUM, Linn.—A genus of Lycopodieæ. This has already been sufficiently characterized under the head of Lycopodiaceæ. There are more than half-a-dozen British species, mostly alpine plants; but *L. inundatum* occurs on bogs in all parts of Britain. The species usually described as *L. selaginoides* has *oosporanges* and *antheridial sporanges*, and belongs to SELAGINELLA.

BIBL. Hook. *Brit. Flora*; Babington, *Man. Brit. Botany*; Francis, *British Ferns*

and their Allies, 5th ed. See also under LYCOPODIACEÆ.

LYGODIUM, Swartz.—A genus of Schizæous Ferns, consisting of beautiful climbing

Fig. 437.

Lygodium reticulatum.

Portion of a leaf, with fertile pinnules. Nat. size.

plants, with conjugate, palmate, lobed or pinnate leaves, having the sessile sporanges in double rows on the teeth of the pinnules

Fig. 438.   Fig. 439.

Lygodium reticulatum.

Fig. 438. Tooth of a pinnule with overlapping indusia. Magn. 20 diams.
Fig. 439. The same, with the indusia removed to show the sporanges. Magn. 20 diams.

(fig. 437), each having a hood-like special indusium (figs. 438, 439).

LYMPHATIC or CONGLOBATE GLANDS.—The structure and functions of these organs are not agreed upon by physiologists.

Each is surrounded by a capsule, consisting of areolar tissue, with numerous scattered fine elastic fibres (nuclear-fibres), and, in animals, unstriated muscular fibres.

The substance of the glands consists of a cortical and a medullary portion.

The cortical portion, which in the larger glands forms a layer about 1·6 to 1·4″ in thickness, exhibits a coarsely granular appearance, visible externally through the capsule. This granular appearance arises from the presence of a large number of septa prolonged from the capsule into the substance of the organ, and dividing it into alveoli; these are about 1-96 to 1-36″ in diameter, and of a rounded or polygonal form; they are more distinct in animals than in man. The septa consist of areolar tissue with a few fine elastic fibres, and numerous delicate spindle-shaped bodies resembling fibro-plastic corpuscles, often anastomosing at their ends.

The contents of the alveoli are greyish white, pulpy, traversed by capillary blood-vessels, and by numerous delicate fibres and plates, composed of spindle-shaped and stellate cells, resembling those found in the septa, but forming a lacunar or spongy tissue. The soft substance consists of free nuclei and rounded cells, resembling those found in the lymph and chyle.

The medullary portion exhibits no septa, but is composed of a plexus of lymphatic vessels closely connected with the efferent vessels, supported by areolar tissue, without elastic fibres, and containing a number of fat-cells.

The afferent lymphatic vessels penetrate the capsule, pass through the septa between the alveoli, and open into their lacunæ, which are not lined with epithelium. From these the lymphatics of the medullary plexus arise, to terminate in the efferent vessel or vessels.

It is supposed by some physiologists that most of the chyle- and lymph-corpuscles are formed in the lymphatic glands, and from a formative blastema poured out by the capillaries of the alveoli.

BIBL. Kölliker, *Mikrosk. Anat.* ii., and the *Bibl.* therein; for the pathology, the works of Förster and Wedl.

LYMPHATICS.—Absorbents or lymph-vessels.

The structure of the lymphatics is much the same as that of the veins, but in some respects it is obscure.

In regard to that of their capillaries, little positive is known. Lymphatics of intermediate and large size consist of three coats. The internal is composed of somewhat elongated epithelial cells, and an elastic reticular layer of longitudinal fibres. The middle coat consists of transverse muscular fibres, with fine elastic fibres also transverse. The outer, areolar coat is composed of longitudinal fibres, with a few reticular elastic fibres, and a larger or smaller number of oblique and longitudinal bundles of unstriated muscular fibres; the latter form a good

distinguishing character of lymphatics from small veins.

The thoracic duct differs somewhat in structure from the lymphatics. Outside the epithelium are some striated layers, next to which is an elastic reticular layer, the fibres being longitudinal; but the entire inner coat is thin. The middle coat consists of an inner very thin longitudinal layer of areolar tissue with fine elastic fibres, and an outer transverse muscular layer, containing also fine elastic fibres. The outer coat contains longitudinal areolar tissue, with elastic fibres and scattered anastomosing longitudinal bundles of muscular fibres.

The valves of the lymphatics agree in structure with those of the veins.

LYNGBYA, Ag.—A genus of Oscillatoriaceæ (Confervoid Algæ), related to *Calothrix* and *Oscillatoria*, distinguished from the former by its stratified habit, from the latter by the long flexile but not oscillating filaments. It contains both freshwater and marine species. Hassall seems to have made strange errors with the plants included under *Lyngbya* in his work on Freshwater Algæ; for *Ulothrix* and *Sphæroplea* belong to a totally distinct group. *L. muralis* (Pl. 4. fig. 10) grows in damp places and in water. *L. copulata*, Hass. probably belongs to the genus. The rest of his species belong apparently to ULOTHRIX. The specific characters are not satisfactory; but we have found what we take to be *L. stagnina*, Kütz. Tab. Phyc. i. pl. 87. fig. 5, and *L. concinnata*, Kütz. *l. c.* pl. 89. fig. 5, in fresh water. *L. speciosa*, *Carmichaelii*, and *ferruginea*, marine species, are figured in Engl. Bot. Supp. Nos. 2926-27 *a* and *b*.

These plants appear to break up into lenticular gonidia; but their reproduction, like that of *Oscillatoria*, is very obscure.

BIBL. Hassall, *Brit. Fr. Alg.* p. 210, pls. 59, 60, 72; Harvey, *Brit. Mar. Alg.* p. 225, pl. 26 E.; Kütz. *Spec. Alg.* p. 279; *Tab. Phyc.* i. pl. 86-90.

LYSIGONIUM. See MELOSIRA.

M.

MACERATION.—The soaking of objects in various menstrua, for the purpose of causing decomposition and solution of portions of structure which are more readily attacked, is an operation frequently had recourse to in the anatomy both of animals and plants. In addition to water, cold and hot, a number of stronger agents are often employed, chiefly oxidizing substances, such as NITRIC ACID, the same with chlorate of potash, &c. Ammonio-oxide of copper dissolves delicate cellulose rapidly, and does not so soon attack woody fibre, &c. See TISSUES.

MACROBIOTUS, Schultze.—A genus of Arachnida, of the order Tardigrada, and family Arctisca.

Char. Head not furnished with appendages ; mouth terminated by a sucker, without palps ; skin soft, with irregular rugæ.

1. *M. Hufelandii* (Pl. 41. fig. 8). Body cylindrical, colourless ; head rounded in front, with minute coloured eye-spots ; sucker, pharyngeal tube, and styles well developed ; œsophageal bulb supported by a solid frame-work of jointed pieces ; legs equal ; claws two, bifid, the point of each again bifid, the movement tolerably quick ; size 1·85 to 1·35".

The most common species ; found upon mosses growing on walls, stones, at the foot of trees, &c.

2. *M. Oberhäuseri.* Dark brown ; colour distributed unsymmetrically in spots, and forming five longitudinal bands ; no eye-spots ; claws three,—one simple, terminal, and forming a short filament—the two others hooked, the interior one double or bifid, the posterior simple ; movement very active ; length 1·100 to 1·85".

3. *M. ursellus.* Claws three, none filamentous.

4. *M. Dujardinii.* Claws two, bifid.

BIBL. Doyère, *Ann. des Sc. Nat.* 2 sér. xiv. xvii. and xviii.; Dujardin, *ibid.* x.

MACROGONIDIA.—A name applied by the Germans to the larger form of ciliated zoospore, found in many Confervoid Algæ, associated with a form much smaller, distinguished as MICROGONIDIA. See ZOOSPORES, and HYDRODICTYON (p. 358).

MACROSPORIUM, Fr.—A supposed genus of Dematiei (Hyphomycetous Fungi), growing upon decaying vegetable matters, corresponding to *Septosporium*, Corda, and *Helmisporium*, Duby. Several species are British. *M. Cheiranthi*, Fr., common on wallflowers and stocks ; *M. Brassicæ*, Berk., on cabbage-leaves ; *M. sarcinula* on gourds ; and *M. concinnum*, on rotting decorticated willow twigs. We have found one species among the OIDIUM of the vine-fungus.

Tulasne asserts that they are stylosporous fruits of a Sphæriaceous genus.

BIBL. Berk. *Brit. Flor.* ii. pt. 2. p. 339; *Ann. Nat. Hist.* i. p. 261, pl. 8. fig. 10, vi. p. 435, pl. 12. fig. 21 ; Fries, *Summa Veget.*

p. 501 ; *Syst. Mycol.* iii. p. 274 ; Corda, *Icones Fung.* i. pp. 175, 176, 188 ; Tulasne, *Ann. des Sc. Nat.* 4 sér. v. p. 109.

Fig. 440.

Macrosporium bulbotrichum.
Magnified 200 diams.

MACROTHRIX, Baird.—A genus of Entomostraca, of the order Cladocera and family Daphniadæ.

Char. Five pairs of legs ; beak directed forwards ; superior antennæ of considerable size, one-jointed, and pendulous from the beak ; inferior antennæ two-branched, posterior branch four-, anterior three-jointed, and with a very long filament arising from the end of the first joint ; a black spot at the root of the superior antennæ.

1. *M. laticornis* (Pl. 14. fig. 25). Shell oval, smooth, anterior margin strongly ciliated ; eye areolar.

Found in ponds.

2. *M. roseus.* Eye without an areola ; superior antennæ longer and more slender than in the above.

Probably a variety of the last. Found in Scotland.

BIBL. Baird, *Brit. Entomostr.* p. 103.

MADOTHECA, Dumortier (*Jungermannia*, L.).—A genus of Jungermannieæ (Hepaticæ), containing two British species, one, *M. platyphylla* (fig. 441), common on walls, rocks, and trees ; the other, *M. lævigata*, found on alpine rocks. The sporange is borne on a short stalk, globose, and bursts by four convex valves, from which the elaters are quite free. The globose persistent epigone is seen in the figure inside the two-lipped perigone.

Fig. 441.

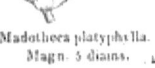

Madotheca platyphylla.
Magn. 5 diams.

BIBL. Endl. *Gen. Plant. Suppl.* i. p. 1341; Hooker, *Brit. Flora*, ii. p. 125, *Brit. Jungermann.* pls. 35, 40, and Supp. pl. 3; Ekart, *Synops. Jungermann.* p. 52, pl. 3. fig. 24, pl. 6. fig. 44.

MAGNESIA, SALTS OF.

Ammonio-phosphate of magnesia or triple phosphate. This salt is frequently met with in animal secretions which have undergone decomposition, also in calculi. The most common forms are prismatic, and figured in the group *a*, Pl. 9. fig. 1; but their varieties are endless. Those of the above group are frequent in decomposing urine, blood, fæces, &c. Those in group *c* are occasional in urine. Those of group *d* are found in the contents of the vesiculæ seminales. The forms *e* and *f* are rare. Fig. 2 *a, b*, represents the so-called penniform crystals, or rather groups of crystals (prisms) occasionally found in urine. Fig. 3 represents the stellate form, occasionally found in urine; sometimes the minute and imperfectly formed crystals of fig. 4 are met with in the same liquid.

The crystals belong to the rhombic system. The prismatic crystals were formerly considered as consisting of a neutral, and the feathery of a bibasic salt; but the composition of the two is the same, and the variation in form depends upon the conditions under which they are produced.

The prismatic forms may be prepared by allowing urine to decompose spontaneously; or by diluting this secretion with water, and gradually stirring-in very dilute solution of ammonia in small quantities at a time; the penniform crystals by adding excess of solution of ammonia to very dilute solutions of the phosphate of ammonia and sulphate of magnesia; and the feathery forms by adding excess of ammonia to urine. The prismatic crystals form a beautiful polarizing object.

Sulphate of magnesia (Epsom salt). When crystallized upon a slide from an aqueous solution, the prisms of this salt, mounted in balsam, form an interesting polarizing object; they are also analytic.

Urate of magnesia. See URIC ACID.

BIBL. That of CHEMISTRY, ANIMAL, and *Phil. Mag.* 1852. iii. p. 373.

MAGNIFYING POWER.—The method of determining the magnifying power of a microscope is given under MEASUREMENT.

MAHOGANY.—The wood of various species of *Swietenia* (Nat. Ord. Cedrelaceæ). Cross sections of this well-known wood form good objects for showing the structure of WOOD with low power.

MAIZE.—Indian corn, *Zea Mays*. L.—One of the family of Grasses producing seeds used as corn. The seeds, or rather caryopses, are remarkably firm, being of a horny texture in the outer part of the substance, while the central mass is more or less brittle and soft. The solidity of the grain results from the outer cells of the albumen being densely filled with starch-grains (Pl. 36. fig. 3), which, by pressure, assume a parenchymatous form and cohere together firmly. In the centre they are loosely packed in the cells, and then are of rounded forms (fig. 5). Figs. 1 to 4 represent successive stages of development of the starch-grains in the protoplasmic mass, originally filling the cells but finally almost wholly displaced. See STARCH.

MALACOSTOMUM, Werneck.—A genus of Rotatoria.

The (three) species correspond to *Notommata* without teeth, but require further examination.

BIBL. Werneck, *Ber. d. Berl. Akad.* 1841. p. 377.

MALPIGHIAN BODIES. See KIDNEY.

MANDIOC or MANIHOT. See CASSAVA.

MANILLA HEMP.—One of the most delicate of vegetable fibres used for textile fabrics, yielded by the liber of the fibro-vascular bundles of *Musa textilis*, a kind of banana common in the Philippine Islands (Pl. 21. fig. 7). It is manufactured into " Manilla handkerchiefs " and " Manilla scarfs," consisting of a delicate muslin. These are often erroneously stated to be made of the fibre of some kind of Pine-apple. See TEXTILE SUBSTANCES.

BIBL. *Hooker's Journal of Botany*, vol. i. 28. 1849.

MARANTACEÆ.—A family of Monocotyledonous Flowering plants, to which belong the true West Indian arrow-root plants (see ARROW ROOT), and the Tous-les-mois plants, species of CANNA. These substances consist of the starch (Pl. 36. figs. 18, 25, & 26) obtained from the tuberous rhizomes of the plants (see STARCH).

Fig. 442.　　　　　Fig. 443.

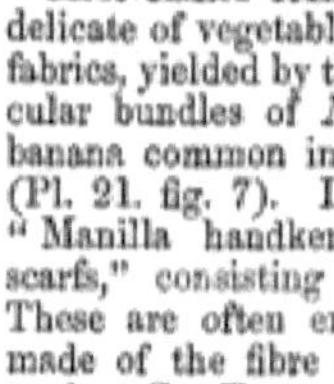

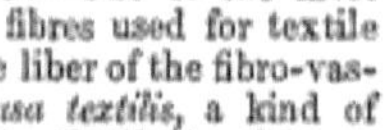

Marattia.

Fig. 442. Side view of a sorus.
Fig. 443. Indusium with the sorus removed.
Magnified 12 diams.

MARATTIA, Swartz.—The typical genus of Marattiaceous Ferns. Exotic (figs. 442 & 443).

MARATTIACEÆ.—A family of Ferns, approaching the Polypodiaceæ in general habit, but more resembling the Ophioglossaceæ in their sporanges, which are destitute of an annulus, and often so fused together as to look like a multilocular sac.

Illustrative Genera.

1. *Angiopteris.* Sporangia in two rows near the apex of transverse veins, distinct, forming linear sori, opening by a slit on the outer side. No indusium.

2. *Kaulfussia.* Sporangia placed on the anastomoses of the veins, radiately connate, forming roundish sori, opening by a slit at the apex.

3. *Marattia.* Sporangia in two rows near the apex of transverse veins, connate, forming oblong sori, gaping transversely by a vertical slit. Indusia connate with the sori (figs. 442, 443).

4. *Eupotium.* Sporangia as in *Marattia*, but pedicellate.

5. *Danæa.* Sporangia in two rows, near the transverse veins, connate into linear sori, opening by a pore. Indusia superficial, encircling the sori (fig. 156, page 206).

MARCHANTIA, Micheli.—A genus of Marchantieæ (Hepaticæ). The most common species, *M. polymorpha,* may be taken as a type at once of this genus and of the family. It is a little plant, not uncommon upon the earth of damp shady courtyards, the borders of springs, &c., extending itself in bright-green thin lamellæ of irre-

dermis, with an intermediate parenchyma; and the lobes are traversed by a kind of midrib. The upper surface is marked by raised lines which cross each other very regularly, leaving between them lozenge-shaped spaces (fig. 444), in the centre of each of which occurs a stoma, leading to an intercellular space in the parenchyma. The stomata of *Marchantia* are circular, and consist of sixteen cells, arranged so as to form four rings, one upon another, each ring being composed of four cells; they may be best explained by comparing them with a chimney composed of four courses of bricks, each consisting of four bricks laid together to enclose a square. The parenchyma is composed of several layers of cells, which contain much chlorophyll. The inferior epidermis is clothed by radical hairs, which exhibit a remarkable spiral marking, arising from the projection of a spirally deposited secondary layer in the interior of the tube.

The fronds do not readily produce sporanges in shady places; but when exposed to the light, these are produced at the ends of the ribs, at the base of the terminal notches of the lobes. The male structures are produced on different plants from the female; but both are borne on peculiar stalked receptacles. The first appearance of one of these receptacles is as a little green papilla surrounded by reddish scales, at the end of one of the principal ribs. As it enlarges, it pushes its way through the scales; and the rib on which it is borne elongates to form a pedicel, on which it is raised up perpendicularly above the surface of the frond,

Fig. 444.

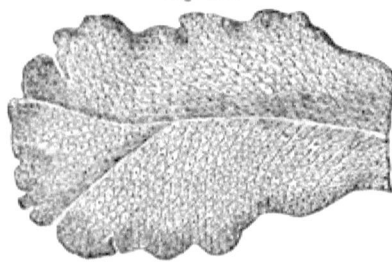

Marchantia polymorpha.
Lobe of a frond.
Magnified 10 diameters.

Fig. 445.

Marchantia polymorpha.
Plant with antheridial receptacles.
Nat. size.

gular lobed outline, attached to the soil by radical hairs arising on the lower surface. The frond presents an upper and lower epi-

ultimately acquiring the form of an expanded cap, in the male receptacles with a sinuate margin (fig. 445), in the female with the border developed into eight or nine thick cylindrical lobes (fig. 446).

Fig. 446.

Marchantia polymorpha.
Plant with fertile receptacles.
Nat. size.

The male receptacle is concave above, with papillæ consisting of the mouths of flask-shaped cavities, in each of which is formed an *antheridium* (fig. 447). These antheridia are oval cellular bodies lodged in the expansion of the cavity, with a long neck projecting upward through the mouth of the flask-shaped excavation. The cells of the interior of the lower part of the an-

Fig. 447.

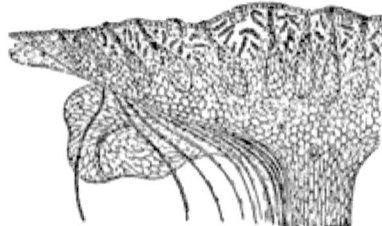

Marchantia polymorpha.
Section through an antheridial receptacle, showing the flask-shaped cavities containing the antheridia.
Magnified 25 diameters.

theridia produce spermatozoids (Pl. 32. fig. 32). The lower surface of the receptacle is clothed by membranous processes and hairs.

The female receptacles are somewhat convex above; and on the under surface of the base of each lobe are found delicate membranous processes with toothed margins. The membranes of each two adjoining lobes form a *perichætium* (fig. 448) alternating with the lobes, concealing between them the *archegonia*, which are at-

tached by their bases, and have their mouths pointing downwards. The archegones of

Fig. 448.

Marchantia polymorpha.
A sporangial receptacle seen from below.
Magnified 5 diameters.

Marchantia are flask-shaped sacs with a long neck (figs. 325–327, p. 347), containing in their cavity a cell (germ-cell), which after fertilization becomes developed into an oval cellular body, the young *sporangium*. In the course of the development of this, it soon fills the cavity of the archegone, which then begins to grow with it, and subsequently forms a loose sac around it—the *epigonium*—finally ruptured at the point, so as to exhibit four or five teeth or valves, which become recurved (fig. 449). Mean-

Fig. 449.

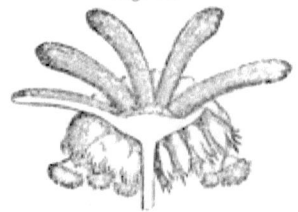

Marchantia polymorpha.
Vertical section of Fig. 448, showing sporanges *in situ*, bursting to discharge the spores and elaters.
Magnified 10 diameters.

while another envelope grows up around the epigone, appearing at first as a mere ring surrounding it (figs. 325–327, p. 347), but ultimately rising up so as to enclose it, remaining open however at the summit; this is the *perigonium*. In its young stages the sporange is a mere oval mass of polygonal cells; but soon may be detected a distinction between a cortical or peripheral layer and the internal mass. The cells of the former remain firmly united into a membrane forming the wall of the sporange. These cells grow so as to assume an elongated form, and when mature exhibit internally a spiral-fibrous secondary deposit (Pl. 32. fig. 35), analogous to that of the cells of the anthers of Flowering plants. The cells of the internal mass present at an early period the appearance of a large number of filaments radiating from the centre of the sporange to the wall. These soon become free from each other; and it may then be perceived that some are of very slender diameter, and others three or four times as thick. The slender ones are developed at once into the long *elaters* (Pl. 32. fig. 36) characteristic of this genus, containing a double spiral fibre, the two fibres, however, coalescing into one at the ends (fig. 37). The thicker filaments become subdivided by cross partitions, and break up into squarish free cells, which are the parent cells of the *spores*, four of which are produced in each (Pl. 38. figs. 10–13). The spores of *M. polymorpha* have but a single coat; and their contents are bright yellow when mature. When they germinate, the contents are converted into chlorophyll; and the growth commences by the production of a tubular process from one side of the spore.

It has been mentioned that *M. polymorpha* does not fruit freely in the shade. Under these circumstances it produces *gemmæ*, consisting of little, compressed, oblong masses of cells, of green colour, capable of reproducing the plant. These are found,

Fig. 450.

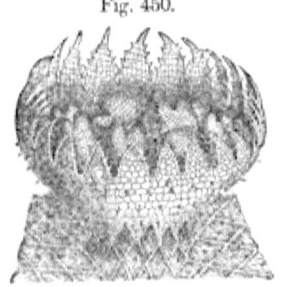

Marchantia polymorpha.
A collection of gemmæ in their involucre.
Magnified 25 diameters.

when mature, in elegant cup-like structures, with toothed borders, sessile on the upper face of the frond (figs. 446, 450). The cup seems to be formed by a development of the superior epidermis, which is raised up and finally bursts and spreads out, laying bare the gemmæ, produced from the internal parenchyma. The gemmæ consist at first of a single cell, which divides so as to present an upper and a lower (stalk-) cell; the upper multiplies until it becomes a cellular mass (fig. 451). The

Fig. 451.

Marchantia polymorpha.
A vertical section of the same, with nascent gemmæ.
Magnified 50 diameters.

development of this structure presents much analogy to that of the sori of the Ferns with their indusia and sporanges.

The *Marchantiæ* also increase by *innovations*, or lobes of the frond becoming detached from those on which they originate.

These plants form most interesting objects of microscopic investigation, in all parts of their structure.

BIBL. Hook. *Brit. Flor.* ii. pt. 1. p. 105; *Engl. Botany*, pl. 110; Mirbel, *Rech. anat. et physiol. sur le Marchantia, Mémoires Acad. Roy. Paris*, xiii. pp. 337, 375; Nägeli, *Wurzel-haare du Marchantia, Linnæa*, xvi. 1842; Henfrey, *Dev. of Spores and Elaters* of *Marchantia, Linn. Trans.* xx. p. 103, pl. 11; Thuret, *Rech. sur les Antheridies, Ann. des Sc. Nat.* 3 sér. xvi. p. 72, pl. 12. figs. 1–5; Gottsche, *Bot. Zeitung*, 1858, *Suppl.*

MARCHANTIEÆ.—A family of Liverworts or Hepaticæ, having broadish, lobed, thalloid fronds, from the bifurcations of which arise stalked receptacles, bearing a number of variously arranged sporanges containing spores mingled with elaters, but destitute of a columella.

British Genera.

1. *Marchantia.* The fructiferous head of the receptacle radiating. Perichætes having from one to six archegonia, alternating with the rays of the fruit-head. Perigone 4–5-

lobed. Epigone persistent. Sporange bursting with teeth, which are at length revolute.

2. *Fegatella.* Fructiferous head scarcely thickened, umbonate. Perichæte absent. Perigones tubular, obliquely split at the apex, connate with each other and confused with the axis. Epigone persistent. Sporange bursting with five or eight teeth, at length revolute.

3. *Rebouillia.* Fructiferous head conical, somewhat 5-lobed. Perichæte wanting. Perigones bursting by a longitudinal slit; distinct, adnate to the axis. Epigone persistent. Sporange bursting irregularly at the apex.

4. *Lunularia.* Fructiferous head of receptacle scarcely thickened. Perichæte wanting. Perigones tubular, truncate, distinct, soldered to the axis. Epigone persistent. Sporanges four to eight, 4–8-valved.

See HEPATICÆ.

MARGARIC ACID and MARGARINE. —The former general ingredient of the fatty matters of both the animal and vegetable kingdom, when crystallized from hot alcohol, forms minute needles, either isolated or in groups (Pl. 7. fig. 16 a). The crystals differ from those of stearic acid, which form lanceolate single or aggregated plates (Pl. 7. fig. 16 b).

Margarine crystallizes from a hot alcoholic solution in fine needles, mostly grouped or branched, sometimes surrounding globules of oleine, or forming bulb-like aggregations of needles (Pl. 7. fig. 15). It is sometimes found crystallized within the cells of fatty tissue (Pl. 7. fig. 15 a).

BIBL. That of CHEMISTRY.

MARGINARIA, Bory. — A genus of Polypodieæ (Polypodioid Ferns), with the naked sori imbedded deeply in the backs of the veins and venules. The sporanges are borne on long pedicels, and are intermixed with articulated paraphyses.

MARGINULINA, D'Orb.—A genus of Foraminifera, of the order Stichostegia, and family Æquilateralidæ.

Char. Shell equilateral, elongate, curved, the first chambers often curved or spiral; chambers globular, partly embracing, the last always convex, often narrowed and prolonged; orifice rounded, mostly placed at the end of the prolongation, not central, but on the same side as the convexity.

Williamson unites this genus with *Cristellaria.*

Some British species, both recent and fossil.

M. pedum, D'Orb. (Pl. 18. fig. 9) ; *M. raphanus,* Ehr. (Pl. 18. fig. 10).

MARSILEA, L.—A genus of Marsileaceæ (Flowerless Plants), growing in mud, by a creeping rhizome, from which arise erect filiform leaf-stalks, supporting a compound four-lobed blade ; at the bases of the leaf-stalks arise also stalked capsules, chambered in the interior, being divided by one perpendicular and many horizontal septa ; in these chambers are found sacs (sporanges) containing the spores. The spores are of two kinds, the larger representing ovules, the smaller pollen; but while the former produce a single archegone in germination, like those of *Pilularia,* the pollen-spores produce numerous vesicles in their interior, which become the parent cells of spermatozoids. The capsules of *Marsilea quadrifolia* have a regular dehiscence when ripe; and the whole mass of the spore-sacs is extruded on a thick gelatinous stalk-like process produced from the interior. As this plant is not native in this country, we do not enter very minutely into its characters, especially as in all essential respects it agrees with PILULARIA.

BIBL. See MARSILEACEÆ.

MARSILEACEÆ.—A family of Flowerless plants possessing a distinct leafy stem ; composed of a small number of plants, of minute dimensions, but of great interest in a physiological point of view. They are all aquatics, some growing in the mud in and around ponds, others floating on the surface of stagnant waters. Known perhaps only to the botanist, they are distinguished from the families to which their reproductive structures ally them most closely, by the much more perfect separation of these from the vegetative structure. They all bear distinct spore-fruits or sporocarps, seated on a stalk arising from the stem. These contain sporanges or spore-sacs, differently arranged in the different genera, but agreeing in this respect, that they contain spores of two kinds, analogous to the two kinds of spore in Lycopodiaceæ, but differing in their mode of development.

Pilularia globulifera is the only British representative of this family ; a description of its organization is given under the head of PILULARIA. It agrees with *Marsilea,* a genus occurring on the continent, in possessing only one kind of sporocarp, which contains spore-sacs, part of which contain *ovulary spores*, part *pollen-spores*,—the principal difference being that the sporocarps are of more complex structure in *Marsilea*. *Salvinia*, consisting of floating aquatic plants, possesses two kinds of sporocarp, which may be called male and female, and the same is the case with *Azolla*; the development of the plants of the last genus, however, has not yet been thoroughly elucidated.

The principal characteristics, in which all these plants agree, consist in the possession of free stalked sporocarps, quite distinct from the leaves, and the production of two kinds of spore, which agree in the history of development. The small spores produce *spermatozoids*, formed in vesicles developed in chambers into which the spores become divided in germination. The large spores, which are more highly organized than those of LYCOPODIACEÆ, produce in germination a *prothallium*, somewhat like that of Lycopodiaceæ, inside the outer coat of the spore, on which is developed a single *archegonium* in *Pilularia* and *Marsilea*, several *archegonia* in *Salvinia*. The conditions in *Azolla* at this stage are unknown. The germ-cell of the *archegonium*, fertilized apparently by the spermatozoids, becomes developed *in situ* into the new leafy plant, which was thus formerly regarded as a product of the simple germination of the spore. More detailed particulars are given under the heads of the genera. The distinctive characters of the genera may be given as follows:

Genera.

* *Stems creeping over mud, rooting; sporocarps of one kind, containing spore-sacs of each kind.*

1. *Pilularia.* Leaves filiform. Sporocarps globular, almost sessile, four-celled, containing the two kinds of spores in distinct sacs.

2. *Marsilea.* Leaves cruciately four-lobed; lobes obcordate. Sporocarps stalked, two-celled, the two cells divided transversely into many smaller cells.

** *Plants floating like Duckweed; sporocarps of two kinds.*

3. *Salvinia.* Leaves opposite, small, glandular, floating. Sporocarps on submerged leafless branches, globular, with a double wall and a central sporophore; some containing racemosely-stalked sacs filled with barren spores, others many simple stalked sacs containing each a solitary fertile spore.

4. *Azolla.* Leaves alternate, imbricated.

Sporocarps submerged, unlike externally:—1. Stalked membranous sacs, irregularly dehiscent, containing stalked sacs filled with barren spores; 2. sessile solitary or twin cellular bodies, each consisting of a highly developed fertile spore, approximating to the condition of an ovule.

BIBL. Bischoff, *Krypt. Gewachse*, Nuremberg, 1828, p. 63; Esprit Fabre, *Ann. des Sc. Nat.* 2 sér. vii. p. 221, pls. 12 & 13; Nägeli, *Zeitschr. für Wiss. Bot.* Heft 1. p. 168; *Ann. des Sc. Nat.* 3 sér. ix. p. 99, pl. 8; Mettenius, *Beitr. z. Kenntn. d. Rhizocarpen*, Frankfort, 1846; *Ueb. Azolla, Linnæa*, xx. (1847); *Ann. des Sc. Nat.* 3 sér. ix. p. 111; Schleiden, *Grundz. d. Wiss. Bot.* 3 ed. p. 104 (transl. *Principles*, p. 203); Meyen, *Beitr. z. Kenntn. der Azollen*, *Nova Acta*, xviii. p. 507; Hofmeister, *Vergleich. Unters.* p. 103, pls. 21 & 22; W. Griffith, *on Azolla, Calcutta Journal of Nat. History*, July, 1844; R. Brown, *on Azolla, Flinder's Voyage, Botany*, 612, pl. x.; Henfrey, *Trans. Brit. Ass.* 1851; *Ann. Nat. Hist.* 2 ser. ix. p. 447.

MASTIGOBRYUM. See HEPATICUM.

MASTIGOCERCA, Ehr.—A genus of Rotatoria, of the family Euchlanidota.

Char. Eye single and cervical; tail-like foot styliform; carapace prismatic, with a dorsal crest.

M. carinata (Pl. 34. fig. 46, side view). Foot as long as the body; aquatic; entire length 1-72".

BIBL. Ehrenberg, *Infus.* p. 400.

MASTOGLOIA, Thwaites.—A genus of Diatomaceæ.

Distinguished by the *Navicula*-like frustules, the hoops of which are furnished with loculi, immersed in a mammillate frond.

Five British species, marine and aquatic.

M. lanceolata (Pl. 42. fig. 22). Valves lanceolate, elliptical, ends acute; loculi 8–30; in brackish water.

M. Danseii = Dickieia Danseii, Thw.

BIBL. Smith, *Brit. Diat.* ii. 63; Thwaites, *ibid.* and *Ann. Nat. Hist.* 1848, i. 171.

MASTOGONIA, Ehr.—A fossil genus of doubtful Diatomaceæ.

Char. Frustules single; valves dissimilar, angular, mammiform, orbicular at the base, free from umbilical processes, not cellular, angles radiating.

The (eight) species are interesting from the structure of the two valves of the frustules differing. Thus in one, *M. crux* (Pl. 43. fig. 23 *a*) the angles and rays are four in one valve, but seven in the other; in *M. actinoptychus* (Pl. 43. fig. 23 *b*) the angles and rays are nine in one valve, and thirteen in the other, and so on. Diameter from 1-1600 to 1-300".

M. hexagona (Pl. 43. fig. 25).

BIBL. Ehrenberg, *Ber. d. Berl. Akad.* 1844; Kützing, *Sp. Alg.* p. 25.

MATONIA, R. Brown. — A genus of Aspidieæ (Polypodioid Ferns) with a curious stalked and imbricate basin-like indusium (figs. 453, 454). Exotic.

Fig. 452.

Fig. 453. Fig. 454.

Matonia pectinata.

Fig. 452. Part of a fertile pinna. Magn. 3 diams.

Fig. 453. Indusium opened at the side, showing thecæ *in situ.* Magn. 25 diams.

Fig. 454. The same with the thecæ removed. Magn. 25 diams.

MAURANDYA.—A genus of Scrophulariaceæ (Dicotyledonous Flowering Plants), the testa of the seed of which is composed of cells with spiral fibrous deposits, forming an elegant microscopic object.

MEASUREMENT and MEASURES.—In this article we shall consider the method of measuring the magnifying power of a microscope, of ascertaining the dimensions of objects, and shall give a sketch of the standard measures in which the dimensions of objects are expressed.

Measurement of the magnifying power of a microscope.—The apparent size which an object will appear to possess under a microscope will vary of course according to the power of the object-glass and of the eyepiece used, and the length of the body of the microscope; and it is a good plan to determine the measurements once for all in the case of the various object-glasses and eyepieces, keeping them written upon a card, so that they may be readily accessible.

The apparatus requisite consists of a micrometer-slide graduated into thousandths of an inch, each tenth division being marked by a longer line; or two separate slides, one graduated into thousandths, the other into hundredths of an inch; and an ivory scale, graduated into inches, tenths, and hundredths.

The simplest method is that by double sight, as it is called. The micrometer-slide is placed upon the stage, the lines brought into focus, and the image of one of the interspaces, as seen upon the stage with the open eye not used in looking through the microscope, is measured with compasses. By then dividing the measure of the image of the space by the known measure of the unmagnified space, the quotient is the required magnifying power. Thus, if the space on the micrometer scale is equal to the 1-100th of an inch, and the image of the magnified space corresponds to 5-10ths of an inch, the space is magnified 50 times : $\frac{5}{10} \div \frac{1}{100} = 50$.

The same result may be obtained with the aid of the camera lucida, by placing the microscope horizontally, and its axis at a distance from the table equal to the distance between the focus of the eyepiece and the stage; the breadth of the image of a division is then measured as before; and this is the best and most certain method.

A most important point in relation to this subject is, that the joint of the microscope shall be furnished with a stop or pin (INTR. p. xiii), by which the body may be placed horizontally at once, so that all objects which are drawn under the same object-glass and eyepiece may be magnified to the same extent, the degree being determined by the second of the above methods.

The obvious use of being acquainted with the magnifying power of a microscope is that objects under examination may be viewed by the same power as that with which figures of them have been made, so that the structure or appearance of the objects in the two cases may be compared. We have elsewhere stated the importance of expressing the magnifying power with which figures of objects have been drawn (INTR. p. xxxix).

In the above estimation of the magnifying power, one dimension only is taken into account, viz. the breadth or diameter ; and this is the ordinary manner in which the magnifying power is taken ; objects are then said to be magnified so many diameters, or so many times linear. But objects are really as much magnified in the other dimension, or in their entire surface ; so that the true expression of the amplification would be given by multiplying that in one direction by that in the other, or by itself, *i. e.* squaring the linear magnifying power. This is called the superficial measurement.

This proceeding, however, offers no advantage, and is not in accordance with custom, either in regard to the microscope or objects in general. It is therefore never used except for fraudulent purposes, to delude the unwary in the purchase of an instrument ; thus supposing a microscope to magnify 40 diameters, $40 \times 40 = 1600$ would express the magnifying power in superficial measure.

Measurement of the size of objects.—This is effected with the aid of a slide-micrometer passed through two slits in the eyepiece above the stop, and at the focus of the upper glass of the eyepiece. The breadth of the spaces between the lines must be such as to give an even and minute fraction of an inch. The value of the spaces will vary with the power of the object-glass and eyepiece, so that it must be determined in each case respectively, and recorded. For measuring small objects, the breadth of the spaces in the eyepiece micrometer may be such that twenty of them correspond to 1-1000th of an inch in the stage-micrometer slide, so that the value of each division will be the 1-20,000th part of an inch. It is seldom that we have to measure objects so small as this ; but the small size is of great advantage, because in most cases it will happen that the margins of the objects will coincide exactly with some of the lines, whereby the chance of error in computation will be avoided. For larger objects, the spaces of the eyepiece micrometer may be coarser.

The method of measuring scarcely requires further explanation. Supposing, however, that the divisions of the stage-micrometer are equal to 1-1000th of an inch, and those of the eyepiece micrometer equal to 1-20,000th of an inch, *i. e.* twenty of them cover one space in the former, an object brought into focus and covering five of the spaces of the eyepiece micrometer, will be 1-4000th of an inch in diameter ; and so for other dimensions.

When the objects are large, the compasses and the ivory scale will suffice for their measurement ; but sometimes this may be conveniently done under a low power, for the 1-100ths of an inch are not very clearly discernible to all eyes.

In measuring objects, they must be covered with thin glass, and not immersed in too much liquid.

It is a matter of great difficulty, under high powers, to adjust accurately the divisions of the eyepiece micrometer to those of the stage-micrometer, or to the margins of objects, by means of the moveable stage ; a very ingenious apparatus has been contrived by Mr. Jackson to overcome the difficulty. It consists of a little brass frame, in which the eyepiece micrometer slides from side to side, the motion being communicated by the end of a screw working against one end of the slide, and resisted at the other by a spring ; and as the magnifying power with which the divisions of the eyepiece micrometer are viewed is small, the adjustment is easily and accurately effected.

Other micrometers, as the 'cobweb-micrometer,' are made ; but as they are very expensive and not necessary, we shall pass them over.

Some authors express the measurement of objects by means of a ruled scale appended to the figures or plates of them, the scale consisting of divisions of a stage-micrometer of known value traced off under the same power as the objects themselves ; or sometimes the divisions are ruled over the figures. These methods are very objectionable, because the size of the objects cannot be ascertained without measuring with compasses and calculation, which is almost as bad as the size being omitted altogether.

Whenever figures of objects are given, the magnifying power with which they are drawn should always be expressed in numbers near the figures. Many or even most authors omit all notice of dimensions, so that whether an object figured be as large as an ox or as small as a mite, is known only to themselves and their friends ; the student will find for himself this to be the greatest difficulty in identifying objects in the study of natural history, because the visible structure of objects varies according to the power under which these are seen. Other writers state the magnifying power in a note in the substance of the book, or in some obscure and inconvenient place.

Measures.—The measures in which the dimensions of objects are expressed should consist of parts of an English inch, and not of a line. On the continent, fractions of a millimetre, of a Paris or French line, and of a Rhenish or Prussian line are used. When fractions of a millimetre are adopted, this is usually denoted by the addition of ^{mm} to the figure or figures. In France the millimetre and the Paris line are both used; in Germany fractions of a line are expressed; but whether this is the Paris line or the Prussian line, we have never seen stated in any of the works, although we believe the Paris line to be generally signified.

The following data will be found useful in reducing the foreign to the English measures :—

A millimetre = 0·0393707 English inch; or (roughly) rather less than 1-25th of an English inch.

A centimetre = 0·393707 Eng. inch; or (roughly) rather more than 1-3rd Eng. inch.

A Paris line = 0·088815 Eng. inch; or rather more than 1-11th Eng. inch, to which vulgar fraction it is nearest.

To convert a foreign into the English measure, the former must be multiplied by its unit value; thus, 0·25^{mm} (millimetre) × 0·0393707 = 0·009842675 Engl. inch. But in most cases a few decimal places only need be observed. In this way, however, we get a rather long sum, which may be avoided by the use of the following Table,

Table for conversion of foreign into English measures.

	Millimetres into English inches.	Old Paris lines into English inches.	Prussian lines into English inches.
1	·039370	·088815	·085817
2	·078741	·177630	·171633
3	·118112	·266445	·25745
4	·157483	·355260	·343267
5	·196853	·444075	·429083
6	·236224	·532890	·51490
7	·275595	·621705	·600717
8	·314966	·710520	·686532
9	·354337	·799335	·77235

in which the numbers in the first (or left-hand) column correspond to the denominations expressed in the uppermost (head) line of the three broader columns, while the fractions opposite these numbers denote their values in parts of the denominations of the lowermost (head) line. Thus, 1^{mm} = 0·039370 Eng. inch; 3^{mm} = 0·118112; 2 Prussian lines = 0·171633 Eng. inch, and so on. In using this Table, the decimal fraction to be converted into parts of an English inch must be broken up into its decimal parts, and each valued separately from the Table; thus, to convert 0·75^{mm} into a fraction of an English inch—

$$0·7^{mm} = 0·0275595$$
$$0·05^{mm} = 0·00196853$$ } (by the Table).

$$0·75^{mm} = 0·02952803 \text{ Eng. inch.}$$

The only circumstance which requires attention in the use of this Table is the position of the decimal point. Thus, in the above measure of 0·75^{mm}, which, when broken up, makes 0·7^{mm} and 0·05^{mm}, if the first value (0·7) had been 7·0, the value in Eng. inch would have been, according to the Table, 0·275595 Eng. inch; but this is 10 times too much, or =7 whole millimetres; hence the shifting of the decimal point, and so on. To express the mode of proceeding by rule,—the decimal point in the fraction of an English inch given by the Table should be shifted to the left, and as many ciphers added as there are decimal places in the foreign measure.

Throughout this work the foot and inch and their fractional parts are expressed for brevity by placing respectively one or two acute accents on their right side; thus, one foot is denoted by 1', and one inch by 1", $\frac{1}{10}$th of an inch by 1-10", &c.

Bibl. That in the Introduction, p. xl; Robertson, *Edinb. Monthly Journ.* 1852. p. 95; Harting, *ibid.* p. 453.

MEDULLA of Plants.—The name applied by the older authors to the pith of

Fig. 455.

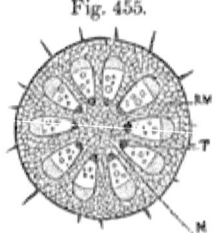

Horizontal section of a yearling shoot of a Dicotyledon. M, medulla; , RM medullary rays; T, medullary sheath. Magnified 25 diameters.

Dicotyledons (fig. 455 M), from a supposed analogy with the *medulla spinalis* of animals,

It affords very excellent subjects for preparing sections of regular parenchymatous tissues, as in the elder, and in the tall annual stems of many of the larger perennial herbaceous plants. It sometimes becomes curiously chambered as it grows older, as in the walnut and the jasmine; very frequently, however, it decays away after a time, leaving the centre of the stem hollow. The same hollow condition occurs early in fistular stems, such as those of the Umbelliferæ, from the pith being torn up by rapid expansion of the wood. The Monocotyledons do not generally possess a definite pith; the cellular mass, in which the isolated FIBRO-VASCULAR BUNDLES are imbedded, answers to a diffused pith, or rather to the pith and medullary rays collectively. It may be seen well in sections of the flowering stem of lilies (fig. 456 M). A more definite medulla occurs in the stem (and in the leaves) of the rushes and sedges, where also the cells are often of most elegant radiating

Fig. 457.

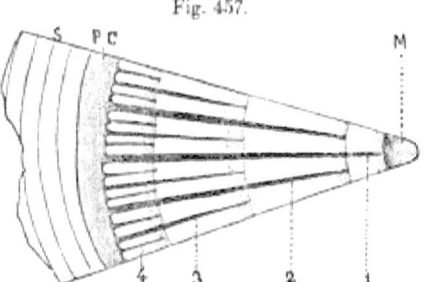

Section of a four years' old shoot of the Cork oak. M, pith; 1, 2, 3, 4, medullary rays of successive years; P. C, liber layers; S, cork layers.

Magnified 20 diameters.

Fig. 456.

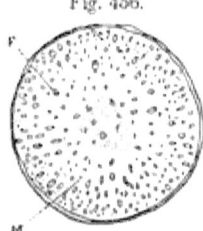

Horizontal section of a flowering stem of a lily. M, medulla; F, fibro-vascular bundles.

Magnified 5 diameters.

forms, leaving large air-canals between them (Pl. 38. fig. 18). The pith of a Dicotyledonous stem loses itself gradually in the terminal bud, where it is confounded with the nascent wood and cortical layers. In this stage its cells possess an active vitality, which, however, is soon lost.

BIBL. General Works on *Structural Botany.*

MEDULLARY RAYS.—The processes of cellular tissue extending out from the pith between the fibro-vascular bundles of a Dicotyledonous stem in the first year of growth (fig. 455 R M), together with additional interposed rays formed between the older in each succeeding annual layer of wood (fig. 457 1, 2, 3, 4). The tissue of these rays generally becomes much compressed during growth; but their size and the degree of development differ much in different cases. In radial sections of Dicotyledonous wood they often appear distinctly to the naked eye, from the direction of their cells being different from that of the woody fibre, and therefore reflecting light differently; this causes the "silver grain" as it is called of oak-panels, &c.; in tangental sections of the trunk, the ends of the medullary rays usually appear as short, more or less regular, narrow streaks.

MEDULLARY SHEATH.—The earliest layer of fibro-vascular tissue developed in a Dicotyledonous stem, consists ordinarily of spiral vessels, these forming the foundation of the wood-bundles (fig. 455 T). As the latter stand in a circle round the pith, their internal vascular layers of course form collectively a continuous cylindrical envelope to the pith; this is called the medullary sheath. It is absent in some Dicotyledonous stems, for example in the Orobanchaceæ.

MEESIA, Hedw.—A genus of Bartramioid Mosses; one species, *M. uliginosa* (= *Bryum trichodes*), certainly British; another, *M. longiseta*, doubtful.

MEESIACEÆ.—A tribe of Bartramioid Mosses, containing two genera, of which there are but few British representatives:

1. *Meesia.* Calyptra dimidiate. Peristome double. External, of sixteen very short, broad, obtuse teeth, with a median line or fissile. Internal: a short membrane produced into sixteen cartilaginous teeth with a median line, or split and perforated; teeth often coherent, with interposed, more or less perfect, mostly irregularly coherent

appendiculiform cilia. Areolation of the leaf of one character.

2. *Paludella.* Calyptra dimidiate. Peristome double, both of sixteen teeth, resembling that of *Bryum,* but the inner without cilia. Inflorescence diœcious. Areolation of the leaves dimorphous, lax and dense.

MEGALOTROCHA, Ehr.—A genus of Rotatoria, of the family Megalotrochæa.

Char. Eyes two, red, sometimes disappearing with age.

Rotatory organ two-lobed or horse-shoe-shaped; teeth in rows.

1. *M. albo-flavicans,* E. (Pl. 35. fig. 1). Colourless and unattached when young, yellowish and grouped in radiant clusters when old; aquatic; length of individuals 1-36''; of the clusters 1-6''.

The ova remain some time attached to the parent by a cord.

2. *M. relata,* Gosse.

BIBL. Ehrenberg, *Infus.* p. 396; Gosse, *Ann. Nat. Hist.* 1851. viii. p. 198.

MEGALOTROCHÆA, Ehr.—A family of Rotatoria.

Char. Neither envelope nor carapace present; rotatory organ simple, notched or sinuous at the margin.

Three genera :

Eyes none.....................1. *Cyphonautes.*
Eyes present
  Eye one.....................2. *Microcodon.*
  Eyes two ....3. *Megalotrocha.*

BIBL. Ehrenberg, *Infus.* p. 394.

MEGAMERUS, Dugès. — A genus of Arachnida, of the order Acarina, and family Trombidina.

Char. Palpi long, free, with a claw; body constricted; coxæ distant; legs ambulatory —femora, especially of the fourth pair, very large, seventh joint short; larvæ hexapod, resembling the adults.

Mandibles forcipate.

Several species. They live in damp shady places, and move rapidly.

M. celer (Pl. 2. fig. 33 : *a,* labium; *b,* palp). Minute; abdomen oblong; the sides narrowed posteriorly, covered with hairs, and with three terminal setæ; labium bifid; mandibles with a moveable, elongated, pointed and curved claw.

Pl. 2. fig. 33 *c,* mandible of *M. roseus.*

BIBL. Dugès, *Ann. des Sc. Nat.* 2 sér. ii. p. 50; Gervais, *Walckenaer's Arachn.* iii. 169.

MELAMPSORA, Cast. — A genus of Uredinei (Coniomycetous Fungi), containing several British species, as the *Uredo*

Euphorbiæ, U. cylindrica, U. Saliceti, and *U. Capræarum* of the British Flora. The plants of this genus have a distinct peridium, and they are remarkable from the Uredo-fruit being produced in autumn, and the proper Melampsora-fructification in the following spring. Their spermogonia have not been observed. To the naked eye they appear as yellow or orange-coloured spots upon the leaves of the plants they infest. See UREDINEI.

BIBL. *Brit. Flora,* ii. pt. 2. p. 385 ; Tulasne, *Ann. des Sc. Nat.* 4 sér. ii. p. 94 *et seq.*

MELANCONIEI.—A provisional family of Coniomycetous Fungi, growing beneath the epidermis of leaves and bark. They are at first little tubercles on the surface of a white mycelium, without an orifice ; subsequently they become hollow and fleshy, and the interior becomes coated with filaments, each terminating in a spore. The tubercles meantime enlarge, raise up the epidermis, and appear there in groups with irregular orifices opening outwards. The conceptacles, which have no proper perithecium, or only an approach to it (as in *Discella*), and are called *nuclei* when young, are closely crowded, and form blackish patches on the leaves or bark; and when mature, the spores are expelled, mixed with filaments in a gelatinous condition, and in the form of threads or ribands. The spores differ in shape.

The objects composing the genera of this group appear from recent observations to be forms belonging to the series of developments of the Ascomycetous Fungi; thus *Cytispora, Nemaspora,* and others are probably the *spermogonia* of Sphæriacei, their supposed spores being *spermatia.* See CONIOMYCETES. Until the exact relations of these structures have been made out, it will be convenient to describe them under their old names and in their old places.

Synopsis of British Genera.

1. *Melanconium.* Sporidia globose, simple, adhering together to form a nucleus, at length breaking out free. Colour black.

2. *Papularia.* Sporidia quite simple, collected in groups under the epidermis of dead plants, set free in a pulverulent patch by the decay of the epidermis.

3. *Stilbospora.* Sporidia septate (the septa always evanescent), full of sporidiola, adhering together into a nucleus, at length breaking out.

4. *Didymosporium.* Like the preceding,

but the sporidia didymous (septate in the middle). Colour black or fuscous.

5. *Cytispora*. Sporidia simple, stick-shaped, minute, contained in a multilocular nucleus, at length opening by a common apical pore and emerging in the form of a gelatinous tendril.

6. *Melasmia*. Sporidia minute, stick-shaped, formed in a flat thin nucleus, which bursts at the apex and extrudes the spores in a gelatinous globule.

7. *Micropera*. Sporidia linear, curved, formed in nuclei bursting by special distant pores, and discharged mixed with jelly.

8. *Ceuthospora*. Sporidia simple, ovate, contained in several globose nuclei seated in a common innate stroma, escaping by a simple laciniate pore.

9. *Nemaspora*. Sporidia simple, spindle-shaped, contained in nuclei associated in a common grumous stroma, and opening by a common pore.

10. *Discella*. Sporidia elongated, simple or uniseptate, stalked, in a nucleus which has a more or less developed perithecium.

11. *Cylindrosporium (Glæosporium)*. Sporidia simple, elliptical, stalked, in a nucleus covered only by the cuticle of the leaf, finally extruded in a gelatinous tendril.

12. *Coryneum*. Sporidia spindle-shaped, multiseptate, stalked, crowded together and breaking out on the surface as a pulvinate disk.

13. *Bactridium*. Sporidia spindle-shaped, multiseptate, transparent at the ends, tufted on a superficial creeping mycelium.

14. *Eriospora*. Sporidia filiform, originally attached in fours upon sporophores, formed in groups of globose nuclei opening by a common pore.

15. *Cheirospora*. Sporidia simple, crowded in tufts at the apex of a filiform sporophore, normally in moniliform rows.

MELANCONIUM, Lk.—A supposed genus of Melanconiei (Coniomycetous Fungi), so called from forming a kind of black rust on branches of trees, reeds, &c. Several species have been found in Britain. The commonest is *M. bicolor*, Nees (*Didymosporium elevatum*, Br. Fl.), on twigs of birch. Fries places also *Cryptosporium vulgare* here. (See CRYPTOSPORIUM.) These plants are forms of Sphæriacei. See CONIOMYCETES.

BIBL. Berk. *Brit. Flora*, ii. pt. 2. p. 357; *Ann. Nat. Hist.* vi. p. 438; Fries, *Summa Veg.* p. 508; Tulasne, *Ann. des Sc. Nat.* 4 sér. v. p. 109.

MELASMIA, Lév.—A supposed genus

of Melanconiei (Coniomycetous Fungi), but apparently only a stylosporous form of RHYTISMA. *M. acerina* occurs on the leaves of the sycamore, forming black spots, sometimes as much as 1-2″ in diameter.

BIBL. Berk. *Ann. Nat. Hist.* 2nd ser. v. p. 456; Léveillé, *Ann. des Sc. Nat.* 3 sér. v. p. 276; Fries, *Summa Veget.* p. 423.

MELICERTA, Schrank.—A genus of Rotatoria, of the family Floscularicæa.

Char. Bodies each in an isolated tubular carapace or urceolus; rotatory organ four-lobed; eyes two, at least when young.

M. ringens (Pl. 35. fig. 3; fig. 4, animal removed from the sheath; fig. 6, jaws). Carapace conical or cylindrical, brownish, composed of numerous rounded or discoidal bodies agglutinated together; body colourless. Aquatic; length of carapace 1-36 to 1-24″.

Frequently found attached to water-plants, especially *Potamogeton crispus*.

BIBL. Ehrenberg, *Infus.* p. 404; Williamson, *Micr. Journ.* 1852; Gosse, *Trans. Micr. Soc.* 1851. iii. 62.

MELOLONTHA, Fabr. (Cock-chafer). —A genus of Coleopterous Insects, of the family Melolonthidæ.

The structure of *M. vulgaris*, the common cock-chafer, has been elaborately studied and described.

BIBL. Suckow, *Naturgeschichte des Maikäfers*; Straus Durckheim, *Considér. général. s. l'Anatomie comparée des Insectes*; Westwood, *Introduction*, &c.

MELOPHILA, Nitzsch (*Melophagus*, Latr.).—A genus of Dipterous Insects, of the family Hippoboscidæ.

Char. Head posteriorly received in an excavation of the thorax; wings and halteres absent; last joint of the tarsus largest.

M. ovinus, the sheep-tick (Pl. 28. fig. 23). Common upon sheep. Antennæ small, sunk in an eye-like cavity of the head; eyes small, oval, resembling two groups of ocelli; setæ three, enclosed in two sheath-like, hairy, unjointed organs (labial palpi), resembling otherwise those of *Pulex*, and arising from the sides of a triangular labium. Legs robust; tarsi with two stout serrated claws, each having at its base a blunt process; accompanying the claw is an elegant feathery tarsal brush; and on the under side of the last tarsal joint is a bilobed pectinate organ.

BIBL. Lyonet, *Rech. s. l'Anatomie et les metamorphoses, &c.* Paris, 1832; Gurlt, *Magaz. f. d. gesammte Thierheilkunde*, 1843. ix.; Westwood, *Introduction, &c.*; Curtis, *Brit.*

Entom. 142; Dufour, *Ann. des Sc. Nat.* 1845. iii; Leuckart, *Fortpflanz. &c. der Pæpiparen.*

MELOSIRA, Ag. (*Gallionella*, Ehr.).— A genus of Diatomaceæ.

Char. Frustules cylindrical, discoidal or subspherical, united into jointed filaments.

Hoops often very broad, to adapt themselves to the breadth of the new frustules. In some species a narrow projecting ridge or keel encircles the valves near their ends. Valves covered with depressions which are mostly very minute and invisible under ordinary illumination; in the side view these sometimes have a radiate arrangement. In some species the margins of the ends (side view) of the frustules have coarse and distinct radiating striæ, their nature undetermined.

This genus has been subdivided—by Ehrenberg and Kützing into *Lysigonium*, in which the keel is present; and *Gallionella* (proper), in which this is absent. Again, by Thwaites into *Aulacosira*, in which the frustules are cylindrical, surrounded transversely by two furrows, with rounded (convex) ends, but no line for division; *Orthosira*, in which the frustules are exactly cylindrical (with flat ends), exhibit the transverse line of division, and have spherical or subspherical internal cavities; and *Melosira* (proper), in which the frustules are convex at the ends, and have the central line for division; including also the varieties in the reproduction (DIATOMACEÆ, p. 219).

Fourteen British species.

* *Marine.*

1. *M. nummuloides*, Kg. (Pl. 13. fig. 5 *a*; *b*, a frustule more magnified). Prepared frustules colourless, a distinct keel present; valves without markings under ordinary illumination; breadth 1-1500 to 1-1200″.

This common species forms long, slightly curved chains, and, on account of the great breadth of the frustules, shows well the various stages of subdivision. The filaments are sometimes stipitate.

2. *M. Borreri*, Grev. Prepared frustules dark brown, ends rounded, entire surface punctate (ordin. illum.), no striæ nor keel present; breadth 1-850 to 1-500″.

3. *M. Dickiei* (*Orthosira Dickiei*, Thw.) (Pl. 13. fig. 15: *a*, front view; *b*, side view). Filaments short, frustules nearly colourless, ends flat, no striæ nor keel (ord. illum.), valves thickened, so as to render the cavity of the frustules rounded; breadth 1-1500 to 1-1200″.

The remarkable sporangia formed in this species (Pl. 6. fig. 9) are noticed under DIATOMACEÆ, p. 219.

** *Aquatic.*

4. *M.* (*Orthosira*) *varians* (Pl. 13. fig. 6, front view; *a*, side view). Frustules colourless, ends slightly convex and striated at the margin (ord. illum.), keel absent; breadth 1-1500 to 1-1200″. The end view of the frustules resembles that of *Cyclotella*.

Formation of sporangia shown in Pl. 6. fig. 8 *a*; *b*, sporangial frustule.

5. *M. arenaria.* Ends of frustules flat and striated at the margin (ord. illum.), the striæ appearing also in the front view; keel absent; frustules broader than long; breadth 1-660 to 1-260″.

6. *M. crenulata*, Kg. (*Aulacosira crenulata*, Thw.; *M. orichalcea*, Ralfs) (Pl. 6. fig. 7 *a* forming sporangia; *b*, *c*, sporangial frustules). Differs from the last in its less diameter, and the frustules being two or three times as long as broad; breadth 1-1400″.

BIBL. Kützing, *Bacill.* p. 52, and *Sp. Alg.* p. 27; Ralfs, *Ann. Nat. Hist.* 1843. xii. p. 346; Thwaites, *ibid.* 1848. i. p. 168; Smith, *Brit. Diat.* ii. 54.

MEMBRANES, UNDULATING.—These are said to be simple membranous bands, one margin only of which is attached, the other being free and exhibiting an undulatory motion. They are allied to and answer the same purpose as cilia. They are described as occurring upon the spermatozoa of salamanders and tritons; as forming longitudinal processes in the watervessels of some Annelida, as the Turbellaria; also as existing in some Infusoria, as *Trichodina*, and some Rotatoria.

Some authors have regarded them as consisting of rows of cilia or a spiral fibre, and not membranes. They are most easily examined in the spermatozoa of the triton, in which we believe the appearance of an undulating membrane arises from the existence of a fibre coiled around the spermatozoa (Pl. 41. fig. 17), and undulating throughout its length. This opinion is based upon the circumstance, that if the coiled fibre be detached from the proper filament of a spermatozoon or spermatozoid, no margins of the (lacerated) membrane can be detected, other than that visible at first, and which really represents the coiled fibre.

This is, however, an interesting subject for further investigation. Siebold, who has paid most attention to it, remarks that *Trypanosoma*, Gruby, a supposed entozoon found in the blood of frogs and fishes, is not an independent animal, but simply an undulating membrane swimming freely.

BIBL. Siebold, *Sieb. & Kolliker's Zeitschr.* Bd. 2. p. 356, and the *Bibl.* therein.

MEMBRANIPORA, Johnst.—A genus of marine Polyzoa, of the family MEMBRANIPORIDÆ.

Eight British species; usually found encrusting sea-weeds, more rarely shells and stones.

M. pilosa (Pl. 33. fig. 18). Orifices of the cells with one long hair, and several spinous teeth. Very common.

MEMBRANIPORIDÆ. — A family of Cheilostomatous Infundibulate Polyzoa.

Distinguished by the expanded, encrusting, stony polypidom, and the horizontal quincuncial cells. Genera :

1. *Membranipora.* Cells open in front, with raised margins.

2. *Lepralia.* Cells closed in front, polypidom spreading circularly.

BIBL. Johnston, *Brit. Zooph.* ; Busk, *Cat. of Mar. Polyz.* (Brit. Mus.) ; Gosse, *Mar. Zool.* ii. 16.

MENIPEA, Lamx.—A genus of Infundibulate Cheilostomatous Polyzoa, of the family Cellulariadæ.

Char. Cells oblong, tapering downwards, not perforate behind, with one or two sessile birds'-heads in front below the orifice. One British species :

M. ternata (*Cellularia ternata*, Johnst.). Cells elongated, greatly tapering downwards, three in each internode, with a stalked operculum protecting the orifice ; operculum expanded, entire, two spines on the upper margin ; anterior birds'-head single.

BIBL. Johnston, *Brit. Zooph.* 335 ; Busk, *Cat. (Brit. Mus.)* 20.

MENISCIUM.—A genus of Grammitideæ (Polypodioid Ferns).

MENISPORA, Pers.—A genus of Mucedines (Hyphomycetous Fungi), one species of which, *M. lucida*, Corda, is recorded as British, growing on decayed wood.

BIBL. Berk. and Broome, *Ann. Nat. Hist.* 2 ser. vii. p. 101 ; Corda, *Icones*, i. pl. 4. fig. 223.

MERENCHYMA.—A name applied by some authors to the form of vegetable cellular tissue where the cells are of circular, ellipsoidal, or irregularly rounded outline ; ordinarily known as "lax parenchyma."

MERIDION, Leibl.—A genus of Diatomaceæ.

Char. Frustules (in front view) wedge-shaped, united laterally so as to form segments of circles or spiral bands. Aquatic.

Frustules in side view obovate, and furnished with coarse transverse striæ visible under ordinary illumination, which extend into the front view.

Kützing distinguishes *Meridion*, in which the frustules form a spiral (helical) band, from *Eumeridion*, in which they form a convolute band.

1. *Meridion circulare*, Ag. (Pl. 13. fig. 7 : *a*, front view ; *b*, side view). Frustules in side view simply obovate, forming a spiral (helical) band or filament ; length of frustules 1-600 to 1-375".

2. *Meridion constrictum*, Kg. (Pl. 12. fig. 28, filament flattened, and frustules (front view) separated by drying ; *a*, convolute filament ; *b*, side view). Frustules in side view constricted near the broad end, attenuate towards the narrow end, and attached to a hemispherical stipes or cushion.

BIBL. Kützing, *Bacill.* p. 41, and *Sp. Alg.* p. 10 ; Ralfs, *Ann. Nat. Hist.* 1843. xii. p. 457 ; Smith, *Brit. Diat.* ii. 5.

MERISMOPÆDIA, Meyen. See SARCINA and GONIUM.

MERMIS, Duj.—A genus of Entozoa.

M. nigrescens resembles *Gordius*, but differs from it principally in the vulva of the female being transverse and situated near the anterior end of the body, whilst in *Gordius* this is placed at the posterior end. Eggs black.

It is found in the newly dug-up damp earth of gardens, and in the intestines of insects.

BIBL. Dujardin, *Ann. des Sc. Nat.* 2 sér. xviii. p. 129, and *Hist. Nat. d. Helminthes*, p. 294 ; Siebold, *Entomolog. Zeitung*, 1842. p. 146 ; Meissner, *Siebold and Kolliker's Zeitschrift*, &c. 1853.

MERULIUS, Hall.—A genus of Agaricini (Hymenomycetous Fungi), distinguished by the veiny or sinuously plicate folds of the hymenium, these folds not being distinct from the flesh of the pileus, and forming angular or serrated pores. *M. lacrymans* is the dry-rot fungus. The mycelium is composed of filaments creeping in the substance of the infected wood, disorganizing and feeding on this as it decays. The fruit is at first white and cottony, forming an effused pileus from 1 to 8" broad ; subsequently ferruginous or deep orange. The irregular folds finally discharge a watery liquid, whence the name.

BIBL. Berk. *Brit. Flora*, ii. pt. 2, p. 129; Sowerby, *Fungi*, pl. 113.

MESOCARPUS, Hassall (*Sphærocarpus*, Kütz.).—A genus of Zygnemaceæ (Confervoid Algæ), with evenly distributed cell-contents, producing in conjugation a cross branch, in which is formed a round spore. It often happens that all the successive members of a long series of cells conjugate with another similar series, so as to produce a ladder-like body, the "rounds" of which are formed of the transverse processes (*trabeculæ*, Kütz.). The only kind of reproduction yet observed is that by the spores formed in the transverse branch from the conjoined contents of two cells; but it is possible that zoospores and encysted conditions of these occur, as in SPIROGYRA and MOUGEOTIA. The stellate encysted bodies found in most of the allied plants have been seen in *M. scalaris* by Thwaites. Thwaites also observed a division of the contents of the spore into four parts, such as occurs in ŒDOGONIEÆ.

1. *M. scalaris*, Hass. (fig. 138, p. 181). Sterile filaments 1-1800 to 1-1440" in diameter, 6 times as long; sporanges oval or round. Hass. pl. 42.

2. *M. depressus*, Hass. Sterile filaments 1-2880 to 1-2400" in diam., 6 to 8 times as long; spores globose or elliptical. Hass. pl. 44. fig. 1.

M. intricatus, Hassall, is apparently the same as *M. scalaris*; all the other forms may be brought under *M. depressus*.

BIBL. Hassall, *Brit. Fr. Alg.* p. 166, pls. 41–45; Kützing, *Sp. Alg.* p. 435; *Tab. Phyc.* v. (*Sphærocarpus*), pls. 5–7; Thwaites, *Ann. Nat. Hist.* xvii. 202.

MESOCENA, Ehr.—A genus of Diatomaceæ, according to Ehrenberg.

The bodies referred to this title consist of single siliceous rings, oval or angular frameworks, without a centre, and mostly with external and sometimes internal spines arising from them. They have no resemblance in structure to the frustules of the Diatomaceæ; they are fossil (marine), and the organic portion is unknown.

Several species are distinguished, which it can be of no interest to describe; the characters are founded upon the form, number of angles and spines.

Whether they are spicula of Echinodermata or not, remains to be decided. Diameter from 1-750 to 1-400".

M. octogona, Ehr., Pl. 19. fig. 1.

BIBL. Ehrenberg, *Ber. d. Berl. Akad.* 1840; Kützing, *Bacill.* 130, and *Sp. Alg.* p. 142.

MESOGLOIA, Ag.—A genus of Chordariaceæ (Fucoid Algæ), with filiform, much-branched fronds, of gelatinous character; the axis of the filaments composed of interlacing longitudinal cells, with gelatinous interposed matter; the periphery of radiating, dichotomous, coloured filaments. The fructification consists of unilocular and multilocular sporanges; the former are ovate sacs (fig. 458) occurring attached to

Fig. 458.

Mesogloia vermicularis.

Peripheral ramuli, unilocular sporanges and the filaments upon which the jointed sporanges arise.

Magnified 50 diameters.

the ramuli of the periphery; the latter are produced by ramifications of other ramuli surrounding them (fig. 458). Both kinds

Fig. 459.

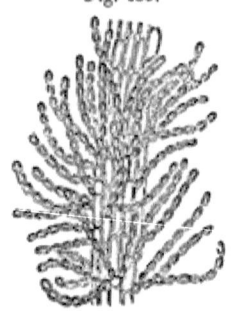

Mesogloia vermicularis.

Portion of a filament.

Magnified 10 diameters.

produce ciliated zoospores, which germinate. *M. vermicularis* (figs. 458, 459), an olive-green or yellowish frond, 6" high, is common on rocks and stones between tide-marks. *M. virescens*, a smaller species, is not uncommon.

BIBL. Harvey, *Brit. Mar. Alg.* p. 47, pl. 10 B; *Phyc. Brit.* pls. 31 & 83; Thuret, *Ann. des Sc. Nat.* 3 sér. xiv. p. 237, pl. 27.

METAXYA, Presl.—A genus of Cyatheous Ferns. Exotic.

METEORIC PAPER. See PAPER, METEORIC.

METOPIDIA, Ehr.—A genus of Rotatoria, of the family Euchlanidota.

Char. Eyes two, red, frontal; foot forked; carapace depressed or prismatic; anterior and upper part of head naked or uncinate; no hood. = *Lepadella* with two frontal eyes.

Lorica closed beneath. The characters are doubtful. In one species, the uncination appears (from Ehrenberg's figures) to arise from the so-called respiratory tube, and in another from the head being taper and curved (*M. triptera*).

M. triptera (Pl. 35. fig. 7). Carapace ovate, accurately trilateral, crested on the back. Aquatic; length 1-288 to 1-144".

Two other species, E., to which Gosse adds two.

BIBL. Ehrenberg, *Infus.* p. 477; Gosse, *Ann. Nat. Hist.* 1851. viii. p. 201.

METZGERIA, Raddi.—A genus of Pelliex (Hepaticæ), comprehending *Jungermannia furcata*, L. and *J. pubescens*, Schrank, growing on trunks of trees, rocks, &c. in very moist places. The fronds of both are linear-dichotomous, membranous, and ribbed. *M. furcata* is hairy beneath, and smooth above; *M. pubescens* hairy on both sides, and larger. In addition to the sporanges, these plants are increased by gemmæ formed in patches on the attenuated lobes of sterile fronds.

BIBL. Hook. *Brit. Flor.* ii. pt. 1. 131; *Brit. Jungermann.* pls. 55, 56 & 73; Endlicher, *Gen. Plant.* Supp. 1. p. 1338; Hofmeister, *Vergleich. Untersuch.* p. 10, pl. 4.

MICA.—This mineral substance, which is often erroneously called talc in the shops, was formerly used for covering mounted objects, but is now replaced by thin glass. It is, however, occasionally useful in applying a red heat to objects, as Diatomaceæ, &c., where it is required not to change the position of the object. It often contains crystalline and crystalloidal inorganic mineral substances, as metallic oxides, &c., of interesting appearance.

Thin plates of mica are used also in bringing out colours in objects with polarized light. See POLARIZATION.

MICRASTERIAS, Ag. — A genus of Desmidiaceæ (Confervoid Algæ).

Char. Cell single, lenticular, deeply divided into two-lobed segments; lobes incisodentate (rarely only bidentate), and generally radiating.

Sporangia spherical, with stout spines (Pl. 10. fig. 12).

Thirteen British species (Ralfs).

1. *M. denticulata* (Pl. 10. fig. 11, undergoing division; fig. 12, sporangium). Cell circular, surface smooth; segments five-lobed; lobes dichotomously divided, ultimate subdivisions truncato-emarginate, with rounded angles. Length 1-113". Common.

2. *M. rotata* (Pl. 10. fig. 13). Cell circular, smooth; segments five-lobed; lobes dichotomously incised, ultimate subdivisions bidentate. Length 1-91". Common.

BIBL. Ralfs, *Brit. Desmid.* p. 68.

MICROCLADIA, Grev. — A genus of Ceramiaceæ (Florideous Algæ), containing one rare British species, *M. glandulosa*, with a dichotomously branched, filiform, compressed frond 1 to 2" high, of a bright rose colour. Its fructification consists of (1) roundish, sessile involucrated favellæ with *spores*, and (2) *tetraspores* (tetrahedrally arranged) imbedded in the ramules.

BIBL. Harvey, *Brit. Mar. Alg.* p. 160; pl. 22 B; *Phyc. Brit.* pl. 29; Grev. *Alg. Brit.* t. xix.

MICROCODON, Ehr.—A genus of Rotatoria, belonging to the family Megalotrochæa.

Char. Eye single; no carapace; foot styliform. Jaws two, each with a single tooth.

M. clavus (Pl. 35. fig. 8). Body campanulate, foot equalling or exceeding the body in length. Aquatic. Length 1-288 to 1-216".

BIBL. Ehrenberg, *Infus.* p. 395.

MICROCOLEUS, Desmaz. (*Chthonoblastus*, Kütz.).—A genus of Oscillatoriaceæ (Confervoid Algæ), with fronds forming strata on moist ground, paths, mud, &c. These plants may be described as bundles of *Oscillatoria*-filaments enclosed in a common gelatinous sheath, which is simple or irregularly dichotomously branched, and forms twisted interwoven masses. The structure of the filaments appears to be identical with that occurring in OSCILLA-

TORIA, described under that head; the filaments oscillate; the mode of origin of the enclosing sheath is obscure, but it would appear to be formed of the gelatinous half-dissolved outer membranes of the enclosed filaments. No formation of spores or gonidia has been described. *M. repens*, Harv. (Pl. 4. fig. 9 *a*, the open end of a sheath), is very common on damp paths, &c., its sheaths are branched; *M. anguiformis*, Harv., occurs on the mud of brackish pools; its sheaths are said to be simple. *M. gracilis*, Hassall, said to be found in similar situations, has no character attached to it.

BIBL. Harvey, *Brit. Mar. Alg.* p. 227, pl. 26 D; *Phyc. Brit.* pl. 249; Hassall, *Br. Freshw. Alg.* p. 260, pl. 70; Kütz. *Tab. Phyc.* i. pls. 54-58.

MICROCYSTIS, Kütz. — A genus of Palmellaceæ (Confervoid Algæ), of which we are unable to identify any British species except *M. æruginosa*, for which see CLATHROCYSTIS, and with some probability the plant described by Mr. Currey under the name of *Monostroma roseum*. The latter consists of a gelatinous body crowded with red gonidia, having at first the form of a closed sac, about 1-3 to 2-3″ in diameter, with a clear central space, subsequently becoming distorted and wrinkled.

BIBL. Kützing; *Linnæa*, viii. p. 342; *Sp. Alg.* p. 208; *Tab. Phyc.* pls. 8, 9; Currey, *Quart. Journ. of Microsc. Sc.* vi. p. 214.

MICROGLENA, Ehr.—A genus of Infusoria, of the family Monadina, E.

Char. Tail absent; body truncated in front, with a single flagelliform filament; a red eye-spot present.

Probably the spores of Algæ.

1. *M. punctifera* (Pl. 24. fig. 43 *a*). Body yellow, ovate, subconical, attenuate posteriorly, red eye-spot accompanied by a blackish frontal spot (in Ehrenberg's figures, some have one, some two red eye-spots). Aquatic; length 1-620″.

2. *M. monadina* (Pl. 24. fig. 43 *b*). Body ovate, equally rounded at both ends, bright green; eye-spot red and single. Aquatic; length 1-1150 to 1-620″.

BIBL. Ehrenberg, *Infus.* p. 25.

MICROGONIDIA. See MACROGONIDIA.

MICROHALOA, Kütz.—A genus of Palmellaceæ (Confervoid Algæ), consisting of microscopic gelatinous patches, floating in water, crowded with minute green gonidia. *M. Icthyoblabe* (quite distinct from CLA-

THROCYSTIS) occurs in Britain, and Hassall's *Sorospora virescens* belongs here.

BIBL. Kütz. *Sp. Alg.* p. 207; *Tab. Phyc.* pls. 6, 7; Hassall, *Brit. Fr. Alg.* p. 326, pl. 78. fig. 8 *a*.

MICROMEGA, Ag.—A genus of Diatomaceæ.

Char. Frustules arranged in longitudinal rows within gelatinous tubes or surrounded by slender curved or crisped fibres—these being enclosed in other gelatinous tubes, forming filiform branched fronds; valves resembling those of *Navicula*. Marine.

Kützing notices the occurrence of sporangia or sporange-like bodies (spermatia) filled with the frustules, within the substance of the sheaths, and formed "from the dilatation of the naviculæ" (frustules); but the exact nature of the process is not described nor understood. This formation of brood-sporangia, as they might be called, would appear to resemble that occurring in the Desmidiaceæ (Pl. 6. fig. 3 A *d*).

Kützing describes twenty-eight species, and divides them into two sections; in one the filaments being slender and capillary, in the other rigid, cartilaginous, and thicker.

M. parasiticum (Pl. 13. fig. 8 : *b*, portion of a filament magnified; *c*, side view; *d*, front view of frustule). Filaments slender, wavy, tufted, cartilagino-gelatinous, yellowish (sometimes brown), much branched, capillary; frustules crowded; length of frustules 1-1380″.

Parasitic upon larger marine algæ.

BIBL. Kützing, *Bacill.* p. 116; *Sp. Alg.* p. 105.

MICROMETER. See INTRODUCTION, p. xxiv, and MEASUREMENT.

MICROPERA, Lév.—A genus of Melanconiei (Coniomycetous Fungi), of which one species is described as British, *M. drupacearum* (*Cenangium Cerasi, junior*, Fr., *Sphæria dubia*, Pers.), growing on dead branches of the cherry-tree. It forms whitish tubercles which split the bark transversely, composed of somewhat cylindrical conceptacles, conjoined at the base, the white mealy ostiole projecting; the linear spores are yellowish and curved at the apex.

BIBL. Berk. and Broome, *Ann. Nat. Hist.* 2 ser. v. 380; Léveillé, *Ann. des Sc. Nat.* 3 sér. v. p. 283; *British Flora*, ii. pt. 2. p. 211.

MICROPYLE (of Animals). See OVUM.

MICROSCOPE.—The first Section of the INTRODUCTION consists of remarks upon the microscope and microscopic apparatus.

MICROSPORON (Gruby) = *Trichophyton* Audouin.

BIBL. Robin, *Hist. Nat. des Végét. Parasites*, 426.

MICROTHECA, Ehr.—A marine organism of doubtful nature, placed by Ehrenberg first among the Rotatoria, and subsequently with the Desmidiaceæ, to neither of which does it seem to bear the least resemblance.

It consists of yellow, flattened, rectangular (side view) bodies, with four equidistant spines projecting from each end; the colour arises from the contents; no transverse line of division; entire length 1-216".

Does it consist of the ovum of some marine animal?

BIBL. Ehrenberg, *Infus.* p. 164.

MELICHHOFERIA, Hornsch.—A genus of Bryaceous Mosses, containing one British species, *M. nitida*, sometimes referred to *Weissia* (fig. 81, p. 108).

MILIOLIDA.—A family of Foraminifera, of the order AGATHISTEGIA.

MILIOLINA, Willn.—A genus of Foraminifera = *Triloculina*, *Quinqueloculina*, and *Adelosina*, D'Orb.

BIBL. Williamson, *Rec. For.* 83.

MILK.—This liquid consists of a solution of caseine and certain salts, holding in suspension minute globules of fatty matter (butter).

The fluid portion possesses no microscopic peculiarities. The globules are very numerous, round, and vary in size from mere molecules to 1-3000 or 1-2000" in diameter. Each is surrounded by a pellicle or coat of caseine, which prevents the globules from fusing into each other. If a portion of a drop of milk be placed upon a slide, and the thin glass cover be moved to and fro, the coat of caseine will be ruptured, the globules of oil will become confluent, and shreds of the coats will be visible. If acetic acid be added, the coats will be acted upon, and the confluence also produced. The same effect occurs naturally in sour milk; hence in this the globules are often much larger than the above dimensions, and irregular in form, frequently becoming elongated and united in twos, so as to bear some resemblance to the young state of a fungus.

The milk first secreted after parturition, called the colostrum, differs considerably from the normal liquid. The fatty globules contained in it vary greatly in size, often being very large, and existing within isolated or aggregated epithelial cells, some of them resembling exudation-corpuscles.

Dr. Peddie's paper on the human milk in relation to medical practice, is well worthy of perusal.

BIBL. Kölliker, *Mikrosk. Anat.* ii.; Donné, *Cours de Microscopie*; Wagner, *Handwörterb. d. Physiologie*, art. *Milch*; Peddie, *Ed. Monthly Journ.* 1840, and the *Bibl.* of CHEMISTRY, Animal.

MILK-VESSELS. See LATICIFEROUS TISSUE.

MILLON'S TEST, or TEST-LIQUID.—This, a strongly acid (nitric and nitrous) solution of proto- and pernitrate of mercury, gives an indication of the presence of proteine or allied compounds by the production of a more or less deep rose-red colour.

The test-liquid is prepared by dissolving metallic mercury in an equal weight of strong nitric acid (sp. gr. 1·4). The acid is first poured upon the metal; gas is copiously evolved; and as soon as the evolution ceases, a gentle heat is applied until the whole of the metal is dissolved. After some hours, the liquid portion is poured off from the crystals which have formed and subsided, and must be kept in a stoppered bottle.

In use, the substance to be tested is immersed in the liquid, either in a tube or upon a slide with a cover, and heat applied over a small flame of a spirit-lamp until boiling occurs. The substance then appears of a red colour if it answers to the action of the test.

Great attention is required to the purity of the substance or body to be tested; otherwise, *e. g.*, a cell-wall might appear to be coloured from the contents consisting of a proteine compound, &c.

The following substances and tissues are coloured by the reagent: albumen, caseine, chondrine, crystalline, epidermis, feathers, fibrine, gelatine, gluten, horn, legumine, proteine, silk, wool.

The following, when pure, are not coloured: cellulose, chitine, cotton, gum (arabic), linen and starch.

BIBL. Millon, *Comptes Rendus*, 1849, or *Chem. Gaz.* 1849. vii. p. 87.

MILNESIUM, Doyère.—A genus of Arachnida, of the order Tardigrada (Colopoda).

Char. Head with two very short palpiform appendages at its anterior and lateral part; mouth terminated by a sucker surrounded by palps; skin soft, transversely furrowed; legs four pairs; rings of the body divided into two segments.

M. tardigradum (Pl. 41. fig. 9). Mouth surrounded by six minute unequal palps, symmetrically arranged, diminishing in size from the upper to the lower part; head rounded in front when the mouth is retracted; eye-spots tolerably large and granular; pharyngeal tube much dilated, styles very small, bulb elongated and pyriform, without an internal framework; body transparent, attenuated at both ends, especially the posterior; skin pale brownish yellow; three anterior pairs of legs nearly equal, the fourth very short, resembling two tubercles, with scarcely a trace of annuliform division; claws four, two terminal, and in the form of elongated filaments hooked at the end, and each supported on a distinct tubercle; two inferior and internal, the anterior divided into three strongly curved hooks, the posterior into two; hooks or terminal filaments of the fourth pair longer than those of the three first. Movement active. Length 1-50 to 1-40″.

BIBL. Doyère, *Ann. des Sc. Nat.*

MIMOSELLA, Hincks.—A genus of Infundibulate Ctenostomatous Polyzoa, of the family Vesiculariadæ.

Char. Polypidom confervoid, jointed, and branched; cells ovate, opposite, with a basal joint; animals with eight tentacles and a gizzard.

M. gracilis. Branches erect, arising from a creeping fibre. On sea-weeds.

BIBL. Hincks, *Ann. Nat. Hist.* viii. 350.

MIRROR OF SŒMMERING. See INTRODUCTION, p. xix.

MISLETOE. See VISCUM.

MITES.—The animals usually included under this indefinite term are species of genera belonging to the order Acarina among the Arachnida.

MNIACEÆ.—A tribe of Mnioideæ (Mosses), of Bryoid habit, but with firm, rigid, and usually undulated leaves, mostly increasing in size toward the summit of the stem.

British Genera.

1. *Cinclidium.* Calyptra conical, dimidiate, small, fugaceous. Peristome double, the external of sixteen short and truncate teeth; the internal composed of a cup-like membrane with sixteen folds, and sixteen foramina opposite the outer teeth, open at the summit.

2. *Mnium.* Calyptra as in *Cinclidium.* Peristome double; exterior of sixteen lanceolate, cuspidate teeth, trabeculate externally and with a longitudinal line, lamellar, fleshy inside, yellowish; interior a membrane with keeled folds, produced into sixteen lanceolate, broad, keeled teeth, with large perforations, connivent like a cupola, surpassing the outer teeth, with two to four intervening cilia.

3. *Georgia.* Calyptra mitriform, plaited. Peristome simple, of four pyramidal cellular teeth.

4. *Timmia.* Calyptra dimidiate-hood-shaped, very fugacious. Peristome double: exterior of teeth like those of *Mnium,* scarcely lamellated, geniculately incurved when dry; interior a hyaline membrane prolonged into numerous nodose filiform cilia, very much appendiculated or rugulose, at first anastomosing together, then free.

MNIADELPHACEÆ.—A family of Pleurocarpous Mosses, with the leaves arranged in four or more series, and composed of parenchymatous cells, mostly equally hexagonal and Mnioid, very smooth, pellucid, destitute of a distinct primordial utricle, the lowest decurrent on the stem at the base, larger, spongy, lax, mostly beautifully dark-tinged, never single, slender.

British Genus.

Daltonia. Calyptra mitre-shaped, bell-shaped, elegantly fringed at the base. Peristome double (*Neckeroid*). External: sixteen narrow, subulate, trabeculate teeth, reflexed when moistened; internal: an equal number of similar cilia, alternating with the teeth, devoid of a basilar membrane.

MNIOIDEÆ.—A family of operculate Mosses, ordinarily of acrocarpous habit, but sometimes pleurocarpous, with broadly oval, spathulate, oval or lanceolate, flattish leaves, having a very prominent, thick dorsal nerve. The base of the leaves composed of somewhat parallelogrammic cells, rounded-hexagonal or with equal walls towards the apex, very full of chlorophyll, or with the primordial utricle mostly very conspicuous, or much thickened, firm, rarely papillose. This family is divided into two tribes:

1. MNIACEÆ. Leaves without appendicular lamellæ, not sheathing at the base. Capsule oval, pyriform or cylindrical, without an annulus.

2. POLYTRICHACEÆ. Leaves mostly sheathing at the base, the internal face mostly lamellated; lamellæ composed of a single layer of cells placed lengthwise on the nerve. Capsule closed by an epiphragm,

without an annulus, mostly angular, apophysate, unequal.

MNIUM, Dill.—A genus of Mniaceous Mosses, of acrocarpous and pleurocarpous habit, including many *Brya* of the British Flora. Among the commonest is *M. hornum* = *Bryum hornum*, L.

MOCHA STONES.—The varieties of chalcedony known under this name contain a number of bodies which have been interpreted by authors to consist of plants, as portions of *Chara*, *Hypnum*, *Confervæ*, *Nostoc*, Desmidiaceæ, &c. The evidence is however very unsatisfactory.

Compare AGATE and FLINT.

BIBL. K. Müller, *Ann. Nat. Hist.* 1843. xi. p. 415.

MOHRIA, Swartz.—A genus of Schizæous Ferns. Exotic (fig. 460).

Fig. 460.

Mohria thurifraga.
A pinnule with sporanges.
Magnified 25 diameters.

MOINA, Baird.—A genus of Entomostraca, of the order Cladocera, and family Daphniadæ.

Char. Head rounded and obtuse; superior antennæ of considerable length, of one piece, and arising from the front of the head near the middle; inferior antennæ large, fleshy at the base, and two-branched, one branch three-jointed, the other four-jointed; legs five pairs.

1. *M. rectirostris* (Pl. 14. fig. 26). Carapace almost straight or but slightly rounded behind. Aquatic.

2. *M. brachiata* or *branchiata*. Carapace greatly rounded behind. Aquatic.

BIBL. Baird, *Brit. Entomos.* p. 100.

MOLECULAR MOTION.—When extremely minute particles of any substance immersed in water or other liquid are examined under the microscope, they are seen to be in a state of vivid motion. A little gamboge or Indian-ink mixed with water will exhibit the phænomenon distinctly enough. The minute particles or molecules are seen to move irregularly, to the right and left, backwards and forwards, as if repelled by each other, until the attraction of gravitation ultimately overcomes the force upon which their motion depends, when they sink to the surface of the slide. This applies to the molecules of those substances which are heavier than water. In the case of those which are lighter than water, or the liquid in which they are immersed, the molecules ultimately become adherent to the thin glass covering the slide.

This motion is in no way connected with evaporation, for it takes place equally when this is completely prevented, just as when it is not. Neither light, electricity, magnetism nor chemical reagents exert any effect upon it. Heat is the only agent which affects it; this causes the motion to become more rapid. Hence it might be attributed to the various impulses which each particle receives from the radiant heat emitted by those adjacent. Or, as it takes place when the temperature is uniform, may it not arise from the physical repulsion of the molecules, uninterfered with by gravitation, hence free to move? The effect of heat would then be explicable, because this increases the natural repulsion of the particles of matter, as in the conversion of water into vapour.

Molecular motion plays a part in some common phænomena. Thus, it prevents turbid water from becoming rapidly clear by repose; by its agency also the disaggregated particles of animal or vegetable matter are diffused throughout the mass of the liquid.

The microscopist should become acquainted with the appearance of particles in molecular motion, as it might give rise to error. Thus particles under its influence might be mistaken for monads; or particles moved by cilia might be regarded as merely exhibiting this molecular motion.

Two circumstances appear most favourable for its production and continuance, in addition to the augmentation of temperature, viz. a very finely divided state of the matter, and the specific gravity of the matter and the liquid in which it is suspended being as nearly as possible coincident.

BIBL. R. Brown, *On Active Molecules, &c.*, *Add. Observ. on the same*, 8vo (*privately printed*); Dujardin, *Observateur au Microscope*; Griffith, *Med. Gaz.* 1843.

MOLGULA, Forbes.—A genus of Tunicate Mollusca, of the family ASCIDIADÆ.

Two British species: *M. oculata*, adherent, bluish or purple, mottled with orange; $2\frac{1}{2}''$ in diameter: and *M. tubulosa*, free, in sand.

BIBL. That of the family.

MOLLUSCA.— Remarks upon certain interesting structures occurring in the Mollusca will be found under TONGUE, SHELL, SNAILS (WATER-), MUSSEL, OYSTER, and OVUM. The calcareous concretions, crystals, and spicula met with in the integument or mantle of some mollusca are curious.

BIBL. Siebold, *Vergleich. Anat.* and the copious BIBL.; Vogt, *Zoologische Briefe*; Adams, *Genera of Recent Mollusca*; Forbes and Hanley, *Brit. Mollusca*; Woodward on *Shells*; R. Jones, *Animal Kingdom*, and *the articles in the Cycl. of Anat. and Phys.*; Turton, *Brit. Shells, by Gray*.

MONACTINUS, Bail.—A genus of Desmidiaceæ.

Distinguished from *Pediastrum* by the marginal cells having one horn only. Species:

1. *M. octonarius.* Marginal cells eight, central none.

2. *M. duodenarius* (Pl. 44. fig. 22). Marginal cells twelve, central three.

BIBL. Bailey, *Smiths. Contribut.* 1853. p. 14.

MONADINA. — A family of Infusoria, according to Ehrenberg's system, but consisting of a heterogeneous group of imperfectly examined bodies (see p. 376).

Char. Carapace absent; no expansions; locomotive organs consisting of one or more flagelliform filaments or cilia at the anterior part of the body.

Ehrenberg distinguishes nine genera:

A. Tail none.
  a. No lips.
    α. Swimming.
      a. No eye-spot.
        1. Single.................1. *Monas.*
        2. Grouped...............2 *Uvella.*

      β. Eye-spot present.
        1. Single.
          * Flagelliform filaments,
            one or two ....3. *Microglena.*
          ** Flagelliform filaments,
            four or five ..... 4. *Chloraster.*
          *** Flagelliform filaments,
            numerous..........5. *Phacelomonas.*
        2. Grouped...............6. *Glenomorum.*
    b. Rolling.....................7. *Desococcus.*
  b. Lips present ....8. *Chilomonas.*
B. Tail present ....9. *Bodo.*

Dujardin's characters are (see p. 377): animalcules without an integument, consisting of a glutinous, apparently homogeneous substance, susceptible of becoming agglutinated to other bodies and so drawn out and altered in form, with one or more flagelliform filaments as locomotive organs, and sometimes lateral or tail-like appendages.

Dujardin divides them thus:

MONADINA.

Isolated.	A single flagelliform filament	arising from the anterior extremity of the body { moving throughout its whole length...... 1. *Monas.*	
		{ thicker and rigid at the base, moveable at the end .... 2. *Cyclidium.*	
		arising obliquely from behind an anterior prolongation .... 3. *Chilomonas.*	
	A second filament, { lateral .... 4. *Amphimonas.*		
	{ posterior .... 5. *Cercomonas.*		
	Two equal filaments terminating the curved angles of the anterior end .... 6. *Trepomonas.*		
	Four equal filaments in front, and two thicker ones behind............................ 7. *Heteromita.*		
	A second filament arising from the same spot as the flagelliform filament, but thicker, trailing and retracting .... 8. *Heteromita.*		
	A filament and vibratile cilia .... 9. *Trichomonas.*		
Aggregate.	Groups always free, revolving .... 10. *Uvella.*		
	Groups originally fixed at the end of a branched polypidom or stalk..................... 11. *Anthophysa.*		

BIBL. Ehrenberg, *Infus.* p. 1; Dujardin, *Infus.* p. 270.

MONADS are species of *Monas*, or of other genera of the family Monadina (Infusoria).

MONAS, Müll.—A genus of Infusoria, of the family Monadina.

Char. See MONADINA.

Ehrenberg describes many species, consisting mostly of the zoospores or lower forms of Algæ, and the young or swarmgerms of Infusoria.

1. *M. vinosa*, E. Ovate, uniformly rounded at each end, of a red-wine colour, motion slow and tremulous. Length 1-12,000 to 1-6000''.

Found upon the sides of glass vessels, in which decaying vegetable matter has been kept, on the side next the light.

The characters of the genus given by Dujardin are:

No integument; form rounded or oblong, variable; no expansions: flagelliform filament single; motion slightly vacillating.

Dujardin describes ten species, which cannot be identified with those of Ehrenberg.

2. *M. lens*, D. (Pl. 24. fig. 44 *a*). Body rounded or discoidal and tubercular. Breadth 1-5200 to 1-1800″.

One of the most common organisms in animal and vegetable infusions. We have found one common in animal infusions (Pl. 24. fig. 44 *b*), perhaps the same as the above, but it possesses usually two filaments; on the left side is one without filaments, but with the body drawn out from adhesion to the slide.

3. *M. attenuata*, D. (Pl. 24. fig. 44 *c*). Body ovoid, narrowed at the ends, nodular, unequal; filament arising from the anterior narrowed portion. Length 1-1000″. Very abundant in stinking films floating on water containing decaying freshwater Algæ.

Bibl. Ehrenberg, *Infus.* p. 3; Dujardin, *Infus.* p. 279.

MONILIA, Hill. See Briarea.

MONOCERCA, Bory, Ehr.—A genus of Rotatoria, of the family Hydatinæa.

Char. Eye red, single, cervical; foot-like tail simply styliform.

Gosse mentions a second eye situated in the breast of one (new) species. Ehrenberg describes three species, to which Gosse adds two.

M. rattus, E. (Pl. 35. fig. 9). Body ovate-oblong; forehead truncate, unarmed; foot styliform, as long as the body. Aquatic. Length 1-120″.

Bibl. Ehrenberg, *Infus.* p. 422; Gosse, *Ann. Nat. Hist.* 1851. viii. p. 199.

MONOCOTYLEDONS. — One of the

Fig. 461.

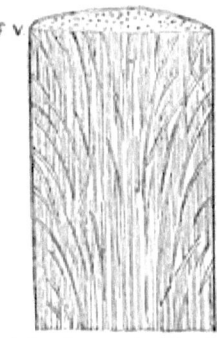

Reduced view of a stem of a Palm, showing the perpendicular and horizontal section, in which the fibro-vascular bundles F. V are seen isolated in the medullary parenchyma.

classes of Angiospermous Flowering Plants, so called from the structure of the embryo contained in the seed, which in a large number of cases is of microscopic dimensions, and always requires the use of the simple microscope for its dissection. Some of the families placed under this head have usually an acotyledonous embryo, as Orchidaceæ, but these possess the character of the class in all other respects. Among the most important of their other characters is the isolated condition of the fibro-vascular bundles forming the woody structures (see Tissues, Vegetable). This character, mostly very evident both in perpendicular and horizontal sections of the stems, is illustrated by figs. 456 & 461.

MONOLABIS, Ehr.—A genus of Rotatoria, of the family Philodinæa.

Char. Eyes two, frontal; tail-like foot with two toes; horns absent.

Two species.

M. gracilis (Pl. 35. fig. 10). Body slender, no cervical process nor respiratory tube; teeth two in each jaw. Aquatic. Length 1-240 to 1-144″.

Bibl. Ehrenberg, *Infus.* p. 497.

MONORMIA, Berkeley.—A genus of Nostochaceæ (Confervoid Algæ), distinguished by its definite, linear, convoluted frond, enclosing a single moniliform filament. It might readily be mistaken for a *Nostoc* if superficially observed; but its convoluted frond is devoid of the common membranous pellicle. The only known British species is *Monormia intricata*, Berk.

This plant occurs in gelatinous masses, each about as large as a walnut and of a reddish-brown colour, floating in slightly brackish ditches. When the spermatic cells are quite mature, the definite outline of the linear frond is almost lost, and there is little to distinguish the plant from *Trichormus*, except the peculiar convolutions of the moniliform filament; the frond then also assumes a greenish tint.

Bibl. Berkeley (*Gleanings of Brit. Algæ*, t. 18); Ralfs, *Ann. Nat. Hist.* ser. 2. vol. v. pl. 8. fig. 1; Harvey, *Phyc. Britann.* t. 256; Hassall, *Brit. Fr. Algæ*, t. 75. fig. 11. *Nostoc intricatum*, Meneghini; *Anabaina intricata*, Kützing, *Tabulæ Phycologicæ*, vol. i. t. 94. fig. 1.

MONOSTEGIA.—An order of Foraminifera, containing those genera in which the shell consists of a single chamber only. Genera:

1. *Gromia.* Shell membranous or cartilaginous (Pl. 24. fig. 13).

2. *Proteonina.* Shell elongate, arenaceous.

3. *Orbulina.* Shell spherical, arenaceo-calcareous (Pl. 18. fig. 11).

4. *Lagena.* Shell oval or fusiform, with a neck, but no internal tube (Pl. 19. figs. 16, 17, 18).

5. *Entoselenia.* Shell as in *Lagena*, but neck usually absent, and an internal tube present (Pl. 18. figs. 19, 20, 21).

BIBL. That of FORAMINIFERA.

MONOSTROMA, Thuret.—A genus of Ulvaceæ (Confervoid Algæ), of which *M. bullosum* (*Ulva bullosa*, Roth) is the type, distinguished from *Ulva* by consisting only of a single layer of cells, and these being roundish (mostly grouped in fours), imbedded in an apparently homogeneous gelatinous membrane (Pl. 5. fig. 1 a). This plant is reproduced by zoospores formed from the cell-contents, and discharged by bursting of the cell-wall (fig. 1 b, c). They have four cilia.

Mr. Currey has described, under the name of *M. roseum*, a plant which we think scarcely referable here, but rather to MICROCYSTIS, Kütz.

BIBL. Thuret, *Ann. des Sc. Nat.* 3 sér. xiv. p. 225, pl. 21. figs. 1-4; *Note sur les Ulvacées, Mém. de la Soc. Scient. de Cherbourg,* ii. p. 1 (1854).

MONOSTYLA, Ehr.—A genus of Rotatoria, of the family Euchlanidota.

Char. Eye single, cervical; tail-like foot simply styliform; carapace depressed.

Four species : three Ehrenberg, and one other, Gosse.

M. quadridentata (Pl. 35. fig. 11). Carapace yellowish, fore part of head deeply cleft into four horns. Aquatic. Length 1-120″.

BIBL. Ehrenberg, *Infus.* p. 459; Gosse, *Ann. Nat. Hist.* 1851. viii. p. 200.

MONOTOSPORA, Corda.—A genus of Sepedonei (Hyphomycetous Fungi), of which one species has been found in England, growing on dead bark of the yew. *M. megalospora*, Berk. and Br. Filaments erect, simple, straight, nearly equal, articulated. Spores terminal, obovate, even, ·0014 to ·00133″ long. Fries regards this genus with doubt.

BIBL. Berk. and Broome, *Ann. Nat. Hist.* 2 ser. xiii. p. 462, pl. 15. fig. 11 ; Fries, *Summa Veget.* 407.

MONURA, Ehr.—A genus of Rotatoria, of the family Euchlanidota.

Char. Eyes two, frontal; foot simply styliform. Carapace somewhat compressed and open beneath.

Two species.

M. dulcis (Pl. 35. fig. 12). Carapace ovate, obliquely truncate and acute behind ; eyes distant. Aquatic. Length of carapace 1-280″.

BIBL. Ehrenberg, *Infus.* p. 474.

MORELS.—Species of *Morchella*, Dill. (Ascomycetous Fungi), having a pileiform receptacle, with a ribbed and lacunose hymenium on the upper side, bearing *asci*.

MORPHIA. See ALKALOIDS, p. 27.

MORPHO, Fabr.—A genus of Exotic Lepidopterous Insects.

M. Menelaus. The scales from the wings of this beautiful insect are sometimes used as TEST-OBJECTS.

MOSSES, MUSCACEÆ.—This order of flowerless plants is distinguished from the Hepaticæ by the vegetative structure and by the sporanges. In one group alone (*Hypopterygiea*) is the stem clothed with leaves, accompanied by amphigastria (stipule-like leaflets), in the manner of the foliaceous Hepaticæ (fig. 355, p. 365) : and here the sporange is a stalked urn-shaped body, with a deciduous lid, and like those of the Mosses generally ; and this Jungermannia-like leafy stem is *erect*, and not procumbent, as in *Jungermannia* itself. In all other Mosses the leaves clothing the stem are arranged in a spiral order around the stem, so as to give the vegetative structure a very characteristic aspect. On the other hand, the Andreaceæ, which have a valvate capsule, have spirally-arranged leaves.

The stem of the Mosses is a slender thread-like or wiry structure, wholly composed of cellular tissue, without vessels ; but the external layer has an epidermoid character, while the central portion is composed of elongated cells. In one section of the Mosses this stem terminates in a sporange, and these are called *Acrocarpous* Mosses ; in others the sporanges spring from lateral branches, and the terminal bud of the stem elongates the stem year after year ; these latter are called *Pleurocarpous* Mosses. In some of the genera the sporanges are borne terminally on short special branches, as in *Sphagnum, Mielichhoferia,* part of *Fissidens, Guembelia fontinaloides* (fig. 289); these are termed *Cladocarpous.*

The leaves are of simple structure, usually composed of a single layer of cells, the forms of which are used as characters by systematic Muscologists. They are either all alike in a leaf, and filled with chlorophyll, and in these cases may be either *parenchymatous* (Pl. 38. fig. 19) or *prosenchymatous* (Pl. 38. fig. 20). In other cases two sorts of cells occur arranged in a peculiar way; some, smaller, containing chlorophyll, form a kind of network, the meshes of which are occupied by large uncoloured cells (see SPHAGNUM and LEUCOBRYUM).

The margins of the leaves are frequently serrated; and the upper surface is occasionally papillose, or covered with rough points. Many of them have one or more distinct nervules, composed of elongated cells, often not reaching the apex of the leaf.

The leaves often differ on different parts of the stem; and we hence have *radical*, *cauline*, and *perichætial* or involucral leaves, the last ordinarily forming a kind of rosette, in the midst of which the reproductive organs are produced. SCHISTOSTEGA exhibits two forms of stem, with two kinds of foliaceous structure : the stems which terminate in a sporange have leaves only at the upper

Fig. 462.

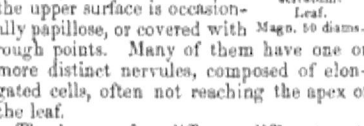

Ephemerum serratum. Leaf. Magn. 50 diams.

Fig. 463.   Fig. 464.

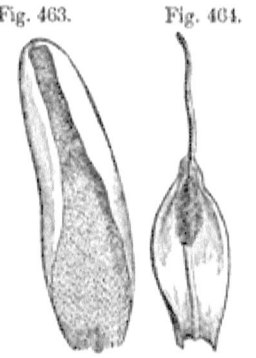

Barbula chloronotus.

Fig. 463. Leaf with cellular filaments at the tip. Magn. 30 diams.
Fig. 464. Leaf with cellular filaments crowded on the midrib, with an awn-like prolongation. Magn. 20 diams.

part, and these arranged in eight rows standing crosswise on the stem, like ordi-

nary leaves; the barren stems have two rows of leaflets arranged in one plane on the stem, like the leaflets of a compound leaf (such as that of the Acacias) of Flowering plants. The stem-leaves of many genera exhibit wing-like structures, hair-like appendages, or peculiar forms of curvature (figs. 242–246, FISSIDENS); others, like certain *Barbulæ* (figs. 463–466), have collections of cellular filaments on the upper side.

Fig. 465.   Fig. 466.

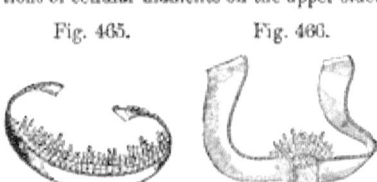

Barbula chloronotus.

Fig. 465. Cross-section of 463. Magn. 50 diams.
Fig. 466. Cross-section of 464. Magn. 50 diams.

The outer leaves surrounding the reproductive organs are called *perichætial*, and sometimes they form the only envelopes; sometimes, however, a few small leaves, differing very much from the above, form the immediate envelopes of the archegones, and these *perigonial* leaves, forming the perigone, are developed *after* the reproductive organs themselves (as is the case also with the *perigone* of the Hepaticæ). The perigonial leaves either overlap and cover-in the reproductive organs, or they are keeled at the base and turned back above, so as to expose the organs of reproduction (POLYTRICHUM).

The young reproductive organs consist of *antheridia* and *archegonia* or *pistillidia*, which are found either together (fig. 467),

Fig. 467.   Fig. 468.

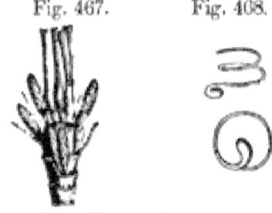

Bryum nutans.

Fig. 467. Inflorescence of antheridia and archegonia. Magn. 25 diams.
Fig. 468. Spermatozoids from antheridia. Magn. 600 diams. (The cilia omitted.)

or on different parts of the same plant, or on different individuals of the same

2 H

species. To these structures the term *in-florescence* is applied. The antherids occur either with the archegones in one perigone (fig. 467) or in the axils of the upper leaves of the stem, which terminates in a perigone containing archegones; or they have a special perigone (fig. 469), either on the same

Fig. 469.

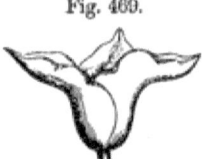

Mnium arcticum.
Antheridial inflorescence.
Magnified 25 diameters.

plant, or on a different one from that which bears the archegones. The antherids are globular, oval (fig. 467), or elongate membranous sacs composed of cellular tissue, filled with minute cellules, which escape by the bursting of the apex of the sac; and these cellules exhibit a fibre coiled in their interior, which circulates rapidly, even before the expulsion from the antherid, and after a time breaks out of its cellule (fig 468, and Pl. 32. fig. 33), and moves rapidly round in the water under the microscope (see ANTHERIDIA). The antherids are generally accompanied by cellular filaments which have received the name of *paraphyses* (fig. 23, p. 51); no physiological office is attributed to these, but the antherids are regarded as male organs.

The *archegone* of the Mosses (figs. 30, 31 (p. 64), 467), like that of the Hepaticæ (excepting *Anthoceros*), is a flask-shaped cellular case, the epigone containing an *embryonal cell* at the bottom of its cavity. This embryonal cell becomes gradually developed by cell-division into a conical body elevated on a stalk, which at length tears away the walls of the flask-shaped epigone by a circular fissure, and carries the upper part upwards as a hood, while the lower part remains as a kind of collar round the base of the stalk (figs. 470–472); the latter is termed the *vaginula* (fig. 473); the cap-like portion carried upwards on the sporange is called the *calyptra* (figs. 470–472). The *sporange*, elevated more or less by the development of its stalk (*seta* or *peduncle*), is gradually converted by internal changes into a hollow urn-like case, usually with a

stalk-like column (*Columella*) running up its centre (figs. 50 (p. 77), 475), the space between the central column and the side

Fig. 470.   Fig. 471.

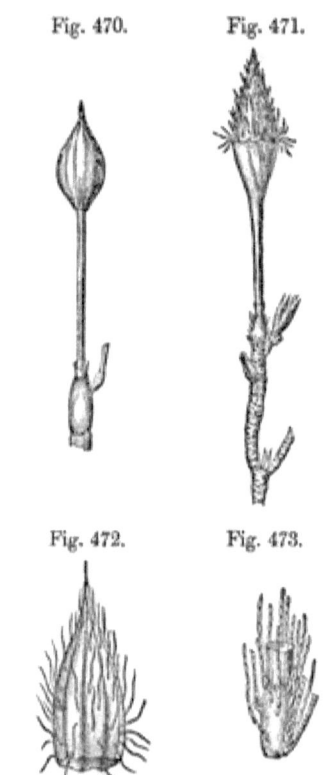

Fig. 472.   Fig. 473.

Fig. 470. Coscinodon pulvinatus. Capsule enclosed in the calyptra, with the vaginule below. Magn. 10 diams.
Fig. 471. Orthotrichum Hutchinsii. Capsule covered by the calyptra, with vaginule below. Magn. 10 diams.
Fig. 472. Ditto. Calyptra. Magn. 25 diams.
Fig. 473. O. stramineum. Vaginule. Magn. 25 diams.

walls becoming filled with free *spores*, which are minute cells with a double coat, the outer of which exhibits elegant markings (see SPORES). In some cases this hollow case does not burst naturally, but the spores escape by its decay (ASTOMUM, fig. 50). In the ANDRÆACEÆ (fig. 11, p. 36) the sporange bursts by vertical slits, so as to be divided into valves, like the Jungermanniæ, and there is no *column* in the sporange here; but the valves do not separate at their summits, and the character of the leafy stem at once distinguishes these Mosses from the Hepaticæ. The ordinary course, however, in the Mosses is the formation of a horizontal slit near the top of the sporange, so that the upper part falls off like a lid (*operculum*, fig. 479).

Fig. 474.   Fig. 475.

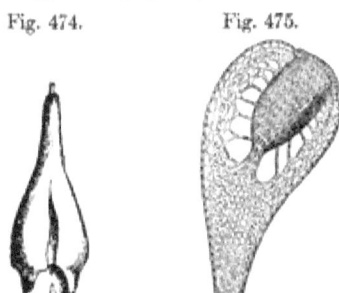

Fig. 474. Tayloria serrata. Dimidiate calyptra. Magn. 25 diams.
Fig. 475. Funaria hygrometrica. Section of young capsule, showing the columella. Magn. 50 diams.

The sporange of the Mosses exhibits a very complex anatomical structure, which we have not space to enter into very mi-

Fig. 476.   Fig. 477.

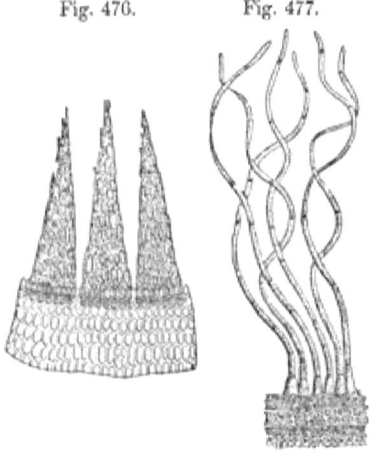

Fig. 476. Coscinodon pulvinatus. Fragment of peristome. Magn. 100 diams.
Fig. 477. Barbula flavipes. Fragment of peristome. Magn. 100 diams.

nutely here: it will suffice to state that the lower part next the peduncle is sometimes enlarged into a thickened mass, called the *apophysis*; sometimes the peduncle is very long, sometimes very short (*Phascum*, fig. 478) so that the sporange is hidden in the perichæte; finally, the mouth may either exhibit a smooth edge (fig. 479), or a single

Fig. 478.   Fig. 479.

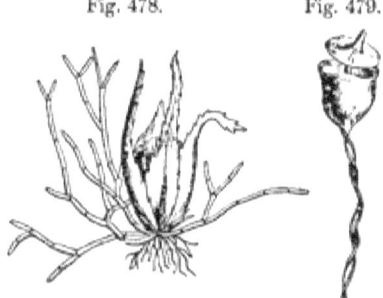

Fig. 478. Phascum serratum. Sessile sporange enclosed by few leaves. Magn. 15 diams.
Fig. 479. Pottia truncata. Operculum separating from the sporange. Magn. 10 diams.

(figs. 476, 477) or double (figs. 483, 484) fringe of very variously constructed teeth, which are of great service in discriminating the genera. When the mouth of the sporange is naked, the Mosses are called *gym-*

Fig. 480.

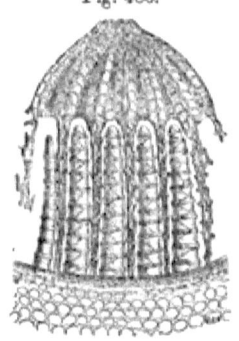

Cinclidium arcticum.

Part of double peristome, the inner processes united into a plaited membrane in the centre.

Magnified 100 diameters.

nostomous, when furnished with only a single row of teeth *aploperistomous*, when with a double row *diploperistomous*. When a double peristome exists, the outer consists of *teeth*, the inner of *processes* or *cilia* (fig. 483) or of both (*Bryum*). The teeth sometimes arise directly from the mouth of the sporange, sometimes are seated on a basal membrane, sometimes connected together irregularly (FUNARIA, fig. 259, p. 302), or by regular bars (GUEMBELLA, fig. 291, p. 325), or the whole of the inner circle may be conjoined entirely (BUXBAUMIA, fig. 93, p. 112) or at the tips (fig. 480) into a membrane, or by a number of cross-bars into an open trellis (fig. 484). The outer rows of teeth are continuations of the inner layers of tissue of the sporange (fig. 481); where an inner circle occurs they are continuations of the spore-sac; the outer wall of the sporange is, as it were, continued by the *operculum*. Ordinarily these do not separate directly from each other when the lid falls off, since one or several layers of elastic cells, forming a ring (*annulus*, fig. 482) round the mouth, split out from between the sporange and its lid, and cause the latter to fall off.

Figure 481.   Fig. 482.

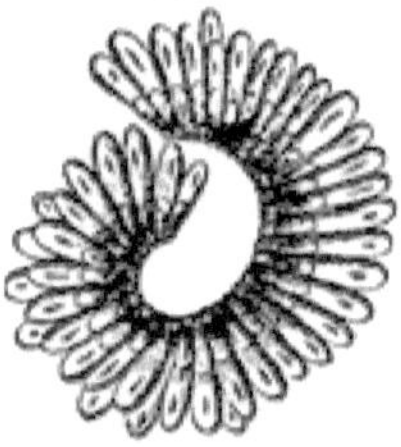

Fig. 483.

Fig. 481. Racomitrium fasciculare. Section of margin of sporange, with a tooth of the peristome. Magn. 100 diams.
Fig. 482. Bryum cæspititium. Annulus. Magn. 100 diams.
Fig. 483. Orthotrichum diaphanum. Portion of double peristome, the outer composed of teeth, the inner of cilia. Magn. 50 diams.

The spores are developed in a distinct spore-sac, which has one layer next the wall of the capsule, and an inner layer next the columella. The top of the columella expands into a kind of pseudo-operculum in

Polytrichum. In Phascaceæ the columella is absorbed.

Allusion has been made to the sexual import of the antherids and archegones; and attention must be directed to the peculiar phænomena exhibited in the reproduction of the Mosses. The *embryo-cell* of the *archegonium* appears to be fertilized by the spiral filaments produced by the *antheridia*; the result here is not the production of a simple plant, but of a sporange or *fruit* which produces a number of spores, each of which may grow up into a new plant.

Fig. 484.

Neckera antipyretica.
Double peristome, the inner composed of teeth united by cross bars, forming a trellis.
Magnified 100 diameters.

The Mosses exhibit a variety of forms of vegetative multiplication. The lower part of the stem often sends out horizontal branches, which root and produce buds (fig. 485), from which arise new leafy stems;

Fig. 485.

Polytrichum undulatum.
Creeping filaments with innovations.
Magnified 5 diameters.

and in this way patches of moss frequently increase to a great size. They also produce confervoid filaments, which exhibit tuberous thickenings, a form of *gemmæ* (figs. 488, 489), which may be detached from each other like bulbils, so as to propagate the plants without any sexual reproductive organs.

Fig. 486.   Fig. 487.

Orthotrichum phyllanthum.
Leaves with gemmæ at the tips.
Magnified 25 diameters.

Gemmæ or minute cellular tubercles, capable of development into new plants, are likewise met with in other situations, as in the axils of leaves, on the surface, the margins (fig. 490), or at the tips (figs. 486, 487) of the leaves or the stems (fig. 491): these are formed of only a few cells at the time when they fall off, and illustrate well the independence of the individual cells forming the organs of these plants, where, under peculiar circumstances, a single cell of the tissue may be developed so as to lay the foundation of a new plant.

In the following arrangement of the Mosses we follow C. Müller. The order Muscaceæ is first divided into two suborders according to the habit of growth :

1. **ACROCARPI.** Mosses with the fruitstalk terminating the stem, or short special branches (Cladocarpi).

2. **PLEUROCARPI.** Mosses with the fruitstalk produced only from lateral buds.

Synopsis of the Families.

ACROCARPI.

* **Schistocarpi.** *Capsule without a lid (operculum), opening by longitudinal fissures.*

I. ANDRÆACEÆ. Capsule splitting into four valves.

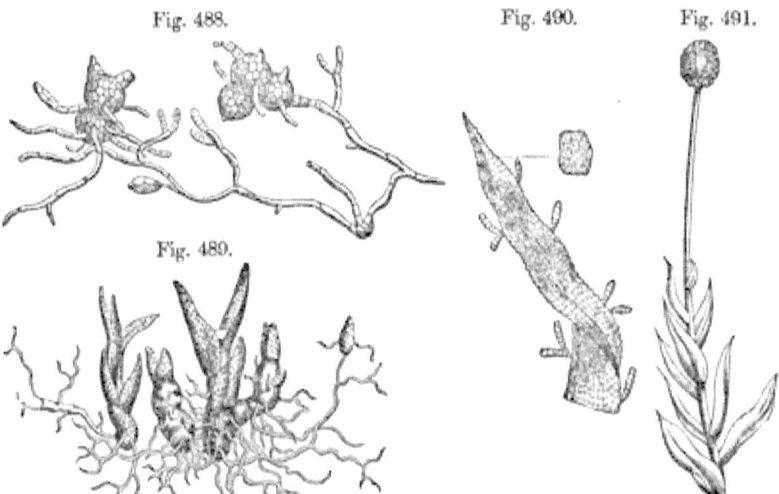

Fig. 488.

Fig. 489.

Hedwigia ciliata.
Creeping filaments with tuber-like gemmæ.
Fig. 488, magnified 50 diameters.
Fig. 489, magnified 20 diameters.

Fig. 490.   Fig. 491.

Fig. 490. Orthotrichum Lyellii. Leaves with marginal gemmæ. Magn. 50 diams.
Fig. 491. Aulacomnium undulatum. Gemmæ in the place of the capsule. Magn. 20 diams.

** **Cleistocarpi.** *Capsule without a lid, bursting open irregularly.*

II. BRUCHIACEÆ. Cells of the leaf (*areolation*) parenchymatous, looser at the base, not papillose, dense.

III. PHASCACEÆ. Areolation of the leaf parenchymatous, dense, filled with chlorophyll, more or less papillose.

IV. EPHEMEREÆ. Areolation of the leaf parenchymatous, everywhere lax, not papillose.

*** **Stegocarpi.** *Capsule bursting by a lid.*

1. Distichophylla. *Leaves arranged in two straight rows.*

a. Leaves regularly vertical.

V. SCHISTOSTEGEÆ.

b. Leaves regularly subvertical.

VI. DREPANOPHYLLEÆ.

c. Leaves horizontal.

VII. DISTICHIACEÆ. Areolation of the leaves parenchymatous, minute; leaves without appendicular laminæ.

VIII. FISSIDENTEÆ. Areolation of the leaves parenchymatous; leaves produced into appendicular laminæ at the back and point.

2. Polystichophylla. *Leaves arranged in three or more straight or alternating rows.*

a. Leaves exhibiting narrow green cells, forming a reticulation between larger diaphanous cells.

IX. LEUCOBRYACEÆ. Leaves composed of several layers of columnar, empty, parenchymatous cells; the 'intercellular' green cells three- to four-angled, interposed between the empty cells in a single curved row.

X. SPHAGNACEÆ. Leaves composed of a single stratum of empty prosenchymatous cells, with intercellular green cells interposed between all the empty cells. Cladocarpous, branches fasciculate.

b. Leaves without 'intercellular' cells.

a. Leaves not papillose.

1. Loosely areolated.

XI. FUNARIOIDEÆ. Areolation of the leaf parenchymatous, lax, containing much chlorophyll.

XII. DISCELIACEÆ. Areolation of the leaves rhomboid-prosenchymatous, destitute of chlorophyll, empty, fuscescent.

XIII. BUXBAUMIACEÆ. Areolation of the leaf hexagonal or polygonal, very minute, dark-coloured, destitute of chlorophyll.

2. Densely areolated.

XIV. MNIOIDEÆ. Areolation of the leaf in parallelograms at the base, round-hexagonally parenchymatous towards the apex; very full of chlorophyll, or more frequently thickened (very rarely papillose).

XV. BRYACEÆ. Areolation of the leaf prosenchymatous, ordinarily rhomboidal, abounding with chlorophyll.

XVI. DICRANACEÆ. Cells of the leaf prosenchymatous, very often intermixed with parenchymatous cells (rarely scabrously papillose), alar basilar cells ordinarily crowded and ventricose, or flat and much more loosely reticulated than the upper cells.

XVII. LEPTOTRICHACEÆ. Cells of the leaf rhombic at the base, rectangular or both mixed further up, smooth, without proper alar cells.

b. Leaves papillose.

XVIII. BARTRAMIOIDEÆ. Cells of the leaves parenchymatous, square, ordinarily nodulose or scabrous with papillæ at the transversal sides, never opake.

XIX. POTTIOIDEÆ. Cells of the leaves parenchymatous, square, ordinarily covered on all sides with papillæ above the base, but smooth and pellucid at the base.

XX. DIPHYSCIACEÆ. Leaves of two kinds: the cauline with the cells densely hexagonally parenchymatous, abounding with chlorophyll, the perichætial leaves with the cells destitute of chlorophyll and more loosely reticulated.

PLEUROCARPI.

1. Distichophylla. *Leaves arranged in two opposite rows.*

XXI. PHYLLOGONIACEÆ.

2. Tristichophylla. *Leaves arranged in three rows, appearing like three, erect, of two forms.*

XXII. HYPOPTERYGIACEÆ. Cells of the leaf everywhere prosenchymatous, equal.

3. Polystichophylla. *Leaves arranged in four or more rows.*

XXIII. MNIADELPHACEÆ. Cells of the leaf parenchymatous, Mnioid.

XXIV. HYPNOIDEÆ. Cells of the leaf prosenchymatous, rhombic or rounded.

BIBL. Hooker, Taylor, and Wilson, *Bryologia Britannica*; Bruch and Schimper, *Bryo-*

logia Europæa; Schimper, *Corollarium, Bryol. Europæa*, 1855; *Flora*, 1856. p. 681; Hedwig, *Theoria generationis*; Bridel, *Bryologia Universa*; Müller, *Synopsis Muscorum frondosorum*; Dillenius, *Historia Muscorum*; Lanzius-Beninga, *Nova Acta*, xxii. p. 555; Hofmeister, *Vergleich. Untersuch.* Leipsic, 1837; *Ber. d. Sachs. Gesellsch. d. Wissensch.* April 1854; *Flora*, 1855. p. 434; Valentine, *Linnean Transactions*, xviii. p. 490.

MOTH, CLOTHES. See TINEA.

MOTHER-CELL, or PARENT-CELL, is the term commonly applied to the cell in the interior of which a new generation of cells is developed.

MOTHER-OF-PEARL. See SHELL.

MOUGEOTIA.—A genus of Zygnemaceæ (Confervoid Algæ), distinguished by the conjugation of the filaments taking place without the formation of transverse processes, the conjugating filaments being geniculately bent. There is still obscurity as to the mode of reproduction of the plants of this genus. According to Vaucher, a spore is formed in one of the conjugating cells, without transfer of contents, and this, germinating *in situ*, breaks out from the parent-cell. This account is probably correct as far as it goes, but does not explain fully the development of the spores. Hassall says the plants are reproduced by zoospores; this has been confirmed by Kützing, who, together with Itzigsohn, has observed the formation of small rounded resting-spores in the joints, which underwent segmentation and developed a number of smaller cells, the ultimate fate of which was not observed. All this tends to prove that the reproduction agrees with that of *Spirogyra*, where we have—1. large conjugation-spores, sometimes germinating *in situ*, producing in some cases new filaments, in others zoospores; 2. zoospores produced immediately from the contents; and 3. what appeared to be encysted forms of these (see SPIROGYRA).

The only satisfactorily established British species of this genus seems to be *M. genuflexa*, Ag. (fig. 139, p. 182). The cells are about 1-720″ in diameter in large specimens (*M. major*, Hass.), and about three or four times as long; in smaller specimens (*M. genuflexa*, Hass., *M. gracilis*, Kütz.) the diameter is about 1-1200″, the length of the cells five or six times greater. The contents of the cells, like those of MESOCARPUS, are mostly evenly distributed.

Mesocarpus notabilis, Hass. (*Sirogonium*

notabile, Kütz.) is an obscure plant, perhaps referable to this genus.

BIBL. Vaucher, *Conferves d'eau douce*, p. 79, pl. 8; Hassall, *Brit. Fr. Alg.* p. 171, pl. 40; Kützing, *Sp. Alg.* p. 43; *Tab. Phyc.* v. pls. 1–3, and 36; Itzigsohn, *Bot. Zeit.* xi. p. 681 (1853).

MOULDS and MILDEWS. — These names are generally applied indifferently to a multitude of Hyphomycetous, Physomycetous and Coniomycetous Fungi, but some of the more common ones are especially distinguished. Thus ordinary 'blue mould' of cheese, &c. is ASPERGILLUS *glaucus*; another still more common blue or green mould is PENICILLIUM *glaucum*; various species of OIDIUM and ERYSIPHE are known as the mildews of the Hop, Vine, Rose, &c. The mildew of wheat is PUCCINIA *graminis*.

MOUNTING. See PRESERVATION.

MOUSE, HAIR OF (Pl. 1. fig. 3; Pl. 22. figs. 27, 28). See HAIR OF ANIMALS and TEST-OBJECTS.

Fig. 402.

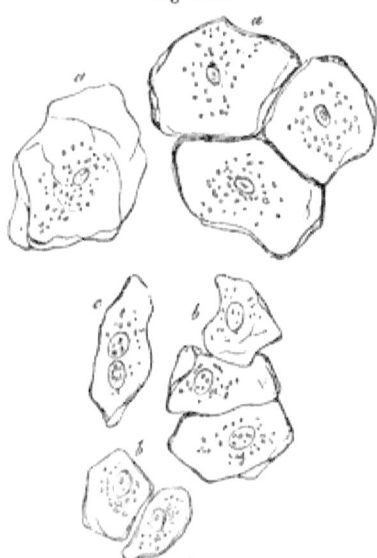

Epithelial cells of the mucous membrane of the human mouth: *a*, large, *b*, smaller cells; *c*, one with two nuclei.

Magnified 350 diameters.

MOUTH. — The mucous membrane of the mouth, which becomes continuous with the skin at the lips, is furnished with very numerous conical or filamentous papillæ resembling those of the skin, sometimes

Fig. 493.

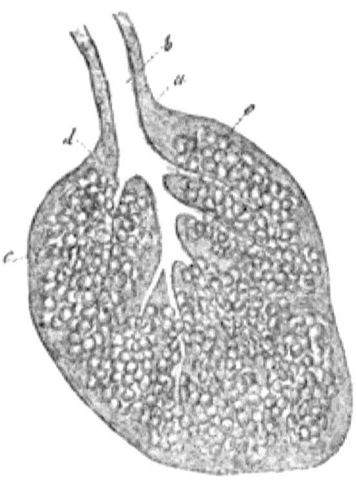

Human racemose mucous gland from the floor of the cavity of the mouth. *a*, areolar coat ; *b*, excretory duct ; *c*, glandular cæca ; *d*, lobular ducts.

Magnified 50 diameters.

simple, at others branched, and a number of mucous glands.

Its epithelium is of the pavement kind, consisting of several layers of delicate cells ; these are roundish in the deeper, flattened and polygonal in the superficial layers.

Fig. 494.

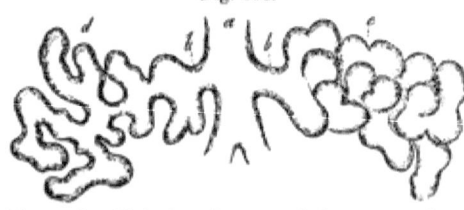

Diagram of two lobular ducts of a mucous gland. *a*, common duct ; *b*, lobular branch ; *c*, glandular vesicles *in situ* ; *d*, the same separated, and the ducts unfolded.

Magnified 100 diameters.

The glands, distinguished according to their situation, as the labial, the buccal, and the palatine glands, are rounded, about 1-36 to 1-6″ in size, and open by short excretory ducts into the mouth. They consist of glandular lobules enveloped in areolar tissue with elastic fibres, the whole being surrounded by a firmer portion or capsule, and a branched duct. The lobules are composed of a number of convoluted canals or lobular ducts, with simple or compound cæca or glandular vesicles, each consisting of a basement membrane, and a single layer of angular epithelial cells. The latter separate

Fig. 495.

Two glandular vesicles of a human racemose mucous gland. *a*, basement membrane ; *b*, epithelium, side view ; *c*, the same in surface view.

Magnified 300 diameters.

very readily ; and then the cæca appear filled with a granular mass.

The ducts of the lobules have a coat of areolar tissue, with networks of fine elastic fibres, and a single layer of cylindrical epithelial cells.

The mucous liquid of the mouth contains, in addition to detached epithelial cells, very transparent corpuscles, about 1-2000 to 1-1500″ in diameter, consisting of a delicate cell-wall, a nucleus, with a number of minute moving molecules. We have figured these among the Test-Objects (Pl. 1. fig. 5). They are called mucous or salivary corpuscles. Kölliker regards them as a form of exudation corpuscles ; and this view is probably correct, for they may occur in the secretion of any mucous surface, and have no special connexion with the salivary glands : we have found them in myriads in the urine.

The secretion of the mouth generally contains also very slender filaments of a fungus (Leptothrix), with species of *Monas*, E., and of *Vibrio*.

BIBL. Kölliker, *Mikr. Anat.* ii.

MUCEDINES.—A family of Hyphomycetous Fungi, forming moulds and mildews upon living or decaying animal or vegetable substances, and contributing to their decomposition, characterized by a flocculent mycelium bearing erect, continuous or septate, simple or branched, tubular pellucid filaments, terminating in single spores or strings of spores, which soon separate from each other, and lie among the filaments of the mycelium. This tribe includes a number of the most interesting of the microscopic fungi, noted for their destructive influence upon organic bodies which they attack. The species of *Botrytis*, *Oidium*, &c. spread with wonderful rapidity as mildews over the herbaceous parts of vegetables and moist vegetable substances generally; in the former situations their spores enter the stomata, their mycelia ramifying among the subjacent cells, and carrying decomposition and decay into all the soft structures. They are most abundantly developed in a close, damp atmosphere. The mycelia of other kinds, as of PENICILLIUM, growing in liquids containing organic matter, or upon decaying vegetable substances, produce remarkable chemical decompositions, causing a fermentation of the medium in which they exist.

See PENICILLIUM and FERMENTATION.

Synopsis of British and nearly allied Genera.

A. Fertile filaments (*pedicels*) simple or branched, terminating in single spores or a very short row.

* *Spores simple.*

1. *Botrytis.* Pedicels erect, septate, branched; branches and branchlets septate; spores solitary, on the tips of the branchlets, which are either racemose, umbellate, cymose (*Polyactis*), paniculate, verticillate (*Acrostalagmus*), spicate (*Haplaria*) or capitate.

2. *Peronospora.* Like *Botrytis*, but the pedicels without septa.

3. *Verticillium.* Pedicels erect, septate, with whorled branches terminating in a solitary spore or a short row of spores.

4. *Acremonium.* Pedicels short, subulate, branches from a horizontal filament, bearing single smooth spores.

5. *Zygodesmus.* Like the last, but with echinulate spores.

6. *Oidium.* Pedicels simple, short, erect, clavate, septate, bearing usually one, sometimes two more or less oval spores.

7. *Fusidium.* Pedicels? Spores elongate, fusiform.

8. *Menispora.* Pedicels erect, septate, bearing fusiform or cylindrical spores, at first joined in bundles.

9. *Sceptromyces.* Pedicels erect, geniculate, verticillately branched; branches short, racemose; spores in grape-like bunches.

** *Spores septate.*

10. *Brachycladium.* Pedicels branched above, septate, moniliform; branches and branchlets forming a sporiferous capitulum; spores transversely septate.

11. *Trichothecium.* Pedicels interwoven in tufts, the central erect, fertile; spores acrogenous, didymous, free, commonly loosely heaped together.

12. *Cephalothecium.* Pedicels simple, continuous, bearing a terminal head of didymous spores.

B. Erect filaments (*pedicels*) terminating in strings of spores.

* *Spores simple.*

13. *Penicillium.* Pedicels erect, septate, penicillately branched above; branches and branchlets septate; strings of spores attached to the tips of the branches.

14. *Sporotrichum.* Pedicels erect, simple, or slightly branched, septate, and articulate, articulations remote, inflated; spores simple, usually found collected in heaps among the filaments.

15. *Briarea.* Pedicels erect, septate, with terminal moniliform chains of spores, crowded into a head.

16. *Gonatorrhodum.* Pedicels erect, septate, with chains of spores in a terminal head and in whorls at the joints.

** *Spores septate.*

17. *Dendryphium.* Pedicels erect, septate, unbranched; strings of spores attached in a bunch to the apex; spores septate.

18. *Dactylium.* Pedicels erect, septate, branched above; strings of septate spores attached singly or in pairs to the apices of the branches.

C. Fertile filaments (*pedicels*), inflated at the tips or at various points in their length, with projecting points or warts on the inflations bearing

* *Simple spores.*

19. *Aspergillus.* Pedicels continuous, erect, simple filaments, inflated into a little head at the summit, bearing moniliform chains of spores, crowded into a capitulum.

20. *Rhinotrichum.* Pedicels erect, septate, sometimes sparingly branched, the apices clavate, cellular, bearing scattered points supporting simple spores.

21. *Papulæspora.* Pedicels short lateral branches from a creeping filament, terminating in cellular heads beset with simple spores on the areolæ.

22. *Rhopalomyces.* Pedicels erect, not septate, terminating in cellular heads, with simple spores on the areolæ.

23. *Stachylidium.* Pedicels erect, articulated, whorled-branched above; branchlets geniculate and articulate; spores subpedicellate, accumulated in little capituliform heads inserted at the tips of the branches.

24. *Gonatobotrys.* Pedicels erect, septate, with joints swollen at intervals, the swollen joints bearing globular heaps of spores on short spines spirally arranged.

25. *Acmosporium.* Pedicels erect, septate, branched above; branches and branchlets forming a cyme, thickened at the apex, and furnished with globular capitules covered all over with points; spores simple, attached on the points of the capitules.

26. *Haplotrichum.* Pedicels erect, septate, terminating above in a continuous, simple, solitary, sporiferous head; spores simple.

27. *Actinocladium.* Pedicels erect, septate, umbellately branched at the summit; spores simple, accumulated at the tips of the branches.

28. *Botryosporium.* Pedicels erect, septate, with short spine-like branchlets above, spirally arranged, and terminating in four or five short points, which support globular heads of spores.

** *Spores septate.*

29. *Arthrobotrys.* Pedicels simple, septate, with joints swollen at intervals, the swollen joints clothed with spines bearing didymous spores, which are collected into globular heaps.

BIBL. See the genera.

MUCOR, Micheli.—A genus of Mucorini (Physomycetous Fungi), forming a common mould of paste, decaying fruits, or other vegetable matters. The general character is that of an interwoven mass of horizontal branched filaments, sending down little root-like ramules and pushing up erect fertile filaments (not septate), which branch at the base in a stoloniferous manner, and thus form loosely grouped tufts. At the summit of the erect filaments, a globular vesicle is formed, which soon becomes cut off by a septum. Its contents become divided by segmentation into a large number of spores; and the septum at the base becomes meanwhile pushed up or protruded into the centre of the vesicle so as to form a kind of "core," called the *columella.* After a time the vesicle (*peridiole*) bursts and discharges its spores; the pressure of the turgid columella apparently hastens the bursting. The dehiscence takes place either by a circular slit just above the base of the columella, leaving this alone, surrounded by a narrow ragged collar

Fig. 496.

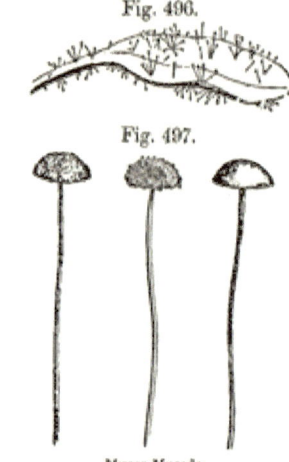

Fig. 497.

Mucor Mucedo.
(*Ascophora*-form.)

Fig. 496. Nat. size, growing on a leaf.
Fig. 497. Single fertile filaments, with the columella collapsed, and fallen like a cap over the end. Magn. 50 diams.

(*Mucor*), or the peridiole bursts above and disappears by solution, and the columella collapses upon the pedicel (*Ascophora*, fig. 497). The membrane of the peridiole of *M. Mucedo* (and perhaps of other species) is clothed with minute spines. The erect filament is sometimes simple, sometimes branched. It appears likely that the columella may become converted into a second peridiole, by being shut off by a septum which is converted into a new columella.

It has been imagined that ACHLYA is only an aquatic form of *Mucor*, and this seems not improbable; however, the experiments we have made on this point have hitherto given negative results.

The species of *Mucor* described by authors are pretty numerous; but we think considerable allowance for variation should always be made in this genus. RHIZOPUS, Ehr. = *Mucor* when distinctly stoloniferous. It seems very doubtful whether HYDROPHORA should be separated from *Mucor*.

* Fertile filaments simple.

1. *M. Mucedo*, L. (figs. 496–497). Mycelium byssoid, peridiole and spores globose, at first white, ultimately blackish. (This includes *Ascophora Mucedo*, Tode.) Extremely common. Sowerby, *Fungi*, pl. 378. fig. 6; Greville (*Ascophora*), *Sc. Crypt. Fl.* pl. 269.

2. *M. caninus*, Pers. Mycelium byssoid, peridiole globose, ultimately yellow or ferruginous; spore globose or elliptic. Very common on excrement of dogs and cats in wet weather. Grev. *Sc. Crypt. Fl.* pl. 305.

3. *M. fusiger*, Lk. Mycelium byssoid. Peridiole globose, ultimately black; spores spindle-shaped. On decaying fungi.

4. *M. clavatus*, Lk. "Mycelium byssoid. Clavate apices of the fertile filaments simply penetrating the globose peridiole; spores globose, at first white, then brown, at length black." On rotten pears. (Possibly only a state of *M. Mucedo*, or the following.)

5. *M. amethysteus*. Mycelium thick, white, closely interwoven. Peridiole at first white, then pale yellow, then crystalline and pure violet, finally violet - black or brownish; "spore globose, filled with globose sporidioles (?)." Fertile filament 1-40" high. On rotten pears with the foregoing.

6. *M. delicatulus*, Berk. Mycelium forming a thin velvety stratum. Very minute, fertile filaments short, peridioles globose, pale yellow; spores globose. On rotting gourds.

7. *M. succosus*, Berk. Mycelium forming small, pulvinate, yellow, spongy masses. Peridiole very minute, globose, yellow, at length olive; columella minute. On dead shoots of *Aucuba*. Berk. *Ann. Nat. Hist.* vi. pl. 12. fig. 15.

** Fertile filaments branched.

8. *M. ramosus*, Bull. Mycelium woolly. Fertile filaments racemose. Peridioles globose, yellow, then bluish-grey or reddish-brown. On rotting fungi. Bulliard, pl. 480. fig. 3.

9. *M. subtilissimus*, Berk. Mycelium creeping, filaments exceedingly slender. Fertile filaments branched, the short patent branches each terminating in a globose peridiole; spores oblong, elliptical. A mildew of onions. Berk. *Hort. Journ.* iii. p. 97. figs. 1–5.

BIBL. Berk. *Brit. Flora.* ii. pt. 2. p. 332; *Ann. Nat. Hist.* vi. p. 433; *Hort. Journal,* iii. p. 91; Fries, *Summa Veg.* p. 487; *Syst.*

Myc. iii. p. 318; Fresenius, *Beitr. z. Mycologie,* 1 heft, p. 4 (1850).

MUCORINI.—A family of microscopic Physomycetous Fungi, constituting the moulds, &c. common on most decaying vegetable and animal substances, consisting of a filamentous mycelium, forming flocks and clouds in or on decaying matters, bearing vesicles (on erect pedicels or sessile) filled with minute sporules, discharged by the rupture of the vesicles (*peridioles*). These plants correspond among the thecasporous Fungi to the Mucedines among the acrosporous or free-spored orders. The peridiole consists of the terminal cell of an erect filament, enlarged (like the head on a pin) into a globular vesicle. At first the cavity of this vesicle communicates with that of the pedicel, but a septum is soon formed; in some genera this septum is flat, in others projecting into the interior of the peridiole like the "punt" of a bottle, forming a hemispherical or cylindrical columella. While this columella rises in the peridiole, the latter becomes filled with spores, forming thus a polysporous sporange, and it bursts to let them escape.

The manner of bursting of the sporange and the form of the central column vary much, and afford generic characters. *Thelactis* presents a remarkable peculiarity: each filament terminates in a sporange containing a great number of spores, while at its base it gives origin to whorls of branches, the terminal cells of which remain sterile.

Syzygites is stated by Ehrenberg to exhibit a phænomenon of conjugation of its branches, like that of the Zygnemaceæ among the Algæ. (See SYZYGITES.)

Some observations have been published by De Bary, tending to show that the genus *Eurotium* only represents certain conditions of *Aspergillus.* From a recent examination of these plants, we have reason to believe that De Bary is mistaken in his conclusions; his account of the early development of the peridiole of *Eurotium* is certainly erroneous. *Eurotium* should properly stand among the PERISPORACEI. (See EUROTIUM.) *Acrostalagmus* is now regarded as a form of TRICHOTHECIUM or BOTRYTIS.

Synopsis of British and allied Genera.

1. *Phycomyces.* Peridiole pear-shaped, separated from the apex of the erect pedicel by an even joint; opening by an umbilicus. Spores oblong, very large. Filaments cæspitose, tubular, continuous, and shining.

2. *Hydrophora.* Peridiole subglobose, membranous, dehiscent, at first crystalline, aqueous, then turbid, and at length indurated, persistent. Columella absent; spores simple, conglobated.

3. *Mucor.* Peridiole subglobose, separating like a cap (leaving an annular fragment attached) from the erect, simple, continuous pedicel, or bursting irregularly; columella cylindrical or ovate, spores simple.

4. (?) *Acrostalagmus.* Peridioles globose, with a columella; at the points of doubly-verticillate branches from an erect pedicel.

5. *Ægerita.* Peridiole spherical, very fugacious; sporidia soon scattered like white meal over the grumous receptacle.

6. *Pilobolus.* Peridiole globular, separating like a cap from the short stalk composed of a single cell, attached on a unicellular ramified mycelium; columella conical; spores very numerous, free in the peridiole.

7. *Syzygites.* Filaments erect, simple, very much branched above, branches and branchlets di- or tri-chotomous, fertile branches forcipate, bearing pairs of opposite internal clavate branches, which subsequently coalesce.

8. (?) *Eurotium.* Peridiole cellular-membranous, sessile, at length bursting irregularly; spores produced by a central cellular nucleus which breaks up into numerous parent cells (*asci*), in which 4–8 minute spores are formed and finally set free; filaments of the mycelium radiating from the base of the peridiole.

Excluded genera.   *Ascophora* = *Mucor*; *Thelactis* = *Mucor?*; *Rhizopus* = *Mucor.*

MUCOUS CORPUSCLES. See MOUTH.

MUCOUS MEMBRANES.—Those internal canals and cavities of the body which open externally, as the alimentary canal, bladder, &c., are bounded by what may be regarded as internal prolongations of the skin, called mucous membranes.

They consist of four layers:—1, an innermost or epithelial layer, corresponding to the cutaneous epidermis; 2, a subjacent structureless basement membrane, which is not always separable and demonstrable; next comes 3, a layer of variable thickness, consisting of areolar and elastic tissue, well supplied with blood-vessels and nerves, often containing numerous small glands, frequently furnished with conical or filiform processes termed papillæ or villi, and sometimes traversed by muscular fibres. These three layers form the proper mucous membrane; and are supported by, 4, an outermost submucous layer or coat, composed of the same elements as the last, but much more lax in structure, and frequently containing fatty tissue.

The mucous membranes are usually very vascular; and injected preparations of them are very beautiful, and to some extent characteristic.

The size and form of the epithelial cells are to a certain extent also characteristic, especially those of the uppermost layer; and a knowledge of the peculiar structure in individual cases is of use in determining the source of morbid mucous products mixed with epithelial cells.

See the special articles.

MUCUS.—Natural mucus contains no essential morphological elements. As ordinarily met with, it often, however, exhibits some epithelial cells, mucous corpuscles, and numerous granules; and the peculiar mucous matter has a striated or fibrous appearance, mostly produced artificially. The abnormal elements are principally those of inflammation.

BIBL. See CHEMISTRY, ANIMAL.

MUD.—The organisms found in mud are very numerous; they consist principally of Diatomaceæ and other minute Algæ. The surface of mud is often covered with yellowish or greenish layers, composed almost entirely of these organisms. The most beautiful and most numerous forms of Diatomaceæ are found in the mud of sea-water, or that of tidal rivers. On exposing a bottle of mud and water to the light, they will rise to the surface of the mud, some adhering to the side of the bottle next the light, and can then be easily separated. The surface of freshwater mud frequently appears of a blood-red colour, from the presence of *Tubifex rivulorum.*

MUREXIDE. See AMMONIA, PURPURATE OF, p. 31.

MURIATE OF AMMONIA. See AMMONIA, HYDROCHLORATE OF, p. 30.

MUSA, Tournef.—A genus of Musaceæ (Monocotyledonous Flowering Plants), comprising the Bananas and Plantains. The fibro-vascular bundles of *Musa* afford examples of spiral vessels with numerous spiral fibres (see SPIRAL STRUCTURES). *Musa textilis* affords the fibre called Manilla hemp (see Pl. 21. fig. 7). See FIBROUS STRUCTURES.

MUSCA, Linn.—A genus of Dipterous Insects, of the family Muscidæ.

It would be of little use to detail the characters of this genus, as they vary so much according to different authors. Among the well-known species (all of which have been formed into new *genera*), we may mention:

1. *Musca domestica*, L., common house-fly. Third joint of antennæ thrice the length of the second; style plumose, eyes reddish brown, front of head white, the rest black; thorax blackish gray with four longitudinal black bands, abdomen blackish brown above, with blackish elongated spots, pale yellowish brown beneath.

2. *M. carnaria*, L. (*Sarcophaga*, Meigen), the flesh-fly. Antennæ feathery; head golden-yellow in front, eyes reddish; thorax gray with black longitudinal lines, abdomen black, with four square white spots on each segment, all the body strewed with black hairs. Viviparous, 1-2″ long.

3. *M. Cæsar*, L. (*Lucilia*, Donov.). No spots, abdomen green, with a metallic lustre.

4. *M. vomitoria*, L. (*Calliphora*, Donov.), bluebottle or blow-fly. Head yellowish, golden or white, eyes brown; thorax black; abdomen shining blue with black stripes and long black hairs.

The larvæ are known as gentles. The ova or larvæ are deposited upon animal or vegetable substances, mostly in a state of decay, upon which they live.

Several parts of the species of *Musca* are of general microscopic interest,—as the proboscis (Pl. 26. fig 29) with its two fleshy lobes (*c*), kept expanded by a beautiful and elastic framework of modified tracheæ; the setæ or lancets (*b*), which are modified maxillæ, sometimes rudimentary, with their palpi (*a*) at the base; the remarkable antennæ (Pl. 26. fig. 20); the elegant tarsus (Pl. 27. fig.7 *a*), with its terminal spine, pulvilli (figs. 7, 8 & 9) and claws; and the rudimentary wings (halteres, INSECTS, p. 387).

5. *Musca pumilionis* (*Chlorops*, Meig.) deposits its eggs in the young wheat-grain, which is consumed and destroyed by the larvæ.

Many other members of allied families of Diptera, commonly known also as flies, are of microscopic interest, on account of their oral setæ or lancet-like organs.

BIBL. Westwood, *Introduction, &c.*; Macquart, *Hist. Nat. d. Ins. Dipt.*; Meigen, *Syst. Beschr. d. bek. eur. zweiflüg. Insect.*; Keller, *Gesch. d. gemein. Stubenfliege.*

MUSCACEÆ. See MOSSES.

MUSCLE.—Muscular tissue forms the greater portion of the flesh of animals.

It occurs in two principal forms; one of which is termed organic, unstriated, or unstriped muscle; the other, voluntary, striated or striped muscle.

Unstriated muscle.—This consists of more or less elongated, somewhat spindle-shaped, narrow fibres (p. 67. fig. 34), having the import of cells, and hence often called fibre-cells. They are, however, solid. Each contains an elongated nucleus, brought to light by the addition of acetic acid, but exhibiting no nucleolus. The fibres are of variable length (from about 1-580 to 1-250″), and 1-5000 to 1-3500″ in diameter. They sometimes exist singly in the midst of areolar tissue; at others they are united into rounded or flattened bundles, and surrounded by an imperfect kind of sarcolemma, composed of areolar tissue with elastic fibres.

They occur most abundantly in the hollow viscera, as the stomach, the intestines, the bladder, and the uterus; but they also exist in other situations, as the spleen, trachea and bronchi, the dartos, the arteries, veins, and lymphatics, the prostate gland, fallopian tubes, urethra, villi of the small intestines, the skin, iris, &c.

Fig. 498.

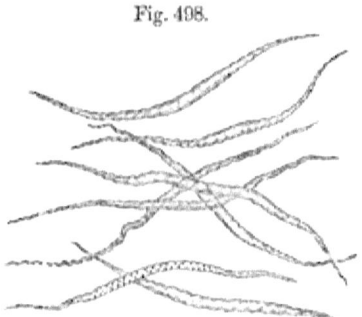

Unstriated muscular fibres from the œsophagus of a pig, after treatment with dilute nitric acid.
Magnified 10 diameters.

Striated muscle.—The structure of striated is more complex than that of unstriated muscular tissue. It consists of a number of very slender fibres, called fibrillæ, connected into bundles, termed primitive bundles or fasciculi, each of which is enclosed in a sheath or sarcolemma. The primitive bundles are again united into secondary and tertiary bundles, the whole being bound together by a connected mass of areolar and

Fig. 499.

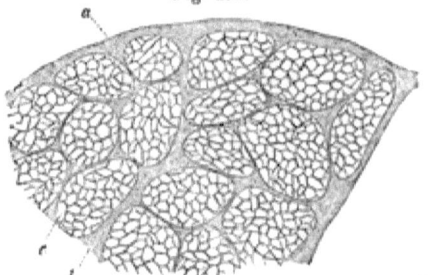

Transverse section of a portion of the sterno-cleido-mastoideus : *a*, outer perimysium ; *b*, inner perimysium ; *c*, primitive and secondary muscular bundles.

Magnified 50 diameters.

Fig. 500.

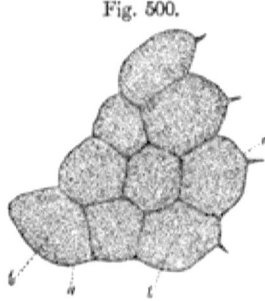

Transverse section of the muscular fibres or primitive bundles of the human gastrocnemius : *a*, sarcolemma and interstitial areolar tissue ; *b*, section of fibrillæ and intermediate substance.

Magnified 350 diameters.

elastic tissue surrounding each of them, and forming the perimysium. This arrangement is best seen in a transverse section (fig. 499).

The primitive bundles are from about 1-1000" to 1-200" in diameter, and of a rounded or polygonal form (fig. 500). Their surfaces are marked by a number of transverse striæ, which forms the most characteristic appearance of the tissue. They also exhibit irregular longitudinal striæ, which are the indications of the component fibrillæ (Pl. 17. fig. 35).

The sheath or sarcolemma, when separated from the muscular substance by treatment with water, acetic acid, and alkalies, in which it is insoluble, forms a structureless, transparent and smooth membrane. It is perhaps most easily seen in the muscle of fishes by simple dissection (Pl. 41. fig. 18).

Fig. 501.

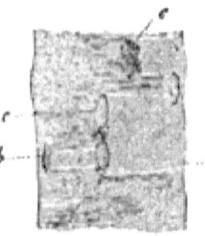

Portion of a primitive bundle treated with acetic acid : *a*, sarcolemma ; *b*, single nucleus ; *c*, twin nuclei surrounded by granules of fat.

Magnified 450 diameters.

On its inner side are numerous spindle-shaped or lenticular nuclei (fig. 501).

The ultimate or primitive fibrillæ in man are about 1-20,000" in diameter, and each exhibits numerous regularly alternating light and dark portions (Pl. 17. fig. 36 *f*) ; the relative positions of the two may, however, be made to change by altering the focus. The ends of the fibrillæ are distinguishable in transverse sections of the primitive bundles ; and their lateral margins are perfectly straight.

Fig. 502.

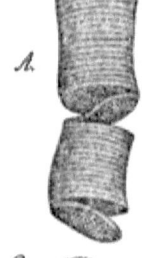

Different views have been taken of the structure of the fibrillæ, and, in fact, of the general structure of muscle. Thus the ultimate fibrillæ have been described as moniliform or beaded (Pl. 17. fig. 36 *c*) ; this appearance, however, arises from an optical illusion, connected either with imperfection in the object-glasses used, viewing the object in too much liquid, or the use of too low an object-glass, and too high an eye-piece.

A, a primitive bundle, magnified 350 diameters, partly separated into disks, side view. *B*, the same, rather more magnified, end view.

It often happens, especially when muscle has been kept in spirit, that it separates transversely into a number of flat disks (fig. 502) ; hence it has been viewed as consisting of these disks. Again, as under certain conditions it separates longitudinally into fibrillæ and transversely into disks, it has been supposed to consist of 'primitive particles' or 'sarcous elements' united end to end as well as laterally. We admit the existence of the primitive fibrillæ as original components of muscle, although there can be little doubt that the fibrillæ are not homogeneous, and of uniform constitution either chemical or physical. On carefully examining them at different foci, it is seen that those portions of isolated fibrils which appear dark when the margins of the fibrils are best in focus, are more highly refractive than the intermediate portions, as shown by the greater luminosity they acquire on altering the focus of the object-glass; and that this focal effect does not arise from a lenticular form of the parts is evident from the straight condition of the margins of the fibrils. Hence these more highly refractive parts probably constitute the proper muscular substance, connected in the direction of their length by a different kind of substance, which becomes brittle under the action of spirit, whilst the former does not; for the line of separation into the disks occurs through the less highly refractive portions. And that these compound fibrils naturally exist is shown by their being distinguishable in a primitive bundle without the use of reagents, or even of mechanical means.

It has also been supposed that the ultimate fibrils are composed of cells arranged end to end; and the appearance represented in Pl. 17. fig. 36 a, which is sometimes met with, might countenance this notion. But whenever it is seen, there is imperfect definition, from the presence of too much liquid, or some other cause; for we have never observed it when the object was properly arranged and examined.

There are other appearances exhibited by the fibrillæ which cannot at present be satisfactorily explained. Thus, sometimes each more highly refractive portion is divided by a dark line, indicating less refraction at that part (Pl. 17. fig. 36 d, taken at the elevated focus); at others the same part appears bounded at each end by a transverse dark line (fig. 36 b), or both parts are traversed mesially by a transverse dark line. In some instances we have noticed a very delicate constriction, which would account for these appearances; but the indication of this we have failed to discover.

The dark portions of the various fibrillæ of the primitive bundles being opposite to each other, gives rise to the coarser dark striæ seen under a low power. But it often happens that by pressure or manipulation this natural relation is destroyed, the direction of the striæ altered, and sometimes those of one bundle are made to alternate with those of the next. Hence arises an appearance of transverse or spiral fibres (Pl. 17. fig. 35); but none such really exist in muscle.

The proper substance of muscle consists chemically of a proteine compound called syntonine, resembling fibrine in several of its properties, but differing from it in the greater action of dilute muriatic acid, &c. By pressing muscle, a liquid is obtained containing some peculiar organic substances. This liquid probably exists between the fibrillæ.

The unstriated and the striated muscular fibres have the same chemical composition.

In regard to the development of muscle, in its earliest stage it consists of nucleated cells; these become fusiform, arranged in rows, and, uniting by their ends, form fibres. The proper muscular substance is then formed within them, as a secondary deposit, from the inner surface of the cells towards the centre, until the whole is solidified.

The muscles are very vascular. The smaller branches of the vessels mostly run parallel to the primitive bundles in the perimysium, and anastomose by transverse or oblique branches.

They are also well supplied with nerves; these mostly terminate in a plexus of looped branches (fig. 503).

Muscle undergoes important changes in disease. Wounds are filled up with areolar or tendinous tissue. In atrophy and fatty degeneration, the bundles become smaller, softer, more readily broken up, the transverse striæ and fibrillæ indistinct, or apparently absent, and contain yellowish or brown pigment-granules, with more or less numerous globules of fat (Pl. 30. fig. 14 a), and sometimes a large number of nuclei or small cells.

The interfascicular areolar tissue is also sometimes increased in amount, and fatty tissue developed in it. Sometimes the muscular substance is partially absorbed, and the sarcolemma contracting, gives the bundles a moniliform appearance (Pl. 30. fig. 14 b). In tetanus, the fibres become varicose and often ruptured, and the striæ closer.

The muscular tissue of the lower Vertebrata, and some of the Invertebrata, agrees essentially in structure with that of man; but the sarcolemma is often much thicker, the fibrillæ larger, and the nuclei contained within the substance of the bundles, and

Fig. 503.

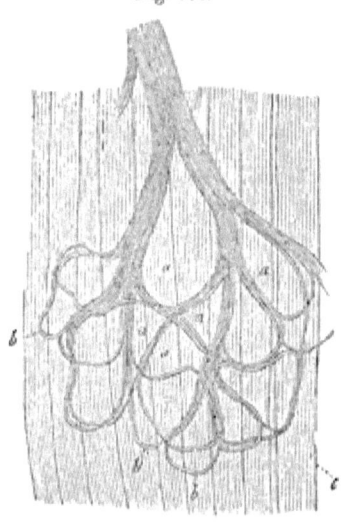

Termination of the branches of a nerve in a portion of the omohyoideus muscle, treated with caustic soda. *a*, meshes of the terminal plexus; *b*, loops; *c*, muscular fibres.

Magnified 350 diameters.

sometimes arranged in regular linear series. The margins of the bundles are also sometimes uneven, and rounded at regular intervals (Pl. 17. fig. 35), giving the appearance of their being surrounded by fibres.

In many of the lower members of the Invertebrata, although the substance of the body is voluntarily contractile, no trace of bundles or fibres can be detected.

To obtain the separate fibrillæ of striated muscle, the tissue should be macerated for about two hours in alcohol. This removes any fatty matter, and renders the fibrillæ more easily separable, by dissection with mounted needles. The fibrillæ are very minute, as we have stated; hence a very small portion of the tissue only should be taken for examination. That of fishes (the cod or the skate), or of reptiles (the frog), is the best for the purpose.

The unstriated muscular fibres are best seen in muscle which has been treated with dilute nitric or muriatic acid (1 part acid to 4 water). This renders them more opaque, and often curiously tortuous or spiral (fig. 502).

BIBL. Kölliker, *Mikrosk. Anat.* ii. and the *Bibl.*; Henle, *Allgem. Anat.*; Bowman, *Todd's Cycl.* iii. art. *Muscle*, and *Phil. Trans.* 1840-41; Donders, *Mulder's Physiolog. Chem.*; Lebert, *Ann. des Sc. Nat.* 3 sér. xiii.; and the *Bibl.* of CHEMISTRY, ANIMAL.

MUSHROOMS. See AGARICUS.

MUSSEL. — The species of Mollusca commonly known as mussels are of interest to the microscopist, on account of their alimentary canal containing Diatomaceæ; the same probably applies also to other marine and aquatic Mollusca, as well as other animals living upon these minute Algæ.

If it be required to obtain the valves only, the entire animal may be dissolved in hot nitric acid, and the residue washed as usual in preparing the Diatomaceæ.

The gills of the common marine mussel (*Mytilus edulis*) are well adapted for the examination of the cilia and ciliary motion.

Mussels also frequently contain the 'nurses' and larvæ (*Cercariæ*) of *Distoma* and other Trematoda (Entozoa).

One of the Acarina, *Hydrachna* (?) *concharum* (or *Limnochares* (?) *anodontæ*), is found in the pallial cavity or beneath the outer lamella of the branchial plates of the Naiadeæ (*Unio*, &c.).

BIBL. Dickie, *Ann. Nat. Hist.* 1848. i. p. 322; Vogt, *Ann. des Sc. Nat.* 3 sér. xii.; and the *Bibl.* of MOLLUSCA.

MUSTARD.—The best mustard consists of the ground seeds of *Sinapis nigra* (Cruciferæ); but those of *S. alba* are largely employed. The structures of these grains are very different from the substances most commonly employed for adulteration,—for example, wheat-flour, which is known by its starch-granules. Inferior samples contain variable quantities of the husk of the seed, which may be detected by the microscope. Mustard is generally coloured artificially, especially when adulterated with white meals, by means of TURMERIC, the peculiar colour-cells of which are readily recognizable.

BIBL. Hassall, *Food and its Adulterations*, p. 123.

MYCOPHYCEÆ.—The name applied by Kützing and some other authors to a collection of obscure vegetable productions, resembling the mycelia of Fungi, but having the habit of Algæ. It includes the *Crypto-*

roccee, Leptomitew, Saprolegniew, and *Phæonemeæ* of Kützing.

BIBL. Kützing, *Sp. Alg.* p. 145; *Phycol.
Generalis,* p. 146.

MYCOTHAMNION, Kütz. — One of
Kützing's genera of Leptomiteous Algæ,
composed of obscure byssoid productions
growing in foul water. Probably the mycelia
of fungi.

MYOBIA, Heyd. See ACARUS, p. 5.

MYRIANGIUM, Berk. and Mont.—A
genus of Collemaceæ (Lichens), forming
small orbiculate patches, radiately plicate
round the edge, with shield-shaped apothecia of the same colour; growing on the
branches of trees. *M. Curtisii* has been
found in the Channel Islands.

BIBL. Berkeley and Montagne, *Ann. des
Sc. Nat.* 3 sér. xi. p. 245; *London Journal
of Botany,* Feb. 1845, p. 72.

MYRIAPODA.—An order of Insects.

Char. Wings absent; legs numerous;
thorax not separated from the abdomen.

These animals are commonly known as
centipedes or millipedes.

The body is usually long, cylindrical
or flattened, and consisting of numerous
rings or joints. The head distinct, and the
jointed legs arranged on each side of the
body throughout its length. A few of them
are broad, short, and flattened, somewhat
resembling wood-lice. The head is furnished
with a pair of antennæ. Behind these are
laterally placed the eyes, which in some are
absent; they consist of mostly a group of
ocelli.

The structure of the trophi varies in the
different genera. The labrum is small, and
usually consolidated with the cephalic plate.
The mandibles (Pl. 28. figs. 25, 26 b) are often
large and powerful, somewhat resembling
those of the spiders, and, like them, traversed
by a canal, through which the duct of a
poison-gland passes. The maxillæ are
smaller, softer, and furnished with two
palpi. The labium (Pl. 28. fig. 26 a) is
often deeply cleft, its anterior and inner
margin elegantly toothed, and to it are
attached the labial palpi (fig. 26 c). In some
the labial palpi and mandibles are absent,
the labium forming a kind of sheath or
suctorial rostrum.

One or two pairs of legs, with a single
claw, are attached to each joint of the body.

The internal structure resembles that of
other insects.

The sexes are separate. The embryo, on
escaping from the ovum, has but few legs,

sometimes three pairs, at others none, the
number being augmented each time the
skin is cast; the same applies to the ocelli.

The Myriapoda live in dark places, beneath the bark of trees, under dead leaves,
stones, &c.

They form very interesting objects when
properly prepared and mounted. The small
ones, when slightly compressed between
two glasses, dried in that position, subsequently macerated in oil of turpentine, and
mounted in balsam, become very transparent, and show the structure beautifully;
the nervous ganglia and cords are often very
distinctly seen in these specimens without
dissection. The abdomen of the longer
specimens should be slit up with fine scis-
sors, and the viscera removed; the integument being gently compressed, and dried as
above.

BIBL. Newport, *Linn. Trans.* xix.; id.
Phil. Trans. 1841; Gervais, *Ann. des Sc.
Nat.* 2 sér. vii.; Leach, *Linn. Trans.* xi.;
R. Jones, *Todd's Cycl. Anat. and Phys.* iii.;
Fabre, *Ann. des Sc. Nat.* 1855. iii. (*Ann. Nat.
Hist.* 1857. xix. p. 162).

MYRIOCEPHALUM, De Not. See
CHEIROSPORA.

MYRIONEMA, Grev.—A genus of Myrionemaceæ (Fucoid Algæ), consisting of minute epiphytic plants, forming patches of
short, erect, simple, jointed filaments, springing from a thin expanded layer of decumbent cohering filaments. They are described
as bearing oblong 'spores;' but these are
probably *sporanges* producing zoospores; and
it is probable that they are accompanied by
septate sporanges, as in *Elachistea.*

1. *M. strangulans,* Grev. Patches convex,
confluent; erect filaments clavate; 'spores'
on the decumbent filaments. Forming dark-
brown dot-like spots on *Ulvæ,* or little rings
round *Enteromorphæ.* Grev. *Sc. Crypt. Flor.*
pl. 300.

2. *M. Leclancherii,* Chauv. Patches orbicular; erect filaments cylindrical; 'spores'
on the decumbent filaments. Forming
patches 1-12 to 1-4″ in diameter (at first like
a *Coleochæte*) on decaying fronds of *Rhodymenia* and *Ulva.* Harv. *Phyc. Brit.* pl. 41 A.

3. *M. punctiforme,* Lyngb. Patches
globose; filaments tapering to the base;
'spores' fixed to the erect filaments near
their bases, and very narrow. Forming
minute patches on *Ceramia, Chylocladia.*
Harv. *l. c.* pl. 41 B.

4. *M. clavatum,* Carm. An obscure species. Hook. *Brit. Fl.* ii. pt. 1. p. 391.

2 I

BIBL. *Op. cit. sup.*; Harvey, *Brit. Mar. Alg.* p. 51, pl. 10 E.

MYRIONEMACEÆ.—A family of Fucoideæ. Olive-coloured sea-weeds, with a tuber-shaped or crustaceous spreading frond, sometimes minute and parasitical. Ovoid unilocular, and filamentous multilocular sporanges attached to the superficial filaments, and concealed among them.

Synopsis of the British Genera.

1. *Leathesia.* Frond tuber-shaped.
2. *Ralfsia.* Frond crustaceous.
3. *Elachistea.* Frond parasitical, consisting of a tubercular base bearing pencilled erect filaments.
4. *Myrionema.* Frond parasitical, forming a flat base bearing cushion-like tufts of decumbent filaments.

MYRIOTRICHIA, Harv.—A genus of Ectocarpeæ (Fucoid Algæ), consisting of minute epiphytic plants, forming tufts of capillary filaments on larger Algæ. The filaments are simple jointed tubes, set all over with minute, simple, spore-like ramules, which again are clothed with very slender, long, articulated filaments. The fructification consists of oval unilocular *sporanges* on the sides of the main axis, producing zoospores; probably also multilocular sporanges exist.

1. *M. claviformis*, Hook. Main filament with quadrifarious ramules, increasing in length upwards. Fronds 1–2″ long, forming tufts on *Chorda lomentaria*. Harv. *Phyc. Brit.* pl. 101.

2. *M. filiformis*, Harv. Main filaments very long, often flexuous, set at irregular intervals with oblong clusters of minute papilliform ramules. Frond 1″ or more long. On *Chorda lomentaria* and *Asperococcus echinatus*. Harv. *Phyc. Brit.* pl. 156.

BIBL. *L. c. sup.*; Harv. *Brit. Mar. Alg.* p. 63, pl. 9 D; *Hook. Journ. Bot.* i. p. 300. t. 138.

MYROTHECIUM, Tode.—A genus of Onygenei (?) (Ascomycetous Fungi).

M. roridum, Tode, a plant of somewhat obscure relations, with a peridium formed of slender filaments, evanescent in the centre, and containing a gelatinous mass of cylindrical sporidia (?); grows on rotting plants, dried fungi, &c.

BIBL. Berk. *Brit. Flor.* ii. pt. 2. p. 323; Fries, *Summa Veg.* p. 448.

MYXOGASTRES.—A family of minute Gasteromycetous Fungi, of curious and interesting structure, characterized by their development from a mucilaginous filamentous matrix, out of which arise sac-like dehiscent peridia, emitting a very remarkable, often reticulated, filamentous structure, bearing the spores.

The Myxogastres grow upon bark of trees, or decayed wood, or on leaves (especially under certain atmospheric conditions), or on the ground; and their evanescent mycelium consists of diffluent mucilaginous filaments of varied form and colour. In proportion as these acquire consistence, there is formed a crust common to the whole mass, divided within into chambers, or a number of individuals appear separate from it and associated on a common thallus. In the first case a single peridium is formed, which may be regarded as a common peridium if we consider the inner cells as partial peridia soldered together, while in the second case each individual has its own peridium. This peridium, sessile or stalked, is composed of one or more membranous, papery, or crustaceous coats; in some cases where there are two coats, the outer is crustaceous and persistent, or it is extremely thin and membranous, and breaks up into deciduous scales. The mode of dehiscence varies. Sometimes an irregular opening is formed at the summit, as in *Physarum*; sometimes the peridium opens like a little box, as in *Craterium* (fig. 145, p. 187); sometimes the upper half falls off, leaving a cup-shaped base, as in *Arcyria*; or the membrane may be very delicate, and break up entirely into little scales, which fall off and leave the *capillitium* with its spores naked, as in *Stemonitis*. The *capillitium* or sporiferous structure is formed of filaments, simple or branched, free and loose, or anastomosing so as to form a network (fig. 147, p. 188); in *Trichia* these have spiral markings, and resemble the elaters of Hepaticæ (Pl. 32. fig. 39). The filaments are often elastic, and when the peridium bursts they rise from the bottom of it, forming a coloured, erect or drooping plume (*Arcyria*). In many species there is a stalk (*columella* or *stylidium*) in the centre of the capillitium. The spores appear to be produced upon these filaments by growing out from them in the manner of basidiospores. They are formed in vast numbers, and lie, when complete, on the branches and in the interstices of the capillitium.

De Bary has recently published an account of the early development of the mycelium of this family, and affirms that the mucilaginous filaments of which it is formed, ex-

hibit a creeping movement and a change-
able form, like what is observed in the
AMŒBÆA; and that the foundation of the
peridia is laid by a quantity of the filaments
crowding together into a common mass.
These statements require confirmation.

Synopsis of British Genera.

* TRICHIACEI. *Primary mucilage conjoin-
ing several distinct peridia. Filaments
of the capillitium free, entwined, elastic,
or almost absent.*

1. *Licea. Peridium* subpersistent, membranous, bursting irregularly. *Spores* in
heaps, with scarcely any *filaments.*

2. *Perichæna. Peridium* persistent, membranous, bursting by a circumscissile slit.
Filaments few, free.

3. *Trichia. Peridium* simple, persistent,
bursting irregularly at the summit. *Filaments* densely interwoven, elastic.

4. *Arcyria. Peridium* simple, membranous, splitting all round at the base, the
upper part very fugacious. *Filaments* densely
interwoven, elastic.

** STEMONITEI. *Primary mucilage connecting several distinct peridia. Filaments conjoined into a network, adnate
or innate.*

5. *Cribraria. Peridium* simple, membranous, the upper part falling off. The
filaments adherent in the interior, at length
expanding into a free network above.

6. *Dictydium. Peridium* simple, subglobose, very delicately membranous, bursting
indeterminately, leaving the *filaments* (innate) forming a cage-like latticed *capillitium.*

7. *Stemonitis. Peridium* simple, globose
or cylindrical, delicately membranous, finally
evanescent. *Filaments* forming a determinate *capillitium*, attached to a bristle-like
central columella, and forming a network
around it.

8. *Diachæa. Peridium* simple, ovate-
oblong, membranous, detached in fragments, leaving a radiately reticulate *capillitium*, with a floccose-grumous pulverulent
axis.

9. *Enerthenema. Peridium* simple, globose, membranous, at length evanescent,
laying bare a conical columella with a cap
at the summit, bearing underneath ascending entwined *filaments.*

*** PHYSAREI. *Primary mucilage spreading widely, passing into many peridia.*

*Filaments adnate, straight, vague. Spores
black.*

10. *Craterium. Peridium* simple, varied,
papery, persistent, closed by a lid, which
finally falls off. *Capillitium* somewhat
chambered, formed of crowded *filaments*, at
length erect.

11. *Physarum. Peridium* simple, variable,
naked, membranous, bursting irregularly.
Capillitium floccose; *filaments* at first joined
into a net or forked.

12. *Didymium. Peridium* double; the
outer bark-like, breaking up into little fur-
furaceous scales or mealy down, the *inner*
membranous, bursting irregularly; *filaments*
vague, adnate to the peridium.

13. *Diderma. Peridium* double; *outer*
crust-like, distinct, brittle, dehiscent, the
inner very delicately membranous, evanescent; *filaments* vague, adnate to the base.

**** ÆTHALINEI. *Primary mucilage producing one peridium.*

14. *Spumaria. Peridium* indeterminate,
crustaceous, divided into cells by regular
ascending folds, and finally falling away.
No internal *filaments.*

15. *Æthalium. Peridium* indeterminate,
fragile, falling away, covered with a floccose
bark externally, cellular internally by means
of *filaments* conjoined into membranous
layers.

16. *Reticularia. Peridium* indeterminate, simple, naked, fugacious, bursting irregularly, laying bare branched, reticulated,
adnate *filaments.*

17. *Lycogala. Peridium* determinate,
composed of a double membrane, membranous, somewhat warty, persistent, bursting
at the summit. *Filaments* adnate on all sides
of the peridium.

BIBL. See under the heads of these
genera; also, for the development of Myxogastres, Schmitz, *Mycologische Beobachtungen; Linnæa*, xvi. 188; De Bary, *Botanische
Zeitung*, 1858, p. 357.

MYXORMIA, Berk. and Br.—A genus
of Phragmotrichacei (?) (Coniomycetous
Fungi), containing one species, *M. atrori-
ridis*, forming minute cup-like bodies, on
dead leaves of grass. It is allied to *Excipula*,
but differs in its concatenate spores being
connected by a slender thread, which frequently breaks off with them; spores very
gelatinous.

BIBL. Berk. and Br. *Ann. Nat. Hist.* 2 ser.
v. p. 457, pl. 2. fig. 9.

MYXOTRICHUM, Kze.—A genus of

Dematiei (Hyphomycetous Fungi), growing on rotten wood, paper, &c. Three species are described as British : *M. cæsium*, Fr. ; *M. chartarum*, Kze. ; and *M. deflexum*, Berk. They form little tufts or downy balls, sending off radiating branched filaments. The spores are described as occurring collected in masses about the base of the threads (?).

BIBL. Berk. *Brit. Flor.* ii. pt. 2. p. 335 ; *Ann. Nat. Hist.* i. p. 260, pl. 8. fig. 9 ; Fries, *Summa Veg.* p. 502 ; *Syst. Myc.* iii. p. 348.

N.

NACCARIA, Endl.—A genus of Cryptonemiaceæ (Florideous Algæ), containing one rare British species, *N. Wigghii*, usually thrown up from deep water. Its rose-coloured frond is 6 to 12" high, and consists of a branched filiform expansion, the central axis being about as thick as a crow-quill, the branchlets quadrifariously alternate and clothed with ramules about 1–12" long. The cells of the main axis and branches of the frond are large and empty in the centre, small and closely packed at the circumference ; the ramules are composed of jointed dichotomous filaments having a whorled arrangement, surrounded by gelatinous matter. The difference between the character of the axes and the ramules is shown in the figure (fig. 504). The spores are borne on branches of the filaments of the ramules, the fertile ramules being swollen in the middle.

Fig. 504.

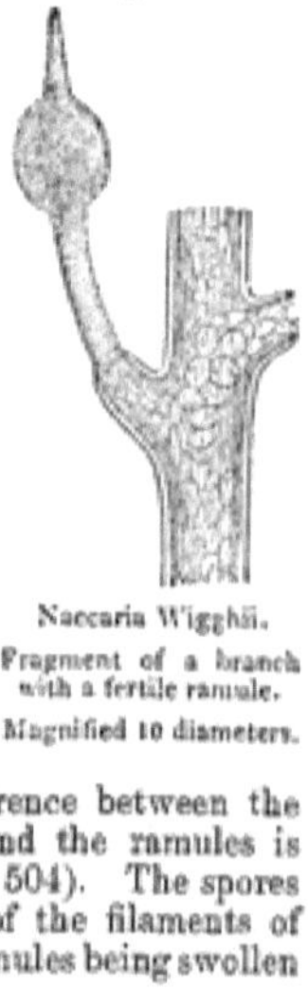

Naccaria Wigghii.
Fragment of a branch with a fertile ramule.
Magnified 10 diameters.

BIBL. Harvey, *Brit. Mar. Alg.* p. 152, pl. 20 D ; *Phyc. Brit.* pl. 38 ; Greville, *Alg. Brit.* pl. 16.

NAIDINA.—A family of Annulata, of the order Setigera.

Char. Body worm-like, annulate or segmented, without suckers or soft leg-like appendages ; segments furnished with partially retractile bristles or setæ, excepting the three or four first ; head distinct from the body.

Animals aquatic, living among aquatic plants, or burrowing in mud. Sexes distinct ; propagation by ova and by spontaneous transverse division. The bristles are moved by muscles, and answer the purpose of legs. They are situated on the upper or under surface of the body, mostly in rows.

Nais, Müll. Four anterior segments without upper bristles.

1. *N. Scotica*, Johnst. Body cylindrical, ends obtuse, the anterior smooth and cylindrical. the portion behind it provided with a double row of thin tufts of prickles, some of them composed of several bristles, shorter than the diameter of the body ; mouth and anus terminal ; no proboscis. Length 1".

2. *N. serpentina* (*Serpentina quadristriata*). Body cylindrical, not flattened in front ; head snake-like, with a produced lower lip ; eyes two, upper bristles subulate, lower forked or uncinate. Length about 1½".

The lower bristles have a globular swelling below the middle ; segments eighty to ninety ; head with four dark transverse bands.

3. *N. proboscidea* (*Stylaria lacustris*). Body cylindrical, flattened in front ; first four segments divided by a stricture from the body, the first, or head, being prolonged into a filiform proboscis ; eyes two ; upper bristles simple, lower forked. Length about 1–2".

Found on the roots of aquatic plants. Middle segments nearly twice as broad as long, regularly decreasing backwards ; upper bristles twice as long as the width of the body, the lower uncinate, with an incisure about the middle.

Chætogaster, Baer. All the segments without upper bristles.

C. vermicularis. Body cylindrical, truncate in front ; eyes none ; mouth terminal : setæ bifid. Length about 1".

Found amongst *Lemna*, in ditches, and in the respiratory chamber of the Lymnæidæ. See TUBIFEX.

BIBL. Schmidt, *Müller's Archiv*, 1846. p. 406 ; Dugès, *Ann. des Sc. Nat.* 2 sér. xv. p. 319 ; Johnston, *Catal. of British Non-parasitical Worms* ; Doyère, *Mém. Linn. Soc. of Normandy*, x.

NAILS.—These organs, which consist of modified epidermic formations, are imbedded posteriorly and laterally in depressions, or are covered at these parts by a fold of the skin. The posterior depression (fig. 505 *d*) is much deeper than the lateral depressions (fig. 506 *c*).

The nail itself consists of the root (fig. 505 *l*), the body (*k*), and the free end (*m*).

The root extends over that part of the matrix furnished with the ridges, and is either entirely lodged in the posterior depression of the cutis, or the crescentic portion of it is exposed. The body of the nail is uncovered except at the sides, which are overlapped by the lateral folds of the skin.

The portion of the cutis (fig. 506 a) to which the under surface o the nail, except that of the anterior free portion, is attached —the matrix or bed—is covered with ridges (fig. 506 a), extending from the posterior part or root of the nail to the convex margin of the white crescentic portion called the lunule, where they become larger and higher, forming plates which run to the end of the matrix. The margins of the ridges and plates are covered with short papillæ. The anterior portion of the matrix of the nail is very vascular.

The under surface of the root and body of the nail is covered with depressions and ridges to adapt itself to those of the matrix.

Two layers are distinguishable in the

Fig. 505.

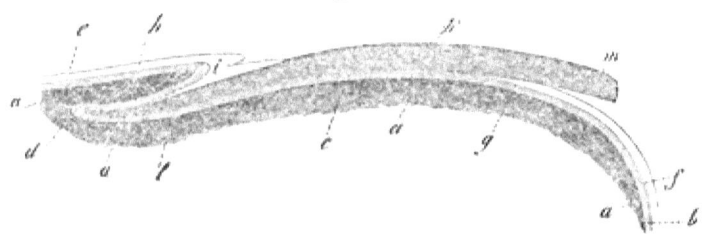

Longitudinal section through the middle of the nail and its matrix. *a*, matrix and cutis of the back and point of the finger; *b*, rete mucosum of the point of the finger; *c*, that of the nail; *d*, that of the bottom of the root-fold; *e*, the same of the back of the finger; *f*, epidermis of the point of the finger; *g*, its origin beneath the margin of the nail; *h*, epidermis of the back of the finger; *i*, its termination at the upper surface of the root of the nail; *k* body, *l* root, *m* free end of the proper nail.

Magnified 8 diameters.

Fig. 506.

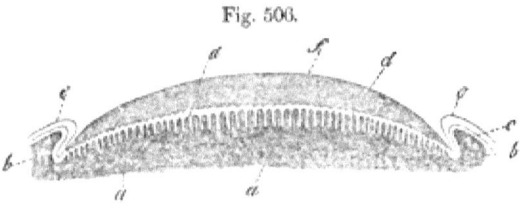

Transverse section of the nail and its matrix. *a*, matrix with its ridges (black); *b*, cutis of the lateral fold; *c*, rete mucosum of the same; *d*, rete mucosum of the nail with its ridges (white); *e*, epidermic layer of cutaneous fold; *f*, proper substance of the nail, with short teeth on its under surface.

Magnified 8 diameters.

nails—an under soft layer (figs. 505 d, 506 c, 507 B), corresponding to and directly continuous with the rete mucosum of the skin, and the upper horny layer forming the true nail (figs. 506 f, 505 k, 507 C). The lower surface of the latter is furnished with small ridges (fig. 507 c), which occupy corresponding furrows in the mucous layer.

In minute structure, the soft layer resembles that of the cutaneous rete, except in the deeper layers of cells being elongated and arranged perpendicularly (fig. 507 b).

The horny portion, or proper nail, consists of epidermic cells, flattened and aggregated into plates or laminæ (fig. 507 C). In the natural state, these cells are undistinguishable, except at the root and the under surface, where the nail is in contact with the mucous layer,—the remainder merely exhibiting shorter or longer dark lines, representing the flattened nuclei, or indicating the existence of the laminæ. But if a section of nail be treated with solution of caustic potash or soda, the nucleated cells swell up, and resume their proper form and appearance.

Fig. 507.

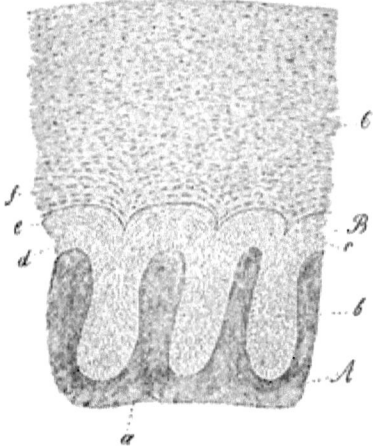

Transverse section of the body of the nail. *A*, cutis of the matrix. *B*, rete mucosum of the nail. *C*, epidermis of the same, or proper nail. *a*, plates of the matrix ; *b*, plates of the rete mucosum of the nail ; *c*, ridges of the proper substance of the nail ; *d*, deeper perpendicular cells of the rete mucosum of the nail ; *e*, upper flattened cells of the same ; *f*, nuclei of the cells of the proper nail.

Magnified 250 diameters.

Fig. 508.

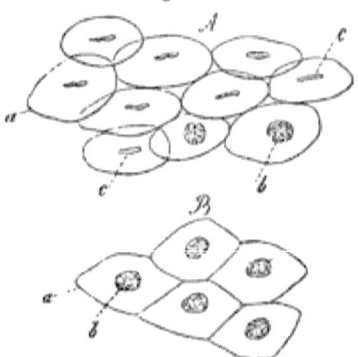

Laminæ of a nail after boiling with solution of caustic soda or potash. *A*, side view. *B*, surface view. *a*, cellmembranes ; *b*, nuclei seen from above ; *c*, the same in side view.

Magnified 350 diameters.

The cutaneous epidermis (fig. 506 *e*) extends for a certain distance into the lateral

and posterior depressions of the skin, covers the anterior portion of the root, the posterior part of the body, and the lateral margins of the nails, terminating in a fine layer, which is, however, nowhere directly continuous with the substance of the nail.

BIBL. Kölliker, *Mikrosk. Anat.* ii. and the *Bibl.* therein.

NAIS, Müll. See NAÏDINA.

NARCOTINE. See ALKALOIDS, p. 27.

NASSULA. Ehr.—A genus of Infusoria, of the family Trachelina.

Char. Body covered with cilia arranged in longitudinal rows ; mouth surrounded by a cone of rod-like teeth ; no proboscis nor ear-like processes.

The gastric sacculi of these animals frequently contain a violet-coloured liquid, derived from the solution of partly digested *Oscillatoriæ.*

1. *N. elegans* (Pl. 24. fig. 45 ; *b*, teeth). Body cylindrical or ovate, somewhat narrowed in front, very obtuse at the ends ; white or greenish. Aquatic ; length 1-144 to 1-120''.

2. *N. aurea* (Pl. 24. fig. 46). Body ovate-oblong, subcylindrical, golden-yellow, very obtuse at the ends. Aquatic ; length 1-120''.

3. *N. ornata.* Brownish-green.

It is questionable how far this genus is different from *Chilodon.*

BIBL. Ehrenberg, *Infus.* p. 338; Stein, *Infus.* p. 248.

NAUNEMA, Ehr.—A genus of Diatomaceæ, no longer retained.

BIBL. Ehrenberg, *Infus.* 233 ; Kützing, *Bacill.* and *Sp. Alg.*

NAVICULA, Bory.—A genus of Diatomaceæ.

Char. Frustules single, free ; valves oblong, lanceolate or elliptical, sometimes with the ends narrowed and produced, rarely constricted in the middle, furnished with a longitudinal line or keel, and a nodule in the middle and at each end ; surface of valves covered with depressions or dots arranged in transverse or slightly radiating rows, producing an appearance of lines, although both dots and lines are often invisible by ordinary illumination.

The valves are usually symmetrical, and the keel median, but in two species the keel is sigmoid and the valves inæquilateral. Sometimes the keel is double. There is mostly a little space between the rows of dots (Pl. 11. fig. 8), so that these readily exhibit transverse lines or striæ by unilateral oblique light ; but sometimes they are pretty uniformly distributed, as in many of the species belonging to the first section of *Gyrosigma*.

The species or forms are very numerous. Kutzing describes 170, some of them, however, belonging to *Pinnularia*, *Gyrosigma*, and other genera. Smith describes thirty-six British species. They may all have been derived from a frustule of a *Schizonema* or *Colletonema* which had escaped from its gelatinous envelope!

The formation of sporangial frustules has been noticed by us in *Navicula amphirhynchus*, and they are contained in a siliceous sporangial sheath or case. The process is sufficiently illustrated by the figures (Pl. 41. figs. 19–24); fig. 19, side view of the parent frustule; fig. 20, front view of conjugating frustules, with young sporangial sheath; fig. 21, empty mature sheath; fig. 22, crushed empty sheath and parent frustules *in situ*; fig. 23, sheath, one parent-frustule and sporangial frustule in front view; fig. 24, sporangial frustule in side view.

1. *N. cuspidata* (Pl. 11. fig. 6, side view; fig. 7, front view; *a*, hoop). Valves lanceolate, somewhat rhomboid, acuminate; aquatic; length 1·350 to 1·200″. Valves slightly iridescent, no striæ by ord. illum.

2. *N. didyma* (Pl. 11. fig. 9). Valves elliptic-oblong, slightly constricted in the middle; marine; length 1·600 to 1·300″. Ends sometimes broadly rounded, and the constriction very deep.

3. *N. rhomboides*. Valves rhomboid-lanceolate; colourless and not striated by ordin. illum.; aquatic; length 1·350″. Striæ 85 in 1·1000″ (Sm.).

4. *N. amphirhynchus* (Pl. 41. fig. 19, side view; fig. 22, front view of conjugating frustules). Valves linear, or nearly so, suddenly contracted near the produced and obtuse ends; aquatic; length 1·500 to 1·250″.

BIBL. Smith, *Brit. Diatom.* i. 46; Kützing, *Bacill.* p. 91, and *Sp. Alg.* p. 60.

NEBALIA, Leach.—A genus of Entomostraca, of the order Phyllopoda, and family Aspidephora.

Char. Antennæ two pairs, large and ramiform; eyes two, stalked; legs twelve pairs, eight branchial and four natatory, carapace large, enclosing head, thorax, and part of abdomen.

N. bipes (Pl. 14. fig. 28). Marine; body yellowish; length 3-8″.

BIBL. Baird, *Brit. Entomostr.* p. 36.

NECKERA, Hedwig.—A genus of Hypnoid Mosses.

Elegant little perennial plants, growing on trunks of trees and shady rocks, having stems pinnately branched, bearing complanate leaves arranged in eight rows.

N. crispa, Dill., found in mountainous districts, is a large moss, with stems 4 or 6″ long or more, growing horizontally from a creeping rhizome.

NECTRIA, Fries.—A genus of Sphæriacei (Ascomycetous Fungi), distinguished from true *Sphæriæ* by the free, membranous, flaccid, brightly-coloured perithecium, the pale papilla, and the gelatinous pale nucleus expelled in the form of a drop or of white flocks; the asci contain eight pellucid spores. The imperfect forms of these plants are described as distinct genera. Thus *Tubercularia vulgaris*, common on bark of dying or dead trunks, and on dead twigs of birch especially, ripens into *N. cinnabarina*; this we have observed, and it is probable that other Coniomycetous forms will require to be reduced in like manner. *Nectria* includes the following *Sphæriæ* of the British Flora: *cinnabarina*, *coccinea*, *ochracea*, *aurantia*, *rosella*, *citrina*, *Peziza*, *sanguinea*, *episphæria*, &c., and several new species are described by Messrs. Berkeley and Broome.

BIBL. Fries, *Summa Veg.* p. 387; Berk. & Broome, *Ann. Nat. Hist.* 2 ser. xiii. p. 467.

NEMALEON, Targioni.—A genus of Cryptonemiaceæ (Florideous Algæ), containing two British species, one, *N. multifidum*, not uncommon on shells and stones near low-water mark. Its frond consists of a somewhat cartilaginous, simple or once or twice dichotomous cord, 3 to 6″ high and 1 to 2″′ in diameter, of a dull purple colour. The cord consists of a dense axis formed of interlaced longitudinal filaments, clothed with horizontal, dichotomously-branched filaments, moniliform and coloured towards the circumference of the cord. The fruit consists of—1. *favellidia*, consisting of globular masses of "spores" attached singly to the filaments of the periphery (MM. Derbès and Solier say that the single cells arising from the filaments each *discharge* one spore from the interior, so that they are sporesacs); and 2. of collections of *antheridia*, consisting of minute hyaline cells seated on the peripheral filaments, exactly corresponding to the spore-sacs, but discharging spermatozoids.

BIBL. Harv. *Br. Mar. Alg.* p. 153, pl. 21 B, *Phyc. Brit.* pl. 36; Derbès and Solier, *Ann. des Sc. Nat.* 3 sér. xiv. p. 274, pl. 35; Thuret, *ibid.* 4 sér. iii. p. 21.

NEMASPORA, Fries.—A supposed genus of Melanconiei (Coniomycetous Fungi), the species of which present two forms, one bearing minute conidia (*Nemaspora*), the other spores (*Libertella*, Desmaz.), and which probably also will be found to exhibit an asciferous form. *N. crocea*, Pers. is common on beech-trees, *N. Rosæ* on roses and lilacs. They are at first minute gelatinous masses of conidia, coherent into a nucleus under the epidermis, devoid of a perithecium; the spores finally exude as a gelatinous tendril; the spores are curved and of an orange-colour. *Nemaspora* consists really of spermogonous fruits, and *Libertella* of stylosporous fruits of Ascomycetous genera.

BIBL. Berk. *Brit. Fl.* ii. pt. 2. p. 355; Fries, *Summa Veg.* p. 413; Desmaz. *Ann. des Sc. Nat.* 1 sér. xix. p. 269, pl. 6. figs. 3–6.

NEMATHECIA.—Wart-like collections of vertical filaments found on the surface of the fronds of the Cryptonemiaceæ (FLORIDEÆ).

NEOTTIOSPORA, Desmaz.—A genus of Sphæronemei (Coniomycetous Fungi), remarkable from the fusiform spores being furnished with three or four terminal threads. *N. Caricum* grows upon dead leaves of sedges, bursting from beneath the epidermis by a circular black orifice, from which an orange-coloured (sometimes olive-coloured) gelatinous mass of spores escapes in the form of a cirrhus. Diameter of conceptacles about 1–80″.

BIBL. Desmazières, *Ann. des Sc. Nat.* 2 sér. xix. p. 346; Berk. & Broome, *Ann. Nat. Hist.* 2 ser. xiii. p. 379.

NEOTTOPTERIS.—A genus of Asplenieæ (Polypodioid Ferns). The exotic fern called *Asplenium Nidus* belongs here.

NEPA, Linn.—A genus of Hemipterous insects.

N. cinerea, the common water-scorpion, is of a dirty brown colour, the body broad and flat, with two long terminal respiratory tubes, the anterior pair of legs stout and greatly elbowed, the posterior formed for crawling and not swimming.

Pl. 26. fig. 26 represents the trophi. The labium (*i*) is three-jointed, with two small lobes between the second and third joints; the four setæ (mandibles and maxillæ) are furnished with teeth, directed towards the free end (and not as shown in the figure); the lingua or tongue (*) is trifid at the apex.

The lateral tracheæ are dilated opposite the thorax to form two internal respiratory

sacs. The eggs are oval, and with seven reflexed filaments at one end.

BIBL. Westwood, *Introduction*, &c.; Dufour, *Rech. s. l. Hémiptères*.

NEPENTHES, L.—A genus of Nepenthaceæ (Dicotyledonous Plants), in which the spiral vessels have four parallel fibres (see SPIRAL STRUCTURES).

NEPHROCYTIUM, Nägeli.—A genus of Unicellular Algæ, perhaps merely decomposing spores of Spirogyra.

BIBL. Nägeli, *Einzellige Algen*, p. 79, pl. 3. fig. 2.

NEPHRODIUM, Schott.—A genus of Aspidieæ (Polypodioid Ferns).

NEPHROLEPIS, Schott.—A genus of Aspidieæ (Polypodioid Ferns).

NEPHROMA, Ag.—A genus of Parmeliaceæ (Gymnocarpous Lichens). *N. resupinata*, Sch. occurs on trees and mossy rocks in subalpine districts. This genus differs from *Peltigera* in the situation of the kidney-shaped apothecia.

BIBL. Hook. *Brit. Flor.* ii. pt. 1. p. 220; *Eng. Bot.* pl. 305.

NERIUM. See STOMATA, and LIBER (p. 416).

NERVES and NERVOUS CENTRES.—The nervous system is usually regarded as consisting of two parts: the nerves, which are divided into the cerebro-spinal and the sympathetic; and the nervous centres, represented by the brain and spinal chord, with which must also be placed the ganglia. These parts are composed essentially either of nerve-tubes, nerve-cells, or of both these elements.

The *nerve-tubes* or primitive nerve-fibres are most numerous in the white portion of the nervous centres and in the nerves. They are slender, soft, cylindrical filaments, varying in diameter from 1–20,000 to 1–1100″. When quite recent, they are transparent and apparently homogeneous (fig. 509, 1), but they really consist of three distinct parts—an enveloping membrane or sheath, a tenacious liquid, and a soft but elastic internal fibre.

The sheath of the nerve-tubes is a very delicate, structureless and transparent membrane (fig. 510, 1 *a*, 2, 3 *a*, 4 *a*); it is not demonstrable in the smallest fibres, although probably always present.

Within the sheath is a hollow cylinder or tube (figs. 509, 3 *b*, 510, 3, 4 *b*), called the white substance of Schwann. It is homogeneous and tenacious in perfectly fresh nerves, but soon after death becomes coagulated, sometimes externally only, giving a double outline to the walls of the nerve-tubes (fig. 510, 2, 3, 4), or becoming granular externally, and remaining liquid internally. It is also easily altered by pressure, sometimes escaping in globules or masses of various form, from the ends or the broken sides of the tubes, at others accumulating at intervals in various parts of the tubes, giving them an elegant varicose appearance (fig. 511).

The third structure exists within the last, in the form of a rounded or flattened, pale,

Fig. 509.

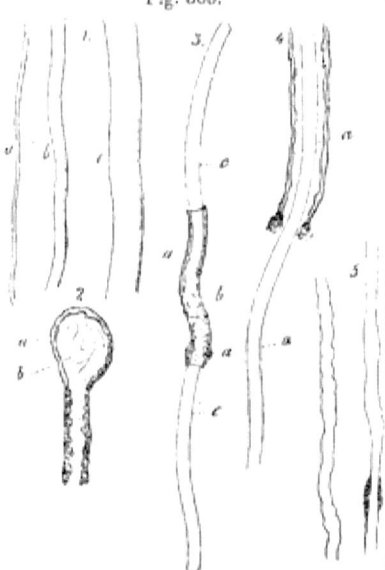

Nerve-fibres. 1. From nerves of the dog and rabbit, in the natural state: *a*, fine, *b*, moderate, *c*, large fibre. 2. From a frog, after the addition of serum: *a*, drop forced out by pressure; *b*, part of the axial fibre contained in it. 3. From the human spinal marrow, treated with serum: *a*, sheath; *b*, white substance with a double outline; *c*, axial fibre. 4. Fibre with double outline, from the human fourth ventricle: *a*, axial fibre. 5. Two isolated axial fibres, with a portion of the white substance adherent to the right-hand one.

Magnified 350 diameters.

elastic band or fibre, occupying the axis of the tube, and called the axial band (figs. 509, 2 *b*, 3 *c*, 4 *a*, 5; 510, 1 *b*).

These three structures of nerve are somewhat difficult of demonstration. The outer sheath may sometimes be shown by pressing the nerve-tube, which forces out the white

substance. Boiling the nerves in absolute alcohol, with the subsequent addition of

Fig. 510.

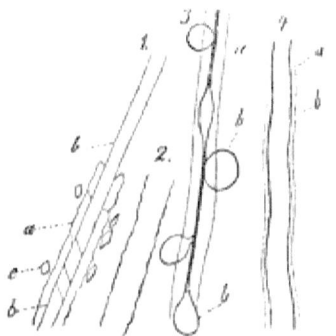

Nerve-tubes. 1. From a frog, after boiling with acetic acid and alcohol: *a*, sheath; *b*, axial band; *c*, crystals of fat. 2. Isolated sheath of a frog's nerve boiled with soda. 3. From the human fourth ventricle, after treatment with soda: *a*, sheath; *b*, white substance exuding in drops: the axial band has been removed in the preparation. 4. Human, treated with soda: *a*, sheath; *b*, white substance; the axial band not visible.

Magnified 350 diameters.

Fig. 511.

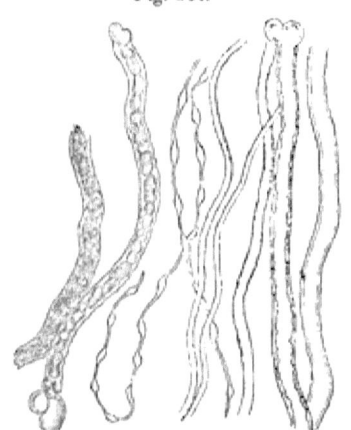

Human nerve-tubes, showing tubes of various sizes; some with a single, others with a double outline; some varicose, others with the white substance in a granular state.

Magnified 350 diameters.

caustic alkali, or in acetic acid, when crystals of fat separate from the white substance (fig. 510, 1), will answer the same purpose. Treatment with strong nitric acid, and afterwards with potash, causes the white substance to exude; and the axial fibre being dissolved, the yellow sheath is left empty and very distinct. Solution of corrosive sublimate has also been recommended. The axial band is best seen in nerves treated with strong acetic acid, cold absolute alcohol, æther, chromic acid, &c.

Chemically the sheath and axial band consist of a proteine compound, and the white substance of a mixture or compound of fat with a proteine substance.

In the cerebro-spinal nerves, the nervetubes are aggregated into bundles, and surrounded by an envelope of areolar tissue, called the neurilemma, in which blood-vessels ramify, thus corresponding with the arrangement of the primitive fibrillæ of muscle. Sometimes, towards the terminations of the nerves, the neurilemma appears as a homogeneous membrane with elongated nuclei.

The nerves rarely branch; they usually terminate in loops.

In the grey, sympathetic, or ganglionic nerves, the fibres of which are sometimes called gelatinous fibres, the nerve-tubes are smaller and paler than those of most of the cerebro-spinal nerves, and scattered through a more copious areolar sheath or neurilemma of mostly longitudinal fibres (Remak's fibres), containing numerous elongated nuclei (fig. 512).

Fig. 512.

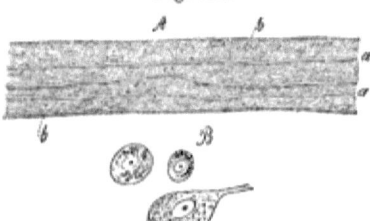

From the human sympathetic. *A.* Portion of a grey fibre treated with acetic acid: *a*, fine nerve-tubes; *b*, nuclei of Remak's fibres. *B.* Three ganglion-globules, one with a pale process.

Magnified 350 diameters.

Nerve-cells, nerve-corpuscles, or ganglion-globules are nucleated cells, most numerous in the cineritious or dark portions of the nervous centres, and in the ganglia, but sometimes met with in the trunks and terminal expansions of nerves, as the retina, &c. They are furnished with a delicate outer coat or membrane (fig. 513, 1 *a*); this is easily seen in the cells of the ganglia, but with difficulty in those of the central organs.

They are rounded, elongate, pyriform, or angular (fig. 513). Some of them are sim-

Fig. 513.

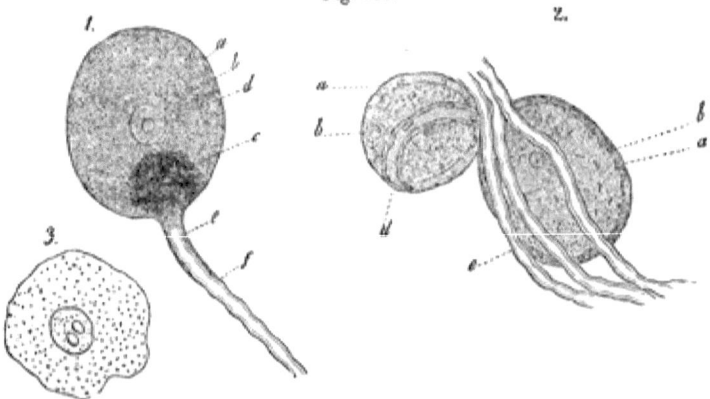

Nerve-cells and fibres from the auditory nerve. 1. Nerve-cell with the origin of a fibre, from the anastomosis between the facial and auditory nerve in the meatus auditorius externus of the ox: *a*, cell-membrane; *b*, contents; *c*, pigment; *d*, nucleus; *e*, prolongation of the sheath upon the nerve-tube; *f*, nerve-tube. 2. Two nerve-cells with tubes from the auditory nerve of the ox: *a*, sheath with nuclei; *b*, cell-membrane; *c*, nucleus; *d*, origin of tube, with nucleated sheath; *e*, tubes. 3. Separate contents of a nerve-cell with a nucleus and two nucleoli.
Magnified 350 diameters.

ple, others furnished with one, two, or more simple or branched processes, by which they are connected with nerve-tubes; hence they are described respectively as uni-, bi-, or multipolar. Their contents are a soft, tenacious, and elastic mass (fig. 513, 3), consisting of a clear, homogeneous, proteine basis, and a number of larger and smaller granules, as well as a nucleus. In size they are very variable, from 1·5000 to 1·500″. The granules are sometimes colourless, at others yellow, brown, or black; and occasionally these are aggregated to form a mass.

Intermingled with the cells in the cineritious matter of the nervous centres, is a finely granular pale substance resembling that within the cells, also aggregations of free nuclei.

The *ganglia* consist of nerve-tubes either separate or united into bundles, intermingled with nerve-cells, from which some of the nerve-tubes arise. The tubes and cells are imbedded in or supported by a stroma of areolar tissue, sometimes homogeneous, at others more or less distinctly fibrous, forming an apparent sheath to the ganglia, and ending in numerous septa, rarely but occasionally forming a distinct envelope to the individual cells; sometimes it consists of elongated, triangular, or spindle-shaped nucleated cells;—in short, corresponding to areolar tissue in various stages of development.

Fig. 514.

Cells from the central grey nucleus of the human spinal marrow.

Magnified 350 diameters.

The nerves are developed from the ele-

Fig. 515.

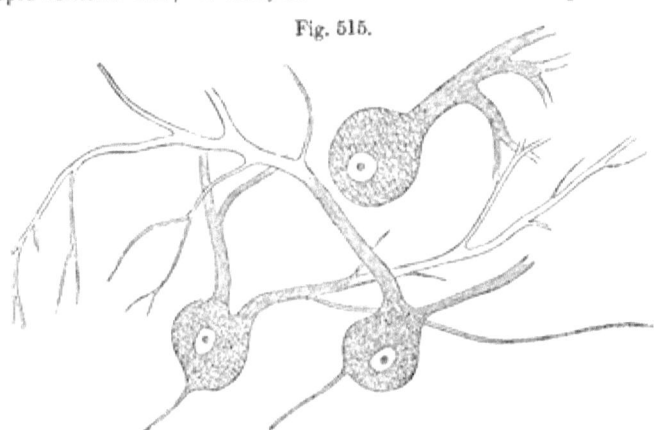

Large cells from the grey cortical layer of the human cerebellum.　Magnified 350 diameters.

mentary embryonic cells, which at first appear rounded or slightly elongated, and somewhat flattened. In their further growth they either retain the primitive shape (fig. 517), or send out persistent lateral processes, so forming nerve-cells or ganglion-globules; or the processes of adjacent cells unite into nucleated fibres, much resembling those of the sympathetic system, in which the white substance and axial fibre of the nerve-tubes are formed as secondary deposits (fig. 518).

In atrophy and degeneration of the nervous elements, the nerve-cells become

Fig. 516.

Fig. 517.

Fig. 518.

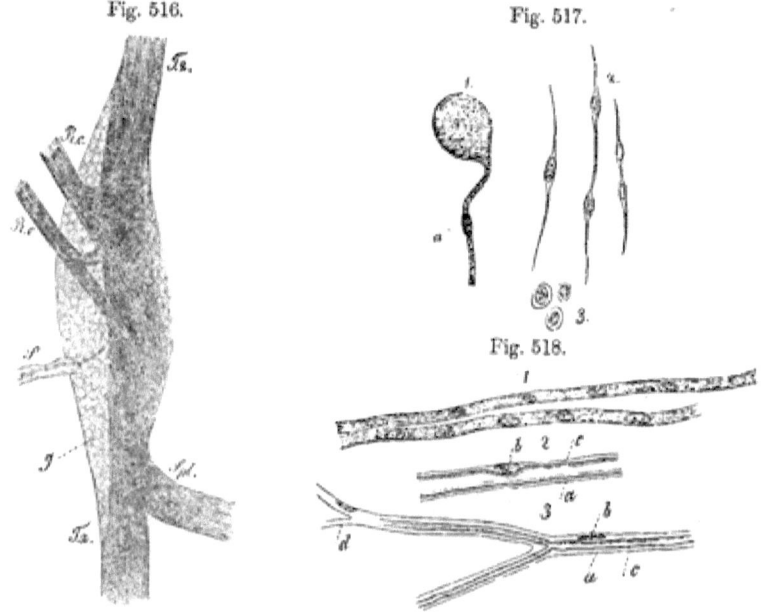

Fig. 516. Sixth thoracic sympathetic ganglion of the left side of a rabbit, seen from behind, after treatment with soda. T. 2, trunk of sympathetic; R.c, communicating branches, each bifurcating; Spl. splanchnic branch; S, ganglial branch, with large and small branches probably going to vessels; g, ganglion-globules and ganglial fibres. Magnified 40 diameters.

Fig. 517. 1. Ganglion-globules from a spinal ganglion of a four-months' human fœtus. a, nucleus in the pale process of the cell. 2. Nerve-tubes in development, from a two months' human fœtus. 3. Cells from the cineritious cerebral substance of the same fœtus.

Fig. 518. 1. Two nerve-fibres from the ischiatic nerve of a four months' fœtus. 2. Nerve-tubes from a newly-born rabbit; a, sheath; b, nucleus; c, white substance. 3. Nerve-fibre from the tail of a tadpole; a, b, c, as above; at d the fibre has still the embryonic character.

loaded with fat and pigment, and the walls of the nerve-tubes thinner, brittle, and the white substance more or less replaced by granules of fat.

Bibl. Kölliker, *Mik. Anat.* 2; Todd, *Cycl. Anat. and Phys.* iii.; Paget, *Brit. and For. Med. Rev.* 1842. xiv.

NEUROPTERA.—An order of Insects, containing the Dragon-flies (Libelluli-dæ), &c.

NEW ZEALAND FLAX. See Phormium and Textile substances.

NICOTHOE, Aud. & Edw.—A genus of Crustacea, of the order Siphonostoma, and family Ergasilidæ.

N. astaci (Pl. 14. fig. 36, fem.) is found upon the gills of the lobster.

The sides of the body are extended into two remarkable lobes, containing the ovaries (a) and the intestinal canal.

Bibl. Baird, *Brit. Entom.* p. 300; Van Beneden, *Ann. des Sc. Nat.* 3 sér. xiii.

NIDULARIACEI.—A small family of Gasteromycetous Fungi, including the Nidularini or bird's-nest-like Fungi, and the Carpoboli, which contain only one conceptacle. They are small and inconspicuous Fungi, growing on the ground among decaying sticks, dung, &c., bearing upon the flocculent mycelium yellow or dull-coloured fruits or receptacles (fig. 519). The external part of the receptacle consists of a more or less globular or ovate *peridium*,

Fig. 519.   Fig. 520.

Cyathus vernicosus.

Fig. 519. A ripe receptacle. Nat. size.
Fig. 520. The same, opened vertically.

which bursts when mature, in the Carpoboli by a lid or by more or less regular slits, in the Nidularini by an orifice which enlarges so that the mouth becomes turned out as a spreading lip around a cup-shaped cavity (fig. 519). The Carpoboli, containing only one conceptacle, project this out with elasticity when ripe. The Nidularini contain many conceptacles lying like eggs in a nest (figs. 519, 520), in *Cyathus* and *Crucibulum* (fig. 521) attached by a funiculus. The structure of the conceptacles is alike in all. The envelope of each is triple (fig. 522); and

Fig. 521.

Crucibulum vulgare.
A conceptacle detached from the receptacle.
Magnified 12 diams.

Fig. 522.

Cyathus vernicosus.

A nearly ripe receptacle, cut open vertically, showing the two halves filled with conceptacles.

Magnified 3 diameters.

they form a cavity lined by delicate filaments which converge towards the centre, where their extremities are expanded into *basidia* crowned by four spores (fig. 523), which are cylindrical and almost sessile. The filaments being of very unequal length, the basidia are intermingled with them in

the cavity of the conceptacle, not forming a definitely marked layer.

Fig. 523.

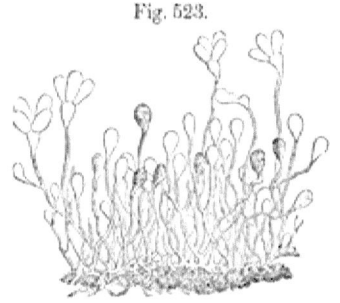

Cyathus striatus.
Basidia and spores from the fertile layer of a conceptacle.
Magnified 250 diameters.

Fig. 524.   Fig. 525.   Fig. 526.

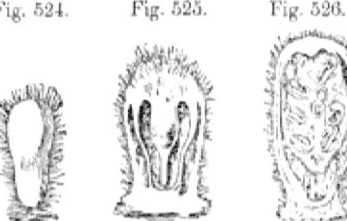

Cyathus striatus.

Fig. 524. Vertical section of a young receptacle. Magn. 10 diams.
Fig. 525. Another, more advanced. Magn. 10 diams.
Fig. 526. Another, still more advanced. Magn. 5 diams.

Synopsis of British Genera.

* CARPOBOLI. *Peridium containing only one conceptacle.*

1. *Atractobolus.* *Peridium* simple, cup-shaped, sessile, closed at first by an umbonate lid. *Conceptacle* spindle-shaped, simple, indehiscent, projected when ripe from the bottom of the *peridium.*

2. *Thelebolus.* *Peridium* simple, sessile, roundish, urceolate-inflated; mouth entire. *Conceptacle* globose, papilliform, protruded from the mouth.

3. *Sphærobolus.* *Peridium* double, each layer bursting in a stellate manner, the internal membrane at length turned inside out, and elastically projecting the globular *conceptacle.*

** NIDULARINI. *Peridium with many conceptacles.*

4. *Crucibulum.* *Peridium* at first globose-

capitate, afterwards crucible-shaped, open at the mouth, exposing numerous disk-shaped smooth *conceptacles*, each with a globular process on the under side prolonged into a long, slender, thread-like funiculus.

5. *Cyathus.* *Peridium* at first obovate or fusiform, sessile or stalked, closed by a veil, afterwards widely open at the mouth, exposing ten to eighteen disk-shaped, thick, fleshy or horny *conceptacles*, umbilicate beneath, and attached to the walls of the peridium by a compound peduncle.

6. *Nidularia.* *Peridium* sessile, subglobose, finally open (without evident veil). *Conceptacles* numerous, disk-shaped, nestling in copious gelatinous mucus, destitute of a funiculus.

BIBL. Tulasne, L.-R. and C., *Recherches sur les Nidulariées, Ann. des Sc. Nat.* 3 sér. i. 41; Schmitz, *Mycologische Beobachtungen, Linnæa,* xvi. 141; Sachs, *Bot. Zeitung,* xiii. p. 823.

NIPHOBOLUS, Kaulf.—A genus of Polypodieæ (Ferns), with elegantly articulated veins and numerous naked sori at the tips of free branchlets.

NITELLA. See CHARACEÆ.

NITOPHYLLUM, Greville.—A genus of Delesseriaceæ (Florideous Algæ), containing about half-a-dozen British species, only two of which are commonly met with. Their fronds are membranaceous, of reticulated (parenchymatous) structure, mostly rosy red, without ribs, or with irregular ribs towards the base. The membranously expanded frond of *N. punctatum*, 4 to 12" high, is either regularly dichotomously divided or parted into two or three principal lobes, which have a border of dichotomous wedge-shaped lobes. *N. lacerum* has the frond 2 to 10" high, much dichotomously divided and marked with flexuous veins, the segments mostly linear, waved or fringed at the margins. The fructification consists of spores, tetraspores, and antheridia. 1. The spores are contained in *coccidia*, sessile on the frond, the spores arising from tufted filaments; 2. the *tetraspores* form distinct scattered spots on the frond; 3. the *antheridia* are minute cellules standing perpendicularly on the surface of the frond, collected into patches, only distinguishable by the help of the microscope.

BIBL. Harvey, *Brit. Mar. Alg.* p. 116, pl. 15 B; *Phyc. Brit.* pls. 202, 203, 247, &c.; Greville, *Alg. Brit.* pl. 12; Thuret, *Ann. des Sc. Nat.* 4 sér. iii. p. 22.

NITRATE OF POTASH. See POTASH, Nitrate of.

NITRIC ACID, or Aquafortis, is useful as a reagent (INTR. p. xxxix, 6), and for separating the organic matter of the Diatomaceæ from the siliceous valves (p. 220), &c.

NITZSCHIA, Denny (*Liotheum*). — A genus of Anoplura.

N. Burmeisteri is the louse of the common swift (*Cypselus apus*).

BIBL. Denny, *Anopl. Monogr.* p. 230.

NITZSCHIA.—A genus of Annulata.

BIBL. Johnst. *Non-parasitic Worms,* 1855.

NITZSCHIA, Hass.—A genus of Diatomaceæ, the name of which should be changed.

Char. Frustules free, single, compressed, usually elongate, straight, arched, or sigmoid, with a longitudinal, not median, external keel (?), and one or more longitudinal rows of puncta; suture in front view of frustules not median.

The valves have no nodules; we have not been able to satisfy ourselves of the presence of the external keel; upon the portions of the valves forming the middle of the side view of the frustules is one or two longitudinal rows of slightly elongate dots or puncta (Pl. 13. fig. 10 *d*), often visible under ordinary illumin.; surface of valves covered with smaller dots, mostly opposite (not quincuncial) (fig. 10 *d*), invisible under ordinary illumination.

The frustules and valves are either linear, lanceolate, or of intermediate forms, sometimes constricted or beaked.

Smith describes twenty-three species, mostly removed from other genera in the systems of Ehrenberg and Kützing.

1. *N. sigmoidea* (Pl. 13. fig. 9: *a,* side view; *b,* front view). Frustules (front view) linear, sigmoid, or arched, truncate; side view straight or nearly so, attenuate, acute; aquatic; common; length 1-75".

2. *N. lanceolata* (Pl. 13. fig. 10: *a,* front view of frustule; *b,* front view of single valve; *c,* side view of frustule). Frustules (front view) straight, lanceolate, ends prolonged, somewhat obtuse; side view narrowly linear-lanceolate, ends acute; marine; length 1-150".

Fig. 10 *a* is too broad; the form of the frustules is best represented by 10 *b*; 10 *d* exhibits the two kinds of markings as seen with the stops, &c.

3. *N. longissima* (*N. birostrata,* Sm.) (Pl. 13. fig. 11: *a,* side view; *b,* front view). Frustules straight, narrowly linear-lanceolate,

ends produced into linear beaks, longer than the intermediate portion ; marine ; length 1-70".

4. *N. acicularis* (Pl. 13. fig, 13 *b*). Frustules linear-lanceolate, sometimes sigmoid, ends beaked and straight ; aquatic, and brackish water ; length 1-300".

5. *N. reversa* (Pl. 13. fig. 12). Differs from the last in having the ends bent at an angle in opposite directions.

6. *N. tænia* (Pl. 13. fig. 13 *b*). Linear or slightly lanceolate, with two spiral markings ; ends somewhat suddenly produced ; brackish water ; length 1-250".

The spiral bands probably arise from the frustules being twisted, and correspond to the sutures ; they are most distinct after a red heat.

BIBL. Smith, *Brit. Diat.* p. 37 ; Hassall, *Freshwater Algæ*, p. 435.

NOCTILUCA, Suriray. — A genus of marine animals, the systematic position and structure of which is doubtful.

N. miliaris is spherical or nearly so, of about the size of a pin's-head, with a tentacle-like, transversely striated, and curved process arising from it, and by means of which it propels itself through the water. The part to which the process is attached is plicate and depressed, so as to render the body somewhat bilobed ; it has no carapace. The body is of gelatinous consistence, and surrounded by a smooth or wrinkled membrane.

It is phosphorescent, rendering the sea luminous by night.

BIBL. Suriray, *Lesson's Acalephæ* ; Quatrefages, *Ann. des Sc. Nat.* 3 sér. xiv. ; Gosse, *Naturalist's Rambles, &c.* ; Krohn, *Wiegmann's Archiv*, 1852 ; Huxley, *Micr. Journ.* 1855 ; Brightwell, *Ann. Nat. Hist.* 1850. vi. ; *Micr. Journ.* v. 185 ; Pring, *Phil. Mag.* 1849.

NODOSARIA, Lamk.—A genus of Foraminifera, of the order Stichostegia, and family Æquilateralidæ.

Char. Shell regular, elongate, straight, rounded or depressed, conical or cylindrical. Chambers globular, distinct, very slightly embracing, and separated by deep constrictions, the last convex, often elongated. Orifice round, minute, situated at the end of a prolongation of the last chamber.

Two recent British species :

N. radicula (Pl. 18. fig. 3) and *N. pyrula* ; and several fossil.

BIBL. That of the order.

NOLELLA, Gosse.—A genus of Infundibulate Ctenostomatous Polyzoa, of the family Vesicularidæ.

Distinguished by the erect, subcylindrical cells, crowded on tubes forming an undefined encrusting mat ; tentacles eighteen, forming a bell. One species :

N. stipitata.

BIBL. Gosse, *Mar. Zool.* ii. 21.

NONIONINA, D'Orb.—A genus of Foraminifera, of the order Helicostegia, and family Nautiloidæ.

Char. Shell equilateral, regular, subcircular, or compressed ; texture sometimes brilliant, vitreous ; mostly perforated ; spire embracing. Chambers arched, in contact at the return of the spire, and at the umbilicus. Orifice a transverse fissure next the return of the spire, and apparent at all ages.

Williamson unites *Operculina* and *Assilina* with this genus.

Four recent species : *N. Barleeana, N. crassula* (Pl. 42. fig. 41), *N. Jeffreysii*, and *N. elegans* ; also some fossil species.

BIBL. That of the order.

NOSTOC, Vaucher.—The typical genus of the Nostochaceæ, distinguished from the allied genera by the definitely formed hardened pellicle or rind enclosing the fronds, which are composed of a gelatinous substance (fig. 527) in which are imbedded

Fig. 527.

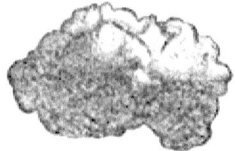

Nostoc commune.

Natural size.

numerous more or less beaded filaments (fig. 528). The filaments are composed of rows of cells (Pl. 4. fig. 7), which increase the length by repeated transverse subdivision ; here and there appear larger cells (*a, c*) which appear brighter than the rest ; these seem to be what Kützing calls the *spermatia* or spermatic cells, but they more resemble the *vesicular cells* of the allied genera. The filaments break up after a time into short fragments, which by cell-division produce new filaments. Thuret has observed this process in *N. verrucosum* (*N. Mougeotii*, Bréb.) ; he states that the pellicle of the frond bursts, allowing the gelatinous mass to escape, and the filaments to spread abroad in the water; these are

Fig. 528.

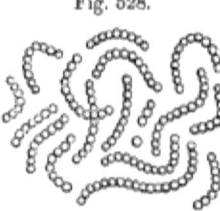

Nostoc cæruleum.
Filaments. Magnified 200 diameters.

seen, by the aid of the microscope, to consist of short straightish pieces, which, as first observed by Vaucher, are endowed with the power of moving slowly along in the direction of their length; after a time they cease to move, and a new gelatinous envelope is   Fig. 529. formed around each piece like a transparent sheath. They soon become enlarged considerably, and then divide in the *direction of the length of the filament* (fig. 529), which becomes so disintegrated that the filament forms a spiral, by the increase of which through further transverse cell-division, the mass becomes confused, until the development of a greater quantity of the gelatinous matter makes the filaments more distinct. The same process was observed in *N. vesicarium*, D.C.; and Thuret considers it likely that this mode of reproduction extends to the other species. We find that the gelatinous fronds break up when kept in water, and the colourless cells become green. Nothing is known of the import of the enlarged, brighter cells.

Nostoc verrucosum.
Filaments multiplying by subdivision.
Magn. 500 diams.

The resemblance of the Nostocs to the species of *Collema* (Lichens) has attracted much attention; and some authors even assert that they are only different forms of the same plants. We do not place much reliance on the statements of Itzigsohn, but the memoir of Sachs on this subject is deserving of attention.

The gelatinous fronds of the British species of this genus are found on damp ground, wet rocks, mosses, &c., and, free or attached to stones, in fresh water.

     * *Frond globose or subglobose.*

1. *Nostoc minutissimum*, Kützing. Frond globose, from 1-30 to 1-4‴; filaments equal, deep æruginous green, densely entangled; periderm growing brown. Kützing, *Tab. Phyc.* vol. ii. pl. 1. fig. 1. Kützing doubtfully refers to the terrestrial form of this, Hassall's *N. muscorum* (*Br. Fr. Algæ*, pl. 74. fig. 4), which grows on calcareous rocks, and among the mosses covering them.

2. *N. lichenoides*, Vaucher. Fronds from the size of a mustard-seed to that of a pea, aggregated and heaped together; filaments equal, loosely entangled, æruginous or olivaceous; periderm pellucid, colourless, firm.

β. *vesicarium*; larger, soft, with a fuscous distinct periderm, mucous within, sometimes hollow. Kützing, *Tab. Phyc.* vol. ii. pl. 2. iv. *N. vesicarium*, Hassall, *Br. Fr. Algæ*, p. 290. Road-side near Perth.

3. *N. sphæricum*, Vaucher. Frond the size of a pea, firm, blackish æruginous or somewhat olive-coloured, soft within; filaments pale green, loosely entangled; periderm firm, colourless or fuscescent, subopaque. Vaucher, *Hist. des Conferves*, xvi. fig. 2; Kützing, *Tab. Phyc.* vol. ii. pl. 3. ii.; Hassall, *Br. Fr. Algæ*, pl. 76. fig. 5. On stones in mountain rivulets. Meneghini states that, when dried and again moistened, it emits a pleasant odour like violets. Hassall thinks it probably an immature form of *N. foliaceum.*

4. *N. cæruleum*, Lyngbye. Frond from the size of a pea to that of a sloe (rarely larger), very soft and slimy, pale æruginous blue; filaments unequal, loosely entwined, joints oblong-elliptical; periderm colourless, pellucid, soft. Lyngbye, *Hydrophytol.* t. 68; Kützing, *Tab. Phyc.* vol. ii. pl. 3. iv.; Hassall, *Br. Fr. Algæ*, pl. 74. fig. 1; 75. fig. 10; 76. fig. 11. Attached to mosses in flowing water or very moist places.

5. *N. pruniforme*, Agardh. Frond the size of a large round plum, deep æruginous green, very soft and watery within; filaments unequal, bright æruginous green, loosely entangled, joints subdepressed, dimidiate; periderm leathery, crystalline. Berkeley, *Gleanings*, t. 19. 2; Kützing, *Tab. Phyc.* vol. ii. pl. 4. iv.; Hassall, *Br. Fr. Algæ*, pl. 76. 3-4; Lyngbye, *Hydroph.* t. 68 A. Fronds unattached, in freshwater pools or rivulets.

** *Frond foliaceous, irregular, or vesicular.*

6. *N. foliaceum*, Agardh. Frond terrestrial, membranous, erect, plaited, olive-green; filaments slender, copious. Hassall, *Br. Fr. Algæ*, pl. 76. fig. 2. On clayey ground constantly moistened by oozing water.

7. *N. commune*, Vaucher (fig. 527, & Pl. 4. fig. 7). Frond terrestrial, gelatinous, subcoriaceous, olivaceous or obscurely green, irregularly plaited; filaments nearly equal, flexuose, colourless or green, loosely entangled, the joints loosely conjoined, distant in one place, geminate in others, subspherical, depressed, marked with a central opaque spot; periderm hyaline, growing brown. Vaucher, *Hist. des Conf.* t. 16. fig. 1; Kützing, *Tab. Phyc.* vol. ii. pl. 6. i.; Hassall, *Br. Fr. Algæ*, pl. 74. 2. *Tremella terrestris*, Dillwyn, *Br. Conferræ*, t. 10. fig. 14. Gravelly soils, garden walks, rocks, barren pastures, &c.; very common in autumn and winter.

8. *N. verrucosum*, Vaucher. Frond bladder-shaped, softly leathery, fuscous-green; filaments spiral, densely entangled, joints globose; periderm gelatinous, soft, green or dirty brown. Vaucher, *Hist. des Conf.* t. 16. fig. 3; Kützing, *Tab. Phyc.* vol. xi. pl. 9. fig. 2; Thuret, *Ann. des Sc. Nat.* 3 sér. vol. ii. pl. 9. figs. 1–4; Hassall, *Br. Fr. Alg.* pl. 75. fig. 1. On stones in streams.

9. *N. variegatum*, Moore. Frond terrestrial, expanded, gelatinous, livid, variable in shape; filaments rather distant; joints oval and variable in size. Hassall, *Br. Fr. Algæ*, pl. 74. fig. 3. On a moist bank in Ireland. A doubtful plant, perhaps referable to a different genus of the Nostochaceæ.

BIBL. The works above quoted; Itzigsohn, *Bot. Zeit.* xii. p. 521 (1854); Sachs, *Bot. Zeit.* xiii. p. 1 (1855); Thuret, *Mém. Société de Cherbourg*, Aug. 1857, *Ann. Nat. Hist.* 3 ser. ii. p. 1.

NOSTOCHACEÆ.—A family of Confervoid Algæ, composed of plants forming gelatinous strata or definitely formed gelatinous balls or masses, either on damp ground or floating at the bottom of water; consisting of minute, unbranched, usually moniliform, microscopic filaments, tranquil or oscillating, imbedded in a mass of mucilaginous or sometimes firmish substance (the amorphous matrix is produced by the fusion of the special gelatinous sheaths of the individual filaments); filaments finally breaking up. Cells of the filaments of three kinds:—1. *ordinary* cells; 2. *vesicular* cells or *heterocysts*, usually large and without granular matter, frequently with erect hairs; 3. *sporangia* or *sporangial* cells, produced by the enlargement of the ordinary cells, globular, elliptical or cylindrical. The reproduction by spores has been observed in *Cylindrospermum* by Thuret, who finds that the *sporangial-cells* produce in their interior one thick-coated spore, which, after a season of rest, germinates and breaks out from the sporange to grow into a new cellular filament.

The genera have been far too much multiplied here; and Kützing's characters are impracticable. The divisions of Ralfs are not all of generic value.

Synopsis of Genera.

1. *Nostoc.* Phycoma or general mass of the plant enclosed by a film formed by the condensation of the surface, determinate, globose or spread out, of variable form, gelatinous or mucous, coriaceous, soft or hard, elastic, slimy, containing simple, curved and entangled, moniliform, colourless or greenish filaments composed of cells which appear solid, imbedded in a continuous amorphous gelatinous matrix; *heterocysts* globose, interstitial, larger than the ordinary joints of the filaments.

2. *Monormia.* Frond or *phycoma* a definite, gelatinous, elongated, linear, spirally curled and convoluted sheath enclosing a single, continuous, moniliform filament; *heterocysts* interstitial; sporanges developed from joints most distant from the vesicular cells.

3. *Anabaina.* Filaments moniliform or cylindrical, often curled, involved in a formless mucous matrix, often forming a floating film, with vesicular cells (*heterocysts*) and sporangial cells.

  * *Without a membranous sheath.*

a. Trichormus. Heterocysts interstitial and terminal. Sporanges at first formed from the cells most distant from the heterocysts.

b. Sphærozyga. Heterocysts interstitial. Sporanges formed from the nearest cells.

c. Cylindrospermum. Heterocysts terminal. Sporanges like the last.

d. Dolichospermum. Heterocysts interstitial. Sporanges without definite arrangement, and of unequal length.

  ** *Filaments not included in a membranous sheath.*

e. Aphanizomenon. Heterocysts none (?).

Sporanges usually simple and of un-equal length.

f. Spermosira. *Heterocysts* interstitial, single, or sometimes in pairs. *Sporanges* as in *Trichormus.*

Exotic genus. Trichodesmium. Filaments straight, short, unbranched, without evident sheaths, in simple separate bundles, in-volved in a matrix of mucus; social, swim-ming in masses. Marine.

BIBL. Ralfs, *on Nostochineæ, Annals of Nat. Hist.* 2 ser. vol. v. 321, pls. 8 & 9; Kützing, *Tabulæ Phycologicæ,* B. i. pp. 91-100. Bd. ii. pls. 1–15; Thuret, *on Nostoc verrucosum, Ann. des Sc. Nat.* 2 sér. t. ii.; *Ann. Nat. Hist.* 3 ser. ii. p. 1; Meneghini, *Monographia Nostochinearum italicarum, Mem. Turin Acad.* ser. 2. v. 1843; Allman, *Micr. Journal,* 1855.

NOTAMIA, Flem.—A genus of Infundi-bulate Cheilostomatous Polyzoa, of the fa-mily Gemellariadæ.

Char. Cells placed back to back, facing opposite directions; tobacco-pipe-shaped bird's-heads above each pair. One species: *N. bursaria* (Pl. 44. fig. 21). An elegant microscopic object.

BIBL. Johnston, *Brit. Zooph.* 294; Busk, *Cat. Mar. Polyz. (Brit. Mus.),* 36.

NOTEUS, Ehr.—A genus of Rotatoria, of the family Brachionæa.

Char. Eyes absent; foot forked (= eye-less *Brachionus*).

N. quadricornis (Pl. 35. fig. 13). Carapace suborbicular, depressed, scabrous, areolate, with four spines in front, and two behind; aquatic; length 1-120 to 1-70″.

BIBL. Ehrenberg, *Infus.* p. 502.

NOTHOLÆNA, Brown.—A genus of Tænitideæ (Polypodioid Ferns).

NOTODELPHYS, Allm.—A genus of Entomostraca, of the order Copepoda.

N. ascidicola (Pl. 14. fig. 22) resembles *Cyclops* in general appearance. The ex-ternal ovary is a single organ, lying across the back of the abdomen; eye single. Marine.

BIBL. Allman, *Ann. Nat. Hist.* xx. p. 1; Baird, *Brit. Entom.* p. 237.

NOTOMMATA, Ehr.—A genus of Ro-tatoria, of the family Hydatinæa.

Char. Free; eye single, cervical; tail-like foot with two toes; rotatory organ simply ciliated.

In some the rotatory organ is extended laterally in an ear- or arm-like form.

Ehrenberg describes twenty-three species, some of which are parasitic, *N. petromyzon*

and *parasita* living within *Volvox globator,* and *N. werneckii* within the vesicles of *Vaucheria*; and divides them into the sub-genera—*Labidodon,* jaws each with a single tooth; *Ctenodon,* jaws each with several teeth.

Notommata granularis is the male of *N. Brachionus.*

Many of the species are large and well adapted for the study of the internal structure.

N. centrura (Pl. 35. fig. 14; 15, jaws and teeth). Body attenuate at each end, foot small and hard; cephalic auricles short; no lateral setæ; aquatic; length 1-36″.

BIBL. Ehrenberg, *Infus.* p. 424; Dujar-din, *Infus.* p. 646.

NOTONECTA, L.—A genus of aquatic Hemipterous insects.

N. glauca (the water-boatman) is com-mon in pools. Its setæ or lancets, and natatorial hind-legs, form interesting micro-scopic objects.

Fig. 530.

Notonecta glauca.
Magnified 3 diameters.

NUCLEUS and NUCLEOLUS OF PLANTS.—The term nucleus is applied in botany to two very different things; first to the central body of the young ovules of Flowering plants, and secondly to a peculiar structure met with in the interior of cells. The first will be described under the head of OVULE; the cell-nucleus and nucleolus, mentioned in the article CELL (*Vegetable*), will be discussed here.

Few parts of the minute organization of plants are more obscure than the structure and function of nuclei; some authors re-gard them as of the highest physiological importance, others consider their import altogether unknown. The nucleus may be observed most easily in the parenchymatous cells of the herbaceous structures and flowers of Monocotyledons (Pl. 36. fig. 28 *b*), or in the young cells of the hairs of Flowering plants generally (Pl. 38. figs. 8, 9 b), or in the embryo-sacs of unfertilized ovules (Pl. 38. figs. 4–6); in such cases the characters are well defined and unmistakeable. It consists of a lenticular body formed of more or less granular substance, apparently not diverse from the PROTOPLASM, with one or more well- or ill-defined bright points or cavities (*nucleoli*) in the interior. Wherever it appears throughout the higher plants, it seems to possess the same characters. Nägeli indeed declares that it is a vesicle; but we believe this to be an error, that real nuclei are ordinarily solid, although bodies akin to them, really hollow, do occasionally occur in the cell-contents. Nägeli, who has investigated the subject of nuclei very extensively, states that they exist in every class of plants, and that in those cases where he failed to find them, there was a probability of their being concealed in the cell-contents. The nuclei of certain plants exhibit very remarkable peculiarities, especially in SPIROGYRA and ZYGNEMA.

Ordinarily, nuclei are found attached to the side of cells, being intimately connected with the PRIMORDIAL UTRICLE, or, whenever this is partially absorbed, forming the centre of the radiating protoplasmic filaments this leaves behind (Pl. 38. fig. 9): sometimes, however, the nucleus is suspended in the cavity of the cell by filamentous processes of protoplasm; in all such cases it forms a kind of centre for the circulation of the protoplasm where this exhibits movement (ROTATION), and it is itself carried about to a certain extent by the currents.

The *nucleoli* (Pl. 38. fig. 8 n) of these larger nuclei are apparently usually solid granules of a transparent substance, but sometimes they appear more like minute cavities.

The nuclei and nucleoli of the lower plants are exceedingly obscure; in a great many cases the so-called nuclei are little different from the nucleoli of the larger forms, occupying to the entire cell-contents the same relation as the nucleoli to large nuclei, for example, in the spores of Lichens (Pl. 29. fig. 7), Fungi, &c. In the lower Confervoid Algæ the nucleus (or nucleolus) appears to be represented by the entire cell-contents (Pl. 3), in which one or more well-defined granules often occur, representing nucleoli; in certain stages, however, a larger granule is met with, coloured by chloro-

phyll, which some regard as a nucleus; this disappears totally at particular epochs, and is replaced by starch-granules or oil-globules. The bright-coloured point, or 'eye-spot,' seen very generally in the Zoospores both of Confervoids and Fucoids, may represent a nucleolus.

Nuclei originate in two ways. The simplest mode is found where they precede free-cell formation, as in the development of the germinal vesicles in the embryo-sacs of Flowering plants. Here the nuclei appear first as globular or lenticular masses, which become gradually defined in the substance of a collection of protoplasm accumulated at the upper end of the cell (Pl. 38. figs. 1–4). This is a spontaneous isolation of a portion of the protoplasm to become the foundation of a new cell. We may compare this with the segmentation of the entire mass of contents of the cells of Confervæ in the formation of Zoospores, which may perhaps be regarded as at first free *nuclei*. In cells multiplying by division, a division of existing nuclei has been observed to take place in certain cases, as in the hairs of *Tradescantia* (Pl. 38. figs. 8 & 9); but in other similar cases of division no nuclei are observed (Pl. 38. figs. 10 & 11). In the case of *Tradescantia*, the oval parent-nucleus fills up the end of the growing cell, so that the division of the nucleus is almost synonymous with the division of the primordial utricle. But in this case, as in the development of cells from free nuclei, as indicated of the germinal vesicles, the cell-membrane in expanding draws away from the nucleus, which remains adherent to or suspended in connexion with a layer of protoplasm lining the cell-wall and forming its primordial utricle. In SPIROGYRA and *Zygnema*, a division of the free suspended nucleus precedes the division of the large primordial utricle.

Mohl describes a division of nuclei as occurring in *Anthoceros*; and most authors who have written on the development of pollen and spores lay great stress on the influence of the nuclei, which they describe; but the import of nuclei in vegetable cells is certainly still a problem. Some believe they are the universal agents of production of new cells, others that they are not the agents of this in any case, but, when present, may be divided with the cells. Others imagine that they are merely the original "mould" of protoplasm on which the cellulose membrane of the nascent-cell is deposited, and which is left unaltered when this expands (the phænomena in *Spirogyra* are opposed to this). Some of those who deny their influence in cell-development believe them to be the vital centres of the cells in which they exist.

They are best seen in very young cells in all cases; in nascent tissues they almost or quite fill the cavity of the young cells. As the cells grow older, their history differs in different cases. Sometimes they persist until the decay of the organ in which they exist. This happens very generally in the cells of the flowers, stems, &c. of Monocotyledons; not unfrequently, in stems and leaves they become converted into starch or chlorophyll-granules. In other cases they have a more definite purpose; for in the vesicles in which are formed the SPERMATOZOIDS of Ferns, Mosses, Hepaticæ, Characæ, &c., these structures appear to be produced by a metamorphosis of the nuclei.

In examining supposed nuclei of plants, especially those of lower cellular organization, tincture of iodine should always be applied, to distinguish starch-granules &c. from true nuclei, which are always coloured deep yellow or brownish by that reagent, besides being coagulated, contracted, and thereby rendered more distinct.

The nuclei of plants require much more investigation.

BIBL. R. Brown, *on Orchidaceæ*, *Phil. Mag.* Dec. 1831; Schleiden, *Phytogenesis*, *Müller's Archiv*, 1838, transl. in *Sc. Memoirs*, ii. p. 281; *Grundzüge*, 3 ed. (*Principles*, p. 568); Nägeli, *Zeitschr. für Wiss. Bot.* (transl. in *Ray Soc. Vols.* 1845 & 1849); Mohl, *Pflanzenzelle* (*Vegetable Cell*), pp. 36 and 51; Hofmeister, *Entsteh. d. Embryo*, Leipsic, 1849. p. 7; Al. Braun, *Verjüngung* (*Ray Soc. Vol.* 1853. p. 175).

NULLIPORES. See CORALLINACEÆ.

NUMMULINA, D'Orb. (*Nummulites*, Lamk.).—A genus of Foraminifera, of the order Helicostegia, and family Nautiloideæ.

Char. Shell equilateral, circular or discoidal, without marginal appendages; spire embracing. Convolutions very close and numerous; the last one always distinct when young, not discoverable in the adult. Chambers small, short, close together, very numerous; the last one prominent in young shells, but indistinct in old ones. Orifice transverse, linear, next the return of the spire, often masked in the old shells.

Williamson unites *Assilina* with this genus. One British species: *N. planulata*

(Pl. 18. fig. 12), recent and fossil; and two other fossil species. The fossil Nummulites, forming mountains &c., are alluded to under FORAMINIFERA (p. 294).

BIBL. That of the order.

NUMMULITES = NUMMULINA.

NYMPHÆACEÆ. See HAIRS (p. 338).

O.

OAT, *Avena sativa* (Nat. Order Graminaceæ, Flowering Plants).—The form of the starch-corpuscles of the oat is very unlike that of the other common corn plants; they consist of numerous small polygonal grains grouped together in roundish or oval masses (Pl. 36. fig. 10). See STARCH.

OBISIDA. See PSEUDO-SCORPIONES.

OBJECT-GLASSES. See TEST-OBJECTS.

OCHLOCHÆTE, Thwaites.—A genus of Chætophoraceæ (Confervoid Algæ), consisting of minute plants growing epiphytically on leaves of grasses, &c. *O. hystrix* occurs both in brackish and freshwater ditches. The minute, dot-like, discoid frond is formed of radiating branched filaments composed of cells, each bearing a very long tubular filament on its back. Fructification unknown. We suspect this plant is closely connected with the lax forms of COLEOCHÆTE.

BIBL. Harvey, *Brit. Mar. Alg.* p. 211, pl. 25 E; *Phyc. Brit.* pl. 226.

ODONTELLA, Ag. — This genus of Diatomaceæ is united with BIDDULPHIA, *Biddulphia* (*Odontella*) *aurita* undergoing spontaneous division, Pl. 14. fig. 9.

ODONTHALIA, Lyngb.—A genus of Rhodomelaceæ (Florideous Algæ) containing one British species, *O. dentata*, which has an irregularly bipinnatifid frond, 3 to 12" long, the main axis and lobes being about 1-4" wide throughout; the colour is deep wine-red, darker when dried. The frond bears marginal, stalked, ostiolate, ovate *ceramidia* with spores; lanceolate *stichidia*, in which are contained two rows of ternate tetraspores; and *antheridia*.

BIBL. Harv. *Brit. Alg.* p. 77, pl. 11 A; *Phyc. Brit.* pl. 34; Greville, *Alg. Br.* pl. 13; Kützing, *Phyc. generalis*, p. 448.

ODONTIDIUM, Kg.—A genus of Diatomaceæ.

Char. Frustules quadrangular, united to form an elongated biconvex filament; linear in front view; valves elliptical with transverse continuous striæ. Aquatic and marine.

Differs from *Denticula* in the elongated

filament, which sometimes, however, consists of only three or four frustules!

Kützing describes fifteen species, two doubtful. Smith describes seven species, two doubtful.

O. turgidulum (Pl. 13. fig. 14: *a*, front view; *b*, side view). Valves lanceolate, obtusish; striæ on each valve six. Aquatic; length of frustules 1-1720 to 1-570".

O. tabellaria, Smith = *Staurosira construens*, Ehr. (Pl. 41. fig. 38).

BIBL. Kützing, *Bacill.* p. 44; *Sp. Alg.* p. 12; Smith, *Brit. Diat.* ii. 15.

ODONTODISCUS, Ehr.—A genus of Diatomaceæ.

Char. Frustules single, lenticular; valves circular, alike, without nodules or apertures, not areolar (under ordin. illum.), but covered with puncta either arranged in radiating rows, or in excentrically curved lines, and with erect marginal teeth.

The puncta are surely the ordinary depressions imperfectly examined. Three species; fossil and in guano.

O. eccentricus (Pl. 43. fig. 52).

BIBL. Ehrenberg, *Ber. d. Berl. Akad.* 1844. p. 73; Kützing, *Sp. Alg.* p. 129.

ŒCISTES, Ehr.—A genus of Rotatoria, of the family (Ecistina.

Char. Single; rotatory organ single, with an entire margin; body attached to the bottom of a fixed cylindrical carapace; eyes two, frontal, red, disappearing in advanced age.

O. crystallinus (Pl. 35. fig. 16). Carapace hyaline, viscid, covered with foreign bodies; aquatic; entire length 1-36".

Jaws each with three teeth.

BIBL. Ehrenberg, *Infus.* p. 392.

ŒCISTINA, Ehr.—A family of Rotatoria.

Char. Animals single or aggregate, attached to the bottom of a gelatinous carapace; rotatory organ single, with an entire margin.

A distinct carapace for each animal.... 1. *Œcistes.*
Carapaces aggregated into a sphere.... 2. *Conochilus.*

BIBL. Ehrenberg, *Infus.* p. 391.

ŒDEMIUM, Fr.—A genus of Dematiei (Hyphomycetous Fungi). *Œ. atrum*, Corda, consists of dense tufts of brown erect fibres, scarcely branched, and without true septa. The roundish "spores" are sessile upon the sides of the erect filaments.

BIBL. Corda, *Sturm's Deutschl. Fl.* 6. pl. 9; Fries, *Systema Mic.* 344; Berkeley and Broome, *Ann. Nat. Hist.* 2 ser. vi. p. 466.

ŒDIPODIUM, Schwägr.—A genus of Splachnaceæ (Acrocarpous, operculated Mosses), sometimes included under *Gymnostomum*. *Œdipodium Griffithianum*, Schwäg., the only species, is remarkable for the peculiarly thickened fruit-stalk, whence the name of the genus is derived.

ŒDOGONIACEÆ.—A family of filamentous Confervoid Algæ, remarkable for the filaments growing by a peculiar mode of cell-division, accompanied by circumscissile dehiscence of the parent-cell, and by the zoospores being formed from the whole contents and bearing a crown of numerous cilia. There are two genera :

1. *Œdogonium*. Filaments unbranched.

2. *Bulbochæte*. Filaments branched and bearing bristle-cells with a bulbous base (fig. 83, p. 110).

BIBL. See the genera.

ŒDOGONIUM, Link. (*Prolifera*, Leclerc, *Vesiculifera*, Hass.).—A genus of Œdogoninceæ (Confervoid Algæ). Some of the *Œdogonia* are among the commonest and most abundant of freshwater Algæ, occurring in every pond, ditch, or stream, and quickly making their appearance in tanks, aquaria, &c. They may generally be recognized at a glance by the dense and uniform green protoplasm, sometimes filling the cells, sometimes (after dividing) leaving half of the cell colourless and devoid of chlorophyll; above all, by the annular striæ occurring at the ends of many of the cells (Pl. 5. fig. 7 *b*, *h*). The cells have each a large parietal nucleus (fig. 7 *a*). The large round interstitial sporangial cell (fig. 7 *g*) is also a very distinctive character. The zoospores also are peculiar, consisting of the entire contents of a cell, therefore very large, and are crowned by a wreath of cilia (Pl. 5. fig. 7 *c*). The filaments are attached, when young, to stones, plants, &c., by root-like processes. These plants, on many grounds, deserve a somewhat close examination. The filaments are composed of rows of cylindrical cells, which multiply interstitially in a very curious manner. When a cell is about to divide, an annular deposit of cellulose occurs around the upper part of the parent-cell. Next the wall of the parent-cell breaks, by a circumscissile dehiscence, just below the cellulose ring. The internal cell elongates and removes the margins of the circular slit from each other, the upper piece of the parent-cell wall being pushed up as a kind of cap on the elongating cell. While the cell is thus being elongated, its primordial utricle becomes divided below the line of dehiscence of the parent-cell; but both the new portions grow, so that the line of division between the two new cells at length rises above the margin of the lower part of the parent-cell. The annular deposit of gelatinous cellulose has meanwhile become stretched or developed over the space left by the separation of the halves of the parent membrane, forming an outer coat to the new cell. After the growth of the lower cell is finished, the upper one begins to elongate, until it attains equal length; it remains poor in protoplasm and chlorophyll while growing, but becomes densely filled when it has attained its full dimensions. The margins or broken ends of the parent-cell wall form the annular striæ seen on the filaments (Pl. 5. fig. 7 *b*, *g*, *h*): at first there is only one at the top of any given cell; but the next dehiscence takes place just below this, giving rise to a second, and so on, until many successive rings are produced at one spot.

The zoospores or ciliated gonidia (fig. 7 *c*) are formed from the entire contents of a cell, and exhibit a large round nucleus; they escape by a circumscissile dehiscence of the wall of the parent-cell (*b*): the filament, however, does not generally become quite broken into two; the portions remain attached by a strip of the side-wall forming a kind of hinge, and the zoospores are not set free directly, but at first are enclosed in a very delicate and almost imperceptible globular envelope, colorable blue by iodine and sulphuric acid, which appears to dissolve very quickly in the water. The zoospores are large, somewhat ovate in form, with a transparent region at one end, whence the numerous cilia arise. When expelled, they move for a time, and then come to rest, attaching themselves to foreign objects by the ciliated end, acquiring a membrane, sending out root-like processes below (*e*), and elongating and expanding above into a longish pear-shaped body. Sometimes the zoospores do not completely extricate themselves from the parent-cell, and then germinate in this way *in situ*, the root-like processes remaining engaged in the parent-cell. Very often they attach themselves upon the parent filament to germinate. The next stage after germination presents two different classes of phænomena: in the one case, as a purely vegetative zoospore, the young plant elongates gradually into a jointed filament by extension and cell-division; in the other it is an *androspore*, and becomes an *antheridial* filament.

The *Œdogonia* produce large resting-spores (*oospores*), which are formed from the entire contents of the uppermost of two cells developed as above described. A rupture of the parent-cell wall takes place at the side during the development of the spore; through the small orifice thus formed the spore-mass becomes fertilized through the agency of the little globular bodies produced in the antheridia (Pl. 45. fig. 17). Ultimately the spore, while increasing in size, retracts itself from the walls of its parent-cell (*oogonium*), and lies free in the cavity, presenting a double coat, the outer of which is thick and tough; its contents acquire a red colour as it ripens. The parent-cell of the spore mostly acquires a globular or elliptical form, and a red or brown colour, appearing like a kind of nodule on the filament; and the ripe spore, of globular, elliptical, or depressed spherical form, is mostly of greater diameter than the ordinary cells (Pl. 45. fig. 21). The ripe spore escapes by the decomposition or dehiscence of the parent-cell; the history of its germination is still involved in obscurity; it is not known whether it germinates directly or first divides into a number of zoospores, as in BULBOCHÆTE.

The antheridial structures of the *Œdogonia* are either formed in the ordinary filaments (Pl. 45. fig. 13), or from dwarf filaments produced from the smaller zoospores or *androspores* (Pl. 45. fig. 19). In either case they consist of one or more very short joints of the filament, formed in the ordinary way, the contents of which divide into two portions. The cells then dehisce and allow the new products to escape, which resemble the vegetative zoospores, but are much smaller. These new bodies, the spermatozoids, make their way through the orifices in the parent-cells of the spores and fertilize their contents (Pl. 45. fig. 20).

The *Œdogonia* appear to be sometimes purely monœcious or diœcious, the single filaments including either both antheridial and spore-cells, or only one kind of organ; but the most common condition is intermediate between these two conditions, the filaments having some joints converted into sporangial cells, others giving birth to the androspores, which germinate into dwarf antheridial filaments (often sessile on or near the sporanges), and these produce spermatozoids. This condition is termed by Pringsheim *gynandrosporous*.

The systematic arrangement of the species

of *Œdogonium* has remained in a state of confusion on account of the variability of the size of the filaments. Pringsheim believes, however, that it is possible to establish specific characters upon perfect fructifying specimens, but not on barren or simply vegetating filaments. The following is his arrangement:—

* *Spores globular.*

† *Sporanges opening by a valvular lid.*

1. *Œ. rostellatum.* Sporange oval, spore globular, not filling the sporange. Antheridia three- to four-celled. Monœcious.

†† *Sporanges opening by a lateral orifice.*

‡ *Monœcious.*

2. *Œ. curvum.* Sporanges compressed vertically, orifice in the middle line; spores completely filling the sporanges, and of the same form. Antheridia three- to four-celled, only one spermatozoid in a cell.

3. *Œ. tumidulum.* Sporange ovate, orifice in the upper half; spore globular, not filling the sporange. Antheridia (mostly) two-celled.

‡‡ *Gynandrosporous.*

4. *Œ. Rothii,* Hass. Dwarf male plant straight, sessile on the sporange, without a spreading base. Sporange ovate, but expanded in the middle; orifice in the middle line; spores compressed vertically, filling the inflated part of the sporange.

5. *Œ. depressum.* Dwarf male plant straight, sessile on the sporange, with a foot and internal antheridia. Antheridium one-celled. Sporange compressed vertically; orifice in the middle line; spores of the form of the sporange, not filling it.

6. *Œ. Braunii,* Kütz. Dwarf male plant a little curved, sessile in the vicinity of the sporange, with a foot, and exterior one-celled antheridium. Sporange oval, inflated in the middle, orifice in the middle line; spore globular, not completely filling the sporange.

7. *Œ. echinospermum,* Al. Br. Dwarf male plant almost straight, sessile on the cell below the sporange, with a foot and outer one-celled antheridium. Sporange oval, orifice in the lower half; spore globular, covered with spines.

** *Spores oval.*

† *Sporanges opening by a valvular lid.*

‡ *Gynandrosporous.*

8. *Œ. ciliatum,* Hass. Dwarf male plant curved, sessile on the sporange, with foot and outer one-celled antheridium. Spores oval, filling the broken portion of the sporange.

†† *Sporanges opening by a lateral orifice.*

‡ *Gynandrosporous.*

9. *Œ. apophysatum,* Al. Br. Dwarf male plant curved, sessile on the cell below the sporange, with foot and outer two-ranked antheridium. Sporange oval, orifice in the upper half; spore filling the sporange up to the cap-like part.

‡‡ *Diœcious.*

10. *Œ. gemelliparum.* Male plants evidently more slender than the female. Antheridia many-ranked; septa of the mother-cells perpendicular to the other septa of the cells. Sporange oval, orifice in the upper half, the spore filling it completely up to the cap-portion. The filaments end in several (up to six) almost hyaline elongated cells, without a terminal bristle.

BIBL. Link, *Hor. physic. berolin.* (1820); Kützing, *Sp. Alg.* p. 364; *Tab. Phyc.* Bd. iii. pl. 33, &c.; Hassall, *Br. Fr. Alg.* p. 195; Thuret, *Ann. des Sc. Nat.* 3 sér. xiv. p. 226; Pringsheim, *Monatsber. d. Berl. Akad.* 1855; *Bau und Bildung der Pflanzenzelle,* Berlin, p. 33, 1854; *Jahrb. f. Wiss. Botanik,* i. p. 1, 1857; Mohl, *Bot. Zeitung,* xiii. p. 689; De Bary, *Soc. des Sc. Nat. d. Friboury,* July, 1856; *Ann. des Sc. Nat.* 4 sér. v. p. 262; *Mus. Senkenb.* 1856. p. 29; Carter, *Ann. Nat. Hist.* 3 ser. i. p. 29.

OIDIUM, Link (*Acrosporium* and *Sporotrichum,* Greville; *Torula,* Corda).—A supposed genus of Mucedines (Hyphomycetous Fungi), but very probably consisting merely of imperfect conditions of plants of more complex nature. The *Oidia* have recently attracted great attention on account of the extraordinary development of the form called *Oidium Tuckeri* on the vines of Europe and the Atlantic islands. This, however, like *O. leucoconium* and others, appears to be only the conidiiferous mycelium of an ERYSIPHE or some allied plant; the particulars of its history are given more at length under VINE FUNGUS. *Oidium lactis* seems also referable to *Torula,* or to the mycelium of PENICILLIUM. *O. abortifaciens,* Lk. is an imperfect state of CLAVICEPS; *O. albicans,* C. Robin, the fungus of APHTHA, is probably referable to some other genus when mature, as *Achorion* should perhaps also be included under *Puccinia*. The objects described as *Oidia* consist of delicate horizontal filaments, creeping over leaves, fruits, or decaying vegetable and animal substances (*O. lactis* at the edges of sour milk, *O. albicans* in the mouth of the human subject), forming an interlaced fleecy coat, the horizontal filaments giving origin to numerous erect (usually short), articulated pedicels, the uppermost cells of which (or several of the uppermost) become expanded into oval bodies (*conidia*) which become disarticulated, and falling upon the matrix, germinate and produce new filaments (Pl. 20. figs. 8, 9).

Oidium leucoconium, Tuckeri, erysiphoides are white; *O. aureum, fulvum, fructigenum,* and others subsequently become coloured.

As we do not regard them as independent organisms, it seems unnecessary to give the characters of the supposed species.

BIBL. Berk. *Hook. Brit. Fl.* ii. pt. 2, p. 349; *Ann. Nat. Hist.* i. p. 263, vi. p. 438, 2 ser. vii. p. 178, xiii. p. 463; *Crypt. Botany,* pp. 300, 308; Fries, *Summa Veg.* 494; Fresenius, *Beitr. z. Mycologie,* Heft i. p. 23, ii. p. 76; Léveillé, *Ann. des Sc. Nat.* 3 sér. xv. p. 109; Grev. *Sc. Crypt. Fl.* pl. 73; Ch. Robin, *Végétaux Parasites,* 2nd ed. p. 488; and the *Bibl.* of VINE-FUNGUS.

OIL.—Oils of various kinds are most abundantly produced by a very large number of plants, and occur to some extent in almost all. For the microscopist, it is convenient to divide them into *essential* and *fixed* oils. The former are special secretions, and occur in the cells of the GLANDS and Glandular HAIRS of the epidermis of those parts of plants exposed to the air and light. Fixed oils are found principally in the cells of tissues still physiologically active in the nutrition of the plants, and they appear in many cases to have a close relation with and to form substitutes for starch. Thus fixed oils occur stored up in the cells of the perisperms or of the cotyledons of certain seeds in which little or no starch is produced, as in the *Papaveraceæ, Cruciferæ, Linum,* the almond, nut, &c. Oil may occur also in the pulp of fruits, as in the olive.

SPORES of Cryptogamic plants and POLLEN-grains are remarkable for the oil they exhibit in their mature condition. It appears to serve as an indifferent or inert form of assimilated nutriment.

Oil occurs in the cavity of cells in the form of minute drops, which may be distinguished mostly, by the experienced microscopist, by simple inspection; but it is often desirable to prove the nature of the globules, which may be done by removing them with æther, or, in the case of pollen, by viewing them in spirit of turpentine or oil of lemons. Potash does not act readily upon oil-globules in the cells of plants.

In certain cases it is convenient to view objects in oil instead of water, in order to render them more transparent; for this purpose oil of lemon or turpentine is usually employed.

OMPHALOPELTA, Ehr.—A genus of fossil Diatomaceæ.

Char. Agrees with *Actinoptychus*; but the upper part of the margin of the valves has a few opposite erect spines.

Four species. Fossil and marine.

O. areolata (Pl. 43. fig. 53).

BIBL. Ehrenberg, *Ber. d. Berl. Akad.* 1844. p. 263; Kützing, *Sp. Alg.* p. 132.

ONCOSPHENIA, Ehr. — A genus of Diatomaceæ.

Char. Frustules single, cuneate in front view; valves equal, uncinate at the apices, with transverse granular striæ; neither vittæ nor nodules present.

O. carpathica. Valves cuneate, laxly striated (ord. illum.), one end turgid, rounded, and straight, the other attenuate and uncinate; aquatic; diameter 1-790".

BIBL. Ehrenberg, *Ber. d. Berl. Akad.* 1845. p. 72; Kützing, *Sp. Alg.* p. 11.

ONION, *Allium Cepa* (Flowering Plants, Nat. Ord. Liliaceæ).—The young bulb of the onion offers a very good and cheap subject for the investigation of the development of spiral vessels, to those who do not object to its odour; other bulbs will do equally well. In the cells of the base of the bulb occur very elegant groups of prismatic crystals (see RAPHIDES).

ONOCLEA, Linn.—A genus of Asplenieæ (Polypodioid Ferns). Indusium very thin, membranous and reticulated. The fertile pinnæ are usually so rolled up as to look like little berries seated on a spike, filled with sporangia. Exotic.

ONYGENEI.—A family of Ascomycetous Fungi, containing a few inconspicuous plants growing upon the feathers of dead birds, or upon cast-off horseshoes. The flocculent spreading mycelium usually produces on its surface little white stalk-like bodies crowned by a globular perithecium. At first erect and thick, these supports become more slender as they elongate, and seem to bend under the weight of the light perithecium (fig. 531). In some species the perithecium is sessile. The perithecium is filled with branching filaments, arising from the walls of its internal cavity, interlacing together and bearing at their free extremities globular cells (*asci*) containing the spores (figs. 533, 535). At the epoch of

Fig. 531.   Fig. 532.

Fig. 533.    Fig. 534.

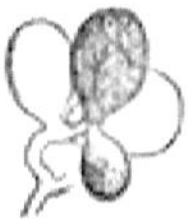

Fig. 535.

Onygenei corvini.
Fig. 531. Plants on a feather. Nat. size.
Fig. 532. Single plant with the perithecium dehiscing. Magn. 10 diams.
Fig. 533. Portion of the sporiferous layer, with asci. Magn. 350 diams.
Fig. 534. Asci detached. Magn. 700 diams.
Fig. 535. Spores. Magn. 700 diams.

maturity the perithecium, originally closed, bursts circularly towards the base, the upper part becoming detached under the form of a more or less regular cap (fig. 532), exposing the spores set free by a solution of the filaments.

British Genus.

Onygena. Perithecium capitate, at length slit round the base, and falling off as an imperforate cap. Asci borne at the free ends of filaments forming an entangled mass in the perithecium, finally free and pulveraceous.

BIBL. Berk. *Brit. Flora,* ii. pt. 2. p. 322; *Ann. Nat. Hist.* vi. p. 432, 2nd ser. vii. p. 184; Tulasne, *Ann. des Sc. Nat.* 3 sér. i. p. 367, pl. 17; *Greville, Sc. Crypt. Fl.* pl. 343.

OOGONIUM. — A term used by some Algologists to signify the parent-cell of a true female spore.

OOLINA, D'Orb. = LAGENA.

OOLITE. — The substance of oolitic rocks consists principally of carbonate of lime, sometimes crystallized, at others granular, and usually abounding in organic remains, as shells, &c. It consists of two parts, one of which forms the matrix, is mostly colourless, often crystalline, and exhibits a number of rounded or oval cavities, each of which contains a nodule or mass of a corresponding form. These nodules give the stone somewhat the appearance of the roe of a fish, hence oolite is sometimes called roestone. The nodules possess rather a granular than a crystalline structure. They are sometimes coloured, hollow, and often exhibit concentric rings like those of calculi, and indicative of the successive deposition of layers. Some kinds of oolite contain grains of sand imbedded in the matrix between the nodules.

Polished sections of oolite form interesting objects; and where the nodules are coloured and the matrix colourless, as in oolite from Bristol, in which the former are red, the beauty of the appearance is increased.

BIBL. Works on geology (see the *Bibl.* of CHALK).

OOMYCES, Berk. and Br. — A genus of Sphæriacei (Ascomycetous Fungi), founded on a minute plant growing upon the leaves of grasses. *O. carneo-albus* (*Sphæria carneo-alba,* Libert) has pale, flesh-coloured, tough receptacles 1-18″ high, marked with the ostioles of 3-7 perithecia closely packed within it, bearing resemblance to the eggs of some insects.

BIBL. Berk. and Broome, *Ann. Nat. Hist.* 2 ser. vii. p. 185.

OOPHORIDIUM. — A term applied to those sporanges of Lycopodiaceæ which contain the larger or female spores.

OOSPORANGE. — A term sometimes applied to the large one-celled sacs producing zoospores in the Fucoid Algæ; also synonymous with OOPHORIDIUM.

OOSPORE. — A term used by some physiologists to indicate a spore which receives impregnation in some way before germination, as in *Œdogonium*; and also applied to the larger form of spore in SELAGINELLA and ISOËTES.

OPALINA, Purk. and Val.—The animals comprised under this title were formerly regarded as Infusoria, among which they were placed; but later researches tend to show that they are imperfectly developed forms or intermediate stages of animals probably higher than the Infusoria. They are microscopic, oval or oblong, colourless, covered with vibratile cilia arranged in regular rows; they contain a nucleus, and exhibit contractile vesicles; but they do not admit colouring matters, nor have they a mouth. In one form, an adhesive suctorial disk has been observed, and in another a hook-apparatus, probably serving the same end. They are parasitic within the bodies and usually the intestinal canal of earth-worms, frogs, *Planariæ*, *Naides*, beneath the gill-plates of *Gammarus*, &c.

O. (*Bursaria*, E.) *ranarum*, P. & V., is figured in Pl. 24. fig. 47.

Dujardin places some of them in his genus *Leucophrys*.

BIBL. Purkinje and Valentin, *De phæn. mot. vibr.*; Schultze, *Beit. z. Naturg. d. Turbell.*; Stein, *Infus.* p. 178, &c.

OPEGRAPHA, Ach.—A genus of Graphideæ (Gymnocarpous Lichens), growing on bark of trees, stones, &c. Besides their linear *lirellæ*, the fronds bear *spermogonia*, in *O. varia* and *O. calcarea* forming black spots on the surface, communicating with little unilocular cavities lined with short linear sterigmata bearing numerous spermatia. Mr. Leighton enumerates fourteen species and numerous varieties in his recent monograph.

BIBL. *Brit. Flor.* ii. pt. 1. p. 147; Leighton, *Ann. Nat. Hist.* 2nd ser. xiii. p. 87, xix. p. 129; Tulasne, *Ann. des Sc. Nat.* 3 sér. xvii. p. 207.

OPERCULARIA, Goldfuss.—A genus of Infusoria, of the family Vorticellina.

According to Ehrenberg's description, *Opercularia* resembles *Epistylis* in being furnished with a rigid (not contractile), branched stalk, but differs in the presence of two kinds of bodies, larger and smaller, attached to the branches, the former being usually situated in the axils. Stein regards the larger bodies as belonging to individuals of an older generation, which attach themselves to the branches as to other foreign bodies, and there secrete a new polypidom. This author would distinguish *Opercularia* by the circular anterior margin or rim (peri-

stome) of the body not being thickened and everted, by no cilia arising from it, and by the presence of a kind of lower lip, formed of a delicate everted fold.

Adapted to the peristome in both genera is a conical plug-like retractile body, fringed with cilia, and flat or convex at the end.

1. *O. articulata*, E. Found adherent to *Hydrophilus piceus* and *Dytiscus marginalis*. Pl. 25. fig. 25, *Acineta*-stage (INFUSORIA).

2. *O. barberina*, St. Found upon *Noterus crassicornis*, a water-beetle.

BIBL. Ehrenberg, *Infus.* p. 286; Stein, *Infus. passim.*

OPERCULINA, D'Orb. — A genus of Foraminifera, of the order Helicostegia, and family Nautiloideæ.

Char. Shell equilateral, oval or discoidal, greatly compressed; spire not embracing, regular, equally apparent on both sides, the convolutions contiguous and rapidly enlarging. Chambers numerous, narrow, the last projecting the whole breadth of the spire. Orifice triangular, next the return of the spire, visible at all ages.

Williamson unites *Operculina* with *Nonionina*.

No recent British species; some fossil unnamed, except one. Pl. 18. figs. 22–28 exhibit the minute structure of the shell of *Operculina Arabica*, Carter.

BIBL. That of the order.

OPHIDOMONAS, Ehr.—A generic name applied to slender, filiform, spiral (helical), *Vibrio*-like bodies, of a brown or red colour, with obtuse ends, and actively moving through the water by means of an anterior flagelliform filament. Ehrenberg places them among the Infusoria, in the family Cryptomonadina, and admits two species, characterized by the difference in colour. One was found in fresh, the other in brackish water. Length about 1-570″, breadth 1-9000″. In some the spire forms only half a turn, in others two and a half turns.

Probably an Alga. Is it the young state of *Spirulina*?

BIBL. Ehrenberg, *Infus.* p. 43, and *Ber. d. Berl. Akad.* 1840.

OPHIOCYTIUM, Nägeli.—A genus of Unicellular Algæ, of which several species are described, not yet noticed in Britain.

BIBL. Nägeli, *Einzell. Alg.* pl. 4 A; Al. Braun, *Alg. Unicell.* p. 52.

OPHIOGLOSSACEÆ. — A family of Ferns, distinguished from all others by the characters both of the vegetative and reproductive structures. The fronds are always divided into two parts, one foliaceous and sterile, and the other fertile, neither being ever rolled up in the form of a crook. The sporanges are destitute of any trace of an annulus, and always split very regularly to discharge the spores. For an account of their germination see FERNS.

Genera.

1. *Ophioglossum.* Sporanges dehiscing transversely, connate on an undivided distichous spike.

2. *Botrychium.* Sporanges dehiscing transversely, arranged on a distichous, secund, bi-, tri-pinnate spike.

3. *Helminthostachys.* Sporanges dehiscing externally, vertically, from the base to the middle, collected in whorls, with crest-like appendages, and stalked, arranged distichously on an elongated spike.

OPHIOGLOSSUM, Linn.—The typical genus of Ophioglossaceous Ferns, represented by the Adder's-tongue Fern, *Ophioglossum vulgatum.*

OPHIOTHECA, Currey. — A form of Myxogastrous Fungi doubtfully separated from ARCYRIA.

BIBL. *Journal of Mic. Science,* ii. p. 240, v. p. 131.

OPHRYDINA, Ehr.—A family of Infusoria, corresponding to Vorticellina with a carapace.

Animals grouped in a gelatinous mass .... 1. *OphRydium.*
Animals { Body attached to the bottom } 2. *Tintinnus.*
of the carapace by a stalk
single { Body not { Carapace stalked .. 3. *Cothurnia.*
stalked { Carapace sessile .. 4. *Vaginicula.*

BIBL. Ehrenberg, *Infus.* p. 291.

OPHRYDIUM, Ehr.—A genus of Infusoria, of the family Ophrydina.

Char. Consists of a colourless, gelatinous, rounded mass, either adherent or free, containing numerous greenish *Vorticella*-like animals imbedded and somewhat radiately arranged within it. Aquatic. Length of extended bodies 1-100''; size of entire mass from that of a pea to that of the fist, and even more.

O. versatile (Pl. 24. fig. 49, portion near the surface; fig. 48, portion expanded by pressure; fig. 50, separate animal). The gelatinous mass or envelope has been described as consisting of separate portions or cells, and again as forming a homogeneous whole. It somewhat resembles and has been mistaken for frog's spawn. The bodies of the animals, when extended, are spindle-shaped, when contracted, oval or nearly spherical; they have a row or ring of cilia at the anterior margin of the peristome, also a lid with a fringe of cilia, as in *Opercularia,* &c. The body exhibits annular constrictions and longitudinal folds, and contains scattered chlorophyll-granules, and a long, narrow, tortuous nucleus. A distinct narrow elongated œsophagus is present. Ehrenberg remarks that at first the individual bodies are united in the centre by filaments, which subsequently disappear. The animals undergo the encysting process, and assume an *Acineta*-form. When they leave the jelly, a posterior ring of cilia is formed, as in *Vorticella,* and the animals swim with the tail first.

This organism bears some resemblance to *Coccochloris* among the Palmellaceæ, yet it appears decidedly animal.

BIBL. Ehrenberg, *Infus.* p. 292; Stein, *Infus., passim.*

OPHRYOCERCINA, Ehr.—A family of Infusoria.

It contains the single genus *Trachelocerca,* E., which corresponds to *Lacrymaria* with a tail. Dujardin unites these two genera; so that the former becomes unnecessary. If the family be retained, it should be called TRACHELOCERCINA.

OPHRYOGLENA, Ehr. — A genus of Infusoria, of the family Colpodea.

Char. Body ciliated all over; a frontal eye-spot present; cilia arranged in longitudinal rows.

Three species, all aquatic. Stein remarks that, on treating these animals with acetic acid, the cilia became converted into a dense network of curved and geniculate hairs, some as long as the body.

1. *O. atra* (Pl. 24. fig. 53). Body ovate, compressed, black, acute posteriorly; eye-spot black, marginal; cilia whitish. Aquatic; length 1-180''.

2. *O. acuminata,* brown; eye-spot red.

3. *O. flavicans,* yellowish; eye-spot red.

Lieberkuhn describes in *O. flavicans* a vibrating membrane contained in a sac-like space, leading from an oral slit; and near the eye-spot a watch-glass-shaped organ; also two contractile vessels, arising close to the mouth, connected with a system of vascular canals ramifying in the outer portions of the body.

Dujardin places this genus in his family Bursarina.

BIBL. Ehrenberg, *Infus.* p. 360; Stein, *Infus.* p. 240; Dujardin, *Infus.* p. 506; Lieberkuhn, *Ann. Nat. Hist.* 1856. xviii. 319.

ORBICULINA, Lamk. — A genus of Foraminifera, of the order Helicostegia, and family Nautiloidæ.

Char. Shell discoidal, equilateral, greatly compressed, very variable according to age; forming an embracing, very regular spire when young, subsequently growing into a more or less perfect disk. Chambers very narrow, curved, and divided throughout their length into a multitude of minute distinct cavities by partitions which are perpendicular and transverse to the spiral coil. Orifices very numerous, round, scattered, arranged in rows longitudinal to the spiral.

No British species.

O. rotella (Pl. 18. fig. 18).

BIBL. That of the order.

ORBITOLITES, Lamarck (*Orbulites*).— A genus of Foraminifera, of the order Cyclostegia. Distinguished by the chambers being arranged in concentric circles.

No recent British species.

O. complanatus (Pl. 18. figs. 16, 17) = *Sorites* and *Amphisorus*, Ehr.

BIBL. Morris, *Brit. Fossils*, xxxix., and the *Bibl.* there given.

ORBULINA, D'Orb.—A genus of Foraminifera, of the order Monostegia.

Char. Shell spherical, hollow. Orifice single, minute, round, without either prominence or rays.

Williamson remarks that the shell is more arenaceous than calcareous.

O. universa. Recent and fossil.

BIBL. That of the order.

ORIBATA, Latr.—This genus has been subdivided, and now constitutes the family Oribatea. The position of three species is, however, doubtful, viz. *Acarus confervæ*, Schr., living in fresh water, and creeping upon Confervæ, &c.; *Oribata demersa*, Duj., aquatic, with a cervical eye, and found upon *Hypnum inundatum*; and *Oribata marina*, a marine species.

We have found one species doubtfully referable to the above, agreeing with the characters of the Oribatea: body brown, tarsi with a single claw, and no caruncle. The individuals were creeping upon broken stems of *Ceratophyllum*.

BIBL. Gervais, *Walckenaer's Apt.* iii. p. 251; Schrank, *Ins. Austriæ*, p. 511; Dujardin, *L'Institut*, 1842. p. 316; Koch, *Deutschl. Crustac.* &c.; Dugès, *Ann. des Sc. Nat.* 2 sér. ii. p. 46.

ORIBATEA.—A family of Arachnida, of the order Acarina.

Char. Body covered by a hard horny envelope; palpi fusiform, 5-jointed; first joint small, second large, inflated and almost half the length of the entire palpus; palpi hairy outside only; mandibles chelate; body often winged. Genera:

1. *Nothrus.* Body elongate, irregularly quadrilateral, with spinous filaments; legs of moderate length, thick.

2. *Belba.* Abdomen distinct from thorax, rounded, inflated; legs long, geniculate.

3. *Galumna.* Abdomen subglobular, depressed, margins of the pseudothorax winged; legs of moderate length.

4. *Hoplophora.* As the last, but winglike appendages absent.

Two doubtful genera: *Sillibano* and *Cœculus.*

BIBL. *Walckenaer's Aptères*, 251; Koch, *Deutschl. Crustac. &c.*; Dugès, *Ann. des Sc. Nat.* ii. 48; Dufour, *Ann. des Sc. Nat.* 1 sér. xxv. 289.

ORTHOCERINA, D'Orb.—A genus of Foraminifera, of the order Stichostegia, and family Æquilateralidæ.

Char. Shell regular; equilateral, conical. Chambers not convex, in apposition, without intermediate constrictions; the last almost flat, and without terminal prolongation, with the single orifice in its centre.

No British species.

O. quadrilatera (Pl. 18. fig. 6).

BIBL. That of the order.

ORTHODONTIUM, Schwägr.—A genus of Bryaceous Mosses, included under *Bryum* by some authors.

BIBL. Wilson, *Bryologia Britann.* p. 218.

ORTHOPTERA.—An order of Insects, containing the grass-hoppers, crickets, &c.

ORTHOSIRA, Thw. See MELOSIRA.

ORTHOTRICHACEÆ. — A tribe of Pottioid Mosses including several British genera.

a. Papillæ distinct, tuberculate, rarely obsolete : peristome mostly pale, rarely orange-coloured.

1. *Zygodon.* Calyptra dimidiate. Peristome wanting, simple (external or internal) or double; external of thirty-two simple, Orthotrichoid, twin or bigeminate-conglutinate, flat, pale, regular, rather fleshy teeth, formed of a single row of cells, spreading or reflexed on drying, and appressed to the capsule as in *Orthotrichum*; internal: eight to sixteen linear, hyaline, more or less connivent, horizontal cilia, or resembling the outer teeth. Capsule pyriform, grooved,

more rarely glabrous, without an annulus.

2. *Orthotrichum*, Hedw. Calyptra campanulate, plaited. Peristome absent, simple, or double. External of thirty-two geminate (sixteen) (fig. 483, p. 468) or bigeminate (eight) (fig. 537) teeth, more rarely of sixteen entire, undivided teeth, granular, fleshy, or brittle, mostly pale, rarely orange-coloured, erect, afterwards reflexed, arising below the mouth of the capsule. Internal: eight or sixteen cilia, simple, hyaline, or (rarely) resembling the teeth. Vaginule ochraceous. Inflorescence monœcious or diœcious. Capsule without an annulus, more or less pyriform, grooved, rarely glabrous; operculum cupitate, conical.

b. Papillæ mostly obsolete, rarely distinct, peristome always coloured, purple, red or orange.

3. *Glyphomitrium*. Calyptra campanulate, large, totally enclosing the capsule, deeply laciniate, plaited. Peristome composed of sixteen short, lanceolate, densely trabeculate, entire teeth, with a central line, approximated in pairs, incurved, arising below the orifice, orange-coloured, smooth (fig. 283, p. 318). Inflorescence monœcious.

4. *Brachystelium*. Calyptra as in the preceding, altogether or almost entirely covering the capsule, mitre-shaped, with long and repeated lacinations, slightly plaited. Peristome like that of *Trichostomum*, the teeth being split more or less, down to the base, into two arms. Inflorescence monœcious.

5. *Guembelia*. Calyptra dimidiate, otherwise like the following (figs. 289-291, p. 325).

6. *Grimmia*. Calyptra mitre-shaped, laciniate, scarcely exceeding the operculum, and smooth, or else shorter. Peristome simple, teeth sixteen, lanceolate, with a median line, trabeculate, often however fissile, hence very polymorphous, more or less split, as far as the middle, into two or four teeth, or into two arms down to the base (fig. 288, p. 324).

ORTHOTRICHUM, Hedwig.—A genus of Orthotrichaceæ (Pottioid Mosses), growing in round tufts, fertile at the summit, on trees and stones, never on the earth. There are numerous British species, which are remarkable for the apophyses (sometimes having stomata) and for the varied character of the outer peristome, the thirty-two teeth of which are variously conjoined, so

as to appear as thirty-two, sixteen, or eight. The calyptra is mostly covered with hair-like processes (fig. 472, p. 466).

Fig. 536.   Fig. 537.

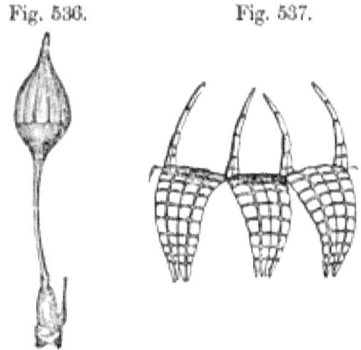

Fig. 536. Orthotrichum pulchellum. Magn. 15 diams.
Fig. 537. Orthotrichum pallens. Fragment of peristome. Magn. 50 diams.

Bibl. Wilson, *Bryologia Brit.* p. 185; Hooker, *Brit. Fl.* ii. pt. 1. p. 57.

OSCILLATORIA, Vauch.—A genus of Oscillatoriaceæ (Confervoid Algæ), distinguished from the allied forms by the simple, rigid, elastic filaments, forming a stratum in a common gelatinous matrix. The filaments are enclosed singly in tubular cellulose sheaths, open at the ends, from which the fragments emerge when they are broken across (Pl. 4. fig. 8). The young filaments or growing extremities are continuous and scarcely striated; but by degrees transverse striæ appear, sometimes very close together, sometimes distant, which striæ indicate a constriction and final fission in the substance of the filament, which, when old, readily breaks at these places. The internal structure of the filament is obscure: it would seem to be composed wholly of protoplasmic substance, the joints not possessing special cellulose coats; but the substance of the filament, although apparently solid, seems sometimes less dense internally, since we have noticed a kind of hour-glass contraction intermediate between the striæ after the action of thick syrup (by endosmose) and after desiccation. The curious rounding-off of the separated ends of dividing filaments (Pl. 4. fig. 8, right-hand figures) seems to depend on some power of expansion of an outer thicker layer of the substance of the filament. The motion of the filaments has been described under Oscil-

LATORIACEÆ. The filaments ultimately break up at the striæ into distinct joints, which may be regarded as *gonidia*. No formation of spores has been observed. A remarkable and unexplained appearance is occasionally observed at the growing ends of the filaments: they appear crowned by a wreath of cilia; but these processes are rigid; no motion of them has ever been seen.

Kützing has multiplied the species beyond all reason, and separated some without good grounds under the name of *Phormidium*. We follow Harvey in the enumeration of the commoner British species; but this genus, like its allies, requires a thorough study of recent specimens. They occur on damp ground, on stones, on mud, in fresh water, running or stagnant, in springs and in brackish water; a few are truly marine. In the following characters the colour of the strata is given as seen by the naked eye, that of the filaments as seen under the microscope.

* In fresh water, or on damp earth, &c.

 a. Stratum æruginous or blue-green.

1. *O. limosa*, Ag. Stratum dark green, glossy, with long rays; filaments green, 1-3300 to 1-3600" in diameter; articulations shorter than the diameter. At the bottom of ditches and pools.

2. *O. tenuis*, Ag. Stratum dark green, thin, with short rays; filaments pale green, 1-4200" in diameter; articulations equalling or half the diameter. In muddy ditches, &c.; at first on the bottom, finally floating to the top.

3. *O. muscorum*, Ag. Stratum dark æruginous-green, 3 or 4" in extent, growing over mosses in rapid streams; filaments 'thickish,' pale blue-green.

4. *O. turfosa*, Carm. Stratum pale verdigris-green, glaucous, 1 or 1½' in diameter, resting on an ochraceous substratum; filaments hyaline, 'very slender.' On floating sods in turf-pits.

5. *O. decorticans*, Grev. Stratum smooth, glaucous-green, membranous, peeling off in flakes; filaments pale bluish-green, 'very slender.' Damp walls, pumps, &c.; common.

 b. Stratum dull green, inclining to purple, black, or brown.

6. *O. nigra*, Vauch. Stratum blackish green (bluish black when dry), with long radii; filaments pale bluish green, 1-2800 to 1-3000" in diameter; joints equalling or

a little shorter than the diameter. Ditches and ponds. Common.

7. *O. autumnalis*, Ag. (Pl. 4. fig. 8). Stratum purplish or greenish black; filaments pale dirty bluish green, 1-4000 to 1-5000" in diameter; joints shorter than the diameter. Damp ground, walls, &c. Common.

8. *O. contexta*, Carm. Stratum glossy black, spreading three feet or more, appearing satiny and striated to the naked eye; filaments pale green, 1-3000" in diameter; articulations largish. On mud; apparently common.

O. ochracea, Grev. is probably the same as *Leptothrix ochracea*.

 ** Marine, or in brackish water.

9. *O. littoralis*, Carm. Stratum bright æruginous-green; filaments deep green, "thicker than in *O. nigra*;" joints one-third the diameter. Pools on the sea-shore.

Other species are described, but without dimensions, so that they are obscure without the aid of figures. See also SYMPLOCA.

BIBL. Harvey, *Brit. Alg.* 1st ed. p. 161; *Br. Mar. Alg.* p. 228; *Phyc. Brit.* pls. 105, 251; Hassall, *Br. Fr. Alg.* p. 244, pl. 70-72; Kützing, *Sp. Alg.* p. 237; *Tab. Phyc.* Bd. 1. pls. 38-44.

OSCILLATORIACEÆ.—A family of Confervoid Algæ, containing organisms of considerable diversity and not very well characterized at present, owing to the obscurity of the reproduction. The genus *Oscillatoria*, with its nearest allies, is composed of cylindrical filaments of protoplasmic substance, invested by a continuous cellulose sheath or tubular cell-membrane. The internal (solid?) filament gradually becomes transversely striated as it increases in age, and subsequently readily breaks across at the transverse lines, and the fragments readily escape from the sheaths, since no cross-walls of cellulose are produced (Pl. 4. fig. 8). These kinds exhibit clearly the remarkable motion from which the family takes its name. They are mostly found upon damp ground, forming wide and irregular strata. *Rivularia* and the allied genera have the joints of the filaments more distinct; and the filaments are coherent into definite fronds, on which they stand erect or radiate from a centre (Pl. 4. figs. 13, 16). The sheaths become complicated in many of these, from the internal multiplication and the persistence of the cellulose sheaths of several generations one within another (see PETALONEMA), often gelatinously swollen up and sometimes decomposed into spiral fibrous structures (Pl. 4. fig. 15; see SPIRAL STRUCTURES). Some of the remaining forms, included here for the present, differ considerably from the above, and are imperfectly understood. *Vibrio* (Pl. 3. figs. 18-21) consists of moniliform filaments without an apparent sheath. *Spirulina* (Pl. 3. fig. 15) has the (solid?) filaments curled spirally; and in the strange plant *Didymohelix* (Pl. 1. fig. 10) two spiral filaments occurred twined together. These last minute forms generally occur imbedded in a gelatinous stratum; but their relation to this is not yet clearly ascertained.

The structure of the Oscillatoriaceæ, judging from *Oscillatoria*, *Microcoleus*, and *Lyngbya*, differs importantly from that of all other Confervoids. The filaments are not composed of rows of cells, but, in the earliest condition, of a cylindrical thread of protoplasm, coloured greyish, green, brown, or purple in different cases. The ends of growing filaments are narrower and devoid of striæ, and have no perceptible cellulose sheath; when a little older, cross striæ appear, consisting of double rows of granules or dots, and the tubular cellulose coat is evident; finally the striæ become distinct lines (see Pl. 4. figs. 8-22). In this stage, external violence will cause the filament to break across at the striæ; and the fragments then slide along inside the cellulose sheath, the broken ends always assuming a rounded form like that of the free extremities (Pl. 4. fig. 8 b). When these fragments slide quite out of the sheaths, the latter appear as continuous tubes (Pl. 4. fig. 8 a), seldom with any cross markings opposite the striæ of the internal mass. In *Lyngbya* the division seems to take place in a peculiar manner, accompanied by an interstitial growth comparable to that of ZYGNEMA. In a well-developed filament, every eighth stria is strongest, the intermediate fourths rather lighter, every second one between them paler still, and the intermediates of these only just marked; while in *Oscillatoria* the striæ seem to be gradually less definite towards the growing apex of a filament. The filaments appear solid as ordinarily viewed; but the endosmose resulting from placing them in syrup or gum-water causes them to contract between the striæ, or to break up into lenticular disks. The ultimate fate of all the filaments seems to be a separation into disks or globular gonidia, by breaking across at the striæ.

In *Microcoleus* (Pl. 4. fig. 9) and many Rivulariæ there would appear to be a transverse multiplication like that occurring occasionally in NOSTOC, as the filaments are found lying side by side in gelatinously decomposed outer (parent) sheaths. The filaments of the Rivulariæ are seated on a large basal cell (Pl. 4. figs. 13, 16, 18), the nature of which is not understood.

The remarkable spontaneous motion of many Oscillatoriaceæ presents a considerable variety of conditions. In *Oscillatoria* and *Microcoleus* the ends of the filaments emerge from their sheaths, the young extremities being apparently devoid of this coat; their ends wave backwards and forwards, somewhat as the fore part of the bodies of certain caterpillars are waved when they stand on their pro-legs with the head reared up. The filaments also emerge from the tubes and break up; and the fragments then exhibit an oscillating movement like that of a balance, together with an advance in a longitudinal direction. *Lyngbya* (Pl. 4. fig. 10) does not appear to oscillate, at all events when in long filaments. *Vibrio*, *Spirulina*, and other forms exhibit only a tremulous oscillation; the same appears to be the case with *Bacterium*; the plant termed *Didymohelix* probably acquires its double-spiral character from the entwining of originally distinct filaments. These last organisms were included by Ehrenberg among the Infusoria; but there is every reason to regard them as vegetables. *Leptothrix* and the allied genera are very imperfectly known, and are only included here from the absence of indications of closer affinities elsewhere; very likely they are mycelial filaments of Fungi.

All these plants occur on damp ground, rocks, or stones, and among Mosses and other Confervæ on rocks, stones, &c., in fresh and salt water, and are allied in some respects to the NOSTOCHACEÆ; but the articulations of the filaments of the latter are all perfect cells with a complete cellulose wall, multiplying by division in the same way as the Confervaceæ.

Synopsis of British Genera.

A. *Oscillatorieæ.* Filaments transversely striated or moniliform, sometimes spirally curled; sheathed, or, in the minute forms, without evident sheaths; exhibiting spontaneous oscillating, creeping, or serpentine motion. Increased by transverse division.

1. *Bacterium* (Pl. 3. fig. 17). Filaments

colourless, extremely small, short, wand-shaped, or longish-oval, with two to four cross striæ, exhibiting a vibratory motion. No sheaths evident.

2. *Vibrio* (Pl. 3. figs. 18–20). Filaments colourless, extremely slender, moniliform, with an active serpentine motion. No sheath evident.

3. *Spirulina* (Pl. 3. figs. 15, 22, 23). Filaments green, very slender, continuous or moniliform, curled into a long helical or screw-like form; oscillating; no sheaths evident, but often a common investing jelly.

4. *Didymohelix* (Pl. 1. fig. 10). Filaments brown, very slender, continuous, curled spirally and twisted together in pairs. Motion?. No evident sheaths, but a common investing jelly.

5. *Oscillatoria* (Pl. 4. fig. 8). Filaments coloured, continuous, transversely striated, readily breaking across, with a proper cellulose sheath, oscillating; collected in strata and imbedded in a common gelatinous matrix.

6. *Microcoleus* (Pl. 4. fig. 9). Filaments as in *Oscillatoria*, but collected in bundles in a common gelatinous tubular sheath, which is dichotomously branched; filaments oscillating.

7. *Cœnocoleus*. Filaments branched, contained with their ramifications within a tough, more or less permanent sheath which bursts irregularly. Filaments annulated.

8. *Symploca*. Filaments as in *Oscillatoria*, but erect and tufted, coherent at their bases, bristling above.

B. *Lyngbyeæ.* Filaments motionless (?), oscillarioid, enclosed in a very distinct sheath, tufted, or forming strata, with or without an enveloping jelly.

9. *Dasyglæa* (Pl. 4. fig. 11). Filaments unbranched, sheathed; older sheaths broad, coalescent outside into an amorphous gelatinous stratum.

10. *Lyngbya* (Pl. 4. fig. 10). Filaments elongated, distinctly articulated, unbranched, with distinct convoluted cellulose tube, but without a gelatinous matrix; (motion creeping?) articulations very close.

11. *Leibleinia*. Filaments short, erect, tufted, unbranched, with distinct cellulose coat, free, without an investing jelly.

C. *Scytonemeæ.* Filaments distinctly articulated, simple or branched, motionless, with distinct articulations and large interstitial (propagative?) cells; sheaths at length softened and swollen, but without a common gelatinous matrix.

12. *Scytonema* (Pl. 4. fig. 19). Filaments cæspitose, or more rarely fasciculate, with a double (lamellar) gelatinous sheath, (mostly) closed at the apex; branches continuous by lateral growing out of the primary filaments, with a knee-like base.

13. *Desmonema*. Filaments branched, more or less coherent, branches of two kinds, primary branches each with a connecting cell at the base, secondary branches without connecting cells; annulated. See TOLYPOTHRIX.

14. *Arthronema* (Pl. 4. fig. 20). Filaments distinctly articulated, simple, in short lengths, overlapping at their ends within the gelatinous sheath.

15. *Petalonema* (Pl. 4. fig. 21). Filaments branched, with the outer sheaths of the single joints expanded upwards and outwards into funnel-shaped bodies, each partly overlapping its successor, forming a common obliquely lamellated and transversely barred gelatinous cylinder.

16. *Calothrix* (Pl. 4. fig. 22). Filaments very closely articulated, tufted, with branches in apposition for some distance, here and there cohering laterally. Sheaths firm, often dark-coloured.

17. *Tolypothrix*. Filaments free, radiantly or fastigiately branched, most distinctly articulated at the bases of the branches; branches continuously excurrent, not in apposition; sheaths thin, hyaline.

18. *Sirosiphon*. Filaments single, double or triple, within a distinct common sheath, very distinctly articulated; branched by lateral budding, the branches divergent.

19. *Schizothrix* (Pl. 4. fig. 17). Filaments branched by division; sheaths lamellated, thick, rigid, curled, thickened below, finally longitudinally divided.

20. *Symphyosiphon*. Filaments erect or ascending, enclosed in lamellated, hard sheaths, concreted laterally at their bases, involved in jelly.

21. *Rhizonema*. Sheath cellular and furnished throughout its length with numerous branched and anastomosing rootlets (?). Filaments distinctly annulated, and interrupted here and there by a connecting cell. Branches in pairs, arising from a protrusion of the filament.

D. *Rivularieæ.* Filaments distinctly articulated, with an enlarged basal cell, mostly attenuated above, connected into definite or indefinite fronds; motionless.

22. *Schizosiphon* (Pl. 4. fig. 13). Basal cells globose, filaments simple, distinctly articulated, mostly attenuated towards the apex, sheathed, sheaths connate into groups, hard, dark-coloured, open and expanded above, and overlapping so as to form a succession of ochreæ which have the free borders slit up into filaments or fringes; also displaying a spiral-fibrous structure in dissolution.

23. *Physactis*. Filaments whip-shaped, torulose at the base, sheathed, sheaths simple, gelatinous; collected into a globose and solid, or subsequently a bullose-vesicular frond; in the globose fronds the filaments radiate from the centre; in the vesicular fronds from the internal (lower) surface of the gelatinous matrix.

24. *Ainactis* (Pl. 4. fig. 15). Filaments branched, articulated, with thin sheaths, collected into a solid pulvinate frond, which is concentrically zoned by the dichotomous branching of the filaments. Sheaths more or less solidified by carbonate of lime; sometimes exhibiting a spiral structure in dissolution.

25. *Rivularia* (Pl. 4. fig. 18). Filaments with an oval basal cell succeeded by one of cylindrical form (*manubrium*), the remainder short, attenuated in diameter upwards (whip-shaped). Sheaths sometimes saccate below, open (not fringed) above; forming a slippery gelatinous frond.

26. *Euactis* (Pl. 4. fig. 16). Filaments whip-shaped, with repeated ochreate sheaths, forming fronds in which they radiate, and, by superposition of successive generations, form concentric layers. The ochreate sheaths are cartilaginous, lamellated, firmly united laterally, dilated upwards (funnel-shaped), decomposed into a fringe at the open edge.

27. *Inomeria*. Filaments whip-shaped, vertical, parallel, with obscure sheaths, everywhere decomposed into very slender filaments; forming crustaceous fronds, becoming stony.

28. *Petronema*. Densely cæspitose, erect, somewhat regularly branched, branches free, with obtuse rounded apices, and each with a connecting cell at the base. Filaments annulated and growing thicker upwards.

F. *Leptothriceæ*. Doubtful Oscillatoriaceæ.

29. *Leptothrix*. Filaments very slender, neither branched, articulated, concreted, nor sheathed.

30. *Hypheothrix*. Filaments unbranched, inarticulate, sheathed, interwoven into a more or less compact stratum.

31. *Symploca*. Filaments unbranched, inarticulate, sheathed, concreted into branches, conjoined at their bases; sheath a simple hyaline membrane.

Excluded Genera.

Stigonema, Ag. See EPHEBE.—*Arthrosiphon*, Ktz. = *Petalonema*.—*Chthonoblastus*, Ktz. = *Microcoleus*. — *Hassallia*, Berk. = *Sirosiphon*.—*Lithonema*, Hass. = *Ainactis*.—*Phormidium*, Ktz. = *Oscillatoria*.—*Symphyothrix*, Ktz. = *Oscillatoria*.—*Spirochæta*, Ehr. = *Spirulina*. — *Spirillum*, Ehr. = *Spirulina*, and also SPERMATOZOIDS of Mosses and Characeæ.—*Spirodiscus*, Ehr. ?

BIBL. See the genera, especially OSCILLATORIA and RIVULARIA, and SPIRAL STRUCTURES.

OSMUNDA, Linn.—A genus of Osmundeæous Ferns, represented in Britain by *Osmunda regalis* (figs. 222, 223, p. 283), the 'Royal or Flowering Fern,' as it is termed, a large and handsome plant, found in damp situations; not common.

OSMUNDEÆ.—A tribe of Polypodiaceous Ferns, characterized by the broad imperfect annulus on the back of the sporanges.

Genera.

1. *Osmunda*. Sporangia borne on metamorphosed pinnules.

2. *Todea*. Sporangia placed on unchanged pinnules.

OTOGLENA, Ehr.—A genus of Rotatoria, of the family Hydatinea.

Char. Eyes three; one sessile and cervical, the two others stalked and frontal.

Neither jaws nor teeth present.

O. papillosa. Body campanulate, turgid, rough with papillæ; aquatic; length 1·96".

BIBL. Ehrenberg, *Infus.* p. 453.

OVA OF ANIMALS.—The germs secreted by the ovaries. When extruded from the body, they are generally termed eggs (EGGS). See OVUM.

OVARY.—The organ in which the ova or germs of the future offspring are formed and temporarily contained.

The ovary consists of an outer fibrous coat, and a parenchyma or stroma.

The outer coat, or tunica albuginea, firm, white, and intimately connected with the subjacent stroma; it consists of interlacing bundles of areolar tissue, with but few fibres of elastic tissue.

2 L

The stroma (fig. 538 e) is composed of nucleated areolar tissue, in which the fibrillæ are mostly indistinct, and in it are imbedded the *Graafian vesicles* or follicles (fig. 538 a).

Fig. 538.

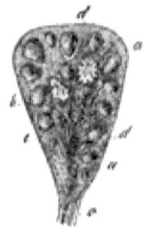

Transverse section of a human ovary at the fifth month of pregnancy. *a*, Graafian vesicle of the under, *b*, of the upper surface; *c*, peritoneal layer continued from the broad ligament of the uterus to the ovary, and becoming fused with *d*, the tunica albuginea; in the centre are two old corpora lutea; *e*, stroma of the ovary.

The vesicles vary greatly in number and size; the largest are generally nearest the surface, and project more or less, so as to give it a nodular aspect. They are round closed sacs (fig. 539). Each possesses two

Fig. 539.

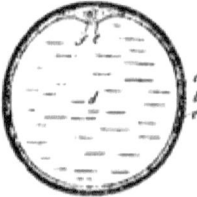

Graafian vesicle of the pig. *a*, outer, *b*, inner layer of the fibrous coat; *c*, membrana granulosa; *d*, liquid contained in the vesicle; *e*, proligerous disk; *f*, ovum with the zona pellucida, yolk and germinal vesicle.

Magnified 10 diameters.

coats; the outer is a fibrous and vascular layer, connected with the stroma by somewhat lax areolar tissue, and which some physiologists consider as consisting of two layers. It is composed of imperfectly developed nucleated areolar tissue, with numerous, somewhat spindle-shaped, formative cells. Lining this is a basement-membrane, which is most distinct in the young vesicles; and within this again is a layer of epithelial cells, constituting the *membrana granulosa* (fig. 539 c). Next the surface of the ovary, this is thickened and projects

inwards, forming the *proligerous disk, e.* Its component cells form several rows; they are roundish-polygonal, about 1-3000" in diameter, with comparatively large nuclei, and frequently contain granules of fat. The ovum is imbedded in this proligerous disk, *e.*

The cavity of the Graafian vesicle contains a liquid resembling the serum of the blood; and in it are found granules, nuclei, and cells, arising from the disintegration of the membrana granulosa.

When the vesicle bursts or is opened, the ovum escapes surrounded by the cells of the proligerous disk and the adjacent part of the epithelium.

In those animals in which the amount of stroma present is small in proportion to the size of the vesicles, the ovaries have a racemose appearance.

In many of the lower animals, the ovaries are tubular, the ova lying closely packed within them.

BIBL. Kölliker, *Mikr. Anat.* ii.; Siebold, *Vergleich. Anat.*

OVULE or OVULUM.—The name applied to the rudiment of the seed of Flowering Plants, produced in the ovary or germen during the development of the flower, fertilized by the pollen-grains when complete, and afterwards converted into a SEED by the development of the EMBRYO and other secondary structures during the conversion of the ovary into the fruit. For the general conditions of the ovules in ovaries, reference must be made to botanical works. The ovules make their appearance upon the placenta as cellular papillæ rising up from its surface, and at first are simple; this first development, the main feature of the organ, is called the *nucleus* (figs. 540–542). In

Fig. 540.　　　　　Fig. 541.

Atropous ovules.

Fig. 540. Young ovule of Chelidonium. *n*, nucleus; *ch*, chalaza.
Fig. 541. Young ovule of misletoe, consisting of a nucleus only.

rare cases this remains naked, but in most instances one or two coats are produced, arising as circular folds near the base, and gradually growing up over the nucleus (fig. 542), leaving only a small passage at the apex, leading down to the point of the nucleus. When two coats are formed (fig. 543), the inner appears first; the outer

Fig. 542.   Fig. 543.

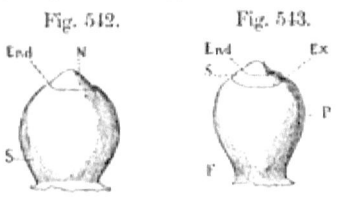

Atropous ovules.

Fig. 542. Young ovule of walnut, consisting of a nucleus *N*, with a single coat *S*; *End* the endostome or micropyle.

Fig. 543. Young ovule of Polygonum. *F*, funiculus; *P*, primine (of Mirbel); *S*, secundine; *Ex*, exostome; *End*, endostome.

Magnified 40 diameters.

originates later and grows up over the inner, and it is generally thicker and more developed. The inner is called the *secundine* by Mirbel, the outer the *primine* (figs. 543, 544, 547 *S, P*). The German writers reverse these names, resting on the true order of development. Some term them the *integumentum internum* and *externum*. The inner is the *tegmen*, the outer the *testa* of R. Brown. The passage at the apex, leading to the nucleus, is called the *micropyle*; sometimes the orifice in the outer coat is distinguished from that in the inner coat, and they are termed respectively *exostome* and *endostome* (fig. 547). While the nucleus and coats are becoming perfected, one of the cells situated near the apex of the nucleus takes

Fig. 544.   Fig. 545.

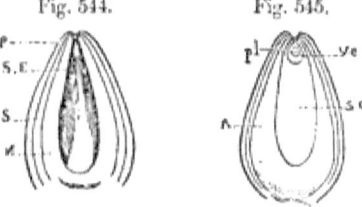

Sections of atropous ovule of Polygonum.

P, primine; *S*, secundine; *N*, nucleus; *SE*, embryosac; *Ve*, *Vi*, nascent embryo.

Magnified 20 diameters.

on a peculiar character, becoming more developed than the rest, and often causing the

absorption of part (or sometimes the whole) of the tissue of the nucleus; it appears at length as a large sac occupying the centre of the ovule; this is the *embryo-sac* (fig. 544). The base of the ovule is pushed up from the surface of the placenta during its development so as to appear at length supported on a stalk of variable length; this is termed the *funiculus* (figs. 543 *F*, 547 *f*); the point of attachment of this stalk to the body of the ovule (marked by a scar when the ripe seed separates) is called the *hilum*. That region of the interior where the lower parts of the coats are confluent with the base of the nucleus, is called the *chalaza* (fig. 546 *C*).

Fig. 546.

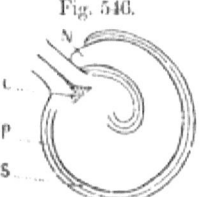

Section of campylotropous ovule of the wallflower. *C*, chalaza; *N*, nucleus; *S*, inner coat; *P* outer coat.

Magnified 20 diameters.

The form of ovules is much affected by excessive development of its constituent parts in special directions before the fertilization. If all parts grow equally, the complete ovule is erect on the placenta, with its hilum and also the chalaza turned towards the latter, and its micropyle at the opposite free end; such an ovule is technically termed *atropous* or *orthotropous* (figs. 541–545). Very frequently an excessive growth takes place at one side of the coats of the ovule, so that the chalaza is carried up and directed away from the placenta, the micropyle being at the same time turned down towards the latter; but as the growth is in the coats of the ovule, the hilum remains at the base, near where the micropyle arrives; such an ovule is termed *anatropous* (fig. 116, p. 140). The hilum is then connected with the chalaza by a ridge (a kind of adherent funiculus) called the *raphe*. In other cases the form becomes altered by the point of the ovule turning down, and the entire structure becoming folded or bent upon itself, without disturbance of the relative positions of the hilum and chalaza, while the micropyle is brought down, as in the anatropous ovule, to the vicinity of the hilum.

This form is termed *campylotropous* (fig. 546). Other conditions occur less frequently, among which is the *amphitropous* form (figs. 550 & 551).

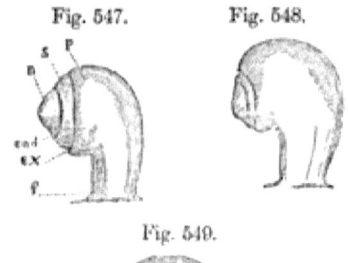

Fig. 547.　　　　Fig. 548.

Fig. 549.

Magnified 40 diameters.

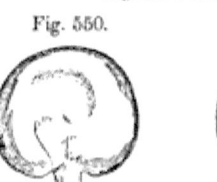

Fig. 550.　　　　Fig. 551.

Magnified 20 diameters.

Amphitropous ovule of Mallow in different stages.

Fig. 551. Section.

During these developments the embryo-sac also undergoes various changes. Sometimes, as in the Orchidaceæ, it expands so as to obliterate all the tissue of the nucleus, and appears like a simple sac enclosed by the coats; in the Scrophulariaceæ and other orders it produces peculiar lobes or pouches at various points; in the Santalaceæ it grows out from the summit of the nucleus, as a free, naked, tubular process, &c.

Up to this point the differences in ovules are such as may be termed secondary; but a primary distinction now comes into view, connected also with a difference in the external conditions, affording grounds for the division of the Flowering Plants into two great classes. In the Coniferæ and Cycadaceæ the ovules are developed upon open carpels, and consequently the micropyle

may receive the pollen-grains immediately, when expelled from the anthers. Plants exhibiting this condition are termed GYMNOSPERMS, or naked-seeded. In the Dicotyledons and Monocotyledons the carpels are always closed up into cases or ovaries, surmounted by a *stigma*, sessile or elevated upon a style, and the pollen, falling upon the stigma, produces there its pollen-tubes, which pass down through what is called the conducting tissue of the style and upper part of the ovary, on to the placentæ, whence they make their way to the micropyles of the ovules. Plants exhibiting these conditions are distinguished as ANGIOSPERMS or covered-seeded.

The next phænomena which characterize the development of the ovules of the Angiosperms may be briefly given as follows. The formation of the embryo-sac has already been described. Shortly before the opening of the flower, in most cases, this sac is more or less densely filled with granular protoplasm, in which a variable number of nuclei may be seen (Pl. 38. figs. 1–7). About the time when the pollen-grains are discharged from the anthers, a number of minute, free, globular protoplasmic bodies may be discovered in the embryo-sac, usually three (more rarely one) of these being crowded into the upper end of the embryo-sac and constituting what are called the *germinal bodies* or *masses* (Pl. 38. fig. 4). Others, which often occur in the embryo-sac, are generally collected near the bottom of the embryo-sac; they are apparently characteristic of particular families only; in some plants they are very large, as in the *Crocus*. About this time the embryo-sac often exhibits asymmetrical growth, forming pouches or processes, sometimes at the summit, sometimes at the base.

When the pollen-grains fall upon the stigma, they produce their pollen-tubes (see POLLEN), which pass down through the conducting tissue, and enter the micropyles of the ovules. When they reach the apex of the embryo-sac, they either stop, often swelling a little, or they pass down a short way over its side (Pl. 38. fig. 5). Not unfrequently two pollen-tubes are found engaged in the micropyle of the same ovule. It is not absolutely known whether the cavities of the pollen-tube and the embryo-sac become actually continuous by absorption of the walls at the point of attachment: it is generally believed not; but we have had occasion to feel some doubt on this point. The essential point of the process is the intermixture of the contents of the pollen-tube with the substance of the germinal body. In the higher Cryptogamia and in the Algæ, the impregnation is of a similar nature; but there the germ-masses are fertilized by the agency of spermatozoids, which make their way to them, either *constituting* or *carrying* the impregnating matter, which in the case of the pollen-tube is a liquid, containing fine granules, but exhibiting no trace of active spermatic bodies.

Soon after the pollen-tube has reached the point of the embryo-sac, one (rarely two, giving rise to POLYEMBRYONY) of the germinal bodies becomes invested by a cellulose membrane (*germ-cell*), and usually changes from a spherical to an oval form, a transverse septum soon dividing it into two. Most frequently the elongation continues, with a successive formation of septa, until the nascent embryo appears as a rounded or oval cellule suspended at the base of a simple confervoid filament (*suspensor*); in other cases the formation of the first transverse septum is followed by the expansion into two globular cellules connected by a narrow neck, the upper, almost devoid of contents, constituting the suspensor (*Potamogeton, Zannichellia*); in *Orchis*, the upper of the first two cells grows upwards and outwards, as a blind septate confervoid filament, through and beyond the micropyle of the ovule. In *Tropæolum* and *Zea*, the suspensor becomes more complex, by formation of perpendicular septa. In all cases the end-cell (*embryonal cell*), at the point of the suspensor, which always appears densely filled with protoplasm, ultimately enlarges, and by segmentation is converted into the *embryo* (Pl. 38. fig. 6).

During the early development of the embryo, the embryo-sac is often found more or less densely filled with free cells formed from its protoplasm (*endosperm-cells*). These are frequently absorbed, and disappear during the growth of the embryo, this ultimately filling the embryo-sac; while in other cases they persist and multiply, forming the ALBUMEN of the seed. In the Nymphæaceæ these cells remain, forming an inner Endosperm or Albumen, in addition to that formed from the body of the nucleus. In other cases (those of exalbuminous seeds) the embryo not only displaces these internal endosperm-cells, but in the course of its growth causes the absorption

of the tissue of the nucleus, and ultimately constitutes the entire seed, enclosed only by the true integuments. The remaining characters are given under ALBUMEN and EMBRYO.

The notion formerly entertained by Schleiden and his followers, that the embryo-cell was formed by the end of the pollen-tube which penetrates the micropyle, is now given up even by Schleiden himself.

Tulasne is in doubt whether the germinal vesicles exist before the pollen-tube enters the micropyle. We have certainly seen them before; but we believe they do not possess a cellulose coat before impregnation. Observations on the ovule of *Santalum album* have led us to conclude that they receive the influence of the pollen while in the state of nucleated protoplasmic corpuscles, analogous to the unimpregnated spores of FUCUS; and this view has since been supported by the later observations of Schacht, although Hofmeister and Radlkofer maintain that the germinal bodies possess a cell-membrane before impregnation.

In the Gymnospermous Flowering Plants (Coniferæ, &c.), the ovule, consisting of a cellular *nucleus* and a single coat, is placed upon an open carpel, and its widely-open micropyle receives the pollen-grain directly. At the period of impregnation, the embryo-sac is a cavity deeply seated in the tissue of the nucleus; it is formed by the coalescence and expansion of several cells (in the Yew there are often at first three embryo-sacs). In the embryo-sac a number of free nuclei soon appear, and numerous free (endosperm-) cells are formed. In many of the Abietineæ this goes on until the spring following the impregnation. Ultimately the embryo-sac is found to have increased to more than twenty times its original size, with the endosperm-cells applied in layers over the inside of its walls, increasing in number until the cavity is filled up. Then a certain number of cells (from three to eight in different genera), situated near the micropyle end, but each in the layer next but one to the wall of the embryo-sac, become enlarged, and the cells intervening between these enlarged ones (secondary embryo-sacs) and the wall of the original embryo-sac become divided, by two perpendicular septa standing at right angles, into four cells. A central intercellular passage then appears at the contiguous angles of these four cells. These new bodies, which closely resemble the archegonia of the LY-

COPODIACEÆ, were called *corpuscula* by Mr. Brown, who discovered them.

Free cells (or perhaps merely protoplasmic masses) are next formed in the secondary embryo-sacs of the corpuscula, several at the upper, one at the lower end. The pollen-tubes now advance, breaking down the tissue of the nucleus, until their points reach the *corpuscula*; and one then makes its way down the intercellular canal of each, to reach its secondary embryo-sac; the free cell (?) at the base of this (*germinal vesicle*) then becomes divided into four collateral cells; these multiply again, and subsequently the cellular body (*proembryo*) so formed breaks through the base of the secondary embryo-sac, and grows down in the substance of the lower part of the nucleus, which is now in a state of semi-solution. The proembryo then separates into four cords (corresponding to its four primary cells); and these filaments (*suspensors*) terminate in rounded cells, each of which is an *embryonal cell*; so that there are now four times as many rudimentary embryos as there are corpuscula. Out of all these, only one ultimately remains and becomes perfectly developed; the rest are absorbed during the ripening of the seed. In the latter, the perfect embryo is found lying in a mass of albumen formed of the nucleus; its *radicle*, developed at the point of junction of the suspensor, never becomes very clearly defined at its extremity, but remains organically continuous with the albumen.

Other points relating to the development of ovules will be found under POLYEMBRYONY, SEEDS, and CELL-formation.

The methods of investigating the development of ovules are simple in their nature, but rather difficult in practice. The ordinary plan is to place an ovule between the thumb and fore finger of the left hand, and with a very sharp lancet cut it into two unequal pieces, in the direction of the axis. The larger of the two being then laid on its flat side on the finger (by the aid of a mounted needle), another slice is made so as to leave a section preserving all the central part of the ovule. This adheres either to the finger or the lancet; and a drop of water should be placed on it to free it; then it may be transferred to a slide with a very fine camel's-hair pencil. Examined under a low power (a half-inch), it will be probably found to require further dissection, with exceedingly fine needles, under a simple lens; sometimes mere pressure is of service. For the minute details, the quarter and eighth object-glasses will require to be applied. We have found ovules which have been kept in spirit easier to dissect; when fresh, the cell-membranes are excessively delicate. It need scarcely be added, that ovules require to be examined in all stages in order to understand their developmental characters; and the student must not be disheartened by the failure of a large proportion of his sections to afford satisfactory observations.

BIBL. R. Brown, *Appendix to King's Voyage*, 1826 ; *Observations on the Orchideæ, &c.*, 1831, *Linnean Trans.* 1833 ; *on Plurality of Embryos, &c., Ann. Nat. Hist.* xiii. p. 368; Amici, *Ann. des Sc. Nat.* 3 sér. vii. p. 193; Brongniart, *Ann. des Sc. Nat.* 1827, 1831; Mirbel and Spach, *Ann. des Sc. Nat.* 2 sér. xx. p. 257 ; Mohl, *Bot. Zeitung*, 1847, 1855; Muller, *ibid.* 1847 ; Schleiden, *Nova Acta*, xix. p. 29; *Grundzüge der Botanik* ; Hofmeister, *Entstehung des Embryo*, Leipsic, 1849 ; *Vergleich. Untersuchung. höher. Crypt. &c.* 1851, 1851, 1855; *Jahrb. der wiss. Botanik*, 1856; *Bulletin Baierisch Akad.* No. 8, 1856; *Flora*, 1857 ; Tulasne, *Ann. des Sc. Nat.* 3 sér. xii. p. 21, 4 sér. iv. p. 65 ; Schacht, *Entw. des Pflanzenembryo; Verhandl. Nederland. K. Inst.* 1850 ; *Beitr. z. Anat. u. Phys.* Berlin, 1854; *Flora*, 1855. p. 145; *Berlin. Bericht*, May 1856; *Jahrb. d. wiss. Bot.* i. 1857; *Botan. Zeitung*, 1858 ; Crüger, *Bot. Zeit.* 1851, 1856; Radlkofer, *Entsteh. des Embryo*, Leipsic, 1856; *Befruchtungsprocess.* Leipsic, 1857 ; *Parthenogenesis, Ann. Nat. Hist.* 2 ser. xx.; Henfrey, *Linnean Trans.* xxi. p. 7, *ibid.* xxii. p. 69 ; *Trans. Brit. Ass.* 1856.

OVUM OF ANIMALS.—Several points in regard to the structure of the ovum, and the nature of the changes which it undergoes at different periods of its development, are in doubt and obscurity.

The first perceptible trace of the ovum existing within the ovary is formed by a very minute granule or globule, not surrounded by a cell-wall. This gradually enlarges; and when it has attained a certain size, being still very minute, a smaller spherical globule forms in its interior. The minute internal globule is the *germinal spot*, and the external globule is the so-called *germinal vesicle*. It appears, however, that in some cases the germinal spot is formed first, and the germinal vesicle subsequently. When these have still further grown, a cell-wall separated by a slight interspace forms around the germinal vesicle, and this inter-space contains a transparent liquid. Minute granules then arise in the liquid, which becomes inspissated, and subsequently a number of globules of sarcode — *yolk-globules*—become perceptible in it ; this mass forms the *yolk*, and the surrounding membrane is the *vitelline membrane*. As the ovum attains further development, al-buminous layers are deposited upon and fused with the vitelline membrane forming the *zona pellucida* or chorion (fig. 552 *a*),

Fig. 552.

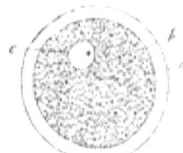

Human ovum from a Graafian vesicle of moderate size. *a*, zona pellucida ; *b*, vitelline membrane and outer boundary of the yolk ; *c*, germinal vesicle with the germi-nal spot.

Magnified 250 diameters.

which appears as a white ring. The yolk-globules are sometimes transparent, or slightly granular, at others they contain one or several vacuoles, and are frequently aggregated into little groups. The yolk, as it approaches maturity, frequently be-comes coloured. It is usually whitish or pale-yellow in the Mammalia, Reptiles, and Fishes ; bright-yellow or reddish in many Birds ; and often green, blue, violet, or red in the Invertebrata. In the yolk of the ova of reptiles and fishes, crystalline plates are met with, consisting of an albuminous substance, allied to Hæmatoidine.

Viewing the ovum as a simple cell, the germinal spot represents the nucleolus, the germinal vesicle the nucleus, the vitelline membrane or zona pellucida the cell-wall, and the yolk the cell-contents.

Some authors consider that the vitelline membrane is formed after the chorion.

The ovum of man and the mammalia differs from that of the lower animals in its remarkably small size, which depends upon the extremely small quantity of yolk enter-ing into its composition. The mature ovum of man and mammalia averages about 1-200 to 1-150" in diameter, being rarely 1-100". Another peculiarity consists in their ova, instead of being in immediate contact by means of their chorion or outer envelope

with the stroma of the ovary, or being loose within the cavity of the latter, as in other animals, being enclosed in distinct larger cells—the Graafian vesicles.

On the escape of the ovum from the ovary, the phænomena which ensue vary according to whether the ovum has been impregnated or not. In both cases the germinal vesicle and spot disappear ; an interspace, filled with albuminous liquid, occurs between the yolk and the zona pellucida ; the ovum becomes covered with cilia, and undergoes a regular motion of rotation ; and certain movements and changes in form of the yolk-substance, which forms Amœba-like processes, have been noticed. In the un-impregnated ovum, decay and decomposi-tion subsequently take place.

The essential part of the process of im-pregnation consists in the penetration of the yolk by the spermatozoa, and their subse-quent solution in it. This takes place either through the micropyles or the radiate canals, or directly into the naked yolk.

In the impregnated ovum, the germinal vesicle soon disappears, the chorion becomes thinner, the ovum grows, and the yolk be-gins to undergo the process of segmentation ; but just before this process commences, one or two globules separate from the substance of the yolk, being apparently pressed out of it, and occupy the interspace between the yolk and the chorion : these globules subsequently dissolve in the liquid.

The process of segmentation has been described under CELL (p. 123) ; but accord-ing to another account, it takes place thus : —At first a notch or slight indentation appears on some part of the surface of the yolk ; this becomes deeper and deeper, so as to encircle the yolk with an annular depression. Soon after the commencement of this, a clear spot appears in the centre of each circumscribed portion of the yolk. The depression becoming deeper, the yolk is divided into two distinct portions. The process is continued in the case of each of these in exactly the same manner, and in that of the segments arising from their subdivision also, each simultaneously ac-quiring a clear spot, until the yolk appears entirely composed of innumerable small bodies, having the appearance of nucleated cells. Finally, these become very minute, and the yolk acquires much the appearance it had before impregnation. Cells then form in the yolk, as in an ordinary blastema, from without inwards, and from the spot originally occupied by the germinal vesicle as a centre; and from these the tissues of the embryo are formed.

According to this description, which is most probably correct, the segmentation is not a process of cell-division or endogenous cell-formation, and the nuclear spots would correspond to portions of the yolk substance from which the granules and globules of sarcode were absent.

In unimpregnated ova, segmentation takes place to a certain extent, but irregularly and incompletely.

In the impregnated ova of some animals, as in some of the Batrachia, most fishes and Cephalopods, the segmentation is only partial, a portion of the yolk remaining as at first.

In some of the Mammalia, the zona pellucida is traversed by very fine radiating lines (canals), which are best seen in the ova immersed in water.

In the lower Vertebrate animals, the ova are often covered by new layers, secreted by the ovaries, as in the Batrachia (frog, &c.), where a thick gelatinous coat is present. In the osseous Fishes, the vitelline membrane is frequently elegantly sculptured, and finely and closely punctate from the existence of minute canals traversing its substance. A second coat is also present, and sometimes a third or albuminous layer. In many of the Cyprinoidea, this layer is represented by small radiate cylinders. In several Fishes, as is so general amongst the Invertebrata, especially Insects (EGGS), the vitelline membrane or chorion exhibits a facetted or sculptured appearance, derived from the impression of the epithelium lining the ovarian passages.

In addition to the fine canals traversing the membranes of the ovum, one or more large canals or apertures are frequently met with resembling the micropyles of vegetable ovules, and receiving the same names. These micropyles are most distinct in the ova of fishes and insects.

The study of ova and their changes is very difficult. The most favourable objects for the purpose exist perhaps in those of the aquatic Mollusca; the ova of insects, as the large species of *Musca*, of species of *Pulex*, &c., are also easily accessible. Some important results have been obtained with the ova of the frog (frog's spawn).

BIBL. Kölliker, *Mikr. Anat.* ii.; Al. Thomson, *Cycl. Anat. &c.*, art. *Ovum*; Vogt, *Physiol. Briefe*; Keber, *De sperm. intr. in ovula*;

Bischoff, *Widerlegung des v. Keber behaup'. Eindringens d. Sperm. in das Ei*; id. *Bestätigung d. von Newport behaupt. Eindring. &c.*, and numerous other memoirs; Newport, *Phil. Trans.* 1851 and 1853; Siebold, *Vergleich. Anat.*; Wagner, *Elements of Physiology*, by Willis; V. Beneden, *Ann. des Sc. Nat.* 3 sér. xiii.; Bruch, *Ueber d. Mikrop. d. Fische*, *Sieb. & Köllik. Zeitsch.* vii. 172; Meissner, *ibid.* vi. pp. 208, 272; Leuckart, *Müll. Archiv*, 1855; Claparède, *Bibl. Univ. d. Genève*, 1855; *Ann. Nat. Hist.* 1856, xvii.; Bischoff, *Sieb. & Köllik. Zeitsch.* vi. 377; Radlkofer, *Befruchtungsprocesse*, Leipsic, 1857.

OVUM OF PLANTS. See OVULE.

OXALATES. See the bases.

OXYGONIUM, Presl.—A genus of Asplenieæ (Polypodioid Ferns). Exotic.

OXYRRHIS, Duj.—A genus of Infusoria, belonging to the family of Thecamonadina.

Char. Body ovoid-oblong, rugose, obliquely notched in front and prolonged into a point; several flagelliform filaments arising laterally from the bottom of the notch.

O. marina (Pl. 24. fig. 54). Body colourless, subcylindrical, rounded behind; marine; length 1-500″.

BIBL. Dujardin, *Infus.* p. 347.

OXYTRICHA, Bory, Ehr.—A genus of Infusoria, of the family Oxytrichina.

Char. Neither styles, hooks, nor horns present. Ehrenberg describes eight species; some are marine, others aquatic.

1. *O. pellionella*, E. (Pl. 24. fig. 52). Body whitish, smooth, slightly depressed, equally rounded at the ends, often somewhat broader in the middle; head not distinct; mouth ciliated; tail with bristles. Aquatic; length 1-720 to 1-280″.

2. *O. gibba*, E. (Pl. 24. fig. 53). Body white, lanceolate, obtuse at each end, ventricose in the middle; ventral surface flat, with a double row of setæ; mouth large, rounded. Aquatic; length 1-240″.

Dujardin places his genus *Oxytricha* among the Keronia, with the characters—body soft, flexible, oval or oblong, more or less depressed, with cirrhi or larger nonvibratile cilia in the form of bristles or styles, but without horns,—and describes nine species, mostly not corresponding to those of Ehrenberg.

The whole requires revision. According to M. Haime, *Oxytricha* is the larva of *Aspidisca*.

BIBL. Ehrenberg, *Infus.* p. 363; Dujardin, *Infus.* p. 416; J. Haime, *Ann. des Sc. Nat.* 3 sér. xix. 109 (or *Carpenter on the Microscope*, p. 483).

OXYTRICHINA, Ehr.—A family of Infusoria.

Char. Carapace absent; alimentary orifices two, neither terminal; body furnished with vibratile cilia and bristles, non-vibratile styles or hooks.

Body depressed; locomotive organs principally situated upon the under surface. Propagation by longitudinal and transverse division, and by the periodical formation of egg-like granules.

The five genera are thus distinguished:

Cilia and bristles present, but no styles nor hooks.

No anterior horns .... *Oxytricha.*
Anterior horns present .... *Ceratidium.*

Cilia present, with styles or hooks, or both.

Hooks present, but no styles .... *Kerona.*
Styles present, no hooks .... *Urostyla.*
Both styles and hooks present .... *Stylonichia.*

BIBL. Ehrenberg, *Infus.* p. 362.

OXYURIS, Rud.   See ASCARIS.

OYSTER (*Ostrea*).—A genus of Lamellibranchiate Mollusca.

The gills of *O. edulis*, the common oyster, show the ciliary movement; but it is not so easily seen in this as in the marine mussel.

The shells of the fry or 'embryo-oysters' exhibit the black cross and an imperfect set of coloured rings with polarized light.

P.

PACHNOCYBE, Berk.— A genus of Stillacei (Hyphomycetous Fungi), somewhat confused at present with *Doratomyces, Corda*, and *Periconia*, Nees. These plants have an erect filiform stem, composed of conjoined filaments, capitulate above, the head being pruinose (not flocculent), with crowded simple spores. The pedicels are mostly brownish or blackish, the spores light-coloured; the entire plants from 1-24 to 1-6" high. Several species occur on rotten wood, stems, &c.

BIBL. Berk. Hook. *Brit. Flor.* ii. pt. 2. p. 333; *Ann. Nat. Hist.* 2 ser. v. p. 465; Fries, *Summa Veg.* p. 467.

PACHYGNATHUS, Dugès.— A genus of Arachnida, of the order Acarina, and family Trombidina.

Char. Palpi conical, last joint scarcely forming a claw; mandibles stout, chelate; body entire, narrowed in front; coxæ distant; legs gressorial, sixth joint very long, seventh very short; anterior legs longest and stoutest.

P. velutinus (Pl. 2. fig. 34), the only species. Found in autumn, under damp stones. Hairs covering the body short, flat, and curved, giving it a velvety aspect. Body inflated, narrowed in front, the narrowed portion with two projecting brownish eyes. Insertions of the legs in two groups, not far distant from each other nor from the median line; second pair of legs shortest; in all the sixth joint very long, the seventh very short and narrow (*b*), as in *Tetranychus, Megamerus*, and *Raphignathus*; claws two, large; rostrum projecting; palpi (*a*) short, about twice the length of the labium; mandibles very large and stout at the base. Movement slow.

BIBL. Dugès, *Ann. des Sc. Nat.* 2 sér. ii. p. 54; Gervais, *Walckenaer's Aptèr.* iii. p. 171.

PACHYMATISMA, Bowk.—A genus of Marine Sponges.

Distinguished by the fleshy, crust-like, not cellular nor elastic mass, covered by a thick skin, and perforated by scattered orifices; the interior beset with siliceous acicular and stellate spicula.

P. Johnstonia.

BIBL. Bowerbank, *Ann. Nat. Hist.* 2 ser. vol. xx. p. 298.

PACINIAN CORPUSCLES. — These curious organs are found as terminations or appendages of the human spinal nerves in the skin and subcutaneous tissue of the palm of the hand, the sole of the foot, the fingers and toes, in the sympathetic semilunar ganglia, the mesentery, &c.

They are elliptical or pear-shaped, whitish, and about 1-25 to 1-6" in diameter. Each consists of from twenty to sixty concentric layers of areolar tissue (fig. 555), separated by interspaces—those between the outer layers being considerable, those between the inner being small. They are filled with a clear serous liquid, contained in largest quantity in the central cavity bounded by the innermost layers. Each is also furnished with a stalk, containing a slender branch of a nerve, which passes from the stalk into the central space, in the upper part of which it terminates frequently in two or three branches, each with a free granular tubercle. The nerve-fibre contains no white substance.

The Pacinian corpuscles are not found exclusively attached to the human nerves, but are met with also on those of many Mammalia, and are very numerous in the skin, the beak, and the tongue of birds.

BIBL. Kölliker, *Mikrosk. Anat.* ii., and the *Bibl.* therein.

Fig. 553.

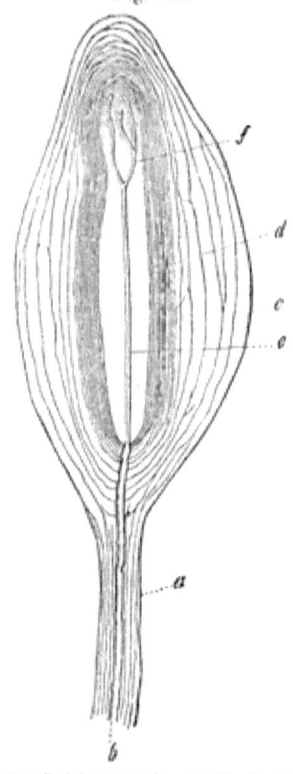

A human Pacinian corpuscle. *a*, stalk ; *b*, nerve-fibre within it ; *c* outer, *d* inner layers of the sheath ; *e*, pale nerve-fibre in the central cavity ; *f*, its branches and termination.

Magnified 350 diameters.

PADINA, Adanson.—A genus of Dictyotaceæ (Fucoid Algæ), containing one species, *P. Pavonia* (fig. 554), found rarely in summer and autumn on the south coast of England. The fan-shaped or reniform fronds grow in tufts, and are 2 to 5″ high, sometimes entire, sometimes cleft (fig. 554). They are marked with concentric zones. The substance is parenchymatous, the number of layers of cells diminishing with the thickness and solidity from the base to the edges. The back of the frond is covered by a layer of cells much smaller than the rest,

forming a kind of epidermis, which ultimately acquires a thickish cuticular layer. The growing edge of the frond is rolled

Fig. 554.

Padina Pavonia.
Frond, one-third natural size.

backwards (circinate) and fringed. The fructification occurs in linear concentric sori, on the coloured zones of the frond. The pear-shaped *spore-sacs* (fig. 555) originate from cells of the epidermal layer, which

Fig. 555.

Vertical section of a frond at a concentric zone, made in a radial direction, cutting through the sorus of spore-sacs and a line of hairs. The indusial layer of cuticle has been removed.

Magnified 50 diameters.

take on special development, and in the course of their growth push up and finally burst through the loosened cuticular layer which originally clothed them, so that the latter forms a kind of indusium like that of the Ferns. The spore-sacs produce each four spores, which separate after their escape from the sac. The zones of the sori alternate with zones composed of tufts of jointed hairs placed in corresponding lines (fig. 555). Thuret states that he has never found *antheridia* hitherto, and he believes that Agardh mistook the hairs or paranemata for them.

BIBL. Harvey, *Brit. Mar. Alg.* p. 37, pl. 6 C ; *Phyc. Brit.* pl. 91 ; Greville, *Alg. Brit.* pl. 10 ; Agardh, *Sp. Alg.* i. p. 112 ; Nägeli, *Neuer. Algensyst.* p. 180, pl. 5 ; Thuret, *Ann. des Sc. Nat.* 4 sér. iii. p. 12 ; Kütz. *Phyc. generalis*, pl. 22 ; Al. Braun, *rejuvenescence, &c. (Ray Soc. Vol.* 1853), *.* 79.

PALMELLA, Lyngbye.—A genus of Palmellaceæ (Confervoid Algæ), of which the best-known example is the common *P. cruenta* (Pl. 3. fig. 3 *a*). This plant, very common on damp walls in shaded places, appears at first in the form of rosy gelatinous patches; these spread and become confluent until the mass extends sometimes over a great extent of surface, as a tough, gelatinous, irregular mass, of the colour and general appearance of coagulated venous blood; when dried up in this state, it forms a horny, somewhat crumbling stratum; if placed in water, portions float to the top in pellucid rosy masses of jelly. In its natural habitats its colour and general appearance become disguised when old by the admixture of *Oscillatoriæ*, and other Confervoid growths.

When placed under the microscope, the frond appears to be composed of a colourless homogeneous jelly, in which are imbedded globular cells, single or in pairs (from division), of a beautiful rose-colour (fig. 3 *a, b*); by the application of reagents, these may be shown to possess a proper membranous coat (*c*). The contents of the cells appear uniformly granular (*b, c*); and it would appear that, besides increasing by division, the cells also burst and discharge their contents, since patches of minute granules occur imbedded in the jelly (lower figs. of *b*), probably destined to grow up into the ordinary cells. No zoospores, nor the remarkable phænomena generally that occur in *Protococcus*, have yet been observed in this, which appears to be a very distinct genus. The jelly of full-grown fronds (which appears to be derived from the gelatinous softening of the coats of the parent cells of the successive generations of cells) is often over-grown and traversed by minute filamentous structures, which at first sight seem to belong to it; but on the application of a high power are found to consist of a very minute Nostochaceous plant, apparently the *Anabaina subtilissima* of Kützing, or *Vibrio Bacillus*, Ehr. (Pl. 3. fig. 21), which we find to occur commonly among the Palmellaceous Algæ.

P. cruenta has received an extraordinary number of generic names: *Tremella, Byssus, Thelephora, Sarcoderma, Phytoconis, Porphyridium, Globulina, Coccochloris,* and *Chaos* (!).

From the examination of specimens of the true "red snow," brought home by Captain Parry (for which we are indebted to Mr. Brown), we incline to regard this as a *Palmella*, distinct generically from the *Protococcus* or *Hæmatococcus placialis* of the German writers, with which it is commonly associated. Our specimens consist of a tough, colourless, gelatinous substance, containing globular cells differing only in size (Pl. 3. fig. 3 *d*) from those of *Palmella cruenta*; and in the jelly occur also abundance of the minute granules or cellules, which are the discharged contents of the larger cells. The red cells of the red-snow plant turn green when exposed to light, if kept moist. An exactly similar plant has been given us by Mr. Oliver, from Crag Lough, Northumberland, in a fresh condition; and we have never been able to detect any moving forms in it. Further particulars are given on this subject under RED SNOW and RUBEFACTION OF WATER, and PROTOCOCCUS.

Other species of *Palmella* are described; but most of them are too imperfectly known to allow of definite characters being given; *P. rosea* is perhaps a good species. The forms with a definite frond formerly placed here (*P. protuberans, botryoides,* &c.) will be found under COCCOCHLORIS.

BIBL. *Eng. Botany* (as *Tremella cruenta*), pl. 1800; Greville, *&c. Crypt. Alg.* pl. 205; Meneghini, *Monogr. Nostoc.* (*Trans. Turin Acad.* ser. 2. v.), pl. 6; Hassall, *Brit. Fr. Alg.* pl. 80; Nägeli, *Einzell. Alg.* p. 66, pl. 4 D (as *Porphyridium*), p. 71, pl. 4 H; Kütz. *Sp. Alg.* p. 211. See also under RED SNOW.

PALMELLACEÆ.—A family of Confervoid Algæ, consisting of gelatinous or pulverulent masses, growing on damp surfaces, in fresh water or in the sea; composed of globular or elliptical cells, either more or less adherent together into a definite or indefinite pseudo-membrane or frond, or loosely aggregated within a definitely or indefinitely formed gelatinous matrix, or loosely coherent in the form of a pulverulent crust. Some authors have imagined that the cells of *Coccochloris* or *Palmella* are attached to filaments included in the gelatinous frond: this seems an error (see PALMELLA). Yellowish or bluish green, or red, often varying from green to red, and *vice versa*, during the course of development. Increased by cell-division into two or four, and by ciliated zoospores. Many exhibit three forms,—1. active; 2. quietly vegetating by subdivision; 3. resting form, with a tough membrane. We include here for the sake of convenience, not only the true Palmellaceæ, where there is a frond composed of a number of cells held together by mucus, but also all those Unicellular Algæ which, from their mode of increase, are found living socially or in masses which appear like Palmelloid plants.

Synopsis of Genera.

* *Plants with a frond composed of colourless gelatinous substance.*

† *Frond amorphous.*

1. *Palmella.* Frond a slimy stratum crowded with rather large globular cells, multiplying by division, green and red (Pl. 3. fig. 3).

2. *Microhaloa.* Frond mucoid, floating in water, densely crowded with minute cells, multiplying by division, green or red.

†† *Frond definite.*

3. *Glæocapsa.* Frond composed of cells enclosed in wide gelatinous coats, enclosed in similar wide gelatinous coats of their parent cells for several generations (Pl. 3. figs. 4 & 13).

4. *Botrydina.* Frond globose, the periphery composed of cells, cohering into a kind of cellular epidermis, the inner cells free (Pl. 3. fig. 9).

5. *Coccochloris.* Frond globose, gelatinous, containing numerous distinct cells, all free (Pl. 3. fig. 6).

6. *Clathrocystis.* Frond gelatinous, at first globose, then hollow, then broken by irregular expansion into a coarse net, finally breaking up; the frond crowded with minute cells, multiplied by division.

7. *Merismopœdia.* Frond very minute, flat, square, gelatinous, containing cells arranged in families of four, sixteen, and sixty-four (Pl. 3. fig. 12).

8. *Urococcus.* Frond composed of streaked gelatinous tubes, formed of the ensheathing parent-cell membranes in a single row, with the cells solitary or binary (from division) in the ends of the tubes (Pl. 3. fig. 7).

9. *Hormospora.* Frond a wide, gelatinous, simple or branched sheath, containing a single row of cells approximated in twos or fours (fig. 336, p. 353).

10. *Tetraspora.* Frond gelatinous, more or less definitely foliaceous, containing cells grouped in fours, ultimately becoming free as zoospores (Pl. 3. fig. 10).

11. *Hydrurus.* Frond toughly gelatinous,

filiform, containing imbedded longitudinal rows of cells (Pl. 3. fig. 8).

12. *Palmodictyon.* Frond gelatinous, filiform, branched; branches dividing and anastomosing into a net, consisting of large vesicular cells, with coloured contents which escape as zoospores.

** *Plants composed of single cells, either solitary or united in small numbers into families (Unicellular Algæ).*

† *Solitary cells.*

13. *Schizochlamys.* Cells free, globular, aggregated in a jelly, each dividing into two or four portions, set free by the parent cell breaking into two or four segments, green.

14. *Chlorosphæra.* Unicellular, free; a large globose cell filled with green contents, ultimately dividing into two cells, in each of which is formed a new cell like the parent, set free by the lateral rupture of the parent-cell membranes (Pl. 45. fig. 4).

15. *Characium.* Unicellular; a minute attached pyriform, fusiform, or subglobose sac, shortly stipitate, containing green protoplasm, which by often-repeated binary division forms a swarm of active two-ciliated zoospores escaping by a lateral or terminal slit (Pl. 45. fig. 1).

16. *Apiocystis.* Unicellular; a simple attached sac with a stout membrane, with green contents, consisting at first of groups of four still gonidia, which subdivide repeatedly, and as the parent sac grows become converted into innumerable active zoospores, which move in the parent sac and then break out in a swarm (Pl. 45. fig. 5).

17. *Codiolum.* Unicellular; an attached, small, long clavate sac, attenuated below into a solid stipe, filled with finely granular green contents, with numerous starch-corpuscles, ultimately converted at once into numerous gonidia, escaping by the rupture of the apex of the sac, gonidia globose (Pl. 45. fig. 6).

18. *Hydrocytium.* Unicellular; an attached, minute, oblong sac, with a short hyaline stalk, with green contents, and a parietal starch-corpuscle. The contents ultimately divided at once into very numerous two-ciliated zoospores, lying on the wall, then moving actively and breaking out in a swarm (Pl. 45. fig. 2).

19. *Ophiocytium.* Unicellular, or more rarely in families; consisting of a minute, elongated-cylindrical, curved or curled sac, with a short stipe, sometimes attached, sometimes free; green contents scattered,

finally organized into eight gonidia, in a single row, at length set free by the circumscissile rupture of the end of the sac (Pl. 45. fig. 11).

†　20. *Sciadium.* At first a minute solitary attached, elongate-tubular, stipitate sac, in which are produced eight gonidia in a single row; the apex of the sac opens by circumscission, and the eight gonidia grow out into tubes like the parent, in an umbel, their stipes remaining inserted; each new tube repeats this development to the fourth or further generations, the last generation from the compound umbel emitting its gonidia as two-ciliated zoospores (Pl. 45. fig. 3).

21. *Chytridium.* Unicellular; parasitic; a minute globular pyriform or urceolate sac, attached by a foot which penetrates into the supporting body (mostly a Confervoid). Cell-contents colourless, at length converted into numerous two-ciliated zoospores, which escape by the dehiscence of a valve-like lid, or by simple rupture of the apex of the sac (Pl. 45. fig. 7).

22. *Pythium.* Unicellular; parasitic; a globular sac living in the interior of the cell of diseased Confervoids, often in groups, contents colourless; sac growing out into a flask-like form, the neck perforating the wall of the nurse-plant and bursting to emit active gonidia (?) (Pl. 45. fig. 8).

For PROTOCOCCUS see VOLVOCINEÆ.— *Hæmatococcus* = PROTOCOCCUS and PALMELLA; *Porphyridium* = PALMELLA; *Chlamidococcus* and *Chlamidomonas* = PROTOCOCCUS; *Sorospora* = GLŒOCAPSA ?; *Cylindrocystis*, Bréb. = COCCOCHLORIS; *Polycystis*, Kutz. = CLATHROCYSTIS; MICROCYSTIS and ANACYSTIS = MICROHALOA ?. Numerous other genera of doubtful value and imperfect character are given by Nägeli (*Einzell. Algen.*), as *Exococcus, Chroococcus, Synechococcus, Stichococcus, Cytococcus, Dactylococcus, Nephrocytium, Dictyosphærium, Glæocystis, Aphanothece, Glæothece, Cælosphærium, Aphanocapsa, Palmodactylon*; by Kützing (*Species Algarum*), as *Botryococcus, Botryocystis, Trichodictyon, Trichocystis, Palmophyllum, Gomphospæria*; *Chlorococcus* and *Pleurococcus* are probably forms of *Protococcus*, or gonidia of Lichens.

Doubtful organism.

Sarcina. Fronds (?) flat, extremely minute, squarish, tough, formed of coherent squarish cells, combined in quaternate groups to the number of eight, sixteen, or sixty-four. Found floating free in the liquid of the human stomach, &c. (Pl. 3. fig. 5).

BIBL. Al. Braun, *Rejuvenescence, &c., Ray Society's Vol.* 1851, *passim*; *Alg. Unicell. Gen. Nova*, Leipsic, 1855; *Ueber Chytridium*, Berlin, 1856; Nägeli, *Einzell. Algen*, Zurich, 1849; Kützing, *Species Algar.* and *Tabulæ Phycolog.* i.; Cohn, *Nova Acta A. L. C. N. C.* xxiv. See also the genera.

PALMODACTYLON, Näg.— A supposed genus of Unicellular Algæ, germinating spores of a Moss ?

BIBL. Nägeli, *Einzell. Alg.* pl. 2. fig. B.

PALMODICTYON, Ktz.—A genus of Palmellaceæ (Confervoid Algæ), described as possessing a frond which appears like a delicate network to the naked eye, of gelatinous texture, and consisting of anastomosing branches, each composed (in *P. viride*) of a single or double row of large vesicular cells, 1-600 to 1-960" in diam. These contain a pair of elliptical green cellules, 1-3000" in diameter, which ultimately escape as active zoospores. This genus appears identical with *Trypothallus*, Hook. and Harvey, and is nearly related to HYDRURUS and TETRASPORA.

P. rufescens, Ktz., doubtfully referred here, is larger; it occurs near Aberdeen.

BIBL. Kützing, *Sp. Alg.* p. 234; *Tab. Phyc.* Bd. i. pl. 31.

PALMOGLŒA, Kütz. (*Cylindrocystis*, Menegh.). See COCCOCHLORIS.

PALMOPHYLLUM, Ktz.—Perhaps a *Prasiola*.

PALUDELLA, Ehr.—A genus of Meesiaceæ, having only one representative, which occurs in Britain, *P. squarrosa* = *Bryum squarrosum*, L.

PALUDICELLA, Gervais.—A genus of Polypi, of the order Bryozoa, and family Paludicellaidæ.

Char. Polypidom fixed, filamentous, diffusely and irregularly branched, coriaceous, consisting of a single row of club-shaped cells arranged end to end; apertures unilateral, tubular, placed near the broad end of each cell; tentacular disk circular, with a single row of free tentacles.

P. articulata. The only species; olive-green; polypes ascidian. Aquatic; diameter of filaments about 1-30 to 1-20".

BIBL. Johnston, *Brit. Zooph.* p. 405; Allman, *Ann. Nat. Hist.* xiii. 331, and *Proc. Irish Acad.* 1843.

PANDORINA, Bory. (Pl. 45. fig. 10).— A genus of Volvocineæ (Confervoid Algæ), which we believe to be synonymous with

Pandorina. It exhibits a great variety of forms, some of which have been described under the name of *P. Morum*, others of *Eud. elegans.* The most characteristic conditions are represented in Pl. 45. fig. 10. *Pandorina* stands midway between *Volvox* and *Stephanosphæra*,—consisting of an ellipsoidal translucent sac of gelatinous consistence, containing, imbedded just below its surface, several zone-like rows of green pear-shaped gonidia, whose two cilia penetrate the gelatinous envelope, and, hanging out free, move the entire organism by their vibration. Two distinct forms occur, one with sixteen, the other with thirty-two gonidia. Where sixteen occur, there are four zones of four gonidia, while where thirty-two exist they stand in four zones of eight, with four at each end (Pl. 45. fig. 10 a and b). The gonidia have a red spot and a vacuole, like those of *Gonium* and *Volvox.* These two forms occur together; and evidently the difference arises simply from an additional binary subdivision of the gonidia in the earlier stages of development from the spore. They are often so numerous as to tinge the water of fresh pools green, like *Volvox* and *Protococcus.* They occur of various sizes, from 1-80" downwards. These forms are multiplied vegetatively by the conversion of each gonidium into a family like the parent, each group acquiring its special envelope and becoming free, apparently by the solution of the parent-envelope.

Two corresponding forms occur with the above, with the sixteen or thirty-two gonidia closely crowded together, instead of standing at wide intervals in the large colourless envelope : it is uncertain whether this form is multiplied vegetatively ; but we have seen its gonidia all converted into resting-spores.

The resting-spores are formed out of all or part of the gonidia of a family, after fertilization by the spermatozoids. The latter are minute, fusiform, ciliated corpuscles, produced in large numbers by subdivision of the substance of some of the gonidia ; they are set free inside the parent-envelope, and make their way to those gonidia which are to become resting-spores. The impregnated gonidia soon acquire a stout special coat, and their originally green contents turn red. They become free by the solution of the parent-envelope. In germination they turn green again, and by repeated division of their protoplasm form the new families of sixteen or thirty-two, constituting the perfect plant.

BIBL. Ehrenberg, *Infus.* p. 53 ; Dujardin, *Infus.* p. 317 ; Henfrey, *Mic. Trans.* 2 ser. iv. p. 46 ; Fresenius, *Mus. Senckenb.* ii. p. 187 (1856) ; Cohn, *Nova Acta,* xxvi. p. 1 ; De Bary, *Bot. Zeit.* xvi., *Supp.* ii. p. 73 (1858) ; Currey, *Quart. Journ. Mic. Soc.* vi. p. 213 ; Carter, *Ann. Nat. Hist.* 3 ser. ii. p. 237.

PANOPHRYS, Duj.—A term proposed to designate certain *Bursariæ*, E., in which the row of larger cilia leading to the mouth, characteristic of *Bursaria*, D., is absent.

Dujardin's specific names are new, although the species are old !

P. fareta, D. = *Bursaria vernalis*, *B. leucas*, and *B. flava* of Ehrenberg.

P. chrysalis (Pl. 24. fig. 55). Marine.

BIBL. Dujardin, *Infus.* p. 491.

PANTOTRICHUM, Ehr.—A genus of Infusoria, of the family Cyclidina.

Char. Body turgid, covered with vibratile cilia. Aquatic.

1. *P. lagenula*, E. (Pl. 24. fig. 58). Body ovate, equally rounded at each end, yellowish ; tegument produced anteriorly in the form of a neck or truncate rostrum ; length 1-1080 to 1-580".

2. *P. volvox*, E. Probably a young *Paramecium* (Dujardin).

3. *P. enchelys*, E. = *Enchelys nodulosa*, D.

BIBL. Ehrenberg, *Infus.* p. 247 ; Dujardin, *Infus.* p. 388.

PAPER.—Only a few general observations can be made under this head. Ordinary paper, as is well known, is generally manufactured from rags of linen or cotton fabrics, so that it consists of a kind of felt of the fibres of cotton or flax ; but other substances, such as straw, for instance, are now coming into use, from the growing scarcity of rags. The manipulation to which the material is subjected, together with the effect of frequent washing in the case of rags, affects the characters of the fibres to some extent ; and the cellulose is in some cases already brought into that state in which iodine colours it blue. The addition of sulphuric acid and iodine always colours the fibres of paper blue ; and care must be taken on this account to avoid errors from the accidental presence of them when blotting-paper is used to absorb these reagents when applied to objects on a slide. The determination of the nature of the filaments of which a paper is composed, by the aid of the microscope, would require a very thorough knowledge of the characters of vegetable fibres, and we should imagine could scarcely be very decisive in most cases, except so far as distinguishing between classes of substances, as between parenchymatous and filamentous or fibrous substances, &c.

Rice-paper, as it is termed, is a totally different material, consisting of thin layers, cut by a peculiar operation, of the pith of *Aralia papyrifera*, a Chinese Araliaceous tree: this consists of parenchymatous cellulose tissue.

Papyrus, consisting of pressed superposed laminæ of the pith of the *Papyrus* plant (*Papyrus antiquorum*, a kind of Sedge), exhibits the lax parenchymatous structure characteristic of similar tissues, such as the pith of Rushes, &c.

PAPER, METEORIC, and AEROPHYTES. —The structure and origin of these substances are the same as that of the so-called natural flannel (FLANNEL). They were formerly regarded as of meteoric origin. They have been observed in some instances to fall from the air, having been wafted perhaps many miles from their place of formation by whirlwinds and hurricanes.

BIBL. Ehrenberg, *Abhandl. d. Berl. Akad.* 1838.

PAPULASPORA, Preuss.—A genus of Mucedines (Hyphomycetous Fungi) consisting of a decumbent articulate mycelium, sending up erect pedicels bearing a cellular head, each cell supporting an oblong spore.

P. sepedonioides has been found on rice-paste.

BIBL. Berk. and Broome, *Ann. Nat. Hist.* ser. 2. xiii. p. 462; Berk. *Crypt. Bot.* p. 305, fig. 69 *b*.

PAPYRUS.—The pith of the stems of the *Papyrus antiquorum* (modern papyrus from *P. syriacus*), cut into slices, which are laid upon one another and pressed so as to form a compact stratum. Sections display the parenchymatous tissue more or less deformed by pressure.

PARAMECIA or PARAMECINA, Duj. —A family of Infusoria.

Char. Body soft, flexible; form variable, usually oblong and more or less depressed; with a lax reticulate integument, through which numerous vibratile cilia pass in regular rows; mouth present.

The organisms included in this family belong to the Ophryocercina, Enchelia, Trachelina, and Colpodea of Ehrenberg.

Dujardin distinguishes the genera thus:

Mouth indistinct or doubtful ..	Body round, prolonged in the form of a neck, with an appearance of a mouth at the end				1. *Lacrymaria.*
	Body oval-oblong, depressed, with a broad lateral orifice, from which a bundle of filaments issues				2. *Pleuronema.*
Mouth lateral ..	with a lip-like appendage	lip longitudinal, vibratile; body oval, depressed, broader behind.			3. *Glaucoma.*
		lip inferior, projecting; body ovoid, sinuous or reniform........			4. *Colpoda.*
	without an appendage	body never globular	oblong, compressed, with a longitudinal oblique fold........		5. *Paramecium.*
			fusiform, greatly elongate and narrowed in front....		6. *Amphileptus.*
			lamelliform, sinuous	mouth with teeth	7. *Chilodon.*
				mouth without teeth	8. *Loxophyllum.*
		Body ovoid or oblong, becoming globular by contraction	mouth with teeth		9. *Nassula.*
			teeth absent................		10. *Panophrys.*
Mouth terminal; body ovoid or oblong, becoming globular by contraction			mouth with teeth		11. *Prorodon.*
			teeth absent..........		12. *Holophrya.*

BIBL. Dujardin, *Infus.* p. 463.

PARAMECIUM, Hill, Ehr.—A genus of Infusoria, of the family Colpodea.

Char. Body covered with cilia; no eye-spot; a papilliform tongue-like process present.

Ehrenberg describes eight species, two being doubtful.

1. *P. aurelia* (Pl. 24. figs. 56 and 57). Body cylindrical, ovate-oblong, rounded or obtuse at the ends, with an oblique longitudinal fold extending to the mouth. Aquatic; length 1-120 to 1-100''.

This common infusorium shows well the curious star-shaped contractile vesicles. Ehrenberg notices in it the periodical occurrence of small black crystalline particles at the anterior end. The depressions on the surface of the integument (Pl. 25. fig. 1) are distinctly seen in the dried animal.

2. *P. chrysalis*, E. (*Pleuronema crassa*, D.) (Pl. 25. fig. 37, undergoing division). Body oblong, cylindrical; oral cilia very long. Aquatic; length 1-240''.

P. Kolpoda, E. = the adult stage of *Kolpoda cucullus*, E.

P. compressum, E. = *Plagiotoma lumbrici*, D.

P. milium, E. = *Enchelys nodulosa* or *triquetra*, D.

Dujardin places this genus with the family Paramecina.

BIBL. Ehrenberg, *Infus.* p. 349; Dujardin, *Infus.* p. 481; Stein, *Infus. passim.*

PARAPHYSES.—The name applied to more or less delicate-jointed, hair-like filaments which occur in small numbers around and between the antheridia and archegonia of Mosses and Hepaticæ (fig. 23. p. 51, fig. 327. p. 347). The same term is applied to simple tubular, more or less clavate cells, occurring in large numbers among the spore-sacs (*asci* and *thecæ*) of the Ascomycetous Fungi and the Lichens (fig. 40. p. 70, fig. 398. p. 418, Pl. 29. figs. 6, 12).

PARASITES.—Under this head are to be included a number of animals and plants infesting other animals and plants, nourished at the expense of their structures or juices. Of the animal parasites, the chief portion belong to the class CRUSTACEA, order SI-PHONOSTOMA; the class ARACHNIDA, family ACARINA; the class Insecta, orders ANO-PLURA and STREPSIPTERA; and the class ENTOZOA.

The Plants parasitic on animals chiefly belong to the class of Fungi, and they are tolerably numerous; but many of the forms which have been described and named are certainly not distinct plants. They will be most conveniently enumerated under the heads of classes of animals infested.

1. *Man and Mammalia.*

On the Skin.—ACHORION *Schœnleinii* and PUCCINIA *favus* (the former probably an earlier stage of the latter), on the hair and in the follicles, in *Favus.* TRICHOPHYTON *tonsurans*, on the hair in *Plica polonica* and *Favus*; this appears to be a *Torula*-like growth, probably not a mature plant. *Tr.? sporuloides*, C. Rob., occurs in *Plica*, and *Tr.? ulcerina*, C. Rob., in the pus of ulcers. *Microsporon Audouinii* occurs in the hair-follicles in *Porrigo decalvans*; *M. mentagrophytes*, on the beard, &c.; *M. furfur*, on the skin of the chest, &c., in *Pityriasis versicolor*. The occurrence of *Mucor Mucedo* on the skin, and of an *Aspergillus* in the external conduit of the ear, must be regarded as accidental.

On the mucous surfaces or in cavities.—SARCINA *ventriculi* in the stomach, &c.; *Torula cerevisiæ* (?), ditto. Various species of LEPTOMITUS, which must be regarded as imperfect mycelial growths, found in almost all the cavities of the body. *Oidium albicans*, Ch. R., the fungus of "*Aphtha*," probably a peculiar condition of PENICILLIUM; *Leptothrix buccalis*, a filamentous growth constant in the tartar of the teeth, probably some allied mycelium.

2. *Birds.*

Various species of ASPERGILLUS have been found in the lungs and air-sacs: their introduction would appear to be accidental. In the eggs of the common fowl, DACTYLIUM *oogenum* occurs not unfrequently, sometimes on the membrane of the yolk, sometimes on the outer membrane, just beneath the shell.—SPOROTRICHUM *brunneum*, Schenk, in the white of eggs, converting it into a brownish gelatinous mass.

3. *Reptiles and Fishes.*

On the skin of Tritons, as of Fishes, ACHLYA is frequently extremely developed; other obscure forms are also enumerated by Ch. Robin. The same author describes the PSOROSPERMLÆ of J. Müller as Algæ allied to the Diatomaceæ; but they appear to be pseudo-naviculæ of GREGARINÆ.

4. *Insects*

are subject to the invasion of various parasitic fungi, among the most remarkable of which is the Muscardine of the Silk-worm, BOTRYTIS *bassiana*, which sometimes occasions enormous loss to the silk-cultivators. This fungus grows in or upon any part of the silk-worm, *Bombyx mori*, in its larva, chrysalis, and imago forms. It is not fully developed until after the death of the insect; but if the spores penetrate the body of a living specimen and this is placed in a damp and confined atmosphere, the germination takes place, and a development of the fungus ensues, which destroys the tissues and organs, finally causing death. It has been developed on many other Lepidoptera which have been inoculated with it; and even the larvæ of certain Coleoptera take it. It is very common to find flies in autumn infested with a fungus, a kind of muscardine of flies this belongs to the genus SPORENDONEMA; its mycelial filaments ramify in the interior of the body, and emerge at the articulations of the segments of the abdomen to bear fruit, killing the fly. A number of so-called genera of Fungi and Algæ have been described by Robin and Leidy as occurring in the intestines, &c. of insects; these appear to us to be imperfect organisms (see ECCRINA, EN-TEROBRYUS, ARTHROMITUS, LEPTOTHRIX, CLADOPHYTUM).—Several species of *Sphæria* infest the larvæ of insects, the mycelium destroying them and gradually completely displacing the internal organs, while the skin retains its shape and dries; the fruit subsequently breaks out from the anterior or posterior extremity (see SPHÆRIA). Some species of ISARIA, described as parasites, grow upon dead insects.

5. *The microscopic parasites of Plants* are very numerous, belonging all to the class of Fungi. Much confusion exists in many works between the true parasites and mere epiphytes; and it is sometimes very difficult to draw any line of demarcation. Among the undoubted parasites are all the genera and species of the family UREDINEI, together with a large portion of the other genera of Coniomycetes, and the Ascomycetous forms to which they mostly belong. Among the Hyphomycetes may especially be cited the genus BOTRYTIS, *B. infestans* being the potato-fungus. FUSISPORIUM, "OIDIUM," &c., form destructive mildews; and among the ASCOMYCETES the ERYSIPHÆ, and especially their mycelia (commonly forming spurious *Oidia*), are well-known pests. Further particulars are given under POTATO-FUNGUS, VINE-FUNGUS, and BLIGHT. The organisms described as Unicellular Algæ, under the names of CHYTRIDIUM and *Pythium*, are parasitic on Confervoids.

BIBL. Ch. Rob. *Hist. Nat. des Végétaux Parasites*, 2nd ed. Paris, 1853; Bærensprung, *Ann. Nat. Hist.* xii.; Siebold, *Wagner's Handwört. d. Phys.*; Hannover, *Müller's Archiv*, 1842; Bennett, *Ed. Phil. Trans.* xv; Küchenmeister, *Parasiten*, 1856.

PARASITIC FUNGI. See PARASITES.

PARENCHYMA. See TISSUES, Vegetable.

PARKERIA, Hooker. — The typical genus of Parkerieæous Ferns. Aquatic; exotic.

PARKERIEÆ. — A family of Polypodiaceous Ferns, consisting of aquatic forms, in which the sporanges are not gathered in sori, and the habit is very different from the majority of Ferns.

Genera.

1. *Ceratopteris.* Sporanges surrounded by a broad, complete, articulated annulus, placed upon longitudinal veins. Spores globose, trifariously streaked.

2. *Parkeria.* Sporanges with an almost obsolete basilar annulus, placed on longitudinal veins. Spores three-sided, concentrically streaked.

PARMELIA, Ach. — An extensive genus of Parmeliaceæ (Gymnocarpous Lichens), characterized by their spreading, lobed, foliaceous thallus, with orbicular apothecia fixed by a central point beneath, growing upon trees, palings, rocks, stones, walls, &c. About thirty British species exist; *P. parietina*, the yellow wall-lichen, is one of the

commonest plants of this family, and furnishes a ready means of observing the structure both of the apothecia and the spermogonia (Pl. 29. figs. 1-3).

BIBL. Hook. *Brit. Fl.* ii. pt. 1. p. 202; *Engl. Bot.* pl. 194, &c.; Schærer, *Enum. Crit. Lich. Europ.* Berne, 1850. p. 33; Tulasne, *Ann. des Sc. Nat.* 3 sér. xvii. pp. 66, 137.

PARMELIACEÆ. — A family of Gymnocarpous or open-fruited Lichens, bearing sessile shields, the borders of which are formed by the surface of the thallus.

British Genera.

* *Apothecia at first veiled, thallus horizontal*: Peltigeri.

1. *Peltigera.* Thallus foliaceous, leathery or membranous, spreading, lobed, with woolly veins beneath. Apothecia somewhat circular, adnate on the upper side of the lobules of the thallus, and having a border formed by this.

2. *Nephroma.* Thallus foliaceous, leathery or membranous, spreading, lobed, naked or hairy beneath. Apothecia circular or reniform, adnate on the under side of the lobules of the thallus, with a border formed by the latter.

3. *Solorina.* Thallus leathery, membranaceous, veined or fibrillose below. Apothecia suborbicular, affixed to the upper surface of the central lobes of the thallus; veil finally forming an evanescent margin.

** *Apothecia at first closed, thallus horizontal*: Euparmeliacei.

4. *Sticta.* Thallus foliaceous, leathery-cartilaginous, spreading, lobed, free and downy beneath, with little cavities or hollow spots, often containing a powdery substance. Apothecia beneath formed of the thallus, to which they are appressed and fixed by a central point, the disk coloured, flat, surrounded by an elevated border formed of the thallus.

5. *Parmelia.* Thallus foliaceous, membranous or leathery, spreading, lobed and stellated or laciniated, more or less fibrous beneath. Apothecia circular, formed by the thallus, fixed by a central point, disk concave, coloured, with an inflexed margin from the thallus.

6. *Urceolaria.* Thallus uniform, crustaceous. Apothecia urceolate, somewhat immersed, the thalline border somewhat distinct.

2 M

7. *Lecanora.* Thallus crustaceous, spreading, flat, adnate and uniform. *Apothecia* circular, thick, sessile and adnate ; disk plano-convex, the border thickish, formed of the crust, and of the same colour.

8. *Physcia. Thallus* cartilaginous, branched and laciniated, the segments free, generally grooved beneath, the margins frequently ciliated. *Apothecia* circular, peltate, formed of the thallus, the disk coloured and surrounded by an inflexed margin derived from the thallus.

*** *Apothecia open from the first, thallus mostly centripetal, vertical or sarmentose, without any hypothallus,* Usnei.

9. *Cetraria.* Thallus foliaceous, cartilagineo-membranous, ascending or spreading, lobed and laciniated, smooth and naked on both sides. *Apothecia* circular, obliquely adnate to the margin of the thallus, the lower portion being free (from the thallus) ; disk coloured, plano-concave, with an inflexed border formed of the thallus.

10. *Roccella.* Thallus cartilaginous, leathery, rounded or flat, branched or laciniated. *Apothecia* circular, adnate to the thallus, the disk coloured, plano-convex, with a border, at length thickened and elevated, formed of the thallus, and covering a black powder concealed within the substance of the thallus.

11. *Ramalina.* Thallus cartilaginous, generally branched and laciniated, somewhat shrubby, generally bearing powdery warts, cottony and compact within. *Apothecia* circular, shield-shaped, stalked and peltate, flat, bordered, entirely formed of the substance of the thallus, and mostly of the same colour.

12. *Cornicularia.* Thallus cartilaginous, branched, subcylindrical, fistulose, or nearly solid and cottony within. *Apothecia* circular, terminal, obliquely peltate, entirely formed of the substance of the thallus, at length convex, more or less bordered and often toothed.

13. *Evernia.* Thallus somewhat crustaceous, branched and laciniated, angled or compressed, cottony within. *Apothecia* circular, shield-shaped, sessile, with the disk concave, coloured, and an inflexed border formed by the thallus.

14. *Usnea.* Thallus somewhat crustaceous, rounded, branched, generally pendulous, with a central thread. *Apothecia* circular, terminal on processes of the thallus, peltate, nearly of the same colour, mostly without a raised border, but ciliated at the margins.

BIBL. See the genera.

PASTE, EELS IN. See ANGUILLULA.

PATELLINA, Will.—A genus of recent Foraminifera, of the order Entomostegia.

Char. Shell trochoid, crenulated on the upper surface. First segments spiral, simple ; later crescentic, each forming about half the circumference, arranged in two opposed alternating series, and subdivided internally by incomplete radiating septa springing from the periphery. Orifice uncertain.

P. corrugata (Pl. 44. fig. 28). Rare.

BIBL. Williamson, *Rec. For.* 46.

PAVONINA, D'Orb.—A genus of Foraminifera, of the order Stichostegia, and family Æquilateralidæ.

Distinguished by the compressed flabelliform shell ; the concentric chambers, the last of which are widest ; and by the round, numerous orifices, arranged in a transverse line along the middle of the last chamber.

No British species.

BIBL. That of the family.

PEARLS.—These well-known bodies are formed as secretions from the mantle of bivalve mollusks, the best being obtained from the Ceylon pearl-oyster or mussel (*Avicula margaritifera*). They occur naturally from the irritation produced by particles of sand accidentally confined between the mantle and the shell ; and they are produced artificially by wounding the mantle with pieces of iron-wire, &c. Their structure agrees with that of the shell of the animal in which they are formed. Sometimes they consist entirely of nacre or pearly matter, arranged in close concentric layers ; at others, the interior exhibits the prismatic structure of shell.

When acted upon by a dilute mineral acid, the lime-salt is removed from the organic cast of the original, which is left.

See SHELL.

BIBL. Hague and Siebold, *Siebold & Kölliker's Journ.* viii. 439 & 445.

PECTINATELLA, Leidy.—A genus of aquatic Polyzoa, of the order Hippocrepia, and family Plumatellidæ.

Char. Polypidom massive, gelatinous, fixed, investing ; orifices arranged in irregular lobate areolæ upon the free surface ; ova lenticular, with a ring and marginal spines.

P. magnifica. Philadelphia. Not yet found in Britain.

BIBL. Leidy, *Proc. Acad. Philadelphia,* 1851 ; Allman, *Freshwater Polyzoa,* 81.

PEDIASTRUM, Meyen.—A genus of Desmidisceæ (Confervoid Algæ).

Char. Cells aggregated into a usually circular, minute disk or flattened star, and generally arranged either in a single or in two or more concentric series; marginal cells bipartite on the outside.

Ralfs describes eleven British species. Interstices of the cells usually hyaline, but in one species (*P. selenæum*) these are greenish.

1. *P. Boryanum* (Pl. 10. fig. 48). Cells arranged in one or more circles around one or two central ones; marginal cells gradually tapering into two long subulate points; notch narrow. Diameter of outer cells 1-2730 to 1-2220''.

2. *P. granulatum* (Pl. 10. fig. 49). Cells six, granular or punctate on the surface; lobes of marginal cells tapering. Diameter of outer cells 1-1850''.

The method of reproduction is noticed under DESMIDIACEÆ, p. 214.

BIBL. Ralfs, *Brit. Desmid.* p. 180; Caspary, *Bot. Zeit.* viii. p. 786, 1850; Al. Braun, *Rejuvenescence, &c., Ray Soc. Vol.* 1853, *passim,* pls. 3 & 4; *Alg. Unicell. Gen. Nova,* p. 64.

PEDICELLARIÆ. See ECHINODERMATA, p. 241.

Pl. 37. fig. 3 represents a pedicellaria from the common star-fish; the stalk is not figured.

The bird's-head processes of the polyzoa (Polyzoa) are probably analogous organs.

PEDICELLINA, Sars.—A genus of Infundibulate Ctenostomatous Polyzoa, of the family Pedicellinidæ.

Char. Those of the family. See PEDICELLINIDÆ (CTENOSTOMATA, p. 193).

The late researches of Prof. Allman have shown that the tentacular disk is bilateral, and that an epistome is present; so that this genus belongs properly to the order Hippocrepia.

Animal bodies globose, with an interrupted circle of short tentacles, curled inwards and not retractile; placed at the ends of erect slender stalks springing from a creeping adherent fibre. Three species :

1. *P. echinata.* Stalks spinous.

2. *P. belgica.* Stalks smooth, inflated about the middle.

3. *P. gracilis.* Stalks smooth, thin and long, not inflated.

BIBL. Johnston, *Brit. Zooph.* 381, and the Bibl. therein; Allman, *Freshwater Polyzoa (Ray Soc.),* p. 19, note.

PEDICELLINIDÆ.—A family of Infundibulate Ctenostomatous Polyzoa; containing the single genus PEDICELLINA.

PEDICULUS, L.—A genus of Anoplurous Insects, of the family Pediculidæ.

Char. Legs all scansorial or prehensile; thorax large, not constricted from the abdomen; abdomen with seven segments; antennæ five-jointed; mouth with a fleshy rostrum.

The species are human lice.

Rostrum retractile, concealed beneath the head, forming a soft tubular sheath dilated at the end, where it is furnished with a double row of hooks, and containing a horny tube formed of four setæ.

1. *P. capitis.* Ashy-white, thorax elongate, quadrate, abdomen ovate, laterally lobed, segments blackish at the margin. Length of male, 1-16''; of female, 1-8''.

2. *P. vestimenti,* body or clothes' louse (Pl. 28. fig. 3). Dirty white, elongato-ovate; head much produced; thorax contracted in front; abdomen with the segments indistinctly indicated. Length about 1-8''.

3. *P. tabescentium,* distemper-louse. Pale yellow; head rounded; antennæ long; thorax large and quadrate; abdomen large, the segments intimately united.

Doubtfully British.

See PHTHIRIUS.

BIBL. Denny, *Anoplur. Monogr.*

PELARGONIUM. See POLLEN, RAPHIDES, and HAIRS.

PELECIDA, Duj.—A genus of Infusoria, of the family of Trichodina.

Char. Body flexible, contractile, oblong, compressed, rounded behind, recurved like a hatchet in front, ciliated all over, and furnished with a mouth, which is either visible, or shown to exist by the presence in the interior of various objects swallowed by the animals.

P. rostrum (Pl. 24. fig. 39) = *Loxodes rostrum,* E., differs from the *Paramecina,* D., by the absence of a contractile integument.

BIBL. Dujardin, *Infus.* p. 403.

PELLIA.—A genus of Pellieæ (frondose Hepaticæ). *P. epiphylla* (fig. 556) is not uncommon in damp shady places, by springs and wells, where it grows rapidly. Its pedicels are silvery-white, and the capsules pale brown; and when the valves are fully expanded, the elaters form an elegant tuft in the middle. The character of the frond varies somewhat according to the degree of moisture of the habitat. The forms called

2 M 2

longifolia and *furcigera*, are now considered to constitute a distinct species, *P. calycina*.

Fig. 550.

Pellia epiphylla.
Magnified 2 diameters.

BIBL. Hooker, *Brit. Jung.* pl. 47; *Brit. Flora,* ii. pt. 1. p. 130; Endlicher, *Gen. Plant. Supp.* i. No. 472–5; Ekart, *Syn. Jung.* p. 63, pls. 7 & 13; *Eng. Bot. Supp.* pl. 2873.

PELLIEÆ.—A tribe of Liverworts or Hepaticæ, nearly allied to the Jungermannieæ in the character of the fructification, but having a lobed thalloid frond, traversed by a mid-nerve, from which the fruit-stalks arise.

British Genera.

1. *Blyttia.* Fructification emerging from the end of the rib below the apex of the frond, at length dorsal. Perichæte 4–5-parted; lobes torn. Perigone herbaceous, tubular, the mouth denticulated. Archegones eight to twenty. Epigone persistent, torn at the summit. Sporange 4-valved. Antheridia dorsal, placed on the rib, covered by dentate incumbent leaflets.

2. *Petalophyllum.* Fructification from the upper surface of the plaited frond. Perichæte broad, bell-shaped and toothed. Perigone wanting. Epigone concealed in the perichæte. Sporange bursting into irregular laciniæ. Elaters often branched.

3. *Fossombronia.* Fructification emerging from the end of the rib below the apex of the frond, at length dorsal. Perichæte obconic bell-shaped, the mouth crenate or dentate. Perigone wanting. Archegones

few. Epigone persistent, torn at the summit. Sporange circumscissile. Antheridia dorsal, situated on the rib, naked.

4. *Metzgeria.* Fructification emerging from the ventral side of the midrib of the frond. Perichæte ventricose, at length bipartite. Perigone none. Archegones few. Epigone persistent, torn at the summit. Sporange four-valved. Antheridia ventral, placed on the rib, covered by incumbent dentate leaflets.

5. *Aneura.* Fructification emerging from the ventral side, near the margin of the frond. Perichæte short, lobed or torn. Perigone wanting. Archegones few. Epigone persistent, torn at the summit. Sporange four-valved. Antheridia immersed in the back of special lobes of the frond.

6. *Pellia.* Fructification emerging from the dorsal side of the frond. Perichæte short, somewhat cup-shaped, the mouth lacero-dentate. Perigone wanting. Archegones several. Epigone membranous, accompanied by a few sterile archegones, at first, at the lower part. Sporange fourvalved. Antheridia immersed in the surface of the frond.

7. *Blasia.* Fructification at first immersed in the rib of the frond, then emerging from the apex. Perichæte and perigone wanting. Epigone membranous, with few sterile archegones, at first, scattered toward the lowest part. Sporange fourvalved. Antheridia immersed in the rib of the thallus, more prominent below, and covered by little dentate scales.

8. *Targionia.* Fructification sessile, inferior, solitary and terminal to the frond. Perichæte two-valved, splitting vertically. Perigone wanting. Epigone delicate, persistent, investing the sporange until maturity, sometimes evanescent above. Sporange bursting by an irregular slit, or into fragments. Antheridia immersed in the rib of the frond below, covered by papillæ.

BIBL. See the genera, and HEPATICÆ.

PELONÆA, Forbes.—A genus of Tunicate Mollusca, of the family Pelonæadæ.

Char. Unattached; feet cylindrical; orifices without rays, on two equal approximate warty eminences at the anterior end. They live buried in mud. Two species:

1. *P. corrugata.* Test deep brown, much elongated, rudely wrinkled transversely.

2. *P. glabra.* Test greenish yellow, smooth, pilose, shorter than the last.

BIBL. Forbes and Hanley, *Brit. Moll.* i. 43.

PELOPS, Koch (*Acarina*).—Is consolidated with GALUMNA.

PELTIDEA, Hoffm. = Species of PELTIGERA and STICTA.

PELTIGERA, Willd.—A genus of Parmeliaceæ (Gymnocarpous Lichens), characterized by a foliaceous, usually leathery thallus, with woolly veins beneath ; the suborbicular shield-like apothecia arising on the upper sides of the lobules.

P. canina, a large Lichen, is extremely common on the ground among moss in woods. Two or three nearly allied species are separated from this by most authors, but with questionable propriety. Three or four others are subalpine.

BIBL. Hook. *Brit. Flora*, ii. pt. 1. p. 218 ; *Eng. Bot.* 2229.

PENEROPLIS, Lamk. — A genus of Foraminifera, of the order Helicostegia, and family Nautiloidæ.

Resembles *Polystomella* in its numerous orifices, and in the chambers consisting of a single cavity ; but differs in the great variation in shape according to age and in different individuals, in the thin texture, and especially in the orifices being situated upon the upper part of the last chamber only, none upon the sides. Williamson describes the orifices as scattered, whilst D'Orbigny says they are in straight lines.

P. planatus. British ; recent ; orifices scattered over the anterior surface of the last chamber.

BIBL. That of the order.

PENICILLIUM, Link.—A genus of Mucedines (Hyphomycetous Fungi), of which the species *P. glaucum* is at once one of the most frequent and the most puzzling plants of the class. This fungus is the commonest of the constituents of the greenish or bluish mould formed on decaying vegetable substances of all kinds, especially on semifluid or liquid matters. On the surface of liquids it forms a kind of dense pasty crust, slimy on the lower surface, and coloured and pulverulent (bearing spores) above. When the upper fertile layer is examined under the microscope, it is found to consist of pedicels terminating in a repeatedly but shortly bifurcated pencil, each ultimate branch of which bears a moniliform row of spores. The ramification of the pedicels is not distinctly represented in fig. 557, but the appearance of the spores is characteristic ; and the ramifications of the sporophores are scarcely perceptible in examples growing on dryish substances. The mode of attachment of the spores is shown in figs. 15 and 16 of Pl. 20. The mycelium consists of interwoven articulated filaments, most extensively ramified. The spores appear whitish, yellowish, greenish, or bluish, according to age : under the microscope they appear opake when mature.

So far there is little difficulty about the history of these plants; and if the spores of the above form are sown on a glass slide, kept moist with an organic liquid, they will germinate and ramify, and under favourable circumstances bear thin penicillate tufts of spores at points which emerge from the nutrient liquid. But this same fructification of *P. glaucum* presents itself invariably under certain circumstances associated with the vinegar - plant and the yeast-plant, toward the close of the ordinary development of these fungi. In common with most observers, we find that the exhaustion of the saccharine matrix of the vinegar-plant is followed in all cases by the appearance of crusts of *Penicillium*-mould on the upper surface, whence it would appear that the vinegar-plant was only the mycelium of *Penicillium*. It was asserted, moreover, many years ago, by Turpin, that *P. glaucum* is the last term of the growth both of the true yeast-plant, *Torula Cerevisiæ*, and of the milk-yeast, *Oidium lactis*. We have found the gelatinous crusts of the vinegar-plant to contain structures which represent *Torula* and *Oidium*, and to grow like them ; and we have also observed, in repeated experiments, that beer allowed to stand until sour, at first appears clothed with a whitish mealy collection of minute vesicles, representing the ultimate stage of *Torula*, and subsequently this gradually gave place to gelatinous matter, which at length covered the whole surface with a tough film, and fruited as *Penicillium glaucum*. Hence it would appear that the yeast-fungus also is merely a vegetative form of *Penicillium* developed under peculiar conditions. More is said on this point under VINEGAR-PLANT and YEAST.

Several species are enumerated ; and we have given under the separate head of COREMIUM a form which is merely a con-

Fig. 557.

Penicillium.

A fertile plume with pencils of spores.

Magnified 150 diameters.

fluent growth of *Penicillium*, producing a compound pedicel.

1. *P. glaucum*, Grev. Mycelial filaments form a crust-like web, spores green or bluish. Greville, *Sc. Crypt. Fl.* pl. 58. fig. 1. *P. crustaceum*, Fries. Extremely common.

2. *P. candidum*, Link. Mycelial filaments woven together, spores white. (Distinct?)

3. *P. sparsum*, Grev. Mycelium lax, spores white. *Sc. Crypt. Fl.* pl. 58. fig. 2. Perhaps not different from the last.

4. *P. fasciculatum*, Sommer. Mycelium scarcely developed, filaments all fertile, trifid at the apex, spores glaucescent.

5. *P. subtile*, Berk. Extremely minute, mycelium creeping, fertile filaments erect, simple or ternate; chains of spores few, spores broadly elliptical. *Ann. Nat. Hist.* vi. pl. 14. fig. 25.

6. *P. roseum*, Lk. Mycelium effused; fertile filaments slightly branched, spores rose-colour.

BIBL. Berk. *Hook. Brit. Fl.* ii. pt. 2. p. 344; *Ann. Nat. Hist.* i. p. 262, vi. p. 437, 2 ser. vii. p. 102; Greville, *loc. cit.*; Fries, *Syst. Myc.* iii. 407; *Summa Vegetabilium*, p. 489. See also under YEAST and VINE-GAR-PLANT.

PENIUM, Bréb.—A genus of Desmidiaceæ.

Char. Cells single, entire, elongated, straight, and slightly or not at all constricted in the middle.

Sporangia round or quadrangular, smooth, not spinous.

At each end of the cells is a rounded space containing moving molecules.

Eight British species (Ralfs).

1. *P. Brebissonii* (Pl. 10. fig. 36). Cells smooth, cylindrical, ends rounded, transverse median band inconspicuous. Length 1-640 to 1-400″.

Common. Sporangium at first quadrate, but finally orbicular; conjugating cells persistent, or remaining permanently attached to the sporangium.

2. *P. margaritaceum* (Pl. 10. fig. 37, empty cell). Cells cylindrical or fusiform, with rounded truncate ends, and covered with pearly granules in longitudinal rows. Length 1-160″.

BIBL. Ralfs, *Brit. Desmid.* p. 148.

PENNATULA, Cuv. (Sea-pen).—A genus of marine Polypi, of the order Actinoida, and family Pennatulidæ.

The spicula form an interesting microscopic object.

BIBL. Johnston, *Brit. Zooph.* 157; Gosse, *Mar. Zool.* i. 34.

PENTASTERIAS, Ehr. (Desmidiaceæ). —The two British species are referred to *Staurastrum*.

PEPPER.—Black pepper consists of the berries of *Piper nigrum*; white and decorticated pepper of the same berries, with the outer part of the coats removed. The cellular tissues of the several lamellæ of the husk, and of the albumen or body of the seed, are tolerably characteristic, and may be known by their appearance under the microscope from the fragments of linseed, mustard, &c. with which peppers are sometimes adulterated. White pepper is fraudulently reduced with flour, which may be detected by the starch-granules—those existing in pepper itself being exceedingly minute particles; the same remark applies to rice and pea-flour, &c. Excessive quantities of the husk-tissue in black pepper denote that the refuse of the decorticated white peppers has been added. (See also CAYENNE).

BIBL. Pereira, *Materia Medica*; Hassall, *Food and its Adulterations*, p. 42.

PERACANTHA, Baird. — A genus of Entomostraca, of the order Cladocera, and family Lynceidæ.

Char. Side view of shell oval, the lower and posterior portion with an acute projection directed backwards and upwards, and, as well as the upper extremity of the anterior margin, beset with strong hooked spines; beak sharp, curved downwards.

P. truncata (Pl. 14. fig. 31). Superior antennæ conical; inferior short, the anterior branch with five setæ, one from first, one from second, and three from last joint; posterior branch with three setæ from the last joint only; intestine convoluted, with one turn and a half; ova two. Aquatic.

BIBL. Baird, *Brit. Entom.* p. 136.

PERANEMA, Duj.—A genus of Infusoria, of the family Euglenia.

Char. Form variable, sometimes nearly globular, at others inflated posteriorly and narrowed in front, where it becomes prolonged into a long flagelliform filament; movement slow, uniform, forwards.

P. globulosa (Pl. 24. fig. 59). Body almost globular, more or less drawn out anteriorly, with oblique wrinkles on the surface; aquatic; length 1-1400″.

BIBL. Dujardin, *Infus.* p. 353.

PERANEMA, Don = *Sphæropteris*, Br.— A genus of Peranemæ (Polypodioid Ferns).

PERANEMEÆ.—A family of Polypo-dioid Ferns characterized by the globose sori being pedunculated or seated on the middle of the superior vein; indusium in-ferior, membranous, splitting into laciniæ.

Genera.

1. *Peranema.* Sori pedunculate, indu-sium cup-shaped, at length splitting into 2–4 lobes; sporanges on a punctiform recep-tacle; veins pinnate.

2. *Diacalpe.* Sori regularly arranged; indusium sessile, spherical, at first closed; sori on a punctiform receptacle, then burst-ing irregularly at the summit.

3. *Woodsia.* Sori regularly arranged; sporanges pedicellate, inserted at the bot-tom of the indusium, which is cup-shaped, and hairy at the margin; veins pinnate.

4. *Hypoderris.* Sori regularly arranged; sporanges on an almost obsolete axis; in-dusium cup-shaped, fringed at the margin; veins anastomosing.

PERICHÆNA, Fr.—A genus of Tricho-gastres (Gasteromycetous Fungi), consisting of little rounded membranous sacs of brown-ish or yellowish colour, generally splitting all round (transversely), and discharging yellow spores and (few) free and elastic filaments. The commonest, *P. populina*, yellowish, and about as large as a mustard-seed, occurs on fallen poplar trees; two others occur in fir-plantations.

BIBL. Berkeley, *Hook. Brit. Fl.* ii. pt. 2. p. 321; Fries, *Syst. Myc.* p. 190; *Summa Veget.* p. 459; Greville, &c. *Crypt. Flora,* p. 252.

Dujardin appends the genera *Chætoglena* and *Chætotyphla* to his genus *Trachelomonas* as uncertain, and arranges the genera *Gle-nodinium* and *Peridinium* as stated under the latter head.

BIBL. Ehrenberg, *Infus.* p. 249; Dujardin, *Infus.* p. 371.

PERIDINIUM, Ehr.—A genus of Infu-soria, of the family Peridinæa.

Char. Those of *Glenodinium* with the ab-sence of the red (eye-) spot.

A flagelliform filament is present as well as the cilia. Some species have horn-like processes.

Eleven species; two (fossil) doubtful. Some of them are phosphorescent.

PERICONIA, Tode.—A genus of Stil-bacei (Hyphomycetous Fungi), apparently nearly related to PACHNOCYBE, but with the stem fistular, and the capitulum vesicular. *P. glaucocephala*, Corda, has been found on rotten linen. Tulasne states that this genus is merely a conidiiferous form of some Hy-poxylous Sphæriacea.

BIBL. Fries, *Summa Veg.* p. 168; Berk. and Broome, *Ann. Nat. Hist.* 2 ser. v. p. 165; Tulasne, *Ann. des Sc. Nat.* 4 sér. v. p. 109.

PERIDERM. See BARK.

PERIDERMIUM, Lk.—A genus of Ure-dinei (Coniomycetous Fungi), distinguished from ÆCIDIUM by the sac-like perithecium bursting irregularly, as if by a circumscis-sile dehiscence. The type of this genus is *P. (Æcid.) Pini*, found on the leaves and bark of Scotch Firs. The spores are covered with very numerous small tubercles. See UREDINEI.

BIBL. Berk. *Brit. Flora*, ii. pt. 2. p. 374; Grev. *Scot. Crypt. Fl.* pl. 7; Tulasne, *Ann. des Sc. Nat.* 4 sér. ii. p. 176, pl. 10; De Bary, *Brandpilze, Berlin*, 1853. p. 72.

PERIDINÆA, Ehr.—A family of Infu-soria.

Char. Body furnished with a membranous carapace, from which a long flagelliform fila-ment issues, and which has one or more fur-rows occupied by vibratile cilia, or exhibits setæ or minute spines upon the surface.

These Infusoria live either in the sea, or in stagnant fresh water; never being found in infusions or decomposing water.

Five genera:

Carapace with rigid setæ or points, but no transverse furrow nor longitudinal crest	Eye-spot present	1. *Chætoglena.*
	Eye-spot absent	2. *Chætotyphla.*
Carapace smooth or rough, and with a transverse ciliated furrow, but no crest	Eye-spot present	3. *Glenodinium.*
	Eye-spot absent	4. *Peridinium.*
Carapace with an incomplete longitudinal crest		5. *Dinophysis.*

1. *P. cinctum* (Pl. 24. fig. 9). Green; not phosphorescent; carapace subglobose, smooth, subtrilobed; no horns. Aquatic; length 1·580″.

2. *P. fuscum* (Pl. 24. fig. 11). Brown; not luminous; carapace ovate, slightly com-pressed, smooth, acute in front, rounded behind; no horns. Aquatic; length 1·430 to 1·290″.

3. *P. tripos* (Pl. 24. fig. 12). Yellowish; splendidly phosphorescent; carapace urceo-late, broadly concave, smooth, with three horns, two very long, frontal and recurved, the third posterior and straight. Marine; length 1·140″.

4. *P. uberrimum*, Allman. Cilia distri-

buted over the whole surface. Length 1-1000 to 1-500″.

Dujardin unites those species of the genera *Glenodinium* and *Peridinium* which have no horns, to form the single genus *Peridinium*, placing those with horns in a genus *Ceratium.*

BIBL. Ehrenberg, *Infus.* p. 252; Dujardin, *Infus.* p. 374; Allman, *Micr. Journ.* iii. 24.

PERIOLA, Fries. — P. *tomentosa*, Fr., described as a Sclerotioid Fungus, is an obscure, irregular, fleshy body, with a white villous surface, found growing on potatoes. It is probably the early form of some unascertained species of fungus.

PERIPTERA, Ehr.—A genus of Diatomaceæ.

Char. Frustules single, compressed; valves dissimilar, one being simply turgid, the other winged or furnished with horns; horns sometimes branched and attached to the extreme margin. Fossil.

Valves not areolar nor punctate under ordinary illumination. Four species. America and Bermuda.

P. chlamidophora (Pl. 41. fig. 41); *P. tetracladia* (Pl. 43. fig. 66); *P. capra* (Pl. 43. fig. 67).

BIBL. Ehrenberg, *Ber. d. Berl. Akad.* 1844. p. 263; Kützing, *Sp. Alg.* p. 25.

PERISPORACEI.—A family of Ascomycetous Fungi, mostly epiphytic and of small size, characterized by producing floccose common receptacles (mostly) radiating from a point, forming patches upon leaves, &c., in the centre of which are developed somewhat globular perithecia, of obscure cellular structure, persistent, bursting at the summit, filled densely with subgelatinous, scarcely diffluent gelatine; sporidia produced in asci, subsequently often effused, simple, free, and mixed with the gelatine in the centre of the perithecium. The mycelia of these plants, bearing conidial structures, have been described as distinct fungi, for example those of *Erysiphe* as *Oidia,* &c. See ERYSIPHE. EUROTIUM probably belongs here.

Synopsis of British Genera.

1. *Lasiobotrys.* Perithecium fleshy-horny, globular, naked, collapsing at the summit.

2. *Capnodium.* Perithecium fleshy, clavate, double (the outer cellular, interior hyaline), mucilaginous, opening by a fringed mouth; asci containing about six spores in two rows.

3. *Erysiphe.* Perithecium membranous,

closed at first, afterwards open, supported on a persistent radiating mycelium, formed of continuous filaments, bifid at their ends. Asci one to eight, paraphyses none; spores definite, ovate.

4. *Perisporium.* Perithecium superficial, at length bursting irregularly. Asci club-shaped, not mixed with paraphyses. Spores numerous, ovate.

5. *Chætomium.* Perithecium superficial, finally open at the mouth, clothed externally with opake hairs. Asci clavate, mixed with paraphyses. Spores simple, ovate.

6. *Ascotricha.* Perithecium thin, at length bursting, clothed with dark, subpellucid, even, obscurely-jointed hairs. Spores simple, contained in linear asci. Superficial, at length free or resting on the investing thallus, black.

PERISPORIUM, Fr.—A genus of Perisporacei (Ascomycetous Fungi), consisting of minute, globular, free, punctiform sacs, with fleshy or waxy walls, seated on an obscure thallus, growing on leaves or stalks; finally bursting and collapsing. The spores

Fig. 558.   Fig. 559.

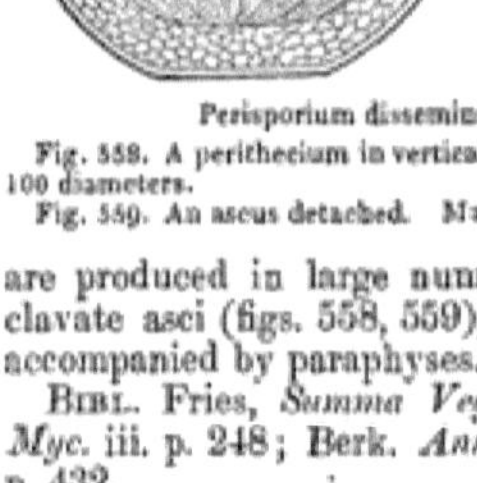

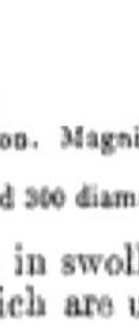

Perisporium disseminatum.

Fig. 558. A perithecium in vertical section. Magnified 100 diameters.

Fig. 559. An ascus detached. Magnified 300 diams.

are produced in large numbers in swollen clavate asci (figs. 558, 559), which are unaccompanied by paraphyses.

BIBL. Fries, *Summa Veg.* p. 404; *Syst. Myc.* iii. p. 248; Berk. *Ann. Nat. Hist.* vi. p. 432.

PERITHECIUM.—The name applied to the special envelope, mostly of different structure from the rest of the thallus or the receptacle, enclosing the "nucleus" of the Angiocarpous Lichens and the Pyrenomycetous Fungi.

PERITONEUM. See SEROUS MEMBRANES.

PERONOSPORA, Ung. See BOTRYTIS.

PEROPHORA. Wiegm. — A genus of

Tunicate Mollusca, of the family Clavelinidæ.

Char. Individuals stalked, roundish, compressed; thorax not marked with granular lines.

P. Listeri. Occurs attached to sea-weeds. Very transparent, appearing on the weeds like little specks of jelly dotted with orange and brown.

BIBL. Forbes and Hanley, *Brit. Mollusca*, i. 28.

PERTUSARIA, DC.— A genus of Endocarpeæ (Angiocarpous Lichens), having an adnate, uniform thallus, spreading over bark, rocks, &c., and bearing wart-like apothecia, finally exhibiting a depressed pore in their centre, leading to the one or several cells containing the thecæ. *P. communis* is very common on trees.

BIBL. Hook. *Brit. Flor.* ii. pt. 1. p. 164; *Engl. Botany*, pl. 677; Leighton, *Brit. Angioc. Lichens*, p. 26, pls. 9–11.

PETALONEMA, Berk. (*Arthrosiphon*, Kutz.).— A genus of Oscillatoriaceæ (Confervoid Algæ), presenting a very remarkable mode of growth. The filaments are branched and cylindrical, with a very evident terete, gelatinous, duplicate sheath (Pl. 4. fig. 21). The inner is thin and follows the filament; the outer presents oblique striæ indicating the interposition of lengths of the outer sheaths one inside another, like a series of nested funnels or conical cups. This appearance is produced by the bursting and expansion of each length of the sheath at the apex alone, to make room for the growth of the new cells of the filament formed at the apex. This structure is analogous to that occurring in URococcus, when each parent-cell membrane bursts at one side only to allow the new one to emerge, thus at length forming a jointed pedicel. The edges of the "funnels" of *Petalonema* sometimes become decomposed into curled filamentous processes.

The filament of *P. alatum* is green and striated, about 1-3000″ in diameter; the inner sheath is yellowish, the outer colourless and 1-400″ in diameter. It forms a brownish stratum on rocks and stones.

BIBL. Berkeley, *Gleanings*, p. 23, pl. 7; Greville, *Sc. Crypt. Fl.* pl. 222; Hassall, *Brit. Fr. Alg.* p. 237, pl. 68. fig. 6; Kützing, *Spec. Alg.* p. 311; *Tab. Phyc.* ii. 28; Al. Braun, *Rejuvenescence, &c., Ray Soc. Vol.* 1853. p. 178.

PETALOPHYLLUM, Wilson.— A genus of Pellieæ (frondose Hepaticæ). *P.*

Ralfsii is an elegant little Liverwort with the frond plaited or lamellated in rays from the origin of the fruit.

BIBL. *Engl. Bot. Supp.* pl. 2874.

PETALS. — The petals of Flowering Plants afford many interesting microscopic objects, in the epidermis, glandular and other hairs, the colour-cells and the veins composed of spiral vessels. Entire petals of small size and delicate character form good objects when dried and mounted in Canada balsam. Those of the smaller Caryophyllaceæ, the ligulate corollas of Compositæ, &c., are well suited for this. The larger kinds are studied by means of sections, like LEAVES.

PETROBIUS, Leach.— A genus of Insects, of the order Thysanura, and family Lepismenæ.

P. maritimus has a general resemblance to *Lepisma saccharina*; but it exercises a leaping movement. The antennæ are longer than the body; of the setæ at the tail, the middle one is longest. The insect is of a blackish-brown colour, and is covered with scales; the legs are yellowish, and the caudal setæ ringed with white; the abdomen is furnished with gill-like processes.

It is found upon the rocky sea-coast.

The scales have been used as test-objects.

BIBL. Gervais, *Walckenaer's Apt.* iii. p. 447; Guérin, *Iconogr. Ins.* pl. 2. fig. 1 *f*; and *Ann. des Sc. Nat.* 2 sér. v. p. 374.

PETRONEMA, Thwaites.— A genus of Oscillatoriaceæ (Confervoid Algæ). *P. fruticulosa* grows as a frustulose olive-brown crust on limestone rocks (not marine), forming little hemispherical masses; the sheaths are thick and cartilaginous, brown above but colourless at the tips, the protoplasma dull green.

BIBL. *Engl. Bot. Supp.* pl. 2959.

PEYER'S GLANDS. See INTESTINES (p. 395).

PEYSSONELIA, Dene.— A genus of Cryptonemiaceæ (Florideous Algæ), consisting of small plants with a depressed lobed thallus (fig. 560), growing over stones, shells, &c., and attached by the whole under surface which produces jointed radical hairs (fig. 561), especially at the thin margins. The thallus is composed of several rows of compact parenchymatous cells, and bears, on the concentrically-marked surface, warts composed of radiating rows of cells, among which occur crucially-divided *tetraspores*. *P. Dubyi* is not uncommon on British shores; it is 1 to 2″ in diameter, roundish at first, ultimately irregularly lobed, colour dull brownish. Thuret has observed *antheridia* on distinct plants of *P. squamosa*, a Mediterranean form; they are jointed filaments collected into wart-like bodies, like those containing the tetraspores. The spores are not described.

Fig. 560.

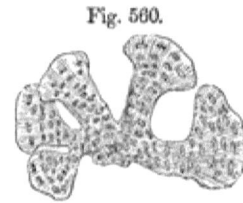

Frond. Nat. size.

Fig. 561.

Peyssonelia squamosa.
Vertical section of a portion through two warts.
Magnified 25 diameters.

BIBL. Harvey, *Brit. Mar. Alg.* p. 144, pl. 14 D; *Phyc. Brit.* pl. 71; Thuret, *Ann. des Sc. Nat.* 4 sér. iii. p. 23, pl. 4.

PEZIZA, Dill.—A genus of Helvellacei (Ascomycetous Fungi), containing numerous species, a large number of which grow upon dead wood, on the ground, among leaves, &c., many brightly coloured. They are at first closed sacs, which burst at the summit, and spread out to form a kind of cup containing asci and paraphyses. Thus they belong to the Discomycetes of some authors.

Fig. 562.   Fig. 563.   Fig. 564.

Peziza furfuracea.
(Small variety.)
Magnified 5 diameters.

Tulasne has recently shown that some of the *Pezizæ* have a secondary fructification consisting of *stylospores*; these forms have been described as species of *Dacrymyces*, a

genus of Tremellini. Other species also produce *spermatia*.

BIBL. Berk. *Brit. Flor.* ii. pt. 2. p. 186; Fries, *Summa Veg.* p. 348; Tulasne, *Ann. des Sc. Nat.* 3 sér. xx. p. 167; Currey, *Quart. Journ. Mic.* Sc. v. p. 124.

PHACELOMONAS, Ehr.—A doubtful genus of Infusoria.

Char. Tail-like process absent; a red (eye-) spot present; mouth (?) terminal, truncate, furnished with eight to ten anterior long cilia or flagelliform filaments.

P. pulcisculus. Body oblong, subconical, attenuate posteriorly, bright green; aquatic; length 1-1150″. Occurs in myriads in pools. Perhaps zoospores of ŒDOGONIUM.

BIBL. Ehrenberg, *Infus.* p. 28.

PHACIDIACEI. — A family of small Ascomycetous Fungi, mostly growing in large numbers on the half-decayed woody parts of plants, or on the ground; consisting usually of dark-coloured indurated or leathery bodies, solitary or connate, or seated on a common base, closed at first, and containing a soft nucleus; the outer case (*perithecium*) subsequently opening widely, and presenting a cavity lined with asci containing spores.

The history of development of these plants is still obscure; for many of them are connected with certain of the Coniomycetes as different stages of one and the same plant. We describe the genera according to the existing classifications, noting the new facts relating to these metamorphic phænomena in the articles on the particular genera.

British Genera.

* *Perithecium open, margined, closed by a lid or veil.*

1. *Patellaria.* Perithecium patelliform, margined, open, covered with a thin veil confluent with the nucleus. Disk at length pulverulent, the annulate asci breaking out.

2. *Tympanis.* Perithecium cup-shaped, margined, open, covered by a thin, evanescent veil. Disk fixed in the receptacle (*proper stratum*), at length dissolved. Asci filiform, fixed.

** *Perithecium (excipulum) at length open, connate with the floccose receptacle. Nucleus discoid, ascigerous, placed on the receptacle.*

3. *Cenangium.* Perithecium entire, leathery-horny, opening by a connivent mouth, distinct from the discigerous stratum. Asci

filiform, persistent, expelling the separate spores with violence.

*** *Perithecium entire, dehiscing by closely connivent slits.*

4. *Lophium.* Perithecium subsessile, elongated, compressed, bursting by a longitudinal slit. Asci erect, fixed, cylindrical, persistent, sporidia simple, rounded. Thallus crustaceous or imperceptible.

**** *Perithecium somewhat dimidiate, at length open, nucleus naked.*

5. *Rhytisma.* Perithecium innate, of irregular form, opening by fragments breaking off into a flexuose slit; nucleus placentiform, persistent. Asci erect, fixed; paraphyses stalked.

6. *Phacidium.* Perithecium roundish, simple, bursting with several teeth at the summit; nucleus disk-shaped, in some degree persistent. Asci erect, fixed; paraphyses stalked.

7. *Hysterium.* Perithecium sessile, oval or elongated, with a longitudinal slit at first closed, afterwards gaping open; nucleus linear, somewhat persistent. Asci erect, fixed; paraphyses stalked.

8. *Labrella.* Perithecium innate, bursting by a longitudinal slit; asci short, broad and obtuse above, attenuated below, mixed with short flexuous paraphyses; spores few, ovate-oblong, occasionally contracted or septate in the middle.

PHACIDIUM, Fr.—A genus of Phacidiacei (Ascomycetous Fungi), containing many species growing on dead leaves, branches, &c. Some of them are common, as *P. dentatum*, on oak-leaves, and *P. Laurocerasi* on the cherry-laurel.

BIBL. Berk. *Brit. Fl.* ii. pt. 2. p. 291; Fries, *Summa Veg.* 360.

PHACUS, Nitzsch, Duj.—A genus of Infusoria, of the family Thecamonadina, D. (Cryptomonadina, E.).

Char. Body flattened and leaf-like, usually green, with an anterior red (eye-) spot, a single flagelliform filament, and covered with a resisting membranous integument, prolonged posteriorly like a tail.

Dujardin distinguishes this genus from *Euglena*, E. by the constancy of the form of the body, which varies every moment in the latter genus.

1. *P. pleuronectes* (Pl. 24. fig. 62). Body oval, almost circular, green, with slightly marked longitudinal furrows, and a tail-like prolongation one-third or one-fourth of its length. Aquatic; length 1-630″.

2. *P. longicauda* (Pl. 24. figs. 3 & 63) = *Euglena longicauda*, E.

3. *P. tripteris.* Aquatic.

4. *P. triquetra* = *Euglena triquetra*, E.

BIBL. Dujardin, *Infus.* p. 334.

PHÆONEMA, Kütz.—A genus of Phæonemeæ.

PHÆONEMEÆ, Kütz. — A family founded on obscure byssoid structures occurring in foul water.

BIBL. Kützing, *Phyc. Generalis*, p. 158; *Spec. Alg.* p. 160.

PHÆOSIPHONIA, Kütz.—A genus of Phæonemeæ.

PHÆOSPORÆ. — A name applied by Thuret to part of the Fucoideæ.

PHALLOIDEI.—A family of Gasteromycetous Fungi, characterized by the protrusion of a large clavate, columnar, stellate body, or globular, hollow, latticed framework, from the summit of the burst peridium. The basidiospores must be observed early here, as they fall off and form a deliquescent mass upon the hymenium when the sporange is mature. The fleshy structure protruded from the dehiscent capsule is composed of spherical cells very loosely connected; the peridium, which is very tough, is composed of closely packed, very slender, filamentous cells.

BIBL. Berkeley, *On the Fructification of Lycoperdon, Phallus, &c., Ann. Nat. Hist.* iv. 155; *Brit. Flor.* ii. pt. 2. p. 226; Rossmann, *Bot. Zeit.* xi. p. 185 (1853).

PHASCACEÆ.—A family of inoperculate Acrocarpous (terminal-fruited) Mosses, of minute dimensions, gregarious or cæspitose, with a simple or branched stem. Leaves oblong, oval, lanceolate or spathulate, concave, with a thick cylindrical nerve; the cells of the leaves parenchymatous, looser at the base, by degrees denser towards the summit, mostly papillose. Capsules mostly obliquely apiculate, with spores larger than in most Mosses, but not so large as in ARCHIDIUM. Columella soon vanishing in the smaller species.

British Genera.

1. *Acaulon.* Plants very dwarf, gregarious. Capsule contained in the closed perichæte. Calyptra mitre-shaped, dimidiate. Inflorescence monœcious (antheridia on a distinct branch at the base of the stem), or diœcious (antheridia terminal on a distinct plant), bud-like.

2. *Phascum.* Plants cæspitose. Perichæte open. Capsule on a longish stalk, and mostly obliquely apiculate. Calyptra dimidiate. Inflorescence monœcious (antheridia terminal in a bud on a distinct lateral branch, or naked and axillary on the fruit-bearing branch), or diœcious.

PHASCUM, L.—A genus of Phascaceæ (Acrocarpous Mosses), which is now subdivided variously by different authors. Wilson separates the earlier *Ph. alternifolium* only, under the name of *Archidium*; foreign authors further distinguish between PHASCUM, ACAULON, EPHEMERUM, and ASTOMUM. Species retained: *Ph. crispum,* Hedw.; *cuspidatum,* Schreb.; *curvicollum,* Hedw.; *rectum,* Smith; *bryoides,* Dicks. *Ph. cuspidatum* is very common on banks, and especially on a gravelly soil.

BIBL. Wilson, *Bryol. Brit.* 32; Hooker, *Brit. Fl.* ii. pt. 1. p. 6.

PHIALINA, Bory, Ehr.—A genus of Infusoria, of the family Trachelina.

Char. Body not ciliated, having a kind of neck crowned with cilia; mouth lateral, without teeth.

1. *P. viridis* (Pl. 24. fig. 61). Body oval, flask-shaped, green, suddenly narrowed in front and gradually behind; neck short. Aquatic; length 1-290″.

2. *P. vermicularis.* White; aquatic.

BIBL. Ehrenberg, *Infus.* p. 333.

PHILODINA, Ehr.—A genus of Rotatoria, of the family Philodinæa.

Char. Eyes two, cervical; tail-like foot with horn-like lateral processes.

Ehrenberg describes seven species; they are all aquatic, and in general structure and appearance closely resemble *Rotifer.*

P. erythrophthalma (Pl. 35. fig. 17). Colourless, smooth, eyes round, processes of foot short. Aquatic; length 1-120 to 1-50″.

P. roseola is reddish, and the eyes oval; *P. collaris* has a projecting cervical ring; *P. citrina* has the middle of the body yellowish; *P. macrostyla* has oblong eyes, and the foot-processes very long; in *P. megalotrocha* the eyes are oval, and the rotatory organs very large; and in *P. aculeata* the body is covered with soft setaceous processes.

BIBL. Ehrenberg, *Infus.* p. 498.

PHILODINÆA, Ehr.—A family of Rotatoria.

Char. No sheath or carapace; rotatory organs two, simple, resembling two wheels when the cilia are in motion.

The body is usually cylindrical, or some-

what spindle-shaped, contractile even so as to form a ball. In certain states of extension it sometimes appears pointed in front, from the presence of a proboscis; in others the two ciliated rotatory organs are protruded.

The animals are capable of swimming by means of the cilia, or of creeping like a leech, the ends of the body being alternately fixed. The tail-like foot is often furnished with horn-like lateral processes and terminal toes.

Ehrenberg distinguishes seven genera.

A. Eyes absent.
  α. Proboscis and horn-like lateral process on the foot present .... } 1. *Callidina.*
  β. Proboscis and horn-like processes absent........................ }
    a. Rotatory organ stalked .... 2. *Hydrias.*
    b. Rotatory organ not stalked .... 3. *Typhlina.*
B. Eyes present.
  Eyes two, frontal.
    Foot with horn-like processes.
      Toes two .... 4. *Rotifer.*
      Toes three .... 5. *Actinurus.*
    Foot without horn-like processes, but with two toes..... ..... } 6. *Monolabis.*
  Eyes two, cervical .... 7. *Philodina.*

BIBL. Ehrenberg, *Infus.* p. 481.

PHILOPTERUS, Nitzsch.—A genus of Anoplurous Insects, of the family Philopteridæ.

Char. Antennæ filiform, five-jointed; maxillary palpi none; mouth with strong toothed mandibles; tarsi with two claws.

The species are very numerous, and have been arranged in six subgenera: *Docophorus, Nirmus, Goniocotes, Goniodes, Lipeurus,* and *Ornithobius.* In some of them there are two moveable organs (trabeculæ) situated in front of the antennæ.

They are external parasites of birds.

P. (*Docophorus*) *communis* (Pl. 28. fig. 5). Chestnut-coloured, shining, with white hairs; head triangular, elongate, anterior portion much produced; trabeculæ very large, curved; posterior femora much incrassated and toothed below. Length 1-16″.

Parasitic upon the Passerina or Insessores.

BIBL. Denny, *Anoplur. Monogr.* p. 62.

PHLYCTÆNA, Desmaz.—A genus of Sphæronemei (ConiomycetousFungi), nearly related to *Septoria,* differing in the absence of a proper perithecium. *P. vagabunda* has been found in Britain.

BIBL. Berk. and Broome, *Ann. Nat. Hist.* 2nd ser. xiii. p. 460; Desmazières, *Ann. des Sc. Nat.* 3 sér. viii. p. 10.

PHLYCTÆNIA, Kg.—A genus of Diatomaceæ.

Char. Frustules those of *Navicula*, enclosed in gelatinous globular cells (masses ?). Marine.

1. *P. minuta.* Cells 1-720 to 1-240" in diameter; length of frustules 1-1200 to 1-600".

2. *P. maritima* (*Frustulia mar.*, E.).

BIBL. Kützing, *Sp. Alg.* p. 96; Ehrenberg, *Infus.* p. 232.

PHLYCTIDIUM, Not. See DISCOSIA.

PHOMA, Fr.—A genus of Sphæronemei (Coniomycetous Fungi), which presents both conidiiferous and ascigerous forms. There are numerous British species, forming small black or brown pustules upon dead leaves, twigs, &c. Tulasne regards this genus as formed by pycnidiiferous states of SPHÆRIA.

BIBL. Berk. *Brit. Flor.* ii. pt. 2. p. 285; *Ann. Nat. Hist.* vi. p. 263; 2 ser. v. p. 368, xiii. p. 459; Fries, *Summa Veg.* p. 421; Tulasne, *Ann. des Sc. Nat.* 4 sér. v. p. 115.

PHORMIDIUM, Kütz. See OSCILLATORIA.

PHORMIUM, Forst.—*P. tenax* is the name of the plant yielding New Zealand Flax. It is a Monocotyledonous Flowering Plant belonging to the order Liliaceæ.

PHOTOGRAPHY. — Microscopic objects may be photographed by the ordinary methods, especially by the collodion process, by arranging the microscope so as to form the optical part of a camera obscura. The old solar microscopes are examples of the principle of such an arrangement. Microscopic cameras have been constructed in which the lens is replaced by a fitting carrying achromatic objectives, with the rod bearing the stage and illuminating apparatus, as in the ordinary stands of compound microscopes. A simpler plan for those who possess a compound instrument and a camera, is to remove the lens of the latter and introduce into its place the eye-end (with the eye-piece removed) of the compound body, placed in a horizontal position; filling up the crevice all round with a piece of black velvet or cloth. Another method, which enables us to dispense with the camera, is to operate in a room darkened by a shutter having an orifice through which the sunlight may be reflected by a mirror placed outside, and received either directly or condensed by a bull's-eye, on the object lying on the stage of the compound microscope placed horizontally, with the eye-piece removed; a screen placed at a suitable distance from the eye-end of the tube receives the image. In operating with this screen, the object should be focused on a sheet of card, and then the light being shut off by covering the eye-end of the tube, a prepared paper or collodion plate be substituted exactly in the same place. Means must be used, by a black cloth or similar contrivance, to shut off all side light between the orifice of the shutter and the objective. In this last process, it is possible to obtain pictures with different parts of the object not lying in the same plane, by separate focusing, applying pieces of card suitably cut to shut off the image at different parts as required. With very minute objects and high powers, the achromatic condenser is used, as well as the bull's-eye.

It is well known that the correction of the objectives for perfect vision is not the best for photographic purposes. With high powers, as the 1-4" objective and upwards, the difference may be neglected, but with lower powers, an adjustment is required. Mr. Shadbolt finds it sufficient to withdraw the objective a little way, by the fine adjustment, from the object, and gives the following data for Smith and Beck's objectives: for the 4-10", withdraw the objective 1-1000"; for the 2-3", withdraw it 1-200"; for the 1½", withdraw it 1-150". Mr. Wenham prefers to place a doubly-convex lens in the place of the back stop of the objective, and advises for the 4-10" and 2-3" objectives, a lens of 5" focus; for the 1½" objective, a lens of 8" focus.

Microscopic photographs are best obtained with solar light; but artificial light has been used—camphene or gas for low powers, the oxyhydrogen light for high powers. A great point is to secure clean preparations, with the object sufficiently flat to allow of being clearly focused all over; this sets a limit to the utility of the process; further, certain objects in which red and yellow, or yellowish-brown colours exist, do not transmit the light, or only imperfectly. It will probably be advantageous to bleach many objects, as, for instance, insects and their parts, by long maceration in turpentine, sections of dark-coloured wood by nitric acid, &c., when they are intended to be photographed.

The purely photographic manipulation cannot be given here, but requires the ordinary skill in photography. Lengthened particulars respecting the application of photography to the microscope are contained in the papers referred to below.

BIBL. W. T. Kingsley, *Journ. Soc. Arts*, May 13, 1853; *Photo. Journal*, i. p. 93; Shadbolt, *Quart. Journ. Mic. Sc.* ii. p. 165; Highley, *ibid.* p. 158; Wenham, *Microsc. Trans.* 2 ser. iii. p. 1.

PHRAGMICOMA, Dumort.—A genus of Jungermannieæ (Hepaticæ), containing one British species, *P. Mackaii (Jung. Mackaii,* Hook.), occurring rarely on trees and rocks, especially on limestone.

BIBL. Hook. *Brit. Jung.* p. 53; Ekart, *Syn. Jung.* p. 59, pl. 9. fig. 72; Endlicher, *Gen. Plant.* Suppl. i. 472–9.

PHRAGMIDIUM, Lk. *(Aregma,* Fr.).— A genus of Uredinei (Coniomycetous Fungi), forming rusts very common on Rosaceous plants. They appear upon living leaves, breaking through from beneath the epidermis, and are chiefly distinguished from PUCCINIA by the number of spores, two to twelve, which are formed on one basidium. *P. bulbosum* is common, forming yellow and brown pulverulent spots on bramble-leaves (see UREDINEI).

Fig. 565.

Phragmidium bulbosum.

Isolated basidium with four catenate spores.

Mag. 100 diams.

BIBL. Berk. *(Aregma), Brit. Flor.* ii. pt. 2. p. 358; Grev. *Sc. Crypt. Flor.* pl. 15; Tulasne, *Ann. des Sc. Nat.* 4 sér. ii. p. 180, pl. 9; De Bary, *Brandpilze,* Berlin, 1853. p. 49, pl. 4; Fries, *Summa Veg.* p. 507; Currey, *Quart. Journ. Micr. Sc.* v. p. 117.

PHRAGMOTRICHACEI.—A family of Coniomycetous Fungi, growing on bark of trees, stems, or more or less dry herbaceous stems and leaves. Their conceptacles are of horny texture, and are little globular or cup-shaped bodies, lined with filaments terminating in simple or septate spores. [In *Excipula* they are membranous.] The conceptacles burst either by a longitudinal slit, or by several radiating slits, or by a circular slit which detaches a lid. In *Excipula* the spores are extruded in a gelatinous mass, but not in the other genera. The objects are perhaps mostly spermogonous forms of Ascomycetous Fungi.

British Genera.

1. *Endotrichum.* Conceptacle innate or immersed, bursting by a longitudinal slit; spores globular, simple.

2. *Schizothecium.* Conceptacle superficial, bursting laterally by a longitudinal slit; spores globular, simple.

3. *Pilidium.* Conceptacle simple, sessile, rounded, bursting from the centre to the margin in several teeth (by a stellate fission); spores spindle-shaped, simple.

4. *Excipula.* Conceptacle cup-shaped, membranous, sessile, naked; spores spindle-shaped.

5. *Dinemasporium.* Conceptacle cup-shaped, membranous, sessile, closed by villi, and at length open; sporigenous layer discoid, dissolving, covered with cylindrical, elongate, abruptly filiform spores.

6. *Myxormia.* Conceptacle thin, cup-shaped, open, formed of elongated cells. Pedicels of the spores delicate. Spores oblong, chained together, at length free, involved in mucus.

7. *Cystotricha.* Conceptacle bursting by a longitudinal slit; pedicels of the spores branched, articulated, somewhat beaded, forming here and there oblong multiseptate spores.

8. *Bloxamia.* Conceptacle very delicate, hyaline, the upper part evanescent, at length forming a rim. Spores quadrate, formed in closely-crowded tubules.

9. *Phraymotrichum.* Conceptacle horny-carbonaceous, breaking out, closed at first, subsequently splitting by a longitudinal fissure; fertile filaments intermixed with inarticulate paraphyses; spores compound and chained in series.

PHRAGMOTRICHUM, Kze.—A genus

Fig. 566.   Fig. 568.

Fig. 567.

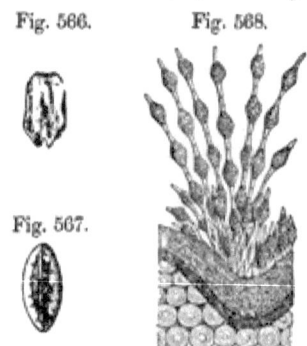

Phragmotrichum Chailletii.

Fig. 566. Scale of a spruce fir-cone, with pustules. Half nat. size.

Fig. 567. A pustule magnified 10 diameters.

Fig. 568. Vertical section across a pustule, showing the chains of spores. Magnified 100 diams.

of Phragmotrichacei (Coniomycetous Fungi). The plants form little tubercles bursting out from beneath the epidermis, and containing filaments arising from a softish fibrous stroma. The filaments (basidia) are interrupted at intervals with cellular spores (fig. 568), which ultimately separate. *P. Chailletii* grows upon the scales of the cones of *Abies excelsa.* Other species grow on the poplar and maple.

Bibl. Fries, *Syst. Myc.* iii. p. 492; *Summa Veg.* p. 474; Kunze, *Myc.* Heft 2. p. 84, pl. 5. fig. 4; Berk. *Crypt. Bot.* p. 327.

PHTHIRIUS, Leach.—A genus of Insects, of the order Anoplura, and family Pediculidæ.

Char. Legs of two kinds, anterior pair formed for walking, posterior two pairs formed for climbing; thorax large, not distinctly separated from the abdomen.

One species, *P. inguinalis* (*Pediculus pubis*). Parasitic upon man. Length 1-10 to 1-20".

The ova are firmly fastened to the hairs by a glutinous secretion; they are urnshaped, and furnished with a lid.

Bibl. Denny, *Anoplur. Monogr.* p. 8; Leach, *Zool. Misc.* iii. p. 65.

PHYCOMYCES, Kze.—A genus of Mucorini (Physomycetous Fungi), of which one species, *P. nitens,* has been found in Britain growing on the walls of oil-cellars. It is an olive-coloured mildew, distinguished from *Mucor* chiefly by the absence of a columella, the pyriform peridiole, and oblong spores; but the entire plants are much larger and of more solid texture. The fertile filaments of *P. splendens,* the only other known species, are as thick as a horse-hair, and 3 to 4" high.

Bibl. Fries, *Syst. Myc.* iii. p. 309; *Summa Veg.* 488; Berk. *Ann. Nat. Hist.* vi. p. 433.

PHYLLOGONIACEÆ. — A family of Pleurocarpous Mosses, distinguished by the peculiar character of the leaves and their arrangement. The leaves are either inserted horizontally or imbricated vertically, clasping, and are composed of very narrow linear parenchymatous cells, appearing almost confluent into a homogeneous membrane, auricled at the base, with minute, parenchymatous, thickened alar cells arranged orbicularly at the auricles, very smooth; the leaves stand in two opposite rows.

This family contains only the single small exotic genus Phyllogonium.

PHYLLOPHORA, Grev.—A genus of Cryptonemiaceæ (Florideous Algæ), consisting of several species, with a red, rigidly membranous, stalked, leaf-like, often dichotomous thallus, the lobes of which are often proliferous; from a few inches to a foot long, growing near low-water mark, or in the sea.

The fructification consists of—1. *favellidia,* scattered over the thallus, containing minute spores; 2. *antheridia,* wart-like bodies composed of radiating moniliform filaments found on distinct plants from the spores; and 3. *tetraspores,* collected into sori either towards the apex of the thallus or on proper lobes.

Bibl. Harvey, *Brit. Mar. Alg.* p. 142, pl. 18 A; *Phyc. Brit.* pl. 191, &c.; Greville, *Alg. Brit.* pl. 15; Derbès and Solier, *Ann. des Sc. Nat.* 3 sér. xiv. p. 277, pl. 37; Thuret, *ibid.* 4 sér. iii. p. 18.

PHYSACTIS, Kütz.—A genus of Oscillatoriaceæ (Confervoid Algæ), nearly related to *Rivularia,* perhaps improperly separated, consisting of aquatic and marine plants, growing on stones, &c., at first globose, and afterwards vesicular and lobed by peripheral growth, accompanied by gradual decay of the originally solid centre. Under this head are included—

1. *P.* (*Rivularia*) *nitida.* Deep olive-green, tufted and lobed, gregarious; fronds from 1-12 to 1" in diameter. (*R. bullata,* Berk.) Marine.

2. *P.* (*Riv.*) *plicata.* Diam. 1-12 to 1-2" in diameter; deep green. Marine.

3. *P.* (*Riv.*) *pisum.* Globose, dirty green, 1-12 to 1-2" in diameter. Aquatic.

Bibl.. Kütz. *Sp. Alg.* p. 332; *Tab. Phyc.* Bd. i. pl. 58, &c.; Hassall, *Br. Fr. Alg.* p. 262; Harvey, *Br. Mar. Alg.* p. 222; Berk. *Gleanings,* pl. 2. fig. 1.

Fig. 571.　　Fig. 569.　　Fig. 570.

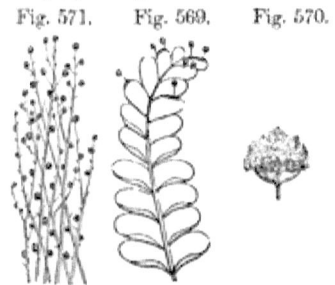

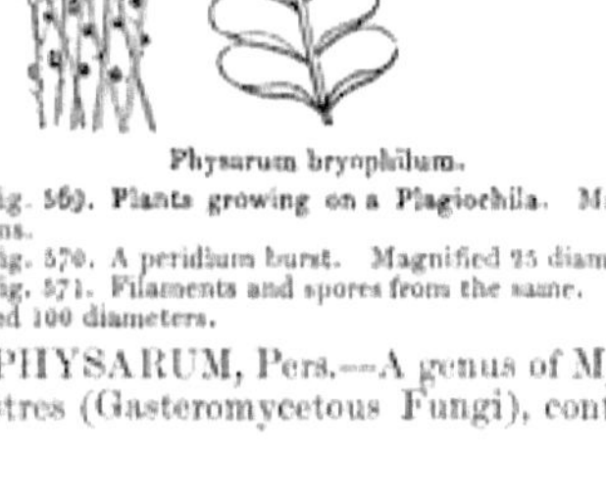

Physarum bryophilum.

Fig. 569. Plants growing on a Plagiochila. Magn. 2 diams.

Fig. 570. A peridium burst. Magnified 25 diameters.

Fig. 571. Filaments and spores from the same. Magnified 100 diameters.

PHYSARUM, Pers.—A genus of Myxogastres (Gasteromycetous Fungi), containing numerous species growing on rotten wood, bark, leaves, &c. They are nearly related to *Didymium* and *Diderma*, but have a simple membranous peridium; the filaments are adnate to the peridium, but in some spores they are very few, approaching to the condition of *Licea*. Some are sessile, others stipitate (fig. 509); the clustered forms (*P. hyalinum* and *utriculatum*) are removed to Berkeley's genus BADHAMIA. *P. album* is common.

BIBL. Berk. *Brit. Flor.* ii. pt. 2. p. 314; *Mag. Zool. and Bot.* i. p. 49; *Ann. Nat. Hist.* vi. p. 431, 2nd ser. xiii. p. 159; Fries, *System. Myc.* iii. p. 127; *Summa Veg.* p. 153; Greville, *Sc. Crypt. Fl.* pl. 40. 310.

PHYSCIA. See BORRERA.

PHYSCOMITRIUM, Bridel.—A genus of Funariaceæ (Acrocarpous Mosses), including many *Gymnostoma* of other authors. *Physcomitrium pyriforme*, Brid. = *Gymnostomum pyriforme*, Hedw. *Ph. sphæricum* is remarkable as having been found only in one year in one locality in Britain.

This species exhibits a pretty structure in a vertical section of the immature capsule, the mass of sporiferous tissue being suspended freely in the middle by cellular threads.

PHYSIOTIUM, Nees.—A genus of Jungermannieæ (Hepaticæ), containing one species, *P. cochleariforme*, a large plant, growing in purple tufts 4 to 6" long, on moors and among rocks in Ireland and the Scotch highlands.

BIBL. Hook. *Brit. Flor.* ii. pt. 1. p. 119; *Br. Jung.* p. 68; *Engl. Bot.* pl. 2500; Ekart, *Synops. Jung.* pl. 5. fig. 40; Endlicher, *Gen. Plant.* Suppl. 1. nos. 472–18.

PHYSOMYCETES.—An order of Fungi composed of microscopic plants of very simple organization, the mycelium being a byssoid or flocculent mass, bearing simple vesicular sporanges (*peridiola*) filled with minute spores. The nature of the membranous wall of the peridioles is not yet well ascertained in all the genera, some authors describing it as merely a veil, others as a perfect sac formed by the expansion of the terminal cell of the filament, which is certainly true in *Mucor*. According to our own observations, the spores are formed by free-cell formation in the peridiole, which ultimately bursts to discharge the spores.

The distinction between the two families seems to depend chiefly on the conditions of the peridioles; but it seems doubtful whether the Antennariei can stand;

ANTENNARIA seems to be merely a form of CAPNODIUM, and PISOMYXA and PLEUROPYXIS are obscure objects of which little is known.

In the Antennariei, the peridioles are sessile on radiating flocci, which sometimes send processes which grow up and surround them, or they are attached to the sides of erect filaments; these filaments form whitish or greyish patches, on the leaves of trees and herbs, bearing a close external resemblance to *Erysiphe*.

The Mucorini are moulds growing on decaying organic matter, the mycelium constituting flocks floating in liquids or overgrowing damp substances, while the delicate spore-sacs or peridioles are borne at the apices of erect stalk-like and often extremely branched filaments. The genus *Syzygites* exhibits a remarkable peculiarity, according to Ehrenberg; for he states that each spore-sac is formed by means of the conjugation of two branches of the ramified fructification (see SYZYGITES).

The later researches on the plants of this group seem to indicate that, as in most of the Fungal Orders, much remains to be cleared up concerning the relations of the forms. See on this subject the article EUROTIUM, which genus, according to De Bary's researches, is associated as merely a second form of fructification, with ASPERGILLUS, upon the same mycelium: recent observations lead us to doubt the accuracy of these views; but this genus should, we think, stand among the PERISPORACEI.

Synopsis of the Families.

1. ANTENNARIEI. Mycelium filamentous, radiating, or erect, bearing sessile, globular, membranous sacs (*peridioles*), filled with ovate spores, discharged by the rupture of the sac at its apex.

2. MUCORINI. Mycelium filamentous, vague, giving off erect simple or branched filaments terminating in vesicular cells (*peridioles*) filled with minute spores; often with a central column in the interior.

BIBL. See the genera. *families*

PHYTELEPHAS, R. and P.—The generic name of the Palm yielding the VEGETABLE IVORY nut.

PHYTOCRENE, Wallich.—An Artocarpaceous tree with wood of very remarkable structure. See WOOD.

PIGGOTIA, Berk. and Broome. — A genus of Sphæronemei (Coniomycetous

Fungi), or perhaps the conidiiferous form of *Dothidea*. *P. astroidea* occurs on the green leaves of the elm, forming irregular round-ish, granulated or wrinkled jet-black patches (sometimes with a yellow border) on the upper surface of the leaf. Perithecia soon confluent, bursting by a lacerated fissure.

BIBL. Berk. and Br., *Ann. Nat. Hist.* 2 ser. vii. p. 95, pl. 5. fig. 1.

PIGMENT. See INTRODUCTION, p. xxix.

PILACRE, Fr.—A genus of Trichogas-tres (Gasteromycetous Fungi).

BIBL. Berk. and Br., *Ann. Nat. Hist.* 2nd ser. v. p. 365, pl. 11.

PILEOLARIA, Cast. See UROMYCES.

PILOBOLUS, Tode.—A genus of Mu-corini (Physomycetous Fungi), consisting of little moulds growing upon dung; bear-ing some resemblance in their structure to *Botrydium* among the Algæ. The plants have a stoloniferous creeping mycelium, from which arise fertile pedicels, each cut off from the mycelium by a septum; the upper part of the pedicel expands into the vesicle, which also becomes shut off by a septum; in the vesicle or peridiole, spores are next developed by free-cell formation, and at the same time the septum becomes pushed up into its interior (as in MUCOR) to form a columella, which ultimately causes the vesicular peridiole to split off by a cir-cumscissile dehiscence just above the sep-tum; it is thrown off with elasticity, en-closing the spores. The development of *P. crystallinus* has been studied by Cohn and Bail. They find the germinating spore to produce a creeping unicellular mycelial por-tion, and next a fruit-pedicel, which soon has the peridiole separated by a septum: thus, in its simplest form, this plant consists of only three cells; subsequently it becomes complex by the root-cell or mycelium pro-ducing numerous stolons. *P. crystallinus* is yellowish at first, the peridiole finally black. *P. roridus*, Bolt., a doubtful species, is smaller and more slender than the last, having an elongated filiform stem.

BIBL. Berk. *Brit. Fl.* ii. pt. 2. p. 231; Fries, *Summa Veg.* p. 487; Cohn, *Nova Acta*, xxiii. p. 492; T. Bail, *Bot. Zeitung*, xiii. p. 630; Currey, *Journ. Linn. Society*, Botany, i. p. 162.

PILOTRICHUM, Pal. de Beauv.—A genus of Hypnoid Mosses, including some *Fontinales* of authors.

1. *Pilotrichum antipyreticum*, C. Müll. = *Fontinalis antipyretica*, L.

2. *P. squamosum*, C. Müll. = *F. squamosa*, L.

3. *P. ciliatum*, C. Müll. = *Anœctangium ciliatum*, Brid., var. γ. *striatum* = *A. ciliatum*, Wilson.

4. *P. heteromallum*, P. d. B. = *Daltonia heteromalla*, H. and T.

PILULARIA, L.—A genus of Marsile-aceous Plants, containing the only British representative of the order—*P. globulifera* (fig. 574). This is an inconspicuous plant growing in mud at the edges of or in pools, having a filiform creeping stem, bearing erect filiform green leaves and delicate ad-ventitious roots, and producing shortly-stalked globular spore-fruits, about the size of a peppercorn. The anatomical structure of the stem and leaves is simple: they are clothed with an epidermis possessing sto-mata; and a cross-section both of the stem and the leaves exhibits a central vascular bundle (of spiral vessels) surrounded by a sheath of brownish cells, while in the deli-cate cellular tissue intervening between the central bundle and the epidermis stands a circle of air-passages separated from each other by simple radiating cellular septa.

Fig. 572.   Fig. 573.

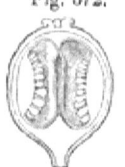 

Pilularia globulifera.

Fig. 572. A vertical section of a spore-fruit. Magni-fied 5 diameters.

Fig. 573. Transverse section of a spore-fruit. Magni-fied 5 diameters.

The spore-fruits are hollow cases with an outer tough cellular coat, and an inner more delicate coat dipping in at four perpendicular lines, as far as the centre, so as to form dissepiments dividing the fruit into four chambers (figs. 572, 573); up the centre of the outer wall of each chamber runs a raised ridge (a kind of placenta), whence arise the sporanges or *thecæ* (fig. 573). These are pear-shaped sacs composed of a very deli-cate cellular membrane. Those in the upper part of each chamber contain a number of minute globular bodies, resembling pollen-grains, immersed in a gelatinous liquid. The sacs in the lower part of the chamber contain only one body or spore, but this of very peculiar form; it nearly fills the theca, is somewhat oval in form, and possesses seve-ral coats.

2 N

The development of the spores, as described by Valentine, is very curious; the small spores are developed in the usual way, by the formation of parent-cells in the theca, which parent-cells subsequently each produce four spores. In the thecæ which have the single large spore, a number of parent-cells are originally produced, and these become divided into four chambers by septa; but then all but one of these decay. This produces four spores; but out of these four only one attains to perfect development, the rest being subsequently dissolved and absorbed to make room for the solitary large spore. This reminds us in some degree of the numerous germs formed in the Gymnosperms (OVULE) and subsequently absorbed. The two kinds of spore in *Pilularia* correspond to the two forms in SELAGINELLA and ISOËTES, and to the pollen and ovules of the Flowering Plants. They are set free by the dehiscence of the spore-fruit,

and lie at first imbedded in the jelly poured out by the thecæ.

In this state the small spores exactly resemble pollen-grains, having an outer granular, and an inner delicately membranous coat,—the outer coat presenting ridges corresponding to the points of contact in the parent-cell. When set free, the spores soon burst at these ridges, and the inner coat is slightly protruded; this next bursts and discharges a number of lenticular cellules, from each of which escapes a ciliated spiral spermatozoid.

The mature large spores (fig. 575) are of oval form, and have a thick outer gelatinous coat composed of prismatic cells standing perpendicularly on an inner glassy coat; the gelatinous coat is perforated at the summit by a funnel-shaped opening through which protrudes a pyramidal elevation of the second glassy coat; the last is lined by a delicate internal coat containing protoplasm,

Fig. 574.   Fig. 575.    Fig. 578.

Fig. 576.

Fig. 577.

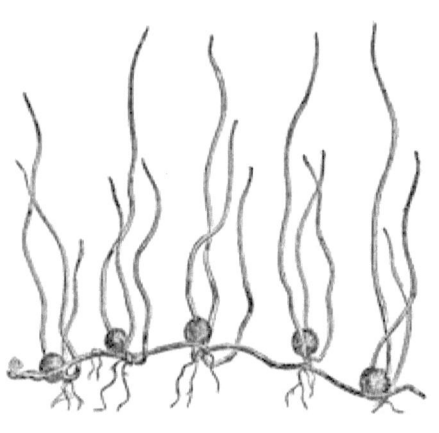

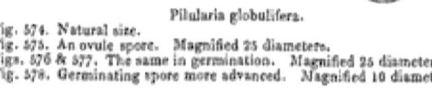

Pilularia globulifera.

Fig. 574. Natural size.
Fig. 575. An ovule spore. Magnified 25 diameters.
Figs. 576 & 577. The same in germination. Magnified 25 diameters.
Fig. 578. Germinating spore more advanced. Magnified 10 diameters.

starch, oil-globules, &c. Soon after the expulsion of the spore, cell-formation takes place inside the pyramidal protrusion of the outer coat, from the cell-contents of the spore. The glassy coat next splits at this point into four teeth, and exposes the cellular structure (*prothallium*), which increases in

size, and acquires a green colour. An archegonium is next formed on this, consisting of a cell (embryo-sac) lying in the substance at the apex, with a canal bordered by four papillose cells leading to it. A spermatozoid fertilizes the free embryo-cell contained in the archegonium; and this becomes developed into a new plant within the substance of the prothallium (fig. 577), sending out a leaf on one side and an adventitious root on the other, tangentially to the surface of the spore. In this stage (fig. 578) the young plant, with the remains of the spore, somewhat resembles a germinating Monocotyledonous seed. Finally, as the young plant increases in size, the remnants of the spore-coat are thrown off.

BIBL. G. W. Bischoff, *Krypt. Gewächse, Rhizocarpeen*, Nuremberg, 1828, pl. 8; Valentine, *Linnean Trans.* xvii.; Schleiden, *Grundzüge*, 3 ed. ii. p. 104 (*Principles*, p. 203); Nägeli, *Zeitschr. f. wiss. Botanik*, Hefte iii. & iv. p. 188 (*Ann. des Sc. Nat.* 3 sér. ix. p. 99); Hofmeister, *Vergleichend. Untersuch.* Leipsic, 1851. p. 103, pls. 21, 22; Mettenius, *Beitr. z. Kenntn. der Rhizocarp.* Frankfort, 1846; Henfrey, *Ann. Nat. Hist.* 2 ser. ix. p. 447; *Trans. Brit. Assoc.* 1851. p. 116.

PINE-APPLE. See BROMELIACEÆ.

PINNULARIA, Ehr.—A genus of Diatomaceæ.

Char. Frustules single, free, longer than broad; front view linear or oblong; valves navicular, elliptical, lanceolate or oblong (side view), with a median line, and a nodule at the centre and at each end, surface exhibiting transverse or slightly radiating striæ or furrows.

This genus differs from *Navicula* in the striæ not being resolvable into dots. They are mostly distinct under ordinary illumination. In some of the species they are absent in the middle, leaving a transverse clear space or band, resembling in appearance the stauros of *Stauroneis*.

Twenty-four British species (Smith).

1. *P. nobilis* (Pl. 11. fig. 1, side view). Valves linear, dilated in the middle and at the rounded ends; striæ coarse. Aquatic and fossil; length 1-100 to 1-70″.

2. *P. viridis* (Pl. 11. fig. 2, side view). Valves elliptical, somewhat turgid, ends obtuse. Aquatic; length 1-500 to 1-220″. Common.

β. Striæ parallel, absent from a transverse band.

3. *P. oblonga* (Pl. 11. fig. 3, side view). Valves linear-oblong, ends rounded. Aquatic and fossil; length 1-120″. Common.

4. *P. radiosa* (Pl. 11. fig. 4, side view; fig. 5, front view). Valves lanceolate, ends somewhat obtuse. Aquatic; length 1-500″. Common.

BIBL. Smith, *Brit. Diatom.* i. p. 54.

PINUS, L.—A genus of Coniferæ (Gymnospermous Flowering plants), presenting many interesting points of structure. The most familiar example is the Scotch Fir (*P. sylvestris*); but a great number of other species are cultivated in this country. For the microscope they yield instructive objects.—in the wood (Pl. 39. fig. 1), composed of peculiarly pitted cells (see CONIFERÆ) and traversed by turpentine reservoirs; in the BARK, which has a kind of false cork; in the development of the Gymnospermous OVULES, and in the structure of the POLLEN-grains.

The wood of species of the genus *Pinus* frequently occurs in a fossil condition, both in coal and silicified (Pl. 19. figs. 29-33).

BIBL. See the articles above cited.

PISOMYXA, Corda (*Bryocladium*, Kze.).—A genus of Antennarei (Physomycetous

Fig. 579.

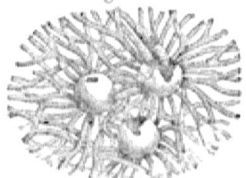

Pisomyxa racodioides.
Magnified 200 diameters.

Fungi), growing upon leaves. Nothing is known of this plant except Corda's description and figure.

BIBL. Fries, *Summa Veg.* p. 406; Corda, *Icones Fung.* i. pl. 6. fig. 292.

PISTILLIDIUM = ARCHEGONIUM, the female reproductive organ of the higher Cryptogamia.

PITH. See MEDULLA.

PITTED STRUCTURES OF PLANTS.—The secondary deposits of cellulose which form the layers of thickening of the walls of vegetable cells are seldom uniform or homogeneous in character. In most, if not in all cases, some special microscopic structure may be distinguished, either by mere inspection or on the application of reagents. These layers, spoken of more particularly as to their nature under SECONDARY DEPOSITS, may be divided into two classes, comprehending pretty accurately all the varied conditions, namely, the *Spiral deposits*, where the secondary layers assume the aspect of fibres applied upon the inside of the cell-wall; and *Pitted* or, as they are often

2 N 2

termed, *Porous deposits*, where layers are applied over the whole internal surface of the cell, which layers present orifices of different characters, leaving the primary membrane bare, and forming in this way a *pit* as viewed from the inside of the cell. When the secondary layers are comparatively thin, their presence is often overlooked; and the pits have thus often been mistaken for orifices or *pores* (figs. 580, 581) in the primary

Fig. 580.   Fig. 581.

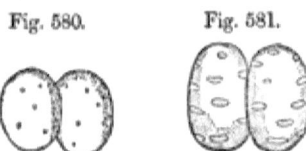

Pitted cells of elder pith.

Magnified 250 diameters.

membrane; but such pores are never originally present; the closure of the pit by the layer of primary membrane may always be demonstrated in young structures; and when orifices really do occur in cell-walls, these arise from the absorption of the primary cell-membrane converting the pit into a pore. The best way of demonstrating that young spotted cell-walls are only pitted and not perforated, is to apply sulphuric acid and iodine for the production of the blue colour in the primary cell-wall.

Simple pits, of no great depth, occur on the slightly thickened walls of most permanent parenchymatous cells; they may be seen in the cells of herbaceous stems, in pith, bark, in the cells of the parenchyma of leaves, &c. (figs. 580, 581; Pl. 38. fig. 14).

In most prosenchymatous wood-cells, or liber-cells, and in the woody cells of the stones or shells of fruits and seeds, the pits are far more clearly evident, and become more and more distinct (Pl. 39. fig. 3) as the layers of thickening increase in number, since by the successive application of these, the pits are deepened (with the contraction of the cavity of the cell) until they become canals or tubular passages radiating from the central cavity (Pl. 38. fig. 23). In these cases it is evidently seen that the pits of adjacent cells and ducts correspond to each other at their outer extremity; and in old tissues, when the primary cell-walls have been absorbed, these coincident pits form tubular canals leading from one cell to another. It has been observed that two or more pits sometimes become confluent in

the later internal deposits, so that the internally simple orifice leads out to several branches corresponding to the original pits on the wall of the cell. In rare cases, simple pits occur on the outer walls of epidermal cells, as in *Cycas* (Pl. 38. fig. 28).

Pits of the above kinds occur on the structures called ducts (see TISSUES, VEGETABLE), formed of cells applied end to end and confluent (fig. 181, page 238). These large pitted tubes, which occur abundantly in most woods, with the exception of that of the Coniferæ, are sometimes termed *bothrenchyma*, signifying *pitted tissue*; but the character not being exclusively applicable to them, the name is bad.

In many pitted ducts, and in the pitted

Fig. 582.   Fig. 583.

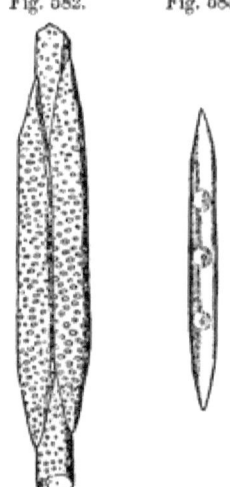

Fig. 582. Pitted ducts of Clematis. Magn. 100 diam.
Fig. 583. Side wall of a cell of Pine, with bordered pits. Magnified 200 diameters.

wood-cells of many plants, especially of the Coniferæ, the pits present a greater degree of complication. The markings on the walls of the wood-cells of most of the Coniferæ, for example, consist of pits surrounded by a broad rim (fig. 583; Pl. 39. figs. 1, 4, 5); the portion within the rim projects somewhat into the cavity of the cell, and appears like a lenticular body attached on the wall; hence the markings were formerly termed the "glands" of Coniferous wood. In reality, however, while the pits themselves resemble ordinary pits, the broad rim, or rather the circular line outside the pit, depends on a condition of the cell-wall outside the membrane, and is merely the outline of a lenti-

Fig. 584.

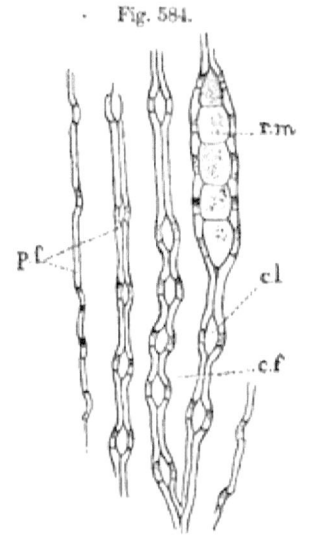

Section of Pine wood at right angles to the pitted walls. *p. f*, walls of a pitted cell ; *c. f*, cavity of a cell ; *c. l*, lenticular cavity between two adjacent pits ; *r. m*, cells of a medullary ray, the pits have no rim here.

Magnified 400 diameters.

cular cavity existing between two adjacent cells, the boundary of which is visible through the wall on account of the transparency of the latter : the nature of this structure is very evident in sections made at right angles to those which show the bordered pits in face (fig. 584 ; Pl. 39. fig. 1 *b*). In most of the Coniferæ the wood is exclusively composed of large elongated prosenchymatous cells, with bordered pits of this character on the side-walls, that is, on the wall standing radially or perpendicular to the bark ; the pits, however, which lie on parts of the wall adjoining the cells of medullary rays, are generally devoid of the rim.

Similar bordered pits occur very generally on the walls of the pitted ducts of Dicotyledons ; but as the wood is here of mixed composition, and the ducts adjoin cells as well as other ducts, independently of the medullary rays, we often find a greater variety of conditions on the wall of the same

duct, which may have bordered pits when adjoining another duct, and simple pits, or pits with a double outline, when adjoining cells. The pits with a double outline (Pl. 39. figs. 15 *b*, & 20) are of different nature from the bordered pits (Pl. 39. figs. 13, 14, 15 *a*, 16, 18), the double outline depending simply on the fact that the later or more internal layers of thickening do not reach the edge of the orifice in the earlier secondary deposits, so that the pit is conical, or rather has sloping edges, the circumference at the primary membrane being rather less than that of the margin next the cell cavity. A peculiar modification of this unequal mode of deposit is seen in company with the true rim or border in many cases (Pl. 39. figs. 14, 16, 18), where the central spot or original pit appears in the middle of a slit running across the circle indicating the border ; this slit indicates the alteration of the shape of the gap in the secondary deposits in the successive layers, and corresponds to the inner margin of the pit, where this has the form of an elongated groove or slit, gradually diminishing to a small round hole towards the primary cell-membrane (Pl. 39. fig. 18 *a*). Sometimes (Pl. 39. fig. 18 *a*, *b*) the two or more slits formed in this way on contiguous pits become confluent. The last condition indicates a transition to the more sparing form of the secondary deposit where it appears as a modification of a spiral fibre or fibres ; and the later secondary deposits of pitted ducts do sometimes actually assume this form, and produce a spiral fibrous layer of thickening inside the layers perforated by pits. This is the case in TAXUS (Pl. 39. fig. 4), in the Lime (Pl. 39. fig. 13), and Mezereon (Pl. 39. fig. 19 *b*), &c.

Hartig and Von Mohl have recently described a peculiar kind of pitted tissue formed of cells, which the former calls *Siebröhren*, the latter *clathrate cells*. They are thin-walled cells occurring associated with the prosenchymatous liber-cells of Dicotyledons, and as forming part of the *vasa propria* of Monocotyledons, having their walls marked with large shallow pits, the membrane of the pits being again very finely punctate or reticulated. Hartig thinks the fine punctations are holes ; Von Mohl doubts this ; but as the points are not more than 1-1000" in diameter, it is difficult to decide this question.

For the guidance of microscopic observers, we may furnish a series of examples in addition to the CONIFERÆ (Pl. 39. figs. 1, 4, 5).

of different kinds of marking on pitted cells and ducts.

A. *Forms where there is no spiral-fibrous secondary deposit.*

a. Bordered pits uniformly distributed, without reference to adjacent structures: *Eleagnus acuminatus, Clematis Vitalba* (Pl. 39. fig. 18).

b. Bordered pits fewer on the walls adjoining cells: *Acacia lophantha, Sophora japonica.*

c. Bordered pits on the walls adjoining ducts, while the walls adjoining wood-cells have few or no bordered pits, and those next the medullary rays have pits without a border: elder, beech, hazel, poplar, alder, plane, apple, &c.

d. Bordered pits on the walls adjoining ducts, but with large pits devoid of a border where adjoining cells: *Cassytha glabella* (Pl. 39. fig. 14), *Bombax pentandrum* (Pl. 39. fig. 15).

e. A modification of the last, where the bordered pits have the form of slits as wide as the ducts when adjoining ducts, while the walls adjoining cells have large pits without a border: *Chilianthus arboreus* (Pl. 39. fig. 17); the vine (in a less striking manner). *Eryngium maritimum* (Pl. 39. fig. 21) exhibits a condition approaching this.

f. Clathrate cells, large thin-walled cells with round, oval, or elongated thinner places (pits) on their walls, the membrane of the pit being finely reticulated or perforated like a sieve. These are found in the liber of Dicotyledons, as in Bignonia, the lime, the vine, elder, pear, &c., and in the central part of the vascular bundles of Monocotyledons, as *Musa, Asparagus,* &c.

B. *Forms where a spiral-fibrous structure is added after the pits.*

g. All the ducts with bordered pits, but the larger ducts with smooth walls, the smaller with a spiral fibre: *Clematis Vitalba, Ulmus campestris, Morus alba.*

h. All the ducts closely pitted, with slender fibres between the rows of pits: *Hakea oleifolia.*

i. The larger ducts with pits, the smaller without; both kinds with spiral fibres on the internal surface: *Daphne Mezereum* (Pl. 39. fig. 19), *Passerina filiformis, Genista canariensis.*

j. The walls adjacent to other ducts pitted, those next cells with very distant pits, or devoid of them; all the walls with fibres: the lime, horse-chestnut, sycamore, cornel, holly, hawthorn, *Prunus Padus, P. virginiana,* &c.

The last set of forms allies these structures to those characterized peculiarly by the SPIRAL-fibrous STRUCTURES; and, as will be indicated there and under SECONDARY DEPOSITS, the smooth layers of thickening, such as those between the pits of *Pinus,* may be made to show a spiral structure by the action of reagents.

For the micro-chemical conditions of these objects, their development and relations, see SECONDARY DEPOSITS; TISSUES, Vegetable: and CELL, Vegetable.

BIBL. Works on Structural Botany; Mohl, *Vegetable Cell,* London, 1852, p. 10; and *Vermischte Schrift.* Tubingen, 1845, pp. 268, 272 (*Linnæa,* xvi. p. 1. 1842), transl. in *Ann. Nat. Hist.* ix. p. 393; *Abh. d. Acad. zu München,* i. 445; *Bot. Zeitung,* xiii. p. 873; and the *Bibl.* of SPIRAL STRUCTURES.

PLAGIOCHILA, Nees and Montagne. —A genus of Jungermanniæ (Hepaticæ), containing a number of British species, viz. *P.* (*Jungermannia,* Hook.) *asplenoides, spinulosa, decipiens, resupinata, undulata, planifolia, nemorosa,* and *umbrosa,* some of which, especially *P. asplenoides* (fig. 585), are among the most frequent and finest plants of the family, its stems growing from 3 to 5″ long.

Fig. 585.

Plagiochila asplenoides.
Magnified 2 diameters.

BIBL. Hook. *Brit. Flor.* ii. pt. 1. p. 111, &c.; *Brit. Jung.* pls. 13, 14, &c.; Ekart, *Synops. Jung.* p. 6 *et seq.* pl. 1, &c.; Endlicher, *Gen. Plant.* Supp. I. No. 473-1.

PLANARIA, Müll.—A genus of Annulata, of the order Turbellaria, and family Planarieæ.

Char. Body soft, flattened, oblong or oval, not jointed, covered with vibratile cilia; neither suckers, bristles, nor leg-like appendages present.

Some parts of the structure of these animals have been noticed under ANNULATA in speaking of the Turbellaria. The mouth is situated on the under surface of the middle of the body, at the end of a retractile proboscis; there is no anus; the mouth leads to a capacious stomach, giving off dendritically branched cæca, somewhat as in one joint of a *Tænia* (Pl. 16. fig. 14). Their motion is continuous and gliding, upon water plants, or the sides of glass jars. The anterior part of the body exhibits a curved row or a single pair of eyes, and sometimes ear-like projections. They multiply by division, and the formation of ova, which are enclosed in a coloured capsule.

Some of the species are very common in pools, and resemble, at first sight, minute leeches. *P. nigra*, which is black, has a row of marginal anterior eyes, and two lateral and one mesial projections; length about 1-2″. *P. brunnea*, dusky-brown, with a dark mesial line; eyes as above; length rather less. *P. lactea*, cream-coloured, tinged with pale reddish brown, truncate in front, with two slight lateral auricles; eyes two or four; length 1-2 to 3-4″. *P. torra*, grey or black; obtuse in front, angles rounded, centre projecting; eyes two, with a white halo; length 1-2″. Of the other species some are marine.

BIBL. Johnston, *Non-parasitical Worms*; Dugès, *Ann. des Sc. Nat.* 2 sér. xv. and xxi.; Œrsted, *System. Eintheil. d. Plattwürmer*; Diesing, *Syst. Helminth.*; Dalyell, *Powers of Creation*, ii.; Schultz, *Naturg. Turbell.*

PLANARIOLA, Duj.—A genus of Infusoria.

Char. Body lamelliform, oblong, variously sinuous and folded at the margin, convex and glabrous above, concave and ciliated beneath.

This genus is placed among the unsymmetrical Infusoria, and has been provisionally founded to contain animals much resembling *Planariæ* in aspect and consistence, but without a mouth or any other external orifice, and only ciliated on the under surface.

P. rubra (Pl. 24. fig. 65). Red, granular, narrowed behind, enlarged in front, and with two ear-like folds. Aquatic, in decomposing vegetable matter; length 1-250″.

BIBL. Dujardin, *Infus.* p. 568.

PLANORBULINA, D'Orb.—A genus of Foraminifera, of the order Helicostegia, and family Turbinoidæ.

Char. Shell fixed, spiral, discoidal, greatly depressed; spire irregular; convolutions very numerous; in the same plane, apparent on both sides; chambers convex above, flat beneath, and moulded upon the body to which the shell is attached; orifice semi-

lunar, next the return of the spire. Foramina coarse.

P. mediterranensis or *vulgaris* (Pl. 44. fig. 29). British; recent and fossil.

BIBL. That of the order.

PLANTAIN. See MUSA.

PLATINUM. — The sodio-chloride of platinum crystallizes in prisms and plates which polarize light; while the potassio-chloride of platinum yields several forms, which do not polarize light. This reaction of the soda-salt has been proposed as a means of distinguishing soda from potash, or detecting minute quantities of the former.

BIBL. Andrews, *Chem. Gaz.* 1852. x. 378.

PLATYGRAMMA, Meyer.—A genus of Graphideæ (Gymnocarpous Lichens), containing two British species.

BIBL. Leighton, *Ann. Nat. Hist.* 2 ser. xiii. p. 393.

PLATYZOMA, R. Brown.—A genus of Gleichenæous Ferns. Exotic.

PLEOPELTIS, Humb. and Bonpl.—An exotic genus of Polypodieæ (Polypodioid

Fig. 586.

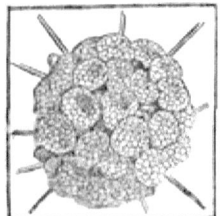

Fig. 587.

Pleopeltis nuda.

Fig. 586. A sorus seen from above.

Fig. 587. Vertical section of ditto.

Magnified 25 diameters.

Ferns), remarkable for the presence of peculiarly formed so-called paraphyses in the sori, performing the function of an indusium. These bodies are peltate, or like minute flat mushrooms or umbrellas expanded over and sheltering the sporanges (figs. 586, 587).

PLEUROCARPI.—MOSSES with lateral fruits.

PLEUROCARPUS, Al. Braun.—A genus of Zygnemeæ.

BIBL. Al. Braun, *Alg. Unicell.* p. 60. note.

PLEUROCOCCUS, Menegh.—A form of *Protococcus*.

PLEURODESMIUM, Kg.—A genus of Diatomaceæ, allied to *Striatella*; but the characters given are very obscure. Marine. Africa.

BIBL. Kützing, *Bot. Zeit.* 1846. p. 248; *Sp. Alg.* p. 115.

PLEUROGRAMMA, Presl.—A genus of Tænitideæ (Polypodioid Ferns). Exotic.

PLEURONEMA, Duj.—A genus of Infusoria, of the family Paramecina.

Char. Body oblong-oval, depressed, with a broad lateral orifice, from which a bundle of long, curved, floating and contractile ciliary filaments issues.

1. *P. chrysalis (crassa)*, D. = *Paramecium chrysalis*, E. (Pl. 24. fig. 66). Aquatic.

2. *P. marina*, D. Has the body somewhat narrower than the last, and is pointed in front. Marine.

BIBL. Dujardin, *Infus.* p. 473.

PLEUROPYXIS, Corda.—A genus of Antennarei (Physomycetous Fungi), grow-

Fig. 588.

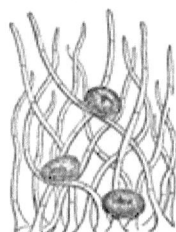

Pleuropyxis microsperma.
Magnified 200 diameters.

ing upon leaves and stems. This and PISOMYXA are imperfectly known.

BIBL. Corda, *Icon. Fung.* pl. 6. fig. 291.

PLEUROSIGMA, Smith. See GYROSIGMA.

PLEUROTROCHA, Ehr.—A genus of Rotatoria, of the family Hydatinæa.

Char. Eyes none; a single tooth in each jaw; foot forked (= *Hydatina* with unidentate jaws).

P. gibba (Pl. 35. fig. 18). Body ovate-oblong, truncate in front; toes small, turgid. Aquatic; length 1-216″.

Other species.

BIBL. Ehrenberg, *Infus.* p. 418; Gosse. *Ann. Nat. Hist.* 1851. viii. 199.

PLEUROXUS, Baird.—A genus of Entomostraca, of the order Cladocera, and family Lynceidæ.

Char. Anterior part of shell prominent above, obliquely truncate below; first pair of legs very large; beak sharp, curved downwards. Aquatic.

1. *P. trigonellus* (Pl. 14. fig. 32). Beak long, sharp-pointed, slightly curved downwards; inferior antennæ short and slender, anterior branch with four setæ, one from the first joint, one from the second, and two from the last; posterior branch with three setæ all arising from the last joint.

2. *P. uncinatus.* Beak curved upwards at the end; three sharp spines at the anterior inferior angle of the shell; inferior antennæ as the last.

3. *P. hamatus.* Beak blunt and strong, slightly curved downwards; first pair of legs with a curved claw at the end. ?Male of *P. trigonellus.*

BIBL. Baird, *Brit. Entomostr.* p. 134.

PLOCAMIUM, Lamouroux.—A genus of Delesseriaceæ (Florideous Algæ), containing one species, *P. coccineum*, the commonest of our red sea-weeds, with a delicate flat feathery thallus, from 2 to 12″ high, growing in bushy tufts on rocks or other Algæ. The fruit consists of—1. *coccidia*, spherical, stalked or sessile tubercles, at the sides or in the axils of the ramules, filled with angular spores; 2. *antheridia*, which occur in inconspicuous flat patches, composed of short erect cells, upon the surface of distinct plants; and 3. *stichidia*, lateral or axillary, simple or branched pods containing a single or double row of linear (transversely parted) tetraspores.

BIBL. Harvey, *Brit. Mar. Alg.* p. 19, pl. 15 C; *Phyc. Brit.* pl. 44; Greville, *Alg. Brit.* pl. 12; Thuret, *Ann. des Sc. Nat.* 4 sér. iii. p. 19.

PLŒOTIA, Duj.—A genus of Infusoria, belonging to the family Thecamonadina.

Char. Body diaphanous, with several longitudinal ribs or keels projecting in the middle, and a rounded perfectly limpid margin. Two anterior locomotive filaments, one flagelliform, the other trailing.

P. vitrea (Pl. 24. fig. 67). Body hyaline, with three or four projecting longitudinal lines in the middle, and some internal granules. Marine; length 1-1200″. Movement slow.

BIBL. Dujardin, *Infus.* p. 345.

PLŒSCONIA, Duj. (Infusoria) = *Euplotes*, Ehr.

PLŒSCONINA, Duj. (INFUSORIA).—This family consists of the family *Euplota*, E., united with the genus *Loxodes*, E.

BIBL. Dujardin, *Infus*. p. 428.

PLUMATELLA, Lamk.—A genus of freshwater Polyzoa, of the order Hippocrepia, and family Plumatellidæ.

Char. Polypidom confervoid, branched, tubular, branches distinct; tentacular disc crescentic; ova elliptical, with a marginal ring, but no spines.

Nine British species.

1. *P. repens.* Polypidom irregularly branched; cells subclavate, without a longitudinal furrow or keel; tentacles about 60; tentacular membrane dentate; ova broad.

a. Adherent throughout.

β. Attached only at the base.

2. *P. fruticosa.* Irregularly branched, attached at the origin only; cells cylindrical, and destitute of furrow, but obscurely keeled; ova elongated.

3. *P. coralloides.* Attached at the base only; tubes dichotomous, densely tufted, destitute of furrow and keel; tentacles about 60; ova broad.

BIBL. Allman, *Freshwater Polyzoa*, 92; *Ann. Nat. Hist.* 1844. xiii. 330; Johnston, *Brit. Zooph.* 402.

PLUMULARIA, Lamk.—A genus of Polypi, of the order Hydroida, and family Sertulariadæ.

Char. Polypidom plant-like, rooted, simple or branched, feathery; cells small, unilateral, usually seated in the axilla of a horny spine; egg-vesicles scattered.

Ten British species.

1. *P. cristata.* Stem simple, a single tube, pinnate; pinnæ alternate; cells close, rim toothed; vesicles gibbous, girt with crested ribs.

2. *P. falcata.* Stem a single tube, waved, branched, branches alternately pinnate; cells close, shortly tubular, rim entire; egg-vesicles oval-oblong. Common.

3. *P. pinnata.* Stem a simple tube, plumous; pinnæ alternate, three on each internode; cells rather distant, campanulate, appressed, rim entire; vesicles pear-shaped, rim toothed.

4. *P. setacea.* Stem a single tube, pinnate; pinnæ alternate, one at each joint; joints ringed; cells very remote, campanulate, rim even; vesicles elliptical, smooth. Common.

In *P. myriophyllum* and *P. frutescens*, the stem consists of several parallel tubes.

BIBL. Johnston, *Brit. Zooph.* 89.

PODAXINEI.—A family of Gasteromycetous Fungi, none of which are found in Britain; they are distinguished from all allied tribes by a solid column in the centre of the sporange.

BIBL. Montagne, *Ann. des Sc. Nat.* 2 sér. xx. 69; Tulasne, *Ann. des Sc. Nat.* 3 sér. iv. 169; Montagne, translated in *Ann. Nat. Hist.* vol. ix.

PODISOMA, Link.—A genus of Uredinei (Coniomycetous Fungi), growing upon

Fig. 589.   Fig. 590.

Podisoma Juniperi.

Fig. 589. Branch of Juniper with clavate fructification protruded from beneath the bark. Nat. size.

Fig. 590. Vertical section through a fruit, showing the filaments terminating in bilocular spores. Magnified 50 diameters.

the living leaves and branches of species of Juniper; the filamentous mycelium creeping beneath the epidermis, and sending up a fleshy, stalk-like, tremelloid body (fig. 589), composed of agglutinated filaments (fig. 590) terminating in bilocular spores (or two spores adherent together), each of the cells having two or four pores, through which the internal membrane is protruded in germination. See UREDINEI.

Four species are described as British, *P. Juniperi-communis*, *P. Juniperi-Sabinæ*, *P. foliicolium* (on the leaves of *J. communis*), and *P. fuscum*, the last occurring upon *Pinus halepensis* and *J. Oxycedrus*.

BIBL. Berk. *Brit. Flor.* ii. pt. 2. p. 302; *Ann. Nat. Hist.* 2 ser. iii. 520; Tulasne, *Ann. des Sc. Nat.* 3 sér. xix. p. 205, 4 sér. ii. p. 186, pl. 10; Fries, *Summa Veg.* 474.

PODOCYSTIS, Bail.—A genus of Diatomaceæ, Cohort Surirelleæ.

Char. Frustules sessile, cuneate; valves convex, obovate, with a median line, transverse continuous, and intermediate granular striæ.

P. americana (Pl. 42. fig. 21). The only species; marine.

BIBL. Baily, *Smith. Contrib.* 1854; Smith, *Brit. Diat.* ii. 101.

PODOCYSTIS, Lév. = *Melampsora*. See UREDINEI.

PODODISCUS, Kg.—A genus of Diatomaceæ.

Char. Frustules single or concatenate, with a marginal stalk; valves circular, convex. Marine.

No markings visible under ordinary illumination.

P. jamaicensis (Pl. 13. fig. 16). Stalk elongate, weak. Diameter 1-840″.

BIBL. Kützing, *Bacill.* p. 51; *Sp. Alg.* p. 26.

PODOPHRYA, Ehr.—A genus of Infusoria, of the family Acinetina.

P. fixa (Pl. 23. fig. 5) is noticed under *Actinophrys pedicellata* (p. 13).

It is doubtful whether this is a distinct organism, or whether it is not a stage of metamorphosis of *Vorticella*. Compare Pl.25. fig. 33.

BIBL. Ehrenberg, *Infus.* p. 305; Dujardin, *Infus.* p. 266; Stein, *Infus., passim.*

PODOSIRA, Ehr.—A genus of Diatomaceæ.

Char. Frustules concatenate, with a lateral stalk; valves circular, punctate, convex. Marine.

Stalk attached to the centre of the valves.

1. *P. hormoides* (Pl. 14. fig. 34). Frustules two to six, depressed-spheroidal, connected by isthmi (stalks); hoops obscurely punctate. Diameter 1-650″.

2. *P. Montagnei* (*Melosira globifera*, Ralfs). Frustules usually two; hoops striate. Diameter 1-600″.

P. ? maculata.

BIBL. Kützing, *Sp. Alg.* p. 26; Smith, *Brit. Diat.* ii. 53.

PODOSPHENIA, Ehr. — A genus of Diatomaceæ.

Char. Frustules attached, sessile, wedge-shaped in front view; ends indented so as to produce a black line (vitta) in the front view; valves convex, obovate, with a longitudinal median line and transverse striæ, but no nodules. Marine.

The striæ consist of rows of dots, sometimes distinct by ordinary illumination, at others not so.

1. *P. Ehrenbergii* (Pl. 13. fig. 17). Frustules, in front view, truncate at the end; valves somewhat acute at the ends. Length 1-240″.

2. *P. Lyngbyei.* Frustules, in front view, truncate at the end; valves rounded at the free end. Length 1-350″.

Three other British species.

BIBL. Smith, *Brit. Diat.* i. p. 82; Kützing, *Bacill.* p. 119; *Sp. Alg.* p. 110.

PODOSPORIUM, Lév. = *Melampsora*. See UREDINEI.

PODURA, L.—A genus of Insects, of the order Thysanura, and family Podurellæ.

This genus has been greatly subdivided. In its extended signification, the characters consist in the thorax being distinct from the

Fig. 591.

Podura.

Magnified about 15 diameters.

abdomen, and in the presence of a forked tail, bent under the abdomen when not in use, and enabling the animals to move by springing or jumping, whence the common name of spring-tails applied to them.

They are of a leaden appearance, and found in shady damp places, as under flower-pots or stones, in cellars, &c., and are about 1-20 to 1-10″ in length. They may be caught by placing a little flour upon a piece of paper in their haunts.

The body is covered with scales (Pl. 1. fig. 12), which are used as test-objects. Those of *P. plumbea*, the so-called common spring-tail, are usually recommended; but we believe that the most common *Podura* is not this species. This is, however, a matter of little importance, because the scales of several species, belonging to even different genera, are exactly similar, both in form and markings.

See SCALES OF INSECTS and TEST-OBJECTS.

BIBL. Gervais, *Walckenaer's Aptères*, iii. and the *Bibl.* therein.

POLARISCOPE.—A term employed to designate a polarizing apparatus, consisting of a polarizer and analyser. See INTRODUCTION, p. xviii.

POLARIZATION OF LIGHT.—The phænomena exhibited by microscopic objects, when viewed by polarized light, are perhaps the most beautiful and interesting of those connected with the use of the microscope. The extreme brilliancy, transparency and variety in the colours developed cannot be equalled, much less can they be represented by illustrations, although the figures in Pl. 31 may give some idea of the manner in which they are arranged in certain objects.

The ordinary arrangement of the parts of the polarizing apparatus scarcely needs description,—the polarizer being placed beneath the object and the analyser above it, the polarizer and analyser usually consisting of two Nicol's prisms, or two plates of tourmaline. Some artificially prepared crystals exert a powerful polarizing action, and may be used either as polarizers or analysers, or as both; among these the salt of QUININE called Herapathite occupies the first place. Others form interesting analysers, some of which have been noticed under ANALYTIC CRYSTALS and DICHROISM.

Numerous salts and other crystalline bodies, which powerfully depolarize the already polarized light, and exhibit beautiful colours, are mentioned under their respective heads; some of these may be enumerated here,—as the oxalate of ammonia, of soda, and of chromium and ammonia; the oxalurate of ammonia, the acetate of copper, chlorate of potash, the prismatic form of the ammonio-phosphate of magnesia, the ammonio-phosphate of soda, the sulphates of cadmium and of magnesia, selenite, salicine, uric acid, &c.

Many animal bodies and tissues also possess considerable depolarizing power,—as horse-hair, portions of feathers, sections of quill, of hoof, horn, &c.

The influence of vegetable structures on polarized light has been long known, but only recently thoroughly investigated, by Von Mohl, whose interesting account we are able to confirm, and a brief notice of it is desirable here. In a communication with which he has favoured us, he recommends the following arrangements as most convenient. As it is desirable to obtain as much light as possible, a glass prism is preferable to the ordinary mirror for illumination; Nicol's prisms are preferable to tourmaline or Herapathite for the polarizer and analyser, and the latter should be as large as possible; further, the light emerging from the polarizer should, if possible, be condensed by an achromatic of large aperture; or the condensation may be effected by a hemispherical flint-glass lens, 5 lines in diameter, having its plane face turned towards the object. The objectives must be of large angular aperture; a power of 4-10″ is sufficient for most objects, but

1-4″, and even 1-8″ objectives, may be made to transmit sufficient light. It is requisite to provide plates of the doubly-refracting substances mica and gypsum, mounted so that they can be inserted between the polarizer and the condenser, and revolved horizontally while so placed. Those of mica are used for detecting weak degrees of doubly-refracting power, being of such thickness as to give a grey field with a white or black object when the prisms cross. The thin laminæ, of which six may be provided, from the thinnest possible up to 1-20″, should be cemented with Canada balsam between glass plates. For obtaining colours, plates of gypsum, similarly mounted, are best: Von Mohl prefers such as give a red field, and provides plates of different thickness, giving the reds of the different orders of Newton's rings.

It is easy to ascertain whether an organic body shows positive or negative colours, by comparing its colour, when seen with a plate of gypsum in a certain definite position, with the colour given under the same circumstances by a strip of glass brought into a state of tension by slight bending, or with the colours of a suddenly-cooled globule of glass. In this way the author determined that the fibres of a spiral vessel displayed negative colours, and the laminæ of a starch-corpuscle positive colours, and then applied these organic structures, by comparison, for ascertaining the properties of other objects. The objects to be examined should be mounted in a liquid or other substance rendering them as transparent as possible, such as concentrated glycerine, Canada balsam, or an essential oil.

When ordinary globular or cylindrical cellular tissues are viewed by cross sections, their substance is seen to be doubly refractive; for when the prisms cross, the circular sections of the cell-walls appear like rings of bright light on a black ground, but with the ring divided into four quadrants by dark stripes, as if a black cross lay over it; when the prisms are placed parallel, the parts of the section previously bright appear dark, and vice versâ, on a bright field. If a section of polyhedral cellular tissue is viewed in the same way, the appearances are somewhat different, since the cut edges are here straight lines, variously inclined towards the prisms; those which are perpendicular to the prisms are invisible, while those standing obliquely are bright in their whole length. In general, cell-membrane acts the more powerfully on the light the denser its substance, and soft collenchymatous tissues are far less powerfully doubly-refractive than wood-cells. When the cells have the walls much thickened, it is common for the primary cell-membrane to be much more powerfully refractive than the secondary layers. The influence of cellulose membranes upon polarized light is not much affected by bleaching them with nitric acid and chlorate of potash (Schultze's reagent). It has been supposed that the remarkable effect produced by the epidermis of *Equisetum hyemale* is attributable to the silex there present; but Mohl finds the action greatly weakened by destroying the organic matter by a red heat. But this heating does not remove the power there, nor in the Diatomaceæ, of which Mohl confirms Bailey's statement, in contradiction to Ehrenberg, that various species of *Navicula*, *Synedra*, *Pleurosigma*, and *Melosira* are decidedly doubly refractive.

Very remarkable phænomena are produced when the polarized light is made to pass through plates of mica or selenite. In the first place, thin plates of mica often allow of the discovery of a doubly-refracting power too feeble to be detected by the prisms alone,—the degree of illumination of the object being slightly different from that of the field on which it is viewed. But the most important matter is the revelation, by the use of the selenite plates, of the existence of positive and negative characters, like those of positive and negative crystals, in the chemically distinct constituents of vegetable tissues.

Let us suppose that between the lower prism and the object is placed a plate of selenite giving a red field, the plate is then rotated so that its neutral axes are at an angle of 45° with the prisms. A section of a cylindrical vegetable cell will be seen to be divided into four quadrants: the two alternate quadrants, whose middle lines correspond to the neutral axes of the selenite, are either blue or green; the other two yellow or red: if the selenite is then rotated so that its neutral axes are perpendicular to the prisms, the colours will be all lost; but on continuing the rotation, they reappear in the reverse order—what was blue appearing yellow, and *vice versâ*. When the walls are rectilinear, all the cell-walls perpendicular to one of the prisms will give the colour of the field, all those which run parallel with one of the neutral axes of the selenite plate, or form no great angle with it, will be blue, those parallel with the other axis yellow.

It is found that vegetable structures fall into two classes in reference to these colours, in one of which classes all layers lying obliquely in the direction of a right-wound screw are tinged blue and yellow, those oblique in the opposite direction yellow or red; in the other class, the colours under the same conditions are just the reverse; so that one class are optically positive, the other optically negative.

The optically negative are the ordinary cell-membranes of the internal organs of plants, whether in their natural condition or cellulose purified by the help of nitric acid and chlorate of potash: collenchyma, horny endosperm-cells, the gelatinous cells of Algæ, &c., all agree in this property. Optically positive colours are given by cell-membranes of periderm and the cuticular layers of epidermal cells. The contrast of the positive and negative colours of the cuticle and other parts of the cell-wall is well seen in the epidermis of *Aloe*. The diversity of colouring under polarized light here corresponds to the diverse behaviour under treatment with iodine after maceration in solution of potash (SECONDARY DEPOSITS).

The longitudinal sections of all behave like the cross sections; but the appearances are not so clear. When side views of the surface of cells are obtained, the phenomena are very varied; but these are best seen in vessels or ducts when the thickening layers are in the form of spiral bands. Thus, if one of the spiral vessels of *Musa* is placed (its spiral somewhat drawn apart) with its long axis perpendicular to one of the prisms, the fibres on the upper side turn to the left, those on the underside towards the right; and when the selenite plate is interposed, they exhibit the complementary colours. When the side walls of cells have obscure striation, as in the cells of Conifers, the liber-cells of Apocyneæ, &c., the membrane gives evidence of its fibrillar structure by the yellow or blue colour developed with the selenite plate. If fibres of a spiral vessel cross at right angles, and they are pressed together, they neutralize one another where they cross: when the prisms are used alone, the crossing points are black, the rest of the fibres white; when the selenite plate is interposed, the crossing points exhibit the colour of the field, and the uncrossed portions of the fibre are blue or yellow according to position.

The vicinity of a round bordered pit, as in the wood-cells of *Pinus*, exhibits a black cross when seen perpendicularly by polarized light. The black cross and the colours exhibited by starch are well known. Chlorophyll does not seem to act on polarized light, nor the primordial utricle of cells, except a trace when contracted by weak alcohol.

The polarization apparatus is exceedingly useful for the detection of crystals (RAPHIDES) in vegetable tissues, when they are so small as to be easily overlooked, and the larger kinds form beautiful objects with, and often without the selenite plate.

BIBL. Herschel, *Encycl. Metropol.* art. *Light*; Pereira, *Lectures on Polarized Light*, *by R. Powell*; Woodward, *On Polarized Light*, Brewster, *Optics*; Erlach, *Mik. Beobacht. üb. organ. Element. bei Polar. Licht*, Müller's *Archiv*, 1847; Von Mohl, *Bot. Zeit.* 1858; *Ann. Nat. Hist.* 3 ser. i. p. 198.

POLLEN.—This name is applied to the coloured pulverulent substance familiar to every one as occurring scattered in the interior of full-blown flowers; it is produced in the anthers, the (usually) stalked club-shaped organs which stand in one or more circles between the floral envelopes and the pistils, and is discharged from them when ripe, in order to fertilize the ovules. When slightly magnified, the pollen of most flowers appears to consist of granules, of different size and colour in different plants; hence the individual particles are called *pollen-grains* or *granules* (Pl. 32). Examination under a sufficient magnifying power shows that the simple or typical forms of pollen - grains are single free cells filled with fluid matter: more complex forms occur in many cases, which, however, may be simply characterized as groups of simple pollen-grains, permanently coherent into definitely-formed groups.

The pollen-grain may be examined as to its form and structure, its contents, and its development.

The forms of simple grains presented in different plants are tolerably varied,—spherical (Pl. 32. figs. 8-10, 22, 23, 25) and elliptical (figs. 6, 11, 29) being perhaps those most common; but besides these, numerous geometrical forms occur, such as tetrahedral (fig. 14), polygonal (figs. 16, 27, 28), cubic (fig. 19). But it must be noted here that the forms frequently vary according as the pollen is viewed dry or in fluid,

since the elliptical and allied forms often expand into a spherical form, when they absorb liquid (figs. 18 & 20 *a*, *b*, *c*). The explanation of this will be given presently. The external appearance is further greatly influenced by minor peculiarities of form, such as ridges, spines and processes of different kinds; these, however, are referable to the structure of the outer coat.

The ordinary structure of the coats or the cell-wall of the pollen-grain is that of a delicate internal cell-membrane, with an outer, thick and resisting layer, which may be regarded as the CUTICLE of the inner or proper membrane of the cell. In a few cases the inner membrane alone exists, as in the cylindrical pollen-cells of *Zostera* and some other aquatic plants. In other cases, the outer or cuticular coat presents a more complex structure, and two, or, it is said, even three layers may be distinguished in it; these, however, seem to be merely a lamination of the outer coat. The conditions in some of the Coniferæ are different from this, and will be alluded to presently. The inner membrane is exceedingly delicate and homogeneous: in ordinary spherical or oval grains it accurately lines the outer coat; in some of those forms which present processes of various kinds, such as *Œnothera*, it seems to us that the inner coat does not extend into these processes in the mature pollen. The outer coat exhibits, as to surface, every variety of appearance, from smooth, through granular and spiny, to pseudo-cellular arising from reticulated ridges; in addition to this, the processes just alluded to give a very peculiar aspect to many kinds of pollen. Besides these, we find in all cases markings appearing like *pores*, or others like *slits* (which become *furrows* when dry), or both together, and these in varying number in different cases. The colour of the pollen presents great differences; although usually yellow, it may be whitish, red (*Verbascum*), blue (*Epilobium angustifolium*), even black (tulip): this colour resides in the outer coat. The outer coat also exhibits, in the majority of cases, a secretion upon its surface, of a viscid character, usually described as oily, but apparently consisting of a viscid matter, not readily soluble in water, remaining from the dissolved parent-cells. It would seem to be the substance which holds together the pollen-grains in those cases where it consists of waxy masses, readily breaking up into small fragments (Ophrydeous Orchids).

In the Onagraceæ the pollen-grains are loosely connected by slender viscid filaments, which appear to be derived from the same source.

The more detailed explanation of the characters of the pores, &c., the projecting processes, and the compound conditions of pollen, will be understood better after a sketch of its development.

The anther, in which the pollen is formed, consists in its younger stages of a minute, solid, cellular papilla or cylindrical body; at an early period a distinction becomes manifest in its cells: a single vertical row, lying in the position of the axis of each pollen-chamber (or loculus), presents a

Fig. 592.　　　　Fig. 593.

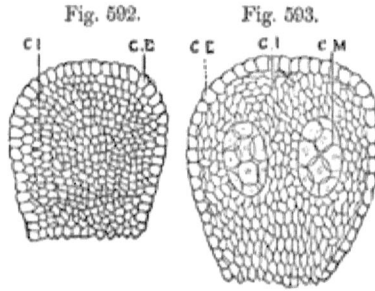

Fig. 594.

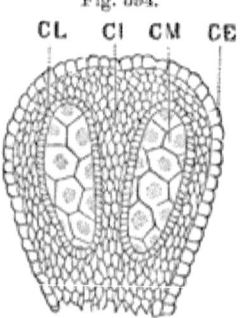

Vertical sections of a cell of a young anther of the Melon, showing the gradual separation of the regions. *C E*, epidermal cells; *C I*, cells of the wall of the anther; *C L*, cells lining the loculi; *C M*, cells from which the pollen is developed.

Magnified 100 diameters.

different aspect, from its cells exceeding the surrounding ones in size; and these rows undergo a special development to produce the pollen-grains, while the surrounding layers are developed into the tissues forming

the coat or wall of the anther, and its midrib or *connective* (see ANTHER). The cells of the primary row multiply by cell-division with the general increase in size of the anther (figs. 592–594), until at length they form relatively large masses of cellular tissue composed of large squarish cells filled with granular contents, well defined as constituting a distinct tissue from the walls of the pollen-chambers. A new change then takes place; the contents of each cell secrete a layer of cellulose, which does not adhere to the wall of the parent-cell to form a layer of secondary deposit, but lies free against it, so that a new free cell is formed within each old one, nearly filling it. The walls of the old cell (forming a connected parenchymatous tissue) then dissolve, so that the new cells become free, no longer merely in their parent-cells, but in a cavity which is to constitute the pollen-chamber or loculus of the anther. These free cells are the *parent-cells of the pollen* of authors. A new phænomenon soon occurs in these. These parent-cells divide into four by ordinary cell-division, either by one or by two successive partings by septa at right angles to each other but both perpendicular to an imaginary axis (as when an orange is quartered), or by simultaneously-formed septa which cut off portions in such a manner that the new cells stand in the position of four cannon-balls piled into a pyramid (tetrahedrally). These new cells are the *special parent-cells* of the pollen; and in each of these the entire protoplasmic contents secrete a series of layers, which in the ordinary course, by the solution of the primary walls of the special

Fig. 595.

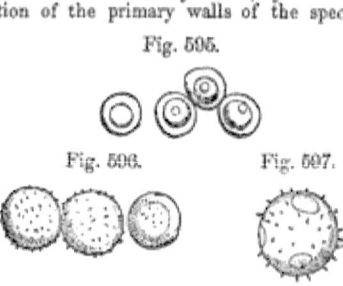

Fig. 596.　　　　　　Fig. 597.

Pollen-grain of the Melon in various stages of development.

Magnified 100 diameters.

parent-cells upon which they were applied, become the walls of free cells, which constitute the simple ordinary pollen-cells.

These subsequently increase in size; and their outer laminæ assume the characteristic form and appearance while free in the chamber of the anther (figs. 595–597).

In referring the peculiarities of many kinds of pollen to circumstances connected with the development, it may be noted, in the first place, that the mode of division of the parent-cells into quarters often influences the ultimate form of the pollen-grain: thus, when the division is by two planes at right angles, the original form of the pollen-grain will be elongated, and the ripe grain will probably be elliptical, while, when the division is "tetrahedral," the grains may retain the form thus produced, or be slightly modified and become polygonal, or, as is more common, they expand more readily than the others into a sphere. But there is no absolute rule here; we find even the tetrahedral and the polar division occur together among the parent-cells of the same anther. In the next place, a compound condition of the pollen-grains (Pl. 32. figs. 7, 17) is readily explicable by referring it to an arrest of the process of subdivision; so that if the walls of the special parent-cell do not dissolve, the pollen-grains will be left in groups of four; and if the parent-cells do not become singly detached in the antecedent process of solution, the grains may be still developed in the same order and manner, and remain connected in greater or smaller masses or groups, each enclosed in its special parent-cell, itself connected with a number of others of the same generation by the persistence of the walls of the cells in which the parent-cells were developed. This explains the compound pollen of the Acacias (Pl. 32. fig. 27), and, as an excessive form, the waxy pollen-masses which occur in the Orchidaceæ and Asclepiadaceæ. It is sometimes stated that the pollen-grains of these compound forms are merely connected together by the viscid substance remaining from the solution of the parent-cells; but this would render such cohesions indefinite in character, instead of being regular; at the same time it will be understood that the solution may have advanced so far that the grains merely hold together slightly, and may readily be separated. This is not the case, however, with the majority of compound pollen-grains. When pollen-grains do become free, the viscidity of their surface is probably referable to the dissolved parent-cells.

The metamorphoses of the outer coat or cuticle of the pollen-grain are very remarkable, and not yet at all understood; the granulations (Pl. 32. figs. 11, 12), spines (figs. 8, 9, 22, 26), reticulations (figs. 13, 23, 27, 28), &c., characterizing mature grains, make their appearance in the interval between the solution of the special parent-cells and the bursting of the anther, while the pollen-grains lie free within the latter; their production is accompanied by a general growth and expansion of the pollen-grain. We have observed that the outer coat is often deposited as a very thick layer inside the special parent-cell, and that when the latter dissolves, the outer coat of the pollen-grain is also in a softened condition, and becomes stretched by the expanding inner coat, finally forming a comparatively thin layer on the ripe grain (e. g. in Tradescantia). The mode of origin of the markings, like those on Spores and on the cuticle of Helleborus, &c. (see Epidermis), is altogether unknown; probably all the cases are referable to one cause.

It has been mentioned that the mature pollen-grain exhibits pores or slits. We believe they should rather be regarded as thinner places in the outer membrane. Their number and position varies much, as will be indicated presently on referring to some of the principal types of form of pollen. The slit-like markings are generally accompanied by a peculiar shrinking of the pollen when dry, the coat collapsing at the thin places, so that grains of this kind appear oval or angular, not clearly exhibiting the slits (which then become furrows); but they swell out, and display the latter clearly when placed in water or dilute acids (Pl. 32. figs. 18 & 20). When the so-called pores exist, they are either like simple pores (Pl. 32. fig. 10), or they may be provided with little disk-like pieces or lids, which fall off and leave them bare when the pollen-tube is formed (figs. 13 & 22). In all cases, however, we believe that the outer coat is extended over the whole surface, and that the slits and dots are merely thinner places; moreover, in certain cases (Leschenaultia, a quaternate pollen) we have seen the thickening layers of the young pollen-grain, inside the parent-cell, exhibit pits (exactly comparable to those of ordinary pitted cells) at the places corresponding to the future pores, and, curiously enough, in some cases at least, the pits of adjacent pollen-cells corresponding, although in the mature expanded compound grains they were far separated. Sometimes the lids are found at the end of short projecting processes (Pl. 32. fig. 22). The pollen of *Œnothera* and allied genera exhibit remarkable conditions, which have been mistakenly described. The form of the grain is that of a depressed sphere with three large equidistant truncated cones projecting pretty nearly in the same plane. The outer coat is thick, except at the ends of the conical masses; and two laminæ are distinguishable (Pl. 32. fig. 14). The outer coat thins off towards the end of each process. It appears to us that the inner coat or true pollen-membrane does not extend into the processes at all, but is globular, and that a semifluid deposit occupies the space between the inner coat and the outer, in the cavity of the tubular processes. Now supposing such a deposit to become hardened and, after circumscissile fission, pushed off as a plate by the advancing pollen-tube, instead of giving way and expanding, we should have the lid occurring in *Cucurbita Pepo* (Pl. 32. fig. 22) and other cases.

In *Mimulus moschatus* (Pl. 32. fig. 24) the slits or furrows are curved, and in *Nymphæa, Pinus*, and other cases, still more complex.

It has been stated that the pollen is the agent of fertilization of the ovules in the Flowering plants. When scattered from the anthers, that portion of the pollen which falls upon the stigma (and frequently other portions falling upon nectaries or secreting surfaces) swell slightly, and germinate, as it were, sending out a delicate tubular process from one or more of the so-called pores or slits (Pl. 32. fig. 30), which processes (the *pollen-tubes*) insinuate themselves between the loosely packed cells of the stigma, and, continually elongating, make their way down the style and along the *conducting tissue* to the ovules. In the Coniferæ the pollen-grains fall directly upon the micropyle of the naked OVULE, and send their pollen-tubes into it. The pollen-tube is produced by the development of the inner or proper coat of the pollen into a tubular filament. When pollen-grains are placed in dilute sulphuric acid or in syrup (sometimes in water), they absorb liquid, swell, and their contents partly exude from pores, &c., either to a slight extent, as a little "hernia," as it were, of the inner membrane, or in large quantity in a worm-like, irregular mass; in the latter case the coagulation of the surface often produces a

pellicular coat. These exuded masses are of course distinct from the true pollen-tubes produced under natural conditions.

The fluid contents of the pollen-grains consist of a granular viscid protoplasm, with minute starch-granules and (apparently) oil-drops, making together what has been called the *fovilla*, which increases in density as the pollen ripens. The starch-granules exhibit molecular motion in the pollen-tube, and still more clearly when they escape by rupture. The granular contents of the pollen-cell, which are always rendered opaque by the action of water, are gradually transferred to the pollen-tube as it elongates.

Connected with this point is the peculiarity exhibited by the pollen of the Coniferæ. In the Abietineæ the form of the granules is very peculiar—elongated, curved, and with bulging ends; and, according to Schacht, a distinct internal cell exists, attached at one side in the cavity of the ordinary pollen-cell, this internal cell dividing and growing out as the pollen-tube when the pollen-grain comes upon the ovule. The pollen of the Cupressineæ is spheroidal; but free cellules appear to be formed in the pollen-tubes during the fertilization. These conditions, which are not yet satisfactorily cleared up, indicate a relation to the spermatozoid-producing spores of the Marsileaceæ, &c., analogous to that between the Gymnospermous ovules and the ovule-spores of those Cryptogamic families.

It has been imagined that the form and structure of the pollen-grains might have some relation to the general structure of the plants, and might serve as an indication of systematic position and affinities. But there appears to be no definite relation; very varied pollen occurs within the limits of the same family, and very similar pollen-grains in families widely distant. There appears, however, to be a certain relation within the limits of *genera*. It may be perhaps generally stated that the Monocotyledons have frequently one pore or furrow; the Grasses often three pores, as is the case with many Dicotyledons, many of which have more, while a large number of the families of the latter division exhibit both pores and slits. As microscopic objects, it is most convenient to class the forms artificially, or according to structure; and we give a brief list of the principal varieties arranged under this point of view.

The pollen-grains of *Zostera, Zanichellia*,

and other submerged aquatic plants, have no cuticle or outer coat; all other known forms possess one or more outer layers.

A. Outer coat without furrows or pores.

　a. Outer coat granular: *Strelitzia Reginæ, Calla palustris, Crocus sativus, &c., Asarum europæum, Laurus nobilis, &c.,* many Euphorbiaceæ.

　b. Outer coat with papillæ: *Canna indica.*

　c. Outer coat with cell-like reticulations: *Ruellia formosa* (Pl. 32. fig. 23), *R. strepens, Tribulus terrestris.*

In *Periploca græca* (Pl 32. fig. 15) and *Apocynum Venetum* (fig. 7) grains of this kind are connected in fours in one plane; in some *Luzulæ* tetrahedrally.

B. Outer coat presenting longitudinal furrows (or folds).

　　* One furrow (the form of most Monocotyledons).

　a. Outer coat finely granular: common in Monocotyledons; among the Dicotyledons, in *Myrica cerifera, Magnolia grandiflora, Liriodendron tulipiferum,* &c.

　b. Outer coat granular, spiny: *Nymphæa alba.*

　c. Outer coat with cell-like reticulations: *Hemerocallis fulva,* and other Monocotyledons.

　d. Outer coat with irregular reticulations: *Alstrœmeria Curtisiana.*

Among the Orchideæ are found quaternate grains belonging to this group.

　　** Outer coat with two furrows: a rare form, occurring in species of *Pontederia* and *Amaryllis, Tamus communis* and *elephantipes, Tigridia pavonia, Calycanthus floridus, &c.*

　　*** Outer coat with three longitudinal furrows.

　a. Outer coat granular. One of the commonest forms: *Quercus Robur, Viola odorata* (Pl. 32. fig. 6).

　b. Outer coat with short spines: *Cactus flagelliformis, Viscum album.*

　c. Outer coat with cell-like reticulations: *Statice* (Pl. 32. fig. 29), various Cruciferæ.

　　**** Outer coat with more than three furrows.

　a. Four: very rare as normal, *Houstonia*

cærulea, Cedrela odorata; occasionally occurring where three is the normal number, as in *Solanum tuberosum.*

　b. Six: some of the Labiatæ and Passifloreæ (Pl. 32. fig. 20), *Ephedra distachya, Heliotropium grandiflorum.*

　c. A larger number of furrows: many Rubiaceæ; e. g. *Sherardia arvensis* (Pl. 32. fig. 18).

The pollen of the Pines is related to this group, also that of *Nymphæa Lotus, Victoria regia,* and other plants, where the furrows or thin places occupy the greater part of the wall, and the outer coat forms only segmental pieces. In *Mimulus moschatus* (Pl. 32. fig. 24) a very remarkable appearance arises from the furrows running in a curved or spiral direction; and analogous conditions are met with in *Thunbergia alata.*

C. Outer coat with pores.

　　* A single pore: Grasses, Sedges, *Typha angustifolia, Sparganium ramosum.*

　　** Two pores: *Colchicum,* and a few other Monocotyledons; also *Broussonetia.*

　　*** Three pores.

　a. Outer coat granular: Dipsaceæ, Urticaceæ, Onagraceæ (here the pores form projecting processes (Pl. 32. fig. 14); and in *Morinda persica* this is still more the case); *Cucumis sativus.*

　b. Outer coat with cell-like reticulations: many Passifloreæ (with large lids, *P. cærulea* (Pl. 32. fig. 13), *alata, &c.*).

　　**** Four pores.

　a. Pores on the equator: *Pistacia terebinthus, Campanula rotundifolia, &c.*

　b. Pores not equatorial: *Passiflora kermesina, Impatiens Balsamina* (Pl. 32. fig. 21) (*Noli-me-tangere*).

　　***** More than four pores.

　† Distributed regularly.

　a. On the equator: *Alnus glutinosa, Ulmus campestris, Collomia linearis, Campanula Speculum.*

　b. All over the grains: *Basella alba* (Pl. 32. fig. 19).

　　†† Scattered irregularly.

　a. Outer coat slightly granular: many Nyctagineæ, Convolvulaceæ, Chenopodiaceæ, Alsineæ, *Alisma Plantago* (Pl.

32. fig. 10), *Plantago lanceolata*, *Ribes nigrum*, *Cactus Opuntia*, &c.

b. Outer coat granular and spiny : *Cucurbita Pepo* (with lids, Pl. 32. fig. 22), Malvaceæ (Pl. 32. fig. 26).

c. Outer coat with cell-like reticulations : *Polygonum amphibium, persicaria, Cobæa scandens.*

Compound porous forms occur in some of the Onagraceæ, and in *Drimys Winteri*, where four grains are conjoined tetrahedrally. In the Mimoseæ groups of eight or sixteen (Pl. 32. fig. 25) occur in various forms. In *Leschenaultia formosa* the grains are quaternate, lying in one plane.

D. Outer coat with both furrows and pores.

   * Grains rounded or depressed, with three depressions, each with a pore : most Dipsaceæ and Geraniaceæ (sometimes only two occur, Pl. 32. fig. 22).

   ** Three furrows and three pores.

a. Outer coat granular ; a very common form among Dicotyledons.

b. Outer coat spiny : most Compositæ.

c. Outer coat with cell-like reticulations ; rare : *Syringa vulgaris*, *Ligustrum vulgare, Grewia occidentalis*, and other species.

   *** Outer coat with more than three furrows, each with a pore. Sometimes abnormally, instead of three, but normally in most of the Boraginaceæ and Polygalaceæ.

   **** Six to nine furrows, three containing a pore : Lythraceæ, Melastomaceæ, Combretaceæ.

   ***** Three or four furrows, with six or eight papillæ : *Neurada procumbens, &c.*

   ****** Three furrows and three papillæ not in the furrows : *Carolinea campestris, &c.*

Related compound forms occur in the Ericaceæ and Epacridaceæ, where the grains are tetrahedrally arranged (Pl. 32. fig. 17). Other aberrant forms occur in which the single grains are cubic or dodecahedral ; and in the Cichoraceæ, polyhedral forms of complicated character are common (Pl. 32. figs. 16, 27, 28).

Mature pollen-grains should be observed dry (as opake and transparent objects), and in water or glycerine ; in some cases, in oil ; treatment with acids is also useful in making out structure. In observing the development of pollen, it is necessary to wet the object with a solution of sugar or gum ; otherwise the appearances are altogether changed through endosmotic action.

Bibl. Mohl, *Bau u. Form. d. Pollenkörner*, Bern, 1834 (transl. in *Ann. des Sc. Nat.* 2 sér. iii.) ; Purkinje, *De cellulis antheris, &c.*, Vratislav. 1830 ; Fritzsche, *Beitr. z. Kenntn. der Pollen*, 1832 ; Hassall, *Ann. Nat. Hist.* viii. p. 92 ; ix. pp. 93 and 544. Mohl's work contains an abstract of the literature up to his date ; since that time notices on the development have been published by Nägeli, *Entwick. des Pollens*, Zurich, 1842, and his papers on Cell-formation translated in *Ray Society's Vols.* for 1846 and 1847 ; Hofmeister, *Botanische Zeitung*, vi. 1848 ; Gieswald, *Linnæa*, xxv. p. 81 (1852) ; Schacht (Coniferæ), *Beitrag z. Botanik*, Berlin, 1854.

POLYACTIS. See Botrytis.

POLYARTHRA, Ehr.—A genus of Rotatoria, of the family Hydatinæa.

Char. Eye single, cervical ; foot absent ; body with six cirrhi or fins on each side. Jaws each with a single tooth.

1. *P. platyptera* (Pl. 35. fig. 19). Body ovato-subquadrate, fins ensiform serrate. Aquatic ; length 1-190″.

2. *P. trigla.* Fins setaceous. Aquatic ; length 1-190″.

Bibl. Ehrenberg, *Infus.* p. 440.

POLYBOTRYA, Humb.—A genus of Acrosticheæ (Polypodioid Ferns). Exotic.

POLYCLINUM, Sav.—A genus of Tunicate Mollusca, of the family Botryllidæ (p. 103).

P. aurantium. Consists of little rounded orange masses, fixed to rocks by a short and thick peduncle.

Bibl. Forbes and Hanley, *Brit. Mollusca*, i. 14.

POLYCOCCUS, Kütz. — Probably belongs to *Protococcus.*

POLYCYSTINA, Ehr. — A group (family ?) of Rhizopoda. They consist of shells of various forms (Pl. 31. figs. 23–31), rounded, conical, oval, radiate, star-shaped, &c., often furnished with spines and other processes, and sometimes constricted so as to give them a jointed appearance. The shells are siliceous, everywhere perforated by coarse, rounded or angular foramina ; and at one end, sometimes at both, is a larger aperture.

They are most abundant as fossils in the rocks of Bermuda; but have also been found in the chalk and marls of Sicily, at Oran in Africa, in Greece, in the tripoli of Richmond in Virginia. A very few have been found recent in mud at the bottom of the sea, near Cuxhaven in the North Sea, and near the South Pole.

The recent shells were filled with an olive-brown organic matter.

Forty-four genera and 282 species have been described by Ehrenberg; and these have recently been added to by Müller.

They form beautiful microscopic objects, viewed by either reflected or transmitted light.

BIBL. Ehrenberg, *Taylor's Scientific Memoirs* (pts. 10 & 11) and *Ber. d. Berl. Akad.* 1846 & 1847 (Schomburgk, *Ann. Nat. Hist.* 1847. xx. 115); Müller, *Abhandl. d. Berl. Akad.* 1858.

POLYCYSTIS, Kütz. See CLATHRO-CYSTIS.

POLYCYSTIS, Léveillé. — A genus of Ustilaginei (Coniomycetous Fungi), including several of the old species of *Uredo*; *P. colchici*, *P. parallela* and *P. Violæ* are British. See USTILAGINEI.

BIBL. Berk. and Broome, *Ann. Nat. Hist.* 2 ser. v. p. 464; Léveillé, *Ann. des Sc. Nat.* 3 sér. v. p. 269; Tulasne, *id.* vii. p. 217.

POLYEMBRYONY.—This term is applied to a phænomenon occurring sometimes regularly, sometimes abnormally, in the development of the ovules of Flowering Plants. In the Angiospermous plants it is usual to find several germinal masses in the unfertilized embryo-sac (see OVULE); but ordinarily only one of these becomes impregnated and developed. Occasionally, however, more than one commences the course of development into an embryo, as in the Orchidaceæ, and more especially in the genus *Citrus*: in most cases all but one become subsequently obliterated; but in the orange this is not the case, and ripe seeds are met with containing more than one embryo. We have met with them in other cases.

Another kind of polyembryony occurs in the Santalaceæ. *Viscum* has two or three embryo-sacs; these may all have their germinal masses fertilized, and the development of the embryos may go on to a certain point until one takes the lead and the others disappear.

In the Gymnospermia (Coniferæ and Cycadaceæ), as described in the article OVULE, there may be one or more (*Taxus*) primary embryo-sacs, in which are produced several *corpuscula*, with secondary embryo-sacs; further, the germinal masses of these, after fertilization, produce suspensors, which branch at their lower ends, and each produce four rudimentary embryos, all but one of them vanishing during the ripening of the seeds. Our space only admits of a brief notice of these interesting phænomena, on which much interesting information will be found in the works referred to below.

BIBL. Meyen, *On Impregnation and Polyembryony* (Berlin, 1840), transl. in *Taylor's Scientific Memoirs*, iii. p. 1; R. Brown, *Ann. Nat. Hist.* xiii. p. 368; Mirbel and Spach, *Ann. des Sc. Nat.* 2 sér. xx. p. 257; Cruger, *Botanische Zeit.* ix. p. 57; Gelesnoff, *Ann. des Sc. Nat.* 3 sér. xiv. p. 189, and the works of Hofmeister cited under OVULE.

POLYGASTRICA.—According to Ehrenberg's system, the Infusoria are subdivided into the Polygastrica and the Rotatoria. The so-called Polygastrica correspond to our Infusoria; the Rotatoria form a distinct class.

POLYIDES, Ag.—A genus of Cryptonemiaceæ (Florideous Algæ), containing one British species, *P. rotundus*, having a branched frond 4 to 6″ high, consisting of repeatedly dichotomous, purplish - brown, solid fibres, about 1-20′ in diameter. The fibres present a central layer of longitudinally arranged filamentous cells, and a cortical layer of perpendicular, dichotomous filaments, formed of elliptical cells internally, terminating at the surface in minute moniliform rows. The fructification consists—1. of *favellæ* bearing spores, contained in superficial wart-like bodies, composed of colourless articulate filaments; 2. tetrahedrally divided *tetraspores*, imbedded in the peripheral filaments of the cortical layer of the frond. Antheridia have not yet been observed.

BIBL. Harvey, *Brit. Mar. Alg.* p. 146, pl. 18 D; *Phyc. Brit.* pl. 95; Greville, *Alg. Brit.* pl. 11.

POLYMORPHINA, D'Orb. — A genus of Foraminifera, of the order Enallostegia, and family Polymorphinidæ.

Char. Shell free, inequilateral, vitreous, oblong or elongate, compressed; chambers often numerous, alternate in two rows, slightly embracing, but always more so on one side than the other; orifice round, at the summit of the last chamber.

Williamson unites the genera *Guttulina* and *Globulina* with this genus.

Two recent British species:

1. *P. lactea* (Pl. 42. fig. 27) = *Guttulina communis, austriaca, Globulina gibba, æqualis* and *tubulosa*, D'Orb.; with five varieties.

2. *P. myristiformis.*

Some also fossil.

BIBL. That of the order.

POLYOMMATUS, Latr. — A genus of Lepidopterous Insects, of the family Lycænidæ.

Char. Antennæ terminated by a contracted knob; tarsal claws minute; wings not tailed.

The (thirteen) species are small butterflies, the upper surface of the wings of a beautiful blue colour, the under side grey or brownish, and with numerous eye-like spots.

The scales upon the under surface of the wings of *P. argiolus* and *P. argus* have been proposed as test-objects. They are of two kinds—one resembling in structure the ordinary scales of insects, the other of a battledore form (Pl. 27. figs. 20 & 21). See SCALES of Insects and TEST-OBJECTS.

The species are figured in Westwood's *British Butterflies.*

POLYPHEMUS, Müll. — A genus of Entomostraca, of the order Cladocera, and family Polyphemidæ.

Char. Head distinct from the body; abdomen long, slender, and projecting externally from the shell.

P. pediculus (Pl. 14. fig. 29). The only species. Aquatic.

BIBL. Baird, *Brit. Entomostr.* p. 111.

POLYPI (Zoophytes). — A class of the Animal Kingdom.

Char. Body rounded or cylindrical, with a distinct mouth, surrounded by retractile unciliated tentacles or radiating lobes; individuals usually aggregate, and furnished with a horny or calcareous external or internal skeleton or polypidom; gemmiparous and oviparous.

The polypes are usually enveloped in an external (Pl. 33. figs. 4 *b*, 12 & 14), or supported by an internal axial skeleton (Pl. 33. fig. 6), called the polypidom or polyparium. This is either horny, leathery or calcareous. Most polypes are united into smaller or larger groups by the polypidom, which often possesses an elegant plant-like form (Pl. 33. fig. 15). The tubular or cup-shaped processes or cavities, in which the body of the individual polypes is contained, form the polype-cells; they are sometimes furnished with a kind of lid.

The structure of the calcareous polypidoms has not been satisfactorily determined. They are usually traversed by vascular canals and appear in some cases at least to consist of spicula aggregated and fused together.

The polypes are rarely free, or capable of fixing themselves by a disk at the base of the body, as in *Hydra*, being usually fixed at the bottom of the polype-cells,—the polypidoms being attached by a rooting base to some foreign body. Imbedded in the outer parts of the soft substance of the body, especially the tentacles, are stinging organs (Pl. 33. fig. 22), resembling in general those of the Acalephæ.

In many, distinct muscles are present, but the fibres are not striated, although frequently exhibiting transverse wrinkles. In some polypes the substance of the body consists entirely of sarcodic substance. In many both the integument, when present, and substance of the body contain scattered calcareous spicula (Pl. 33. figs. 7, 27 & 28).

The alimentary apparatus consists of mouth and a simple gastric sac, the food being admitted and the undigested portion rejected from the single aperture, excepting in one genus, where the anus is separate.

The oral orifice is usually surrounded by a ring of contractile arms or tentacles, which are hollow internally and communicate with the cavity of the abdomen; but sometimes the tentacles are distributed over the surface of the body.

The simple gastric sac is usually separated from the cavity of the body; whereby a larger or smaller abdominal cavity is formed, which is almost always prolonged into the hollow arms, and in many polypes living in colonies passes into the canals traversing the interior of the polypidom, so that the abdominal cavities of the individual polypes are all brought into connexion by these canals. Sometimes longitudinal partitions run like a mesentery from the outer to the inner surface of the abdominal walls, thus dividing the abdominal cavity into chambers. The bottom of the gastric cavity provided with one or more spontaneously closeable openings, by which it communicates with the abdominal cavity. The gastric cavity appears covered with a very delicate ciliated epithelium, which is continued through the gastric apertures into the abdominal cavity, and here not only covers the outer surface of the stomach and the septa, but also the inner surface of the abdominal walls, the cavities of the arms and the canals of the polypidom.

The walls of the stomach are variously coloured, white, yellow, or brown, from the presence of aggregations of pigment-cells (liver - cells) in the gastric walls, which most probably perform the function of a liver, as there is no glandular appendage corresponding to a liver present.

A peculiar circulation takes place in almost all polypes, by the to-and-fro motion of a nearly transparent liquid containing minute colourless corpuscles, in the abdominal cavity. The liquid ascends thence to the apex of the hollow tentacles, whence it returns to the abdominal cavity. In the colonial polypes this circulation continues through the canals which traverse the polypidoms, from one abdominal cavity to the other. The motion is produced by very delicate ciliated epithelium lining the abdominal cavity, the hollow tentacles, and the canals of the polypidom.

The propagation of the polypes takes place in three ways: by spontaneous division, which is mostly longitudinal and rare; by the formation of gemmæ or buds, which is very common, the individuals either separating or remaining attached; and by the formation of ova. Most of the gemmæ become developed into ordinary polype-cells, and so produce the growth of the compound organism. But in many polypes, some of them grow into larger cells, of different forms from the common polype-cells, constituting the so-called ovarian vesicles, capsules, ovisacs, or bulbules (Pl. 33. figs. 14 b, and 16 b). In these, the gemmæ which are developed within them, and which are often called ova, gradually become bell- or disk-shaped, and assume the form of Acalephæ (*Coryne, Campanularia*, &c.), and on escaping from the vesicles, they swim about freely, subsequently either becoming directly developed into new polypes, or acquiring sexual organs and producing ova.

In other (simple) polypes, distinct spermatic and ovi sacs occur in the parent animals; either together in the same animal, and external (*Hydra*), or separately in different individuals, and internal (*Actinia, &c.*).

The ovum-embryo of the polypes is usually more or less elongate-oval, coated with cilia, and moves about on its long axis like an infusorium. After a short time it fixes itself to some object; the cilia then disappear, and the tentacles of the polypes are protruded. Many of these polypes then increase by gemmation, thus forming new colonies.

The formation of coral-reefs and islands by the skeletons of polypes is well known.

The class Polypi is divided thus:

Order 1. **Hydroida** (Hydrozoa). Internal cavity simple; reproductive organs external. Families:

1. TUBULARIADÆ. Bodies naked or enclosed in a horny tubular envelope; ovisacs or gemmules bud-like, growing from the base of the tentacles. Marine.
2. SERTULARIADÆ. Bodies contained in cup-like sessile cells, situated on a horny polypidom; egg-germs in scattered deciduous capsules. Marine.
3. CAMPANULARIADÆ. As the last, but cells stalked. Marine. Genera, CAMPANULARIA, LAOMEDEA.
4. HYDRAIDÆ. Bodies single, naked. Freshwater.

Order 2. **Actinoida** (Helianthoida and Asteroida, *Johnston*). Internal cavity enclosing the stomach, and divided by radiate septa; germs internal.

Suborder 1. **Actinaria** (Helianthoida). Fam.:

1. ACTINIADÆ. ACTINIA, &c.
2. LUCERNARIADÆ.
3. ZOANTHIDÆ.
4. CARYOPHYLLEADÆ.

Suborder 2. **Alcyonaria** (Asteroida). Fam.

1. PENNATULIDÆ. PENNATULA.
2. ALCYONIDÆ. ALCYONIUM, &c.
3. GORGONIADÆ. GORGONIA, &c.

BIBL. Johnston, *British Zoophytes*; Siebold, *Vergl. Anat.* 25; Wagner, *Icones Zootomicæ*; Farre, *Phil. Trans.* 1837; v. Beneden, *Mém. s. les Campanulaires*, and *Rech. s. les Tubulaires*; Vogt, *Zool. Briefe*; Owen, *Hunterian Lectures*, i.; Lister, *Phil. Trans.* 1834; Couch, *Corn. Fauna*; Hancock, *Ann. Nat. Hist.* 1850. v. 173; Desor, *Ann. des Sc. Nat.* 3 sér. xii.; Dana, *Report on Zoophytes*; Gosse, *Mar. Zool.* i. 15; M.-Edwards and Haime, *Ann. des Sc. Nat.* 1848. ix.

POLYPODIACEÆ.—An order of Ferns, divided into six families by the characters of the sporanges.

Synopsis of the Families.

1. POLYPODIOIDEÆ. Sporanges numerous, united in sessile sori, and divided into two equal parts by a vertical annulus.
2. CYATHÆEÆ. Sporanges numerous, united in sori on a salient axis; with a somewhat oblique annulus.
3. GLEICHENIEÆ. Sporanges united in

fours into sori, and surrounded by an oblique annulus, like a turban.

4. PARKERIEÆ. Sporanges not united in sori, and divided into two equal parts by a more or less extensive vertical annulus.

5. OSMUNDEÆ. Sporanges united in sori, and covered on the back by a broad and imperfect annulus.

6. SCHIZÆEÆ. Sporanges united in sori, and crowned by an annulus that looks like a skull-cap with radiating streaks.

POLYPODIEÆ.—A tribe of Polypodioid Ferns :

Illustrative Genera.

　● *Veins pinnate.*

†. *Margins of the fertile fronds not recolute.*

1. *Polypodium,* L. Sori globose, seated on the apex or the back of veins or venules.

2. *Marginaria.* Sori globose, immersed deeply in the backs of veins or venules.

3. *Pleopeltis.* Sori globose, seated on the backs of veins and venules, with peltate paraphyses concealing the sporanges.

††. *Margins of the fertile fronds recolute.*

4. *Struthiopteris.* Sori globose, seated on the backs of veins and venules.

** *Veins anastomosing, without free veins in the areolæ.*

5. *Dictyopteris.* Sori globose, seated on the anastomosing venules. Venules anastomosing in irregular hexagonal spots.

*** *Veins anastomosing, with free veins in the areolæ.*

6. *Niphobolus.* Sori globose, seated on the apex of the venules. Venules very much branched, forming transverse rhomboid spots; secondary venules arising from the transverse venules, and bearing the sori at their apices.

POLYPODIOIDEÆ.—A family of Polypodiaceous Ferns, of large extent, broken up into tribes and genera, which are characterized by peculiarities generally requiring a more or less powerful lens to distinguish them. In certain cases, where the venation of the leaves, and the relation of this to the fructifying points, are in question, it is found very convenient to scrape off the sori of pinnules and place them in spirits of turpentine or oil, between two slips of glass, for examination with a low power under the microscope by transmitted light. The general arrangement of the sori, with the *indusium,* in very minute forms, is best observed as an

opaque object, with a low power, and a lieberkuhn or side condenser; if held in the mounted forceps, the pinnule can be turned about and thoroughly examined.

Synopsis of the Family.

A. *Without an indusium.*

1. ACROSTICHEÆ. Sporangia scattered over the whole surface.

2. TÆNITIDEÆ. Sori linear, extending to the areolæ of the leaves.

3. GRAMMITIDEÆ. Sori linear, confined to the veins or veinlets.

4. POLYPODIEÆ. Sori at the apices of veins.

5. VITTARIEÆ. Sori in the grooved margin, which simulates an indusium.

B. *With an indusium.*

6. ADIANTEÆ. Sori linear, marginal, at the apices of veins, indusium spurious, formed by the revolute margin.

7. DICKSONIEÆ. Sori globose, apical, indusium lateral, two-valved.

8. DAVALLIEÆ. Sori apical, inframarginal, indusium one-valved.

9. ASPLENIEÆ. Sori on the veins, indusium persistent, lateral, the margin free.

10. ASPIDIEÆ. Sori subglobose, indusium with a central or excentric point of attachment, free all round.

11. PERANEMEÆ. Indusium inferior, ultimately lobed or ciliated.

BIBL. See FERNS.

POLYPODIUM, Linn. — A genus of Ferns with naked sori, of which there are several indigenous representatives, *P. vulgare,* the Oak-Fern, being one of our commonest species. Exceedingly well adapted for examination of the structure of the sori and sporanges in this family.

POLYPOREI.—A family of Hymenomycetous Fungi, characterized by bearing basidiospores clothing tubes, pores, or pits, on the under side of a stalked or sessile *pileus,* or fleshy cap or disk. The basidiospores are seen by horizontal sections from the undersurface of the pileus. (See BASIDIOSPORES and HYMENOMYCETES.)

BIBL. Berkeley, *On the Fructification of Hymenomycetous Fungi, Ann. Nat. Hist.* i. 81; Léveillé, *Sur l'Hymenium des Champignons, Ann. des Sc. Nat.* 2 sér. viii. 324.

POLYSELMIS, Duj.—A genus of Infusoria, of the family Euglenia.

Char. Oblong or variable in form, with several anterior flagelliform filaments, and a single red eye-spot.

Probably the zoospore of a Confervoid Alga.

P. viridis (Pl. 24. fig. 68) resembles a *Euglena* of an oblong form with the ends rounded; one of the filaments is longer than the three or four others which surround its base. Aquatic; length 1-650".

Bibl. Dujardin, *Infus.* p. 370.

POLYSIPHONIA, Grev.—An extensive genus of Rhodomelaceæ (Florideous Algæ), with cylindrical, more or less articulated fronds, the joints consisting of a circle of longitudinally arranged cells surrounding a central cell (like the wood-bundles of a young Dicotyledonous stem surrounding the pith), so that the transverse section presents the appearance of a rosette; the number of peripheral cells varies among the 300 different species of this genus, from four to twenty-five. The British forms mostly have four and six. In some of the species a kind of rind is formed subsequently, by a growth from the base of the joints analogous to that which occurs in Batrachospermum and Callithamnion. The fructification consists of—1. *ceramidia*, attached to the sides of branches, containing numerous pear-shaped spores; 2. *tetraspores* on distinct plants, formed in the swollen central cell of distorted branches (fig. 598); and 3. *antheridia*, elongated whitish sacs, collected in great numbers at the summits of the branches, accompanied by a dichotomous hair, and sometimes prolonged into a hair-like process at the summit. Nägeli describes the spermatozoids as consisting of a spiral filament. Thuret disagrees with this, and states that they are merely hyaline globules, about 1-5000" in diameter. The British species are placed in two subgenera: *Oligosiphonia*, where there are but four or rarely five peripheral cells, and *Polysiphonia*, where there are six or more. Twenty-six species are described, many of which are common.

Fig. 598.

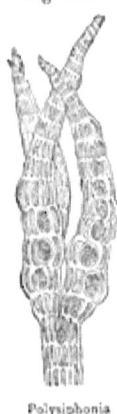

Polysiphonia nigrescens.

Distorted ramuli containing imbedded tetraspores.

Magn. 50 diams.

Bibl. Harvey, *Brit. Mar. Alg.* p. 82, pl. 12 A; Thuret, *Ann. des Sc. Nat.* 3 sér. xvi. p. 16, pl. 6; Nägeli, *Zeitschr. f. wiss. Botan.* Heft 3 and 4 (1846). p. 207, pls. 6 & 7.

POLYSTOMELLA, Lamk. (*Geoponus*, Ehr.).—A genus of Foraminifera, of the order Helicostegia, and family Nautiloidæ.

Char. Shell free, regular, equilateral, constant in form, compressed, often dorsally keeled; *spire* embracing; *chambers* with a single cavity, straight or arched, meeting at the umbilicus and furnished with transverse pits between the sutures or over them. *Orifices* numerous, arranged along the margin of, or forming a triangle at, the upper part of the last chamber.

D'Orbigny asserts the existence of apertures in the lateral pits of the last chambers, which Williamson denies. Two British recent species:

1. *P. crispa* (Pl. 18. fig. 19) = *P. crispa, flexuosa, antonina, regina, josephina,* and *aculeata,* D'Orb.; also fossil.

2. *P. umbilicatula* (Pl. 18. fig. 20) = *Geoponus stella-borealis,* Ehr.

Bibl. D'Orbigny, *For. d. Vienne,* 121; Williamson, *Recent Foram.* 39; Morris, *Brit. Fossils,* 40.

POLYTÆNIUM, Desv.—A genus of Tæniitideæ (Polypodioid Ferns). Exotic.

POLYTHALAMIA. See Foraminifera.

POLYTOMA, Ehr.—A genus of Infusoria, of the family Monadina (Hydromorina).

P. uvella (Pl. 24. fig. 69, undergoing division), the only species, is oblong or oval, obtuse at the ends, colourless, furnished with two flagelliform filaments; it has no carapace. Aquatic; length 1-2200 to 1-900"; size of body when the division is nearly complete, 1-400".

Bibl. Ehrenberg, *Infus.* p. 24.

POLYTRICHACEÆ. — A tribe of Mnioideæ (operculate Mosses of usually Acrocarpous habit).

Genera.

1. *Catharinea.* Calyptra narrowly hood-shaped, subscabrous at the apex, rather hairy within. Peristome simple, composed of thirty-two teeth, arising from a narrow, cellular, basilar membrane, ligulate, membranous, white, with many percurrent, reddish, inarticulate filaments, somewhat incurved, scarcely hygroscopic, firm. Columella dilated at the apex into a drum-like epiphragm. Capsule equal. Inflorescence monœcious or diœcious.

2. *Polytrichum.* Calyptra dimidiate, but appearing campanulate on account of a quantity of very close hairs descending from it as a long villous coat; otherwise resembling the preceding genus.

POLYTRICHUM, Dill. — A genus of Polytrichaceous Mosses, variously defined by different authors. In the British Flora, it includes the forms separated in this work under CATHARINEA, which in the 'Bryologia Britannica' are divided between *Atrichum* and *Oligotrichum*. The species of *Polytrichum* comprised in our definition are distributed in the same work under *Pogonatum* (those with a round capsule and thirty-two teeth) and *Polytrichum* proper (those with a square or prismatic apophysate capsule (fig. 600), and usually twice as many teeth). *P. commune* is one of our finest Mosses, common on heaths, moors, and mountain tracks, varying somewhat under the different physical conditions. The stems are from 6" to 1' long, and the fruit-stalks 2" or 3". The

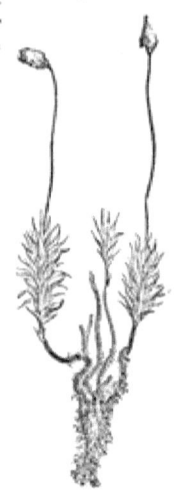

Fig. 599.

Polytrichum commune.

Plants in fruit.

One-half natural size.

stems are almost of woody texture, the leaves large and firm. The calyptra is densely covered with hairs. Wilson remarks that the true structure of the sporange and columella of Mosses may be most easily learned from the study of this genus. The columella (figs. 601, 603) is seen to be separated from the spores by an inner layer of the sporangial membrane. The diaphragm attached to the apices of the teeth of the peristome is the dilated apex of the columella (fig. 603). The peristome (fig. 602) is composed of ligulate obtuse teeth, connected by a membrane at the base, continuous with the inner layer of the wall of the capsule. These plants are also exceedingly well adapted for the examination of the male inflorescence and spermatozoids. They are all diœcious, and the male plants (fig. 604) are readily distinguishable by the cup-shaped inflorescence, composed of scale-like leaves and paraphyses surrounding a number of subulate sacs constituting the *antheridia*. The male flowers of *P. commune, juniperinum,* &c., are found everywhere on heaths in spring.

The antheridia may be readily extracted under a simple lens, and when placed in water

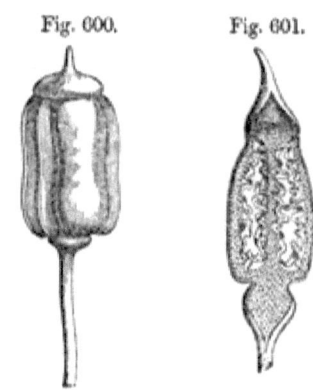

Fig. 600.   Fig. 601.

Polytrichum commune.

Capsule with operculum. Magnified 10 diameters.   Section of young capsule, showing the plaited sporangial membrane.

under the compound microscope, soon (if ripe) burst at the summit and discharge the spermatozoids; these usually escape still enclosed in their parent cells, which when

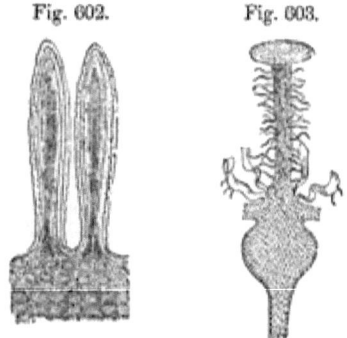

Fig. 602.   Fig. 603.

Polytrichum commune.

Fragment of peristome. Magn. 100 diams.   Columella with section of the apophysis. Magn. 25 diams.

first discharged cohere in a gelatinous mass, but the ciliated spermatozoids (Pl. 32. fig. 33) escape and swim actively in the water. They require at least an eighth object-glass for examination; and the cilia are seen most clearly after drying the object, or treating with tincture of iodine.

Fig. 604.   Fig. 605.

Polytrichum commune.

Male inflorescence.   Innovation from male inflorescence.
One-half nat. size.   Magn. 5 diams.

BIBL. Wilson, *Bryol. Britann.* p. 205 *et seq.*; Thuret, *Ann. des Sc. Nat.* 3 sér. xvi. p. 26, pl. 14.

POLYZOA or BRYOZOA.—A class of Animals, belonging to the subkingdom Mollusca.

Char. Polypiform, aggregate; individual bodies microscopic, contained in horny or calcareous cells, often connected by tubular stems, forming a usually branched polypidom; mouth surrounded by long, ciliated, uncontractile tentacles; alimentary canal folded, mouth and anus separate, but near each other. Marine and aquatic.

The Polyzoa were formerly associated with the Polypes, to which in general structure and appearance they bear considerable resemblance. Leuckart places them between the Annulata and Rotatoria.

They are found everywhere on the seashore, either rooted to or forming a crust upon submerged rocks, stones, shells, &c. The polypidom, sometimes called cenœcium or polyzoary, is usually of a whitish or brownish colour, of a horny or calcareous texture, and consists either of cells or cups simply aggregated (Pl. 33. figs. 17, 20), or connected by tubular stems, and often arranged in elegant plant-like forms (Pl. 33. fig. 5 *a*). Sometimes the cells are immersed in a structureless jelly.

The cells are lined with a delicate membrane (*endocyst*), which terminates at the base of the tentacles, to be reflected upon the alimentary canal; this possesses a minutely cellular structure. The polyzoal cells are of various forms, mentioned under the genera, and they are often furnished with bristles or spines. At or near the distal end of each cell is the orifice, through which the tentacles and more or less of the body of the animals is protruded. In the marine or Infundibulate order, the structure of the cell-mouth is used as a character,—those in which it is terminal and simple (Pl. 33. fig. 30) forming the Cyclostomata, and those in which it is subterminal, curved, and furnished with a moveable lid, the Cheilostomata (Pl. 33. fig. 5 *b*); whilst in the Ctenostomata there is a comb-like circular fringe of bristles connected by a membrane surrounding the cell-orifice, visible when the body is partly protruded.

Curious appendages are found attached mostly to the cells of the polypidoms. The first are called bird's-head processes or *avicularia* (Pl. 33. figs. 5 *b**, and fig. 26). They consist of a body (fig. 26 *f*), a hinge- or lower-jaw-like process (fig. 26 *e*), and a stalk (*f*). They are attached by the stalk to the interior of a round hollow process, projecting slightly from the surface of the polypidom (fig. 26 *a*). The body is divided by an oblique ridge (fig. 26 *d*) on its inner surface into two chambers. The lower portion is moved up and down by an elevator and depressor muscle (fig. 26 *c*). During life the motion is constant; and it continues long after the death of the animal. These bodies appear analogous to the pedicellaria of the Echinodermata.

The second kind, called *vibracula*, consist of a hollow process (fig. 5 *d*, *b*), from which a vibrating filament (fig. 5 *d*, *d*) projects. The interior of the process is filled with a contractile substance which moves the filament.

The body is usually oblong or elongate. At its anterior end is a ring or disk (*lophophore*), upon which the tentacles are placed; this is perfect in the Infundibulata, but deficient at one part, or horse-shoe shaped in the Hippocrepia (Pl. 33. figs. 3 *e* & 9). The tentacles are hollow, closed at the end, uncontractile, coated externally with cilia on the sides next each other, and communicate with the cavity of the body, through apertures in the disk. In most of the Hippocrepia, the tentacles are surrounded at the base by a transparent cup-like membrane (*calyx*), prolonged somewhat upon each tentacle, and mostly dentate at the margin.

Digestive System.—The mouth is situated in the middle of the tentacular disk (Pl. 33. fig. 3 c), and is closeable in the Hippocrepia by an epiglottis-like hollow valve (*epistome*), which is absent in the Infundibulata; at the base of this valve is an aperture which perforates the disk to open into the abdominal cavity. The mouth terminates in a pharynx (Pl. 33. fig. 5 e, f) and œsophagus (fig. 18*, b, d) often of considerable length, which is sometimes succeeded by a strongly muscular gizzard. Next comes the stomach (figs. 5 e, b*, 18*, f), often very capacious, and with an appendix (fig. 18* e), and finally the intestine (fig. 18* g), which terminates outside, but close to the disk (fig. 5 e, c). Thus the alimentary canal is bent upon itself, the two orifices being very near each other.

The alimentary canal consists of three coats: an inner rugose, composed of cells with brownish contents, and representing a liver; a middle, composed of colourless nucleated cells; and an outer, thin, cellular coat, probably containing muscular fibres. The mouth and more or less of the upper portion of the alimentary are ciliated.

The walls of the cavity of the abdomen, the interior of the disk and of the tentacles all communicate, and are filled with a clear liquid, in which irregular particles float, and in which a constant rotatory motion exists, produced partly by muscular action, and partly by cilia. This liquid corresponds to a chylaqueous fluid, and performs the chyliferous, sanguiferous and respiratory functions; for there are no distinct respiratory organs nor blood-vessels.

The muscular system is well-developed, the fibres being transversely striated; the principal arising from the bottom of the cells, and being inserted into the sides of the œsophagus, so as to exert a retracting action upon the body.

The nervous system consists of an oval ganglion attached to the œsophagus, and giving off branches to the tentacles, alimentary canal, &c.

Reproduction.—The Polyzoa are propagated by gemmation, and by the agency of sexual organs.

Two kinds of gemmation occur. In the first, the gemmæ are developed externally from the parent-cells, and usually near the orifice, but often from the stem; these gemmæ, on attaining their full development,

remain attached to the parent, thus forming the compound organism. In the second, they are formed internally, upon the funiculus, afterwards becoming free within the abdominal cavity, from which they escape at an orifice near the disk, according to Van Beneden, although this is denied by Allman. The latter kind, which are often called ova, have an external hard coat, exhibiting the appearance of a marginal ring, and are often of a dark colour. Their development is not dependent upon impregnation; and they seem to correspond to the winter ova of the Entomostraca, &c.: Allman proposes the name *statoblasts* for them. The sexual organs, which usually exist together in the same cells, consist of a roundish ovary, attached by a short peduncle near the orifice of the cells; whilst the testis is a roundish irregular mass attached to the funiculus. The ova, which are first set free in the abdominal cavity, are ciliated and swim freely.

The Polyzoa are divided into two orders:

1. HIPPOCREPIA (*Phylactolæmata*, Allman). Tentacular disk horseshoe-shaped or bilateral, mouth with an epistome. Mostly aquatic.

2. INFUNDIBULATA (*Gymnolæmata*, Allman). Disk circular, or nearly so, epistome absent. Mostly marine.

The synopsis of the suborders is given under the respective heads, excepting that of the Cyclostomata, which is omitted, and may find place here.

Suborder CYCLOSTOMATA (see INFUNDIBULATA). Two families:

1. *Tubuliporidæ.* Polypidom calcareous, massive, circular, or lobed or divided dichotomously; cells long and tubular, orifice round, prominent, and unconstricted.

2. *Crisiadæ.* Polypidom plant-like, jointed, branched; cells tubular, in one or two rows; orifices round, alternately facing opposite sides.

BIBL. Johnston, *Brit. Zooph.* 253; Busk, *Catal. of Marine Polyzoa (Brit. Mus.)*; Siebold, *Vergleich. Anat.* 25; Farre, *Phil. Trans.* 1837; Dumortier and Van Beneden, *Mém. de l'Acad. de Bruxelles*, 1850; Vogt, *Zool. Briefe*, i. 246; Lister, *Phil. Trans.* 1834; Couch, *Corn. Fauna*; Hancock, *Ann. Nat. Hist.* 1850, v.; Leuckart, *Van d. Hoeven's Zoologie (Nachträge)*, 47; Allman, *Freshwater Polyzoa*; Gosse, *Mar. Zool.* ii. 1.

POMPHOLYX, Gosse.—A genus of Rotatoria, of the family Brachionæa.

BIBL. Gosse, *Ann. Nat. Hist.* 1851. viii. p. 203.

PONTIA, Fabr.—A genus of Lepidopterous Insects, of the family Papilionidæ.

This genus contains some of the commonest butterflies, as *P. brassicæ*, the large-cabbage butterfly; *P. rapæ*, the small-cabbage butterfly; and *P. napi*, the green-veined white butterfly.

The form and structure of certain scales existing upon the under side of the wings of the males are curious; and the markings were formerly found so difficult to render distinct, that the scales were used as test-objects.

In the male *P. brassicæ* the upper surface of the anterior wings is free from spots, whilst in the female there are two black spots in that situation. The peculiar scales are represented in Pl. 27. fig. 24; fig. 26 exhibits a portion of the wing with the ordinary scales.

In *P. rapæ* and *P. napi* the anterior wings of the males have a single spot upon the upper surface, whilst there are two upon each wing in the females. The peculiar scales bear considerable resemblance in the two species (Pl. 27. fig. 23 *a*, scale of *P. rapæ*; fig. 23 *b*, portion of wing, showing the points of attachment of the two kinds of scales).

The scales may be separated by gently pressing the under surface of the wings against a slide.

See SCALES of insects and TEST-OBJECTS.

BIBL. Westwood, *Brit. Butterflies*.

POPPY.—The seeds of Poppies (*Papaver*, L., Nat. Order Papaveraceæ) are elegant opaque objects under a low power, the testa being pitted so as to produce a reticulated surface (Pl. 31. fig. 14).

POROSITY OF BODIES.—That all bodies are porous to a greater or less degree, allowing vapours and gases to pass through their substance, is an established fact in physics and physiology. The passage of solid particles, also, as charcoal and sulphur, through certain organic tissues in which no apertures have hitherto been detected, as the skin and mucous membranes, has recently been attested by several observers.

M. Keber believes that he has detected the existence of pores in all bodies of whatever kind; these he finds in the dots, streaks and irregular markings from 1-11,000 to 1-45,000″ in diameter, visible in minute and thin scrapings and fragments of (dry) solids, as particles of dust, scrapings from a piece of bladder, &c. This view does not require a serious refutation. Of evidence that the markings are pores, there is none; and on examining a thoroughly cleaned and thin piece of the membrane of a vegetable cell, we do not perceive anything corresponding to pores. If the true pores are ever detected by the microscope, there can be little question that they will exhibit a beautifully regular arrangement; whereas the so-called pores of the author are totally devoid of definite arrangement.

BIBL. Keber, *Mikrosk. Untersuch. üb. die Porosität d. Körper*, and *Phil. Mag.* 1854. pp. 287 and 370.

POROUS STRUCTURES OF PLANTS.—What are ordinarily called porous tissues in vegetable anatomy are described in accordance with their real nature under the head of PITTED STRUCTURES. True pores do, however, occur in the walls of vegetable cells, from secondary or ultimate changes in their character. They are seen in the cells of the leaves of *Leucobryum* and *Sphagnum* (see SPHAGNACEÆ). Other regular orifices are produced in the walls of the cells of many of the zoospore-producing Confervæ, as *Conferva*, *Cladophora*, *Enteromorpha*, &c. (see Pl. 5). The wall of the sporangial cell of *Achlya* presents analogous openings; and according to Cohn, pores are produced in the spore-cells of SPHÆROPLEA to admit the spermatozoids. The pits and the interstices between reticulated fibrous secondary deposits are often changed into true holes in old cells; but this is a result of decay of the primary membrane; it takes place very early, however, at the contiguous ends of SPIRAL-fibrous and PITTED CELLS coalescing to form ducts, changing the septum formed by the adjoining ends into a kind of grating, or irregularly torn diaphragm.

BIBL. See the heads referred to in this article.

PORPHYRA, Ag.—A genus of Porphyraceæ (Florideous Algæ), with an expanded, membranous, shortly-stalked frond, composed of a single layer of cells approximated in fours, the contents of purple or red colour. Fructification consisting of—1. scattered sori of oval *spores*; 2. *tetraspores* (crucial) immersed in the frond; and 3. *antheridia*, on the same or distinct plants. *P. laciniata* and *vulgaris* are common on our coasts.

BIBL. Harvey, *Brit. Mar. Alg.* p. 261, pl. 25 A; Thuret, *Mémoires de la Société de Cherbourg*, ii. 1854; *Ann. des Sc. Nat.* 4 sér.

iii. p. 5; Derbès and Solier, *Supplément aux Comptes Rendus*, i.

PORPHYRACEÆ.—A tribe of Florideous Algæ (according to Thuret), of low organization, forming Ulvoid membranous fronds or strata of Confervoid filaments, of a purple or red colour. They are placed among the Ulvaceæ by most authors, but differ in the absence of the zoospores and, according to Thuret, the presence of tetraspores and antheridia. They are marine,—*Porphyra* growing on rocks and stones, *Bangia* the same, or parasitic upon *Zostera*, Algæ, &c.

British Genera.

1. *Porphyra*. Frond plane, membranous, very thin, of a purple colour, with oval spores in sori, and tetraspores (square) scattered all over the frond.

2. *Bangia*. Frond filiform, tubular, composed of numerous radiating cells in transverse rows, enclosed within a continuous hyaline sheath.

PORPHYRIDIUM, Näg. = *Palmella cruenta?*

PORRIGO. See FAVUS.

POTASH, AND ITS SALTS.

Caustic Potash.—The strength of the solution may be that of the Liq. Potassæ of the Pharmacopœia. But we prefer a stronger solution made with 1 drachm of the *potassa fusa* or stick-potash of the shops, and 1 fluid oz. of water. The solution should be allowed to settle, and the clear portion poured off into one of the test-bottles (INTR. p. xxiii).

Some remarks are made upon the action of potash in the INTR. p. xxxviii, and others under the heads of the tissues, &c. On treating organic substances with this reagent, the cystic-oxide-like crystals of the carbonate (Pl. 6. fig. 7*) will frequently be formed.

Chromates of Potash.—The bichromate is used in the preparation of the chromate of lead for injection. Its crystals polarize well. The neutral chromate is also sometimes used for preparing injections.

Nitrate of potash, nitre, or saltpetre.—This salt is dimorphous: it usually crystallizes in six-sided prisms with dihedral summits, or in other forms belonging to the right-rhombic prismatic system. But sometimes it assumes the form of obtuse rhombohedra, resembling those of nitrate of soda, and referable to the rhombohedric system.

The crystals exhibit very beautifully the phænomena of ANALYTIC CRYSTALS.

BIBL. That of CHEMISTRY.

POTTIA, Ehr.—A genus of Pottiaceous Mosses, including some of the *Gymnostoma* and *Weissiæ* of Hedwig and others. Wilson separates as *Anacalyptæ* the species with a peristome (fig. 606).

Fig. 606.

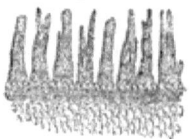

Pottia cæspitosa.

Fragment of peristome.

Magnified 50 diameters.

POTTIACEÆ. — A tribe of Pottioid Mosses.

Synopsis of Genera.

1. *Pottia*. Calyptra dimidiate. Peristome simple or wanting; if present, composed of lanceolate articulate teeth, simple or with a longitudinal line, rugulose and somewhat fleshy.

2. *Trichostomum*. Calyptra dimidiate. Peristome simple, sixteen teeth split to the base into two cilia, or irregularly and therefore into more than two, erect, stiff, and not twisted.

3. *Barbula*. Calyptra dimidiate-hood-shaped. Peristome simple, ciliiform; cilia thirty-two, solitary or approximated in pairs on a more or less exserted basilar membrane, split into two cilioles behind, very long, articulate-rugulose, twisted to the left, rarely to the right, in one or several spires, hygroscopic. Cells of the operculum and calyptra twisted in the same way.

4. *Ceratodon*. Calyptra dimidiate. Peristome simple; teeth sixteen, connate at the base into a cellular membrane, split into two long, nodosely articulated, dark-coloured arms, paler on each side, densely trabeculated at the lower part. Capsule thick-skinned, shining, nodding, with a somewhat nodose collum; annulate.

5. *Weissia*. Calyptra dimidiate. Peristome simple or wanting; if present, composed of sixteen lanceolate or subulate, entire or cribrose, equidistant teeth.

POTTIOIDEÆ.—A family of operculate Mosses belonging to the Acrocarpi, but sometimes Pleurocarpous by innovating branches. Leaves of very varied form, with a terete nerve; cells parenchymatous, perfectly hexagonal or squarish six-sided, always looser at the base, sometimes very lax, more or less pellucid, often exceedingly transparent, large, fragile, rigid, foraminate, bearing on the upper side solitary papillæ or several confluent papillæ (hence often truncate and tuberculate at the apex), placed in the middle of the cell; cells mostly full of chlorophyll, sometimes with a primordial utricle, often very small and thickened. Capsule erect, rarely inclined, oval, elliptic or pear-shaped oblong, smooth or striate, the operculum mostly conical or beaked.

This family is divided into three tribes:

1. CALYMPERACEÆ. Basilar cells of the leaves rigid, hyaline, often very brittle, more or less ample, empty, distinctly foraminated.

2. POTTIACEÆ. Basilar cells of the leaves soft, pellucid, longer, mostly empty, rarely containing a persistent primordial utricle.

3. ORTHOTRICHACEÆ. Basilar cells of the leaves with only the very lowest soft, the upper mostly thickened, rarely pellucid and normal.

PRASIOLA, Meneghini.—A genus of Ulvaceæ (Confervoid Algæ), separated from *Monostroma*, Thuret, by the arrangement of the quadrigeminate cells of the frond in lines, with wide intercellular walls: from *Ulva* by the existence of only a single layer of cells, and from both by the absence (?) of a reproduction by zoospores; from *Schizogonium* by the frond consisting of expanded plates. The species are included under *Ulva* (the terrestrial forms) in the *Brit. Flora* and Harvey's *Algæ*, ed. 1. They have recently been examined by Jessen, who finds the fronds proliferous at the margins; the 'spores' he describes as consisting of motionless cells formed of the entire contents of the cells of the frond, set free by the solution of the parent-cell. The reproduction of this group seems to us to require further investigation. Jessen includes here the British species, *P. calophylla, crispa, furfuracea*, and a form which he names *P. stipitata*, differing from the last chiefly in the narrowly wedge-shaped, stipitate character of the frond: probably the three last constitute only varieties of one species.

BIBL. Jessen, *Prasiolæ Monograph.* Kiliæ, 1848; Harvey, *Brit. Alg.* ed. 1. p. 171; Hassall, *Brit. Freshw. Alg.* p. 297, pls. 77, 78; Kütz. *Sp. Alg.* p. 472.

PREPARATION of microscopic objects for examination and preservation.—Some remarks on the former point will be found in the INTRODUCTION, p. xxviii; and under many of the general articles, such as DIATOMACEÆ, COAL, OVULE, &c., special directions are given. A few general remarks may be offered in this place. The parts of bodies are separated by means of the mounted needles under a dissecting microscope, or by means of sections, according to the nature of the views which it is desired to obtain. With regard to the former operation, it need be observed merely that it is usually to be performed under water, in a watch-glass, glass cell, or other convenient holder.

The preparation of sections is a more complicated process. Soft parts of animals are best sliced by means of a Valentin's knife; but firmer structures, such as horn, may be cut with a sharp razor. Vegetable structures in general are sliced with a razor, which must be kept very sharp, and rubbed on a strop frequently while in use, and always before putting it away. Fresh stems, thick leaves, &c., may be simply held in the fingers; thin objects, such as leaves, petals, &c., are best placed in a split cork, the halves of which are kept together by insertion in the neck of a vial or a test-tube, which at the same time serves as a handle. Sometimes it is advantageous to immerse objects, especially soft or very small ones, in thick mucilage of gum-arabic, and to allow this to dry until tough enough to be cut by the razor; the slices are freed from gum by immersion in water. Dry objects, such as wood, dried leaves, seeds, &c., must be softened by soaking in water before slicing. Small firm objects, such as seeds, are most easily sliced when fixed in a bit of white wax or stearine, which may be done by placing them on the surface of the latter, and stirring them into the substance melted by the application of a hot wire. Most slices of vegetable objects are obscured by air-bubbles engaged in the intercellular passages, &c. In old wood and similar objects the air is readily driven out by heat; in fresh structures, where heat may coagulate or dissolve matters, the air may be allowed to dissolve or escape by itself, which requires time, or may be removed by exhaustion. A substitute for a regular air-pump may prove useful to the microscopist, consisting of a piece of thick and stout glass tube, closed at one end, containing a tight-fitting piston, with a valve opening upwards; the object being placed in water (or other liquid) at the bottom, a single raising of the piston, or at all events, two pulls, will draw out all the air, and the water will take its place. This apparatus may be used also for saturating dry objects with oil of turpentine (for mounting in balsam), or with oil, to produce transparency.

Sections of woods, &c. which are to be mounted in liquids, should be soaked for some little time in spirit or turpentine, to remove resins, &c. A special apparatus is made for slicing such objects; but this is not of much use except when large numbers of very perfect sections of the same kind are required for purposes of sale, &c.

It need scarcely be said that sections require to be made in various directions in studying objects by these means. Thus stems should be sliced horizontally, and perpendicularly both parallel to the medullary rays and at right angles to them, &c. When working with high powers, it is necessary to be on our guard against appearances of striation or fibres which may be produced by the fine notches in the cutting instrument.

The structure of laminated shells, &c. may often be seen in fragments broken off by the point of a knife. But sections of shell, bone, &c. are best made by sawing off thin pieces with a frame-saw having a watch-spring blade, grinding them down upon a water-of-Ayr or some other stone, and polishing them upon a clean leather-hone or strop with putty-powder and water, finally upon a dry hone alone.

Sections of very hard substances, as agate, &c., are so easily made by jewellers, that a description of the process is scarcely necessary. They are made by means of a circular iron plate, made to rotate by a lathe, its margins being coated with a mixture of oil and diamond dust. They are then ground upon a plate of metal with emery-powder and water, and polished upon a flat surface of pitch with putty-powder and water.

In grinding and polishing sections of hard structures, it is often requisite to cement them to a slide with Canada balsam, heat being applied until the balsam has become so hard as to fix the section firmly to the slide. As soon as one side has been polished, the section is removed from the slide, the balsam being rendered soft by heat, the polished side cemented to the glass, and the other side polished. The balsam may afterwards be separated from the section by maceration in oil of turpentine, æther, &c.

PRESERVATION of microscopic objects.—Under this head we shall consider the arrangement of microscopic objects for permanent preservation, or the MOUNTING of them, as it is called, supposing that they have been prepared (PREPARATION) in such manner as to render this desirable. We shall first notice—

Dry objects, or those which exhibit their structural peculiarities in the dry state. These are sometimes mounted alone, at others when immersed in some preservative compound.

1. In the dry and uncovered state, they are occasionally mounted upon disks of cork, leather, or pasteboard, the surface upon which the object is to be placed being blackened by a coating of very fine lamp-black mixed with warm size or gum-water, or by a piece of dull black paper pasted upon it; the simplest way of making the disks is to paste black paper upon thick soft leather, and cut out the disks with a punch, like gun-wads. The object is fastened to the disk with a little solution of marine glue in naphtha, or with gum. The disks are sold in the shops. They are usually transfixed with a pin, by which they may be fixed in the forceps under the microscope, and may be fastened to the bottom of a box lined with sheet-cork when not in use. The advantage of this plan is its simplicity; its greater disadvantage, however, is that the objects are liable to injury, and become covered with dust. It answers very well for common objects, seeds, minute lichens, &c.; but when the objects are of value, they should be mounted in a cell.

2. The cell may be made of a square piece of card-board or pasteboard, of suitable thickness, with a hole punched in the middle, fastened to a slide by marine glue or Canada balsam; the object being fixed to the slide by a little of either of the above cements, and a thin glass cover cemented to the card-board. Or the whole may be fastened together with paste: first a piece of black paper upon the middle of the slide, then the perforated square, next the object, and lastly the cover. The square of pasteboard may be replaced by a glass ring, a perforated square of glass, or a piece of sheet gutta percha.

3. When the objects are minute or very thin, the square of pasteboard may be dispensed with, and they may be mounted thus: they are to be laid upon a slide, and a cover of thin glass placed upon them; a piece of

paper larger than the cover, with a portion cut from the middle larger than the object, is then covered with paste, and a minute or two allowed to elapse, that the paper may become thoroughly imbued with it, the superfluous paste being removed with the paste-brush; the paper with the pasted side downwards is then laid upon the cover and the adjacent portions of the slide, and gently pressed with a cloth, that it may be accurately applied to the glass surfaces. The whole is then allowed to dry. The principal point in this process is the complete removal of the superfluous paste before the paper is applied. If this be not effected, it will be drawn by capillary attraction between the cover and the slide, and reaching the object, will spoil it.

4. A very secure method of mounting dry objects which are not altered by heat, consists in laying a ring or square of black japan upon a slide, the thickness of the layer being adapted to that of the object, and applying a pretty strong or long-continued heat until the cement becomes perfectly hard when cold. The object is next placed within the ring, a cover laid on, and heat applied until the cement becomes liquid. Gentle pressure then brings the cement and the margins of the cover into contact; and when the cement becomes cold, the cover is firmly fixed to the slide.

5. Another method of fastening the cover to the slide is by the use of electrical cement and balsam (CEMENTS, p. 135, 5 b) mixed with 1 or 2 parts of tallow.

6. Many dry objects can be well preserved by—

Mounting in Canada Balsam.—When this is to be done, care must be taken that they are thoroughly dry; otherwise they will acquire a milky appearance, from being surrounded by minute drops of water. Some objects in drying curl up or become deformed, although their minute structure may not be essentially changed; this may be prevented by confining them between two slides tied together with thread, or held together by india-rubber rings, sealing-wax applied at the two ends, or by a folded strip of brass with the ends riveted. If the objects be of tolerable size, they are then soaked in oil of turpentine kept in an ointment-pot covered with a lid, for some hours, or even days, until the air is entirely displaced from them by the turpentine. The latter will often also remove the colouring matter from some objects, as parts of insects,

which may or may not be desirable; hence the duration of the process must vary accordingly. A clean slide is then warmed over the flame of a spirit-lamp, or upon a stove, and some clear balsam placed in the middle of it, and rendered more liquid by further gentle heat; the object is then carefully removed from the turpentine with forceps, drained, and laid upon the warm balsam. Some more balsam is then allowed to fall from the warmed wire (BALSAM) upon the object, and when this is well covered with it, a warmed cover is gently laid upon its surface. The superfluous balsam then escapes at the sides of the cover; and this should be aided by gentle pressure. The slide is next maintained at a gentle heat upon a warm mantelpiece, or a piece of tin-plate (INTR. p. xxiv), until, when allowed to cool, the balsam is perfectly hard. As soon as this is the case, the superfluous portions are cut away or scraped off with a knife, the surfaces of the glasses cleaned from any residue by a cloth wetted with oil of turpentine, and some sealing-wax varnish applied to the edges of the cover and the adjacent portions of the slide.

7. The success of the operation depends mainly upon two circumstances, viz. the object having been thoroughly dried, and the exclusion of air-bubbles. The former constitutes no difficulty, time being all that is required; but the latter requires that the object shall previously have been thoroughly moistened with the turpentine, and that the balsam shall have been added to the object, when laid in the balsam upon the slide, before so much of the turpentine has evaporated as will allow air to enter any minute cavities in the object. The heat applied should also be gentle; and if the direct flame of a spirit-lamp be used, its application should be made rather to some portion of the slide near that upon which the object is placed, than directly beneath the object. If much heat be applied, bubbles of the vapour of the turpentine will often disfigure the object for a time; but these will vanish as the object becomes cool.

If air-bubbles have found their way into the object, the slide must be macerated in oil of turpentine until the balsam is dissolved and the object liberated, and a fresh mounting made.

8. If the object be large, it must be mounted in a cell. A glass ring (sold in the shops) of suitable thickness must first be cemented to the slide by balsam; more bal-

sam is then added until the cavity is filled, the object next added, and the cover applied.

9. If the object be minute, its removal for maceration in the turpentine is not requisite, and might entail the loss of the object. It must then be laid upon a slide, a drop or two of turpentine added, and the whole warmed until no air-bubbles are visible. The cover is then removed, most of the turpentine drained off, balsam added from the warmed wire, and the cover applied as before; or balsam may be placed upon the slide near the margin of the applied cover, and, on applying a continued gentle heat, it will find its way under the cover, and replace the turpentine as it evaporates.

10. If air-bubbles remain in parts of a minute object, a cover should be applied, turpentine added, and the slide held over a lamp until the turpentine boils, and the bubbles disappear on cooling. The cover is then removed, most of the turpentine allowed to evaporate, the balsam added, and the cover re-applied.

11. *Gum and Glycerine.*—Objects which cannot be conveniently dried may be mounted in a solution of gum-arabic in glycerine; the manipulations are much the same as with balsam, except that no heat is required.

12. *Mounting in liquid.*—The structure of many objects is so altered by drying, that they require to be mounted in some preservative liquid. These, if of considerable size, must be mounted in glass cells.

13. The cells may consist of glass rings, *i.e.* portions cut transversely from pieces of glass tubes, of various sizes, according to the dimensions of the objects. In using these, the ring is first warmed in the flame of a spirit-lamp, being held by steel forceps; one of the ground surfaces of the ring is then covered with marine glue or balsam previously melted in the same flame; the surface of the slide to which the ring is to be cemented is then heated in the flame, and whilst it is hot, the surface of the ring coated with the melted cement is applied to it, and the ring pressed firmly, so as to displace the superfluous portions. When cold, these are to be removed with the point of a knife; sometimes a little solution of potash, oil of turpentine, or naphtha is required for this purpose. The cell is then complete, excepting the lid or cover, which consists of a circular plate of thin glass, of slightly less diameter than that of the outer margin of the glass ring. The cell is now to be

filled with the preservative liquid, the object placed in it, and the cover applied, being made to slide over the upper surface of the ring, so as to displace any excess of liquid, and prevent the admission of air-bubbles. If the quantity of liquid at first put into the cell be not sufficient, more must be added, until slight excess is present; the superfluous portions may be removed by a piece of blotting-paper, and the margin of the cover and ring very carefully wiped clean with a silk handkerchief, so that the surfaces may be free from all traces of the preservative liquid. The exposed parts of the upper surface of the glass ring, and the adjacent margins of the cover, are then to be coated lightly with one of the liquid cements, by means of a camel's-hair pencil; and when the first coat is dry, another must be laid on, so that the edges of the cover and the adjacent parts of the glass ring may be firmly cemented together, and the cell completely closed, so that no evaporation of the contained liquid can take place.

The important points in this process are, that the heated cement used to fasten the ring to the slide must accurately coat every portion of the two surfaces in apposition, and that the surfaces to which the liquid cement is applied must be perfectly clean and dry, so that the cement may come into contact with the surfaces of the glass.

14. When the objects are very large, the rings may be conveniently replaced by cells constructed of slips of glass, arranged so as to constitute four sides of a box, the bottom of the box being formed by the slide, and the top by a plate of thin glass: the pieces should be cemented together by marine glue.

15. Smaller cells may be made with marine glue, melted, dropped upon a slide, and flattened whilst warm with a piece of wetted glass, the superfluous portions and central portion cut away with a knife: should the marine glue become loosened from the slide, it may be re-fastened by heat; and if the upper surface be not perfectly flat, it may be made so by grinding with emery-powder and water upon a plate of metal or upon a stone.

Minute objects may be mounted in liquid, in a variety of ways, the choice of which will vary according to the option of the microscopist. They are generally mounted in shallow cells, the sides of which are formed by varnish.

16. The old method consisted in placing

the object upon a slide, adding a drop or two of the preservative liquid, applying the glass cover, adding more of the liquid, or removing excess with blotting-paper, until the space between the slide and cover is accurately filled, then applying to the margin of the cover and the adjacent portions of the slide a coat of some liquid cement, as gold-size, black japan, &c. Objects thus mounted keep well for a time; but the cement soon apparently runs into the space between the cover and the slide, and the object becomes spoiled. It is often requisite, however, to mount an object in this way, which may be lying upon a slide, perhaps in some peculiar position which it is important for it to retain; when this is the case, the electrical cement with balsam and tallow (PRESERVATION, § 5) should be used; and there is less fear of change, provided spirit be not used as the preservative liquid.

17. Whenever it is possible, then, a cell-wall should be previously formed, by laying a ring or square of one of the liquid cements upon the slide with a camel's-hair pencil, and applying a continued heat until it becomes thoroughly hard when cold. The cements generally used are—black japan; gold-size with which a little finely powdered litharge has been well mixed, immediately applied, as it soon hardens; sealing-wax varnish; solution of marine glue in naphtha, or of Canada balsam in æther, or the balsam alone. If the upper surfaces of the rings or squares formed of these compounds, when thoroughly dry and hard, be not perfectly flat, they may be made so by grinding alone, or with emery and water, upon a piece of metal, marble, or a stone. The object is then placed in the cell, the preservative liquid added, and the cell closed as above described.

The following are the most important preservative liquids and compounds :—

Thwaites's liquid is thus prepared: to 16 parts of distilled water add 1 part of rectified spirit, and a few drops of creosote sufficient to saturate it; stir in a small quantity of prepared chalk, and then filter. With this liquid mix an equal measure of camphor-water, and before using, strain through fine muslin. Used by Mr. Thwaites for preserving freshwater Algæ, as having but little action upon the endochrome.

Ralfs's liquid.—Prepared with bay-salt and alum, of each a grain, distilled water 1 oz.; dissolve. Forms a readily prepared

substitute for the former, in the preservation of the Algæ (Desmidiaceæ).

Acetate of alumina.—1 part of the salt to 4 parts of distilled water. Mr. Topping finds this the best preservative for delicate vegetable colours.

Distilled water.—Very often used for preserving Algæ; but perhaps camphor-water would be better.

Camphor-water is prepared by digesting distilled water with a lump of camphor.

Spirit and water.—Proof-spirit may be prepared by mixing 5 measures of rectified spirit with 3 of water. It is frequently used for preserving animal structures, organs, injections, &c. Delicate preparations may be kept in a mixture of 1 part of spirit with 5 parts of water. Dilute spirit should never be used as a preservative when it can possibly be avoided, on account of its action upon the cements.

Creosote water is prepared by filtering a saturated solution of creosote in rectified spirit, mixed with 20 parts of water. It is recommended for preserving preparations of muscle, cellular tissue, tendon, cartilage, &c.

Arsenious acid.—A preservative liquid is made of this substance by boiling excess of the acid with water, filtering the solution, and adding 2 parts of water. It is a very good preservative of animal tissues.

Corrosive sublimate.—Harting recommends a solution of this substance as the best preservative for the corpuscles of the blood, nerve, muscular fibre, &c.; the strength of the solution must vary from 1 part in 200 to 500 of water, according to the nature of the object. Thus the blood-corpuscles of the frog require 1-400, those of birds 1-300, of mammals 1-200.

Salt (chloride of sodium) and water, 5 gr. to the ounce, was long since recommended for the preservation of tissues, but is not much used, because fungi are apt to grow in it, which might, however, be prevented by saturating it with camphor by digestion. M. Corti has found "a tolerably concentrated solution" the best preservative for the delicate structures and nerve-cells of the internal ear.

Carbonate of potash.—1 part dissolved in from 200 to 500 of distilled water, is a good preservative of the primitive nerve-tubes.

Arsenite of potash.—1 part dissolved in 160 of water has been found useful for preserving the primitive nerve-tubes.

Glycerine.—We have found this the most valuable of all liquids for vegetable preparations, which may be closed air-tight or not at pleasure. Dissections covered with a glass may be left in it from day to day, remaining unchanged and always ready for examination. Objects may be mounted in it as with chloride of calcium.

Glycerine and Gum.—Pure gum-arabic 1 oz., glycerine 1 oz., water 1 oz., arsenious acid 1½ grain; dissolve the arsenious acid in the water, then the gum (without heat), add the glycerine, and incorporate with great care to avoid forming bubbles.

Canada balsam (See BALSAM, Canada). —When rendered thinner by digestion with a little æther at a gentle heat, it forms a liquid cement.

Gum-water (see CEMENTS, p. 135, § 14). —The solution should be very thick, so as to flow with difficulty from the end of a wire. It may be used like balsam, but without heat. The residue is very apt to crack when dry; this may be prevented by applying a thick coating of varnish around its margin.

Chloride of calcium (CALCIUM, chloride of).—Objects may be mounted in this solution without closing the cell, by pasting two narrow strips of paper transversely upon a slide, leaving a greater interval than the breadth of the object; the latter is then laid upon the slide, a small quantity of the solution added, and a cover applied. The solution must not touch the paper. The cover may be fixed to the paper on the slide by the electrical cement with balsam and tallow. It is best, however, to close the cell.

Chloride of zinc.—This is perhaps the best preservative of animal tissues for microscopic examination known. It exerts a slight coagulating action; but this is not sufficient to impair seriously the peculiarities of the objects, and the large portions of all structures which may require to be subsequently examined should be kept in it. The strength must vary according to the softness of the tissues. The best ordinary strength is in the proportion of 20 grains of the fused chloride to 1 oz. of water, or 400 grains to the pint. A lump of camphor should be kept floating upon the surface of the solution in the stock-bottle.

Goadby's solutions.—These are of three kinds. The first (A) is made with—bay-salt (coarse sea-salt) 4 oz., alum 2 oz., corrosive sublimate 2 grains, boiling water 1 quart. This is too strong for most purposes, and is only to be employed where great astringency is required to give form and support to delicate structures.

The second (B) is made with—bay-salt 4 oz., alum 2 oz., corrosive sublimate 4 grains, water 2 quarts. This is recommended for general use, and as best adapted for permanent preparations. Mr. Thwaites uses it for marine Algæ; but we have found chloride of calcium answer for this purpose, and it is much more secure. Schultze recommends it for preserving *Medusæ*, Echinodermata, Annelid larvæ, Entomostraca, Diatomaceæ, Polythalamia, and Polycystina, both the hard and the soft parts; and advises the use of glycerine afterwards to produce transparence.

When carbonate of lime exists in the preparations, as in the Mollusca, the following (C) should be used:—take of bay-salt 8 oz., corrosive sublimate 2 grains. water 1 quart. Marine animals require a stronger liquid (D) of this kind, made by adding about 2 oz. more salt to the last.

Deane's compound.—This is made with— gelatine 1 oz., honey 5 oz., water 5 oz., rectified spirit ½ oz., and 6 drops of creosote. The gelatine is soaked in the water until soft, and then added to the honey, which has been previously raised to a boiling-heat in another vessel; then boil the mixture, and when it has cooled somewhat, add the creosote mixed with the spirit; lastly, filter through fine flannel.

When about to be used, the compound must be slightly warmed, and the object placed in a drop upon a previously warmed slide. The cover is then to be breathed upon and applied, taking care to exclude air-bubbles; a coating of black japan or Brunswick black around the margin completes the whole.

Chromic acid. See p. 153.

Soluble glass.—This compound, which is a solution of silicate of soda or potash, or of both, promises to become one of the best preservative liquids. It is used as glycerine, and in the course of a day or two becomes perfectly hard, retaining a beautiful glass-like transparency. Unfortunately all our specimens have become opake, on account of the formation of crystals, apparently from the presence of too much alkali. When properly prepared, it will undoubtedly surpass all other preservatives, on account of its durability and extremely low refractive power, which scarcely exceeds that of water.

Remarks.—It may be well to make a few general remarks upon the selection and use of the preservative liquids, and the method of mounting objects.

That preservative liquid should always be chosen which exerts least action upon the structure of the object which it is required to preserve.

When drying the object does not destroy its peculiar structure, and the object is not very transparent, balsam should be used.

If the structure be destroyed by drying, and the object be not impaired by endosmosis, the chloride of calcium or glycerine is best. Other circumstances may render these preservatives desirable: thus, the minute parts of the mouth of the Acarina are best seen and preserved in balsam, whilst the general form of the body is best retained when the animals are immersed in chloride of calcium or glycerine.

Objects to be mounted in a preservative liquid should be placed in a watch-glass; if existing in water, as much of this as possible should be poured off, or removed with a pipette or blotting-paper, and the preservative liquid added, and this operation repeated that the water may be entirely displaced. The use of spirit should always be avoided if possible, because, although slowly, yet surely, it will act upon the cement used to close the cell.

If objects be mounted according to the method described in § 15, p. 576, the electrical cement and tallow compound should be used; for if black japan or gold size be made use of, the objects will certainly be spoiled.

The liquid cements used to close the cell should be applied in several layers, each being allowed to dry before the next is applied.

The preservative liquid must not be capable of exerting any action upon the cements used in making or closing the cell.

If chloride of calcium or glycerine be used as the preservative liquid, when the first coat of liquid cement used to close the cell has become dry, the slide and cover should be washed gently with a sponge and distilled water, then dried with blotting-paper or a silk handkerchief, and the next coat of varnish applied.

The deeper the cell, the less the chance of the object being spoiled.

As soon as objects are mounted, the slides should be labelled with a square or circular piece of paper pasted upon them, the name and other particulars being expressed in writing. The name, &c. may also be written upon slides with a diamond; but the paper labels should always be used, otherwise much time will be lost in searching for and distinguishing particular objects in the cabinet.

BIBL. Treatises upon the Microscope; Harting, *Het Mikroscop, Edinb. Monthly Journ.* 1852, or *Ann. Nat. Hist.* 1852. x. 311; Reckitt, *Ann. Nat. Hist.* 1845. xvi. 242; Berkeley, *ibid.* 1845. xvi. 104; Ralfs, *Brit. Desmid.*; Smith, *Brit. Diatom.*; Corti, *Siebold and Kölliker's Zeitschr.* iii. 134; Griffith, *Ann. Nat. Hist.* 1843. xxi. 113; Tulk and Henfrey, *Anatomical Manipulation,* 1844. p. 128; Goadby, *Amer. Journ.* xiii. 15; Davies, *Naturalist's Guide*; Welcker, *Aufbewahrung Mikroskop. Objecte*; Mohl, *Botan. Zeit.* xv. p. 249.

PRIMORDIAL UTRICLE (*utriculus primordialis, Primordialschlauch*). — This name has recently come into general use, at the suggestion of Mohl, to indicate a peculiar portion of the contents of the cellulose sac constituting a vegetable cell. By that author it is regarded as a distinct structure; by others its separate existence is doubted, while recently it has been proposed by Pringsheim to transfer the name to a structure different in its nature from that which Mohl has described as his primordial utricle. As the formations comprehended under this name are of great importance in the development of vegetable cells, a little detail must be entered into in explaining this subject.

If a cell of the pulp of any succulent fruit, a cell of yeast, or cells in sections taken from the delicate nascent tissues of any growing part of plants, are placed in water, the entire contents will soon be seen to retract from the cellulose wall, leaving a clear space, filled with transparent liquid, between the latter and a sharply-defined line bounding the contracted or coagulated contents (Pl. 38. figs. 1, 2, 10–12). The addition of tincture of iodine makes the conditions still more clear. If the parent cells of pollen-grains or spores are treated thus, just before the development of the cellulose wall of the special parent cells (see POLLEN), the four portions of the contents of the parent cell contract and separate, and each portion, containing its own granular structures and nucleus, appears bounded by a well-defined line (fig. 607). This well-defined line presents in this condition the appearance of a delicate membrane or pellicle enclosing the entire contents. The action of acids, or spirit, and iodine, reveals the existence of a similar set of conditions in all actively vegetating cells; and in most

2 P 2

cases a more or less thick viscous layer of the protoplasm is found lining the cellulose

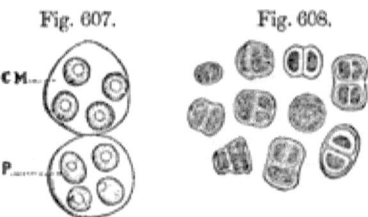

Fig. 607.   Fig. 608.

Fig. 607. Parent cells of pollen-grains just after the separation of the contents into four portions, treated with iodine. *C M*, the parent cell. *P*, the protoplasmic portions, each with a nucleus and a well-defined outline at the surface of the primordial utricle. Magnified 250 diameters.

Fig. 608. Cells of Protococcus multiplying. The green granular contents are bounded by the definite outline of the primordial utricle; the primary and secondary cellulose parent-cell membranes are represented as separated from each other. Magnified 400 diameters.

wall before the application of the reagents. Since the line indicating the boundary of the contents cannot be distinctly seen until the contents have retracted from the cellulose wall, and since the protoplasm is always coagulated by the action of the reagents, it is a subject of discussion whether the film forming the well-defined line on the surface of the contracted contents is a true structure, or only a pellicle produced by the coagulation of the surface of the protoplasm, just as a "skin" forms over size, or other similar substances when they dry up in the air. There is great ground for believing the latter view to be correct, but the term *primordial utricle*, as used by Mohl, is applied to the protoplasmic layer lining the cellulose wall, whether it be merely a gelatinous investment in its natural condition, or a true membrane, because this formation, whether a membrane or merely a layer of viscid protoplasm, exerts in any case a special and most important function. Among the principal reasons for doubting the independent existence of a pellicular nitrogenous membrane, are the following facts: —Very young cells often appear filled with a dense protoplasm (young cells of antheridia of Cryptogamia, embryo-sacs of many flowering plants, cells about to produce zoospores in the Confervoids, &c.), which may produce numerous new cells by merely breaking up into separate portions; and thus the function of the primordial utricle is shared by the entire mass of contents.

Young cells of nascent tissues, presenting this condition at first, acquire the so-called primordial utricle afterwards, simply by the dense contents becoming excavated, as it were, as the cell-wall expands, and following this in its growth, so that the originally dense homogeneous mass becomes a hollow sphere with the centre occupied by watery cell-sap; in other cases the originally homogeneous protoplasm becomes excavated by numerous water-vesicles, and thus honeycombed, until it forms a mere reticulation of protoplasmic threads upon the wall or stretched across the cavity. But the point is by no means clear at present. Indeed, the protoplasmic layer lying upon the wall of the cell presents a complex arrangement of parts in some cases: A. Braun correctly distinguishes three layers in *Hydrodictyon*. there are three in *Chara*, where the intermediate one contains the chlorophyll-granules, and the innermost forms the circulating mass; a distinct layer is left after the discharge of the zoospores in *Cladophora*, &c. Pringsheim has lately asserted that he has coloured blue by Schultze's reagent the outermost layer of the pellicular structures detached from the cell-wall by acids, &c. in the Confervæ; and hence he assumes that Mohl's primordial utricle is really the most recently-formed of the layers of cellulose belonging to the permanent cell-wall, and that this is formed by a chemical transformation of the superficial stratum of the protoplasm. Possibly the last cellulose layer of thickening may be brought away from the wall by reagents; but it would cause a confusion of ideas to call this the *primordial utricle*, even if it be the pellicular structure seen under some circumstances by Mohl and others. The term properly applies to the formative stratum of all independently vitalized masses of protoplasm, capable of secreting layers of cellulose, which in the cavities of parent cells form layers of thickening or septa, or, in a free condition the primary walls of new and independent cells. Thus, as explained under the head of CELL-formation, the primordial utricle or formative protoplasmic layer is the active agent in cell-division, and the layer forming the surface of the isolated portions of contents of parent cells produces the new cell-wall in all cases of free cell-formation, whether taking place in parent cells, or as in the case of the zoospores of Algæ, after escape from the latter.

In many of the Algæ, some of the individual cells regularly exist for a certain period as masses of protoplasm devoid of a cellulose coat, as, for example, the spores of *Fucus* and its allies, and the active zoospores of Confervoids; and these bodies, although presenting a well-defined outline, do not appear to have a properly developed membrane on the surface, which merely appears to be denser than the semifluid central portion. These bodies withdraw themselves evidently from the definition of a vegetable cell as ordinarily given; and even the existence of a protoplasmic pellicle upon the surface of the *primordial utricle* cannot be shown; nevertheless they constitute all the essential living part of a vegetable cell, and indicate most clearly the undoubted fact that the cellulose walls, that is to say all the really solid and permanent portions of vegetable structure, are mere skeleton or shell for the protoplasmic or nitrogenous structures. Cohn has proposed for the independently vitalized masses of 'cell-contents' the title of *primordial cells*; and they do correspond to many of the forms of the 'cells' of animal tissues, and of the 'unicellular' animal organisms, AMŒBA, &c.; but none of these are really *cells* according to the original idea; hence the transfer of names causes confusion. Were not the name *nucleus* already taken for the supposed centre of vitality of these bodies, it would be applicable, as would be that of *cytoblast*; but as these are occupied, the name of *protoplast*, or, as Huxley proposes, *endoplast*, might be adopted, and certainly would be preferable to calling the bodies " primordial cells."

The relation of the " primordial utricle " or formative nitrogenous layer, to the SECONDARY DEPOSITS of cell-walls, is not yet clearly ascertained. Crüger has recently asserted their essential agency in producing these, as will be noticed under that head and under SPIRAL STRUCTURES.

The protoplasmic substances indistinguishably connected with the so-called *primordial utricle*, are also the active agents in the ROTATION or circulation of the cell-contents. Further relations of these nitrogenous matters are also dwelt upon under CHLOROPHYLL and STARCH.

BIBL. Von Mohl, *Botan. Zeit.* ii. p. 273 (1844), transl. in *Taylor's Scient. Mem.* iv. p. 91; *Vermischte Schrift.* p. 302; Henfrey, *Ann. N. H.* xviii. p. 364; Nägeli, *Zeitschr. f. wiss. Bot.* Heft 1 (1844), & 3, 4 (1846), transl. in *Ray Soc. Vols.* 1845. p. 215, & 1849. p. 94;

Alex. Braun, *Verjüngung, &c.* (trans. in *Ray Soc. Vol.* 1853. p. 121 *et seq.*); Cohn, *Nova Acta*, xxii. p. 605, transl. in *Ray Soc. Vol.* 1853. p. 517; Pringsheim, *Bau. u. Bild. d. Pflanzenzelle*, Heft I. Berlin, 1854; Hartig, *Botan. Zeitung*, xiii. p. 393 *et seq.* 1855; Crüger, *ibid.* p. 601; Mohl, *ibid.* p. 689.

PROEMBRYO.—The term applied to the structure first produced from the germinal vesicle of Flowering Plants, after impregnation, consisting of the suspensor and the embryonal cell at its extremity. The proembryos of the Gymnosperms are especially remarkable (see OVULE). The same term is often incorrectly applied to the PROTHALLIUM, the cellular structure first produced in the germination of the spores of the higher Flowerless Plants. In the MOSSES this is a Confervoid expansion (fig. 478, page 467), upon which buds are formed from which arise the leafy stems; in the FERNS the prothallium (figs. 236-9, page 285) is a *Marchantia*-like body, upon which are developed archegonia and antheridia; in the LYCOPODIACEÆ and MARSILEACEÆ (figs. 576, 577, p. 546) the prothallium is produced within the coats of the ovule-spore.

BIBL. See the heads referred to.

PROROCENTRUM, Ehr.—A genus of Infusoria, of the family Cryptomonadina.

Char. Eye-spot absent; carapace smooth, terminating in a point or tooth in front; a single flagelliform filament present. Marine.

1. *P. micans* (Pl. 24. figs. 70 & 71). Ovate, compressed, attenuate behind, dilated in front. Length 1-430″. Luminous.

2. *P. viride.*

BIBL. Ehrenberg, *Infus.* p. 44; *Ber. d. Berl. Akad.* 1840. p. 201.

PRORODON, Ehr.—A genus of Infusoria, of the family Enchelia.

Char. Body covered with vibratile cilia, truncate in front; mouth with a cylinder of teeth. Aquatic.

P. teres (Pl. 24. fig. 72). Body ovate, terete, white. Length 1-140″.

Two other species, one of them green.

Dujardin places this genus in the family Paramecina.

BIBL. Ehrenberg, *Infus.* p. 315, and *Ber. d. Berlin Akad.* 1840. p. 201.

PROSENCHYMA. See TISSUES, Vegetable.

PROSTHEMIUM, Kunze.—A genus of Sphæronemei (Coniomycetous Fungi), growing upon the branches of trees, forming circular depressed spots; the perithecia enclose erect articulated filaments bearing radiating tufts of two or three septate spores (fig. 609). *P. betulinum* occurs upon the bark of the branches of the birch-tree.

Fig. 609.

Prosthenium betulinum.

Spores and paraphyses seen in a vertical section of fruit.

Magnified 200 diams.

BIBL. Berkeley, *Brit. Flor.* ii. pt. 2. p. 297.

PROTEACEÆ.—A family of Dicotyledonous plants, mostly from New Holland or the Cape, shrubs or small trees (*Banksia, Grevillea, Hakea,* &c.), of remarkably rigid, evergreen habit. The coriaceous leaves are well suited for the study of the epidermal structures; and the stomata have interesting peculiarities (see STOMATA). The epidermis is often scurfy with scattered hairs, some of which are of curious forms (Pl. 21. fig. 29).

PROTEONINA, Williamson.—A genus of recent Foraminifera, of the order Monostegia.

Char. Shell free, irregular, fusiform or compressed, at first slightly convoluted at one end, arenaceous; *orifice* irregular in size and form, terminal. Two species.

1. *P. fusiformis.* Oblong, fusiform, variable, coarsely arenaceous and granular; length $\frac{1}{16}''$.

2. *P. pseudospiralis.* Compressed, thin, at first somewhat spiral; length $\frac{1}{16}''$.

BIBL. Williamson, *Rec. Foram.* (*Ray Soc.*), 1.

PROTEUS.—An old name applied to certain Infusoria, as *Amœba,* &c.

PROTHALLIUM. See PROEMBRYO.

PROTOCOCCUS, Ag.—A genus of Volvocineæ (Confervoid Algæ), at present very imperfectly known, since without a tolerably complete history of the development of the forms it is impossible to distinguish the true species of *Protococcus* from the young states of the more complicated Palmellaceæ, and even from the germinating gonidia of the Lichens. As we have limited it, *Protococcus* includes those unicellular Algæ which in the aquatic state consist of single zoospore-like bodies, with a more or less evident gelatinous cellulose envelope through which the two cilia protrude. They move actively, and are multiplied by division during the active state. Finally, they settle down into a resting-stage; and they may then increase by vegetation so as to form granular patches. Mostly, however, those which settle down turn red and acquire a thick coat, passing through a stage of rest before they germinate again, apparently requiring to be dried up first. When they germinate, they frequently produce many generations of *still* forms before the active ciliated forms reappear, especially when placed on damp surfaces, and not in water. When placed in favourable circumstances, the resting forms (even after several years) recommence the course of vegetation, reacquiring the green colour by degrees, in the course of several generations of vegetative cells. The contents of the red form appear to consist partly of oil-globules; in the green form the protoplasmic substance is coloured by chlorophyll, and at a certain stage contains starch.

We have traced *P. viridis* through all these stages, as represented in Pl. 3. fig. 2 *a–g*: a most elaborate monograph of *P. pluvialis* has been written by Cohn, which is far too extensive to be analysed here, but goes to establish the same conclusion, that the genus *Hæmatococcus* is founded on states of *Protococcus.* The *P. viridis* of our figures is undoubtedly *Chlamidomonas,* one of Ehrenberg's genera of Polygastrica, synonymous with *Diselmis,* Dujardin. This form appears at first sight nearly allied to *Euglena*; but there are striking differences in the appearance and movements of the active forms, and the "vegetative" forms are somewhat different. It may be remarked, however, that the zoospores of *Protococcus viridis,* allowed to dry upon a slide, often turn red and look just like small *Astasiæ* (Pl. 3. fig. 2 *g*).

We have remarked under PALMELLA, that the Polar red snow appears to be a Palmella (Pl. 3. fig. 3 *d*), although this species has been called *Protococcus* and *Hæmatococcus nivalis*; and it appears to us that Shuttleworth and others have confounded this with *Protococcus pluvialis.* Hassall's species of *Hæmatococcus,* nos. 8 to 19, with the exception of *H. vulgaris* (*Chlorococcum*) (Pl. 3. fig. 1), are probably congeneric with our *P. viridis.* We find it impossible to extricate the British forms from their confusion; the Palmellaceæ require a thorough study in a living state. Meneghini's definitions of the genera will not hold; and Kützing has multiplied species indefinitely.

Our *P. viridis* makes its appearance commonly on damp earth, sand, &c., forming a greenish coat of no perceptible thickness; and the zoospores (*Chlamidomonas*) occur constantly in standing pools in spring and autumn, tinging the surface of the water bright green, and, as they settle to rest, forming a kind of green scum at the margins (constituting the *green matter* of Priestley). Cells of resting-form 1-2400″ in diameter. *P. pluvialis* colours water red in like manner; it occurs on mountains, especially in melted snow-water. Cells of resting-form 1-1250 to 1-625″ in diameter. Similar colorations, however, are produced by various other organisms (see WATER).

It may be observed that when the active forms of *P. viridis* and *P. pluvialis* divide without coming to rest, they produce forms which are undistinguishable from many of Ehrenberg's species of Polygastrica. When they acquire a loose cellulose coat before losing their cilia, they represent *Gyges*; at other times they resemble *Chlorogonium, Urella, Polytoma, Monas, Bodo*, &c.

BIBL. Harvey, *Brit. Alg.* 1 ed. p. 180; Hassall, *Brit. Fr. Alg.* p. 321, &c., pls. 76–82; Meneghini, *Trans. Turin Acad.* 2 ser. v. p. 1; Cohn, *Nova Acta*, xxii. p. 605 (abstr. in *Ray Soc. Vol.* 1853. p. 514); Von Flotow, *Nova Acta*, xx. p. 414; Alex. Braun, *Verjüngung, &c.* (*Ray Soc. Vol.* 1853. p. 206 *et seq.*); Nägeli, *Einzelliger Algen, passim*; Kützing, *Spec. Alg.* p. 196; *Tab. Phyc.* i. pls. 1–6. See also under RED SNOW.

PROTOMYCES, Unger.—A genus of Ustilaginei (Coniomycetous Fungi), growing in the intercellular passages of leaves and leaf-stalks. According to De Bary, these Fungi consist of ramified filaments creeping between the cells of soft tissues, and swelling up at intervals (apparently where they meet an intercellular space large enough), to form globular spores: a filament with several spores in course of division appears like a varicose tube; it is septate, however, and when the globular spores are mature, they have a double coat; in *P. macrosporus*, the diameter of the ripe spore is about 1-5000″. When advanced in age, the mycelium appears to be wholly converted into spores, which become free. The existence of these Fungi is rendered more or less evident externally by warty projections of the epidermis, finally bursting. Unger describes four species: *P. macrosporus* occurring on *Ægopodium* and *Angelica*; *P. endogenus* (*Galii*), occurring on *Galium mollugo*; *P. microsporus* on *Ranunculus repens*; and *P. Paridis* on *Paris quadrifolia*. De Bary found a species on *Menyanthes*, with oval spores 1-800″ long and 1-1300″ broad.

BIBL. Unger, *Exanthem. der Pflanz.* p. 341; De Bary, *Brandpilze*, p. 15, pls. 1 & 2; Léveillé, *Ann. des Sc. Nat.* 3 sér. viii. p. 374; Tulasne, *ibid.* vii. p. 112; Fries, *Summa Veg.* p. 517.

PROTOPLASM.—The name applied by Mohl to the colourless or yellowish, smooth or granular viscid substance, of nitrogenous constitution, which constitutes the formative substance in the contents of vegetable cells, in the condition of gelatinous strata, reticulated threads, and nuclear aggregations, &c. It is the same substance as that formerly termed by the Germans "*Schleim*," which was usually translated in English works by "mucus" or "mucilage" (see PRIMORDIAL UTRICLE, and CELL, Vegetable).

PROTOZOA.—This term was proposed by Siebold to designate a group of invertebrate animals, characterized by the absence of distinct organs, the form and simple organization being reducible to a cell.

Siebold included in it the Infusoria and the Rhizopoda, the latter consisting of the Amœbæa, Arcellina, and Foraminifera.

If the above definition be adopted, it must be remembered that the cell may be represented by the cell-contents only; and these we believe to constitute the essential part of a cell.

BIBL. Siebold, *Vergleich. Anat.* iii.; Lieberkuhn, *Siebold und Kölliker's Zeitschr.* viii. 307.

PSEUDOGONIDIA.—A term applied to bodies appearing in the interior of cells of Algæ, which are obscure in their nature, being either metamorphosed and isolated masses of protoplasm or parasitic bodies, resembling monads. They are apparently connected with the objects called CHYTRIDIUM and PYTHIUM.

BIBL. Cienkowski, *Pringsheim's Jahrb. d. Botanik*, i. p. 371.

PSILONIA, Fr.—A genus of Sepedoniei (Hyphomycetous Fungi), consisting of little compact tufts of twisted filaments, at first covering the fusiform, globose, or oval spores, which arise from the wart-like protuberances on the central filaments, and soon become free. They are found on dead wood or on reeds.

BIBL. Berk. *Brit. Flora*, ii. pt. 2. p. 353; *Ann. Nat. Hist.* ser. 2. viii. p. 179; Fries, *Summa Veg.* p. 495.

PSILOTEÆ.—A family of Lycopodiaceous plants, distinguished by their many-celled sporanges, varying much in habit and external appearance.

Synopsis of Genera.

1. *Psilotum.* Sporangessessile, three-celled, bursting imperfectly into three valves by a vertical crack, filled with mealy spores.

2. *Tmesipteris.* Sporanges sessile, three-celled, bursting imperfectly into two valves by a vertical crack, filled with mealy spores.

3. *Isoëtes.* Sporanges imbedded in the bases of the leaves, and adnate at the back, not valvate, with several transverse septa; containing two kinds of spores (in distinct sporangia).

Fig. 610.

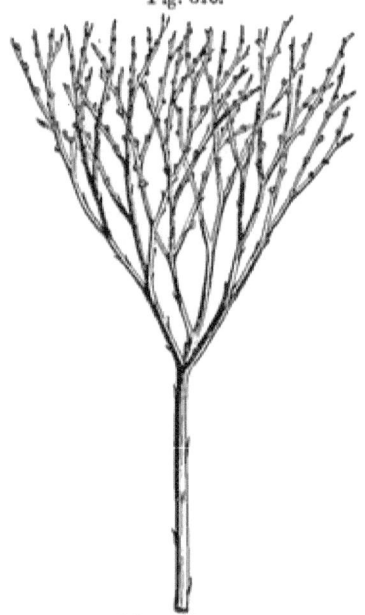

Psilotum triquetrum.
Nat. size.

PSILOTUM, Swartz. (*Lycopodium nudum*, L.).—An exotic genus of Psiloteæ (Ly-

copodiaceæ), remarkable for their trilocular capsules and minute leaves (fig. 611).

Fig. 611.

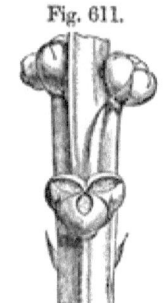

Fragment of a branch of Psilotum triquetrum.
Magnified 10 diameters.

PSOROPTES (Gervais).—A genus of Arachnida, of the order Acarina, and family Acarea.

Char. Body soft, depressed, with rigid hairs beneath, and on the legs.

Parasitic upon the horse (and other mammalia?).

P. equi (Pl. 2. fig. 18), itch-insect of the horse. Found upon the scaly crusts formed upon the body. Mandibles each terminated by two teeth, and not chelate; palpi three-jointed, and adherent to the labium; ventral surface covered with parallel undulating rugæ; at the end of the body are two fleshy lobes, terminated by a tuft of setæ.

BIBL. Hering, *Nov. Act. N. Cur.* xviii. 585; Gervais, *Walckenaer's Aptères*, iii. 266; Dujardin, *Obs. au Micr.* 147.

PSOROSPERMLÆ.—These bodies were discovered by J. Müller, and appear to represent the pseudo-naviculæ of the *Gregarinæ* of fishes.

They are microscopic, oval, depressed, or discoidal corpuscles, with or without a tail, exhibiting no movements, and consisting of a tolerably firm outer coat, containing one or two oblong contiguous vesicles at that end of the body opposite the tail. They are about 1-2500 to 1-2000″ in length, and are contained in immense numbers in minute cysts, in almost every part of the body of fishes, as upon the gills, in the muscles, and between the coats of the eye, in the swimming-bladder, &c. Sometimes they are imbedded in a ramified sarcodic mass.

Diameter of the cysts on the pike 1-50 to 1-25″; of the corpuscles, length 1-2000″, breadth 1-3500″.

BIBL. Müller, *Archiv*, 1841. 477, 1842.
193; Creplin, *ibid.* 1842. p. 61; Dujardin,
Helminthes, 643; Leydig, *Müll. Archiv*,
1851. 221 (*Microsc. Journ.* 1853. i. 206);
Ch. Robin, *Végétaux Parasitiques, &c.*, 2 ed.
p. 291.

PTERIS, Linn.—A genus of Adianteæ
(Polypodioid Ferns), represented by one
indigenous species, *Pteris aquilina*, common
Brake Fern.

Fig. 612.

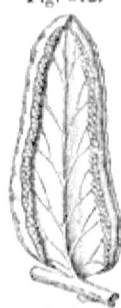

Pteris.
A pinnule with marginal indusiate sori.
Magnified 10 diameters.

PTERODINA, Ehr.—A genus of Rotatoria, of the family Brachionæa.

Char. Eyes two, frontal; foot simply
styliform. At the end of the tail-like foot
is a suctorial disk; jaws with the teeth
either arranged in a row, or two teeth only
in each.

Three species; two aquatic, one marine.

P. patina (Pl. 35. fig. 20). Testula membranous, orbicular, crystalline, roughish
near the broad margin; a depression present between the rotatory lobes. Aquatic;
length 1-120".

BIBL. Ehrenberg, *Infus.* p. 516.

PTEROPTUS, Dufour.—A genus of
Arachnida, of the order Acarina, and family
Gamasea.

Char. Body depressed; last joint of palpi
longest; legs stout, with short joints.

P. vespertilionis (Pl. 2. fig. 39). Found
upon bats. Several species have been described; but the subject requires revision.

BIBL. Gervais, *Walckenaer's Aptères*, iii.
227; Dufour, *Ann. des Sc. Nat.* xvi. 98,
xxv. 9; Koch, *Deutschlands Crustac.*

PTERYGONIUM, Sw. — A genus of
Mosses. See NECKERA.

PTILIDIUM, Nees.—A genus of Jungermanniæ (Hepaticæ), containing one ele-

gant British species, *P. ciliare*, frequent on
heaths and rocks in subalpine districts, but
rarely found in fruit.

BIBL. Hooker, *Brit. Flor.* ii. p. 126; *Brit.
Jung.* pl. 65; Ekart, *Synops. Jung.* pl. 5.
fig. 36.

PTILOTA, Ag.—A genus of Ceramiaceæ
(Florideous Algæ), with flat feathery fronds
a few inches high; of a deep red colour,
growing on *Laminariæ* or *Fuci*, or on rocks
between tide-marks. The fructification
consists of—1. clustered roundish *favellæ*
containing spores, terminating the ultimate
pinnules, and surrounded by an involucre
of subulate ramuli, or naked; 2. tetrahedral
tetraspores on short pedicels fringing the
pinnules. Antheridia have not been observed.

BIBL. Harvey, *Brit. Mar. Alg.* p. 159,
pl. 22 A; *Phyc. Brit.* pl. 70; Greville, *Alg.
Brit.* pl. 16; Nägeli, *Neuere Algensystem*,
pl. 6. figs. 38-42.

PTYGURA, Ehr.—A genus of Rotatoria,
of the family Ichthydina.

Char. Eyes none; no hairs upon the
body; tail-like foot cylindrical, and simply
truncate.

Teeth three in each jaw; anus situated
at the end of the tail-like foot.

P. melicerta (Pl. 35. fig. 21). Body terete-
clavate, turgid in front, hyaline; mouth
with two little hook-like horns; cervical
process single and smooth. Aquatic; length
1-144".

Ehrenberg questions whether this is not
a young form of another genus.

BIBL. Ehrenberg, *Infus.* p. 387.

PUCCINIA, Persoon.—A genus of Uredinei (Coniomycetous Fungi), containing
numerous parasitical species, growing upon
the leaves and other herbaceous parts of the
higher plants, forming "mildews" and, with
their Uredinous forms, "rusts," &c. These
Fungi have received considerable attention
lately from Tulasne, De Bary, and others;
and it appears that the genera *Uredo* and
others have no distinct existence, but are
preparatory forms of *Puccinia* and other
genera noticed under UREDINEI. In the
article ÆCIDIUM we have described the
twofold reproductive structures, namely the
spermogonia and the perithecia (figs. 5 & 6,
p. 17; Pl. 20. figs. 1-4), producing respectively the spermatia (supposed to have the
office of spermatozoids) and the spores. In
Puccinia three forms of reproductive organs
occur: first, spermogonia, analogous to those
of *Æcidium*; then the forms called Uredines

(chiefly of the supposed genus *Trichobasis*), producing globular unilocular bodies, shortly stalked, and with transparent walls, but with yellow or orange-coloured contents; and lastly the true *Pucciniæ*, containing bilocular spores borne on short stalks, and having a dark-brown integument. The latter present remarkable phænomena in germination, which may be best observed in those which sprout without becoming detached from the matrix, such as *P. graminis*, which however remain quiescent until the spring following their development, while *P. Glechomæ, Buxi, Dianthi*, and others germinate in the same summer. The bilocular spores have each one pore (analogous to the pores of POLLEN-grains), from which extends a filamentous process, ultimately giving rise to four short processes, each terminating in a pointed process bearing a *sporidium*, of more or less curved elliptical form. About the time when these fall off, the filament bearing the four processes becomes divided by septa into four chambers, but then appears to die. The sporidia germinate and produce a filament, which, instead of becoming the basis of a mycelium, reproduces a sporidium smaller than the first. More is said respecting these remarkable organisms under the head of UREDINEI.

The *Pucciniæ* present the following general characters:—The *spermogonia* rare, scattered on either face of the infested leaf, with an immersed, ostiolate peridiole, bearing long cilia at the mouth; pale, orange, or blackish in colour. The *Uredinous* fruits are scattered or grouped in circles, devoid of a proper peridium, but surrounded sometimes by thickish cylindrical paraphyses, very rarely connected below into a membrane, forming a kind of ciliated peridium; the *stylospores* are round and mostly spinulose, with three or four equidistant pores. The *Puccineous* fruits are also scattered or grouped in circles, sometimes containing only their proper spores, sometimes with Uredinous spores intermixed, destitute of a proper peridium, but, like the *Uredines*, having sometimes a false envelope formed of confluent paraphyses; their *spores*, forming the chief distinctive character of the genus, are *bilocular*, oblong or globose, rounded-obtuse or acuminate at the apex, smooth or spinulose, the upper loculus with a pore at its summit, the lower with a pore at the upper end of one side (next the septum).

These plants occur commonly on the Grasses and many other herbaceous plants, often changing colour during the summer, being yellow or orange when the Uredinous spores are ripe, and afterwards blackish when the Puccineous form is mature.

The species are very numerous; but some of those formerly included under this name are now removed to other genera, such as *Uromyces, Triphragmium*, &c. (See URE-DINEI.) *P. graminis* is common on corn and other grasses (*Mildew*); among the other frequent species are *P. Caricis, Polygonorum, Menthæ, Anemones, Buxi*, &c. Ch. Robin describes a *Puccinia*, apparently on the authority of Ardsten, a Swedish physician, found upon the human head in FAVUS. From his description it appears to be a true *Puccinia*, and should hold its place (*P. Favi*, Ardst.) among the species. But what is more remarkable, it occurs together with *Achorion Schœnleinii*, the latter presenting itself as a constituent of the cups or crusts, while the *Puccinia* occurs afterwards on the desquamations of the epidermis. This appears to warrant (from what we know of the species parasitic on vegetables) the opinion that the ACHORION is merely the spermogonial form of the *P. Favi*.

BIBL. Berk. *Brit. Flor.* ii. pt. 2. p. 303; *Ann. Nat. Hist.* vi. p. 439; *ibid.* 2 ser. v. p. 462, xiii. p. 461; Tulasne, *Ann. des Sc. Nat.* 3 sér. vii. p. 12; *ibid.* 4 sér. ii. p. 77, 138 & 182; Léveillé, *ibid.* 3 sér. viii. p. 369; De Bary, *Brandpilze*, p. 36; Fries, *Summa Veg.* p. 513; Robin, *Végétaux parasit.* 2nd ed. p. 613, pl. 14. fig. 13.

PULEX, Linn. (Flea).—A genus of Insects, of the order Siphonaptera (Suctoria or Aphaniptera), and family Pulicidæ.

Char. As there are only the single family and genus in the order, the characters of the latter are distinctive.

Head small (Pl. 28. fig. 9), compressed, rounded above, truncate in front, in some species with an inferior pectinate fringe of blackish-brown teeth; eyes one on each side, round, simple, smooth; behind each eye is a cavity or depression, at the bottom of which the antennæ are attached; antennæ (figs. 9 *a*, 12) four-jointed, their form varying in the different species, the third joint very minute, and forming the cup-shaped base of the terminal joint or piece, which in some species is furnished with numerous transverse incisions, representing as many distinct joints; in some the antennæ extend out of the depression, and are carried erect.

Oral appendages (Pl. 28. fig. 9 e) composed of several parts : 1. (Pl. 26. figs. 32 d, 33 d) The uppermost is single, and consists of a thin, flattened seta, coarsely toothed on the upper surface, and traversed throughout its entire length by a canal, upon the walls of which a very slender trachea runs, and from which very minute canals, terminating at the end of the little teeth, are given off. This is the suctorial organ, and perhaps corresponds to the labrum, but is sometimes considered as the lingua or ligula. 2. (figs. 32 f, 33 f) Two quadrangular, narrow, and elongated plates, each furnished with longitudinal ribs, and with fine teeth ; these are the lancets or scalpella, and correspond to the mandibles. 3. (Pl. 26. fig. 32 g) Two somewhat triangular or leaf-like plates, the maxillæ ; to which are attached—4. (Pl. 26. fig. 32 h ; Pl. 28. fig. 9 d) Two nearly cylindrical four-jointed maxillary palpi. 5. (Pl. 26. fig. 32 k ; fig. 33 k) Two labial palpi, in the form of sheaths, four-jointed, thickened at the back and membranous at the margin ; these palpi arise from near the apex of—6. (Pl. 26. fig. 33 l) A small membranous labium, with the still smaller mentum (Pl. 26. fig. 33 m) at its base.

Thorax composed of three segments, each consisting of an upper (Pl. 28. fig. 9 c) and a lower piece (f f, that of the metathoracic segment is not lettered) ; from the lower arise the corresponding legs. The two posterior segments of the thorax are each furnished with a pair of plates, the hindermost of which is longest, and nearly covers the sides of the first and part of the second abdominal segment (fig. 9, behind f, f) ; these represent rudimentary wings.

The legs are large, especially the hinder ones, and adapted for leaping. The first joint or coxa (g) is very thick ; the second or trochanter (h) is very small ; next come the femur (i), the tibia (k), and lastly the five-jointed tarsus (l), which is terminated by two curved and denticulate claws, with a lobe or heel at the base.

The abdomen of the female has nine distinct rings, the first seven of which are each furnished with a pair of stigmata (a), and consist of horny arches with membranous margins. The eighth arch, which has no membranous margin, is strengthened by a horny band furnished with fine hairs, to protect the orifice of the last stigma. The ninth and last segment, called the pygidium (fig. 9 ×, and Pl. 1. fig. 13), is somewhat kidney-shaped or two-lobed, folded on the dorsum, and exhibits twenty-five to twenty-eight stiff and longish bristles, implanted in the centre of as many disk-like areolæ, each of which is ornamented with a ring of rectangular or somewhat cuneate rays. The portions of the pygidium between the areolæ are studded with minute spines. The end of the abdomen in the female (Pl. 28. fig. 9) is more rounded or ovate than that of the male (fig. 13), which is somewhat turned upwards.

In some species the segments of the thorax and abdomen are furnished with a posterior pectinate fringe.

The alimentary canal is short and straight; the stomach cylindrical ; the small intestine as long as the stomach, and the large intestine short. Four short and broad Malpighian vessels open into the lower orifice of the stomach ; and the ducts of two round salivary vesicles unite to a single canal ascending in a coiled form on each side of the œsophagus towards the mouth.

The eggs of the flea are white, elongated and viscid outside. The larvæ have no legs ; they are elongated, resembling minute worms, and very active, coiling themselves into a circle or spiral, and serpentine in their movements. The head is scaly, without eyes, and supporting two very minute antennæ ; the body has thirteen segments, with small tufts of hairs, and at the end of the last are two little hooks.

The species are numerous (twenty-five, Gervais) ; but their characters are not well defined. One species (P. terrestris) is said to exist under brush-wood ; and one (P. Boleti) in Boleti.

1. P. irritans, human flea. Pitch-brown ; head shining, smooth, pectinate fringe absent ; legs pale ; femora of posterior legs with hairs inside ; second joint of the tarsi of the anterior pair of legs and first joint of posterior tarsi longest. Tarsal joints, in respective order of greatest length : anterior, 2, 5, 1, 3, 4; posterior, 1, 5, 2, 3, 4 (Bouché). We have never been able to find a flea with the above relative length of the joints of the anterior tarsi.

2. P. felis, cat's flea (P. canis, Bouché; P. irritans, Dugès) (Pl. 28. fig. 9). Pale pitch-brown; head naked, shining, smooth, with delicate scattered dots; coxæ and femora almost naked; fifth joint of anterior tarsi and first joint of posterior tarsi longest. Tarsal joints: anterior, 5, 2, 1, 3, 4; posterior, 1, 5, 2, 3, 4.

3. P. canis, flea of dog and fox (Pl. 28.

fig. 10, head) (*P. felis*, Bouché). Pale pitch-brown; head shining, smooth, punctate behind; lower part of head and protothorax with a pectinate fringe; posterior tibiæ much expanded at the end; fifth joint of anterior and first of posterior tarsi longest. Tarsi: anterior, 5, 2, 1, 3, 4; posterior, 1, 2, 5, 3, 4.

4. *P. gallinæ*, fowl's flea. Pitch-brown, with shining, smooth, elongated head; protothorax with a pectinate fringe; first joint of all the tarsi longest. Tarsi: anterior and posterior, 1, 2, 5, 3, 4.

5. *P. martis*, flea of the marten and dog. Postero-inferior margin of head and protothorax with pectinate fringe; tarsi as in *P. canis*.

6. *P. sciurorum*, flea of the squirrel. Head naked; pectinate fringe on protothorax, none upon the abdomen. Tarsi: anterior, 1, 5, 2, 3, 4; posterior, 1, 2, 5, 3, 4.

7. *P. erinacei*, flea of hedgehog. Head naked, mesothorax with a fringe. Tarsi: anterior, 5, 2, 1, 3, 4; posterior, 1, 2, 5, 3, 4.

8. *P. talpæ*, Curtis, flea of mole (Pl. 28. fig. 24).

9. *P. columbæ*, pigeon's flea. Protothorax with pectinate fringe, none upon the abdomen; antennæ of male erect, those of the female lying in the depression.

10. *P. penetrans*, the chigoe or jigger. The females burrow in the skin of the feet; and the ova, undergoing development, enlarge the parent-abdomen to the size of a pea, causing severe inflammation, &c. Rostrum very long. Tropical.

11. *P. vespertilionis*, flea of the bat (Pl. 28. fig. 11, head).

BIBL. Westwood, *Introduction, &c.*, ii. 489; Bouché, *Nov. Act. Nat. Cur.* 1835. xvii. 501; Dugès, *Ann. des Sc. Nat.* 1832. xxvii. p. 165; Gervais, *Walckenaer's Apt.* iii. 362; Denny, *Ann. Nat. Hist.* 1843. xii. 315.

PUNCTARIA, Greville.—A genus of Punctariaceæ (Fucoid Algæ), containing three (one doubtful) British species, *P. latifolia, plantaginea* and *tenuissima*, growing on rocks and stones, consisting of membranous, olive or brown, ribless fronds, 4 to 12" long, 1 to 3" broad, having a shield-like organ of attachment at the base. The fructification consists of *sori* scattered all over the fronds in minute distinct dots, composed of roundish sporanges (producing zoospores) intermixed with paraphyses; these sporanges are called *spores* in most works. No other form of fructification has yet been observed.

BIBL. Harvey, *Brit. Mar. Alg.* p. 41, pl. 8B; *Phyc. Brit.* pls. 8, 128, 148; Greville, *Alg. Brit.* pl. 9.

PUNCTARIACEÆ.—A family of Fucoideæ. Root a minute naked disk; frond cylindrical or flat, unbranched, cellular; with ovate *sporanges* intermixed with jointed threads in groups on the surface.

Synopsis of the British Genera.

1. *Punctaria.* Frond flat and leaf-like. *Sporanges* scattered or in sori.

2. *Asperococcus.* Frond membranous, tubular, either cylindrical or compressed. *Sporanges* in dot-like sori.

3. *Litosiphon.* Frond cartilaginous, filiform, subsolid. *Sporanges* scattered, almost solitary.

PUS.—Popularly known as "matter." One of the products of inflammatory exudation.

Its general properties are too well known to require description. Pus consists of an albuminous liquid, containing a number of minute corpuscles in suspension. These consist of molecules and granules, composed of proteine-compounds, fat or the earthy phosphates; globules of fat of very various sizes; and the proper pus-corpuscles. Pus-corpuscles (Pl. 30. fig. 4) are spherical, from $\frac{1}{2500}$ to $\frac{1}{2000}$" in diameter; presenting a granular appearance on the surface, and containing a number of larger or smaller granules and a small quantity of liquid. The granular appearance of the surface arises from the internal granules pushing out, as it were, the cell-wall; for it disappears when the cell-wall is distended and separated from the granules by the action of water or very dilute solution of potash. When treated with acetic acid, the cell-wall and granules become excessively transparent, and ultimately vanish (Pl. 30. fig. 5), leaving from one to five, generally two or three, round or oval nuclei, which mostly present a dark margin and light centre, giving them a cupped appearance, indicating a diminution of refractive power in the centre, arising from either a depression on the surface or the existence of a vacuole. The cupped centre is sometimes seen in the nuclei without acetic acid, after the action of water only.

In the pus of chronic abscesses, unhealthy ulcers, &c., the corpuscles are often few, deformed and mixed with numerous granules of proteine, fatty and calcareous matters, crystals of cholesterine, of the ammonio-phosphate of magnesia, and sometimes monads and vibrios; exudation-corpuscles are occasionally present also.

Pyoid corpuscles. — Under this term, Lebert describes a modification of pus-corpuscles, consisting of a tolerably transparent envelope, enclosing from eight to ten or more small globules (Pl. 30. fig. 6). Acetic acid does not alter them, or at most only renders them slightly more transparent. The small globules are composed of a proteine-compound; for they are soluble in potash.

BIBL. That of CHEMISTRY, Animal; and Lebert, *Phys. Pathologique.*

PUSTULIPORA, Blainville.—A genus of Infundibulate Cyclostomatous Polyzoa, of the family Tubuliporidæ.

Char. Polypidom erect, cylindrical; cells half-immersed, arranged on all sides; orifices prominent.

Two British species: *P. proboscidea,* and *P. deflexa.* The latter common on shells from deep water.

BIBL. Johnston, *Brit. Zooph.* 278; Gosse, *Mar. Zool.* ii. 8.

PYCNIDIA.—A term applied by Tulasne to the receptacles enclosing *stylospores* in the LICHENS and FUNGI.

PYCNOPHYCUS, Kütz.—A genus of Fucaceæ (Fucoid Algæ), containing one British species, *P.* (FUCUS) *tuberculatus,* removed from *Fucus* on account of its cylindrical frond, the compact cellular substance of the receptacles, and the ramified fibrous pseudo-root. The fructifications, formed at the ends of the dichotomous lobes of the frond, are of elongated form, cylindrical, more or less tuberculated, and exhibit numerous pores opening from conceptacles containing *spore-sacs* and *antheridia* (together), resembling in general those of *Fucus.* The spore-sacs are collected at the bottom of the conceptacles, the antheridia at the upper part. For the details respecting the spores and spermatozoids, see FUCUS.

BIBL. Harvey, *Brit. Mar. Alg.* p. 18, pl. 2 A; *Phyc. Brit.* p. 89; Decaisne and Thuret, *Ann. des Sc. Nat.* 3 sér. iii. p. 5, &c., pl. 1; Thuret, *ibid.* xvi. p. 10.

PYOID CORPUSCLES. See PUS.

PYRAMIDIUM, Bridel.—A genus of Funariaceæ (Acrocarpous Mosses), allied to *Funaria* in habit, but differing in important points.

Pyramidium tetragonum, Brid. = *Gymnostomum tetragonum,* Schwägr.

PYRENOMYCETES.—That portion of the Ascomycetous and Coniomycetous Fungi having a closed, nuclear fruit; standing opposed to the Discomycetes, with open fruits, like the Angiocarpous and Gymnocarpous Lichens.

PYRENOTHEA, Fries.—A genus of Limboriæ (Angiocarpous Lichens), containing a number of species separated from *Verrucaria,* Ach., on account of the spores being free in the perithecia and not developed in thecæ. The bodies taken for spores are, however, spermatia contained in spermogonia, the sporiferous perithecia being apparently unknown (see LICHENS).

BIBL. Leighton, *Brit. Ang. Lichens,* p. 65; Tulasne, *Ann. des Sc. Nat.* 3 sér. xvii. p. 217.

PYRULINA, D'Orb.—A genus of Foraminifera, of the order Helicostegia, and family Turbinoidæ.

Char. Shell glossy, smooth, free; spire short, indistinct. *Chambers* half-embracing, close; the last acuminate in front; with the round *orifice* at the end.

P. acuminata has been found fossil.

BIBL. D'Orbigny, *Mém. Geol. Soc. of France,* iv. 43; Id. *For. Foss. d. Vienne,* 101; Morris, *Brit. Foss.* 40.

PYTHIUM, Pringsheim.—A supposed genus of parasitic Unicellular Algæ, the true nature of which is however yet doubtful.

P. entophytum (Pl. 45. fig. 8) occurs in this country in diseased cells of Confervoid Algæ. It consists of minute flask-shaped bodies, taking the place of the proper cell-contents, finally pushing the neck-like portion through the wall of the cells, outside of which it bursts and discharges active (?) molecules, which Pringsheim regards as gonidia. Pringsheim describes another species which grows upon insects in water, in the manner of *Achlya,* and he refers this genus to the family Saprolegnieæ.

BIBL. Pringsheim, *Jahrb. d. wiss. Bot.* i. p. 289; Carter, *Ann. Nat. Hist.* 2 ser. xvii. p. 101; Henfrey, *Trans. Mic. Soc.* New Series, vii. p. 26; Currey, *Mic. Journal,* v. p. 211.

PYXIDICULA, Ehr.—A genus of Diatomaceæ.

Char. Frustules single, free or sessile; valves circular, convex, hoop absent.

Twenty-two species have been described; one aquatic, one marine, the remainder fossil, found in America.

Some of them do not appear to differ from *Coscinodiscus* and *Cyclotella,* except in the greater convexity of the valves.

1. *P. major* (Pl. 19. fig. 13). Valves coni-

cal, regularly punctate. Diameter 1-420";
aquatic.

2. *P. adriatica.* Fr. sessile; valves nearly
hemispherical, free from markings (ord. ill.).
Upon marine Algæ. Diam. 1-000".

3. *P. minor* = *Cyclotella operculata.*

The bodies represented in Pl. 19. fig. 12,
found in flint, have been described as *P.
globator*, Pritch. (not *P. globosus*, Ehr.); they
do not, however, appear to belong to the
Diatomaceæ.

Kützing places *Stephanopyxis* and *Xanthiopyxis* here.

BIBL. Ehrenberg, *Infus.* 165, and *Ber. d.
Berl. Akad.* 1844 & 1845; Kützing, *Bacill.*
51, and *Spec. Alg.* xxi.; Pritchard, *Infusoria*, 432.

PYXINEÆ.—A family of Gymnocarpous
Lichens, characterized by a horizontal foliaceous thallus, mostly fixed by the centre,
an orbicular disc, with the excipulum
distinct from the thallus, closed at first and
superficial.

Genera.

1. *Umbilicaria.* Apothecia orbicular,
somewhat concave, adnate, covered by a
black membrane, the disk at length tubercled,
with a border of its own substance.

2. *Gyrophora.* Apothecia orbicular, sub-
scutelliform, sessile and adnate, covered by
a black membrane, the disk marked with
concentric circles or folds, with a border of
its own substance.

Q.

QUILL.—The quill of feathers possesses
considerable polarizing power; the coloured
bands are, however, so broad that they are
better seen with the naked eye.

See FEATHERS.

QUININE. See ALKALOIDS, p. 28.

Iodo-disulphate, sulphate of iodo-quinine,
Herapathite.—This salt is prepared by dissolving disulphate of quinine in strong acetic
acid, warming the solution, dropping into it
an alcoholic solution of iodine carefully in
small quantities at a time, and placing the
mixture aside for some hours, when the
crystals separate.

They dissolve in the heated mother-liquor,
also in hot alcohol, being again deposited on
cooling; but they are not soluble in cold
alcohol or æther.

They are so easily decomposed and altered
that they are with difficulty mounted. This
may, however, be effected by cautiously
neutralizing the excess of acid in the mother-
liquor by solution of ammonia, taking care
not to precipitate the excess of the disulphate
of quinine; a portion of the liquid containing the crystals is then transferred to a slide,
the liquid removed with blotting-paper, and
the crystals dried in a current of cold air.
They are then mounted in Canada balsam
rendered thin with æther, heat being avoided.

The crystals are of a pale olive-green
colour (Pl. 7. fig. 17), and possess a more
intense polarizing power than any other
known substance. The play of colours presented when they are rolling over each other
whilst contained in a watch-glass, forms a
very beautiful sight, the colours varying
according to the relative positions of the
crystals to each other; and when the latter
cross each other at a right angle, complete
blackness is produced.

Dr. Herapath, who discovered this beautiful salt, has also described a method of
making crystals of sufficient size to replace
tourmalines or Nicol's prisms. The ingre-
dients are,—as pure disulphate of quinine as
can be obtained, that from Messrs. Howard
and Kent being best; strong acetic acid, of
sp. gr. 1·042; proof-spirit, composed of
equal bulks of rectified spirit of sp. gr. ·837
and distilled water; and tincture of iodine,
made by dissolving 40 grains of iodine in
1 oz. of rectified spirit. The proportions are:

Disulphate of quinine.. 50 grains.
Acetic acid .... 2 fluid ounces.
Proof-spirit .... 2 fluid ounces.
Tincture of iodine .... 50 drops.

The disulphate of quinine is dissolved in the
acetic acid mixed with the spirit, the solution heated to 130° F., and the tincture of
iodine immediately added in drops, the
mixture being constantly agitated.

The compound should be prepared in a
wide-mouthed Florence flask or matrass; and
the temperature should be maintained for a
little time after the addition of the iodine,
so that the solution may become perfectly
clear, and of a dark sherry colour. It should
then be set aside to crystallize in a room of
a uniform temperature of 45° to 50° F., and
kept from vibration. The latter may be
effected by suspending the flask by the neck
with strong string, attaching this to a horizontal cord stretching across the room from
one wall to the other; or placing the flask
on a steady support, lying upon a pillow.
The large crystalline plates form upon the
surface of the liquid, where they are allowed
to remain for twelve to twenty-four hours,
until they have acquired sufficient thickness.

The flask is then carefully removed without shaking, and rested upon a gallipot. A circular cover is then fastened by its edge to the end of a glass rod with a little wax or marine glue, and passed beneath one of the crystalline films, the adherent mother-liquor removed with blotting-paper, and the film allowed to dry in a room at a temperature of 45° to 50° F. The cover and film are then placed under a cupping-glass or small bell-glass, with a watch-glass containing a few drops of tincture of iodine. The time required for the iodizing may be about three hours at 50° F., or less if the temperature be higher.

The film is then covered with a solution of Canada balsam in æther, saturated with iodine by warming with a few crystals of this substance, and allowing it to cool.

Other films are removed and mounted in the same manner. Should the films not separate from the original liquid at the end of six hours, this must be heated with a spirit-lamp until the deposited crystals are dissolved, a little spirit and a few drops more tincture of iodine added, and the liquid again set aside.

If the film appear black when removed on the cover, it is crossed by an adherent or interposed crystal, which must be carefully removed.

These crystals are sold ready mounted, and may be purchased at a very small cost.

Dr. Herapath proposes the production of the crystals of the quinine-salt as a very delicate test for the presence of quinine. A test-liquid is first made with 3 drachms of acetic acid, 1 drachm of rectified spirit, and 6 drops of dilute sulphuric acid. A drop of this is placed upon a slide and the alkaloid added, and when it is dissolved, a very minute quantity of tincture of iodine added ; after a time the salt separates in little rosettes.

BIBL. Herapath, *Phil. Mag.* 1852. iii. 161, iv. 186, and 1853. vi. 171 & 346; Haidinger, *ibid.* 1853. 284.

QUINQUELOCULINA, D'Orb.—A genus of Foraminifera, of the order Agathistegia, and family Multiloculidæ.

Char. Shell inequilateral, globular or compressed, sometimes angular, of the same form at all ages; *chambers* aggregated on five opposing faces, embracing so that five only are apparent, their cavities simple ; *orifice* single, with a tooth.

Several British species, both recent and fossil.

Williamson unites this genus with *Miliolina.*

Q. seminulum (Pl. 42. fig. 10) = one form of *Miliolina seminulum*, Will.

BIBL. That of the order.

R.

RACODIUM, Pers. See ANTENNARIA.

RADULA, Dumort.—A genus of Jungermannieæ (Hepaticæ), containing one British species, *R. complanata* (fig. 613),

Fig. 613.

Radula complanata.
Leafy shoot with an immature and a burst capsule.
Magnified 5 diameters.

common upon the trunks of trees, everywhere, forming orbicular pale-green patches closely appressed to the bark.

BIBL. Hook. *Brit. Jung.* pl. 81 ; *Brit. Flor.* ii. pt. 1. p. 120 ; Ekart, *Syn. Jung.* pl. 4. fig. 31 ; Endlicher, *Gen. Plant,* Supp. 1. No. 472–13.

RALFSIA, Berk.—A genus of Myrionemaceæ (Fucoid Algæ), containing one British species, *R. verrucosa* (*R. deusta*, Berk.), forming dark-brown Lichen-like patches, 1 to 6″ in diameter, on rocks between tide-marks. The fronds are at first orbicular and concentrically zoned ; they are composed of densely-packed, vertical, simple, jointed filaments. The fruit is formed in wart-like patches, and consists of obovate sporanges attached to the bases of vertical filaments.

BIBL. Harvey, *Brit. Mar. Alg.* p. 49. pl. 10 D.

RAMALINA, Ach.—A genus of Parmeliaceæ (Gymnocarpous Lichens), containing several British species, forms of shrubby habit, mostly growing upon the trunks of trees, bearing orbicular - peltate apothecia, nearly of the same colour as the thallus. *R. fraxinea, fastigiata,* and *farinacea* are common.

BIBL. Hook. *Brit. Flor.* ii. pt. 1. p. 228; Tulasne, *Ann. des Sc. Nat.* 3 sér. xvii. p. 192, pl. 2. figs. 13–15.

RANA, Linn. See FROG.

RAPHIDES.—This name was first applied to the minute needle-shaped crystals occurring in great abundance in the tissues of many plants; but it is now used in general application to all the crystalline formations contained in vegetable cells. The crystals occur either solitary or grouped, and sometimes the groups are formed on a peculiar stalked matrix projecting into the cavity of enlarged cells, forming the organs called *cystolithes.*

There are few plants of the higher classes which do not contain raphides; they are very abundant in the herbaceous structures of the Monocotyledons generally, and especially those of the Araceæ, Musaceæ, Liliaceæ, &c.; they also abound in the Polygonaceæ, Cactaceæ, Euphorbiaceæ, Urticaceæ, &c., among the Dicotyledons. They are usually found only in the interior of the cavities of cells, but in some cases they occur in the intercellular cavities, perhaps, however, accidentally. They may occur in almost any part, but are found most extensively in the stems of herbaceous plants (Monocotyledons in general and Cactaceæ); they also occur in the bark and pith of many woody plants (lime, vine); leaves likewise frequently contain them in vast quantity (Araceæ, Musaceæ, Liliaceæ, Iridaceæ, Polygonaceæ); also sepals (Orchidaceæ, Gemaniaceæ); in the rhubarbs, and also in Umbelliferæ, they occur extensively in the roots, for instance in the carrot; and they abound in autumn in the base of the bulbs of the onion and other Liliaceæ. Raphides are very readily discovered and clearly seen in tissues, by the aid of the polarizing apparatus.

The form of the needle-shaped raphides is usually that of a square prism, with pyramidal ends. These ordinarily occur lying parallel in bundles (fig. 614); another common form is that of rectangular or rhombic prisms with oblique or pyramidal ends; the smaller of these often present themselves in groups radiating from a centre (fig. 615). Prisms of similar or of six-sided forms, octohedra, rhombs, &c., also occur solitary or few together (Pl. 39. fig. 28), the larger ones sometimes nearly filling the cavity of the cells in which they lie. The cells containing the bundles of acicular raphides in the Araceæ also contain a viscid sap, which causes them

to burst, through endosmose, when placed in water, and discharge the crystals. Turpin erroneously described these as organs of a special nature, under the name of *Biforines.*

Raphides most frequently consist of oxalate of lime, especially in the Cactaceæ, Polygonaceæ, &c.; carbonate of lime seems to stand next in the order of frequency, then

Fig. 614.   Fig. 615.

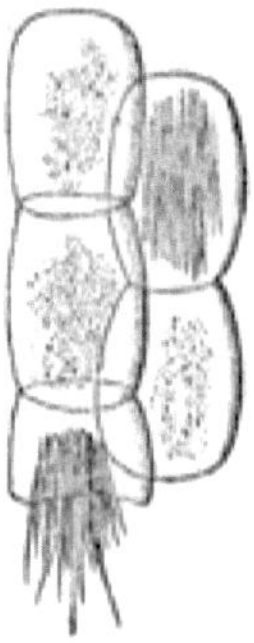

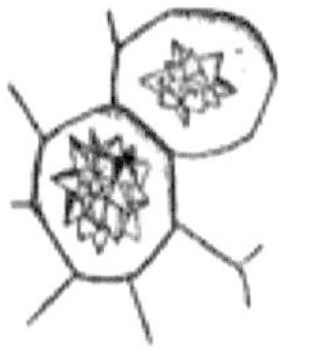

Fig. 614. Parenchymatous cells of the stem of Rumex, containing bundles of raphides. Magnified 400 diams.
Fig. 615. Parenchymatous cells of the stem of Beta, with groups of raphides. Magnified 400 diams.

sulphate and phosphate of lime. Their composition may be ascertained by the appropriate tests for these salts. It is sometimes difficult to determine the form accurately, on account of the small size; it is found advantageous to mount well-cleaned and partly crushed crystals in Canada balsam, also to view them rolling over in alcohol (INTRODUCTION, p. xxix).

The peculiar crystalline structures called by Weddell *cystolithes,* occur most abundantly in the families of the Urticaceæ (including Moreæ) and the Acanthaceæ. They ordinarily consist of a stalked, clavate, and globose, or irregular linear body, suspended in a greatly enlarged cell, most frequently situated beneath the epidermis of the leaf (Pl. 39. figs. 26, 27); but they also occur in deeper-seated regions. Their nature and development has been followed by several observers; and they are found to consist of a cellulose matrix with carbonate of lime crystallized in a kind of efflorescence upon the surface. They appear to originate by a little papilla or column of secondary deposit, at the upper end of the cell, which increases by successive concentric layers of cellulose applied on the lower surface, leaving a short stalk-like portion, which remains uncovered and also free from the crystals which gradually sprout out from the thickened head. The crystals may be removed by the action of acid, and then the matrix assumes a blue colour with sulphuric acid and iodine. Payen imagined the thicker portion encrusted by the crystals to be composed of numerous cellules, each producing a crystal: this is erroneous. The *cystolithes* vary in form; the clavate kinds may be best observed, in *Ficus elastica* (Pl. 39. fig. 27) and other species, in vertical sections of the leaf; globular forms are found in *Parietaria officinalis* (fig. 26) and the Hop; in species of *Pilea* they are linear or crescentic, and suspended by the convex edge.

BIBL. Lindley (and E. Quekett), *Introd. to Botany*, 4th ed. i. p. 97; Turpin, *Ann. des Sc. Nat.* 2 sér. vi. p. 5; Raspail, *Chemie organique*; Morren, *Bull. Acad. de Bruxelles*, vi. No. 3; Meyen, *Müller's Archiv*, 1839. p. 255; *Ann. des Sc. Nat.* 2 sér. xii. p. 257; Schleiden, *Grundzüge*, 3rd ed. pp. 168, 341; *Principles*, pp. 6, 122; Weddell, *Ann. des Sc. Nat.* 4 sér. ii. p. 267; Schacht, *Beitr. z. Anat. und Phys.* 1854. p. 212; Unger, *Ann. d. Wiener Museum*, i. 1844; *Anat. und Phys. d. Pflanz.* 1855. p. 123; Payen, *Mém. sur l. dével. d. végétaux*, Paris, 1844; Quekett, *Trans. Mic. Soc.* new ser. i. p. 20.

RAPHIGNATHUS, Dugès.—A genus of Arachnida, of the order Acarina, and family Trombidina.

Char. Palpi with an indistinct claw; mandibles represented by two short setæ inserted upon a fleshy bulb, concealed by a broad labium; body entire; coxæ contiguous; legs but little attenuate at the ends, anterior longest, last joint longer than the others.

1. *R. ruberrimus* (Pl. 2. fig. 35 *a*, labium with mandibles and a palp; *b*, a mandible). Body oval, slightly depressed, smooth, and almost free from hairs, rostrum forming a conical process; eyes two, dark red, one on each side at the anterior part of the body; labium triangular, concave; setæ accompanied by a more slender hair-like process; palpi large, inflated, claw of the 4th joint very short. Size minute! Found under stones and on plants.

2. *R. hispidus.* Form of that of the preceding; body velvety, with two posterior papillæ.

BIBL. Dugès, *Ann. des Sc. Nat.* 2 sér. i. 22, ii. 55; Gervais, *Walckenaer's Aptèr* iii. 172.

RATTULUS, Lamarck.—A genus of Rotatoria, of the family Hydatinæa.

Char. Eyes two, frontal; tail-like foot simply styliform; neither cirrhi nor fins present. Teeth indistinct.

R. lunaris (Pl. 35. fig. 22). Eyes distant from the anterior margin; foot decurved, lunate. Aquatic; length 1-288″.

BIBL. Ehrenberg, *Infus.* p. 448.

REAGENTS. See INTRODUCTION, pp. xxxvii and xl.

REBOUILLIA, Raddi. — A genus of Marchantieæ (Hepaticæ), founded on the *Marchantia hemisphærica*, Linn., characterized by the conical or flattened, 1–5-lobed stalked receptacle (fig. 616), the perigone being adherent to the lobes of the

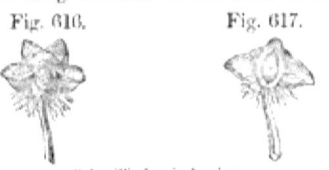

Fig. 616.   Fig. 617.

Rebouillia hemisphærica.
Female receptacles, with the perigone burst.
Fig. 616, seen from above; fig. 617, from below.

Magnified 2 diameters.

receptacle on the under side, opening by a slit (fig. 617); perichæte none, and the globose sporange bursting irregularly. The antheridia are imbedded in sessile, creascent-shaped disks. The fronds are rigid, with a well-marked midrib, green above, purple beneath. It grows on moist banks, or by the side of mountain streams.

BIBL. Hook. *Brit. Flor.* ii. pt. 1. p. 108; G. W. Bischoff, *Nova Acta*, xvii. p. 1001, pl. 69. fig. 1; Endlich. *Gen. Plant.* No. 468.

RECEPTACLES FOR SECRETIONS. See SECRETING ORGANS of Plants.

RED SNOW.—The remarkable phænomenon known under this name has been the subject of very extensive investigation, and it is well known to be the result of the enormous development of a microscopic organism related to *Protococcus* or *Chlamidococcus viridis*. We are inclined to believe that more than one form is comprehended at present under the name of *Protococcus* or *Hæmatococcus nivalis*; for our specimens of Arctic red snow (for which we are indebted to the kindness of Mr. R. Brown) appear to belong to the same genus as *Palmella cruenta*, as first indicated by Mr. Brown, and confirmed by Sir W. J. Hooker. Dr. Greville's figures of the Scotch plant closely resemble this; but the continental plants, described by Mr. Shuttleworth and others, would seem congeneric with *Protococcus* (*Chlamidococcus*, Braun, *Chlamidomonas*, Ehr.), since they produce active zoospores, the forms which Shuttleworth described as distinct infusoria, as species of *Astasia*. Nearly connected with this continental snow-plant, if not identical, is the *Protococcus pluvialis*, described so elaborately by Dr. Cohn, which moreover appears to be synonymous with the *Disceræa purpurea* of Morren.

The following is a description of the red snow (brought home by Capt. Parry) from our own observation. It may be noticed as remarkable, that after being kept so many years in a moist state in a stoppered bottle, the structure appears almost unchanged, the only difference being the assumption of a green colour on the surface of the masses when exposed to light. Frond an indefinite gelatinous mass densely filled with spherical cells, about 1-1200″ in diameter (Pl. 3. fig. 3 *d*); cells with a distinct membrane, their contents consisting of numerous tolerably equal granules, red or green (see above). Between the large cells lie patches of minute red granules (as in *Palmella cruenta*, Pl. 3. fig. 3 *a*, *b*), apparently discharged from the large cells. Bauer and Greville both describe this as the mode of propagation of the plant; but it is probable that the cells also increase by division when actively vegetating. Like the rest of the unicellular Algæ, this plant requires a new and thorough investigation; for no characters are of any service without a complete history of the development. We subjoin references to the most important papers on this subject. See also WATER, Coloration of.

BIBL. R. Brown, *Appendix to Ross's First Voyage*, London, 1819; Bauer, *Quarterly Journal of Lit. Sciences and Arts*, vii. p. 222; Agardh, *Nova Acta*, xii. p. 2; *System. Alg.* p. 13; DeCandolle, *Bibl. univ. de Genève*, 1824; Nees v. Esenbeck, *German ed. of R. Brown's Works*, i. p. 571 (abundant citations of older writers); Hooker, *Append. to Parry's Second Voyage*; Greville, *Sc. Crypt. Fl.* pl. 231; Shuttleworth, *Bibl. univ. de Genève*, Feb. 1840; Desmazières, *Ann. des Sc. Nat.* 2 sér. xvii. p. 91; Meyen, *Wiegmann's Archiv*, 1840. i. p. 166, transl. in *Ann. Nat. Hist.* vii. p. 245; Morren, *Hydrophytes de Belgique*, *Mém. Acad. Bruxelles*, xiv. 1841; Von Flotow, *Nova Acta*, xx. p. 11; Cohn, *Nova Acta*, xxii. p. 605.

RED SPIDER.—The insect so called by gardeners is a GAMASUS.

REPRODUCTION.—Some observations upon reproduction are made under the respective heads of the classes, orders, and families to which the organisms belong. See also CELL and OVUM.

RESERVOIRS FOR SECRETIONS IN PLANTS. See SECRETING ORGANS of Plants.

RETE MUCOSUM. See SKIN.

RETEPORA, Lamk.—A genus of Infundibulate Cheilostomatous Polyzoa, of the family Escharidæ.

Char. Polypidom leafy, reticular, fragile; cells on one surface only, short, and not prominent. Two British species:

1. *R. reticulata.* Wavy and convolute, upper side warty and very porous.

2. *R. beaniana.* Umbilicate, funnel-shaped, wavy; interspaces unarmed.

BIBL. Johnston, *Brit. Zooph.* 353; Gosse, *Mar. Zool.* 18.

RETICULARIA, Bull. — A genus of Myxogastres (Gasteromycetous Fungi), characterized by the indeterminate, thin, simple peridium, bursting irregularly, with the branched, shrubby, reticulated capillitium adherent to it. Several species are British; they are rather large plants, growing over recently felled timber or on hollow trees, rails, &c.

BIBL. Berk. *Brit. Flor.* ii. pt. 2. p. 308; Fries, *Summa Veg.* p. 449; *Syst. Mycol.* iii. p. 83.

RETINA. See EYE, p. 275.

RHABDITIS, Duj. See ANGUILLULA.

RHABDONEMA, Kütz. — A genus of Diatomaceæ.

Char. Frustules tabular, depressed, compound, fixed by a stalk arising from one of the angles, with interrupted vittæ (front view), vittæ capitate; valves transversely striate, striæ extending into the front view, and forming numerous longitudinal series.

Marine; upon Algæ. Striæ visible under ordinary illumination; the dark lines or vittæ correspond to more or less complete internal septa; frustules connected with each other by gelatinous cushions (isthmi).

Conjugation and the formation of sporangia have been observed in one species.

1. *R. arcuatum* (*Striatella arcuat.*, Ralfs) (Pl. 13. fig. 18). Vittæ in two marginal rows, isthmi convex. Length 1-300″.

2. *R. minutum* (*Tessella catena*, Ralfs). Vittæ in two marginal rows; transverse striæ faint. Length 1-1200 to 1-900″.

3. *R. adriaticum.* Vittæ forming four rows (interrupted in the middle, and again between the middle and the margin on each side); transverse striæ distinct; isthmi concave. Length 1-480 to 1-170".

BIBL. Kützing, *Bacill.* 126, and *Sp. Alg.* 115; Ralfs, *Ann. Nat. Hist.* xi. 455, and xii. 104; Smith, *Brit. Diat.* ii. 32; West, *Micr. Journ.* 1858. 186; Arnott, *Micr. Journ.* 1858. 91.

RHAPHIDOGLŒA, Kütz.—A genus of Diatomaceæ.

Char. Frustules navicular, arranged in radiating crowded rows in a globose gelatinous mass. Marine.

R. micans (Pl. 14. fig. 11). Rows of frustules irregular, obsolete; valves linear-lanceolate, subulate, somewhat acute. Length 1-140".

Three other species.

BIBL. Kützing, *Bacill.* 10; id. *Sp. Alg.* 97.

RHAPHONEIS, Ehr.—A genus of Diatomaceæ.

Char. Frustules single, quadrangular, navicular; valves without a median aperture (nodule?); median sutural line longitudinal. Marine. = *Doryphora* without a stalk.

Eleven species.

BIBL. Ehrenberg, *Ber. d. Berl. Akad.* 1844. 74; Kützing, *Sp. Alg.* 49.

RHINOTRICHUM, Corda.—A genus of Mucedines (Hyphomycetous Fungi), growing upon dead wood, characterized by erect, simple or sparingly divided, fertile filaments, the last joint of which is clavate and covered with minute spines, scattered or in transverse rows, bearing single spores. Two (new) British species are described by Berkeley and Broome.

BIBL. Corda, *Icones Fung.* i. fig. 232; Fries, *Summa Veg.* p. 501; Berkeley and Broome, *Ann. Nat. Hist.* 2nd ser. vii. p. 177, pl. 7, xiii. p. 462, pl. 16.

RHIPIDOPHORA, Kütz.—A genus of Diatomaceæ.

Char. Those of *Licmophora*, except that the frustules are each furnished with a distinct stipes; but as this is not always the case, the character is of little or no value. Marine.

Three British species (Smith); twelve others (Kützing).

R. paradoxa (Pl. 13. fig. 19). Stipes filiform, dichotomous; frustules in front view broadly wedge-shaped, somewhat acute at the base. Length of frustules 1-540 to 1-480".

RHIZOCLONIUM, Kütz.—A genus of Confervaceæ (Confervoid Algæ), distinguished by the decumbent habit and the short, root-like character of the branches.

Kützing includes here many of our British Confervæ:

1. *R. rivulare,* C. Filaments simple, diam. 1-900", fine bright-green bundles 2 to 3 feet long; in streams and rivers; common (Dillwyn, pl. 39).

2. *R. tortuosum,* Dillw. Filaments simple, diam. 1-800", rigid, curled and twisted, forming large strata; in salt-water pools; abundant (Dillwyn, pl. 46).

3. *R. arenosum,* Carm. Filaments simple, diam. 1-1000 to 1-1800"; in dirty-green strata; sandy sea-shores.

4. *R. obtusangulum,* Lyngb. (Pl. 5. fig. 12). Filaments branched, diam. 1-1400"; pale-green, stratified; sandy sea-shores.

5. *R. riparium* (*Jürgensii,* Kütz.). Filaments branched, diam. 1-1400 to 1-1800". Apparently not distinct from the preceding. On sandy sea-shores; not uncommon (*Engl. Botany,* pl. 2100).

6. *R. implexum,* Dillw. Filaments simple, diam. 1-2000"; bright green; forming large strata, on mountain rocks (Dillw. *C. implexa,* tab. B).

7. *R. arenicolum,* Berk. (*Kochianum,* Kz.). Filament 1-2000 to 1-2400"; mountain rocks (Berkeley, *Gleanings,* pl. 13. fig. 3).

BIBL. Harvey, *Brit. Mar. Alg.* p. 206, pl. 24 F; Kütz. *Sp. Alg.* 385; *Tab. Phyc. Brit. Flora,* ii. pt. 1. p. 354; Dillwyn, *Brit. Confervæ.*

RHIZONEMA, Thw.—A genus of Oscillatoriaceæ (Confervoid Algæ) = *Dictyonema,* Kütz. This curious plant (*R. interruptum*) differs from its allies by the gelatinous sheath being composed of distinct cells and furnished with branched root-like processes, which anastomose freely. The cell-contents are deep blue-green, with occasional yellowish interstitial cells.

BIBL. Thwaites, *Eng. Bot. Supp.* pl. 2954; Kütz. *Sp. Alg.* p. 321; *Tab. Phyc.* ii. pl. 40. fig. 5.

RHIZONOTIA, Ehr.—A genus of Diatomaceæ, of obscure structure.

BIBL. Ehrenberg, *Ber. d. Berl. Akad.* 1843. 139.

RHIZOPHORACEÆ.—A family of Dicotyledonous plants, to which belong the celebrated Mangrove-trees of the tropics. They are remarkable for the general occurrence of a ramified form of *liber-cell* (Pl. 39. fig. 31). The long woody radicles pushed out by the fruits, while still attached to the parent tree, contain a vast quantity of these ramified cells with very thick walls.

RHIZOPODA, Duj., or better, Pseudopoda, E.—A subdivision of the animal kingdom, comprising, according to Dujardin and Ehrenberg, the Arcellina (with Dujardin's genera *Euglypha, Gromia,* and *Trinema*) and the Foraminifera.

In Siebold's arrangement, it contains the Amœbæa, the Arcellina, and the Foraminifera.

The essential characters are the gelatinous structureless composition of the body, and the locomotive organs consisting of variable retractile root-like processes (false legs).

BIBL. Dujardin, *Infus.* p. 240; Ehrenberg, *Infus.*; Siebold, *Vergl. Anat.* 11.

RHIZOSELENIA, Ehr.—A doubtful genus of Diatomaceæ.

Char. Frustules elongate, subcylindrical, marked with transverse or spiral lines, ends oblique or conical, and with one or more terminal bristles; marine and fossil.

Four British species: *R. styliformis, R. imbricata, R. setigera,* and *R. alata.* Ehrenberg and Kützing describe six other species.

R. alata (Pl. 42. fig. 43); *R. americana* (Pl. 41. fig. 46), imperfect at the lower end. The British species were obtained from *Salpa, Ascidia,* and *Noctiluca.*

BIBL. Ehrenberg, *Abh. d. Berl. Akad.* 1841. 291; Kützing, *Sp. Alg.* p. 24; Brightwell, *Micr. Journ.* 1858. 94.

RHODOMELA, Ag.—A genus of Rhodomelaceæ (Florideous Algæ), containing two tolerably common British species, with feathery, inarticulate, branched fronds, the branches composed of concentric layers of oblong, colourless cells, with a cortical layer of minute coloured cells. Colour of *R. lycopodioides* purplish brown, becoming black; height 4 to 18″. Colour of *R. subfusca* brownish or reddish; height 4 to 10″. The *ceramidia* are stalked on the ramuli, occurring in summer; the *stichidia,* with tetrahedral tetraspores, occur in a similar situation in winter; the *antheridia* (observed in *R. subfusca*) also occur in tufts in the same position.

BIBL. Harvey, *Brit. Mar. Alg.* p. 78, pls. 11, 13; Tulasne, *Ann. des Sc. Nat.* 4 sér. iii. p. 20.

RHODOMELACEÆ.—A family of Florideous Algæ. Red or brown sea-weeds, with a leafy or filiform, areolated or articulated frond, composed of polygonal cells. *Fructification*: 1. *Conceptacles (ceramidia)*

external, ovate or urn-shaped, furnished with a terminal pore, and containing a tuft of pear-shaped spores; 2. *antheridia,* borne in tufts in similar situations; 3. *tetraspores* immersed in distorted ramuli or in lanceolate receptacles (*stichidia*), usually in rows.

Synopsis of the British Genera.

1. *Odonthalia. Frond* flattened, linear, with an obsolete midrib, pinnatifid, alternately inciso-dentate.

2. *Rhodomela. Frond* cylindrical, inarticulate, opaque. *Tetraspores* contained in pod-like receptacles (*stichidia*).

3. *Bostrychia. Frond* cylindrical, inarticulate, dotted; the surface-cells quadrate. *Tetraspores* in terminal pods.

4. *Rytiphlœa. Frond* cylindrical, inarticulate, transversely striate. *Tetraspores* in pod-like receptacles.

5. *Polysiphonia. Frond* cylindrical, articulated wholly or in part; the branches longitudinally streaked. *Tetraspores* in distorted ramuli.

6. *Dasya. Frond* cylindrical, the stem inarticulate; the ramuli articulated, composed of a single string of cells. *Tetraspores* in pod-like receptacles (*stichidia*), borne by the ramuli.

RHODYMENIA, Grev.—A genus of Rhodymeniaceæ (Florideous Algæ), containing seven British species, beautiful, brightly-coloured sea-weeds, growing on rocks or larger Algæ, having a flat membranous or somewhat leathery frond, ribless and veinless, of parenchymatous texture. Most are not more than 2″ high, but *R. laciniata* and *palmata* grow to 10″ and 18″. The colour is mostly rose- or blood-red. The *coccidia* are formed on the lacerated margins or the tips of lobes of the frond. The *tetraspores* form cloudy spots along the margin, or are scattered, tetrahedrally divided. The *antheridia* likewise form patches on the surface of the frond (observed in *R. Palmetta* and *palmata*).

BIBL. Harvey, *Brit. Mar. Alg.* p. 124, pl. 16 A; Thuret, *Ann. des Sc. Nat.* 4 sér. iii. p. 19, pl. 3.

RHODYMENIACEÆ. — A family of Florideous Algæ. Purplish or blood-red sea-weeds, with an expanded or filiform inarticulate frond, composed of polygonal cells; occasionally traversed by a fibrous axis. Superficial cells minute, irregularly packed, or *rarely* arranged in filamentous series. *Fructification*: 1. *Conceptacles (coccidia)* external or half-immersed, globose or hemispherical, imperforate, containing beneath a thick envelope a mass of spores affixed to a central column; 2. *antheridia* collected in flat patches or sori; 3. *tetraspores* either dispersed through the whole frond, or collected in indefinite cloudy patches.

Synopsis of the British Genera.

* Frond flat, expanded, leaf-like, dichotomous or palmate.

1. *Stenogramme.* Conceptacles linear, riblike.

2. *Rhodymenia.* Conceptacles hemispherical, scattered.

** Frond compressed or terete, linear or filiform, much branched.

3. *Sphærococcus.* Frond linear, compressed, two-edged, distichously branched, with an obscure midrib.

4. *Gracilaria.* Frond filiform, compressed or flat, irregularly branched; the central cells very large.

5. *Hypnea.* Frond filiform, irregularly branched, traversed by a fibro-cellular axis.

RHOPALOMYCES, Corda.—A genus of Mucedines (Hyphomycetous Fungi), nearly

Fig. 618.　　　　　　Fig. 619.

Rhopalomyces nigra.

Fig. 618. Tufts on wood. Nat. size.

Fig. 619. Fertile filaments. Magnified 200 diameters.

allied to ASPERGILLUS, but having the spores single (fig. 619), and not in moniliform series. The single spores are borne on minute spines (fig. 619, left-hand head). They are mildews growing over decayed wood, matting, dung, &c. Two (new) British species are described by Berkeley and Broome, found growing together.

BIBL. Berk. and Broome, *Ann. Nat. Hist.* 2 ser. vii. p. 96, pl. 5.

RHUBARB.—Garden rhubarb (*Rheum undulatum*, and other species) affords in the large edible petioles, excellent specimens of SPIRAL-fibrous STRUCTURES, spiral, an-

nular, and reticulate vessels and ducts: these are readily isolated by the help of a needle from a fragment of cooked rhubarb placed in water on a slide. The petioles and leaves likewise contain bundles of acicular RAPHIDES. The roots also contain special receptacles for a characteristic secretion.

RHYNCHOLOPHUS, Dugès. = *Erythræus*, Latreille (not Dugès). A genus of Arachnida, of the order Acarina, and family Trombidina.

Char. Palpi large, free; labium penicillate; mandibles ensiform, very long; body entire; coxæ very remote, legs palp-like, *i. e.* dilated at the end, the posterior longest.

Species numerous; found in woods, under leaves, and in mosses.

R. cinereus (Pl. 2. fig. 40: *a*, labium with palp; *b*, tarsus; *c*, plume of labium more magnified; *d*, mandible).

BIBL. Dugès, *Ann. des Sc. Nat.* 2 sér. i. 30; Gervais, *Walckenaer's Arachnid.* iii. 175; Koch, *Deutschlands Crust. &c.*

RHYNCHOPAGON, Werneck (Rotatoria) = *Diglena* with a bilobed rostrum! Two species.

BIBL. Werneck, *Ber. d. Berl. Akad.* 1841. p. 377.

RHYTISMA, Fries.—A genus of Phacidiacei (Ascomycetous Fungi), growing upon the leaves of trees and shrubs, forming dark patches or spots on the surface, breaking through the epidermis with little scales or irregular fissures. *R. acerinum* is exceedingly common, forming large black spots on the leaves of the sycamore and maple; the thecasporous fruit is perfected (on the dead fallen leaves) in spring; MELASMIA *acerina*, which occurs in autumn, appears to be a preparatory form of this plant. *R. salicinum* is common on willow-leaves.

BIBL. Berk. *Brit. Flor.* ii. pt. 2. p. 290; Grev. *Sc. Crypt. Fl.* pl. 118; Fries, *Summa Veg.* 370; Tulasne, *Comptes Rendus*, March 31, 1852 (*Ann. Nat. Hist.* 2 ser. viii. p. 118).

RICCIA, L.—A genus of Riccieæ (Hepaticæ), consisting of minute green thalloid productions growing upon damp ground or floating on water, distinguished from the allied forms by the capsules being immersed in the substance of the frond, destitute of perichæte and perigone, while the archegone permanently encloses the sporange as an adherent epigone, bearing a persistent style-like neck (figs. 621, 622). The antheridia are globose sacs contained in special cavities, the orifices of which, narrowed into a neck, project as short processes from the surface (cuspides). The epigone being adherent to

Fig. 620.

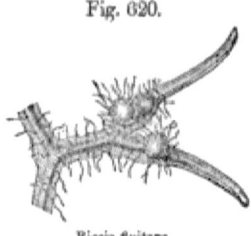

Riccia fluitans.

Lower surface of a fragment of the frond, with three imbedded sporanges projecting, their orifices being on the upper surface.

Magnified 5 diameters.

the sporange, the spores appear to lie immediately in the cavity of the former when

Fig. 621.   Fig. 622.

Riccia fluitans.

Fig. 621. Vertical section through the frond and sporange contained in its substance.

Fig. 622. Sporange with persistent epigone, extracted from the frond.

Magnified 25 diameters.

ripe; they are unaccompanied by elaters, and escape by irregular rupture of the epigone. Several species occur in Britain.

* Terrestrial.

1. *R. glauca*, L. Frond without membranous scales below, fleshy, ovate-oblong, two- to three-lobed, 1-2 to 1" in diameter, the divisions dichotomous, growing in orbicular tufts, surface smoothish, punctate, glaucous green. On banks.

2. *R. crystallina.* L. Differing from the last chiefly in larger size and lighter colour, and having large cavernous air-cells opening widely on the upper surface. Damp mould.

** Aquatic.

3. *R. fluitans*, L. (fig. 620). Fronds without scales below, 1-2 to 2" long, repeatedly forked, segments linear, notched at the ends; when placed on damp earth it produces radical hairs (fig. 621-2). Stagnant water.

4. *R. natans*, L. Fronds with long reti-

culated scales below, obcordate, 1-2" long, or with the two lobes again divided; scales of the lower surface purple. On stagnant pools.

Bibl. Hook. *Brit. Flora*, ii. pt. 1. p. 102; Bischoff, *Nova Acta*, xvii. p. 909; Lindenberg, *ibid.* xviii. p. 361; Hofmeister, *Vergleich. Untersuch.* p. 43, pl. 10.

RICCIEÆ.—A tribe of Liverworts or Hepaticæ, consisting of delicate, green, membranous fronds, spreading on the ground or floating on water. The fruits are always sessile on the frond, more or less imbedded in its substance according to the thickness; the spores are unaccompanied by elaters.

Synopsis of British Genera.

1. *Sphærocarpus.* Archegones dorsal, on a lobed membranous frond, sparingly aggregated. Perichæte obtusely conical or pear-shaped; perforated at the summit, continuous with the frond. Perigone wanting. Epigone crowned by the deciduous style. Sporange at length free, indehiscent.

2. *Riccia.* Archegones immersed in the frond, scattered, neither emergent nor exposed on the surface until burst. Perichæte and perigone indistinguishable. Epigone crowned by the enlarged, long, persistent style, adherent to the sporange. Sporange bursting irregularly.

RICE.—This grain is produced by the grass called *Oryza sativa.* The seed is remarkable for the hard character of the albumen, which is explained at once when we examine a section under the microscope (Pl. 36. figs. 12 & 13). The cells are filled with very small starch-grains, which are packed so closely that they assume a parenchymatous form, and present the appearance of a continuous tissue (as in maize). The cohesion of the starch-granules is the cause of the peculiar grittiness of rice-flour. See Starch.

RIMULINA, D'Orb.—A genus of Foraminifera, of the order Stichostegia, and family Æquilateralidæ.

Char. Shell regular, equilateral, elongate, curved; *chambers* slightly globular, oblique, partly embracing, without constrictions, the last convex; *orifice* a lateral longitudinal fissure, occupying almost the entire length of the last chamber on the same side as the convexity.

Not British.

Bibl. That of the order.

RIND.—This word is used to denote a structure intermediate between epidermis and bark,—a compound structure consisting of several or many layers of cells and even of distinct forms of tissue, but not presenting the characteristic kinds and mode of arrangement which occur in true BARK.

RIVULARIA, Roth.—A genus of Oscillatoriaceæ (Confervoid Algæ), subdivided by Kützing, and restricted to the forms in which there is a distinct *manubrium* or elongated cell next to the globular basal cell. As thus defined, it contains only a few aquatic species, the rest being transferred to PHYSACTIS, EUACTIS and allied genera.

1. *R. angulosa*, Roth. Frond floating, globose, dirty green; manubria oblong and curved, or oblong-ovate and abbreviated; filaments torulose at the base, interruptedly articulated at the apex. *Eng. Bot.* 968.

2. *R. Boryana*, Kg. (Pl. 4. fig. 18). Frond globose, greenish brown; manubria large; sheaths ventricose, colourless, with plaited constrictions; filaments moniliform or interruptedly articulate, flagelliform. Frond as large as a cherry. β *flaccida*, smaller, filaments flaccid, not interrupted. The following two are given as doubtful: *R. botryoides*, Carmichael, and *R. plana*, Harvey.

3. *R. plicata*, Harv. Frond densely gregarious, compresso-plicate, often hollow and ruptured, dark green; filaments spuriously dichotomous, attenuated.

BIBL. Kützing, *Sp. Alg.* p. 336; *Tab. Phyc.* ii. pls. 67, 68; Harvey, *Brit. Alg.* 1 ed. p. 150; Hassall, *Brit. Fr. Alg.* p. 262, pl. 64; *Eng. Bot. Supp.* pl. 2911.

ROBERTINA, D'Orb.—A genus of Foraminifera, of the order Entomostegia, and family Asterigerinidæ.

Char. Shell free, spiral, oblong; spire oblique, turriculate; *chambers* divided by a partition; *orifice* comma-shaped, on the side of the last chamber.

No British species.

BIBL. That of the order.

ROBULINA, D'Orb.—A genus of Foraminifera, of the order Helicostegia, and family Nautiloidæ.

Char. Shell regular, equilateral, subcircular, greatly compressed, keeled, texture vitreous, brilliant; *spire* always embracing; *chambers* elongate, uniting at the umbilicus on the return of the spire. *Orifice* a triangular longitudinal fissure, placed at the carinal angle of the chambers.

Williamson unites this genus with *Cristellaria*; D'Orbigny remarks, however, that it differs from the latter in the form of the orifice, the more perfect spiral coil, the more regular nautiloid form, and in its umbilical disk, which is almost always very distinct.

Some British species, both recent and fossil.

R. cultrata (a form of *Cristellaria calcar*, Willn.) (Pl. 18. fig. 37).

BIBL. That of the order.

ROCCELLA, Ach.—A genus of Parmeliaceæ (Gymnocarpous Lichens), growing on maritime rocks, remarkable as furnishing the dye called orchil or archil. *R. tinctoria* and *R. fusiformis*, the British species, grow only in the extreme south of England.

BIBL. Hook. *Brit. Flor.* ii. pt. 1. p. 225; *Engl. Botany*, pls. 211, 728.

RŒSTELLA, Rebent.— A genus of Uredinei (Coniomycetous Fungi), closely related to ÆCIDIUM, and presenting similar spermogonia and perithecia; the chains of spores of the *Rastelieæ*, however, present a peculiarity,—having a sterile joint, forming an isthmus of variable length, between each spore: the peridium bursts irregularly; or (in *R. cancellata*) the teeth cohere more or less for a time, so as to form a kind of lattice. This genus includes *Æcidium cornutum*, *laceratum*, and *cancellatum* of older authors, growing respectively on the leaves of the mountain-ash, hawthorn, and pear. See ÆCIDIUM and UREDINEI.

BIBL. Berk. *Brit. Flor.* ii. pt. 2. p. 373; Greville, *Sc. Crypt. Fl.* pls. 180, 209; De Bary, *Brandpilze*, Berlin 1853. p. 73; Tulasne, *Ann. des Sc. Nat.* 4 sér. ii. pp. 132, 173; Fries, *Summa Veg.* p. 510.

ROSALINA, D'Orb. (= *Rotalia*, Lamk. and Ehr. part).—A genus of Foraminifera, of the order Helicostegia, and family Turbinoidæ.

Char. Shell depressed or trochoid, the last chambers rugose or coarsely perforated; *spire* apparent above, arched or conical; *chambers* depressed, often keeled; *orifice* slit-like, placed at the umbilical angle, and continued from one chamber to the other.

Distinguished from *Rotalina* by the central orifice placed underneath nearly all the end chambers, instead of being situated on the side of the last only.

Williamson unites the two genera.

Species numerous, both recent and fossil. *R. beccarii* (Pl. 18. fig. 36) = *Rotalia becc.*, Ehr., and *Rotalina becc.*, Willn. Common in sea-sand and attached to sea-weeds.

BIBL. That of the order.

ROTALIA, Lamk. Ehr. = ROSALINA and ROTALINA.

ROTALINA, Lamk. (*Rotalia*, Lamk. and Ehrenb. part).—A genus of Foraminifera, of the order Helicostegia, and family Turbinoidæ.

Char. Shell depressed or trochoid, finely foraminated, often keeled; *spire* depressed, truncate or conical; *chambers* depressed, often keeled; *orifice* a longitudinal fissure, next the last coil but one, occupying a part only of the last chamber. Periphery generally without marginal appendages, and with or without a central disk.

Distinguished from *Rosalina* by the orifice being next the return of the spire and only outside the last chamber, instead of being at the umbilicus and continued from chamber to chamber; and from *Truncatulina* in the orifice not being continued on the side of the spire.

Williamson unites *Rosalina* and *Rotalina* D'Orb.).

Species numerous, both recent and fossil; some common in chalk.

R. Haidingerii (Pl. 18. fig. 21).

BIBL. That of the order.

ROTATION.—This term is usually employed in botanical works to denote peculiar flowing movements of the protoplasm within the cavity of vegetable cells; and it is useful to retain the word for all the cases of the kind, in order to avoid confusion of these phænomena with the general circulation of the sap. The term "circulation of the cell-sap" is, however, often used instead of rotation, and especially in reference to the cases where it exhibits numerous distinct currents.

The rotation or circulation of the protoplasm presents itself in two types, namely—1. a rotatory movement of a layer of protoplasm investing the entire internal surface of the cell, as in CHARA, &c.; and 2. a radiating movement of the protoplasm in slender currents, from the nucleus out over the remainder of the cell, with a return flow towards the nucleus; but as the nucleus itself shifts in the latter type, as in the former, the two kinds are scarcely definitely distinguishable. They may, however, be spoken of separately.

The rotation in *Chara* (and *Nitella*) has been long known; a similar movement occurs in many water-plants, such as *Vallisneria*, *Hydrocharis*, *Anacharis*, *Stratiotes*, *Sagittaria*, *Potamogeton*, *Ceratophyllum*, &c., where it is seen best in the more delicate foliaceous structures, such as young leaves, stipules, or sepals, or in the young rootlets.

It has also been observed in the fruit-stalks of *Blasia pusilla*, and some other Hepaticæ; but general rotation has not yet been observed in other land-plants.

In the Characeæ the wall of the cells is lined with chlorophyll-granules, leaving two oblique or spiral striæ bare (fig. 125, p. 145); these striæ indicate the boundaries of the ascending and descending currents (marked by arrows). The moving substance is a viscid semifluid layer lying within the chlorophyll-layer, and itself surrounding the watery cell-sap occupying the centre of the cell. This layer, forming a kind of gelatinous sac, moves in a spiral course up one side of the cell and down the other, the motion being rendered very evident by chlorophyll- and other granules imbedded in it; these appear to be carried along passively by the stream, the larger slowly, the smaller with greater rapidity. In *Vallisneria*, *Anacharis*, &c. the chlorophyll-granules and the nucleus are imbedded in and moved with the flowing protoplasm. If long cells of *Chara* are bent or tied round by a ligature, the circulation is not stopped, but takes place independently in each half. If a cell of *Chara* is cut across, the protoplasm of the current flowing towards the cut surface escapes at once, but that of the current flowing away, goes on to the end of the cell, turns round, and then flows towards and out from the wound.

The size of the stream seems to be in inverse proportion to the length of the cell, decreasing as the latter acquires its full development. The rapidity of the current varies according to the age of the plant and the activity of its vegetation. It is most rapid in hot weather and in sunshine. Artificial elevation of temperature in the water in which the plant grows, up to a certain point, hastens the movement; a heat above 80° Fahr., however, retards it for a time. A temperature of 112° Fahr. kills the plant, as also does a cold of about 20°. Darkness appears merely to exert effect through its influence on the activity of the vegetation. Keeping *Chara* in water exhausted of air does not stop the rotation until the plant dies. Most chemical reagents seem to exert no special action; only lime-water appears to stop it in a few moments. A solution of sugar, or gum, or milk greatly hastens the rotation in *Vallisneria*, so that the protoplasm is moved on in waves; but the primordial utricle finally dissolves, and the movement ceases. Passing an electric current through the cell stops the current for a time; but it recovers itself, just as occurs after any mechanical interference. If several cells are injured by cutting or pricking, the whole rotation stops in young plants, but it gradually returns as before in the uninjured cells. Pressure interrupts or stops the motion for a time only; when removed, the current is gradually restored; but actual injury to the cell stops it for ever.

The rotation which takes place between the external surface of the green layer and the outer cell-membrane in *Closterium* and other DESMIDIACEÆ appears to be of the same kind as the above.

The circulation in reticular currents, first observed by Mr. Brown in the hairs of the stamens of *Tradescantia*, appears to exist far more extensively, if it be not even a universal phænomenon. It has been observed in the Confervoideæ, Fucoideæ, Florideæ, Lichens, Fungi, Hepaticæ, Equisetaceæ, Lycopodiaceæ, and Ferns, and in the most varied families of Flowering plants. It is seen most easily in young tissues, especially such as can be prepared readily without much mechanical injury; for example, in hairs, cells of the pulp of fruits, cells of the germen of Onagraceæ, of the labellum of Orchids, &c. It generally exhibits the following characters:—In the middle or at one side of the cell occurs a large heap of protoplasm, in which is imbedded the nucleus; from this protoplasm more or less slender filaments run out over the cavity of the cell, and, as these contain numerous fine granules, a flowing movement which takes place becomes evident by the change of place of the granules. Attentive examination shows that these flow out from the central mass, and return to it, and, moreover, that the currents change their form and direction, and, lastly, that the nucleus itself moves. This rotation cannot be observed in very young cells when the cavity is densely filled with protoplasm; but Hofmeister states that he has seen the entire primordial utricle rotate in the special-parent cell of the spore of *Phascum cuspidatum*. As the young cells increase in size, vacuoles are formed in the protoplasm, filled with watery sap; and these enlarging and becoming confluent, leave the protoplasm in the form of a reticulated mass.

The cause of the motion is quite unexplained; but it is evidently related to the movements exhibited by free protoplasmic bodies, such as ZOOSPORES, SPERMATOZOIDS, the free filaments of OSCILLATORIA,

&c. It has been stated to be dependent on the action of cilia; but we believe this is totally erroneous, and that it is rather referable to a common cause with the motion of cilia themselves. It has been well compared with the movements of the body of *Amœba*, which bear considerable resemblance to some kinds of the reticular rotation. The relation existing here is further borne out by the fact of pulsating vacuoles existing in *Volvox*, *Gonium*, &c., just like those in the Infusoria.

The rotation in *Chara* may be observed by simply placing portions of the plant on a slide in water. The unencrusted species are of course most favourable; but the growing points of the others are tolerably transparent. In *Vallisneria*, detached fragments of leaves, or even horizontal sections of the leaf, may be used; in *Anacharis* entire leaves or sepals may be detached and observed. Hairs are frequently more or less covered with a viscid secretion, which retains air-bubbles about them; in such cases, it is often useful to dip them for an instant in alcohol, and then place them in water.

BIBL. Varley, *Trans. Soc. of Arts*, xlviii. (1832); *Mic. Trans.*; Slack, *Trans. Soc. Arts*, xlix.; Dutrochet, *Comptes Rendus*, 1837. p. 775; Becquerel, *ibid.* p. 784; Meyen, *Pflanzenphys.* ii. p. 206; A. Braun, *Richtungsverhältnisse der Saftströme*, Berlin Bericht. 1852; Göppert and Cohn, *Bot. Zeit.* vii. p. 665 (1849); Unger, *Sitzungsber. d. Wien. Akad.* viii. p. 32; Mohl, *Bot. Zeit.* iv. p. 73 (1846); *Ann. Nat. Hist.* xviii. p. 1; Hofmeister, *Vergleich. Unters.* p. 73; Osborne, *Mic. Journal*, iii. p. 54 (1854); Branson, *ibid.* iii. p. 260 (1855); Wenham, *ibid.* p. 250; Henfrey, *Ann. Nat. Hist.* 3 ser. i. p. 419.

ROTATORIA or ROTIFERA.—A class of the Animal Kingdom.

Char. Microscopic, transparent, aquatic animals; legs absent; anterior portion of the body furnished with a retractile, often lobed disk, upon which are placed usually vibratile cilia, when in motion presenting the appearance of one or more revolving wheels; alimentary canals usually distinct, with a dental apparatus, and two orifices; reproduction by ova.

Body covered with a firm and usually smooth skin or integument, sometimes presenting indications of segments; often more or less enclosed in a carapace (CARAPACE), which is either secreted by the skin, by the alimentary canal, or by a special secreting organ. In some species the skin is furnished with hairs or rigid bristles.

In most, there is a tail-like process at the posterior end of the body called the foot-like tail, tail-like foot, or false foot; this is jointed, and can often be contracted and extended like a telescope; it does not form a direct prolongation of the end of the body, but arises from and is situated upon the ventral aspect. It is often terminated by a suctorial disk, or a pair of claw- or toe-like processes.

Distinct muscular bands are present, longitudinal, circular, &c.; these sometimes present transverse striæ, but it is doubtful whether they agree with those of the fibres of the higher animals.

The rotatory disk or wheel-organ varies greatly in structure, the varieties forming characters of the families, &c.

Its margin is usually furnished with one or two rows of vibratile cilia; sometimes these are replaced by bundles of non-contractile elongate cilia (Pl. 34. fig. 32), or the rotatory organ is divided into tentacle-like processes, upon which cilia are placed (Pl. 34. fig. 25).

The rotatory disk is the principal organ of motion, by means of the cilia of which the animals swim through the water; some of the Rotatoria, however, move in a leech-like manner, by alternately fixing the toe-like processes and the anterior end of the body, which in some forms a kind of proboscis (Pl. 34. fig. 1).

The nervous system is not well known. It appears to consist of a cervical ganglion and branches given off in various directions.

In many of the Rotatoria, eyes are present, mostly red. These appear to have a cornea and a lens. They sometimes disappear in the adult animals; and as their number, position, &c. are used as characters, when absent in the adults, they must be looked for in the young or the ova, either within the carapace or adherent to the body.

Alimentary apparatus.—Behind the mouth is sometimes a distinct conical pharynx, but nearly always a rounded muscular gizzard containing the jaws and teeth. In the pharynx are occasionally seen two undulating lines, presenting a flickering appearance, the indications of cilia or undulating membranes. The jaws are constructed mostly after two forms. In one of these, they consist of two knee-shaped pieces (Pl. 34. fig. 24),—to the posterior portion of which muscles are attached, whilst the anterior, which

passes inwards at a right or obtuse angle to the former, ends in a single point or in several teeth (fig. 26). In the other, the jaws have the form of stirrups (Pl. 34. fig. 17), with their bases turned towards each other, upon which two or more teeth are placed. A third single or compound intermediate piece forms a support (Pl. 34. figs. 24, 26), upon which the food acted upon by the jaws is triturated. In some species the jaws and teeth are very complex in their arrangement.

The alimentary canal is usually short and straight, but sometimes curved. Its walls are very thick, and lined with ciliated epithelium. The stomach forms a distinct expansion (Pl. 34. fig. 27 c); this is succeeded by an intestine, the termination of which corresponds to a cloaca, receiving the expelled contents of the reproductive organs and so-called water-vessel system, and opening at the base of the foot. In some Rotatoria, a second expansion or stomach is situated below the upper one.

The walls of the stomach and intestine frequently contain brown or yellow cells, representing a liver. And at the commencement of the stomach are two or more cæcal appendages, probably corresponding to a pancreas (Pl. 35. figs. 14, 34).

In the male Rotatoria, the alimentary canal is entirely absent.

Vascular system.—Distinct blood-vessels are apparently not present in the Rotatoria; but on each side of the body, in most of them, runs a narrow straight or wavy band, containing a slender vessel (Pl. 34. fig. 18 a; Pl. 35. fig. 14 b). Anteriorly, these vessels give off branches, the terminations of which are not well known. By some they are said to open into the abdominal cavity, by others to terminate as cæca. Attached to the walls of these lateral tubes, or situated within them, are pear-shaped or oval corpuscles (Pl. 34. fig. 18 a; Pl. 35. fig. 14 c), which exhibit a flickering appearance from the action of cilia connected with them; and which open into the cavity of the abdomen. Posteriorly, the tubes terminate in an actively contractile sac, which opens into the cloaca. In regard to their function, these tubes have been variously viewed, as water-vessels, testes, and kidneys. Ehrenberg considered them as connected anteriorly with a certain projecting organ (Pl. 35. fig. 14 a), situated usually in the cervical region (Pl. 34. fig. 3; Pl. 35. fig. 17), denominated the calcar or respiratory tube, and terminated by a retractile tuft of non-vibratile cilia (Pl. 35. fig. 5 a). They have no relation, however, with this, which corresponds to an antenna.

Beneath the integument of the Rotatoria, a kind of irregular circulation, varying with the motions of the body, or a simple molecular movement of minute granules, has been noticed. These granules are probably situated in the abdominal cavity; in which also sarcodic globules, sometimes free, at others connected by filaments, have been observed.

Reproduction.—The Rotatoria are propagated by means of sexual organs, and are unisexual. The female organs consist of one or two longer or shorter ovarian sacs or ovaries, situated towards the posterior end of the body in the abdominal cavity, the oviduct terminating in the cloaca, or at a distinct vulva. The ova are of an oval form, and are sometimes smooth externally and soft; at others they correspond with the winter-ova, being larger, darker, and the outer coat thick and hairy or tubercular.

The testis is situated at the posterior part of the body, and consists of a wedge-shaped body, with a muscular duct opening externally.

The ova sometimes remain adherent to the cloaca for a time, and in a few instances they are hatched within the ovary.

Many of the Rotatoria are remarkably tenacious of life; and some of them are stated to have revived after having been kept dry for several years.

The families of the Rotatoria are thus distinguished :—

Ciliated margin of rotatory disk simple or continuous.
Margin entire. *Holotrocha.*
　Carapace absent............ 1. Ichthydina.
　Carapace present .... 2. Œcistina.

Margin undulate or excised. *Schizotrocha.*
　Carapace absent.. .... 3. Megalotrochæa.
　Carapace present .... 4. Floscularieæ.

Rotatory disk divided or multiple.
Divided into several parts. *Polytrocha.*
　Carapace absent........... 5. Hydatinæa.
　Carapace present .... 6. Euchlanidota.

Divided into two parts. *Zygotrocha.*
　Carapace absent.. .... 7. Philodinæa.
　Carapace present .... 8. Brachionæa.

See ALBERTINA.

They are found wherever water exists, provided it be not in a state of putrefaction,—thus in pools, on moist earth, mosses, in gutters, &c., and even in the cells of mosses and algæ.

BIBL. Ehrenberg, *Infusoria*; Dujardin, *Infus.*; Siebold, *Vergleich.Anat.*; Dalrymple, *Phil. Trans.* 1849. 331; Huxley, *Trans. Micr.*

Soc. 1852. i. 1; Williamson, *Micr. Journ.* i. 1; Pritchard, *Infusorial Animalc.*; Valenciennes, *Ann. des Sc. Nat.* 1850; Vogt, *Zool. Briefe*, i. 210; id. *Siebold und Kölliker's Zeitsch.* vii. 193, and ix. 284; Cohn, *ibid.* vii. 431; Leydig, *ibid.* vi. 1, and *Müll. Archiv*, 1857. 404; Gosse, *Trans. Micr. Soc.* iii.; id. *Ann. Nat. Hist.* 1856. 333; Van d. Hoeven, *Zoolog.*, and Leuckart, *Nachträge.*

ROTIFER, Cuv.—A genus of Rotatoria, of the family Philodinæa.

Char. Eyes two, situated upon the proboscis; foot furnished with lateral horn-like processes, and with two terminal toes, giving its end a bifurcate appearance.

R. vulgaris (Pl. 35. fig. 23). Body fusiform, white, gradually attenuated towards the foot. Aquatic; length 1-48 to 1-24".

This is one of the commonest of the Rotatoria, and has long been known as a favourite microscopic object under the popular name of the wheel-animalcule. The anterior and upper part of the body terminates in a proboscis, ciliated at the end, and upon which the eyes are placed; the two rounded lobes of the rotatory organ are placed laterally. Behind, and at the root of the proboscis, is the calcar.

In *R. citrinus*, the middle of the body is yellowish, the horns of the foot long, and the eyes round. In *R. macrurus* the body is suddenly narrowed into a long foot. In *R. tardus* the body is gradually attenuated, but somewhat deeply constricted into segments. The species are all aquatic.

BIBL. Ehrenberg, *Infus.* p. 484.

ROTIFERA. See ROTATORIA.

RUBEFACTION OF WATER. See WATER.

RUCKERIA.—A genus of Compositæ. The pericarp possesses HAIRS of an interesting structure.

BIBL. Decaisne, *Ann. Nat. Hist.* vi. p. 257 (trans. from *Ann. des Sc. Nat.* 2 sér. xii. p. 251).

RUELLIA.—A genus of Acanthaceous Plants. The testa of the seed of *Ruellia formosa* exhibits a peculiar kind of HAIR (Pl. 21. fig. 21).

RUST OF PLANTS. See BLIGHT.

RYE.—The grain of *Secale cereale.* See STARCH.

RYTIPHLŒA, Ag.—A genus of Rhodomelaceæ (Florideous Algæ), containing four British species, mostly common, having pinnately-branched, filiform or compressed fronds, transversely striate and reticulated: the articulate axis is composed of a circle of large elongated tubular cells surrounding a central cell, the whole enclosed by a kind of rind of several layers of small coloured cells. Colour mostly dull-red or brown. Fronds from 2" to 4" or 6" high. The *ceramidia* occur scattered on the ramules of some plants; the *antheridia* tufted in the same situations on others; and *tetraspores* (tetrahedral) occur imbedded in a double row in *stichidia*, borne on distinct plants.

BIBL. Harvey, *Brit. Mar. Alg.* p. 80, pl. 11 D; Grev. *Alg. Brit.* pl. 13; Derbès and Solier, *Ann. des Sc. Nat.* 3 sér. xvi. p. 275, pl. 35. figs. 11 & 12; Thuret, *ibid.* 4 sér. iii. p. 20.

S.

SACCOGYNA.—A genus of Jungermanniæ (Hepaticæ) founded on the *Jungermannia viticulosa* of Linnæus; it is remarkable on account of the subterraneous fleshy perianth, in which character and in habit it is allied to *Calypogeia*. It is found among mosses, especially in alpine districts.

BIBL. Hook. *Brit. Flor.* ii. pt. 1. p. 121; *Brit. Jung.* pl. 60; Ekart, *Syn. Jung.* pl. 1. fig. 6; Endlicher, *Gen. Plant.* Supp. 1. No. 472-23.

SACCULUS, Gosse.—A genus of Rotatoria, of the family Ichthydina.

Char. Eye single, frontal; body free from hairs, and without a foot; rotatory organ a simple wreath; alimentary canal very large; jaws set far forward, apparently consisting of two delicate, unequal, lateral pieces, and a slender central portion, very evanescent; eggs attached behind after deposition.

S. viridis. Length 1-150"; aquatic.

BIBL. Gosse, *Ann. Nat. Hist.* 1851. viii. 198.

SAGEDIA, Fries.—A genus of Endocarpeæ (Angiocarpous Lichens), consisting of a few anomalous plants, closely related to *Endocarpon* and *Verrucaria*.

BIBL. Leighton, *Brit. Angioc. Lichens*, p. 21.

SAGENIA, Presl.—A genus of Aspidieæ (Polypodioid Ferns). Exotic.

SAGO.—Farinas obtained from a variety of tropical plants are known by this name; but the true East Indian sagoes are extracted from the central part of the trunks of Palm-trees belonging to the genus *Sagus*, natives of the Moluccas. In Pl. 36. fig. 23, is figured the starch of a sago obtained from the Museum at Kew; but it is uncertain whether this is the produce of a *Sagus*. Its grains resemble those of some East Indian Arrow-roots (Pl. 36. fig. 18). See STARCH.

SAGRINA, D'Orb.—A genus of Foraminifera, of the order Enallostegia, and family Textularidæ.

Char. Shell regular, equilateral, conical; *chambers* globular, regularly alternate at all ages, partly embracing; *orifice* round, at the end of a prolongation of the last chamber.

S. rugosa, and some unnamed species, British; fossil.

BIBL. That of the order.

SALICINE.—The alkaloid of the willow and poplar.

The so-called circular crystals of this substance (Pl. 31. fig. 9) form a beautiful polarizing object. The largest crystals are obtained by fusion.

SALICORNARIA, Cuv.—A genus of Infundibulate Cheilostomatous Polyzoa.

Char. Surface divided into rhomboidal or hexagonal spaces by ridges surrounding the cells; avicularia disposed irregularly. One species:

S. farciminoides. On old shells, &c. from deep water, not uncommon.

BIBL. Johnston, *Brit. Zooph.* 355; Busk, *Cat. of Mar. Polyz.* (*Brit. Mus.*) 16.

SALICORNARIADÆ.—A family of Infundibulate Cheilostomatous Polyzoa.

Char. Polypidom erect, branched, jointed; branches cylindrical, dichotomous, with the cells on all sides. One genus:

SALICORNARIA.

SALIVARY GLANDS.—These organs, consisting of the parotid, the submaxillary, and the sublingual glands, agree in structure with the racemose mucous glands (MOUTH), of which they may be regarded as aggregations.

Their ducts consist of areolar tissue, with numerous very dense networks of elastic tissue. Wharton's duct contains unstriped muscular fibres.

The salivary corpuscles are noticed under MOUTH (p. 472).

SALPINA, Ehr.—A genus of Rotatoria, of the family Euchlanidota.

Char. Eye single, cervical; foot forked; carapace closed on the ventral surface, and furnished with spines or horns at the ends. Aquatic.

The carapace resembles a three-sided box with convex sides, flat and closed beneath, and often scabrous.

S. redunca (Pl. 35. fig. 24). Carapace with two curved horns in front upon the ventral surface, smooth, posterior end with three horns; dorsum cleft, gaping. Length of carapace 1-216 to 1-144".

Five other species.

BIBL. Ehrenberg, *Infus.* p. 409.

SALPINGIA, Coppin.—A genus of Infundibulate Cheilostomatous Polyzoa, of the family Eucratiadæ.

Char. Erect, branched; cells elongate, with spines and trumpet-shaped processes; orifice lateral. One species:

S. Hassalii. On filamentous *fuci*; rare.

BIBL. Coppin, *Ann. Nat. Hist.* 1848. ii. p. 273.

SALTS. See CRYSTALS.

SALVIA, L.—An extensive genus of Flowering plants of the Nat. Ord. Labiatæ, including common sage, and many species cultivated for the beauty of their flowers. They are interesting to the microscopist both on account of the Glandular hairs, containing the essential oils, and the spiral-fibrous structures found in the HAIRS of the pericarp (Pl. 21. fig. 23) and the hairs of the stigma.

SALVINIA, Mich.—A genus of Marsileaceæ, growing floating on the surface of stagnant water (not British). They are distinguished from MARSILEA and PILULARIA also by bearing two distinct kinds of spore-fruits, one kind producing only ovule-spores, the other only pollen-spores, which exhibit analogous phænomena in their germination to those described under PILULARIA. See that head and MARSILEACEÆ.

BIBL. That of MARSILEACEÆ and PILULARIA.

SAND, BRAIN-.—Brain-sand, or the acervulus cerebri, is found in the pineal gland and the choroid plexus, sometimes also in the pia mater, the arachnoid membrane, and the walls of the ventricles.

It consists of single, or aggregated and nodular, rounded, dark bodies, 1-2500 to 1-200″ in diameter, sometimes also forming club-shaped, cylindrical, or reticular masses. Chemically it is principally composed of carbonate and, phosphate of lime, and, like other concretions, leaves an organic cast of the original form, after the salts have been removed by a dilute acid.

Fig. 623.

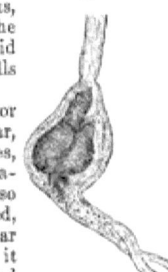

Brain-sand from the pineal gland, in bundles of areolar tissue.

Magn. 350 diams.

BIBL. Kölliker, *Mikrosk. Anat.* ii.

SAND, SEA.—This often contains interesting microscopic objects, as Foraminifera, spicules of sponges, minute shells of the Mollusca, or their fragments, portions of the skeleton of the Echinodermata, &c.

The various bodies may be separated from the washed and dried sand with a mounted bristle (INTR. p. xxii).

The sand or powder which may be separated by pressing or shaking newly imported sponges, and which is sometimes called sponge-sand, is very rich in the above organic bodies, especially the Foraminifera.

SAP.—A name vaguely applied to the watery juices contained in living plants. Sap flowing from wounds may contain various organized substances, such as starch-granules, chlorophyll- or protoplasmic globules, also raphides; but it cannot be said to have any proper microscopic characters.

SAPROLEGNIA, Nees. See ACHLYA.

SAPROLEGNIEÆ. See CONFERVOIDEÆ, p. 176.

SARCINA, Goodsir.—A curious organism, placed provisionally among the Palmellaceæ (Confervoid Algæ) from considerations relating to its apparent structure, but which in its habitat and general characters would appear more nearly related to the Fungi. *Sarcina ventriculi* (Pl. 3. fig. 5 *a* and *b*) is a body found sometimes in great abundance in vomited contents of the stomach of the human subject, also in the stomach after death, where no disorder had appeared during life; in the urine, fæces, in the pus of pulmonary abscess, &c.; it has also been found in the stomach of the rabbit. It ordinarily consists of minute square, oblong, or even irregular masses, of considerable consistence, composed of four, eight, sixteen, sixty-four, or more squarish cells contained in a tough transparent frond, apparently composed of the cell-membranes of these cells. The cells are always most closely connected in groups of four, which stand a little more apart from each other in the secondary groups of sixteen; these again have a stronger line of demarcation between them when they are collected in tertiary groups of sixty-four (Pl. 3. fig. 5 *a*, *b*). The size of the primary cells (nuclei of Ch. Robin) appears to vary slightly; we find their diameter about 1-16,000″; they have a slight brownish tint, which imparts a colour to the whole mass. Iodine colours the fronds brown; alcohol contracts them a little. Nitric acid does not dissolve them, even when heat is applied. Alkalies cause the fronds to break up into their constituent components. The plant appears to increase by the division of the contents of its ultimate cells into four and the formation of a new membrane around each portion, the groups remaining attached a longer or shorter time according to circumstances. The history of this remarkable production requires further elucidation; it is evidently not connected with any special derangement of the stomach, as was formerly supposed; and its occurrence is now known to be much more common than was at one time imagined.

Ch. Robin places *Sarcina* in Meyen's genus *Merismopædia*; but from its habit and general character, *Sarcina* would appear to be rather referable to the Fungi.

Mr. H. C. Stephens has described what he regards as a second species of *Sarcina*, which he found upon calcined ox-bones, giving them a red colour. The cells of this are about half the size of those of *S. ventriculi.*

BIBL. Goodsir, *Edinb. Med. and Surg. Journ.* 1842. p. 430; *Anat. and Path. Obs.* Edinb. 1845. pl. 8. figs. 1 & 3; Busk, *Microsc. Journal*, 1843; Virchow, *Archiv f. Path. Anat.* i. p. 264; Simon, *ibid.* ii. p. 331; Wedl, *Path. Histol.* 753; Schlossberger, *Archiv f. Phys. Heilkunde*, 1846. p. 747-768; C. Müller, *Bot. Zeit.* v. p. 273 (1847); Nägeli, *Einz. Alg.* p. 2; Ch. Robin, *Végétaux Parasit.* 2nd ed. p. 331; Lehmann, *Phys. Chemie*; Bennett, *Lectures on Clin. Med.* 1851. p. 214; Funke, *Atlas der Phys. Chem.* pl. 7. fig. 4; Rossmann, *Flora*, 1857. p. 641; Stephens, *Ann. Nat. Hist.* 2 ser. xx. p. 514.

SARCOCHITUM, Hass. — A genus of Infundibulate Ctenostomatous Polyzoa, of the family Alcyonidiadæ.

Char. Encrusting, covered with perforate prominences in which the cells are immersed; ova scattered singly throughout. One species:

S. polyoum. On *Fucus serratus.*

BIBL. Hassall, *Ann. Nat. Hist.* 1851. vii. 484.

SARCODE.—A term applied by Dujardin to the gelatinous, homogeneous, diaphanous proteine substance occurring abundantly in very young animals, the larvæ of insects, embryos of the Vertebrata, worms, zoophytes, &c., and representing the fibro-areolar tissue of the higher and adult animals. It appears to constitute the whole of some of the lower animals, as the *Amœbæ.* It may be readily studied when exuding from around the body of the intestinal parenchymatous worms, as the *Distoma, Cysticercus, Tænia,* &c., or almost any of the Infusoria, placed alive in water between two plates of glass. In the course of a short time, the bodies of the animals are seen to be bordered with a row of projecting diaphanous globules (Pl. 25. fig. 2 a), frequently more or less pressed together, which after a time become separated and float in the liquid, especially if it be shaken. Spherical cavities or vacuoles are soon perceptible in these globules of sarcode (Pl. 25. fig. 2 b), the nature of which is readily determined by comparing the refraction of the light at their circumference with that at the circumference of the globules themselves; for on elevating the object-glass, the centre of the vacuoles becomes darker, and the centre of the globules becomes brighter; whilst on approximating the object-glass, the reverse takes place. The spontaneously produced cavities or vacuoles continue to enlarge and increase in numbers, until some of them appear perforated in all directions. Ultimately the globules become so altered by the action of the water, that they form a thin granular or wrinkled layer, resembling coagulated albumen.

The protoplasm of vegetable cells appears to correspond to the sarcode of animal structures. In certain cells it exists in two forms as regards density, the outer portion being firmer than the inner; or it may become entirely liquid. In many of the lower organisms, and probably most cells in their youngest state, it is glutinous, and in the former permanently remains so.

When existing in cells and the lowest animals, it appears to constitute the essential part of their structure, and is capable of performing all the functions carried on by the tissues of the higher or more perfect organisms. It also appears that the cell-theory, in so far as it attributes the principal importance to the cell-wall, is founded upon error; the cell-wall merely forming a protection to the sarcode or primordial utricle of plants, and the sarcode or protoplast as it might be called of animals, enabling them to carry on their essential functions uninterrupted by surrounding influences.

BIBL. Dujardin, *Infus.* p. 35.

SARCOPTES, Latr.—A genus of Arachnida, of the order Acarina, and family Acarea.

S. scabiei (Acarus scabiei) (Pl. 2. fig. 16). The itch-insect of man.

Body soft, white, oval-oblong or rounded; ventral surface with transverse and undulating rugæ; dorsal surface with marginal irregularly concentric rugæ, the central space with numerous short and conical papillæ and stouter but short protuberances or spines arising from an annular base; at the sides and upon the surface of the body are also scattered setæ. Head small, somewhat narrowed in front; mandibles toothed. Anterior two pairs of legs separated from the posterior by a considerable interval; legs short, the anterior two pairs with acetabula or adhesion-disks and five-jointed, the posterior three-jointed, the last joint terminated by a long seta and without acetabula. Length of female 1·100 to 1·75″.

The females burrow in the skin, in which the oval eggs, 1·120″ in length, are laid; these are hatched in about ten days, and the young have only six legs.

Male only about half the size of the female, and with acetabula to the hindermost pair of legs.

There is no question that the irritation produced by these mites and their ova is the cause of the itch.

They should be searched for at the bottom of one of the burrows, which are often visible to the naked eye; the ova are frequently present in the pustules. They are most easily found by examining the skin with a power of fifty to seventy diameters, attached to a firm but moveable arm, and with the aid of a good bull's-eye condenser.

The entire animals may be preserved in glycerine or solution of chloride of calcium; the parts of the mouth should be dried and mounted in Canada balsam.

Other imperfectly examined or doubtful species occur upon animals, as the dromedary, the chamois, the dog, sheep, rabbit, &c.

See DEMODEX and PSONOPTES.

BIBL. Bourguignon, *Traité, &c., de la Gale* (abstract in *Ed. Monthly Journ.* 1852. lx.); Gervais, *Walckenaer's Insect. Aptères*, iii. 268, and *Ann. des Sc. Nat.* xv. 9; Hering, *D. Kratzmilben d. Thiere, Nov. Act. Nat. Cur.* xviii. 573; Dugès, *Ann. des Sc. Nat.* 2 sér. iii. 245; Wedl, *Pathol. Histolog.* 798.

SARCOSCYPHUS, Corda.—A genus of Jungermannieæ (Hepaticæ). *S. Ehrharti* (*Jung. emarginata*, Ehrh.) is a remarkable species, of dark purple, almost black colour, growing frequently in wet places, on rocks of mountainous districts.

BIBL. Hook. *Brit. Flor.* ii. pt. 2. p. 114; *Brit. Jung.* pl. 27; Ekart, *Synops. Jung.* pl. 7. fig. 56, and pl. 13. fig. 113; Endlicher, *Gen. Plant.* Supp. i. nos. 474–1.

Fig. 624.　　　　Fig. 625.

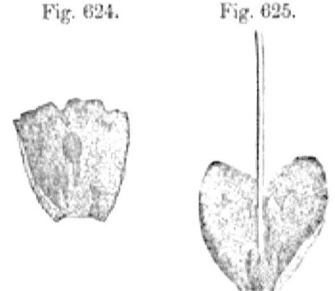

Sarcoscyphus Ehrharti.

Fig. 624. Perichæte and perigone opened, showing the young sporange emerging from the epigone. Magnified 25 diameters.

Fig. 625. Perichæte and perigone opened, showing the base of the seta surrounded by the epigone. Magnified 10 diameters.

SARGASSUM, Ag.—A genus of Fucaceæ (Fucoid Algæ), gulf - weeds, known from the allied sea-weeds by its stalked globular air-vessels. The receptacles are small, linear, and mostly clustered at the base of branches, and pierced by numerous pores leading to *conceptacles* containing spore-sacs and clusters of antheridia (see FUCACEÆ).

BIBL. Harvey, *Brit. Mar. Alg.* p. 14, pl. 1 A; Greville, *Alg. Brit.* pl. 1.

SCALES OF FISHES. — These bodies were formerly regarded as epidermic formations, analogous to the nails, &c. of the higher animals, which later observations have shown not to be the case.

Each scale is contained in a distinct sac of the skin or cutis, covered externally with its pigment-layer and epidermis. The cutis itself consists of interlacing fibres of areolar tissue with formative cells. The pigment-layer is composed of elegant pigment-cells with long processes. Immediately above the upper suface of the scales lies a very fine membrane, distinct from the cutis, in which the impressions of the irregularities of surface existing upon the scales are visible.

In some fishes, as the eel, the scales do not project beyond the surface; hence the eel is commonly supposed to possess no scales. They are easily seen, however, in a dried piece of the skin, mounted in balsam, covered by the skin with its pigment-cells

(Pl. 17. fig. 19), the whole forming a very beautiful object.

In many of the common cycloid fishes, as the roach, dace, &c., the scales project posteriorly from the surface, carrying before them the thinner and closely applied outer layer of the cutaneous sac, whilst the anterior portion of the sac extends into or is formed by the under portion of the cutis. In these fishes also, the portion of the cutis situated beneath the posterior projecting portion of the scales, contains a large number of very thin and minute crystals, to which the silvery lustre of the skin is owing, and which often exhibit very beautifully the colours of thin plates.

The signification of the various parts of structure of the scales has not been satisfactorily determined; hence we must confine our remarks to simply pointing out the structural peculiarities.

Most scales consist of two portions,—an under, composed of numerous layers made up of very fine fibres taking various directions, and best seen by scraping away the upper portion of the scale after maceration in dilute acid (Pl. 17. fig. 11 a). The upper portion consists of concentric plates, the margins of which give rise to the concentric lines so frequently seen in the scales (Pl. 17. figs. 6, 10, 22, 23, &c.). These lines correspond to the margins of the layers, and often present a nodular or crenate appearance (Pl. 17. fig. 11 b); and towards the middle of the scales they are frequently interrupted and irregularly curved (Pl. 17. fig. 11 c). The substance of the upper portion appears to be structureless.

In a transverse section, the projecting margins of the laminæ belonging to the upper portion of the scale are seen as so many teeth (Pl. 17. fig. 12).

Many scales also exhibit radiating lines (Pl. 17. fig. 23), corresponding to furrows in the upper portion of the scales; these are sometimes closed above, so as to form tubes, and have been regarded as nutritive canals.

Near the centre of some scales, as those of the perch, are numerous rounded corpuscles or solid bodies, imbedded in the substance of the upper portion of the scales (Pl. 17. figs. 6 a & 7). At the posterior portion of the same scales, are often seen spine-like processes (Pl. 17. figs. 6 b & 9), with rounded or angular bodies, resembling the last in appearance, arranged in rows at their bases (Pl. 17. fig. 8).

The scales of the eel appear to be principally composed of similar bodies, differing only in form, and arranged in concentric rows (Pl. 17. figs. 20 & 20 a). They are solid, impregnated throughout with calcareous matter, which is left after incinerating the scales, retaining the original form of the bodies (Pl. 17. fig. 21).

In the scales of some fishes, particularly those of extinct genera and species, lacunæ and canaliculi resembling those of bone (Pl. 17. fig. 1 c), with Haversian canals, are met with. A vitreous or enamel-like layer, having the structure of dentine, is also met with in the form of an external coating.

The structure of the spines or spine-like scales of the skate is curious. The larger of them consist of a button-like base, surmounted by a sharp process (Pl. 17. fig. 3). The outer and lower part of the base is opake-white, and consists of an imperfectly fibrous tissue with large areolæ (Pl. 17. fig. 37). The spine is hollow, the cavity being continuous with that of a rounded body, partly immersed in the white substance (Pl. 17. fig. 3 a). The cavity is filled with a pulp, consisting of lax areolar tissue with minute cells; whilst its walls are composed of a hard substance traversed by branched canals resembling those of dentine (Pl. 17. fig. 4). The substance of the smaller spines (Pl. 17. fig. 2) exhibits the same dentinous structure (fig. 5).

Pl. 17. fig. 10 represents one of a longitudinal row of scales extending along the middle of the side of the body of most fishes, and traversed by a tube (a), formerly supposed to give exit to the mucous secretion of the surface, which view has lately been thrown into doubt. The tubes are visible to the naked eye, and produce the lateral line, as it is called.

The scales of fishes contain a large amount of inorganic matter, composed principally of phosphate of lime, but mixed with the carbonate. The organic basis consists of a cartilaginous substance.

Some years since, M. Agassiz founded a classification of fishes upon the structure of the scales, having found that with differences in the scales, other great and important distinctions were in harmony. The system has been found of eminent service to the geologist; although later researches have shown that scales presenting the characteristics of those belonging to fishes of different orders in this system, have been found upon the same fish.

The arrangement was as follows:—
Scales enamelled.

Ord. 1. Ganoid fishes. Those the skin of which is regularly covered with angular thick scales, composed internally of bone, and externally of enamel. Most of the species are fossil, the sturgeon and bony pike being recent.

Ord. 2. Placoid fishes. Skin covered irregularly with large or small plates or points of enamel. Includes all the cartilaginous fishes of Cuvier, except the sturgeon ; as examples may be mentioned the sharks and rays. Many are fossil.

Scales not enamelled.

Ord. 3. Ctenoid fishes. Scales horny or bony, serrated or spinous at the posterior margin. Contains the perch and many other existing species, but few fossil.

Ord. 4. Cycloid fishes. Scales smooth, horny or bony, entire at the posterior margin; as the salmon, herring, roach, and most of our edible and freshwater fishes.

Most of the fossil fishes belong to the first two orders, and most of the recent to the third and fourth.

BIBL. Agassiz, *Rech. sur les poissons fossiles, Ann. des Sc. Nat.* 2 sér. 14; Mandl, *Ann. des Sc. Nat.* 2 sér. xi. xii. xiii. & xiv.; Heusinger, *Histolog.* ii. 226 ; Stannius, *Vergl. Anat.* ; Peters, *Müller's Archiv*, 1841. ccix. ; Müller, *Wiegmann's Archiv*, 1843. 298 ; Reade, *Ann. Nat. Hist.* 1838. ii. 191 ; Vogt, *Zoolog. Briefe*, ii. ; Williamson, *Phil. Trans.* 1849. p. 435.

SCALES OF INSECTS.—The fine dust which adheres so readily to the fingers on handling a butterfly or moth, consists of a number of microscopic flattened bodies, called scales or feathers, upon which the beautiful colours and opacity of the wings depend, the membranous wing itself being transparent and colourless.

These scales have always been favourite microscopic objects, both on account of the beauty and variety of their forms, and the curious markings found upon them. The manner in which they are attached is best examined in the wing of a butterfly. Each has a narrow portion at its base, forming a pedicle or stalk. The stalks are implanted into small and short tubes or cups (Pl. 27. fig. 23 b), denominated the squamuliferous tubes, the orifices of which are directed backwards. Around the points of attachment of the cups to the wings, the surface exhibits a number of irregularly radiating rugæ or folds of the upper membrane of the wing (Pl. 27. fig. 26). The cups are arranged in more or less regular transverse rows.

The scales are variable in form, both in different insects and in different parts of the same insect, being oval, oblong, cordate, obcordate, or cuneate, &c. (Pls. 1 & 27); sometimes they are filiform or capillary (Pl. 27. fig. 27). Their free end is rounded, truncate, toothed, or terminated by a number of hair-like processes; and they are arranged like the tiles of a roof, overlapping each other (Pl. 27. fig. 26).

The interesting markings seen upon the scales vary considerably in different insects.

The most common, as seen by transmitted light, are longitudinal, simple, continuous, parallel or slightly radiating dark striæ or lines (Pl. 1. figs. 6, 7, 8, 9 a). These are met with upon the scales of nearly all butterflies, and many other insects. In some insects the striæ are not simple and continuous, but are made up of rows of smaller striæ in twos or threes meeting at an angle (Pl. 27. figs. 28 b, 30 & 31). In others they are composed of a number of bead-like dots, or are interrupted, still preserving their general longitudinal direction (Pl. 27. fig. 24) ; or they are slightly undulate or irregular, and give off short lateral branches (Pl. 27. figs. 23 a & 29). In others, again, they present dilatations in certain parts of their course (Pl. 27. figs. 20 & 21).

These longitudinal striæ consist of elevations or ridges upon the surface, probably representing folds of the upper layer or membrane of the scale. They often project slightly from the free end of the scale (Pl. 27. figs. 3 & 22) ; and when moistened, bubbles of air may not unfrequently be found imprisoned between the surface of the scale and the cover, which, being confined between two of the ridges, assume an oblong form. They sometimes contain air, which may be displaced by liquid (Pl. 27. fig. 21). We have never been able to detect tracheæ in these folds or in the scales. A minute conical point or spine sometimes occurs in each of the dilatations when present (Pl. 27. fig. 20 a).

In the scales of *Podura* (Pl. 1. fig. 12), the striæ consist of longitudinal rows of minute wedge-shaped bodies.

In addition to the longitudinal striæ, on most scales, especially when examined by unilateral oblique light, are seen a number of minute transverse striæ (Pl. 1. figs. 7 & 9 a). These are neither indications of ridges nor depressions, but arise from the existence of

2 R

a number of pigment-granules situated between the two layers of the scale; and the appearance of striæ has the same origin as that in the case of the valves of the Diatomaceæ. This point is best examined in brown or other dark-coloured scales. If perfectly direct (*i. e.* not oblique) light be transmitted through one of these scales, the transverse striæ vanish, their place being occupied by the distinct and isolated granules of pigment (Pl. 1. fig. 9 *b*); the scale should also be immersed in balsam or liquid, to diminish the effects of the refraction arising from the inequalities of the surface of the scale. On then transmitting unilateral oblique light through the scale, the appearance of transverse striæ may be easily produced.

The colours of the scales of insects arise partly from iridescence, partly from the presence of pigment; in general, the brilliant colours depending upon the former, and the more sombre hues upon the latter. The darkness of the longitudinal striæ is caused by refraction; for scales containing no pigment appear perfectly white by reflected light, although the striæ may be very dark.

Upon certain scales, other irregular, more or less transverse curved striæ exist (Pl. 27. figs. 3 & 22); these appear to consist of wrinklings or folds of the under membrane of the scale.

In examining the scales of insects, they should be viewed both in the dry state and immersed in water or oil of turpentine, and both by transmitted and reflected light. When the insects are pressed against the slide to remove the scales, a number of globules of oil adhere simultaneously to the slide; and when the cover is applied, the scales often become partially or entirely covered with the oily matter, producing an appearance as if the upper layer of the scale were removed, and rendering the markings so pale and indistinct as to be apparently absent. The appearance of transverse striæ is best produced by turning the mirror to one side, so as to reflect unilateral light.

A brief notice of some interesting insects in respect to the structure of their scales is given under the individual heads, as CURCULIO, LEPISMA, MORPHO, PODURA, POLYOMMATUS, PONTIA, TINEA, &c.

See also TEST-OBJECTS.

BIBL. Westwood, *Introduction, &c.*, and *British Butterflies*; Deschamps, *Ann. des Sc. Nat.* 2 sér. iii. p. 111; Bowerbank, *Entomol. Mag.* No. 23. p. 304; Craig, *Phil. Mag.* 1839. xv. p. 279; Dujardin, *Obs. au Microscope*;

Ratzeburg, *Die Forst - Insekten*; Siebold, *Vergleich. Anat.*

SCALES OF PLANTS.—Under the head of HAIRS, mention has been made of scales (*lepides*) occurring on the epidermis of plants. They consist of flat, usually more or less circular plates of cellular tissue, the cells presenting a radiated arrangement from the centre, by which they are ordinarily attached; the margins are usually toothed or fringed more or less regularly by the prolongation of the free ends of the cells. They are closely related to stellate hairs, such as those of ivy, of *Deutzia* (Pl. 21. figs. 26, 27), &c., and may be regarded as more highly developed forms of these. They are particularly remarkable on the epidermis of certain plants which exhibit a kind of scurfy surface, for example the Eleagnaceæ (fig. 626), the Bromeliaceæ, some Rhododendra, and the lower surface of the leaves of many ferns; they must be distinguished in the last case from the *ramenta* of the stems, which are attached by the base, and not by a central pedicle.

Fig. 626.

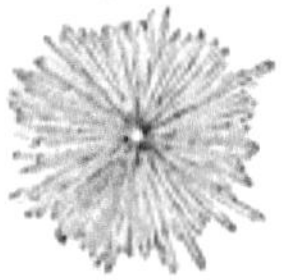

Scale of the epidermis of Hippophaë rhamnoides. Magnified 50 diams.

BIBL. See HAIRS and EPIDERMIS.

SCARIDIUM, Ehr.—A genus of Rotatoria, of the family Hydatinæa.

Char. Eye single, cervical; rotatory organ armed with a hooked bristle in front; foot forked, very long, adapted for leaping. Lateral processes of jaws bifurcate, so as to present two teeth each.

S. longicaudum (Pl. 35. fig. 27). Foot as long as or longer than the body, toes shorter than the foot. Aquatic; length 1-72".

BIBL. Ehrenberg, *Infus.* p. 439.

SCENEDESMUS, Meyen.—A genus of Desmidiaceæ.

Char. Cells fusiform or oblong, arranged side by side in a single row of from two to ten, after division forming two alternating rows; division oblique; terminal cells often lunate, or with a bristle at each end.

Six species (Ralfs).

1. *S. quadricauda* (Pl. 10. fig. 50). Cells generally four, oblong, rounded at the ends, in a single row, terminal cells with a bristle at each end. Common; length of cells 1-1120".

2. *S. obliquus* (Pl. 10. fig. 51). Cells elliptico-fusiform, after division arranged in two distinct and generally oblique rows, end cells lunate. Length 1-1670".

3. *S. obtusus* (Pl. 10. figs. 53 & 54, just after division). Cells three to eight, ovate or oblong, all alike, arranged in one row, or after division alternately in two rows. Common; length 1-2330 to 1-1960'.

BIBL. Ralfs, *Brit. Desmid.* p. 189.

SCEPTRONEIS, Ehr.—An obscure genus of fossil Diatomaceæ.

BIBL. Ehrenberg, *Ber. d. Berl. Akad.* 1844. p. 264.

SCHISMA.—A genus of Jungermannieæ (Hepaticæ), founded on a rare British form, *S. (Jung.) juniperina, β europæa*, found among rocks on the mountains of Scotland, Ireland, and Wales. It grows 3 to 6″ high, and is rarely found in fruit.

BIBL. Hook. *Brit. Flor.* ii. pt. 1. p. 124, *Brit. Jung.* pl. 4; Ekart, *Syn. Jung.* pl. 8. fig. 62; Endlicher, *Gen. Plant.* Supp. 1. No. 472-17.

SCHISTOSTEGEÆ.—A family of operculate Acrocarpous (terminal-fruited) Mosses of gregarious habit. Stem naked below, foliaceous in two manners above; sometimes frond-like or fern-like, composed of leaves attached vertically and connected at the base, with dense areolations consisting of rhomboidal prosenchymatous pellucid or green cells; sometimes with small leaves, like those of other Mosses, horizontal and arranged quincuncially. All the leaves nerveless and flat. Capsule without an annulus, very minute, globular-oval, with a very small convex operculum (figs. 627-630).

British Genus.

SCHISTOSTEGA. Calyptra cylindrically bell-shaped. Inflorescence diœcious, plants similar.

The only species of this genus, the elegant

Fig. 627.

Schistostega osmundacea.

Leaves of barren branches. Magnified 50 diameters.

little *Sch. osmundacea*, Web. and Mohr (*Sch. pennata*, Hook. and Taylor), occurs here and there in Great Britain. The name was

derived from what appears to have been an erroneous observation of Hedwig, who de-

Fig. 628.   Fig. 629.   Fig. 630.

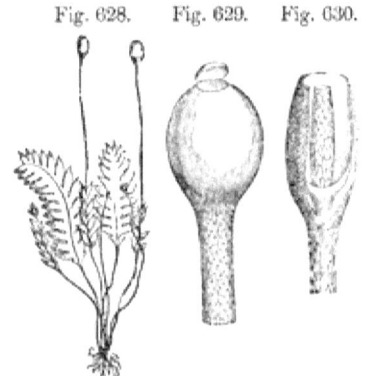

Schistostega osmundacea.

Fig. 628. A plant or fruit. Magnified 10 diameters.

Fig. 629. Open capsule with operculum. Magnified 50 diameters.

Fig. 630. Young capsule opened, showing the columella. Magnified 50 diameters.

scribed radiating fissures in the operculum, which do not exist in living specimens. The germinating confervoid prothallium of this moss was described by Bridel as an alga, under the name of *Catoptridium smaragdinum*; Agardh described it as a *Protococcus (smaragdinus)*; and it was long supposed to be phosphorescent: this appears to be an error: *Schistostega* grows on the roofs of sandy caves and similar places; and the luminous appearance seems to arise from the condensation and reflexion of the little daylight admitted, by the pellucid convex cellules of the prothallium.

SCHIZÆA, Smith.—A genus of Schizæous Ferns of curious and elegant structure. Exotic (figs. 631, 632).

SCHIZÆEÆ.—A tribe of Polypodiaceous Ferns, with sporanges in the form of a top, and crowned by a radiated cap-like 'annulus,' which hardens at maturity, splitting the case.

Illustrative Genera.

1. *Aneimia.* Sporangia twin, sessile in two rows, on lateral lobes of the leaf, contracted into a many-times paniculate immarginate rachis, naked, splitting longitudinally outside. No indusium.

2. *Schizæa.* Sporanges sessile in two or four rows in linear membranous-margined

lobes, pectinately opposite or digitate at the apex of the leaf, set among hairs, splitting longitudinally on the outside. No indusium.

Fig. 631.

Fig. 632.

Schizæa dichotoma.

Fig. 631. A fertile pinna. Magnified 5 diameters.

Fig. 632. A pinnule with sporanges. Magnified 25 diameters.

3. *Lygodium.* Sporangia sessile, alternately biseriate on marginal lobes of the leaf, splitting longitudinally, each veiled by a scale-like hood-shaped indusium adhering transversely to the nerves.

4. *Mohria.* Sporangia sessile in one row, close to the margin of the leaf, splitting longitudinally on the outside. A spurious indusium formed by the revolute margin of the leaf.

SCHIZOCÆNA.—A genus of Cyathæeæ (Polypodiaceous Ferns).

SCHIZOCHLAMYS, A. Br.—A genus of Palmellaceæ (Confervoid Algæ). *S. gelatinosa* has been found on the Continent, growing on aquatic plants or floating free, in little gelatinous masses composed of globular green cells, 1-2000″ in diameter, surrounded by a hyaline cell-membrane. The remarkable peculiarity in this genus is the splitting of the hyaline membrane into two or four equal parts by regular, clean dehiscence, the internal cell-mass becoming divided at the same time or remaining unchanged. By frequent repetition of this splitting (the internal cell acquiring a new coat each time), the cell becomes surrounded by a number of fragments of the old coats, held together by a gelatinous matter.

Bibl. A. Braun, *Verjüngung, &c.* (*Ray Soc. Vol.* 1853. p. 181. pl. 2); Kützing, *Sp. Alg.* p. 891.

SCHIZOGONIUM, Kütz.—A genus of Ulvaceæ (Confervoid Algæ), nearly related to *Prasiola*, distinguished by filiform fronds, which, when young, present only a single row of cells, but subsequently, by collateral subdivision, have two, four, or eight parallel rows. Of the species given by Kützing, the following appear to be British:

1. *S. murale* (*Bangia relutina*, Ktz., olim)

Fig. 633.

Schizogonium murale.

Filaments of frond in various stages of development.

Magnified 300 diameters.

(fig. 633). Fronds of a single row of cells 1-2400 to 1-2160″ in diam.; double, 1-1440 to 1-1200″; triple, 1-720″: cells half as long as broad, dull green. On damp earth.

2. *S. percursum* (*Enteromorpha*, Ag.). Frond with a double row of cells, 1-1200 to 1-900″ in diam.; length of cells equal to the breadth; bright or pale green; collapsed when dry. Marine.

3. *S. lætevirens* (*Bangia*, Harv.). Frond with a simple row of cells, 1-1800 to 1-1440″ in diam., rigid; with a double row, 1-600″; bright or yellowish green. Marine.

Bangia lacustris, Harv., is given as a doubtful species.

BIBL. Kütz. *Sp. Alg.* p. 350, *Tab. Phyc.* ii. pls. 98, 99; Harvey, *Brit. Alg.* 1 ed. p. 172, and *Br. Marine Alg.* p. 211.

SCHIZOLOMA, Gaudichaud.—A genus of Davallieæ (Polypodioid Ferns). Exotic.

SCHIZONEMA, Ag.—A genus of Diatomaceæ.

Char. Frustules short, resembling those of *Navicula*, aggregated in longitudinal rows in a filiform, branched, slender and lax gelatinous frond. Marine.

Sporangia (spermatia: see MICROMEGA) external, simple, sessile upon the filaments.

Kützing describes thirty-eight species, three of which are doubtful; Smith describes seventeen as British.

S. Dillwynii (Pl. 14. fig. 12). Frond hyaline, tufted, wavy, lubricous, bright green, much branched; end branches short, numerous, patent, attenuate, and somewhat acute; frustules towards the base of the frond remote and scattered, towards the ends crowded, oblong-truncate in front view; valves lanceolate, 1-1020″ in length.

Compare HOMŒOCLADIA, MICROMEGA, and RHAPHIDOGLŒA.

BIBL. Kützing, *Bacill.* p. 111, and *Sp. Alg.* p. 97; Smith, *Brit. Diat.* ii. 71.

SCHIZOSIPHON, Kütz.—A genus of Oscillatoriaceæ (Confervoid Algæ), containing *Calothrix scopulorum, fasciculata,* and perhaps other species of Harvey's 'Manual.' Another British species has also been described by Caspary, *S. Warreniæ* (Pl. 4. fig. 13). This last plant extends over large surfaces of maritime rocks, in tufts of variable size, from 1-4 to 1-2′ in thickness, of dull blackish-green colour. The erect filaments are fastigiately branched (*a*), the basal cell of the branches broader and hemispherical (*c*); the ochreal sheaths are obscure (*b*), frequently exhibiting a spiral-fibrous structure in decay (*d, e*); the apices of the branches are much attenuated.

BIBL. Kütz. *Sp. Alg.* p. 326, *Tab. Phyc.* ii. pl. 47 *et seq.*; Harvey, *Brit. Mar. Alg.* p. 224; Caspary, *Ann. Nat. Hist.* ser. 2. vi. p. 266, pl. 8.

SCHIZOTHRIX, Kütz.—A genus of Oscillatoriaceæ (Confervoid Algæ), of which two British species, growing over maritime rocks, have been described.

1. *S. Creswellii* (Pl. 4. fig. 17). Tufts 1-2 to 3-4″ high, olive-coloured; filaments curled, 1-3600″ in diameter at the base, 1-12000′ at the summit, in twisted bundles, penicillately corymbose above.

2. *S. Smithii* (*Coleonema*, Thw.). Stratum dense, dirty red; filaments closely entwined, more or less laterally concreted, 1-9600 to 1-8400″ in diameter; sheaths lax, multiplicate, the internal prolonged and exserted.

BIBL. Kütz. *Sp. Alg.* p. 320, *Tab. Phyc.* ii. pl. 40; Harvey, *Brit. Mar. Alg.* p. 223, pl. 26 B, *Phyc. Brit.* pl. 190.

SCHULTZE'S TEST.—This was originally proposed by Pettenkofer as a test for bile; but Schultze found that it reacted also with several other substances, and especially the proteine compounds. In this application it is often of use in discriminating one kind of tissue or substance from another. It consists in treating the matter with strong sulphuric acid, and then adding a little syrup. The characteristic reaction is the production of a purplish-red colour. The best method of proceeding is to wash the substance in question, then to moisten it with a drop of syrup, and finally to add the acid.

The tissues and substances affected by it are muscular tissue, both striated and unstriated; nerve-tubes and cells; the corpuscles of blood, pus, and mucus; epithelial and epidermic scales; hairs; feathers; horn; whalebone; and the cellular portions (cell-contents?) of Fungi and Algæ.

Those in which the reaction is not produced are areolar tissue, elastic tissue, gelatine and chondrine, chitine, silk, cellulose, gum, starch, and vegetable mucus.

BIBL. Schultze, *Liebig's Annalen*, 1849, abridged in the *Chem. Gaz.* viii. 98.

SCHULZE'S TEST.—This consists of a solution of chloriodide of zinc, used as a test for cellulose, which it colours blue.

The original directions given for its preparation are indefinite; they are as follows:—dissolve zinc in muriatic acid, evaporate the solution with excess of zinc until it acquires the consistence of syrup, and dissolve in this enough iodide of potassium to saturate it; iodine is then added, and the solution diluted with water if necessary.

Radlkofer recommends zinc to be dissolved in muriatic acid, the solution to be evaporated at a temperature but little above that of boiling water, when a liquid of about 2·0 sp. gr. is obtained. This is diluted with water until its sp. gr. is 1·8; if its original sp. gr. was 2·0, 12 parts by weight of water must be added to 100 parts of the solution. In 100 parts of this liquid, 6 parts by weight of iodide of potassium are to be dissolved at a gentle heat, and the mixture heated with excess of iodine until the latter is no longer dissolved, and violet fumes become perceptible over the liquid.

This reagent has the consistence of strong sulphuric acid, and is pale yellowish-brown. It must be kept in a well-stoppered bottle.

BIBL. Schulze, *Flora*, 1850. p. 643; Schacht, *Das Mikroskop*, pp. 30 & 197; Radlkofer, *Liebig's Annal.* xciv. 332, or *Chem. Gaz.* 1855. xiii. 372.

SCIADIUM, Al. Braun. — A genus of Unicellular Algæ (Pl. 45. fig. 3) found in fresh water. The young plant is attached to foreign bodies, and consists of a cylindrical cell (*a*), in which are produced eight gonidia; the top of the cylinder falling off like a cap, the gonidia emerge and form an umbel of similar cylinders (*b*), the bases of which stick in the primary cell. Each new cell repeats the process, so as to form a compound umbel; but the gonidia of the third generation (*c*) are set completely free, and become the primary cells of new families.

BIBL. Alex. Braun, *Alg. Unicellul.* p. 48, tab. 4; Currey, *Microsc. Journ.* vi. p. 212.

SCLEROTICA. See EYE (p. 273).

SCLEROTIUM, Tode.—A large collection of fungoid structures were formerly gathered together under this name, among others the preparatory form of the ERGOT fungus. They are all now regarded as consisting of the *mycelia* of fungi in an imperfect state. The *sclerotioid* state exists when the mycelium forms hard tubercular masses. Analogous masses of mycelial structures occur, in a pulpy condition, in the Vinegarplant; in a filamentous condition in those fungi forming large masses of barren *byssus*, &c.; in other cases, as in some of the Myxogastres, the structure is membranous.

BIBL. Léveillé, *Ann. des Sc. Nat.* 2 sér. xx. p. 218; Berkeley, *Hort. Journal*, iii. p. 97; Fries, *Summa Veg.* p. 477.

SCOLEX. See TÆNIA.

SCOLOPENDRIUM, Smith, *Hart's-tongue.*—A genus of Asplenieæ (Polypodioid Ferns), represented by the indigenous species *Sc. vulgare* (fig. 221, p. 282).

SCRUPARIA, Oken. See EUCRATEA.

SCRUPIADÆ. See EUCRATIADÆ.

SCRUPOCELLARIA, Van Beneden (*Cellularia*, Johnst., part).—A genus of Infundibulate Cheilostomatous Polyzoa, of the family Cellulariadæ.

Char. Cells with a vibraculum behind, and a sessile avicularium at the upper and outer angle; orifice spinous. Two species.

1. *S. scruposa.* Cells without an operculum. Common on Algæ, &c.

2. *S. scrupea.* Cells with a stalked reniform operculum.

BIBL. Johnston, *Brit. Zooph.* 336; Busk, *Ann. Nat. Hist.* 1851. vii. 83.

SCURF OF ANIMALS.—Consists of aggregations of dry and flattened epidermic scales, sometimes containing globules of fatty matter.

SCUTULA, Tulasne.—A genus of Coccocarpeæ (Gymnocarpous Lichens), parasitic, found upon *Peltigera canina.*

BIBL. Tulasne, *Ann. des Sc. Nat.* 3 sér. xvii. p. 118.

SCYPHIDIA, Duj.—A genus of Infusoria, of the family Vorticellina.

Char. Body oblong or campanulate, narrowed at the base, very contractile, covered with a reticular integument.

S. rugosa (Pl. 24. fig. 74). Body with oblique striæ or rugæ, not numerous. Aquatic; length 1-550″.

SCYTONEMA, Berk.—A genus of Oscillatoriaceæ (Confervoid Algæ), especially distinguished by the mode of branching of the filaments. We can only make out with certainty one British species of the genus as now restricted, *S. Myochrous* (Pl. 4. fig. 19), which grows in alpine bogs and rivulets, and is composed of decumbent filaments interwoven into a dark-brown stratum.

BIBL. Harvey,*Brit. Alg.* 1 ed. p. 155; Hassall, *Brit. Fr. Alg.* p. 235, pl. 68; Kützing, *Spec. Alg.* 303, Tab. Phyc. ii. pl. 16 *et seq.*

SEBACEOUS FOLLICLES or GLANDS.—These organs exist pretty generally in the skin, and secrete a fatty matter. They are mostly seated close to the hair-follicles, into which their ducts usually open. They vary in form, some being simple pouches or depressions of the skin, whilst in others the deeper part of the pouch is branched, so as to constitute a true racemose gland. The narrower portion, or duct, is variable in diameter; it usually opens into the hair-follicle, rather above its middle, but sometimes upon the surface of the skin itself.

Each gland consists of an outer coat of areolar tissue, forming a more or less thick membrane in proportion to the size of the gland; this is derived either from the hair-follicle, or the cutis, according to the situation of the gland. It is lined by layers of roundish or polygonal, epidermic or epithelial cells, the outermost of which are closely connected, so as to form one or more membranous layers, and contain few or no globules of fat; whilst the inner ones are larger, and almost filled with these globules.

Fig. 634.

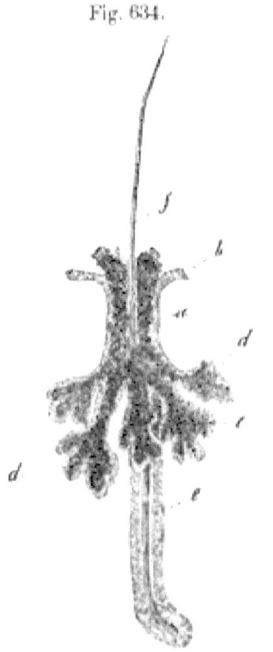

Compound sebaceous gland, from the nose, opening upon the surface with a hair-follicle. *a, b, c*, as in the next figure ; *d*, lobules of the compound gland; *e*, hair-follicle (root-sheath) ; *f*, the hair.

Magnified 50 diameters.

The development of the sebaceous glands commences at the end of the fourth or in

Fig. 635.

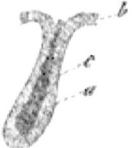

Simple sebaceous follicle, from the nose. *a*, glandular epithelium, continuous with *b*, the rete mucosum ; *c*, contents of the gland, consisting of cells containing fat, with free fatty matter.

Magnified 50 diameters.

the fifth month. The glands at first consist of solid depressions or outgrowths of the

Fig. 636.

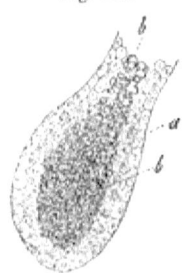

Glandular vesicle of a sebaceous gland. *a*, epithelium continuous with the glandular cells *b*, containing fat.

Magnified 250 diameters.

Fig. 637.

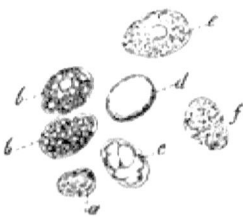

Cells from the glandular vesicles and the sebaceous secretion. *a*, small nucleated cell, containing but little fat, and resembling an epithelial cell ; *b*, cells abounding in fat, without evident nuclei ; *c*, cell in which the fat-globules are becoming confluent ; *d*, cell containing a single drop of fat ; *e, f*, cells from which part of the fat has escaped.

Magnified 350 diameters.

Fig. 638.

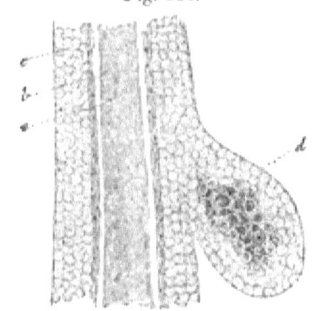

Development of the sebaceous follicles in a six-months' fœtus. *a*, hair ; *b*, inner root-sheath ; *c*, outer root-sheath ; *d*, radimentary follicle.

Magnified 250 diameters.

rete mucosum of the skin, or the inner root-sheath of the hairs; the inner cells then become filled with fat, loosened, and are finally evacuated through that part of the immature gland which in its subsequent development forms the duct.

Fig. 639.

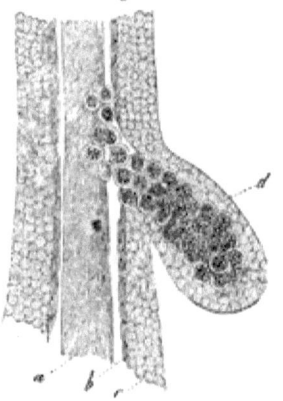

a, b, c, d, as above, but in a more advanced stage. Magnified 250 diameters.

BIBL. Kölliker, *Mikroskop. Anat.* i. 180, and the *Bibl.* of that article.

SECONDARY DEPOSITS, or LAYERS, OF VEGETABLE CELLS.—The structures known by this name are spoken of under the head of CELLS, in a general point of view, and in detail under PITTED and SPIRAL STRUCTURES. A few remarks may be given here, connecting the phænomena included under the last two heads.

It is well known that the original or *primary* cell-wall, the layer of cellulose by which the cell first becomes really constituted as a closed membranous sac, is, so far as our present instruments enable us to judge, devoid of detailed structure ; it is a homogeneous pellicle. This has a power of extension by interstitial nutrition, which leaves no traces in the perfect membrane, enabling the cell to increase in size. But the increase in solidity is effected by a different process, leaving distinct evidences of its occurrence, namely by an application of successive thin layers of cellulose membrane, more or less completely all over the inside of the primary membrane, giving the cell-wall a laminated character, either evident in the natural condition, or capable of being demonstrated by the aid of maceration or corrosive applications.

No cell which is to form part of a perma-

nent tissue remains long without receiving secondary layers upon its walls. In certain cases the wall exhibits in its natural state merely the laminated structure, without any markings (Pl. 38. fig. 24) ; but in the majority of cases, where the secondary deposits are considerable, these layers exhibit markings of very peculiar characters. As a general rule, the layers present themselves under two different types, according to the extent to which they cover the primary membrane. In one case they are applied as a general layer over the wall, absent merely at dot-like or slit-like points, where they leave the primary wall uncovered, and thus give rise to a *pitted* condition as seen from the inside of the cell. Successive layers leaving the same spots bare, the pits become gradually deeper, and form canals running through the thick cell-wall to the primary membrane (see PITTED STRUCTURES) (Pl. 38. fig. 23).

Another curious condition of the secondary deposits has been pointed out by Hartig and von Mohl, where large patches or spots upon the cell-wall left bare by the thicker secondary layers, become coated with a thin layer perforated by minute orifices, as if riddled with holes, or reticulated ; this is described as *clathrate tissue* under PITTED STRUCTURES.

In the other case, the secondary deposits are more sparing in quantity, and are applied over lines forming a definite pattern upon the primary membrane, in which a spiral course in the direction of the long axis of the cell is more or less evident : infinite modifications of this type occur, which are treated of under the head of SPIRAL STRUCTURES (Pl. 39. figs. 7, 9).

In certain less common cases we find the earlier secondary layers exhibiting the pitted character, while others later-formed produce spiral-fibrous thickening, as in *Taxus,* the lime, and other cases (see PITTED STRUCTURES) (Pl. 39. figs. 4, 13, 19 *b*).

The last-mentioned cases point to a relation between the spiral-fibrous and the pitted layers, which appears really to exist, for in a great number of cases it is possible to distinguish a spiral structure in the membranous layers of pitted cells or even of cells where the layers of thickening merely exhibit the laminated structure without any pits or fibrous markings. Thus, in the liber-cells of the Apocynaceæ (Pl. 39. fig. 30), the thickened walls appear under a low power homogeneous, while under sufficient magnifying power, and especially by the help of acids, we may detect an evident though delicate spiral structure. The action of acids reveals a similar spiral arrangement of the constituent molecules, in the cotton hair (Pl. 21. fig. 1), and in most liber-cells (Pl. 21. figs. 2, 5, 25), in many wood-cells, as of *Pinus*, &c. The membranes forming the sheaths of many of the Oscillatoriaceæ (Pl. 4. figs. 13 *d*, *e*, 15) exhibit a spiral-fibrous structure when undergoing dissolution; and an analogous condition may be detected by the help of reagents pretty generally in the cell-walls of the tubular Confervæ. All these phænomena seem to indicate a fundamental identity in secondary layers of all kinds, to which we direct attention under SPIRAL STRUCTURES; but it is convenient in practice to keep the PITTED and the SPIRAL-fibrous structures distinct.

The mode of formation of the secondary deposits is not clearly known at present: some imagine them to be precipitated from the cell-sap upon the walls; others, and apparently with more reason, believe that they are attributable to the agency of the PRIMORDIAL UTRICLE, continuing its action after the formation of the primary membrane. Crüger goes so far as to consider the spiral markings, &c. as dependent on the ROTATION-currents of the protoplasm. These points require further investigation. There can be little doubt of the mistaken character of Trécul's recent view, which regards the spiral and other fibrous thickenings as folds of the primary wall thrown inwards.

The secondary deposits appear to be always composed of some modification of cellulose. Mohl has investigated this point very thoroughly; and we have followed him over much of the ground. The cellulose, however, loses its distinctive character with age, either by infiltration with foreign matters, or by a slight chemical metamorphosis, so that old secondary layers do not readily become blue when sulphuric acid and iodine are applied; but as a general rule the cellulose reaction may be obtained by using a preliminary treatment. All internal structures, such as wood-cells, liber-cells, stones of fruits, &c., should be boiled in nitric acid, washed, dried, and tincture of iodine applied; then, if again dried and wetted with water, they turn blue: external structures, such as epidermal cells, cork, and the like, require a similar boiling, but with solution of potash.

Secondary deposits present a considerable difference in their consistence and degree of development in different cases. In most wood- and liber-cells they are abundant in quantity, in some cases almost filling up the cavity (Pl. 38. fig. 27); here they are hard, and appear to be in that state of the cellulose-compound which may be distinguished as *lignine*. The same condition prevails in the stones of fruits, bony shells, the "grit" of pears, &c.; and the less abundant secondary substance of spiral-fibrous tissues appears to be in the same state. The secondary layers of parenchymatous cells are usually rather soft and elastic, and often turn blue with sulphuric acid and iodine alone; those of the collenchymatous tissue beneath the epidermis of many herbaceous plants, such as the Chenopodiaceæ, &c., are abundant in quantity, but of somewhat cartilaginous texture. Those of the larger Algæ, and of the thallus of the larger Lichens, approach to the same condition, while the fleshy and horny ALBUMEN of many seeds contains abundant deposits of analogous character (Pl. 38. figs. 21-23); in the latter the composition is sometimes of *amyloid*, approaching starch, stained blue by iodine alone, and more or less soluble in dilute sulphuric acid. The secondary layer of epidermis and corky layers differs again, being usually more sparing in quantity, but very firm and elastic, and strongly resisting decomposing agents; the composition appears to be of that modification of cellulose called *suberine*.

BIBL. *Gen. Works on Structural Botany*; Mohl, *Vegetable Cell*, London, 1852. p. 10, *Botan. Zeit.* p. 97 (1847) (Transl. in *Taylor's Scientific Memoirs*, 2nd ser. i. p. 95); Schacht, *Pflanzenzelle*, Berlin, 1852; Crüger, *Bot. Zeit.* xiii. p. 601. 1855; Trécul, *Ann. des Sc. Nat.* 4 sér. ii. p. 273; Wigand, *Intercellular-substanz u. Cuticula*, Brunswick, 1850; Mulder, *Phys. Chemistry*, Edinburgh, 1849. p. 347.

SECRETING ORGANS OF PLANTS; RESERVOIRS OR RECEPTACLES for SECRETIONS.—The structures falling under this head have been in part treated of under the heads of GLANDS and LATICIFEROUS TISSUE; but there still remain certain organs of analogous character, which could not be properly included under either of the above. The name of receptacle or reservoir for peculiar secretions is ordinarily applied to groups of cells, of variable, but most frequently elongated prismatic form, containing special secretions, either in their cavities or effused into their intercellular passages, traversing in the form of cords or bundles the parenchymatous or prosenchymatous tissues. They are almost special characteristics of families, and by no means frequent; the Coniferæ, the Cycadaceæ, the Aloineous Liliaceæ, the Polygonaceæ, Compositæ, Umbelliferæ, Amygdaleous Rosaceæ, Leguminosæ, &c., afford striking examples.

In the Coniferæ the turpentine-reservoirs are very remarkable; and to a certain extent they render it possible to determine the genus by their arrangement. In *Pinus* they consist of bundles of elongated thin-walled cells, running through the wood parallel to the axis of the stem. These thin-wall cells are densely filled with turpentine; in some cases the cells of the medullary rays are likewise filled with turpentine, and, besides these, perpendicular intercellular passages; the latter form of turpentine-canal is chiefly met with in the bark. Turpentine-canals also exist in the leaves of the Coniferæ, the scales of the cones, &c.

The reservoirs of the Aloes are bundles of prismatic cells accompanying the vascular bundles of the leaves and stems. The colouring matter of the root of rhubarb is contained in cells of imperfect medullary rays. The structure of the balsam-reservoirs of the myrrh tree, &c., has not been thoroughly studied. The resin- and oil-canals of the Umbelliferæ are of great importance; but the former, chiefly occurring in the roots, are imperfectly known. The oil-reservoir of the fruits (*vittæ*) consists of elongated excavations in the cellular tissue, filled with oil. Canals containing odoriferous oils occur in some of the Compositæ. Resin-canals occur also in the common lime.

Gum-canals, consisting of simple or branched intercellular passages with a special coat of small (secreting?) cells, occur in the leaf-stalks of Cycadaceæ, the bark of the *Amygdaleæ*, in the stems of the Malvaceæ, Cactaceæ, &c. Structures of similar nature contain the milky juices of certain plants, as of the Anacardiaceæ; and these appear to be different from the ordinary LATEX vessels.

BIBL. Meyen, *Secretions-Organe der Pflanzen*, Berlin, 1837. p. 18; Unger, *Anat. und Phys. der Pflanzen*, 1855. p. 204.

SECTIONS. See PREPARATION (p. 573).

SEEDS.—These are interesting objects for microscopic examination in respect to many different characteristics. Among

these may be mentioned first the variety of beautiful markings upon the surface, which render almost all seeds, like the elytra of beetles, interesting opaque objects for observation with a low power. A few striking forms are represented in Plate 31. figs. 14–18; and we give a list of kinds easily to be obtained.

Hypericum.	Datura.	Maurandya.
Lychnis.	Nicotiana.	Hyoscyamus.
Stellaria.	Petunia.	Sempervivum.
Reseda.	Sedum.	Limnocharis.
Lepidium.	Saxifraga.	Silene (Pl. 31.
Nigella.	Capparis.	figs. 16, 17).
Erica.	Elatine.	Dianthus (Pl. 31.
Anagallis.	Gesnera.	fig. 14).
Orobanche.	Begonia.	Papaver (Pl. 31.
Linaria.	Delphinium.	fig. 14).
Chironia.	Scrophularia.	Digitalis (Pl. 31.
Gentiana.	Antirrhinum.	fig. 18).
Mesembryanthemum.		

The following are well seen when mounted as transparent objects in Canada balsam.

Parnassia.	Pyrola.	Saxifraga.
Drosera.	Monotropa.	Rhododendron.
Orchis.	Hydrangea.	

The *testa* or outer skin of some of the latter (also *Begonia*), when removed from the seed and viewed with a high power, exhibits elegant pitted cells. The surface of the seed of *Cobæa* is mealy with little scales consisting of pyriform cells containing a spiral fibre (Pl. 21. fig. 20).

The surface of various seeds, such as *Collomia*, *Ruellia* (and the pericarp of many seed-like fruits, such as that of *Salvia*, *Senecio*), present remarkable forms of HAIRS.

The 'stones' of plums or cherries, the so-called shell of the Cocoa-nut and similar fruits, exhibit remarkably thick SECONDARY DEPOSITS.

The examination of the structure of ripe seeds is a matter of great importance in botany. The investigation will vary much according to circumstances. Where seeds are large, the microscope is only required for the examination of their tissues; but small seeds must be examined by dissection with needles under the simple microscope, or by sections, which are most easily made by fixing the softened seed into a piece of wax. Seeds have two coats, the *testa* and *tegmen*, or external and internal membrane, and, according as the seed is or is not albuminous, an albumen enclosing the embryo, or an embryo of larger size immediately invested by the coats. The characters of the ALBUMEN and EMBRYO will be found under these heads, as also other particulars under OVULE. Embryos are either Monocotyledonous or Dicotyledonous; sometimes, however, the two cotyledons are soldered together more or less completely; in the Coniferæ and certain genera of Dicotyledonous Angiosperms, as *Schizopetalum*, the cotyledons appear to be four, six, or more in number; but the recent observations of M. Duchartre go to show that there exist only two—bifid, trifid, or multifid cotyledons. In other cases, as in *Orchis*, the embryo remains imperfectly developed, and appears as a mere cellular mass in the ripe seed before germination; this is destitute of albumen; but in *Orobanche* an amorphous embryo is found imbedded in the albumen.

BIBL. General works on Botany.

SEGESTRELLA, Fr.—A genus of Verrucarieæ (Angiocarpous Lichens), containing one doubtful British plant, the *Lecanora thelostoma* of the *Brit. Fl.*

BIBL. Leighton, *Brit. Angioc. Lichens*, p. 34; Hook. *Brit. Fl.* ii. pt. 1. p. 189.

SEIROSPORA, Harv.—A genus of Ceramiaceæ (Florideous Algæ), containing one rare species, *S. Griffithsiana*, a little crimson feathery sea-weed, composed of single articulated tubes, the joints of which are traversed by articulated filaments. The spores are unknown; but the *tetraspores*, which serve to distinguish this plant from the *Callithamnia*, occur in terminal beaded strings, being formed out of the ramuli.

BIBL. Harvey, *Brit. Mar. Alg.* p. 170, pl. 23 C.

SELAGINELLA, P. de Beauv.—A genus of Lycopodiaceæ, distinguished from *Lycopodium* by the presence of two kinds of spores and the dissimilar habit. This genus includes only one of our native Clubmosses, *S. spinosa* (*Lyc. selaginoides*); but most of the so-called *Lycopodia*, now so extensively cultivated in Wardian cases, fernhouses, &c., belong to this division (fig. 430. p. 436). The principal particulars relating to these plants, especially the remarkable history of the reproduction by the spores, are given under LYCOPODIACEÆ.

BIBL. See LYCOPODIACEÆ.

SELENITE.—This well-known mineral substance consists of crystallized hydrated sulphate of lime. Its crystals belong to the oblique prismatic system; and the colours exhibited by thin laminæ, into which they may be easily split, are very beautiful under polarized light. Polarizing crystals and

organic substances, in which the thickness is not suited to the production of distinct colours under the polariscope, may be made to exhibit them by placing a plate of selenite beneath the object. For this purpose the plate is usually kept mounted in Canada balsam.

BIBL. That of POLARIZATION.

SELIGERIA.—A genus of Leptotrichaceous Mosses, including certain *Weissiæ* and *Gymnostoma* of authors.

SELLIGUÆA, Bory.—A genus of Grammitideæ (Polypodioid Ferns). Exotic.

SENDTNERA, Woods.— A genus of Jungermannieæ (Hepaticæ), mostly tropical, one species of which, *S. (Jung.) Woodsii*, occurs rarely in the mountains of the S.W. of Ireland (devoid of fruit).

BIBL. Hook. *Brit. Flor.* ii. pt. 1. p. 126; *Brit. Jung.* pl. 66; Ekart, *Synops. Jung.* pl. 12. fig. 108; Endlicher, *Gen. Plant.* Supp. 1. No. 472-16.

SENECIO.—The surface of the achænia or seed-like fruits of the common groundsel (*Senecio vulgaris*) are sparingly clothed with HAIRS of a peculiar character. These appear to consist of two semicylindrical cells applied together by their flat faces, so as to form a kind of tube with a vertical septum. When placed in water they expand somewhat, and the contents are expelled from the ends, consisting of an indistinctly spiral-fibrous structure, which untwists and expands, by the absorption of water, to twice or three times the length of the hairs, in a manner comparable in some degree to the behaviour of the contents of the hairs of ACANTHACEÆ.

BIBL. Leighton, *Ann. Nat. Hist.* vi. p. 259.

SEPEDONIEI.—A family of Hyphomycetous Fungi, consisting of a heterogeneous assemblage of imperfectly known genera, and differently defined by different authors. Those genera we have included in our list are enumerated in Lindley's 'Vegetable Kingdom;' but Fries includes *Oidium* and others. The general character of the family is, that the plants produce spores lying immediately upon the filaments of mycelium, or upon short pedicels.

Synopsis of British Genera.

1. *Artotrogus*, Entophyte. Filaments creeping, persistent; spores springing from the middle of the filaments, simple, at length free, spinous.

2. *Sepedonium*. Filaments woolly, sep-

tate, evanescent; spores globose, connate, scabrous, stipitate, solitary, at length heaped together.

3. *Fusisporium.* Spores fusiform or cylindrical, glued together in heaps resting on the gelatinous matrix.

4. *Epochnium.* Spores heaped together, oblong, apiculate, septate, adnate to the matrix, interwoven with the effused, entangled, slender filaments of the mycelium.

5. *Psilonia.* Spores simple, pellucid, not glued together, at first covered by the converging filaments of the mycelium.

6. *Monotospora,* Entophyte. Filaments creeping, evanescent; spores globose, solitary, terminal, at length free.

7. *Asterophora.* Filaments creeping (over larger Fungi); spores on short ramules, vesicular, stellate.

8. *Acrospeira.* Filaments creeping, ramuli branched, the fertile terminating in a spiral coil, composed of about three joints, one of which swells into a rough-coated spore.

9. *Zygodesmus.* Filament creeping, branched, with short ramuli bearing echinate spores, the pedicels with a peculiar lateral indentation looking like a joint.

SEPEDONIUM, Link.—A genus of Sepedoniei (Hyphomycetous Fungi), containing two species, growing upon decaying Fungi. *S. chrysosperma* has golden-yellow spores, *S. roseum* red ones. The first is common.

BIBL. Berk. *Brit. Flor.* ii. pt. 2. p. 350; Fries, *Summa Vegetab.* p. 497; Grev. *Sc. Crypt. Flor.* pl. 198.

SEPTONEMA, Corda.—A genus of Torulacei (Coniomycetous Fungi), related to *Torula,* and connecting this in some measure with *Dendryphium.* *S. spiloma,* forming green tufts on old rails, has been found in Guernsey. Several species are recorded as French by Léveillé, one forming patches on vine-leaves, the others on the potato. The chains of septate spores soon break up.

Fig. 640.

Septonema viride.
Magnified
200 diameters.

BIBL. Corda, *Icones,* i. & ii.; Fries, *Summa Veg.* 504; Léveillé, *Ann. des Sc. Nat.* 3 sér. ix. 261; Berkeley and Broome, *Ann. Nat. Hist.* 2nd ser. v. p. 461; Berk. *Lond. Journ. Bot.* iv. t. 12. fig. 5.

SEPTORIA, Fr.—A genus of Sphæronemei (Coniomycetous Fungi), but probably in reality consisting of preparatory forms of *Sphæriæ.* They grow upon the leaves of plants, the fusiform septate "spores" oozing out from a pore in the form of a tendril.

S. Ulmi and *S. Oxyacanthæ* are common; several other species are recorded.

BIBL. Berk. *Brit. Flor.* ii. pt. 2. p. 356; Berk. and Br. *Ann. Nat. Hist.* 2nd ser. v. p. 379, xiii. p. 460; Fries, *Summa Veg.* p. 426; Tulasne, *Ann. Nat. Hist.* 2nd ser. viii. p. 117, 4th ser. v. p. 115.

SEPTOSPORIUM, Corda. See MACROSPORIUM.

SEROUS MEMBRANES.—These consist of the same elements arranged in the same number of layers as in the MUCOUS MEMBRANES. The thickness of the layers, however, is considerably less; the fibrous elements are finer; and the epithelium forms a single layer only of polygonal cells.

BIBL. Kölliker, *Mikrosk. Anat.* ii.; Todd and Bowman, *Physiolog. Anat. &c. of Man.*

SERTULARIA, Linn.—A genus of Polypi (Zoophytes), of the order Hydroida, and family Sertulariadæ.

Char. Polypidom plant-like, and fixed by its base, variously branched, the branches formed of a single tube, denticulated or serrated with the cells, and jointed; cells alternate, semi-alternate or opposite, biserial, sessile, urceolate, short, with everted apertures; ovarian vesicles scattered.

Many of these elegant zoophytes, which would at once be referred to the vegetable kingdom by any casual observer, are commonly found on the sea-coast, either loose or attached to shells, sea-weeds, &c.

There are eighteen British species.

1. *S. rugosa* (Pl. 33. figs. 11 & 12). Cells alternate, one to each joint, ovate, transversely wrinkled; mouth narrow, with four small teeth at the rim.

Common upon *Flustræ, Fuci,* &c. at low-water mark.

2. *S. pumila* (Pl. 33. figs. 13 & 14). Cells opposite, approximate, shortly tubular, the top everted, with an oblique somewhat mucronate aperture; vesicles ovate.

Common on Fuci near low-water mark.

3. *S. operculata* (Pl. 33. figs. 15 & 16). Cells opposite, inversely conical; aperture patulous, obliquely truncate, pointed on the outer edge, and with two small lateral teeth; vesicles obovate.

Common on Fuci near low-water mark.

BIBL. Johnston, *Brit. Zoophytes,* p. 61.

SERTULARIADÆ.—A family of Polypes, of the order Hydroida.

Char. Bodies contained in cup-like sessile cells, situated on a horny polypidom; egg-germs contained in scattered deciduous capsules. Marine. Seven genera:

1. *Halecium.* Polypidom plant-like; stem consisting of several parallel tubes; cells shallow cups, on opposite sides, alternate, one under each joint.

2. *Sertularia.* Plant-like; stem simply tubular, branched, jointed; cells vase-like, alternate or in pairs, on opposite sides, with everted rims.

3. *Reticularia.* Polypidom an investing network of horny tubes, immersed in a homogeneous horny crust; cells short curved projections of the tubes, with simple round orifices.

4. *Coppinia.* Parasitic, massive, hairy; cells long, tubular, often curved, arising at irregular distances (generally at the angles of junction) out of a cellular basis, the apertures of the cells or spaces of which are often themselves covered in by a lid perforated by a small tubular orifice.

5. *Thuiaria.* As *Sertularia*, but the cells closely pressed to, or imbedded in the surface of the stem and branches.

6. *Antennularia.* Simple or branched, jointed, with slender hair-like whorled branchlets; cells small cups on the inner side of the branchlets; egg-vesicles seated in the angles.

7. *Plumularia.* Simple or branched, feathery; cells small, usually in the angles formed by horny spines on the inner side of the branches; egg-vesicles scattered.

SHEEP-TICK. See MELOPHILA.

A species of *Trichodectes* (*sphærocephalus*) is also found as a louse upon sheep.

SHELL OF ANIMALS.—In this article we shall notice the various substances comprised under the term shell, in its common acceptation.

Egg-shell.—As an example of the structure of the egg-shell of birds, we may select the shell of the egg of the common fowl.

This is lined internally by a loosely adherent layer of a thin yet firm albuminous membrane, called the membrana putaminis. It consists of a number of very slender fibres, interlacing in various directions. In imperfectly formed or soft eggs, as they are called, the fibres present thickenings at irregular intervals, resembling, on the whole, the nuclear fibres of elastic tissue with the remains of their formative cells still visible.

On macerating the shell in dilute muriatic acid, an outer layer of this membrane, inseparably adherent in the natural state to the inner surface of the shell, may be detached.

The membrane may be heated to boiling in solution of potash without undergoing solution, and is insoluble in acetic acid; but it is coloured by Schultze's test.

The substance of the shell consists of numerous masses of secretion, or protoplasts, impregnated with calcareous matter. In soft eggs, these form rounded, loosely adherent masses (Pl. 37. fig. 12), may easily be detached from the surface of the egg, and contain but little calcareous matter; whilst in the perfect egg they are somewhat angular from mutual pressure, and abound in calcareous granules having an imperfectly radiating arrangement (Pl. 37. fig. 13); this is most easily perceived in the inner portions of the shell.

The structure of the shell of the ostrich presents a curious variety. In a section parallel to the surface (Pl. 37. fig. 14) the protoplast structure is distinctly visible (although omitted in the figure), but the calcareous matter is arranged in the form of triangular plates, often fused together, and leaving angular interspaces. The perpendicular section is represented in Pl. 37. fig. 15. The former section constitutes an interesting polarizing object.

Tortoise-shell.—This substance is an epidermic formation, structurally resembling horn, in so far as it consists of epidermic cells flattened and united into numerous superimposed plates. The long-continued action of solution of potash (from twenty-four to forty-eight hours), and the subsequent addition of water, are necessary to resolve tortoise-shell into its component cells.

Shells of the Mollusca.—The structure of these shells varies in the different orders, &c. of the class; and a knowledge of the respective varieties has been used as an aid to the recognition of fossils, and the determination of the affinities of the genera, families, &c.

In the bivalve Mollusca, two kinds of structure may be distinguished, an outer prismatic or fibrous, and an inner laminated.

The outer prismatic portion consists of flattened masses or plates of crowded polygonal prisms, placed sometimes perpendicularly, sometimes obliquely to the surface of the inner layer. These prisms are transparent, and polarize light, possessing a crystalline structure, although their forms are not crystalline but those resulting from mutual pressure. Transverse sections of the prismatic structure exhibit a cellular appearance (Pl. 37. figs. 4 & 11 *a*); and a somewhat similar appearance is presented by perpendicular sections (Pl. 37. figs. 5 and 11 *b*). The prisms are pretty easily separable in the lines of mutual contact, and often form several superimposed strata. They frequently contain pigment, either uniformly diffused through their substance, or in granules. They also sometimes appear transversely striated.

The inner laminated portion, which sometimes constitutes the entire shell, is either white or presents the brilliant iridescent tints of nacre or mother-of-pearl. It is often called the nacreous portion, or nacre, and when polished forms the mother-of-pearl of the shops. Under the microscope it exhibits a number of fine lines or grooves, running in various directions, and probably corresponding to the edges or intersections of the strata or laminæ of which this portion of the shell is composed; and it is to the interference of light ensuing at the surfaces of these grooves that the iridescent colours are usually owing.

In some shells there are tubes traversing the substance perpendicularly (Pl. 37. fig. 7) or obliquely, or forming branched horizontal channels (Pl. 37. fig. 9 *a*, *b*); in the latter case they are sometimes connected with rounded cavities (Pl. 37. fig. 9 *a*).

In some Gasteropoda, as *Cypræa*, the outer portion of the shell consists of three layers of similar prismatic structure, but with the prisms in each layer in alternately contrary directions. The same may be seen in some of the outer layers of oyster-shell, except that the prisms are nearly horizontal or slightly oblique. But in the Acephala generally, the structure corresponds to the inner portion of that of the Cephalophora.

Shell consists of an organic basis, in which calcareous matter, principally composed of carbonate of lime, is deposited; and by digesting it with dilute muriatic acid, the latter may be removed, an organic cast of the original being left. On treating a thin plate of nacre in this way, Dr. Carpenter found that the iridescent colours remained visible until the membrane was stretched and the supposed folds obliterated, when they vanished; hence this author concludes

that the edges of the folds were the cause of the interference of light producing the colours. It appears to us, however, objectionable to this view, that the same structure and colour are produced by laminated calcareous and organic matter artificially formed; that they are also present after the edges of the folds must have been ground away, as in sections; and that the colours, in the instance mentioned, might have been those of a thin plate, and some of the colours of iridescent shell are known to be those of thin plates. It may be stated here that Dr. Carpenter considers the lines or striæ in nacre to be produced by the edges of folds of a single layer of membrane, arranged so as to lie over each other in an imbricated manner. The same author views the shell of the Mollusca as corresponding to the epidermis of the higher animals, calcified.

The outer prismatic layers of shell are secreted by the borders or margins of the mantle, whilst the inner laminated portions arise from the outer surface. The growth of shell is not uninterrupted or constant, but periodical; hence the laminated arrangement of its constituents.

In some portions of the shell of the oyster, &c., the calcareous matter assumes the form of distinct rhomboidal or hexagonal crystals (Pl. 37. fig. 10). These appear to be deposited in the inner laminated portion; and when detached, they leave angular spaces corresponding to them in form. In the tooth of the shell of *Mya*, groups of radiating prisms are present, forming an elegant microscopic object.

The prisms existing in the outer portion of shells have been supposed to represent cells filled with calcareous matter; they have also been regarded as consisting of aggregations of epidermic cells, the transverse striæ (in *Pinna*) corresponding to thickenings of the cell-membranes where the layers come into contact; and the folded membrane has been compared to a basement membrane. It is probable, however, that shell should be regarded as a simple secretion from the mantle, and as corresponding in structure to egg-shell.

Shell of the Crustacea.—The hard portion of the integument of the Crustacea, alluded to at p. 189, possesses a laminated structure, corresponding to periods of growth, and giving rise to the appearance of transverse parallel lines in a perpendicular section (Pl. 37. fig. 16). The substance is traversed by numerous straight or slightly wavy, very slender tubes (Pl. 37. fig. 16), resembling those of dentine.

Shell of Echinodermata.—The perforated structure of the homogeneous basis forming this substance has been already noticed (p. 241). In the spines of *Echinus, Cidaris,* &c., the calcareous network consists of slender fibres with large areolæ at intervals, arranged in a somewhat regular pattern, and traversing a solid homogeneous substance, which is thus divided into a number of ribs or pillars. The transverse section of these is seen in Pl. 37. figs. 6 & 6 *a*.

Dr. Carpenter regards the calcareous network as corresponding to the fibrous structure of the cutis of the higher animals, calcified. This view does not, however, account for the intervening substance.

The method of procuring sections of shell is noticed under PREPARATION (p. 574).

BIBL. Carpenter, *Trans. of the British Association,* 1844 & 1847; *Ann. Nat. Hist.* 1843. xii. 376; Gray, *Phil. Trans.* 1833; Deshayes, *Todd's Cycl. of Anat., &c.,* iv. 556; Bowerbank, *Trans. Micr. Soc.* 1844. i.; Lavalle, *Ann. des Sc. Nat.* 3 sér. vii.; Siebold, *Vergl. Anat.*; Brewster, *Phil. Trans.* 1814, and *Optics,* 1853; Woodward, *On Shells.*

SIDA, Baird (*Daphnia,* auct.).—A genus of Entomostraca, of the order Cladocera, and family Daphniadæ.

Char. Anterior branch of inferior antennæ two-jointed, posterior three-jointed and with a row of spines at its anterior margin; legs six pairs.

S. crystallina (Pl. 14. fig. 27). The only species. Aquatic.

Daphnella belongs here.

BIBL. Baird, *Brit. Entomostr.* p. 107.

SIDEROLINA, Lamk.—A genus of Foraminifera, of the order Helicostegia, and family Nautiloidæ.

Resembles *Nummulina,* except that the shell has elongated appendages at the circumference, interrupting internally the succession of the chambers, which pass on each side of them.

No British species.

BIBL. D'Orbigny, *Foram. Foss. de Vienne,* 116.

SIDYNUM, Sav.—A genus of Tunicate Mollusca, of the family BOTRYLLIDÆ.

S. turbinatum. Amber or orange. On the under side of shelving rocks.

BIBL. Forbes and Hanley, *Brit. Moll.* i. 13.

SILK.—This valuable substance is secreted in Insects by two glandular organs, described under INSECTS, *Spinning Organs.*

The fibres of which it is composed are cylindrical or somewhat flattened, solid, tolerably highly refractive, and free from structural markings of any kind.

Chemically, silk consists of a proper silk-cylinder, consisting of fibroine and forming the principal part of the fibres, surrounded by a coat of albumen, upon which is a layer of gelatine. The fibres also contain a small quantity of fat and colouring matter.

Fibres of silk may easily be distinguished from those of linen or cotton by the application of Millon's or Schultze's test, both of which colour the silk, but neither of them the linen or cotton. The test for cellulose is equally applicable to the same purpose.

BIBL. That of CHEMISTRY.

SIPHONACEÆ. — A family of Confervoid Algæ, either marine, aquatic, or growing on damp ground; characterized by the individual fronds being composed of large branched cells, the contents of which, expelled in various forms, serve for the reproduction. The fronds mostly have a more or less compound character, either from regular ramification, or by a kind of stoloniferous multiplication at the base of the cells; and in *Hydrodictyon,* which seems best placed in this family, the cells are always connected together by their extremities, so as to form a net-like frond. In the majority of the genera the cell-contents are green; in *Achlya,* however, they are brownish or almost colourless. The modes of reproduction exhibit considerable diversity, and are probably still imperfectly known in most of the genera. *Codium, Bryopsis,* and *Achlya* are reproduced by the discharge of the contents of certain cells in the form of numerous small ciliated zoospores. *Vaucheria* is increased by large elliptical solitary zoospores, covered with vibratile cilia; in *Hydrodictyon,* the cell-contents are converted into a multitude of ciliated zoospores, which unite to form a new net or frond before leaving the parent-cell; while in *Botrydium* the cell-contents are said to be discharged in the condition of motionless gonidia; but we imagine this point is not quite certain. In addition to the gonidial reproduction, spores have been discovered in *Achlya* and *Vaucheria,* and will probably be found in the rest. In *Achlya* these occur in special lateral sporangial branch-cells. In *Vaucheria* they also occur in special branch-cells, here however accompanied by antheridial cells, which produce spermatozoids, fertilizing the sporangial cell. From the fact that orifices have been observed in the wall of the sporange of *Achlya*, it is possible that an impregnation occurs there also. Spores have not yet been observed in the other genera; but it is to be expected that they will be found in them also. More particular details on the very interesting genera of this somewhat heterogeneous family will be found under their respective heads.

Synopsis of British Genera.

1. *Codium.* Filaments green, branched, closely interwoven into a spongiform frond, producing biciliated zoospores in sporangial cells borne on the sides of the erect clavate branches. Marine.

2. *Bryopsis.* Filaments green, free, pinnately branched, producing two- or four-ciliated zoospores in the extremities of the branches. Marine.

3. *Vaucheria.* Filaments green, more or less branched, continuous, producing in their apices large solitary zoospores covered with cilia; also bearing lateral globose sporangial cells and hook-like antheridial cells ("horns"). Marine or aquatic, and still more commonly on muddy ground, damp garden-pots, &c.

4. *Botrydium.* Frond a spherical green vesicle seated on a ramified filamentous base, the cavity of the whole continuous, the ramified base producing new vesicles (sporanges) by stoloniferous growth. Multiplied by the granular contents of the vesicle discharged by a rupture at the summit. On damp (mostly clayey) ground subject to floods.

5. *Hydrodictyon.* Frond a green bag-like net, with usually pentagonal open meshes, formed of cylindrical cells connected by their ends. Reproduced by ciliated zoospores formed in the "link"-cells, uniting together and forming a perfect miniature net before escaping from the parent-cell.

6. *Achlya.* Filaments colourless or light brownish (like the mycelia of Fungi), free, slightly branched; producing numerous biciliated zoospores in the apices of the filaments, and spores in globose lateral sporangial cells. On dead flies, fishes, or sometimes on decaying vegetable matter in water.

See also PYTHIUM.

BIBL. See the genera.

SIPHONOSTOMA (Parasita, or Pœcilopoda).—An order of Crustacea.

Char. Body often almost entirely enclosed in a buckler, consisting generally of one, sometimes of two pieces; mouth suctorial; legs formed for walking or prehension, or partly branchiferous and fitted for swimming. Parasitic upon fishes, &c.

These animals (Pl. 14. figs. 7, 23, 24, 36, and Pl. 15. fig. 1), which often present the most extraordinary forms, are found mostly affixed to the gills of fishes by means of hooks, arms, or suckers, arising from or consisting of modified foot-jaws. In some, the cephalothorax is distinct from the abdomen, and the head is more or less distinct from the thorax; whilst in others the body presents more of a worm-like form, is occasionally ringed or segmented, and sometimes exhibits simple or branched lateral lobes or processes. The antennæ are mostly rudimentary. Flattened elytriform dorsal appendages are sometimes present. The rostrum is conical, tubular, and furnished with two setaceous or styliform mandibles. The alimentary canal is straight, without a gastric expansion, and its orifices at the two ends of the body. In some, branchial plates form the respiratory organs; but in most the same office is performed by the skin.

The sexes are distinct, although they are not known in all the species. The males are smaller than the females. The ova are often attached to the lower part of the body of the females, either contained in external ovaries, or simply glued together by the secretion from a special gland, and forming long, cylindrical, straight or convolute appendages. The young animals have but few legs, swim freely, and frequently resemble the young of *Cyclops.*

BIBL. Baird, *Brit. Entomostr.*; M.-Edwards, *Hist. Nat. Crust.* iii.; Siebold, *Vergleich. Anat.*

SIROCROCIS, Kütz. — Probably the mycelium of a fungus.

BIBL. Kützing, *Sp. Alg.* p. 153.

SIROGONIUM, Kützing. *S. notabile* = *Mesocarpus notabilis*, Hass.; *S. sticticum* = *Spirogyra* (*Zygnema*, Hassall) *stictica*; *S. breviarticulatum* = *Spirogyra curvata.*

SIROSIPHON, Kütz.—A genus of Oscillatoriaceæ (Confervoid Algæ), which should perhaps have been placed under the older name of HASSALLIA. This genus is principally distinguished by the solitary branches passing off from the sides of the rather rigid filaments, the branches arising from longitudinal division and lateral growth of interstitial cells. The plants are found on wet moors, rocks, &c. Two species seem to be established—*S. ocellata* (Pl. 4. fig. 12), and *S. compacta*; others appear doubtful.

BIBL. Hassall, *Brit. Fr. Alg.* p. 231, pls. 77, 78; Kützing, *Spec. Alg.* p. 315, *Tab. Phyc.* ii. pls. 36, 37.

SKELETON LARVA.—The larva of *Corethra plumicornis*, a dipterous insect, of the family Tipulidæ.

It is very transparent, and shows well the internal structure.

BIBL. Westwood, *Insects*, ii. 515; Pritchard, *Micr. Illustr.* 50.

SKIN OR INTEGUMENT OF ANIMALS.—

Three parts are distinguishable in the skin: an outer or cellular, forming the epidermis; an inner fibrous, or cutis vera; and an internal or subjacent, known as the subcutaneous cellular tissue. The two former constitute the skin proper.

The cutis vera or corium (fig. 641 *c*) consists of areolar and elastic tissue, with fat-cells, blood-vessels, nerves, absorbents, and unstriated muscular fibres. The fibres of the areolar tissue are variously interlaced and united into interwoven bundles, forming a tolerably dense and firm tissue, with small areolæ, and sometimes presenting laminæ. The elastic tissue is less abundant than the areolar, and consists of networks of finer or coarser fibres.

Fig. 641.

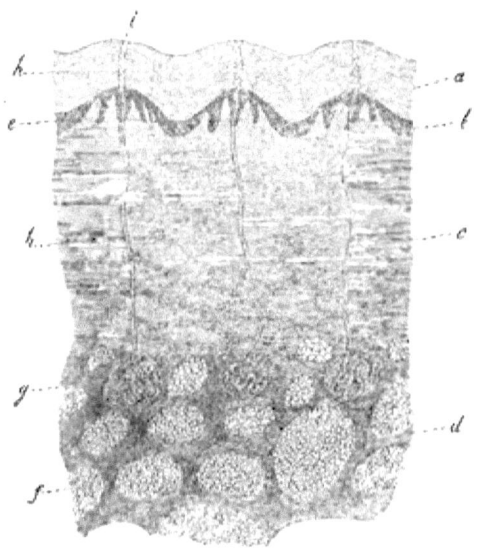

Fig. 642.

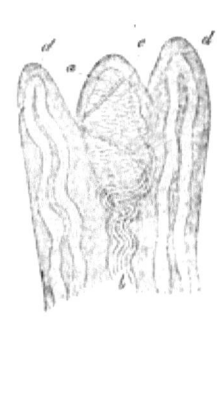

Fig. 641. Perpendicular section of the skin of the under surface of the end of the thumb, through three furrows. *a*, cuticle; *b*, rete mucosum; *c*, cutis vera; *d*, upper part of subcutaneous tissue; *e*, papillæ of the cutis; *f*, fatty tissue; *g*, sudoriparous glands; *h*, sudoriparous ducts; *i*, orifice of the latter. Magnified 20 diameters.

Fig. 642. Papillæ from the skin of the under part of the end of the finger. *a*, axial body; *b*, nerve; *c*, its terminal loop; *d*, *d*, loops of capillary blood-vessels. Magnified 250 diameters.

The outer surface of the cutis gives off a number of conical processes or papillæ (fig. 641 *e*), which are frequently bifid, lobed, or arise several from a common base. In many parts of the skin they are arranged in more or less regular rows. The areolar tissue of

the papillæ is often homogeneous, especially in the median portion, where in certain papillæ it forms an oval transparent body (fig. 642 *a*), surrounded by a layer of imperfectly developed elastic tissue, consisting of spindle-shaped cells and fibres taking a

2 s

horizontal or circular direction, and giving the oval bodies a transversely striated or laminated appearance. These oval or axial bodies, as they are called, have been supposed to be connected with sensation,—an assumption which Kölliker has rendered at least improbable. The papillæ are traversed by the terminal loops of the cutaneous capillaries (fig. 642 *d*) and nerves (fig. 642 *c*).

The cutis is continuous beneath with the subcutaneous cellular or properly areolar tissue (fig. 641 *d*), which is of a much more lax texture than the cutis, presenting large areolæ filled with fatty tissue (fig. 641 *f*).

The cutis is everywhere covered externally by the epidermis, which is a semitransparent coat, containing neither vessels nor nerves, moulded as it were upon its surface (fig. 643) and filling up the intervals between its papillæ (fig. 644). The variously arranged lines seen upon its outer surface are depressions corresponding to those existing upon the cutis between its rows or groups of papillæ.

The epidermis consists entirely of nucleated cells; and two distinct layers are

Fig. 643.

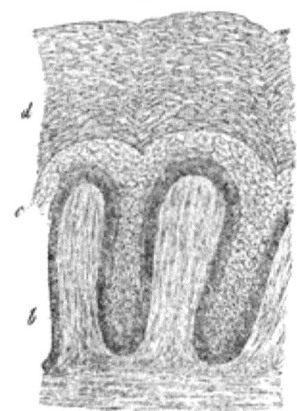

Perpendicular section of the skin of the Negro. *a*, papillæ of the cutis ; *b*, deepest and most intensely coloured layer of elongated perpendicular cells of the rete mucosum ; *c*, upper layer of the rete ; *d*, cuticle.

Magnified 250 diameters.

Fig. 644.

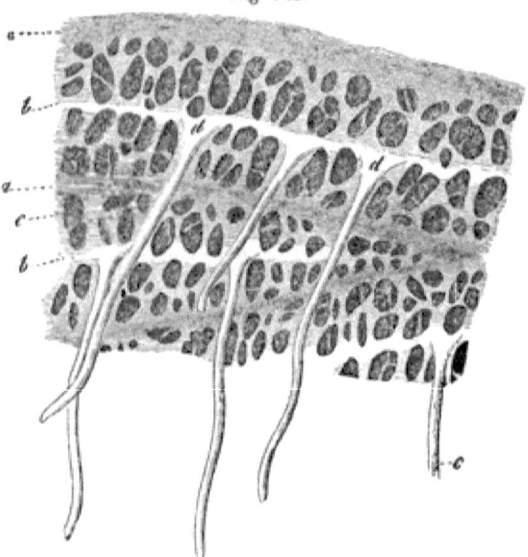

Under surface of the epidermis of the palm of the hand. *a*, ridges corresponding to the furrows between the ridges of the cutis ; *b*, ridges corresponding to the furrows between the rows of papillæ ; *c*, suduriparous ducts ; *d*, their broad insertions in the epidermis ; *e*, depressions corresponding to the papillæ.

Magnified about 20 diameters.

recognized in it (fig. 643), an inner forming the rete mucosum (fig. 643 c), and an outer or cuticle (fig. 643 d). The rete mucosum is softer than the cuticle, and is frequently of a brownish colour, from its cells, especially the deepest, containing granules of pigment. These cells are not all of the same form, those immediately applied to the cutis being somewhat elongated and arranged perpendicularly upon its surface (fig. 643 b), the next being roundish, and those nearest the cuticle becoming longer, horizontally flattened, and polygonal from mutual pressure (fig. 643 c).

The cells of the cuticle are colourless, flattened, often wrinkled or folded, and correspond to the pavement epithelium of the mucous membranes. Between the epidermis and the cutis is situated a basement membrane, which is rarely distinguishable.

In the examination of the skin, sections

Fig. 645.

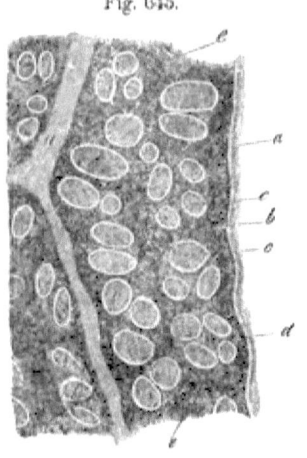

Section of the skin of the heel parallel to the surface, through one entire ridge of the skin and part of two others; showing the arrangement of the papillæ in rows corresponding to the ridges of the cutis. a, cuticle between the ridges; b, rete mucosum; c, papillæ; d, portion of the rete mucosum between papillæ arising from a common base; e, sudoriparous ducts.

Magnified 60 diameters.

must be made with Valentin's knife, and these treated with acetic acid, solution of potash, dilute nitric acid, &c. The blood-vessels are well seen as regards general arrangement in injected preparations, some of which, as those of the pulp of the finger,

form very beautiful objects. The epidermis is easily separated by maceration.

The integument of animals is noticed under the respective heads of the classes.

It must be remarked that the terms epidermis and cuticle are generally used synonymously.

BIBL. Kölliker, *Mikrosk. Anat.* i., and *Gewebelehre*; Krause, *Wagner's Handwörterbuch d. Physiol.* ii. 127; Weber, *ibid.* iii.; Todd and Bowman, *Phys. Anat.* &c.

SLIDES. INTRODUCTION, p. xxi.

SMARIS, or SMARIDIA, Latr.—A genus of Arachnida, of the order Acarina, and family Trombidina.

Char. Palpi slender, inserted upon a retractile rostrum; mandibles sword-shaped; body entire, narrowed in front; coxæ stout, distant, the anterior articulated to a fixed eminence upon the body; legs palpatorial (used also as palpi), the anterior longest.

S. papillosa (Pl. 2. fig. 36; *a*, mandible). Body vermilion-coloured, broader in front, depressed, covered with short cylindrical papillæ rounded at the end.

Found upon the trunks of trees, and in moss.

Fusiform scales replace the papillæ upon the legs, palpi, and rostrum.

Several other species are found in moss, upon fallen leaves, and on the *débris* left after inundations.

BIBL. Dugès, *Ann. des Sc. Nat.* 2 sér. i. 16 & 34; Gervais, *Walckenaer's Apt.* iii. 173.

SMUT. See UREDO.

SNAILS, WATER-.—Most microscopic observers, ever anxious to determine the unknown cause of the curious circulation or rotation (ROTATION) taking place in certain water-plants, as *Vallisneria, Anacharis,* &c., keep these growing in large glass vessels, as confectioners' jars, or other reservoirs (Vivaria). These plants, and the sides of the vessels, are, however, very apt to become overgrown and obscured by Confervoid Algæ (as *Œdogonium*), Palmellaceæ, &c., which may be prevented by keeping water-snails in the water, as species of *Lymnœus, Physa, Bithynia, Planorbis,* &c. The latter are best for this purpose (the shell is flat-spiral). If Desmidiaceæ, Diatomaceæ, Infusoria, &c. are to be preserved, the snails must be carefully excluded, because many of these are consumed by them, and will not live, as the bottom of the vessels soon becomes covered, when snails are kept, with a load of excrement. The characters of the

2 s 2

snails are too long to be given here. The gelatinous masses of ova are found adhering to water plants.

See the *Bibl.* of MOLLUSCA.

SNOW.—The various forms presented by ice or crystallized water in the form of snow constitute beautiful although fugitive microscopic objects.

The crystals belong to the rhombohedric or hexagonal system. Several hundreds of forms have been observed, and many of them figured. Among them may be mentioned hexagonal or dodecahedral plates, hexagonal prisms, single, arranged in a stellate form, or terminated by rectangularly placed plates or secondary groups of needles, hexagonal pyramids, &c. The angles of these forms frequently constitute secondary centres, around which other similar or dissimilar forms are aggregated. By some authors these forms are regarded as skeleton crystals.

See also RED SNOW.

BIBL. Scoresby, *Account of the Arctic Regions*; Kämtz, *Meteorologie*; Glaisher, *Micr. Journ.* 1855. iii.; Naumann, *Elem. d. Mineralogie*.

SODA.—Kölliker recommends a solution of caustic soda, in preference to potash, for the resolution of some of the tissues into their component elements. We have been unable to detect any marked difference between the action of these two solutions; and the former has the disadvantage of lifting the stopper from the bottle by the crystallization of the carbonate formed, so that it is with difficulty preserved.

Pl. 6. fig. 15 represents the crystals of oxalate of soda; and fig. 19 those of the nitrate (UREA).

SODIUM, CHLORIDE OF, or common salt.—The crystals of this salt belong to the regular system. The most common form is the cube terminated by quadrangular pyramids or quadrangular pyramidal depressions, rectangular tables, &c. Schmidt endeavours to show that the primary form of the crystals is the octohedron, and that the cubes are twin octohedra. The crystals do not polarize light.

BIBL. Schmidt, *Entwurf ein. allg. Untersuch. &c.* p. 90, and the *Bibl.* of CHEMISTRY.

SŒMMERING, MIRROR OF.—INTRODUCTION, p. xix.

SOLORINA, Ach.—A genus of Parmeliaceous Lichens, intermediate between *Peltigera* and *Sticta*. *S. crocea* and *S. saccata* occur in mountainous districts.

SORITES, Ehr. = *Orbitolites*, Lamk. part. *S. orbiculus* (Pl. 18. figs. 16, 17) = *Orbitolites complanatus*, Lamk.

SOROSPORA, Hass.—A genus of Palmellaceæ (Confervoid Algæ) not clearly distinguished from *Glæocapsa* and *Protococcus*.

BIBL. Hassall, *Brit. Freshw. Algæ*, p. 309.

SORUS.—The name applied to the aggregation of sporanges of the FERNS; sometimes applied also to the groups of spores in the Florideous Algæ.

SPATHIDIUM, Duj.—A genus of Infusoria, of the family Leucophryina.

Char. Body oblong, thicker and rounded behind; thinner, broader, and obliquely truncate in front.

S. hyalinum (*Leucophrys spathula*, E.) (Pl. 24. figs. 75 & 76). Hyaline; anterior margin with irregularly arranged minute black points.

Ehrenberg figures a row of cilia at the anterior end of the body.

BIBL. Dujardin, *Infus.* p. 458.

SPERMATIA.—The minute corpuscles supposed to represent spermatozoids in the LICHENS (Pl. 29. figs. 3, 15, 16) and FUNGI (Pl. 20. figs. 2, 3, 4).

SPERMATOZOA or SPERMATOZOIDS OF ANIMALS.—The form of the spermatozoa varies in different animals (Pl. 41); but they usually consist of a rounded or oval body or head, to one end of which is appended a moveable filament. This is their form in man and in the Mammalia generally.

In Birds, the body is sometimes cylindrical, sometimes spiral or presenting a zigzag outline.

In Reptiles the body is usually cylindrical and straight, sometimes spiral; but in some of them the straight or slightly undulating terminal filament is surrounded by a spiral filament, which some observers have regarded as an undulating membrane (Undulating MEMBRANES).

In Fishes, the spermatozoa are usually very small, and the body round, although in some the body is spiral.

In the Invertebrata, a distinct body and terminal filament are present in some, whilst in others each spermatozoon represents a simple filament tapering at the ends. In some of these the body seems to exist in the form of a short cylinder or rod; in others the spermatozoa are represented by simple cells, or cells with radiating processes.

The curious filaments one of which is represented in Pl. 14. fig. 20, we found within the body of a *Cypris*. There were several together, in those containing as well as in those not containing ova, and they consisted of two spiral fibres. We have little doubt that they are spermatozoa; but they resist the action of a boiling solution of potash, which renders other spermatozoa invisible or dissolves them. They bear some resemblance to the elaters of *Trichia*.

The exact manner in which the spermatozoa are developed is not agreed upon.

According to Kölliker's observations, they are developed within cysts or (epithelial?) cells contained in the tubuli testis, or other form of seminal organs. A number of nuclei or globules arise within these, in each of which a spermatozoon is afterwards found lying coiled up. On the solution or rupture of the globules, the spermatozoa become free within the cysts. In some animals the spermatozoa are formed in bundles, the bodies and filaments lying parallel with and opposite each other.

According to Reichert and Quatrefages, the transparent and homogeneous spermatogenous masses undergo a process of segmentation analogous to that occurring in the ovum, reducing them to a granular state, the filaments being subsequently formed.

Most spermatozoa exhibit active movements produced by the action of the filament, whence they were formerly considered as independent living animals. This notion is now abandoned, the movements being undoubtedly comparable to those of the ciliated zoospores of the Algæ, or the ciliated epithelial cells of animals. They are much increased by the addition of solution of caustic potash.

In some animals tubular sheaths are secreted around the masses of spermatozoa whilst contained in the seminal apparatus, and called spermatophores. These, when discharged from the organ, are fixed by the male to the posterior end of the body of the female by means of a glutinous secretion.

The spermatozoa are the essential fertilizing elements of the liquid in which they are contained. See Ova.

Spermatozoa may be best examined and preserved by washing them with distilled water, and drying them upon a slide.

BIBL. Kölliker, *Mikrosk. Anat.* ii. 393; id. *Siebold and Kölliker's Zeitschr.* vii. 201; id. *Beitr. z. Kenntn. d. Geschlechtsverhältnisse, &c. d. wirbel. Thiere*; Siebold, *Vergl. Anat., passim*; Czermak, *Siebold und Kölli-*

ker's *Zeitschr.* ii.; Wagner, *Todd's Cycl. of Anat. &c.* iv., art. *Semen*; id., *Physiology, by Willis*; Leuckart, *Wagner's Handwörterb. d. Phys.* iv. 819; Beneden, *Anat. Comparée*; Dujardin, *Observ. au Microsc.*; and the *Bibl.* of Ovum.

SPERMATOZOIDS, or ANTHEROZOIDS.—The terms applied to the structures produced in the antheridia of the Cryptogamia, regarded as analogous to the spermatozoa of animals, and as the agents of fertilization of the germ-cell. In the Marsileaceæ, Lycopodiaceæ, Equisetaceæ, Ferns (Pl. 32. fig. 34), Mosses (Pl. 32. fig. 33), Hepaticæ (Pl. 32. fig. 32), and Characeæ (Pl. 32. fig. 31), they are ciliated spirally-coiled filaments, exhibiting very active spontaneous motion. In the Fucoïd Algæ, they are globular cells bearing two unequal cilia moving actively. In the Florideæ they are minute globular cells, and neither cilia nor movement have been certainly demonstrated. In the Lichens and Fungi the SPERMATIA (Pl. 20. fig. 4; Pl. 29. fig. 15) appear to represent the spermatozoids of the other classes, and they seem to be devoid of spontaneous movement. The details respecting these bodies are given under their respective classes.

BIBL. Thuret, *Ann. des Sc. Nat.* 3 sér. xiv. p. 214, and xvi. p. 5. See also under the families.

SPERMOGONIA.—The supposed antheridial structures of LICHENS (Pl. 29. figs. 2, 13, 16) and FUNGI (Pl. 20. figs. 1 and 4).

SPERMOSIRA, Kützing.—A genus of Nostochaceæ, growing in salt marshes, containing two British species; known from the other genera by the disk-shaped or lenticular cells; but the filaments are liable to be mistaken for a *Nostoc* in the young state.

1. *Spermosira litorea*, Kützing. Filaments 1-3600″ thick, straightish, æruginous; ordinary cells confluent, very short; sporangial cells at first green, depressed-spheroidal, 1-3600″ in diameter, granulate, fuscous when mature; vesicular cells transversely elliptical, not wider than the ordinary cells. Kützing, *Tab. Phyc.* vol. i. pl. 100. fig 3; Harvey, *Phyc. Brit.* pl. 93. fig. C, *Manual of Br. Algæ*, 2 ed. pl. 27 E. In muddy brackish ditches.

2. *S. Harveyana*, Thwaites. Filaments much curved; cells nearly as long as broad; sporangial cells exactly spherical, almost twice the diameter of the ordinary cells; vesicular cells subquadrate, rather longer

than wide, about as wide as the ordinary cells. Harvey, *Phyc. Brit.* pl. 173 C. In muddy brackish ditches.

BIBL. As above.

SPHACELARIA, Lyngb.—A genus of Ectocarpaceæ (Fucoid Algæ), containing a number of species, two of which, *S. scoparia* and *S. cirrhosa*, are common. They have jointed, rigid, distichously branched, feathery filamentous fronds, of an olive colour, a few inches high, and are especially characterized by the *sphacelæ* formed at the ends of the branches, which consist of an expanded terminal cell containing a granular mass. This structure appears to represent the antheridium of these plants; for Pringsheim has observed the conversion of the granular mass into one or more large free cells, the contents of which are after a time converted into ciliated spermatozoids, ultimately discharged through a tubular process breaking its way out at the side of the *sphacela*. The spores (or spore-sacs?) are borne at the sides of the branchlets, apparently on distinct plants.

BIBL. Harvey, *Brit. Mar. Alg.* p. 55, pl. 9 B; Pringsheim, *Bericht. Berlin. Akad.* March 1855.

SPHÆRIA, Hall.—A genus of Sphæriacei (Ascomycetous Fungi), now somewhat reduced from its ancient limits, but still containing a vast quantity of species, which it is impossible to treat satisfactorily within our limits. The forms vary chiefly in regard to the perithecia, which are sometimes only covered by a veil, and hence appear superficial on the matrix, while in other cases they are imbedded in the matrix, only evident externally by the black papilla, which is permanent, becoming indurated, and opening by a pore to discharge the spores in a fine powder. Many of the immersed kinds are only evident externally as minute black points or dots upon the surface of the leaf, stem, &c., which they infest; others are exposed freely when mature, breaking out from beneath the epidermis. Sometimes they are solitary, sometimes associated in small or large numbers, distinct or confluent. *S. quaternata* (fig. 646) is an example of the occurrence of free perithecia grouped together, mostly in fours; being decumbent, their ostioles are collected together, and they perforate the bark by a little black rugged tubercle. This is common on beech-trees. *S. convergens* (figs. 647, 648) is an analogous form. *S. elongata* (figs. 655–657) affords an example of those species which are at first

immersed and adnate, and finally burst forth and become nearly free.

Fig. 646.

Sphæria quaternata.
Three groups growing on a piece of beech-wood.
Magnified 20 diameters.

For species now separated from this genus see CLAVICEPS, HYPOXYLON, XYLARIA, HYPOCREA, and NECTRIA.

Certain points of great interest have lately been ascertained respecting this genus and its allies, which are mentioned under the heads of the family and other genera, namely

Fig. 647.   Fig. 648.

Sphæria convergens.
Magnified 20 diameters.

Fig. 649.

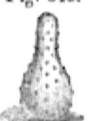

Sphæria verrucosa.
Magnified 20 diameters.

the coincidence and evident connexion between true species of *Sphæria* and various Coniomycetous Fungi; for just as *Melasmia* is a precursory form of *Dothidea*, *Tubercularia* of *Nectria*, &c., *Cytispora*, *Septoria*, and other forms precede *Sphæria*, and many distinct stylosporous forms are associated, usually described as belonging to distinct genera, such as *Stilbospora*, *Sporocadus*, *Sphæropsis*, &c. Thus these plants seem to produce three kinds of reproductive organs, as is now known to be the case with the Uredinei, viz.—1. a form analogous to the *spermogonia* of the Lichens (in *Sphæria* represented by *Cytispora*, &c.); 2. an ascophorous fruit, the perithecium of the true *Sphæria*; and 3. a stylosporous fruit, representing the genera *Stilbospora*, *Sporocadus*, &c.

S. Laburni has been found by Tulasne to

exhibit all these stages, namely perithecia containing asci, surrounding a cytispore, with other conceptacles on the same stroma resembling the perithecia, but lined with stylospores instead of asci. Berkeley and Broome also describe the existence of the perithecia of *Sphæria inquinans* and the conceptacles of *Stilbospora macrosperma* on the same stroma (Pl. 20. figs. 25–28).

It is stated by Tulasne that the 'spermatia' of the cytisporous forms may be contemporaneous with the stylospores or basidiospores, but they always precede the ascospores in their development; hence there is ground for supposing that they represent the spermatozoids of the higher Cryptogamia. With regard to the relations of the stylospores, it is possible that they are merely modifications of the ascospores; but it would appear probable that they must be regarded as real gonidial structures, for which it may be desirable to retain Fries's name of *conidia*, just as that of *tetraspores* is retained among the Florideous Algæ. Attention should be directed here to the complete correspondence between the series of forms of these genera and those of the UREDINEI, where, as in PUCCINIA, we have the *spermogonium* (cytispore), the *uredo* (stylosporous fruit), and the *perfect fruit* (perithecium). See also CONIOMYCETES.

Mr. Currey has recently published some extensive observations on the spores of the *Sphæriæ*.

BIBL. Berk. *Brit. Flor.* ii. pt. 2. p. 232; *Ann. Nat. Hist.* i. p. 205, vi. p. 360, 2 ser. v. p. 374, vii. p. 186; *Hook. Journ. Bot.* iii. p. 319; Fries, *Summa Veg.* p. 388, *Syst. Mycol.* ii. p. 319; Tulasne, *Ann. des Sc. Nat.* 3 sér. xv. p. 375 (*Ann. Nat. Hist.* 2 ser. viii. p. 117), 4 sér. v. p. 108, viii. p. 35; Currey, *Mic. Journ.* iii. 263 (1855), *Linnean Trans.* vol. xxii. p. 257.

SPHÆRIACEI.—A family of Ascomycetous Fungi, containing a vast number of parasitic plants, mostly of minute dimensions, growing upon leaves, stems, bark, wood, &c., and sometimes on the bodies of insects. The essential distinctive character lies in the globular, ovate, or flask-shaped conceptacle or *perithecium*, containing asci, which ultimately opens by a pore at its summit to discharge the spores. These perithecia occur either solitary or in groups on an indistinct matrix, growing out from the epidermis of leaves, &c. (*Sphæria*), or they are immersed in a tubercular stroma (*Nectria*), while in the larger forms the stroma

becomes developed into an erect clavate or bushy structure, of a fleshy or horny consistence, the perithecia being imbedded in the superficial layer of this, and opening by pores on the surface. Much remains to be done in reference to the history of this family, not merely on account of the polymorphous characters of the ascophorous forms, but from the circumstance that it has recently been shown, as was suspected before, that there is a relationship existing between them and the supposed genera of Coniomycetous Fungi of similar habit. These last are in fact mostly forms of Sphæriaceous Fungi, as is indicated under the heads CONIOMYCETES, ASCOMYCETES, DOTHIDEA, SPILÆRIA, CYTISPORA, SEPTORIA. Our treatment of this family is very imperfect, the knowledge of them being confined to few persons, and much of it lying scattered in fragments.

Synopsis of British Genera.

* Stroma erect.

1. *Clariceps.* Stroma simple, clavate; perithecia superficial, in a distinct layer at the summit of the clavate stroma; asci tubular, spores very long, multiseptate.

2. *Xylaria.* Stroma simple or branched; perithecia spread all over, often wanting at the summit, black; asci eight-spored, spores uniseptate.

3. *Thamnomyces.* Stroma branched, shrubby, or stalk-like; perithecia formed from the stroma, more or less naked; asci tubular; spores simple, ovate.

** Stroma between erect and horizontal.

4. *Poronia.* Stroma cup-shaped, stipitate or sessile, margined; perithecia in the disk, superficial; ostioles even slightly prominent.

*** Stroma horizontal.

5. *Hypocrea.* Stroma distinct from the matrix, tubercular; perithecia immersed; asci filiform; spores simple or uniseptate.

6. *Hypoxylon.* Stroma distinct from the matrix, at first covered with a floccose mealy veil; perithecia black; asci linear-clavate; spores subseptate, expelled in a cloud of black powder.

7. *Diatrype.* Stroma partly formed from the matrix, not distinct; perithecia deep-seated, produced into a long neck, and frequently a beak; spores simple and pellucid.

8. *Dothidea.* Perithecia indistinguishable from the stroma; asci collected into a glo-

bose nucleus with a neck above, leading to an ostiolate papilla.

Fig. 650.

Fig. 651.

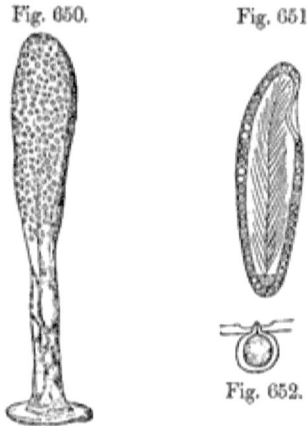

Fig. 652.

Xylaria guianensis.

Fig. 650. A stroma. Nat. size.
Fig. 651. Vertical section of the same. Nat. size.
Fig. 652. Section of a perithecium. Magnified 10 diameters.

Fig. 653.

Fig. 654.

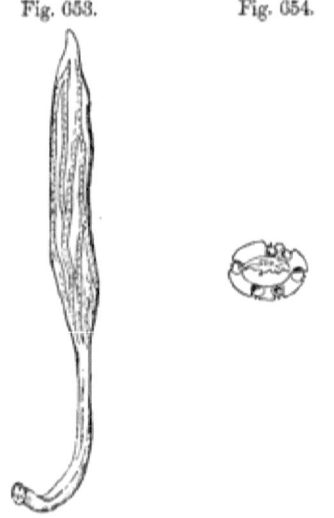

Xylaria grammica.

Fig. 653. Nat. size.
Fig. 654. Horizontal section. Magnified 5 diameters.

**** *Stroma wanting; the perithecia often seated on a tuberculose, crustaceous, byssoid, macular mycelium.*

9. *Nectria.* Perithecia free, membranous, flaccid, brightly coloured, with a pale papilla, nucleus pale ; asci eight-spored ; spores pellucid.

10. *Oomyces.* Perithecia erect, several contained in a shining sac, free towards the upper part ; ostiole punctiform ; asci linear ; spore filiform, very long.

11. *Sphæria.* Perithecia black, papilla covered by a veil or by the matrix, sometimes beaked, indurated, ostiolate, black ; asci usually eight-spored ; spores usually septate, discharged as a powder.

Fig. 657.

Fig. 655.

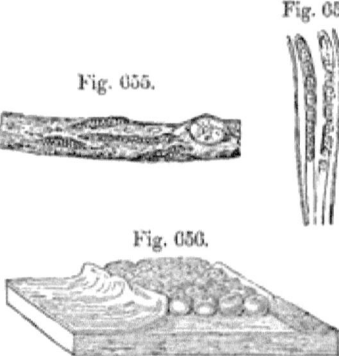

Fig. 656.

Sphæria elongata.

Fig. 655. Erumpent lines of perithecia. Nat. size.
Fig. 656. Portion of one in end view. Magnified 20 diameters.
Fig. 657. Asci and paraphyses from a perithecium. Magnified 200 diameters.

SPHÆROCARPUS, Kütz. = STAUROCARPUS.

SPHÆROCARPUS, Mich. — A genus of Ricciæ (Hepaticæ). *S. terrestris* (fig. 658) is a minute Liverwort growing on the ground, especially, it is said, in clover-fields. The fronds are from 1-4 to 1-2″ long, palish green, very thin and membranous, the lower surface adhering to the ground by radical hairs. The middle part of the upper surface bears a quantity of fruits, which consist at first of archegonia and antheridia, like those of other Liverworts, surrounded by a cup-like open perichæte (?), which gradually grows up over the fertilized archegonium and closes at the top, so as to form a pyriform sac, presenting an orifice at the summit. The archegonium ripens into a globular sporange, containing spores without elaters, crowned by a curious little styliform process. The spores are discharged by irregular rupture. The walls of the sporange are composed of simple parenchymatous cells, with-

Fig. 658.

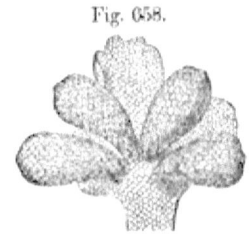

Sphærocarpus terrestris.

A frond with perichætes containing sporanges;
one cut open.

Magnified 10 diameters.

out spiral-fibrous layers. While the sporange is ripening, the perichæte enlarges into a loose, obconical, green, membranous sac, through the thin walls of which the globular sporange is visible (fig. 658).

BIBL. Hook. *Brit. Flor.* ii. pt. 1. p. 103; Bischoff, *Nova Acta*, xiii. p. 150; Lindenberg, *ibid.* xviii. p. 496; Fitt, *Hooker's Journ. of Bot.* vi. p. 287 (1847).

SPHÆROCOCCUS, Stackh.—A genus of Rhodymeniaceæ (Florideous Algæ), containing one British species, *S. coronopifolius*, having a flat, linear, distichously branched frond of crimson colour and cartilaginous texture, of fan-like outline; parenchymatous, with an internal denser rib and cortical layer; 6 to 12" long. The upper branches have their margins set with minute tooth-like processes, about 1-24" long, in some of which the spherical conceptacles are imbedded.

BIBL. Harv. *Brit. Mar. Alg.* p. 128, pl. 16 B; Greville, *Alg. Brit.* pl. 15.

SPHÆROIDINA, D'Orb.—A genus of Foraminifera, of the order Agathistegia, and family Multiloculidæ. See AGATHISTEGIA.

Not British.

S. austriaca (Pl. 42. fig. 9).

SPHÆROMPHALE.—A genus of Trypetheliæ (Angiocarpous Lichens), nearly related to *Verrucaria*.

SPHÆRONEMA, Fr. — A genus of Sphæronemei (Coniomycetous Fungi), characterized chiefly by the spores which emerge from the pore becoming glued together into a firm globule. The species which grow upon the surface of decaying plants are probably only forms belonging to Sphæriaceous genera.

BIBL. Berk. *Brit. Flor.* ii. pt. 2. p. 281; *Ann. Nat. Hist.* vi. p. 363, *ibid.* 2nd ser. v. p. 371; Fries, *Summa Veget.* 400.

SPHÆRONEMEI.—A family of minute Coniomycetous Fungi, growing on bark, or more or less dry stems or leaves, characterized by the conceptacle ordinarily bursting by a pore or *ostiole*, or a lid, to extrude, in most cases, a gelatinous ball of filaments mixed with spores. From recent observations it appears that the genera of this order do not consist of independent species, but are forms which occur in combination with Ascomycetous forms to complete the whole development of an individual,—the Sphæronemeous genera constituting the stylosporous or conidial fruits of Sphæriacei, &c., corresponding perhaps to the tetraspores found in the Florideous Algæ, which also possess proper spores (see SPHÆRIA).

Synopsis of British Genera.

1. *Coniothyrium.* Conceptacle free, membranous, opening by an irregular pore at the summit; spores globular.

2. *Leptostroma.* Conceptacle innate, subumbonate in the centre, dimidiate, at length falling off, leaving a very thin disk.

3. *Phoma.* Conceptacle ostiolate, very thin, innate, immersed, rounded, with a simple pore; spores oblong, simple.

4. *Leptothyrium.* Conceptacle operculate, innate, shield-shaped, not radiate-fibrous; spores spindle-shaped, simple.

5. *Actinothyrium.* Conceptacle operculate, innate, shield-shaped, radiate-fibrous; spores spindle-shaped, simple.

6. *Microthecium.* Conceptacle indehiscent, membranous, immersed, endophytic; spores simple.

7. *Cryptosporium.* Conceptacle membranous, opening irregularly at the summit; spores spindle-shaped, simple.

8. *Sphæronema.* Conceptacle horny, innate-superficial, more or less produced into a neck, ostiole simple; spores oblong, simple.

9. *Acrospermum.* Conceptacle leathery externally, fleshy within, elongate-clavate, ostiole simple; spores stick-shaped, simple.

10. *Diplodia.* Conceptacle horny, innate-superficial or immersed, perforated by a pore or irregularly opened or ostiolate, ostiole more or less produced; spores ovoid

or ellipsoid, double, then halved into compressed-ternate semi-ellipsoid sporules.

11. *Hendersonia.* Conceptacle fleshy, superficially innate or immersed, perforated by a pore, opening irregularly or ostiolate, ostiole more or less produced; spores globose, cylindrical, or discoid.

12. *Septoria.* Conceptacle horny, innate-immersed, rounded, ostiole simple; spores cylindrical, septate.

13. *Vermicularia.* Conceptacle bristly, depressed, bursting irregularly; spores minute, linear.

14. *Neottiospora.* Conceptacles immersed; spores appendaged at one end with short hyaline threads.

15. *Prosthemium.* Conceptacle horny, immersed, ostiole simple; spores transversely septate, verticillate at the apex of their filaments.

16. *Asteroma.* Conceptacle very small, slightly prominent, close, subconfluent, seated on more or less distinct radiating fibrils.

17. *Angiopoma.* Conceptacles free, membranous, somewhat horny, cup-shaped, dehiscing by a circular mouth, provided with a fugacious epiphragm; spores affixed at the base, stalked, septate.

18. *Discosia.* Conceptacles innate, somewhat carbonaceous, at length collapsed and plicate, ostiole perforated; spores fusiform, produced at both ends into a thread-like point.

19. *Piggotia.* Conceptacles very irregular, thin, obsolete beneath, confluent into a rugulose patch, bursting by an irregular crack; spores on short stalks, largish, obovate, somewhat constricted towards the base.

20. *Phlyctæna.* Conceptacle spurious, formed by the blackened epidermis; spores fusiform, cuspidate, septate, emerging accompanied by a gelatinous mass.

21. *Glœosporium.* Conceptacle absent; spores covered only by the cuticle, which separates; spores stalked, longish, elliptical, simple, exuding a gelatinous tendril.

22. *Dilophosphora.* Conceptacle immersed in a spurious stroma, covered, perforated by a pore; spores cylindrical, continuous, crowned at both ends with radiating filiform appendages.

23. *Sphæropsis.* Conceptacle spherical, immersed, subinnate, astomous, at length (by the separation of the epidermis) bursting by circumscissile dehiscence or irregularly. Spores simple.

SPHÆROPHOREÆ. — A family of Angiocarpous or closed-fruited Lichens, characterized by their apothecia formed in the swollen points of the thallus, bursting irregularly; containing the genus:

SPHÆROPHORON. — *Thallus* erect, shrubby, externally crustaceo-cartilaginous, internally solid and cottony. Apothecia terminal, spherical, the perithecium, formed of the thallus, closed, dehiscing irregularly. Nucleus globular, internally floccoso-cartilaginous, the discharged (black) sporidia crowded in the circumference.

1. *S. coralloides* (fig. 305. p. 418) is not uncommon on sand-rocks, among mosses.

2. *S. compactum* is less common. The *spermogonia* have only been discovered as yet in the latter; they occur at the ends of the more delicate branchlets of the thallus.

Bibl. Hook. *Brit. Flor.* ii. pt. 1. p. 236; Leighton, *Brit. Angioc. Lichens*; Tulasne, *Ann. des Sc. Nat.* 3 sér. xviii. p. 209, pl. 15.

SPHÆROPLEA, Ag.—A genus of Confervaceæ of uncertain position, but probably allied to the Chætophoraceæ. It is characterized chiefly by the formation of the spores. The plants consist of simple jointed filaments with long articulations, at first containing green colouring matter excavated by large vacuoles, producing a banded appearance (Pl. 5. fig. 14 *a*), the contents finally resolving themselves in the fertile cells into numerous spinulose globular spores' arranged in longitudinal rows (*b*), which become red when ripe.

The development of the spores of *S. annulina* has been observed by several authors; and Cohn has recently published an account of the formation of spermatozoids in distinct cells, exercising a fertilizing function. The filaments (which always terminate in pointed hair-like ends) present, when actively vegetating, the excavated or banded appearance of the green contents above noticed; the vacuoles separating the bands have a proper, colourless, mucilaginous coat. When about to produce spores the regularity of the bands vanishes, the vacuoles multiply in number in the substance of the bands, and the contents present the appearance of a green *froth* with starch-granules scattered through it. After a time a number of green corpuscles (the spores) appear in the median line of the cell; these assume a stellate shape, with radiating threads of protoplasm connecting them together; they soon appear in pairs, separated by transverse false septa formed by the flattened vesicles of the vacuoles. The spores gradually become better defined, and the false septa disappear; then the young spores present themselves as globular bodies, devoid at this time of a cellulose coat. From two to six minute orifices are perceptible at this time in the partially softened wall of the parent cell. While these phænomena are occurring in some of the cells, a different change takes place in others. The green bands assume a reddish-yellow colour, their starch disappears, and they are gradually converted into myriads of short stick-shaped bodies, which break apart and "swarm" in vast numbers, filling the whole cell, moving actively in all directions. The gelatinous coat of some of the vacuoles sometimes remains intact; and these then lie free in the cavity of the cell, and are often carried about by the rapid motion of the corpuscles. Orifices are meanwhile formed in these cells also, through which the stick-shaped bodies (spermatozoids) escape into the water. Their length is about 1-3000″. Their hinder end now appears somewhat swollen, and they bear two long cilia on the pointed beak—in fact resembling the *microgonidia* of the other Confervoids. Cohn states he has seen them accumulate around the orifices of the spore-cells, enter into the cavities of these, and swarm about in the interior, in considerable numbers, at length adhering to the young spores. The spores then acquire a membrane, and under this a second, which is at first smooth, but afterwards presents a spinulose or stellate appearance; the first coat is then thrown off, and a third, smooth coat appears under the stellate coat, closely investing the contents. These conditions resemble those of the spores of SPIROGYRA and other Confervoids; *Spirogyra*, however, retains the outer coat until germination. The green contents of the spores ultimately turn red. Their size and number in a cell vary much.

Cohn has also observed the germination of these spores, which is interesting in several respects. Their ordinary size is from 1-1200 to 1-1500″; and they present, as above mentioned, two coats, the outer elegantly marked; most authors describe it as stellate; Kützing asserts that it is spirally folded. The real fact is, that it is plaited in the direction of 'meridians' from pole to pole, and thus appears stellate when seen at either pole, marked with lines when seen sideways. The spores do not appear to germinate until the spring following their production. The red contents begin to assume a green colour from the surface inwards,

divide into two, then into four or eight portions, which break out from the spore-cell, and swim about as free biciliated zoospores, of globular or shortly cylindrical form, from 1-2280 to 1-1680″ long, either bright red or particoloured red and green, the point bearing the cilia, however, always colourless. After a time they become coated with a cellulose membrane, cease to move, and grow into a spindle-shaped body, the ends prolonged into hair-like points. The growth appears to be always in the middle, the hair-like points remaining; thus the spindle-shape is retained until the length reaches 1-24″ or more, and the first septum appears in the middle of the filament.

S. annulina (Pl. 5. fig. 14) appears to be the only well-known form. It is a rare Conferva, growing on flooded fields; it does not seem to have been recorded in Britain.

For *Sph. crispa* and *punctata*, see ULOTHRIX.

BIBL. Kütz. *Sp. Alg.* p. 302, *Tab. Phyc.* iii. pl. 31; A. Braun, *Verjüngung, &c.* (*Ray Soc. Vol.* 1853, p. 105); Cohn, *Bericht. Berlin. Akad.* May 1855; *Ann. des Sc. Nat.* 4 sér. v. p. 187; *Ann. Nat. Hist.* 2 sér. viii. p. 81; Cienkowski, *Bot. Zeit.* xiii. p. 777.

SPHÆROPSIS, Lév.—A genus of Sphæronemei (Coniomycetous Fungi), growing upon stems, &c., apparently only stylosporous forms of Sphæriaceous genera.

BIBL. Fries, *Summa Veget.* p. 419; Tulasne, *Ann. des Sc. Nat.* 4 sér. v. p. 115.

SPHÆROSIRA, Ehr. See VOLVOX.

SPHÆROZOSMA, Corda.—A genus of Desmidiaceæ.

Char. Filamentous; filaments flat, fragile, their component cells closely united by means of minute (glandular) processes, and deeply divided on each side into two segments.

1. *S. vertebratum* (Pl. 10. fig. 9, front view; fig. 10, side view). Cells about as long as broad; connecting processes oblique, one on each side. Length of cell 1-1430″.

Not uncommon.

2. *S. excavatum.* Cells longer than broad; connecting processes sessile, two on each side. Length of cell 1-2570″.

After separation the cells conjugate; sporangia elliptical.

BIBL. Ralfs, *Brit. Desmid.* p. 65.

SPHÆROZYGA, Agardh (*Anabaina*, Bory, Brébisson).—A genus of Nostochaceæ, differing from the allied genera only in the microscopic characters of the filaments, the sporangial cells being separated by vesicular cells. As the sporangial cells are developed from the ordinary cells, and this gradually, the vesicular cell will appear at certain epochs to have a sporangial cell on one side and an ordinary cell on the other; but this arises merely from the fact that the sporangial cells are developed singly and successively, first one on one side of the vesicular cell and then one on the other, and so on, to whatever number of adjacent sporangial cells there may be developed on either side of the vesicular cell; and those nearest the latter will therefore always be the largest, until the whole have acquired the full size. Ralfs describes seven British species.

* Filaments moniliform: sporangia elongated, not turgid.

1. *S. Carmichaelii*, Harvey. — Filaments with tapering extremities; ordinary joints distinct, subquadrate; sporangial cells oblong; vesicular cells spherical.—Ralfs, *Ann. Nat. Hist.* 2 ser. v. pl. 8. fig. 7; Harvey, *Phyc. Brit.* pl. 113 A; *Brit. Mar. Algæ,* 2nd ed. pl. 27. fig. D.

Belonia torulosa, Carmichael; *Sphærozyga compacta,* Kützing, *Phyc. Generalis. Anabaina marina,* Brébisson; *Cylindrospermum Carmichaelii,* Kützing, *Sp. Alg.* 204, *Tab. Phyc.* i. pl. 90.

Var. *tenuissima,* with very slender filaments. Forming a tender, very thin stratum of a dark or bluish-green colour, on the damp soil of salt-marshes flooded at springtides, more rarely in brackish ditches or upon decaying marine Algæ.

The best distinctive marks of this species are the " subacute extremities combined with the short filament and littoral habit."

2. *S. Jacobi,* Agardh. — Filaments elongated, their ends usually attenuated; ordinary cells subspherical; vesicular cells spherical; sporangial cells oblong or cylindrical. —Ralfs, *l. c.* pl. 8. fig. 8; *Eng. Bot.* 2826. fig. 2. Forming thick, bluish-green, gelatinous masses, from which the filaments issue in long rays. Fresh water.

3. *S. elastica,* Agardh.—Dissepiments conspicuous; ordinary cells quadrate; vesicular cells elliptic; sporangial cells cylindrical, truncate.—Ralfs, *l. c.* pl. 8. fig. 9. *Cylindrospermum elongatum,* Kütz. *Tab. Phyc.* i. pl. 90. fig. 3. Forming a tender stratum, of a deep bluish colour, in bogs.

** Filaments moniliform; sporangia turgid, much broader than the ordinary cells.

4. *S. Broomei,* Thwaites.—Filaments elongated; ordinary cells suborbicular; vesicular cells barrel-shaped or elliptic; sporangial cells elliptic, catenate.—Ralfs, *l. c.* pl. 7. fig. 10. Forming a firmish bluish- or yellowish-green stratum in brackish ditches.

5. *S. Berkeleyana,* Thwaites.—Ordinary cells spherical or slightly compressed; vesicular cells spheroidal, compressed, as broad as the large, turgid-elliptic, sporangial cells. —Ralfs, *l. c.* pl. 8. fig. 11. In brackish ditches.

6. *S. Mooreana,* Ralfs.— Ordinary cells subspherical; vesicular cells barrel-shaped, much narrower than the large, broadly elliptical sporangial cells.—Ralfs, *l. c.* pl. 8. fig. 12. An Irish species.

*** Dissepiments obscure; cells longer than broad.

7. *S. leptosperma* (Kützing).—Filaments elongated, not constricted at the dissepiments; ordinary cells longer than broad, confluent; vesicular cells elliptic; sporangial cells linear.—Ralfs, *l. c.* pl. 8. fig. 13. *Cylindrospermum leptospermum,* Kützing, *Tab. Phyc.* i. pl. 90. fig. 2. Forming large shapeless gelatinous masses in still waters, varying from deep green to yellowish green, or, when the filaments are comparatively few, nearly colourless. Distinguished especially by the "confluent ordinary cells with obscure dissepiments."

BIBL. As above.

SPHAGNACEÆ.—A family of Cladocarpous Mosses, of peculiar habit, growing on bogs, &c., distinguished especially by the mode of branching, the structure of the leaves, sporanges, and antheridia, and by the absence of roots, except in the early stages of growth.

The stem of the *Sphagna* is composed of three layers of cells,—a cortical, a medullary, and a prosenchymatous layer intermediate, which finally becomes somewhat woody. The primary axis is indefinite in its growth; the lateral axes, sterile or fertile, are annual. The secondary axes are fasciculate, and being pendent or recurved upon the stem, they fulfil in some measure the function of roots. The leaves are remarkable for the cellular structure, being composed of two kinds of cells, namely, narrow and elongated cells filled with chlorophyll, conjoined into a kind of network, the meshes of which are occupied by large hyaline cells. The hyaline cells contain, in all but one exotic species, a spiral or annular secondary deposit (Pl. 39. fig. 25) characteristic of this family. These large cells also become opened by regular circular pores at a certain stage of growth.

The inflorescence is monœcious or diœcious. The antheridia are produced singly in the axils of perigonial leaves at the club-shaped tips of short branches. They are pedicellate and roundish, like those of the Liverworts; they produce biciliated spermatozoids. The archegonia are found about four together, sessile, in a tuft of perichætial leaves occupying the axis of a fascicle of branches; the receptacle subsequently elongating into a peduncle, bearing a globular capsule, entirely surrounded by the calyptra; the calyptra is ruptured near the middle, the lower part persistent and continuous with the fleshy vaginule, within which the capsule is seated on a bulb-like pedicel; peristome none; operculum flattish, thrown off with elasticity. Spore-sac wanting; columella short, not reaching the mouth of the capsule. Spores apparently of two kinds, some enclosed four together in parent cells, others smaller, sixteen in one mother cell; the former fertile, the latter sterile, occurring either together or in distinct capsules.

British Genus.

Sphagnum, Dill. Character that of the order. Nine species occur in Britain, some common on every bog, distinguished by their brilliant yellow-green colour and the wet, spongy character of the beds they form. The leaves are very interesting microscopic objects.

BIBL. Wilson, *Bryologia Brit.* p. 14; Schimper, *Ann. des Sc. Nat.* 4 sér. i. p. 313.

SPHAGNOCETIS, Nees.—A genus of Jungermannieæ (Hepaticæ), containing one species, *S. (Jung.) Sphagni*, an elegant little plant growing over *Sphagnum* and other mosses on bogs; attaching itself by long radicles, numerous on the under side of the procumbent, nearly simple stem. The gemmiferous branches only have amphigastria.

BIBL. Hook. *Brit. Flor* ii. pt. 1. p. 113; *Brit. Jung.* pl. 33, and Suppl. pl. 2; Ekart, *Syn. Jung.* pl. 6. figs. 43 & 48.

SPHENELLA, Kütz.—A genus of Diatomaceæ.

This genus appears to consist of the detached frustules of *Gomphonema*.

Kützing describes seven species.

S. vulgaris (Pl. 14. fig. 19).

BIBL. Kützing, *Bacill.* 83, and *Sp. Alg.* 62.

SPHENOSIRA, Ehr., Kütz.—A genus of freshwater Diatomaceæ. DIATOMACEÆ, § 41, p. 224.

S. catena (Pl. 13. fig. 26). Not British?

BIBL. Kützing, *Sp. Alg.* 68.

SPHINCTOCYSTIS, Hass. (*Cymatopleura*, Sm.). A genus of Diatomaceæ.

Char. Frustules free, single; in front view linear, with undulate margins; valves oblong or elliptical, sometimes constricted in the middle. Aquatic.

Valves with coarse, transverse or nearly transverse, rounded elevations appearing as dark bands, an interrupted median line, coarse marginal dots and transverse striæ, but neither alæ nor nodules.

Five British species.

1. *S. solea* (Pl. 12. fig. 23). Valves linear-elliptic, narrowed on each side towards the middle, transverse striæ evident; extreme length 1-216″.

Undulations six. Common.

β. Much shorter, undulations four, ends apiculate.

2. *S. elliptica* (Pl. 12. fig. 24). Valves broadly elliptic or elliptic-oblong, striæ obscure, undulations four or five; length 1-280″.

Common.

3. *S. hibernica.* Valves broadly elliptic, acuminate, undulations three; length 1-250″.

BIBL. Hassall, *Brit. Freshw. Algæ*, 436; Smith, *Brit. Diat.* i. 36; Kützing, *Sp. Alg.*

SPHINCTRINA.—A genus of Calycieæ (Gymnocarpous Lichens), with their stalk-like excipula and scarcely distinguishable thallus, growing on leaves or on other Lichens.

BIBL. Leighton, *Ann. Nat. Hist.* 2 ser. xix. p. 132.

SPICULA (plural of *spiculum*).—In some of the Invertebrata, firmness is given to the body by a rudimentary external skeleton consisting of a number of curiously shaped microscopic bodies, many of which are of a needle-like form, often containing a cavity, and denominated spicula. They are met with in endless variety of form in sponges (Pl. 37, the lettered objects), where they usually consist of silex. They also occur in the Echinodermata (Pl. 37. figs. 1 *h, i, k, l*, and 19 *a, b, c*), the Foraminifera (Pl. 18. fig. 24), and in the Mollusca, in these instances being calcareous.

There can scarcely be doubt that spicula

are homologous with the elements of shell; but little or nothing is known of their development.

Spicula form very interesting microscopic objects, on account of their remarkable forms.

To prepare them, the animal substance in which they are contained should be boiled with nitric acid if they are composed of silex, and with dilute solution of potash if they consist of lime-salts. They may be preserved by mounting in Canada balsam.

They are commonly met with in sea-mud.

SPIDERS. See ARACHNIDA and ARANEIDA, and for Red Spider, GAMASUS.

SPILOCÆA, Fr.—A genus of Torulacei (Coniomycetous Fungi). *S. Pomi* occurs upon apples, in contiguous effused patches, from which the epidermis separates in fragments, exposing the simple globular spores, adherent to each other and to the matrix.

BIBL. Berk. *Brit. Flor.* ii. pt. 2. p. 360; Fries, *Summa Veget.* p. 482.

SPINES OF ANIMALS.—These are properly stout rigid and pointed processes of the integument, formed externally by the epidermis, and internally of a portion of the cutis or corresponding structure; but the term is frequently applied to stout rigid and pointed processes of the epidermis only.

See HAIRS, and the notices of the structure of the integument under the heads of the various classes.

SPIRACLES or STIGMATA of animals. —The external orifices of the tracheæ of Insects and Arachnida. The respiratory tubes of these animals have no communication with the mouth, but terminate externally in orifices situated upon the surface of the thorax or abdomen. These are mostly rounded or elliptical (Pl. 28. figs. 3, 7, 8, and 9 *a*), sometimes in the form of small clefts, and are often furnished with a kind of moveable valve, or bounded by a thickened rim; sometimes a sieve-like structure (Pl. 27 fig. 34) prevents the admission of foreign bodies, or they are surrounded by hairs or scales effecting the same purpose.

They are often situated at the lateral and upper portions of the abdomen, at the posterior, lateral, and upper part of the thorax, &c.

See ARACHNIDA, INSECTS, and the heads of the genera.

SPIRAL STRUCTURES OF PLANTS.— Among the most elegant of the microscopic objects furnished by the Vegetable Kingdom are the various forms of the secondary deposits upon the walls of cells, vessels, and ducts, &c., which present the appearance of fibres coiled into perfect spirals, or of spiral fibres either with the coils detached and forming rings, or with the coils more or less connected by cross-pieces, producing a reticulated structure.

Under the head of SECONDARY DEPOSITS it is stated that this spiral-fibrous deposit may be taken as the character of a group of structures to be contrasted with those structures described as PITTED, and that the essential distinction in the nature of these two groups lies in the greater extent to which the primary wall is covered in the pitted structures. This is not quite absolute in reference to all spiral-fibrous structures, as in the true unrollable spiral vessels and similar organs the coils of the spiral fibres are often closely in contact, although not adherent to each other. It has been stated that the various forms of the open spiral, annular, and reticulated deposits are modifications of the simple close spiral; but this must be understood only in a morphological sense, since there is no actual change of condition ensuing with age, as has been assumed by some authors, the fibrous layers being always originally deposited on the primary wall in the form and pattern which they ultimately possess. There appears to be no real opening of the spirals or breaking up into rings, in consequence of the expansion of the primary wall to which they are attached.

It will be convenient, in the first place, to speak of the distinct well-marked structures ordinarily known as spiral cells and vessels, occurring in the stems, leaves, &c. of the higher plants, before describing certain other forms found in special organs, and to reserve to the end some points relating to the ultimate constitution of the secondary membranes of cells. Spiral structures are usually divided into *true spiral, annular, reticulated,* and *scalariform* organs.

Spiral cells and vessels are perhaps the most generally diffused of the forms. The name spiral vessel is given to elongated cylindrical cells tapering to a point at both ends, with a spiral-fibrous deposit lining the primary wall (fig. 650, and Pl. 30. figs. 8, 11, 12); the spiral fibre may be either single, as is most common, double (fig. 659); or a number of fibres may run parallel (*Musa, Nepenthes, Zingiberaceæ, Marantaceæ*).

These spiral vessels occur as the first vascular formation outside the pith (MEDULLARY SHEATH) in almost all the Dicotyledons (fig. 660), and as the first vascular forma-

Fig. 659.　　　　　　　　Fig. 660.

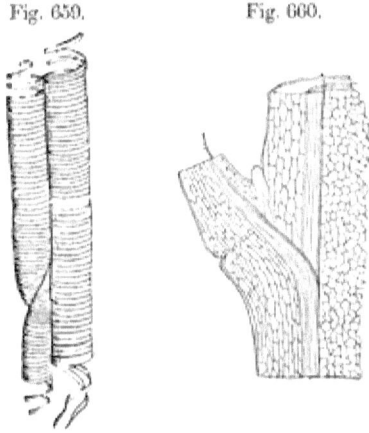

tion in the vascular bundles of the stems of Monocotyledons; also of all other vascular bundles, forming the ribs or veins of petioles, leaves, bracts, sepals, petals, &c. In the internal organs they can only be observed in sections, or when extracted by maceration; in delicate vessels and petals they may often be observed through the transparent epidermis. The coiled spiral fibre is mostly elastic enough to bear stretching open like a wire spring; in this case the primary wall is torn between the coils, and its ragged edges may sometimes be detected. The uncoiled fibres are often seen still unbroken when a hyacinth or similar leaf is broken across and the pieces gently drawn apart. *Annular* vessels closely resemble the preceding, except that the fibrous deposits are in the form of detached rings (fig. 661); they are the rarest forms; they are especially remarkable in the Equisetaceæ. The *reticulated*, again, have irregular spiral coils or rings connected more or less by perpendicular or oblique bars (fig. 662, and Pl. 39. fig. 9) into a network; these two modifications are usually of larger

diameter than the true spiral vessel, and the reticulated larger (also of later origin in the organs) than the annular. However, mixed forms occur not uncommonly, partly annular, partly spiral or reticulated (fig. 663).

Fig. 661.　　　Fig. 662.　　　Fig. 663.

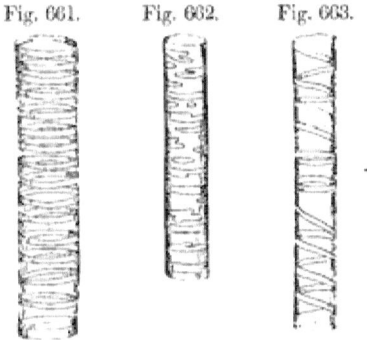

They are found in similar situations, but generally do not extend into the more delicate organs. Spiral, annular, and reticulated vessels may be prepared in most beautiful forms and large size from portions of the leaf-stalk of rhubarb, of the stem of the garden balsam, the melon, &c.

Spiral and other vessels are usually simple at first (branched *spiral* vessels do occur, more rarely), but ordinarily unite together by a kind of fusion; the conical extremities overlap to a certain extent (fig. 659), and thus the articulation is more or less oblique. This fusion is much more evident and complicated in roots, rhizomes, and abbreviated stems, than in stems with developed internodes. The elementary cells are then generally much shorter, and the vessels formed from them branch out in various directions through the tissue. This is very well seen in the roots of many herbaceous plants, such as the dandelion, chicory, &c., and at the point of origin of the vascular bundles of adventitious roots generally.

The above-mentioned confluent spiral vessels pass insensibly into the *ducts*, which are similar confluent rows of cells forming parts of the solid wood of stems, composed of cells with flat ends applied together. They may resemble in their markings the preceding forms, but in their varied conditions form a series leading towards the PITTED DUCTS. The *scalariform* vessels or ducts (fig. 664, and Pl. 39. fig. 10), so called from the ladder-like markings, are a very regular form of the reticulated type; this regularity appearing to depend, however, upon the relation between the markings of the adjacent organs. In the PITTED DUCTS we find the pits only opposite to other pits, therefore on the sides adjacent to other ducts or to cells; in the scalariform ducts a spiral-fibrous deposit is conjoined into a network by vertical fibres placed opposite the intercellular passages or the meeting angles of contiguous cells or ducts, leaving regular slit-like spaces opposite the cavities of the adjacent cells. This form is especially characteristic of the Ferns; but it occurs also commonly in the Dicotyledons in a less regular form, passing quite insensibly into PITTED DUCTS, as in the wood of *Eryngium maritimum* (Pl. 39. fig. 21). The scalariform vessels of Ferns are often slightly unrollable.

Fig. 664.

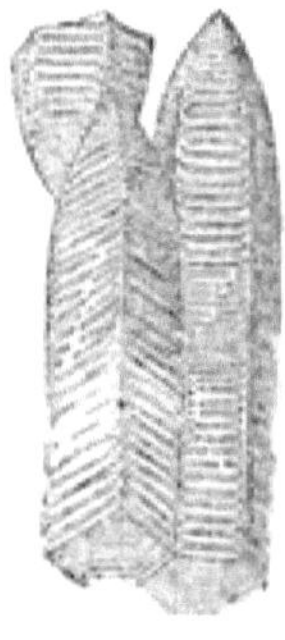

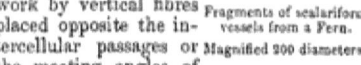

Fragments of scalariform vessels from a Fern. Magnified 200 diameters.

It is mentioned under PITTED STRUCTURES, also, that a combination of the two types sometimes occurs in the same cell. This is the case in the ducts of the Lime, Mezereon, and other plants (Pl. 39. figs. 4, 13, & 19).

Besides the generally-diffused spiral and other vessels and ducts above described, cells, properly so called, that is, such as never become elongated very greatly in one particular direction, belonging to particular organs and plants, present the same kind of markings. The ducts and vessels, indeed, in many cases are formed of very short cellular elements; but these may be distinguished from proper cellular tissue characterized by spiral secondary deposits. Under this head may be cited first certain *wood-cells*. In the Cactaceæ, the prosenchymatous tissue of the stem presents remarkable spiral and annular cells, in which the fibre becomes so much thickened that it projects like a riband set with its edge against the

cell-wall (Pl. 39. fig. 7). The wood of the Misletoe (figs. 665, 666) also exhibits spiral-fibrous cells; that of the Yew (TAXUS) is composed of true spiral-fibrous cells and others with bordered PITS and an internal spiral-fibre in addition (Pl. 39. fig. 4). In the stems of the Leguminosæ, parenchymatous portions occur in the midst of the wood, the cells of which exhibit spiral fibres (*Ulex, Spartium*). The cellular tissue near the surface of the roots of the epiphytic Orchids (Pl. 39. fig. 6) affords another example, as also some of the subepidermal cells of the leaves (fig. 667). The layers of

Fig. 665.   Fig. 666.   Fig. 667.

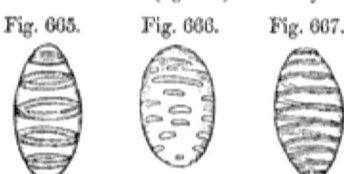

Fig. 665. Annular-fibrous cell from the stem of Misletoe. Magnified 200 diameters.

Fig. 666. Cell intermediate between reticulated and pitted, from the Misletoe. Magnified 200 diameters.

Fig. 667. Spiral-fibrous cell from the leaf of an Orchid. Magnified 200 diameters.

cells lining the ANTHERS of Flowering plants are characterized by most varied patterns of spiral markings (Pl. 32. figs. 1–5); in these cells, moreover, we sometimes see the connexion between the fibrous and homogeneous deposits well illustrated, as the cells may have one or more sides marked with spiral fibres, while the remainder of the wall is covered with a continuous layer. A similar structure, generally with perfect spiral fibres, occurs in the walls of the sporanges of *Jungermannia, Marchantia* (Pl. 32. fig. 35), and other Liverworts. With these are nearly connected the structures called ELATERS, which are found mixed with the spores in the same plants. These are tubular cells containing a single or double elastic spiral fibre (Pl. 32. figs. 36–38), exactly analogous to the spiral vessel in structure. Elaters of similar nature occur even among the Fungi, as in the sporange of TRICHIA (Pl. 32. figs. 39, 40). The elaters of the Equisetaceæ (fig. 205, p. 265) are of different character, consisting of four short filaments with clavate ends, attached at one side of the spore and originally coiled round it, ultimately unrolling with elasticity. They appear to be formed by the deposition of a spiral-fibrous layer on the wall of the parent cell of the spore, within which the true (single) spore-membrane is formed, unadherent; and when the spore is ripe, the spiral-fibrous layer splits up and starts away from the inner coat. An elegant spiral and annular fibrous structure is also met with in the large cells of the leaves of the SPHAGNACEÆ (Pl. 39. fig. 25); this is exactly analogous to the similar deposits in the higher plants. Spiral layers are found, less distinctly, in the radical hairs growing from the lower surface of the frond of MARCHANTIA. Nägeli regards them as folds of an inner layer of membrane; but they appear to be regular secondary deposits.

Lastly, the hairs and similar epidermal appendages sometimes exhibit spiral-fibrous deposits. An unrollable spiral fibre is beautifully arranged in the cells forming the mealy coating of the seed of Cobœa scandens (Pl. 21. fig. 20). The seeds of many of the Acanthaceæ (Pl. 21. figs. 21 & 24), Collomia (Pl. 21. fig. 22), the pericarp of some of the Labiatæ (Pl. 21. fig. 23) and Compositæ (SENECIO) bear tubular hairs, consisting of cells with a spiral or annular fibre in their interior (see HAIRS of Plants). The structure of the hairs of Collomia, Ruellia, &c. has been much discussed, but it seems very simple: they appear to consist of a short tubular cell, upon the wall of which a closely coiled elastic spiral-fibrous layer is deposited; during the ripening of the seed the primary membrane undergoes a metamorphosis into a substance related to amyloid (or bassorin?), which softens and swells up when placed in water, allowing the spiral fibre to extend itself (Pl. 21. figs. 21, 22 b, c). Sulphuric acid and iodine give the swollen gum-like envelope a purplish tint.

Another and less distinctly marked spiral arrangement of the substance of the cell-walls occurs in the form of cracks or gaps in certain of the layers of the secondary deposits, running more or less round the cell, appearing like irregular spiral streaks; these are sometimes present in the earlier secondary layers and not in the later, so that the "cracks" are covered in by the latter and converted into canals in the substance of the cell-wall. These occur in the wood-cells of Hernandia sonora, in the prosenchymatous cells of the vascular bundles of Caryota urens, Phœnix, Metroxylon, and probably in other cases. Something similar may be detected in the wood-cells of Pinus

(Pl. 39. fig. 1), especially after treatment with boiling nitric acid. In liber-cells a spiral texture is far more generally evident. In Vinca, for instance (Pl. 39. fig. 30), and other Apocynaceous plants, a delicate spiral striation of the wall is evident in its natural state, beautifully regular in its arrangement; a similar appearance may often be detected in the walls of thickened hairs, especially when acids are applied, as in Cotton (Pl. 21. fig. 1 b), particularly in gun-cotton (fig. 1 c); sometimes with intermediate slits, as in Urtica (Pl. 21. fig. 8), &c.; and by boiling with nitric acid, a minute spiral-fibrous structure may be detected in the secondary layers of the liber-cells of very many plants, as of Flax (Pl. 21. fig. 2 b, c), Coir (Pl. 21. fig. 5 a, b), Bœhmeria (Pl. 21. fig. 2 b, c), &c. All these spiral structures belong to the secondary deposits of the cells; they are mostly distinguishable from those previously described by being thinner places or lines left bare, instead of being lines of deposit.

We have observed a somewhat similar spiral streaking of the walls of Hydrodictyon, depending on slits in certain of the laminæ. Some of the genera of Oscillatorineæ, as Ainactis (Pl. 4. fig. 15 b) and Schizosiphon (Pl. 4. fig. 13 d, e), also present a spiral-fibrous decomposition of their cellulose coats when old; and we have seen a spiral marking on the wall of Cladophora, as described by Mitscherlich. Agardh has recently stated that he detected a complicated spiral-fibrous structure in the cell-wall of Confervæ, extending, however, from one cell to another; and he regards this as a proof of the spiral structure of primary cell-membrane generally; and he says he has likewise detected an analogous spiral-fibrous structure in the primary cell-wall of the structures of the Phanerogamia. With regard to the fibrillous structure of the walls of the Confervoids, this appears comparable with that we have described in the liber-cells, especially of Vinca; and apparently a delicate spiral structure of this kind exists in all cell-membranes which have received thickening layers; but in reference to the coarse interlaced fibrils figured by Agardh, we believe there is an error of observation. If cells of the fruit of the white snow-berry (Symphoricarpus) are allowed to dry upon a slide, they fall into minute creases, often running spirally; if boiled in nitric acid, they are cleared of adhering protoplasm, &c., and minute creases or folds of the same

2 T

kind are produced in greater abundance; but a very careful examination and observation of the *ends* of the folds, their irregular directions, &c., and especially when coloured with iodine, has convinced us that in this case no real spiral structure exists, although at first sight the appearance is very deceptive. These fine folds must not be confounded with the delicate striation above alluded to. This striation, however, existing as it does so generally, raises an interesting question as to whether the *secondary membranes* are always composed of delicate fibrils. Crüger asserts that they are, and declares that he has resolved every form of secondary deposit into primitive fibrils, in liber-cells, wood-cells, parenchymatous cells, pitted cells, and also the large fibres of the spiral vessels, &c., the broken ends of which he represents as split up into a kind of brush of fibrils; these however cannot be isolated so as to trace their course; and the most we can say is that the membrane often tears most readily in the direction of the striæ; and in some liber-cells, moreover, the secondary deposits tear readily into perpendicular fibrils after maceration (Pl. 21. fig. 26 c). The delicate striation of the membranes of the Confervæ and slightly thickened liber- or parenchyma-cells of many Flowering plants form a desirable object of investigation for those accustomed to the delicate observation of the markings of the valves of the Diatomaceæ. The use of reagents, such as nitric acid and solution of potash, boiling, maceration, and other means must be employed for this purpose, controlled always by a careful observation of the structures in their natural state and in different stages of development. It is not impossible that all secondary deposits may prove, as Meyen assumed, to have a fibrous constitution, and true *membrane* to be confined to the primary walls. One set of layers, however, seem always to resist the endeavour to resolve them into fibrils, namely those of the horny and fleshy ALBUMEN of seeds.

As to the mode of the formation of spiral secondary deposits, little is certainly known at present. Crüger attributes them to spiral circulation of the secreting protoplasm over the cell-wall in the position of the future fibres. We believe this to be a somewhat speculative notion. Others have asserted that they are formed by gradual collocation of visible granules; this is certainly an error. We have observed the gradual formation of the spiral band in the elater of *Marchantia*, where it is at first a faint spiral trace with indistinct edges; as it grows thicker, the edges become more and more defined, and it is produced originally in the exact position and pattern which it subsequently retains. Trécul has lately published an elaborate memoir, reviving an old notion that the spiral and other fibrous markings are folds of membrane thrown inwards from the cell-wall. We believe this to be altogether a misconception.

The actively moving spiral filaments or SPERMATOZOIDS of the Ferns, Mosses, Characeæ, &c., have nothing in common, except the spiral form, with the structures described in this article; they belong to the protoplasmic structures or *cell-contents*, as is also the case with the spirally-arranged green contents of SPIROGYRA; while this article refers exclusively to cellulose structures belonging to the *cell-wall*.

See also CELL, Vegetable; SECONDARY DEPOSITS; PITTED STRUCTURES; and TISSUES, Vegetable.

BIBL. General works on Vegetable Anatomy. Schleiden, *Ann. Nat. Hist.* vi. p. 35 (from the *Flora*, 1839); *Taylor's Scient. Mem.* ii. p. 281 (from *Müller's Archiv*, 1838); *Principles*, p. 42; Griffith, *Ann. Nat. Hist.* x. p. 109; E. Quekett, *Trans. Mic. Soc.* i. p. 1; *Ann. Nat. Hist.* xv. p. 495; Mohl, *Verm. Schrift.* p. 285 (*Ann. des Sc. Nat.* 2.sér. xiv. p. 242); *Vegetable Cell*, London, 1852, p. 14; *Botan. Zeitung*, xi. p. 753 (1853); Agardh, *De Cell. Vegetab.* Lund. 1852; Crüger, *Botan. Zeit.* xii. pp. 57, 833 (1854); xiii. p. 601 (1855); Caspary, *Bot. Zeit.* xi. p. 801 (1853); Trécul, *Ann. des Sc. Nat.* 4 sér. ii. p. 273; Schacht, *Pflanzenzelle*, Berlin, 1852; *Bot. Zeit.* viii. p. 697 (1850); Unger, *Linnæa*, xv. p. 385 (1841); Meyen, *Pflanzenphysiologie*, i.; Mitscherlich, *Ann. Nat. Hist.* ser. 2. i. p. 436.

SPIRILLINA, Ehr.—A doubtful genus of marine Infusoria, of the family Arcellina.

Char. Shell siliceous, porous, forming a flat spiral.

S. vivipara. Shell microscopic, hyaline, smooth, containing numerous embryo shells. Found in America.

BIBL. Ehrenberg, *Abhandl. d. Berl. Akad.* 1841. pp. 402, 422.

SPIRILLINA, Ehr., Willmson.—A genus of Foraminifera, of the order Monostegia.

Char. Shell consisting of a single elongated chamber, coiled into a flat close spiral; orifice simple, as wide as the tube.

Four recent British species : *S. foliacea, perforata, arenacea,* and *margaritifera* ; also some fossil.

BIBL. Williamson, *Rec. For.* ; Morris, *Brit. Foss.* p. 42.

SPIRILLUM, Ehr.—A genus of Vibrionia.

Char. Consisting of a colourless, tortuous, contractile but not extensile filament, or a cylindrical spiral.

These organisms, found in infusions and decomposing liquids, are very interesting objects on account of the remarkable character of their corkscrew-like movements. They multiply by transverse division, separating into two portions while in motion. They are jointed (or septate ?), but the joints are not always easy of detection. They are insoluble in boiling potash. Their structure is best examined when they are preserved in a dry state. It is difficult to know where to place them in a system ; but they are apparently nearest related to the Oscillatoriaceous Algæ. They are very different, however, from SPIRULINA, to which they have been compared. *Spirillum bryozoon* consists of the spermatozoids of Mosses.

1. *S. tenue.* Filament slightly tortuous, indistinctly jointed ; spiral of three or four turns ; movement active ; length 1-1000″ ; diam. 1-12,000″.

2. *S. undula.* Filament very tortuous, distinctly jointed ; spiral of óne or one and a half turns ; length 1-1500″ ; diam. 1-20,000″.

3. *S. volutans* (Pl. 3. fig. 23). Filaments very tortuous, distinctly jointed ; spiral of three, four, or more turns ; length 1-1400″ ; diam. 1-14,000″.

4. *S. plicatile* (*Spirochæta plicatilis*, Ehr.) (Pl. 3. fig. 22). Filament very long ; coils very numerous ; movement undulating ; length 1-180″ ; diam. 1-12,000″.

BIBL. Ehrenb. *Infus.* p. 84 ; Dujardin, *Infus.* p. 223.

SPIROCHÆTA, Ehr.—*S. plicatilis* = *Spirillum plicatile.*

SPIROCHONA, Stein.—A genus of Infusoria, of the family Vorticellina.

S. gemmipara (Pl. 25. fig. 35) is found upon the branchial plates of *Gammarus pulex*, where also its remarkable *Acineta*-form (Pl. 35. fig. 36) occurs.

S. Scheutenii is met with upon the feathery setæ arising from the terminal joints of the post-abdominal legs of *Gammarus*.

BIBL. Stein, *Die Infus.*

SPIRODISCUS, Ehr.—Under the name *S. fulcus*, Ehrenberg places among the Infusoria, in the family Vibrionia, a brownish organism, consisting of a short discoidal or much-flattened helical spiral, 1-1200″ in diameter, and found in Siberia. It exhibited a slow movement. Ehrenberg's figure greatly resembles that in Pl. 32. fig. 34 (the upper two), without the cilia, and magnified 200 instead of 400 diameters.

BIBL. Ehrenberg, *Infus.* p. 86.

SPIROGYRA (*Zygnema*, Agardh in part) (fig. 668).—A genus of Zygnemaceæ (Confervoid Algæ), mostly very elegant, and all very interesting on account of their structure and modes of development. They are green filaments, floating unattached in standing fresh water. They consist of jointed tubes (that is, rows of cylindrical cells), sometimes of considerable size, in the interior of which the green colouring matter is arranged in one or more spiral lines running round the walls, these spiral lines presenting bright points at intervals along their course (Pl. 5. figs. 17, 26, 27). The green lines consist of bands of protoplasm coloured green by chlorophyll ; the bright points are in some stages composed of globules of similar substance, but generally they are occupied by starch-granules imbedded in the protoplasm ; smaller starch-granules also occur at certain stages throughout the green band. A remarkable lenticular nucleus is also present, suspended in the centre of the cell by threads of protoplasm running out to the primordial utricle lying against the cell-wall. Sometimes this nucleus is placed with its faces towards the side wall (*S. nitida*, Pl. 5. fig. 26) ; sometimes it appears to be placed with its faces

Fig. 668.

Spirogyra communis.
Fragments of two
filaments conjugating.
Magnified 200 diameters.

looking up and down, as it presents the appearance of a narrow ellipse when seen sideways (*S. pellucida*, Pl. 5. fig. 27). The laminated structure of the cell-walls is also curious, but will be better understood after a sketch of the mode of development.

The attractive appearance of the *Spirogyræ* and the easily observed phænomenon of conjugation have caused much attention

2 T 2

to be paid to this genus; and many points of their history have been determined. The cells composing the filaments all multiply simultaneously when the plant is growing, each becoming twice its length and dividing into two. It has been certainly observed by A. Braun and Pringsheim that the division is preceded by a division of the nucleus. From this interstitial mode of growth it is evident that the walls of the cells of plants actively vegetating must soon become composed of a number of layers belonging to distinct generations of cells. Thus, supposing we have an original cell a, this encloses its progeny, two cells a^2 & b, and when these divide again and come to enclose respectively a^3 & c and b^2 & d, the parent-cell a, stretched to *four* times its original length, still encloses the whole. The laminæ belonging to the respective generations do not become very intimately blended, for by maceration we may cause the outer membranes to soften and dissolve, and set free the younger cells intact. The older membranes seem to have become thinner by stretching, or by solution, midway between their septa, since on maceration we may often see them give way in the middle, and the young cells slip out from them, leaving them as short hyaline tubes with a diaphragm in the middle. The ends of the cells of some species generally present a curious appearance, which might be compared with the "punt" of a bottle, only it is a *circular fold* thrown in from the cross septum. It is attributed to the excessive growth of the membrane of the young cells, confined in space by the outer parent-membrane. The filaments of *Spirogyra* are consequently very instructive in reference to vegetative cell-formation. In some cases the half-dissolved parent-cell membranes form a delicate but well-defined gelatinous coat on the tube (Pl. 5. fig. 27 *s*).

The reproduction of this genus exhibits, besides the proper conjugation, other phænomena, the import of which is not yet fully determined. The conjugation itself has been observed by almost every microscopist. It consists essentially in the production of papillary elevations on the contiguous walls of the cells of two filaments lying side by side; the growth of these papillæ until they come in contact; and their coalescence so as to form a canal of communication between the two cells (fig. 668, Pl. 5. fig. 18). When this is accomplished, the contents of one of the cells (the contents of both having meanwhile lost their characteristic arrange-

ment on the cell-walls) pass over through the cross tube into the other cell, when the contents of both become blended and form an elliptical free body (Pl. 5. fig. 18), which acquires cellulose integuments and becomes a *spore*, lying free in the parent cell. This process is accompanied by the death of the parent filaments, conjugation often taking place in the majority of the cells: the spores are sometimes set free by decay of the parent-cell wall; but very often the latter remains undissolved until the germination of the spore (Pl. 5. fig. 19). A modification of this mode of conjugation occurs in some cases, apparently as an abnormal process, for it has been observed (Braun) taking place in those species which conjugate as above. It occurs in solitary filaments, in which two contiguous cells produce papillæ at the adjoining ends, growing towards each other and coalescing, the contents of one of the cells thus passing into the next cell of the same filament. A. Braun calls this "chainlike" conjugation, in contradistinction to the "ladder-like" conjugation above described. As the two forms occur associated, Kützing's genus *Rhynchonema* and others founded upon this are of doubtful value.

The ripe spore presents the appearance of an elliptical body enclosed in three membranous coats, the outer of which is of delicate texture and separated by an interval from the next, which is brownish and of firm texture. The inmost coat, or true spore-membrane, is again delicate. The spores appear to rest through the winter after they are formed, and to germinate in spring, in which process the middle coat of the spore splits at one end, longitudinally, opening by two valves to allow the inner to grow forth, which bursts through the outermost sac, in the form of a tube (Pl. 5. fig. 19) which soon acquires the characteristic appearance of the parent plants. The contents of the spore are brown and homogeneous during the stage of rest (fig. 21); in germination they become green again, and arrange themselves in the spiral bands (fig. 22), which become more distinct as the cell elongates.

Certain other occurrences take place in the cell-contents of the *Spirogyra*, the relation of which to the reproduction is not so clear as the above. In filaments in an unhealthy condition, about to decay, such as are often seen when a collection of them is placed in a jar of water to keep for examination, it is not uncommon to see the green contents gradually lose their spiral arrangement and break up into a number of globular portions (Pl. 5. fig. 28); we have sometimes observed these rolling over slowly in the cell. In one case we have observed the contents converted into sixteen distinctly organized biciliated zoospores (Pl. 5. fig. 20), differing only from the ordinary zoospores of the Confervoids in the almost total absence of colour. They were somewhat crowded in the cell, and moved lazily about in it, the cilia vibrating. It is still more common to observe the contents of decayed filaments converted into encysted globules (Pl. 5. figs. 24, 25), which would appear to be a kind of resting-form of the zoospores. These globules, which have a tough spinulose coat, have been observed by Pringsheim as produced from the contents both of ordinary cells and (abnormally?) from the contents of a large spore (Pl. 5. fig. 23); the latter case might give colour to the idea that this was a sporange, had not its germination been observed. Pringsheim has further noticed that actively moving zoospores are produced from the small encysted bodies; perhaps these may fulfil an antheridial function. Carter has observed in the cells of *Spirogyra* the bodies constituting the genus *Pythium* of the German authors, and apparently connected with the zoospore-like bodies just described (see PYTHIUM). We are compelled to treat this subject somewhat briefly, but must direct attention to the relations of the CONJUGATION to that of the DESMIDIACEÆ, and those of the large spores and smaller globules to the similar bodies in the Desmidiaceæ and in the Volvocineæ, as well as in the other Confervoids.

The species of *Spirogyra* have been greatly multiplied by authors. The peculiar fold projecting from the septum appears to us to depend upon age and activity of growth; and the length of the joints depends greatly on the stage of growth, as they continually divide into two equal parts.

Spiral band single.

1. *S. tenuissima.* Vegetating filaments 1-3000" in diam.; joints four or five times as long; spiral band open; spore oblong-elliptical (Hassall, pl. 32. figs. 9, 10).

2. *S. longata.* Filaments about 1-1000" in diam.; joints six or eight times as long; spiral lax; spores oblong-elliptical (Hass. pl. 31. fig. 304, pl. 28. figs. 3, 4?).

3. *S. inflata* (*S. gustroides*, Kütz.). Fila-

ments 1-1680" in diam.; joints four or five times as long; turns of spiral about five; fertile cells ventricose; spores oblong elliptical (Hass. pl. 32. figs. 6, 7).

4. *S. communis* (fig. 668). Filaments 1-1440 to 1-1200" in diam.; joints two or three times as long; turns of spiral four, broad; spores elliptical (Hass. pl. 28. figs. 5, 6).

5. *S. quinina* (Pl. 5. fig. 17). Filaments 1-600" in diam.; joints once and a half or twice as long; turns of spiral broad and dense; spores elliptical (Hass. pl. 28. fig. 2). Varies to some extent in the length of the joints, which are sometimes twice to seven times as long.

Spiral bands two.

6. *S. decimina.* Filaments 1-720" in diam.; joints two or four times as long; spiral bands lax, crossing so as to present the appearance of a row of the letter X (Hass. pl. 23. figs. 3, 4).

7. *S. elongata.* Filaments 1-1320 to 1-1200" in diam.; joints ten times as long; spiral bands lax (Berkeley, *Gleanings*, p. 12, fig. 2).

Spiral bands numerous.

8. *S. nitida* (Pl. 5. fig. 26). Filaments 1-360" in diam.; joints twice or three times as long; spiral bands four, dense, closely veiled; spores elliptical (Hass. pl. 22. figs. 1, 2).

9. *S. maxima.* Filaments 1-200 to 1-300" in diam.; joints equal, once and a half or twice as long; spiral bands lax; spores globular (Hass. pls. 18, 19).

10. *S. bellis.* Filaments 1-480" in diam.; joints equal or twice as long; spiral bands two or three, lax; spores somewhat globose; var. β, spirals condensed (Hass. pl. 24).

11. *S. pellucida.* Filaments 1-840' in diam.; joints four or six times as long; spiral band lax and slender; fertile cells ventricose; spores globose (Hass. pl. 25).

12. *S. rivularis.* Filaments 1-2040" in diam.; joints three or four times as long; spiral bands four, broad, dense (Hass. pl. 27).

13. *S. curvata* (*Sirogonium sticticum* and *breviarticulatum*, Kütz.). Filaments 1-720" in diameter, joints four or five times as long; spiral bands three or four, slender; conjugation direct, without a cross branch, approaching *Mougeotia* (Hassall, pl. 26. figs. 1, 2).

BIBL. Hassall, *Brit. Freshw. Alg.* p. 135;

Kützing, *Sp. Alg.* p. 437, *Tab. Phyc.* v.;
Pringsheim, *Flora*, xxxv. p. 465, 1852 (*Ann. Nat. Hist.* 2 ser. xi. p. 210); Al. Braun, *Verjüngung* (*Ray Soc. Vol.* 1853, *passim*); Meyen, *Pflanzenphysiologie*, iii. p. 422; Vaucher, *Conferves*, p. 37; Agardh, *Ann. des Sc. Nat.* 2 sér. vi. p. 197.

SPIROLINA, D'Orb.—A genus of Foraminifera, of the order Helicostegia, and family Nautiloidæ.

Char. See HELICOSTEGIA.

S. austriaca (Pl. 18. fig. 15).

BIBL. See the order.

SPIROLOCULINA, D'Orb.—A genus of Foraminifera, of the order Agathistegia, and family Miliolida.

Char. Shell regular, equilateral, compressed, oblong, oval, or elongated; *chambers* concentric on two opposing faces, in the same plane, not embracing, all apparent and with simple cavities; *orifice* single, situated alternately at the two ends of the longitudinal axis, simple or with a tooth, almost always prolonged into a tube.

S. depressa (Pl. 42. fig. 5). The only British species; recent and fossil.

a. rotundata. Section of chambers round, ridges absent.

β. cymbium. Shell elongate, narrow; chambers sigmoid.

BIBL. That of the order.

SPIRORBIS, Daudin, Lamk.—A genus of Annulata, of the order Setigera, and family Amphitritæ.

The elegant little milk-white flat spiral shells of *S. nautiloides* (*communis*) (Pl. 44. fig. 30) are frequently met with upon *Fucus serratus*, &c. The animal has six pinnate branchial filaments and a pedunculate operculum.

SPIROSTOMUM, Ehr.—A genus of Infusoria, of the family Trachelina.

Char. Body ciliated all over, oblong or cylindrical and elongated, without a neck; mouth spiral, with neither teeth nor a tremulous lamina.

S. ambiguum (Pl. 24. figs. 77, 78). Body cylindrical and elongated, colourless, obtuse in front, truncate behind, prolonged anteriorly beyond and above the mouth. Aquatic; length 1-12″.

S. virens. Body oblong, green. Aquatic; length 1-120″.

Dujardin gives the characters — Body cylindrical, greatly elongated, and very flexible, often twisted, covered with cilia arranged upon the oblique or spiral striæ of the surface; mouth situated laterally beyond the middle, at the end of a row of larger cilia;—the genus consisting of *S. ambiguum*, E., and *S.* (*Uroleptus*, E.) *filum*, *S. virens* being placed as *Bursaria spirigera*.

BIBL. Ehrenberg, *Infus.* p. 332; Dujardin, *Infus.* p. 514.

SPIROTÆNIA, Bréb.—A genus of Desmidiaceæ.

Char. Cells single, elongated, cylindrical or fusiform, straight, entire, not constricted, ends rounded; endochrome spiral.

Division oblique. In one species the endochrome is spiral at first, subsequently becoming uniform.

1. *S. condensata* (Pl. 10. fig. 59). Endochrome forming a single broad band. Length 1-208″. Common.

2. *S. obscura.* Endochrome at first forming several spiral threads, afterwards uniform. Length 1-240″.

BIBL. Ralfs, *Brit. Desmid.* 178.

SPIRULINA, Link.—A genus of Oscillatoriaceæ (Confervoid Algæ), consisting of minute spirally coiled filaments immersed in a gelatinous matrix, having an oscillating motion; forming extensive strata in lakes, brackish water, &c. The intimate structure and development of these curious organisms are not yet well understood; they are supposed to increase by the filaments breaking across; in some the filament appears continuous; in others it has striæ, like the *Oscillatoriæ* (appearing beaded when badly defined). It does not appear that Ehrenberg's and Dujardin's genus SPIRILLUM consists of species referable to this genus. Several British species are described.

1. *S. Jenneri* (Pl. 3. fig. 16). Filaments with striæ, 1-6000″ in diameter, usually of eight or ten coils, forming a thin æruginous stratum.

2. *S.* (?) *Thompsoni.* Filaments striated, of rarely more than four coils, then about 1-50″ in length (from the figure, the diameter would appear to equal 1-2000″ at least), forming a greenish, then pale blue, finally ferruginous stratum. *Anabaina spiralis*, Thompson, *Ann. Nat. Hist.* v. p. 84.

3. *S. tenuissima.* Filaments not striated, with close coils; coils 1-9500″ in diam., pale æruginous, forming a pellicle of a rich green colour, ultimately ferruginous (Ralfs, *Ann. Nat. Hist.* xvi. pl. 10. fig. 1; Harvey, *Brit. Mar. Alg.* pl. 27 C). In brackish pools.

4. *S. Hutchinsiæ.* Filaments not striated, with close coils; coils from 1-6000 to 1-1080″ in diam.; forming an æruginous

stratum in the sea (Kützing, *Tab. Phyc.* i. pl. 37. fig. 2).

5. *S. oscillarioides* (Pl. 3. fig. 15). Filaments not striated ; coils 1-7200'' in diam. ; lax. Among Oscillatorieæ in stagnant pools.

Spirillum minutissimum and *rupestre,* Hassall, probably belong here ; but the former may be *Spirillum volutans* of Ehrenberg. These organisms require further investigation.

BIBL. Kützing, *Sp. Alg.* p. 236, *Tab. Phyc.* i. pl. 37 ; Hassall, *Brit. Fr. Alg.* p. 277, pl. 75 ; Harvey, *Brit. Mar. Alg.* p. 229, pl. 27 ; *Phyc. Brit.* pl. 105 ; Thompson, *Ann. Nat. Hist.* v. p. 81 ; Ralfs, *Ann. Nat. Hist.* xvi. 308, 2nd ser. viii. p. 205 ; Cohn, *Nova Acta,* xxiv. ; Stitzenberger, *Hedwigia,* i. p. 32, pl. 5 ; Crouan, *Mém. d. Soc. d. Cherbourg,* ii. p. 38 (1854).

SPLACHNACEÆ.—A family of Funarioideæ (Acrocarpous operculated Mosses), of broad and densely tufted habit, mostly found upon dung, with a very much branched, loosely-leaved stem (fig. 669). Inflorescence

Fig. 669.   Fig. 670.

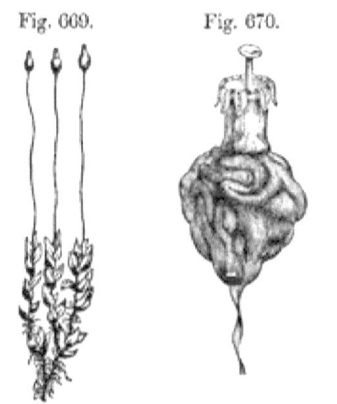

Splachnum vasculosum.

Fig. 669. Nat. size.
Fig. 670. Ripe capsule open, dried, and the apophysis shrivelled. Magnified 20 diameters.

hermaphrodite, diœcious, rarely monœcious. Antheridial flower a capituliform, terminal bud. Antheridia large, club-shaped, rather curved. Archegonia narrow, long-apiculate. Peristome, if present, of regularly lanceolate, neither obtuse nor tmbeculate, twin, rufescent, rather fleshy teeth. Columella ordinarily projecting (fig. 670). Capsule on an apophysis (fig. 673), mostly furnished with stomates.

British Genera.

1. *Œdipodium.* Calyptra soft, longish-narrow, split almost to the summit, obtuse, somewhat lacerated at the base. Capsule subglobose, very loosely reticulated, soft, with a very long collum arising from a gradually thickened fruit-stalk, the mouth naked. Columella dilated at the apex. Inflorescence monœcious.

Fig. 671.   Fig. 672.   Fig. 673.

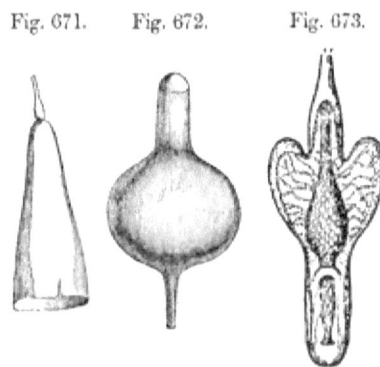

Splachnum vasculosum.

Fig. 671. Calyptra. Magnified 20 diameters.
Fig. 672. Young capsule and apophysis. Magnified 20 diameters.
Fig. 673. Vertical section of an unopened capsule with its spongy apophysis. Magnified 20 diameters.

2. *Tetraplodon.* Calyptra smallish, hood-shaped, split to the middle, operculate, delicate. Capsule apophysate, oval-cylindrical. Apophysis obconical, obovate, or sub-ovate. Columella scarcely dilated at the apex. Peristome of sixteen double teeth approximated in fours, lanceolate, formed of two rows of cells, connate in pairs at the base, reflexed when dry, erect, incurved when moist, much shorter than the capsule. Antheridial flower sessile in the axil of a leaf, or terminal in a little special branch, in a capituliform bud.

3. *Tayloria.* Calyptra inflatedly conical, erect, split at one side, constricted at the base, lacerated or erose all round the margin. Peristome arising below the orifice of the capsule, of sixteen or thirty-two teeth ; teeth single, approximated in pairs or coherent, often very long ; when moist incurved and involuted, when dry (in the ripe capsule) reflexed, appressed to the capsule or tortuously bent down ; very hygroscopic. Inflorescence monœcious. Co-

lumella mostly free, exserted from the ripe capsule, flattish-apiculate.

4. *Dissodon.* Calyptra inflatedly conical, erect, slit at one side, constricted at the base and torn or erose. Peristome arising at the orifice of the capsule. Teeth thirty-two, connate, in eight bigeminate or sixteen geminate teeth, lanceolate, smooth, transversely articulate, connivent into a depressed cone when moist, subincurved when dry. Inflorescence perfect or monœcious. Columella included or exserted, flattish.

5. *Splachnum.* Calyptra conical, rather small, entire or slit here and there at the base. Peristome of sixteen teeth, composed of a double row of cells, lanceolate, largish, yellowish, approximated in pairs and to some extent conglutinated, when dry reflexed and appressed to the capsule, when moist erect and incurved at the apex. Inflorescence dicœcious, rarely monœcious. Columella ordinarily emerging, capitate.

SPLACHNUM, Linn. — A genus of Splachnaceæ (Acrocarpous operculate Mosses), remarkable for the large apophysis, often umbrella-shaped. *S. ampullaceum,* Linn., not uncommon on the dung of animals on bogs, is a very handsome moss, with purple or red capsules. *S. vasculosum* (figs. 669–673) is less common, occurring only in high mountain districts.

SPLEEN.—This organ appears to occur exclusively in the Vertebrata. The spleen is covered externally by the peritoneum, except at the hilus, where the vessels are connected with it.

Beneath the peritoneal tunic is a thin, semitransparent, firm, fibrous coat, which at the hilus accompanies the vessels, and forms sheaths around them.

The spleen is traversed by fibrous processes, bands or trabeculæ (fig. 674), which arise from the inner surface of the fibrous coat and from the outer surface of the vascular sheaths, and, being connected with each other, form a number of irregular meshes or areolæ, in which are situated the splenic corpuscles and the spleen-pulp.

The fibrous coat and the trabeculæ consist of ordinary areolar tissue, with mostly parallel fibres, traversed by networks of fine elastic fibres. In certain animals, as the dog, cat, pig, &c., the fibrous coat and trabeculæ contain also unstriped muscular fibres. These do not occur in man, unless they are represented in the microscopic trabeculæ by peculiar wavy fibres, about 1-500" in length, with lateral or stalked nuclei (fig. 675). Some of these are found enclosed in cells (fig. 676), from which they become liberated by the action of water.

The splenic or Malpighian corpuscles (fig. 677) are white rounded bodies, imbedded in the spleen-pulp, and attached to the smallest arteries. They vary in size from 1-120 to 1-36", and cannot always be

Fig. 674.   Fig. 675. 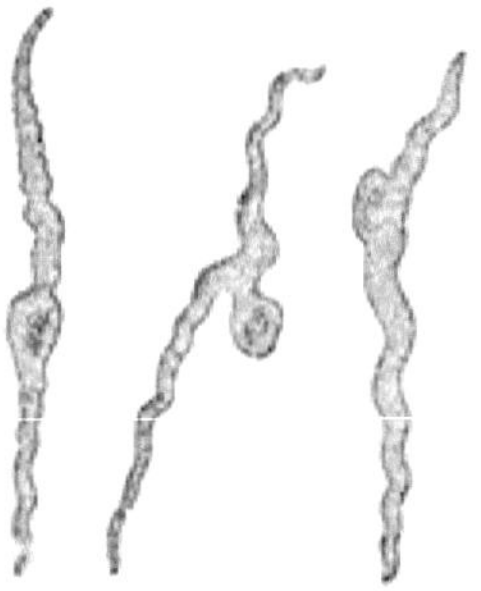   Fig. 676.

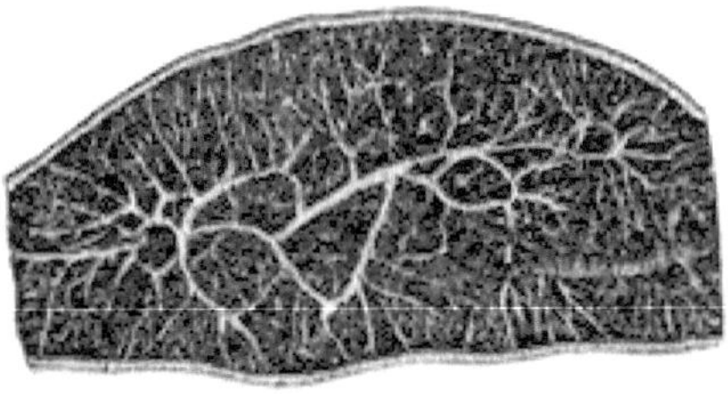

Fig. 674. Natural size. Portion from the middle of the spleen of an ox, washed; showing the bands and their arrangement.

Fig. 675. Peculiar fibres from the pulp of the human spleen, belonging to the microscopic trabeculæ. Magnified 350 diameters.

Fig. 676. One of the same enclosed in a cell. Magnified 350 diameters.

detected. They are either placed upon the sides of the arterial branch, or situated in the angles of their bifurcation.

The splenic corpuscles consist of an enveloping membrane (fig. 678 *a*) composed of areolar tissue with fine reticular elastic fibres, and derived from the arterial sheath. They are traversed by capillaries and filled with a tenacious grey mass, consisting of an albuminous liquid, with cells 1-3000'' in diameter, containing one or two nuclei, and free nuclei (fig. 104, p. 122). Sometimes the cells contain globules of fat or blood-corpuscles; and occasionally free blood-corpuscles are met with.

Thes pleen-pulp forms a soft reddish mass, and consists of three elements, microscopic trabeculæ, fibres or bands, parenchyma-cells, and the smaller blood-vessels. The trabeculæ agree in structure with the larger ones. The fibres or bands are the terminations of the sheaths of the vessels; they are indistinctly fibrous, and free from elastic tissue. The parenchyma-cells resemble those in the splenic corpuscles. Extravasated blood is so frequently met with in the parenchyma that its presence may be regarded as normal; and the blood-corpuscles are found enclosed

Fig. 677.

Fig. 678.

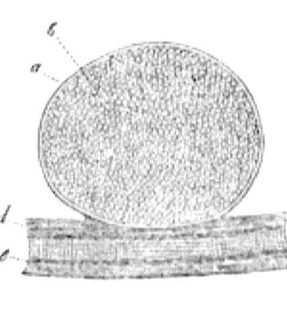

Fig. 677. Portion of a small artery from the spleen of a dog, with one of the branches covered with Malpighian bodies. Magnified 10 diameters.
Fig. 678. Malpighian corpuscle from the spleen of an ox. *a*, wall of the corpuscle; *b*, contents; *c*, wall of the artery upon which it is situated; *d*, its sheath. Magnified 150 diameters.

in cells, from one to twenty in each, or surrounded by a transparent substance, their contents exhibiting various changes in colour and consistence. The arteries terminate in elegant tufts or penicilli, becoming continuous with a mesh-work of capillaries.

The blood-corpuscles from the blood of the splenic vein frequently contain crystals of hæmatoidine.

In the examination of the spleen, the trabeculæ are best seen after washing away the pulp with water; the splenic corpuscles by tearing the spleen, or boiling it; either in the pig or ox. The cells containing blood-corpuscles must be searched for in the pulp unacted upon by water. The muscular fibres are most evident in the smaller trabeculæ,

especially after treatment with dilute nitric acid (one part to five parts of water).

BIBL. Kölliker, *Mikrosk. Anat.* ii. 253, and *Todd's Cycl. Anat. &c.*, art. *Spleen*; Gray, *A. Cooper's Prize Essay*; Saunders, *Goodsir's Annals of Anat. &c.* 1851, i.; Crisp, *On the Spleen.*

SPONGIÆ (Sponges).—A class of Animals, belonging to the subkingdom Radiata.

Char. Form variable; fixed by a kind of root at the base, or encrusting; consisting of a soft gelatinous mass, mostly supported by an internal skeleton composed of reticularly anastomosing horny fibres, in or among which are usually imbedded siliceous or calcareous spicula; or sometimes the spicula alone form the skeleton.

The horny fibres forming the skeleton of sponges, which may be well seen in any common sponge, are cylindrical, and variously united, so as to form a coarse network with roundish or angular microscopic meshes. In addition to these generally diffused meshes or intervals, large (to the naked eye) rounded apertures (oscula) are scattered over the surface of most sponges, leading into sinuous canals permeating their substance in every direction; and between these are other smaller apertures, just visible to the naked eye, also the orifices of canals, which traverse the substance and communicate with the oscular canals.

In the living sponge this skeleton is covered with a glairy or gelatinous, colourless, amorphous substance, resembling that of which the *Amœbæ* are composed, but sometimes more liquid; the proportion of which is variable in the different genera. This substance appears to be composed of minute masses, those on the surface being furnished with long and very slender vibratile cilia; and during life, by means of these, water entering by the smaller apertures, and reaching the oscular channels, is expelled from the oscula in currents, which may be rendered visible by sprinkling a little finely powdered charcoal over them. If detached portions of this gelatinous substance are examined under the microscope, they exhibit *Amœba*-like processes in motion.

The fibres have been described as solid and as tubular. Those of the common sponges appear under the microscope to be solid; but when treated with sulphuric acid, it is easily seen that they consist of two parts, an outer tubular portion, which is contracted in length by the acid, and an inner cylindrical thread, which is not so contracted, but usually becomes elegantly wavy or spiral from flexion, frequently also partly protruding from the cavity of the outer portion in broken fibres, and resembling Pl. 21. fig. 22.

The spicula are of various forms (Pl. 37, the lettered figures), and either scattered through the substance or arranged in bundles forming spurious fibres; sometimes projecting more or less from the surface (Pl. 37. fig. 8). In some sponges they are absent, and in one genus they are replaced by gravel. There is some obscurity about the gravel, however, for its particles are described as being uncrystalline, and as neither siliceous nor calcareous!

In some sponges an external membrane is present; and this has been observed to exhibit a reticular or cellular appearance, from the presence of fine reticular fibres.

Sponges are mostly marine, rarely aquatic. In the natural state they possess lively colours, which appear in some instances to arise from the presence of granules of colouring matter, probably chlorophyll, in others from iridescence. They usually grow in groups upon rocks, shells, polypes, seaweeds, &c.

A vascular system has been described as existing in some marine sponges, consisting of anastomosing tubes or vessels enclosed in a membranous sheath surrounding the horny fibres, and containing minute corpuscles; but the existence of this system is problematical.

Sponges appear to be propagated in four ways: by gemmation, from the interior of the canals; by the formation of ciliated gemmules (swarm-spores); by the formation of true sexual ova; and by the production of bodies analogous to "winter-ova."

The ciliated gemmules, which are not of general occurrence, are yellowish, oval, narrowed at one end, and covered, except at this part, by vibratile cilia. They are mostly formed in spring, and after swimming about for a time, become fixed to some suitable spot and undergo development.

Of the other reproductive bodies, one kind consists of roundish or ovate masses, containing spicula and resembling the parent in structure, either lying loose in its substance or adherent to the horny fibres, and escaping at its death and solution, to acquire maturity.

The bodies resembling winter-ova are round or ovoid, with a funnel-shaped depression on the surface communicating with the interior. At first these lie in a cavity formed by condensed surrounding substance; subsequently a membrane presenting a hexagonal reticular structure is formed around them, upon which a crust of spicula is afterwards deposited. When expelled from the body of the parent, they are motionless; they then swell up, burst, and the minute locomotive germs escape. These now exhibit *Amœba*-like processes, and take on an independent life.

The true ova are oval, and scattered through the general substance; they have a distinct outer membrane, with a germinal vesicle and spot. The spermatozoa occur in minute cells, also diffused through the substance.

Sponges are probably nourished by enclosing Algæ, &c. in their substance in the same manner as *Amœba*. This has been seen to take place in the case of the young animals developed from the winter-ova.

The genera and species have been so loosely and unintelligibly characterized, that the descriptions would be useless to any microscopic observer.

BIBL. Johnston, *Brit. Sponges*; Grant, *Edinb. New Phil. Mag.* 1827; Hogg, *Ann. Nat. Hist.* 1841. viii. 3, and 1851. vii. 190; Bowerbank, *Trans. Micr. Soc.* 1840. i.; Carter, *Ann. Nat. Hist.* 1848. i. 303, 1849. iv. 81, and 1856. xviii.; Dobie, *Ann. Nat. Hist.* 1852. x. 317; Huxley, *ibid.* 1851. vii. 370.

SPONGILLA, Lam.—A genus of fresh-water sponges.

Two British species, *S. fluviatilis* and *S. lacustris*.

Found attached to stones, old wood-work, &c. in still or slowly running waters; green or grey.

See SPONGLÆ.

BIBL. Johnston, *Brit. Sponges*, 149, and the *Bibl.* therein; Carter, *Ann. Nat. Hist.* 1849. iv. 81, and 1857. xx. 21; Lieberkuhn, *ibid.* 1856. xvii. 403.

SPONGIOLES.—Many works on vegetable physiology still retain the old error that the extremities of roots are devoid of epidermis, and that the tissue then presents an open spongy character, whence the name of *spongioles* applied to the absorbing apices of roots. So far is this from being a correct account of the conditions, that, in reality, not only is the surface completely invested with a continuous epidermis, but the growing point and principal absorbing surface is found a little above the absolute extremity, which is pushed forward by interstitial growth. On the ends of developing roots (including those which break out from the interior of stems), especially remarkable in the Duck-weed, exists a kind of cap formed of tissue rather denser than that of the substance of the apex of the rootlet. This cap either persists in this form, and is then carried forward (like the calyptra on a moss-capsule) as a distinctly defined cap, called a *pilorhiza*, or the dense layer at the end of the root is gradually disintegrated; but in both cases it undergoes constant renewal by cell-division just behind the point. Many young roots, especially such as grow in a moist medium, are clothed with numerous radicle hairs, which on superficial examination

might lead to the idea that the end was of a spongy character. The cells of the extremities of the aerial roots of Orchids, &c., and

Fig. 679.

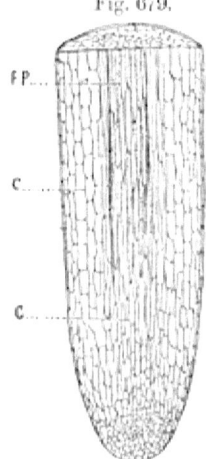

Longitudinal section of the rootlet of an Orchis.

C, C, Cellular tissue (cambium) in which development is still going on. *F P,* Fibro-vascular bundles gradually becoming organized from above downwards.

Magnified 500 diameters.

of various water-plants, contain sufficient chlorophyll to give them a green colour.

BIBL. Trécul, *Ann. des Sc. Nat.* 3 sér. vi. p. 303; Garreau and Brauwers, *Ann. Nat. Hist.* 1859. iv. p. 201; Henfrey, *Journ. of Agric. Society of England*, January 1859.

SPORANGIUM and SPOROCARP.—The term sporangium is applied to the structure immediately enclosing the spores of the Cryptogamia. The different forms and conditions are described under the classes of Flowerless plants. Sporocarp or spore-fruit is the name given to the capsules or similar organs which contain the sporanges of the Marsileaceæ (see PILULARIA).

SPORENDONEMA, Desm. — A supposed genus of Sepedoniei (Hyphomycetous Fungi). It is a very common occurrence in autumn to find the house-fly, dead, adhering to walls, window-panes, &c., firmly fixed by its proboscis, and with its legs spread out; thus differing from dead flies in general, which have the legs contracted. In about twenty-four hours after death, a kind of fleshy substance, of a white colour, is found in the form of a ring projecting out between each of the rings of the abdomen; and in a day or two after, the whole will be found dried, and the surface of the wall or glass lightly covered in a semicircle, at about 1-2 to 1" from the fly's abdomen, with a cloud of whitish powder. The whitish fleshy substance is found on examination to consist of a vast number of short erect filaments growing out from the interior of the fly's body, between the rings; these filaments contain large oil-globules, often arranged in a row; and their having been mistaken for spores gave origin to the name *Sporendonema*, applied to this fungus. Cohn has lately described its growth somewhat minutely, and changed the generic name to *Empusa*, or rather *Empusina*, the first of these names being already occupied. He correctly states that the vertical filaments terminate in the abdomen in a continuous, often branched tube, and consist therefore of a single tubular cell. The upper free end, however, becomes cut off by a septum, and the terminal cell acquires a campanulate form and a darkish colour; when ripe, it is thrown off with elasticity, and a number of these form the white cloud above mentioned. Cohn endeavoured in vain to make them germinate; and nothing like them was found in the cavity of the abdomen of numerous flies, in which the filaments were traced in their earlier stages. From our own observations, we rather incline to regard them as *peridioles* or spore-cases, comparable perhaps to that of *Pilobolus*; or they may be stylospores, like some of those of the Uredinei, which after a stage of rest produce an intermediate mycelial structure, and then give birth to the ripe spores.

The most remarkable point about this fly-fungus, to which, however, Cohn does not allude, is the circumstance that when the body of the fly with the rings of fungi freshly developed is placed in water, ACHLYA *prolifera* is almost always, if not always, produced, and apparently from the filaments which in the air produce the bell-shaped deciduous body above described. We find the *Achlya* with its ciliated zoospores, and later with its globular sporanges filled with spores, apparently representing an aquatic form of the *Sporendonema* or *Empusina*.

Several points require yet to be cleared up, especially the ultimate history of the spore-like body of the *Empusina*-form; and the relation between this plant and the *Achlya* is not quite demonstrated.

Cienkowski has recently confirmed the view that *Achlya* is an aquatic form of the present plant; but A. Braun denies this; he

states that he has found a second species of *Empusina* on the common gnat (*Culex pipiens*).

Sporendonema Casei, Desm., is referable to TORULA.

BIBL. Berk. *Brit. Flora*, ii. pt. 2. p. 350; Fries, *Syst. Myc.* iii. p. 435, *Summa Veget.* p. 494; Varley, *Trans. Mic. Soc. Lond.* iii.; Cohn, *Nova Acta*, xxv. p. 299; Berk. and Broome, *Ann. Nat. Hist.* 2nd ser. v. p. 460; Cienkowski, *Bot. Zeit.* xiii. p. 801; Al. Braun, *Alg. Unicell.* p. 105.

SPORES, SPORULES, SPORIDIA, and SPORIDIOLA.—A number of nearly connected terms are applied to the various organs which either really or apparently represent, in the Flowerless Plants, the *seeds* of the Flowering classes. The names have been mostly applied with a view of marking slight distinctions between organs supposed to be homologous. Of those placed at the head of this article, the first only should be retained, the second being merely a useless diminutive of it, and the third and fourth being superseded by the more definite nomenclature now applied to the reproductive bodies of the Cryptogamia.

It may be desirable perhaps here, if merely for the sake of explaining the exact meaning of words constantly used in this work, to pass in review the various structures comprehended under the general name of Spore.

The definition of the word spore itself, as commonly used, may be stated thus:—a reproductive body, thrown off by a Flowerless plant to reproduce its kind, and containing no embryo at the moment when cast off by the parent. It is evident from this how lax is its application.

The highest of the Flowerless plants, the Marsileaceæ and the Lycopodiaceæ, produce two kinds of spore, one destined to produce spermatozoids, the other archegonia and ultimately embryos growing up into new plants. These are now sometimes distinguished as *pollen-spores* and *ovule-spores* or *oospores*; the latter are large sacs with complicated outer membranes, the former simple cells with a double coat, like pollen-grains (see PILULARIA, ISOËTES, and LYCOPODIACEÆ).

The Ferns and the Equisetaceæ produce only one kind of spore, a simple cell with a double coat, the outer of which is generally elegantly marked in the former (figs. 232-235, p. 284), and is split up into elastic filaments in the latter (fig. 205, p. 265). In germinating, this spore produces a kind of thallus (figs. 236–239, p. 285), on which antheridia and archegonia ultimately appear, and an embryo is formed, fertilized, and developed (see FERNS and EQUISETACEÆ).

In the above cases the spores are always formed in sporanges of various kinds, developed directly from the axis or the leaves by a process of vegetative growth.

In the Mosses and Liverworts the spores are mostly of one kind (an obscurity exists as to the nature of the difference between the two kinds in SPHAGNACEÆ), consisting of a cell with a single or (generally) double coat, like a pollen-grain. The spores unlike those above-mentioned are formed in sporanges which are the product of fertilized archegonia, and more resemble the *fruits* of Flowering plants. The spores of Mosses germinate by emitting the inner coat as a Confervoid filament (fig. 680), which usually branches and gives origin to numerous stem-buds. The spores of the Liverworts exhibit many modifications in the first stages of germination, as illustrated by the accompanying figures (figs. 681–683); the Marchantieæ and other frondose kinds grow at once into thalloid fronds (see MOSSES and HEPATICÆ).

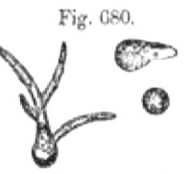

Fig. 680.

Spores of a moss germinating.

Magn. 160 diams.

The systematic position of the Characeæ

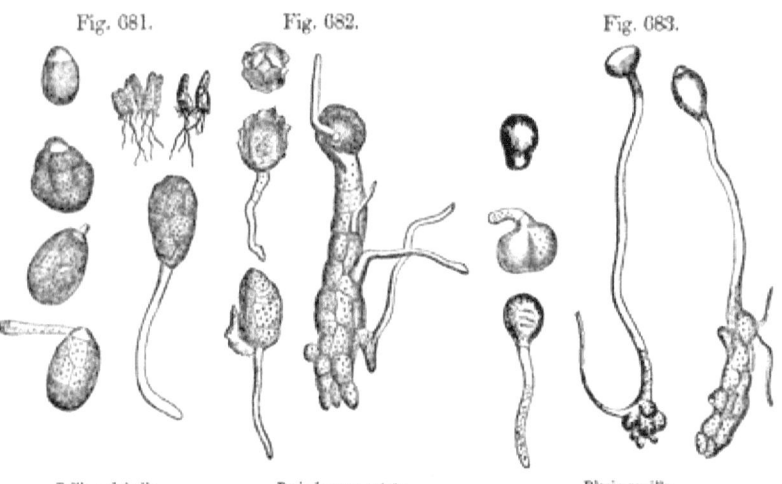

Fig. 681.   Fig. 682.   Fig. 683.

Pellia epiphylla.   Preissia commutata.   Blasia pusilla.

Spores of Hepaticæ germinating.   Magnified 200 diameters.

is perhaps still an open question; but there can be little doubt of the analogies between these reproductive bodies and those of the other Cryptogamia. There is no sporange here, nor apparently any archegonia. The *globule* (figs. 121–2, p. 145) produces antheridia giving birth to spermatozoids. The *nucule* (fig. 120, p. 144) appears to be a spore (see CHARACEÆ).

In the Lichens, only one kind of organ has been termed a *spore*, namely the reproductive cells formed in the thecæ (Pl. 29. figs. 6 & 12), which are known to reproduce the plant when thrown off by the parent. Two other kinds of body connected with the reproduction occur; these, the *gonidia* (Pl. 29. figs. 2, 3) and the *spermatia* (see LICHENS), have fortunately obtained and preserved distinctive appellations. The spores are simple cells or septate tubes, with a double membrane.

In the Algæ much confusion still exists, not only between different kinds of spore, but even between spores and sporanges; and this is not easily cleared away, since in certain cases the organs appear really capable of serving as one or the other, according to circumstances; the true spores are always simple cells with a double or triple coat.

In the Florideæ, the characters of the structures seem pretty clear: we find spores (fig.693, p. 656), TETRASPORES (figs. 248–50, pp. 289, 290), which appear to represent the gonidia of the Lichens, and spermatozoids (see FLORIDEÆ). Among the olive-coloured sea-weeds (Fucoids), the FUCACEÆ and DICTYOTACEÆ produce spores and spermatozoids; but in the majority of the families, only a totally different mode of reproduction is known. The plants produce ovate sacs (commonly called spores) and chambered filaments; from both are discharged actively moving ciliated cells, corresponding exactly to the ZOOSPORES of the Confervoids. Thuret now regards the *oosporanges* and *trichosporanges* (fig. 458, p. 456), as he called these sacs and filaments respectively, as merely different forms of one kind of structure. But it seems possible that true *spores* may be discovered, even indeed that the oosporanges may be parent cells sometimes of zoospores and sometimes of spores.

In the Confervoids we find true spores in very many cases, produced generally after some process of fertilization or of CONJUGATION, in special cells (fig. 668, and Pl. 5. figs. 16 & 18; Pl. 6. figs. 1–5). But the "spores" thus produced, while they sometimes germinate into new filaments, also sometimes produce numerous bodies of different kinds, connected in some way with reproduction; this is the case in SPIROGYRA (Pl. 5. fig. 23), perhaps also in CLOSTERIUM and other instances. Besides the *spores* proper, we have also in this family ZOOSPORES —the actively moving ciliated bodies which are regarded as *gonidia* and are further divided into *macrogonidia* and *microgonidia* (see HYDRODICTYON), the latter of which may perhaps have the function of spermatozoids (see SPHÆROPLEA and VAUCHERIA).

In the Fungi the greatest confusion exists in the nomenclature. The Agarics and their congeners produce free naked cells at the tips of short filaments, whence they

Fig. 684.

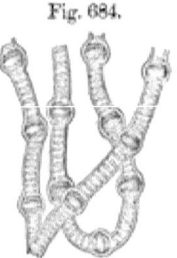

Nodularia spumigera.

Filaments with sporangial cells containing quaternate spores.

Magnified 200 diameters.

ultimately fall off, to reproduce the plant; these are called *spores* or *sporules*, or distinctively BASIDIOSPORES (figs. 53–55, p. 83). There is no essential difference between them and the spores produced by the Hyphomycetes, either singly or in rows or capitula (BOTRYTIS, figs. 77, 78, p. 104; figs. 685, 686; and Pl. 20. figs. 5, 6, 15, 16) at the ends of erect filaments; these

Fig. 685.   Fig. 686.

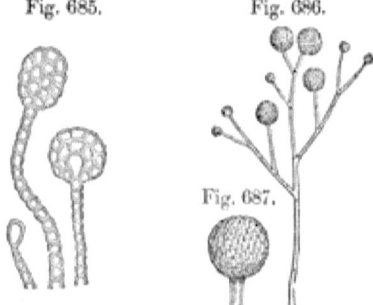

Fig. 687.

Fig. 685. Mystrosporium Stemphylium, Corda (Stemphylium, Fries). Magn. 200 diameters.

Fig. 686. Stachyobotrys atra. Fertile filament with heads of acrogenous spores. Magnified 200 diameters.

Fig. 687. A head of spores. Magn. 500 diameters.

again appear to pass almost insensibly into the *conidia* or reproductive cells produced by the breaking up of the mycelium, either wholly or in part, into free cells capable of continuing the growth (TORULA, Pl. 20. fig. 7, and OIDIUM, Pl. 20. fig. 8): on the other hand, the *spermatia* (Pl. 20. figs. 2, 3, 4), such as occur in some of the Coniomycetous forms of the Pyrenomycetous and Discomycetous Fungi, are closely related, as far as structure goes, to the conidia of *Torula,* &c. and the spores of the Hyphomycetes; while the *stylospores* of the UREDINEI and TREMELLINI produce bodies resembling them, and still more like the basidiospores of the Agaricini. The stylospores, another free form of spore, may be regarded probably as compound organs, formed of a row of cells contained in a persistent parent cell: it is surmised that they are merely metamorphosed asci (see SPHÆRIA and STILBOSPORA, Pl. 20. figs. 25–8); yet their mode of occurrence would lead to the idea that they are a distinct kind of organ. Lastly, we have the *ascospores* or *thecaspores* (fig. 42, p. 70), closely resembling those of the Lichens, consisting of free cells with a double coat, developed free in the cavity of a parent cell or sac. In the *British Flora* the terms *sporule* and *sporidium* are used synonymously in the sense of *spore*, and are applied to basidio-spores, ascospores, stylospores, and to the bodies (found in *Cytispora*, *Tubercularia*, &c.) called by Tulasne spermatia. The term *sporidiola* is applied apparently to nuclei or granular masses occurring in the cavities of spores, or to the separate portions of contents of imperfectly septate stylospores.

With regard to the homologies of the above structures, the *spermatia* are supposed

Fig. 688.　　　　　Fig. 689.

to represent spermatozoids; the *conidia* are regarded as corresponding to gonidia of Lichens; the stylospores are also connected with these through the medium of the tetraspores of the *Florideæ*.

In conclusion, a reference may be made to descriptions and figures like those given (figs. 688, 689) of *free* spores resting on the matrix and among the filaments. Such characters are totally out of date in the present state of science, and simply serve as indices of points requiring further investigation.

BIBL. See under the heads of the classes of Cryptogamic Plants.

SPORIDESMIUM.—A genus of Torulacei (Coniomycetous Fungi), growing upon bark, wood, &c. The character of the spores appears to vary in different species; sometimes they are simply septate, sometimes cellular (fig. 690).

Fig. 690.

Sporidesmium paradoxum. Spores sessile on the matrix. Magnified 200 diameters.

BIBL. Berk. and

Fig. 688. Leptotrichum glaucum. Free spores among the filaments of the matrix. Magnified 200 diameters.
Fig. 689. Fusarium herbarum. Free spores resting on the matrix. Magnified 200 diameters.

Broome, *Ann. Nat. Hist.* 2nd ser. v. p. 459, xiii. p. 460; Fries, *Summa Veg.* p. 506; Corda, *Icones Fung.* i. ii. &c.; Fresenius, *Beitr. z. Mycol.* Heft 2. p. 50.

SPOROCADUS, Corda. See HENDER-SONIA.

SPOROCHISMA, Berk. and Br.—A genus of Torulacei (Coniomycetous Fungi), containing one species, *S. mirabile*, forming a black velvety stratum on rotten beech-wood.

BIBL. Berk. and Broome, *Ann. Nat. Hist.* 2nd ser. v. p. 461; *Gardener's Chronicle*, 1847. p. 540; Fresenius, *Beitr. z. Mycol.* Heft 2. pl. 6.

SPOROCHNACEÆ.—A family of Fucoideæ. Olive-coloured, inarticulate seaweeds, whose unilocular and septate sporanges are attached to external jointed filaments, which are either free or compacted together into knob-like or warty masses.

Synopsis of British Genera.

* *Sporanges attached to pencilled filaments issuing from the branches* (Arthrocladieæ).

1. *Desmarestia.* Frond solid or flat, dichotomously branched.

2. *Arthrocladia.* Frond traversed by a jointed tube, filiform, nodose.

3. *Stilophora.* Frond filiform, tubular or solid, branched; sporanges arising from necklace-shaped filaments collected in wart-like groups upon the frond.

** *Sporanges produced in knob-like receptacles composed of whorled filaments compacted together* (Sporochneæ.)

4. *Sporochnus.* Receptacles lateral, on short peduncles.

5. *Carpomitra.* Receptacles terminal, at the tips of the branches.

SPOROCHNUS, Ag.—A genus of Sporochnaceæ (Fucoid Algæ), containing one British species, *S. pedunculatus*, having a filiform, solid, cellular main axis (containing a central cord of dense tissue) bearing long slender branches arranged in a somewhat pinnate manner and clothed at intervals with elliptical fertile ramules, consisting of an axis densely covered with whorled horizontal branching filaments bearing ovoid *sporanges*, and terminating in a deciduous pencil of byssoid filaments. Main stem 6 to 8" long, olive-brown, changing to yellow-green on exposure.

BIBL. Harvey, *Brit. Mar. Alg.* p. 25,

pl. 5 A; Greville, *Alg. Brit.* pl. 6; Thuret, *Ann. des Sc. Nat.* 3 sér. xiv. p. 238.

SPOROCYBE, Fries.—A genus of Dematiei (?) (Hyphomycetous Fungi), growing on dead sticks, decaying stems, &c., forming usually a blackish stratum. Several British species are recorded. They have a rigid, septate, simple or branched peduncle, ending with a capitate head clothed with

Fig. 691.   Fig. 692.

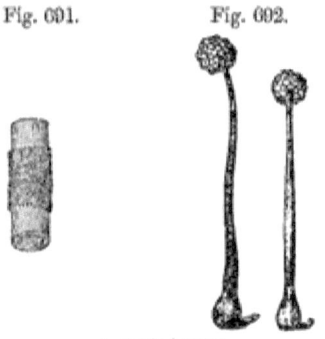

Sporocybe bulbosa.

Fig. 691. Stratum upon a stick. Nat. size.

Fig. 692. Two fertile peduncles, crowned with heads of spores. Magnified 160 diameters.

spores (figs. 691, 692). This genus is synonymous with *Periconia*, Corda. *Periconia*, Tode, is an obscure form, not well understood.

BIBL. Berk. *Brit. Flor.* ii. pt. 2. p. 333; *Ann. Nat. Hist.* vi. p. 433, pl. 13; Fries, *Summa Veget.* p. 467; *Syst. Mycol.* iii. p. 340.

SPOROTRICHUM, Link.—A genus of Mucedines (Hyphomycetous Fungi), growing on decaying vegetable substances, dung, &c. The forms referable to this genus, according to the character, include a very heterogeneous assemblage; indeed the character, which omits the nature of the original attachment of the spores, is worth nothing. Fries has separated a genus TRICHOSPORIUM, including a number of species with distinctly acrogenous spores; this includes *S. nigrum* and *S. geochorum* of the *Brit. Flora*. The remainder are placed by him among the Sepedoniei, under *Sporotrichum* and another genus which he calls *Physospora*. These genera are very obscurely known, so much resembling mycelia with detached conidia scattered on them.

BIBL. Berk. *Brit. Flor.* ii. pt. 2. p. 346; Fries, *Summa Veg.* pp. 492, 495, 521; Greville, *Sc. Crypt. Flor.* pl. 108. figs. 1, 2.

SPUMARIA, Pers.—A genus of Myxogastres (Gasteromycetous Fungi), the peridia of which are divided internally into chambers by ascending folds, and in *S. alba* are either sessile and pass above into torn white laminæ, or are stipitate and divided, and form corniculate peridioles bursting above; the latter is probably the perfect form. The whole plant looks at first like white froth; it grows on grasses, &c., generally at a little height from the ground.

BIBL. Berk. *Brit. Fl.* ii. pt. 2. p. 309; Greville, *Sc. Crypt. Fl.* pl. 267; Sowerby, *Fungi* (*Reticularia*), pl. 280; Fries, *Summa Veg.* p. 449.

SPUTUM.—We omitted to notice under EXPECTORATION the occurrence of fibrinous casts of the smaller bronchi and pulmonary air-cells in the expectoration of pneumonia. They are best seen on mixing the sputa with water, forming dichotomous cylinders with rounded enlargements. They consist of fine filaments, and are mostly covered with granule-cells, and are generally met with between the third and the seventh day.

BIBL. Remak, *Diagnost. u. Pathogene. Untersuch. &c.*, or *Edinb. Monthly Journ.* 1847. vii. 350.

SPYRIDIA, Harv.—A genus of Ceramiaceæ (Florideous Algæ), containing one British species, *S. filamentosa* (fig. 693), having a dull - red, cylindrical, filiform, much - branched frond, consisting of a chambered tube, the articulations of which are short, and the walls of which are composed of small angular cells. It arises from

Fig. 693.

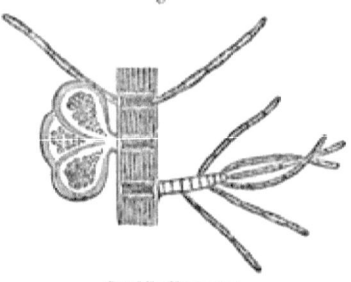

Spyridia filamentosa.

Fragment with a favella and ramules.

Magnified 25 diameters.

a broadly expanded disk. The branches are clothed with setaceous ramules. The *favella* are stalked, gelatinous, and lobed, surrounded by a few ramules, and contain two or three masses of spores. The *tetraspores* occur attached to the ramules. *Antheridia* have not yet been observed.

BIBL. Harvey, *Brit. Mar. Alg.* p. 166, pl. 22 D.

SQUAMELLA, Bory, Ehr.—A genus of Rotatoria, of the family Euchlanidota.

Char. Eyes four, frontal; foot forked.

1. *S. oblonga* (Pl. 35. fig. 29). Carapace depressed, elliptical, or ovate-oblong, hyaline; toes slender, long. Aquatic; length 1-216''.

2. *S. bractea.* Toes short and thick. Aquatic.

BIBL. Ehrenberg, *Infus.* p. 479.

STACHYLIDIUM, Link.—A genus of Mucedines (Hyphomycetous Fungi), nearly related to *Botrytis*, distinguished apparently only by the subpedicellate spores. Fries states that these are developed within a fugacious veil (?). BOTRYOSPORIUM *diffusum*, Corda, is included here by most authors. *S. bicolor* and *S. terrestre*, having quaternate sporiferous branches at the upper joints of the erect, simple filaments, grow upon decaying herbaceous plants and rotten sticks.

BIBL. Berk. *Brit. Flor.* ii. pt. 2. p. 341; Fries, *Summa Veg.* p. 490; Greville, *&c. Crypt. Flor.* pl. 257.

STAMENS.—The fertilizing organs producing the POLLEN, surrounding the pistil in perfect Flowering plants, or occurring alone in the barren flowers of the monœcious and diœcious genera. Stamens present a great variety of interesting points for examination under a simple microscope with a low power, in their forms, appendages, pores, &c. For the compound microscope they afford good material for the study of development of cells in the pollen, the POLLEN-grains themselves, and the spiral-fibrous tissue of their ANTHERS.

STARCH.—This substance, with the exception of the protoplasm the most generally diffused of all the products met with in the interior of vegetable cells, occurs in the form of transparent granules, of varied size and form and in varying quantity, in all classes of plants but the Fungi. It has been stated that it exists sometimes in a diffused or formless condition; but this seems questionable. All starch-grains appear when newly-formed as minute spherical bodies, and very many never advance beyond this stage; but a considerable proportion of the grains, in all cases where the starch becomes an important and considerable element in the cell-contents, increase in size, and acquire a more or less definite form, diverging from the spherical, and often characteristic of the particular plant in which the grain is produced. The grains in a single cell mostly vary very much in size, on account of their different degrees of development; but the full-grown characteristic grains of the same species of plant agree tolerably well in size. One of the most remarkable peculiarities of starch is the fact that it assumes a blue colour when iodine is applied to it, which in most cases affords a ready means of detecting its presence. The smallest grains are almost too minute to measure, and even their determination by the application of iodine is sometimes unsatisfactory; the largest grains, such as those of *Canna* and the potato, for example, attain a length of more than 1-400''.

The starch-granule is a definitely organized structure, although its existence in relation to that of the cell is transitory. It consists of assimilated food, deposited in a definite form insoluble in the ordinary cell-sap, through a process of organization analogous to that by which the development of the cell itself is effected. It is related closely with the cellulose structures of the cell-wall through the remarkable secondary layers found in the ALBUMEN of certain seeds, composed of the substance called *amyloid*, which sometimes takes a blue colour when iodine is applied to it, and, like starch, is ultimately dissolved and removed to furnish material for development.

The structure of the starch-granule has formed the subject of much debate, which, however, seems to have originated rather through considerations relating to the development than from a difficulty in observing the complete objects. Very minute granules, as above stated, appear as solid globules; but when the granules acquire appreciable dimensions, concentric lines may be observed, more or less distinctly in different cases, which lines increase in number with the increase of size, in many cases, however, soon becoming excentrical from the preponderating growth of one side of the granule. In freshly extracted granules the original centre mostly appears solid or with a minute black point; but if the starch is dry, the centre appears hollow, sometimes is even occupied by air; and some starch-grains, as in *Iris pallida, florentina*, &c., have a large cavity. If strong alcohol is applied

2 U

to fresh grains, the abstraction of water likewise produces a hollow in the central point of growth; and in all these cases, cracks not unfrequently run out towards the surface. The point in question, the starting-point of growth, solid or hollow as the case may be, is sometimes called the *hilum* or the *nucleus*: the former term arose out of the mistaken hypothesis of its being a point of attachment to the cell-wall; the latter term is admissible in a general sense as merely indicative of its precedence in age of the general mass of the grain. It is sometimes asserted that this point or nucleus is a pore or funnel-shaped cavity; but this is altogether a mistake, as may be readily proved by gently roasting a few starch-granules of the potato on a slide, and observing how the expanding air blows up the dextrine into which the starch is changed, in the form of a bubble or bladder. Sometimes small granules occur in the potato with a large cavity and thin walls.

The lines seen in the starch-granules are the boundaries of superimposed layers of its substance; sometimes these are very distinct, sometimes very faint; often more distinct lines appear at intervals in the series of the same granule (Pl. 36. fig. 21), and in these cases even a thin vacancy, or in the dried granules a stratum of air, seems to exist between the layers. The markings have been described as "folds" on the starch-granules; but their dependence on the existence of the concentric layers is beyond doubt. They are seen in the proper relative positions when the granules are rolled over in all directions beneath the microscope; their relative numbers and forms correspond to the size and stage of development of the granules in the same plant; and other characters connected with the physical structure confirm the conclusions from simple inspection.

Starch is usually stated to be unaffected by *cold water*, and this is generally the case; but if the granules of *Tous-les-mois* are crushed before placing them in water, so as to expose the internal substance, the water is sometimes absorbed by the inner layers, and these swell up considerably without the outer layers being affected. When starch-granules are *heated* (*dry*) gradually upon a slide, until some of them assume a yellowish colour, either the air-bubble above-mentioned appears—occasionally with a partial separation of the concentric layers through expansion of the films of air existing between

them, while other parts become fused,—or the general shape remains unchanged, and the striæ gradually vanish, becoming melted into a mass, as it were, the starch itself being converted into dextrine. When starch-granules are *heated in water* to the boiling-point, they usually soften and "blow-up" into a large sac, the inner part softening first, and pushing out the more superficial; if the sac bursts, the inner substance sometimes partly escapes in the form of cloudy flocks, but is not dissolved. *Diluted sulphuric acid* acts somewhat in the same manner as hot water; but if stronger acid is allowed to attack the granules locally or partially by flowing in from one side upon the object, very remarkable appearances present themselves: the acid touching certain parts of the granule first, or acting most quickly on softer portions, causes the softening internal layers to expand and bulge out the external layers at particular points (like *herniæ*) until the entire grain is softened, when these coalesce and the whole expands into a thin sac. Gradual action of the acid causes a more uniform expansion, which is usually accompanied by a sudden crack running out from the nucleus into the substance (indicating the abstraction of water?), followed almost immediately by a collapse of the wall above this crack, and a sudden expansion of the whole into a sac or an irregular gelatinous film. *Solution of potash* produces much the same effect as dilute sulphuric acid.

All the above appearances indicate that the starch-granule is composed of concentric "shells" of a substance of the same nature, but less dense and more rich in water in the interior layers, firmer, less hydrated, and more resisting in proportion to the distance from the starting-point of growth or nucleus. With polarized light, moreover, the starch-granule exhibits a black cross, and with a plate of selenite a beautiful coloured system, especially well seen in large grains like those of the potato or *Tous-les-mois* (Pl. 31. fig. 4).

But the recent observations of Nägeli and others go to prove that there exists a still greater complication. They find that prolonged treatment with saliva and some other agents will remove the substance coloured blue by iodine, leaving the granule, with its striæ more distinct, capable of resisting acids and alkalies.

Pure starch is coloured blue by iodine, whether in its natural state or softened by hot water, the depth of the colour depending on the quantity of iodine; where much is added, the colour is almost black. When dilute sulphuric acid has been added previously, the colour is rather purple than blue, especially the faint tinge given at first by weak solution of iodine. When the starch grains are heated dry, the colour given by iodine changes, proportionately to the violence of the action, from blue to purple, red-wine colour, and finally brown. The best application is the solution of iodine in iodide of potassium; and this should be used very weak in investigation of starch.

Starch-granules occur either isolated (Pl. 36. figs. 8 & 21), or in groups (figs. 7, 10, 11) (in the latter case mostly with flat faces, so as to fit together into round, oval, or similar forms), or packed closely in the parent cell in such numbers that they press upon each other and appear like parenchymatous cells (Pl. 36. figs. 3 & 12). In the actively vegetating parts of plants, starch-granules occur very generally imbedded in the green globules called CHLOROPHYLL-granules, either singly or in groups; this is seen especially well in the cells of the Confervaceæ, of the Hepaticæ, the prothallia of Ferns, in the leaves of aquatic plants, such as *Vallisneria*, in autumn, &c. The free granules occur more particularly in the colourless organs of plants—in tubers, rhizomes, roots and the cambium region in the season of rest, in the endosperm of ovules, or the ALBUMEN or cotyledons of seeds, &c. The parenchymatously-grouped granules are found in the albumen of seeds, especially of maize and rice. The comparison of the states and of the course of development of the crowded granules of maize throws much light upon the manner in which starch-granules are formed.

In the first place, two rival doctrines exist as to the order of development of the parts of the granule. Most authors assert that the granules grow by the superposition of layers from within outwards, consequently that the outermost layers are the youngest. Other authors, especially Nägeli, comparing the granule to a cell, assert that the layers are formed internally, the older ones expanding *pari passu* to make room for them. There can be no doubt that the first view is correct. In the next place a variety of notions have been put forth as to the origin of the starch-granule and its relation to the rest of the contents of the cell, especially the chlorophyll. It is curious to note the

error into which earlier observers fell from the want of the guiding thread furnished by a knowledge of the function of the protoplastic structures connected with the primordial utricle. The idea that the starch-granule sprouted out from the cell-wall corresponded with the original view of the origin of the septum in cell-division, while the hypothesis that starch is developed from chlorophyll, and the contrary notion that starch-granules form the nuclei of chlorophyll-granules, both rest on actual phænomena, in which, however, the chlorophyll proper (that is, the mere green colouring matter) bears no important share.

The development of the starch-granule is very beautifully illustrated in the gradual ripening of the seeds of Maize; and in imperfect seeds, different parts of the same grain often afford various stages of growth. The figs. 1–4 of Pl. 36, show the gradual formation of the starch-granules by deposition from the internal surface of *vacuoles in the protoplasm* filling the cell, exactly in the same way as the primordial utricle secretes cellulose layers upon its outer surface. Fig. 28 shows minute starch-granules originating in the same way in the protoplasm-current connected with the nucleus in the white lily; and Crüger, who first published this view in a decided form, has shown that the large granules, with an excentric "hilum," originate in a similar position, and owe the excentricity of their form to the fact of their remaining imbedded at one (the thicker) end in the protoplasmic threads of the primordial utricle, while the small free end is gradually pushed out further from the nutrient mass. The existence of starch-granules in chlorophyll-masses is thus clearly enough accounted for, now that we know the chlorophyll-globules to consist of masses of protoplasm coloured green by the presence of an extremely small quantity of a substance acquiring a green colour under the influence of light. Starch originates in vacuoles in this as in any other protoplasm. The *groups* of granules are formed through the simultaneous origin of a number, in vacuoles excavated in one large globule of chlorophyll or colourless protoplasm. We have traced this in the fronds of the Hepaticæ. These brief remarks must suffice on this part of the subject; and further details must be sought in the very copious literature which exists.

It remains to speak of the diversities of form and size of the large and perfect granules in different plants. A glance at Plate 36 will give some idea of these; and an inspection of the individual figures will show how remarkably the characteristic forms may vary in nearly related plants, even genera of the same family, as is the case with the ordinary Cereal grains. Thus in Maize (figs. 1 to 6), where the small grains are, as usual, originally roundish or oval (fig. 6), they gradually press upon one another and become polygonal; in the cells of the centre of the grain, where they are less densely packed, remaining with obtuse edges and angles (fig. 5), in the cells of the horny outer part of the grain, where they adhere more or less firmly together, forming angular parenchymatous masses (fig. 3). The central cavity is large here. In the grain of Wheat we find delicate, transparent, lenticular granules (fig. 8), the striæ faint; in Barley (fig. 9) they are more irregularly discoid, with a thickened edge, the striæ obscure; while in the Oat (fig. 10) the granules are of very small size, but of angular forms and packed together in large numbers, so as to form roundish masses with a smooth surface, which readily break down into their components when pressed; the separate segments all exhibit their separate black crosses in polarized light. In Rice (fig. 12) we find somewhat similar conditions to those in Maize; but the granules are much smaller and more firmly united, whence the gritty character of rice-flour. In the Potato the starch-granules are found larger (fig. 21) than any of the above; they are numerous and loosely packed in the cells (fig. 20). Among the more remarkable forms of starch are the large grains of the *Cannæ* (fig. 25), *Musa* (fig. 24), and most of the Zingiberaceæ (fig. 19). Some East Indian Arrowroot (fig. 18) has compound grains of large size (mostly detached in the prepared farina). True West Indian Arrow-root, from *Maranta arundinacea*, is represented in fig. 26. Various other kinds are illustrated in Pl. 36. *Dieffenbachia Seguina* (Araceæ) has remarkable lobed granules.

Starch-granules are usually isolated by slicing the tissues in which they exist, and washing them out. When they are to be observed *in situ*, either delicate transparent structures (as in the Cryptogamia) must be selected, or sections very carefully made. The cells filled with starch of the potato (Pl. 36. fig. 20), &c., may be isolated by macerating the structures in water for a day or two. Starch-granules may be preserved for

a certain time in glycerine; but they are, perhaps, best taken fresh from a store of dry granules, when required for examination.

BIBL. *Rapport sur Payen, Persoz, &c., Mémoires des savans étrangers (Paris Acad.),* v.; Poggendorff, *Annal. d. Chem. u. Pharm.* xxxvii. p. 114 (1836); Fritzsche, *ibid.* xxxii. p. 129 (1834); Payen, *Ann. des Sc. Nat.* 2 sér. x. p. 5; *Mém. Paris Acad.* viii. p. 209; Meyen, *Pflanzenphys.* i. p. 180; Mulder, *Physiol. Chemist.* (Edinburgh, 1849), p. 208; Bischoff, *Bot. Zeit.* ii. p. 385 (1844); Münter, iii. p. 193 (1845); C. Müller, *ibid.* 833 (*Ann. Nat. Hist.* xvii. p. 73); Nägeli, *Zeitschr. f. wiss. Bot.* p. 149 (1844), iii. p. 117 (1846), *Ann. Nat. Hist.* xvii. p. 185, *Ray Soc. Vol.* 1849. p. 183; *Die Stärkekörner,* 1858; Schleiden, *Grundz. der Bot.* 3rd ed. p. 177 (*Principles,* p. 10); Mohl, *Vermischt. Schrift.* p. 449, *Ann. Nat. Hist.* 2nd ser. xv. p. 371, *Botanische Zeitung,* xvii. p. 225; Martin, *Phil. Mag.* 2nd ser. iii. p. 277; Busk, *Microsc. Trans.* 2nd ser. i. p. 58; Allman, *Micr. Journ.* ii. p. 163; Cruger, *Bot. Zeit.* xii. p. 41 (1854) (*Micr. Journal,* ii. p. 173); Kützing, *Grundz. d. Phil. Bot.* i. p. 261; Lindley, *Introd. to Botany,* 2nd ed. p. 111; E. Quekett, *Ann. Nat. Hist.* xvii. p. 193; Raspail, *Ann. des Sc. Nat.* vi. (1825) and vii. (1826); Grundy, *Pharmaceutical Journal,* April 1855; Caspary, *Ueb. Hydrillen, Jahrb. f. wiss. Botanik,* i. p. 448; Trécul, *Ann. des Sc. Nat.* 4 sér. x.

STAURASTRUM, Meyen.—A genus of Desmidiaceæ.

Char. Cells single, constricted at the middle; end view angular or circular, with a lobato-radiate margin, or rarely compressed with a process at each end.

Sporangia generally spinous and often globose.

Thirty-eight British species (Ralfs).

1. *S. dejectum* (Pl. 10. fig. 26). Segments smooth, lunate or elliptical, constricted portion very short; end view with inflated awned lobes. Common; length 1-830″.

2. *S. margaritaceum* (Pl. 10. figs. 28, 29). Segments rough, tapering at the constriction, and with short lateral processes; end view with five or more short, narrow, obtuse rays. Length 1-1176″.

3. *S. gracile* (Pl. 10. fig. 30). Segments rough, elongated on each side into a slender process terminated by minute spines; end view biradiate. Length 1-770 to 1-540″.

BIBL. Ralfs, *Brit. Desmidiaceæ,* p. 119.

STAUROCARPUS, Hassall (*Staurospermum,* Kütz.).—A genus of Zygnemaceæ

(Confervoid Algæ), growing in (boggy) freshwater pools; distinguished by the remarkable quadrate spore formed in the cross-branch produced by conjugation. Hassall enumerates six species. He speaks of, but does not describe or figure the spores of *S. cærulescens* filled with "zoospores." Thwaites, however, saw the spores of *S. gracilis* resolved into four portions; and possibly these may become converted into zoospores like the spores of BULBOCHÆTE. Probably, however, they germinate directly, as in SPIROGYRA.

1. *S. glutinosus.* Filaments 1-1800 to 1-1560″ in diameter, bluish green, lubricous; spores four-sided, with the angles rounded (Hass. pl. 47. fig. 1).

2. *S. cærulescens.* Filaments about the same size as the last; spores cruciate, with obtuse lobes (Hass. pl. 47. fig. 2).

3. *S. quadratus.* Filaments 1-2400″ in diameter, spores between square and globose (Hass. pl. 48. fig. 1).

4. *S. virescens.* Filaments 1-3240 to 1-3000″ in diameter; spores cruciate, emarginate (Hass. pl. 48. fig. 2).

Fig. 694.

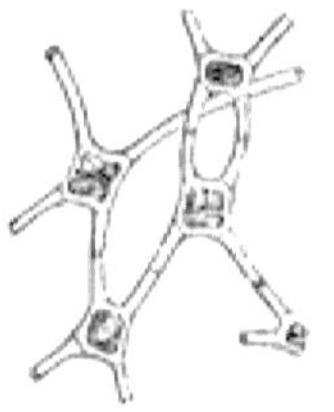

5. *S. gracillimus.* Filaments 1-4200 to 1-3000″ in diameter; spores acutely quadrangular (Hass. pl. 49. fig. 2).

6. *S. gracilis* (fig. 694 and Pl. 5. fig. 16). Filaments thicker than in *S. gracillimus;* spores cruciform (Hass. pl. 49. fig. 1). Perhaps the same as the preceding.

Staurocarpus gracilis.
Conjugating filaments with spores (or sporanges).
Magnified 100 diameters.

BIBL. Hassall, *Brit. Fr. Alg.* p. 176; Kützing, *Sp. Alg.* p. 437; *Tab. Phyc.* v. pls. 8 & 9; Thwaites, *Ann. Nat. Hist.* xvii. p. 202; Ralfs, *Brit. Desmidieæ*, p. 146; Al. Braun, *Verjüngung, &c. (Ray Soc. Vol.* 1853. p.287).

STAURONEIS, Ehr.—A genus of Diatomaceæ.

Char. Frustules resembling those of *Navicula*, but the median nodule expanded into a transverse band or stauros.

Striæ resembling those of *Navicula*, or intermediate between those of *Navicula* and *Pinnularia*; often invisible by ordinary illumination.

The species or forms are numerous; Kützing describes forty, Smith admits ten British species.

1. *S. phœnicenteron* (Pl. 11. fig. 43). Valves lanceolate, gradually attenuated towards the somewhat obtuse ends; stauros reaching the margins of the valves; striæ faint. Aquatic; common; length 1-170″.

2. *S. pulchella* (Pl. 11. figs. 44, 45). Valves oblong, ends obtuse; frustules in front view, broadly linear, constricted in the middle, and rounded-truncate at the ends; striæ distinct; stauros not reaching the margins. Marine; length 1-70″.

BIBL. Ehrenberg, *Ber. d. Berl. Akad.* 1843; Kützing, *Bacill.* p. 104, and *Sp. Alg.* p. 89.

STAUROPTERA, Ehr. — A genus of Diatomaceæ, including those species of *Stauroneis* in which Ehrenberg was enabled to detect the transverse striæ; it is no longer retained.

STAUROSIRA, Ehr.—A doubtful genus of Diatomaceæ.

S. construens (Pl. 41. fig. 38) = *Odontidium tabellaria*, Smith.

BIBL. Ehrenberg, *Mikrogeologie;* Smith, *Brit. Diat.* ii. p. 17.

STEARIC ACID.—The crystals of this fatty acid are represented in Pl. 7. fig. 16 b.

BIBL. See that of CHEMISTRY.

STEMONITIS, Gled.—A genus of Myxogastres (Gasteromycetous Fungi), consisting of little, somewhat stamen-shaped plants, either separate or fasciculated, growing on rotten wood, &c. They appear at first in the form of a mucilaginous flocculent expansion (fig. 695), from which the

Fig. 695.

Stemonitis ferruginea.
Mycelium overgrowing decaying pine-leaves.

membranaceous peridia grow up (fig. 696). Many of these remain abortive, others are raised upon stalks, ripen, and, on the separation of the fugacious peridium, display themselves somewhat in the form of DIACHÆA, but with a bristle-like columella and no remains of the peridium. The flat, cylindrical or globose, reticulated capillitium is penetrated partly or through its whole length by a columella continuous with the peduncle ; the spores are inter-

Fig. 606.

Stemonitis ferruginea.
Immature (fasciculate) peridia arising from the mycelium.

spersed in the reticulations of the capillitium. Capillitium and spores mostly of blackish colour. There are numerous British species ; *S. fusca* is common. See ENERTHENEMA and DIACHÆA.

BIBL. Berk. *Brit. Flor.* ii. pt. 2. p. 317 ; *Ann. Nat. Hist.* i. p. 257, vi. p. 431, 2nd ser. v. 366 ; Greville, *Sc. Crypt. Fl.* pl. 170 ; Fries, *Summa Veg.* p. 455 ; *Syst. Myc.* iii. p. 150.

STENOGRAMME, Harv.—A genus of Rhodymeniaceæ (Florideous Algæ), containing one very rare British plant, *S. interrupta*, characterized by stalked, flat, fan-shaped fronds, more or less divided dichotomously into riband-like lobes, 3–5" high, of a clear, pinky-red colour. It is composed of a central layer of large globular cells, with a kind of rind of small cells. The *conceptacles* form a sort of sorus or dark line resembling a rib, up the centre of each fertile lobe.   Tetraspores and antheridia unknown.

BIBL. Harv. *Brit. Mar. Alg.* p. 123, pl. 15 D.

STENTOR, Oken.—A genus of Infusoria, of the family Vorticellina.

Char. Body conical or trumpet-shaped, free, or sessile and attached by the narrow base ; covered with cilia ; anterior portion widened and fringed with a marginal row of longer cilia, with a spiral row of cilia extending from it to the mouth. Aquatic.

These Infusoria are among the largest and the most beautiful of the class. The body is very contractile and liable to variation in form, often becoming ovate, oblong, or globular. The so-called nucleus is moniliform or strap-shaped. The encysting process has been noticed in some of the species.

According to Lachmann, in *S. Mülleri, polymorphus,* and *Rœselii,* near the plane of the ciliary disk is a large contractile vesicle ;

from which a longitudinal vessel runs to the posterior extremity of the animal, and an annular vessel round the ciliary disk, close under its row of cilia ; the longitudinal vessel has several dilatations.

1. *S. Mülleri* (Pl. 25. fig. 3).   Body colourless unless from containing foreign coloured particles, with a fringe of cilia or a ciliated crest extending from the mouth to near the middle of the body ; nucleus moniliform.   Length 1-24″.

2. *S. Rœselii.* Differs from the former in the nucleus being very long, but unjointed.

3. *S. polymorphus.* Green, nucleus moniliform, no lateral crest.

Three other species.

Dujardin places this genus in the family Urceolarina.

BIBL. Ehrenberg, *Infus.* p. 261 ; Stein, *Infus., passim.*

STEPHANOCEROS, Ehr.—A genus of Rotatoria, of the family Flosculariæa.

Char. Eyes single ; rotatory organ divided into five tentacle-like lobes, furnished with whorls of vibratile cilia ; body attached by the base to a cylindrical hyaline carapace.

S. Eichhornii (Pl. 35. fig. 25).   The only species. Aquatic ; length 1-36″. This beautiful animal uses the lobes of the rotating organ to catch its prey, in the manner of *Hydra.* At *a* (fig. 25) are seen the tremulous bodies, above which is a row of roundish globules, called by Ehrenberg nervous ganglia.

BIBL. Ehrenberg, *Infus.* p. 400.

STEPHANODISCUS, Ehr.—A doubtfully distinct genus of Diatomaceæ.

Char. Frustules discoidal, single ; valves circular, alike, not areolar (under ordinary illumination), and with a fringe of minute marginal teeth. Aquatic.

S. berolinensis has the valves finely radiate, with mostly thirty-two teeth, and is 1-1150″ in diameter. *S. Niogaræ* (Pl. 43. fig. 26) ; *S. lineatus* (fig. 27) ; *S. sinensis* (fig. 28) ; *S. Ægyptiacus* (fig. 29) ; *S. Bramaputræ* (fig. 29*).

These species should be referred to *Coscinodiscus* or *Cyclotella.*

BIBL. Ehrenberg, *Ber. d. Berl. Akad.* 1845. lxxii. ; Kützing, *Sp. Alg.* p. 21.

STEPHANOGONIA, Ehr.—An obscure genus of fossil Diatomaceæ.

Char. Frustules resembling those of *Mastogonia,* but with the apices of the valves truncate, angular, and spinous.

Two species found in Bermuda and North America. *S. polygona* (Pl. 43. fig. 30).

BIBL. Ehrenberg, *Ber. d. Berl. Akad.* 1844. p. 264 ; Kutzing, *Sp. Alg.* p. 26.

STEPHANOPS, Ehr.—A genus of Rotatoria, of the family Euchlanidota.

Char. Eyes two, frontal, foot forked ; carapace depressed or prismatic ; anterior part of body expanded so as to form a frontal hood.

Jaws each with a single tooth.

S. cirratus (Pl. 35. fig. 28). Carapace with two posterior spines. Aquatic ; length 1-240''.

S. muticus has the carapace without spines posteriorly, and the eyes have not been recognized ; whilst *S. lamellatus* has three posterior spines.

BIBL. Ehrenberg, *Infus.* p. 478.

STEPHANOPYXIS, Ehr.—A genus of Diatomaceæ = *Pyxidicula*, in part.

STEPHANOSPHÆRA, Cohn.—A genus of Volvocineæ (Confervoid Algæ), not yet observed in Britain. *S. pluvialis* is nearly related to *Pandorina*, consisting of a large hyaline globe with eight biciliated green cells, placed at equal distances on the equator.

BIBL. Cohn, *Sieb. & Kóllik. Zeitschr.* iv. p. 77 (1852) (*Ann. Nat. Hist.* 2nd ser. x. p. 321, pl. 6) ; *Nova Acta*, xxvi. pt. 1 ; *Microsc. Journal*, vi. p. 131.

STEREOCAULON, Ach.—A genus of Lecidineæ (Gymnocarpous Lichens), so called from the solid character of the branched bushy thallus. *S. paschale*, the most distinct species, is abundant on rocks and stones on mountainous districts. The thallus is grayish and rough, the apothecia conglomerated, blackish brown. The spermogonia occur in little brown heads, near the apothecia.

BIBL. Hook. *Brit. Flor.* ii. pt. 1. p. 237 ; Tulasne, *Ann. des Sc. Nat.* 3 sér. xvii. p. 197 ; *Engl. Bot.* pl. 282.

STEREONEMA, Kütz. — A supposed Alga of the family Phæonemeæ (Kützing), stated by Cohn, however, to consist of the decaying stalks of ANTHOPHYSA.

BIBL. Kützing, *Sp. Alg.* p. 100.

STERIGMATA.—The term applied by Tulasne to the filaments forming the pedicels of the spermatia in the FUNGI (Pl. 20. figs. 2, 3).

STICHIDIA.—Pod-shaped processes of the fronds of Florideous Algæ, containing the tetraspores imbedded in them (fig. 157, page 207).

STICHOCOCCUS, Nägeli. See PALMELLACEÆ.

STICHOSTEGLA.—An order of Foraminifera.

Char. Shell composed of chambers arranged end to end in a single straight or slightly curved row.

Fam. I. ÆQUILATERALIDÆ. Shell free, regular, equilateral.

    * *Orifice single.*

Gen. 1. *Glandulina* (Pl. 42. fig. 40). Shell straight, round ; chambers embracing, no constrictions ; orifice central, round, at the end of a prolongation.

2. *Nodosaria* (Pl. 18. fig. 3). As the last, but chambers not embracing, and with constrictions.

3. *Orthocerina* (Pl. 18. fig. 6). Shell straight, round, no constrictions ; orifice central, round, no prolongation.

4. *Dentalina* (Pl. 42. fig. 18). Shell curved, round ; orifice central, round.

5. *Frondicularia* (Pl. 42. fig. 29). Shell compressed, flabelliform ; orifice round, central.

6. *Lingulina.* Orifice central, forming a transverse fissure.

7. *Rimulina.* Orifice marginal, a longitudinal fissure.

8. *Vaginulina* (Pl. 42. fig. 33). Shell compressed ; chambers oblique ; orifice round, marginal, no prolongation.

9. *Marginulina* (Pl. 42. fig. 9). Shell crosier-like ; orifice marginal, round, with a prolongation.

    ** *Orifices numerous.*

10. *Conulina.* Shell conical ; orifices scattered over the last chamber.

11. *Pavonina.* Shell compressed, flabelliform ; orifices in a single line.

Fam. II. INÆQUILATERALIDÆ. Shell fixed, inequilateral, irregular.

12. *Webbina.* The only genus.

BIBL. D'Orbigny, *Dict. Univ.* v. 666 ; id. *For. Foss. de Vienne*, 25 ; Morris, *Brit. Fossils* ; Williamson, *Rec. Foram.* (*Ray Soc.*).

STICTA, Ach.—A genus of Parmeliaceæ (Gymnocarpous Lichens), with a tough, foliaceous thallus, growing over rocks and trunks of trees, mostly in mountainous districts. *S. pulmonaria* forms large shaggy fronds of olive-green colour when fresh, pale-brown when dry, pitted and reticulated ; the apothecia mostly marginal, red-brown. The spermogonia of this genus occur scattered on the upper surface, mostly near the ends of the lobes.

BIBL. Hook. *Brit. Flor.* ii. pt. 1. p. 208; Tulasne, *Ann. des Sc. Nat.* 3 sér. xvii. p. 169, pl. 1; *Engl. Bot.* pl. 572.

STICTEI, Fries.—A group of Helvellacei (Ascomycetous Fungi), containing several genera of plants, growing on wood, branches of trees, &c., bursting through from beneath the bark when mature. *S. (Cryptomyces*, Berk.; *Propolis*, Fr., *S. Veg.) versicolor* (figs. 697–699) is common on

Fig. 697.   Fig. 699.

Fig. 698.

Sticta versicolor.

Fig. 697. An open disk, emerged on the surface of wood, having an irregular border.
Fig. 698. Vertical section of the same.

Magnified 20 diameters.

Fig. 699. Asci and paraphyses from the last. Magnified 200 diameters.

wood; the upper surface of the open fruit is white, and at length mealy.

BIBL. Berk. *Brit. Flora.* ii. pt. 2. p. 214; *Ann. Nat. Hist.* vi. p. 359; Fries, *Summa Veg.* p. 372.

STIGEOCLONIUM, Kütz.—A genus of Confervoid Algæ, doubtfully referred to Confervaceæ, growing mostly in brooks, and composed of delicate branched filaments, drawn out into delicate hyaline points; attached to stones and forming masses of a sinuous or lubricous character. The jointed filaments are composed of short cells, possessing bright green contents; the entire contents of a cell are converted into a single zoospore (with four cilia) and discharged (Pl. 5. fig. 5), and the cell-wall is so delicate that it generally vanishes at the same time. Many species are described by Kützing, formerly regarded as members of the genus DRAPARNALDIA, which differs in the number of zoospores produced in each cell, and in possessing large primary fila-

ments with lateral tufts of delicate ones, resembling those of *Stigeoclonium* (fig. 179, p. 238). We select the most distinct of the British forms.

1. *S. protensum* (Pl. 5, fig. 5). Tufts of filaments 1-36 to 1-60″ high, very much branched and elongated; primary filaments 1-1800″ in diameter, joints equal or three times as long as long (*Drap. condensata*, Hassall, pl. 11. fig. 1).

2. *S. tenue.* Tufts about 1-36 to 1-72″ high; primary filaments 1-2160″ in diameter; torulose; set above with numerous tufts of abbreviated branchlets (*Drap. tenuis*, Hass. pl. 11. fig. 2).

3. *S. elongatum.* Filaments very slender; primaries 1-2880″ in diameter; branches erecto-patent, often opposite, subramulose, flagelliform; all the joints three or five times as long as broad (*Drap. elongata*, Hass. pl. 10. fig. 3).

4. *S. nanum.* "Filaments highly mucous, very slender, sparingly branched, branches acuminate, not usually ciliated (produced into a filiform end); cells rather broader than long" (*Drap. nana*, Hass. pl. 10. fig. 4).

BIBL. Kützing, *Sp. Alg.* p. 352; *Tab. Phyc.* iii. pls. 1–11; Hassall, *Brit. Fr. Alg.* fig. 118; Thuret, *Ann. des Sc. Nat.* 3 sér. xiv. p. 223, pl. 18; *Engl. Bot.* Suppl. No. 2913.

STIGMA.—The part of the pistil of Angiospermous Flowering Plants, upon which the pollen rests to produce its pollen-tubes, and where the orifices exist leading to the cavity of the ovary. It is situated either at or near the summit of the style or its branches, or, when this is absent, it is sessile on the ovary. The surface of the stigma is clothed with papilliform or short tubular cells, from which a saccharine secretion exudes at the period when the ovules are prepared to receive the influence of the pollen-grains. In this fluid the pollen-grains produce their tubes, which make their way between the papillæ to descend through the conducting tissue of the style to the placenta (Pl. 32. fig. 30). These papilliform cells in a young state often form favourable subjects for the study of the protoplastic cell-contents, and also of the fluid colouring matter. The forms of the stigma are exceedingly varied and sometimes very elegant, and some of those covered with coloured hairs form beautiful microscopic objects. In the family of Compositæ, its characters are used for the systematic division of the numerous genera.

STIGMATA OF ANIMALS. See SPIRA-CLES.

STIGMATEA, Fr. See DOTHIDEA.

STIGONEMA, Ag.—A supposed genus of Scytonemeous Oscillatoriaceæ (Confervoid Algæ), founded upon what has proved to be the thallus of a genus of Lichens. See EPHEBE.

STILBACEI.—A family of Hyphomycetous Fungi, growing upon decaying animal or vegetable matter, or on bark or leathery leaves. Characterized by a wart-shaped receptacle, composed of conjoined filamentous or hexagonal cells and spores borne singly on the apices of free filaments. Some of the Fungi here included are heterogeneous and imperfectly studied; for example, *Tubercularia* and *Fusarium* are apparently only imperfect states of other Fungi, while the more distinct genera appear to be referable to the family Dematiei.

Synopsis of British Genera.

1. *Stilbum.* Receptacle stalked at the base, clavate or capitate at the summit, composed of coalescent, densely crowded, parallel filaments; spores simple, arising singly at the apices of free filaments.

2. *Pachnocybe.* Receptacle stipitate, clavate, floccose, the filaments twisted, the head finally pruinose, with simple spores.

3. *Periconia.* Receptacle stalked at the base, clavate or capitate at the apex, composed of coalescent, densely crowded, parallel filaments, or cellularly fleshy; spores simple, crowded on simple sporophores arising at the summit (and on the stalk, Fries).

4. *Tubercularia.* Receptacle wart-shaped, globular or stalked, fleshy, composed of continuous sterile, and thread-like beaded fertile filaments. Finally indurated, floccose, with the spores scattered over it, or falling into powder.

5. *Periola.* Receptacle cellular, sessile; fertile filaments abbreviated, torulose, mixed with septate lax sterile filaments.

6. *Volutella.* Receptacle wart-like, cellular, compact, with long rigid bristles; spores spindle-shaped, septate, on continuous short filaments, arising all over the receptacle.

7. *Fusarium.* Receptacle wart-like, cellular, gelatinous; spores spindle-shaped, simple, somewhat curved, borne on simple filaments arising all over the receptacle, and forming a discoid stratum.

8. *Illosporium.* Receptacle wart-shaped, subgelatinous, diffluent; spores simple, pellucid, generally with a hyaline envelope, borne on short filaments.

9. *Epicoccum.* Receptacle wart-shaped, cellular, for the most part seated on an effused patch; spores four-sided, cellular, attached singly to very short, continuous filaments.

BIBL. Berkeley, *Crypt. Botany*, p. 311.

STILBOSPORA, Pers. — A supposed genus of Melanconiei (Coniomycetous Fungi), but apparently only consisting of stylosporous fruits of *Sphæriæ*. These grow upon wood, sticks, &c., breaking forth on the surface without any distinct perithecium, consisting of a nucleus composed of agglutinated (septate) stylospores (see SPHÆNIA).

Fig. 700.

Stilbospora macrosperma.

Group of conceptacles breaking forth on a fragment of wood; nat. size. The detached spores on the right-hand magnified 150 diameters.

BIBL. Berk. *Brit. Flor.* ii. pt. 2. p. 356; *Ann. Nat. Hist.* vi. p. 355; *Hooker's London Journ. of Bot.* iii. p. 322; Fries, *Summa Veg.* p. 508; Fresenius, *Beitr. z. Myc.* Heft ii. p. 63; Tulasne, *Ann. des Sc. Nat.* 4 sér. v. p. 109.

STILBUM, Tode.—A genus of Stilbacei (Hyphomycetous Fungi), containing a considerable number of species, forming little shining mildews, sometimes brightly coloured, on decaying wood, herbaceous plants, Fungi, &c. The stalk-like stroma differs in character, being sometimes villous, sometimes glabrous and rigid, sometimes pellucid and soft; it is formed of conjoined filaments, the free ends of which bear the spores in a capitulum, which finally exhibits a gelatinous character.

BIBL. Berk. *Brit. Flor.* ii. pt. 2. p. 330; *Ann. Nat. Hist.* vi. p. 432, pl. 12; *ibid.* 2nd ser. v. p. 465; Fries, *Summa Veget.* p. 460.

STILOPHORA, J. Ag. — A genus of Sporochnaceæ (Fucoid Algæ), included by some authors among the Dictyotaceæ. There are two British species, *S. rhizodes* and *S. Lyngbyei*, characterized by a branched, filiform, at first solid, afterwards tubular frond, the former 6 to 24″, the latter 2 to 4″ long, arising from a small naked disk. The fructification consists of little wart-like bodies scattered all over the frond, composed of tufts of moniliform filaments, at the bases of which are attached either pyriform unilocular, or tubular septate sporanges. Thuret states that the specimens of *S. rhizodes* found a certain distance above low-water mark appear mostly to bear septate, those always under water simple sporanges, and those in an intermediate position exhibit both. The plants of the first kind are of paler colour than those of the second.

BIBL. Harvey, *Brit. Mar. Alg.* p. 39, pl. 7 C; Greville, *Alg. Brit.* pl. 6; Thuret, *Ann. des Sc. Nat.* 3 sér. xiv. p. 238, pl. 38.

STING OF INSECTS.—The well-known sting of the female or so-called neuters of Hymenopterous Insects, as the honey-bee, the humble-bee, the hornet, the wasp, &c., appears to the naked eye to be a single needle-like organ; but when examined under the microscope, it is seen to consist of three pieces—a short, stout, cylindrico-conical outer piece or sheath (Pl. 27. fig. 14 *a*), cleft throughout its length on the under surface and obtuse at the end, within which are partly contained two long elbowed setæ or lancets (Pl. 27. fig. 15, one of them), thickened and furnished with teeth directed backwards near the end of one margin, the other margin sharp and cutting. These setæ play within the sheath, being partially protrusile and retractile, as is the sheath itself. The poison-apparatus consists of two glandular elongated sacs, either simple (Pl. 27. fig. 14 *e*, *f*), or branched as in the humble-bee, &c., and terminating by one (fig. 14 *d*) or two ducts, in a muscular reservoir (fig. 14 *c*), from which an excretory duct runs to the base of the sheath of the sting.

The irritation produced by the sting of one of these insects needs no remark. It does not, however, serve a merely defensive purpose, but is used also to paralyse the prey, so that it may be kept in store for future use.

The sting represents a modified ovipositor.

BIBL. Lacaze-Duthiers, *Ann. des Sc. Nat.* 3 sér. xii. xiv.; Westwood, *Introduction,&c.*; Siebold, *Vergl. Anat.*

STINGS OF PLANTS.— These are epidermal structures, consisting of large hairs, with a bulbous base more or less included in a cellular coat, and attenuated upwards. In the sting of the nettle the apex is expanded into a little bulb, which is broken off when the sting is lightly touched (Pl. 21. fig. 8). Young stings exhibit the ROTATION. Stings occur not only in the nettles (*Urtica*), but in the cultivated

Fig. 701.

Stinging hair of Nettle.
Magn. 20 diams.

Loasaceæ (*Loasa*, *Bartonia*, &c.), and of much larger size in some exotic Urticaceæ and Euphorbiaceæ.

See HAIRS, page 339.

STOMACH.—The glands which secrete the gastric juice are tubular glands, perpendicularly placed beneath the surface of the mucous membrane, and extending as deeply as the muscular coat of the stomach.

They vary in length from 1-60 to 1-12", are cylindrical, somewhat narrowed towards the closed end, which is rounded or somewhat inflated. The lower third is wavy or

Fig. 702.

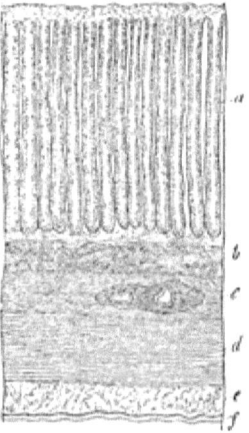

Perpendicular section of the pyloric portion of the stomach of a pig. *a*, glands; *b*, muscular layer of the proper mucous membrane; *c*, submucous tissue with the orifices of divided vessels; *d*, transverse muscular layer; *e*, longitudinal ditto; *f*, serous coat. Magnified 30 diameters.

spiral, especially in the glands occupying the pylorus; some of them also give off a cæcal branch.

The gastric glands consist of a delicate basement membrane, lined in the upper third with cylindrical epithelium, the lower portion being filled with large, pale, polygonal, finely granular cells, not arranged in a laminated form.

In many animals the gastric glands are of more complicated structure than in man, and two distinct kinds exist, in one, secreting mucus, the tubes being lined with cylindrical epithelium; whilst in the other, which secretes gastric juice, rounded epithelial cells occur, and the walls are expanded at intervals.

Closed follicles resembling the solitary glands of the small intestines are met with in the stomach; they are, however, inconstant and variable in number.

Fig. 703.   Fig. 704.   Fig. 705.

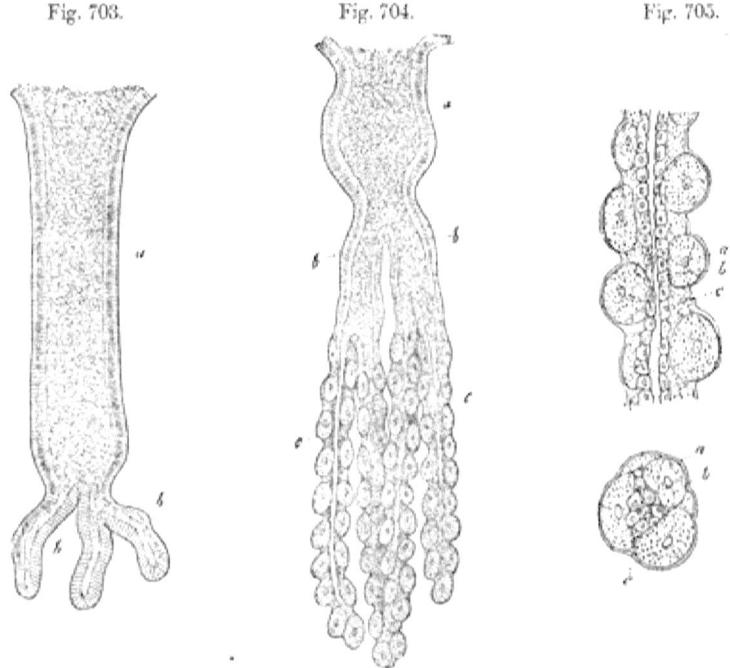

Fig. 703. Gastric gland with cylinder-epithelium, from the pylorus of a dog. *a*, principal cavity; *b*, tubular processes arising from it.   Magnified 60 diameters.

Fig. 704. Gastric gland from the middle of the stomach. *a*, principal cavity; *b*, primary, and *c*, terminal branches arising from it.   Magnified 60 diameters.

Fig. 705. Portions of a terminal branch, the upper representing a longitudinal, the lower a transverse section. *a*, basement membrane; *b*, large cells in close apposition with it; *c*, smaller epithelial cells surrounding the cavity. Magnified 350 diameters.

The stomach is lined by cylindrical epithelium.

BIBL. Kölliker, *Mikrosk. Anat.* ii. p. 137, and the Bibl. therein; Todd and Bowman, *Phys. Anat. &c.*

STOMATA (plural of STOMA).—This name is applied to the structures which constitute the passages of communication, through the EPIDERMIS of plants, from the intercellular passages to the external air. They occur almost exclusively on the green parts of plants, and are absent from the epidermis of roots, also on the surface of all structures growing under water. The lowest classes which present them are the Liverworts and Mosses, where, however, they are limited to a few kinds, and in the former present a peculiar organization. In the Ferns they are distributed just as in the Flowering Plants, where they occur principally upon the leaves (fig. 706), especially upon the lower face, but extend also over the green shoots, the parts of the flower (fig. 200, page 262), and even into the interior of cavities, as on the epidermis of the *rephon* of Cruciferæ (wallflower), and still more remarkably, on the epidermis of seeds (skin of the walnut).

In the Liverworts the stomata occur on the fronds and receptacles of certain genera

(*Marchantia*, *Fegatella*, &c. &c.). In *Marchantia* (fig. 447, p. 444), they are somewhat circular orifices in the epidermis, guarded by cells arranged in three or four tiers. In the Mosses they are met with on the apophyses or thickened summits of the setæ bearing the capsules, as in *Funaria* (fig. 262, page 303). The structures here resemble those in the higher plants, as is the case also with those on the leaves of the Ferns.

Fig. 706.

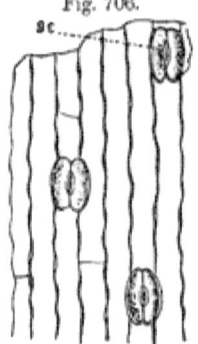

Epidermis of the White Lily with stomata, at (lower surface).

Magnified 100 diameters.

In the Flowering Plants the perfect stomata appear as roundish or sometimes squarish chasms in the epidermal layer, occurring regularly at the meeting angles or sides of four or more epidermal cells, the chasm forming an orifice leading down to a subepidermal intercellular space, and guarded a little below the upper edge, more deeply, or even at the bottom, by (usually) two semilunar cells, applied together by their flat faces, but not coherent, their convex surfaces adhering firmly to the sides of the epidermal gap. According as the two stomatal cells or "pore-cells" or "guard-cells" are distended or collapsed, their flat faces approach or retreat from each other, in the latter case leaving a slit-like orifice leading from the outer passage into the subepidermal space. Sometimes the "guard-cells" are four in number, in which case they either form two tiers, as upper and lower (Proteaceæ, *e. g. Hakea*, *Protea*, &c.), or they are in the same line and parallel, forming inner and outer "guard-cells" (*Ficus elastica*). In certain coriaceous leaves the stomata are placed on the sides of pits excavated beneath the surface of the leaves, as in *Dasylyrion oblongifolium* and *Nerium Oleander*.

A considerable difference exists between the appearances presented by vertical sections of the epidermis of leaves made so as to pass through the stomata. In young leaves the guard-cells are little, if at all below the general level of the epidermis; and the same is the case with the perfect forms in various herbaceous plants in which the leaves are of membranous texture. In other cases, as in the Hyacinth, *Iris*, *Narcissus*, *Equisetum*, &c., the guard-cells are found at a very early period quite beneath the layer of epidermal cells, attached as it were *under* the passage communicating with the air. The same occurs very frequently in the stomata of coriaceous leaves, as in *Aloe* (Pl. 39. fig. 22), *Ficus*, *Cycas*, *Hakea*, *Protea*, &c. In other instances, also in leathery leaves, the "guard-cells" appear more or less elevated *above* the general level of the epidermal cells, as in some species of *Leucadendron*, *Grevillea*, &c. It is important to observe that in the cases where the "guard-cells" are sunk in the orifice of the epidermis, the upper margin of the orifice, formed by the borders of the surrounding epidermal cells, sometimes becomes elevated and even converted into a kind of perforated dome (Pl. 39. fig. 22), by development of the cuticular layers (see EPIDERMIS). This might be mistaken for the stoma itself. The same cuticular substance is often developed in mature leaves, not only down over the walls of the stomatal passage, but over the guard-cells, and from thence more or less into contiguous intercellular passages. This may be observed in *Euphorbia Caput-Medusæ*, *Helleborus niger* and *viridis*, *Betula alba*, *Asphodelus luteus*, and *Cereus*, some *Aloes*, &c. Gasparrini obtained these connected processes of cuticular substance, in the form of an isolated coherent piece, by boiling epidermis in nitric acid, which dissolved the adjoining cell-walls: these he mistook for peculiar organs, and called them *cistomes*. Dr. Hooker has described a remarkable form of stomata in the parasitical plant *Myzodendron*.

In those plants in which the epidermis becomes infiltrated with siliceous matter, the walls of the stomatal pore and the "guard-cells" become imbued with it, and a siliceous skeleton of the structure remains after the organic matter has been removed by nitric acid and burning (Pl. 39. fig. 29). This is readily seen in the Equisetaceæ, especially *E. hyemale*, also in the Grasses.

The mode of development of the stomata appears to be uncertain. Mohl and other authors assert that the "guard-cells" originate from one of the cells of the subepidermal tissue, which is pushed up into a vacancy formed by the separation of the epidermal cells at certain points. This cell is said to be next divided into two, which become free from each other in the line of the new partition then formed. Nägeli and others assert that the guard-cells are originally constituent cells of the epidermal layer, which become subsequently displaced downwards (or upwards), and undergo special development analogous to that just described. Dr. Garreau has recently described this mode of development as occurring in *Tradescantia*. We believe it is the correct view, at all events in some cases; but the appearances are certainly difficult to explain on this plan in the Iridaceæ, Equisetaceæ, and some other plants.

The stomata are generally largest upon succulent leaves, smallest on hard and leathery kinds; their form and number are most varied, both in different plants and on different parts of the same plant. They abound most on the lower face of leaves; but it has been mentioned that they are not found on submerged organs, and on floating leaves they occur only upon the upper face. The larger kinds are more scattered on a given surface, the smaller occur closer together (this depends, of course, on the general character of the epidermal and subjacent tissue). The numbers have been estimated upon the surfaces of many leaves, of which a few examples may be given: thus a square inch contains, in

	Upper surface.	Lower surface.
Carnation	38,500	38,500
Garden Flag	11,572	11,572
House-leek	10,710	6,000
Tradescantia	2,000	2,000
Misletoe	200	200
Holly	0	63,600
Lilac	0	160,000
Vine	0	13,600
Laurestinus	0	90,000

BIBL. *General Works on Struct. Botany*; Krocker, *De Epidermide*, Vratisl. 1833; Mohl, *Verm. Schrift.* pp. 245, 252; *Bot. Zeit.* iii. p. 1 (*Ann. Nat. Hist.* xv. p. 217); *Bot. Zeit.* xiv. p. 697 (*Ann. des Sc. Nat.* 4 sér. vi. p. 162); Nägeli, *Linnæa*, xvi. p. 237. 1842; Mirbel, *sur Marchantia, Mém. Acad. Roy. France*, xiii.; Gasparrini, *Nuove ric. s. strutt. d. Cistomi*, Naples, 1844; Garreau, *Ann. des Sc. Nat.* 4 sér. i. p. 213; J. D. Hooker, *Flora Antarct.* i. p. 291; Golding Bird, *Proc. Linn. Society*, i. p. 260; Stocks, MS.

STONES OF FRUITS, such as cherries, plums, &c., afford excellent materials for sections, showing extreme development of the woody SECONDARY DEPOSITS of vegetable cells.

STREPTOTHRIX. See AMBER.

STRIARIA, Grev.—A genus of Dictyosiphonaceæ, nearly related to Punctariaceæ (Fucoid Algæ), having a branched, filiform, tubular frond, arising from a shield-shaped naked disk. The walls of the tube are mem-

Fig. 707.

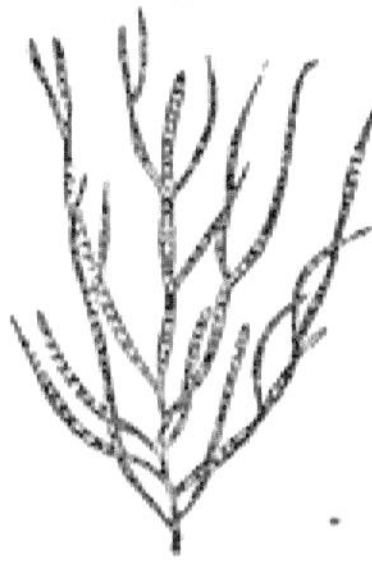

Fig. 708. 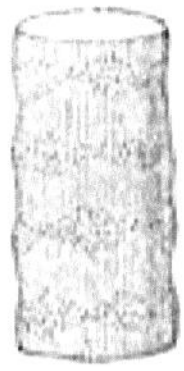　　　　　Fig. 709.

Striaria attenuata.

Fig. 707. Part of a frond. One-third of the nat. size.
Fig. 708. A fragment with sori. Magnified 5 diams.
Fig. 709. Section of a fertile branch, with sori. Magnified 25 diameters.

branous, and the cavity without septa. *S. attenuata* (fig. 707) grows from 3 to 12" high. The branches are attenuated towards each end, and marked with rings consisting of clusters of simple sporanges ("spores") (fig. 708), sometimes accompanied by filaments (fig. 709). Colour pale olive.

BIBL. Harv. *Brit. Mar. Alg.* p. 41, pl. 8 A; Grev. *Brit. Alg.* fig. 9.

STRIATELLA, Kütz.—A genus of Diatomaceæ.

Char. Frustules with a stipes attached to one angle, depressed, tabulate; with longitudinal uninterrupted vittæ, apparently thickened at each end. Marine.

The vittæ appear as dark lines; no transverse striæ are visible under ordinary illumination.

S. unipunctata (Pl. 13. fig. 20). Frustules in front view quadrangular, often broader than long, lateral margins subulate; valves narrowly lanceolate; stalk elongate, simple, filiform and thickish. Length of frustules 1-450 to 1-280″.

Compare the other genera enumerated under Striatelleæ (DIATOMACEÆ, p. 225).

BIBL. Kützing, *Bacill.* p. 125; *Species Algarum*, p. 114.

STRIGULA, Fries.—A genus of Limborieæ (Angiocarpous Lichens), containing one British species, *S. Babingtonii*, growing on the leaves of box and other evergreens. The thallus is subepidermal; the asci contain eight cymbiform triseptate spores.

BIBL. Leighton, *Brit. Angioc. Lich.* p. 70, pl. 30. f. 4; Berk. *English Botany*, Supp. pl. 2957.

STRONTIA on STRONTIAN.—The crystals of the sulphate of this earthy base are figured in Pl. 6. fig. 18, to contrast with those of the sulphates of baryta and lime.

STRUTHIOPTE-RIS, Willden. — A genus of Polypodieæ (Ferns), with the margins of the fertile leaves rolled up so as to conceal the sori, which are without a true indusium. *Str. germanica* (fig. 710) is of large size; and the fertile fronds, distinct from the sterile, if cursorily examined, might lead to the reference of this plant to the Osmundeæ or "Flowering ferns."

Fig. 710.

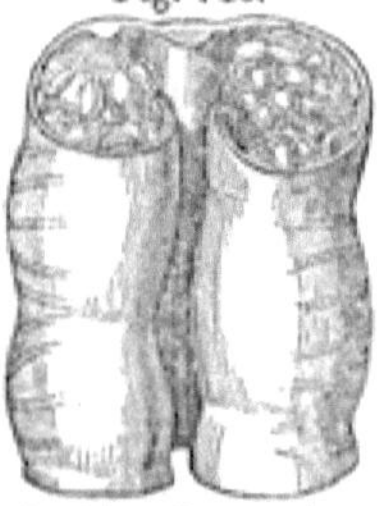

Struthiopteris germanica.

Portion of a pinna with the rolled margins covering the sori.

Magnified 40 diameters.

STRYCHNINE, or STRYCHNIA. See ALKALOIDS, p. 28.

STYLOBIBLIUM, Ehr.—A genus of fossil Diatomaceæ.

Char. Frustules circular, single, compound; valves contiguous, in a single row, like the leaves of a book, the inner ones with a large median aperture (?), the outer not being perforated but sculptured.

S. clypeus (Pl. 43. fig. 50 *a*, *b*); *S. divisum* (fig. 50 *c*); *S. eccentricum* (fig. 50 *d*). It is uncertain whether the so-called inner valves are merely hoops, or the valves of imperfectly separated frustules; also whether they are perforated or not, for neither Ehrenberg nor Kützing can be relied on for distinguishing a perforation, as evidenced by their erroneous description of the structure of the valves of *Pinnularia*, *Grammatophora*, and many other Diatomaceæ.

Three species are described, occurring in America and Siberia. The sculpturings upon the outer valves consist of radiating or excentric curved lines.

BIBL. Ehrenberg, *Ber. d. Berl. Akad.* 1845; id. *Mikrogeologie, &c.*; Kützing, *Sp. Alg.* p. 116.

STYLONICHIA, Ehr.—A genus of Infusoria, of the family Oxytrichina.

Char. Body ciliated, and furnished with styles and hooks.

In this genus, transverse and longitudinal division, gemmation, and the encysting process have been observed.

1. *S. mytilus* = *Kerona mytilus*. D. (Pl. 24. figs. 27, 28). Body white, hyaline at each end, flat, oblong, slightly constricted in the middle, dilated at the oblique fore part. Aquatic; length 1-240 to 1-100″.

2. *S. pustulata* = *Kerona pustul.* D. (Pl. 24. fig. 26). Body white, turbid, oblong, with a median ventral band of hooks. Aquatic; length 1-144″.

3. *S. histrio* (Pl. 24. fig. 29). Body white, elliptic-oblong, hooks aggregated into an anterior heap; no setæ. Aquatic; length 1-290 to 1-220″.

4. *S. lanceolata* (Pl. 24. fig. 30). Body lanceolate, pale green, obtuse at the ends; ventral surface flat; hooks acervate near the mouth; styles none. Aquatic; length 1-140 to 1-120″.

Two other species.

BIBL. Ehrenberg, *Infus.* p. 370; Stein, *Infus.* p. 172.

STYLOSPORES. —Stalked spores of Coniomycetous Fungi, usually compound or septate, then probably consisting of a row of independent spores connected by an adherent parent sac—thus, structurally, metamorphosed asci; they are sometimes appendaged above (fig. 711) (see SPORES and CONIOMYCETES).

Fig. 711.

Stylospores of Pestalozzia.

Magnified 200 diameters.

STYSANUS, Corda, = CEPHALOTRI-CHUM.

SUCCINIC ACID.—This acid, which occurs in amber, in all fermented liquids, and in the contents of *Echinococcus* cysts, is pretty soluble in water, readily in hot but with difficulty in cold alcohol, and but little in æther.

The crystals belong to the oblique prismatic system, and are represented in Pl. 7. fig. 21.

BIBL. That of CHEMISTRY.

SUDORIPAROUS GLANDS. — These organs secrete the perspiration.

They are found in most parts of the skin, but in variable numbers in different localities. Thus it has been estimated that 417 exist in a square inch of the skin of the back of the hand, 1093 in an inch of the outside, and 1123 in the inside of the fore-arm, and 2736 in an inch of the palm of the hand.

Each gland consists of a long tube coiled into a knot near the closed end, which is situated in the subcutaneous cellular tissue, and forms the gland proper, and a straight, undulate, or spiral duct, which traverses the skin perpendicularly, to terminate upon its surface between the papillæ.

Fig. 712.

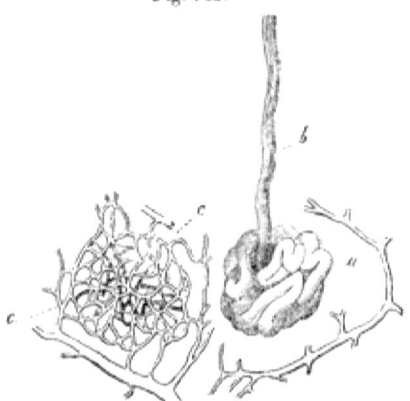

Fig. 713.

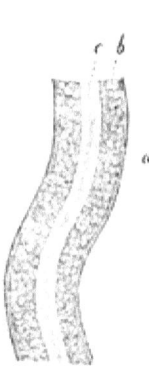

Fig. 712. A sudoriparous gland, with its blood-vessels.　*a*, proper gland; *b*, duct; *c*, blood-vessels of a gland. Magnified 35 diameters.

Fig. 713. Portion of the tube forming a sudoriparous gland from the hand.　*a*, areolar coat; *b*, epithelium; *c*, cavity. Magnified 350 diameters.

In the glands of the axilla, the portion of the tube forming the gland proper is branched, and sometimes the branches anastomose.

The coiled portion or proper gland is surrounded and permeated by an elegant plexus of capillaries; and some of them are surrounded by a capsule of areolar tissue with spindle-shaped cells.

The tube of the glands exhibits two forms of structure. In one of these there is an outer coat of indistinctly fibrous areolar tissue with elongated nuclei, sharply defined internally by probably a basement membrane, this being lined with one, two, or more layers of polygonal pavement-epithelial cells, mostly containing fat-globules and pigment-granules.

In the other form, the fibrillation of the areolar coat is tolerably distinct, the fibres longitudinal, sometimes also with an inner,

Fig. 714.

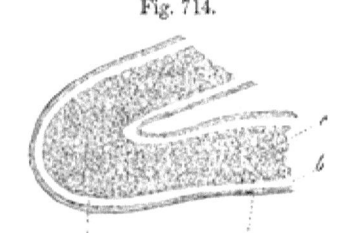

Portion of a tube with a muscular coat, from the scrotum. *a*, areolar tissue; *b*, muscular layer; *c*, epithelial cells, filling the tube and containing yellow granules. Magnified 350 diameters.

delicate transverse layer, and both containing nuclear elastic fibres; and within this coat is a layer of longitudinal, unstriped muscular fibres.

The portion of the ducts traversing the cuticle is spiral.

It is by no means an easy matter to obtain the sudoriparous glands in the entire state. The skin of the palm of the hand or the paw of a dog is best for the purpose; and before making sections with a Valentin's knife, the structure should be macerated in a mixture of 1 part nitric acid and 2 of water, or in solution of carbonate of potash.

BIBL. Kölliker, *Mikrosk. Anat.* ii.; Todd and Bowman, *Physiolog. Anat. &c.*

SUGAR.—This substance is liable to fraudulent adulterations; and the coarser kinds of brown sugar contain many impurities, such as Acari, fragments of the cane, &c. Starch and flour are used to whiten and give dryness to inferior moist sugar; and these may be detected by the microscope (STARCH).

The crystals of sugar of milk are represented in Pl. 6. fig. 12, and those of diabetic sugar in Pl. 6. fig. 13.

BIBL. Hassall, *Food and its Adulterations*, p. 12, and the Bibl. of CHEMISTRY.

SULPHUR. See LIME, *sulphate of* (p. 427).

SURIRELLA, Turpin.—A genus of Diatomaceæ.

Char. Frustules free, single, ovate, elliptical, oblong, cuneate or broadly linear in front view; valves with a longitudinal median line or a clear space, the margins winged, and with transverse or slightly radiating canaliculi or tubular striæ.

It appears that in the valves the margins of the depressions are fused together to form tubular channels open at the ends.

Kützing describes fifty-six species or forms, Smith twenty as British.

1. *S. bifrons* (Ehr. 1833 = *S. biseriata*, Bréb. and Smith) (Pl. 13. fig. 22). Frustules in front view broadly linear, with rounded angles; valves elliptic-lanceolate, somewhat obtuse; alæ and canaliculi distinct. Aquatic; length 1-180 to 1-96″.

2. *S. gemma* (Pl. 13. fig. 21). Frustules ovate; valves elliptic-ovate; canaliculi narrow, inequidistant. Marine; length 1-240″.

3. *S. splendida.* Frustules ovato-cuneate, ends rounded; valves ovato-lanceolate; alæ and canaliculi distinct. Aquatic; length 1-160″.

Compare TRYBLIONELLA, and see DIATOMACEÆ (p. 220).

BIBL. Smith, *Brit. Diatom.* i. p. 30; Kütz. *Bacill.* p. 59, and *Sp. Alg.* p. 34.

SWARMING.—This term has been applied by the Germans, from comparison with the swarming of bees, to the remarkable oscillating crowding movements of the zoospores of Confervæ, &c., while free in the cavity of the parent-cell, and preparing to break forth. The zoospores are hence often called "swarming-spores." See HYDRODICTYON.

SYMBOLOPHORA, Ehr.—A genus of Diatomaceæ.

Char. Frustules single, disk-shaped, with incomplete septa radiating from the solid angular centre, and intermediate bundles of radiating lines. Marine and fossil.

S. Trinitatis (Pl. 19. fig. 6). Valves with a triangular umbilicus, the transparent margins of which are crenulate, the rest of the disk covered with six bundles of very fine radiating lines. Diameter 1-220″. America.

S. acuta (Pl. 43. fig. 54); *S. micrasterias* (fig. 55); *S. pentas* (fig. 56).

Five other species.

BIBL. Ehrenberg, *Ber. d. Berl. Akad.* 1844. p. 74; Kützing, *Sp. Alg.* p. 131.

SYMPHIOTHRIX, Kütz. = OSCILLATORIA.

SYMPHYOSIPHON, Kütz.—A genus of Oscillatoriaceæ (Confervoid Algæ), growing on the ground, &c. *S. (Scytonema,* Lyngb.) *Bangii* grows among mosses; it is of blackish colour, tufted and bristling, the filaments from 1-9600 to 1-7200″ in diameter.

BIBL. Kütz. *Sp. Alg.* p. 324; *Tab. Phyc.* ii. pl. 44. f. 1.

SYMPLOCA, Kütz.—A genus of Oscillatoriaceæ (Confervoid Algæ), perhaps not distinct from *Symphyosiphon.* Kützing includes here *S. Ralfsiana* = *Osc. Friesii* of British authors, *S. lucifuga* = *Oscill. lucifuga,* Harv., and *S. hydnoides* = *Calothrix hydnoides,* Harvey.

BIBL. Kütz. *Sp. Alg.* p. 270; *Tab. Phyc.* i. pl. 74–76; Harvey, *Brit. Alg.* 1st ed.

SYNALISSA.—A genus of Collemaceæ (Gymnocarpous Lichens), somewhat resembling *Lichina,* but with open apothecia.

BIBL. Berk. *Crypt. Bot.* p. 407.

SYNAMMIA, Presl.—A genus of Grammitideæ (Polypodioid Ferns). Exotic.

SYNAPTA, Eschsch.—A genus of vermiform Echinodermata, of the order Apoda. The species of *Synapta,* which are not

British, are of special microscopic interest, on account of the presence in their skin of remarkable anchor-shaped calcareous spicula, the bases of which play in perforated plates. These are situated upon minute papillæ of the skin, and serve to aid in locomotion and adhesion.

These bodies have been formed into genera and species of Polygastric Infusoria by Ehrenberg, the perforated plate constituting a *Dictyocha*.

BIBL. V. d. Hoeven, *Zoologie*, i. p. 150; Vogt, *Zool. Briefe*, i. p. 168; Quatrefages, *Ann. des Sc. Nat.* 2 sér. xvii. p. 19.

SYNCHLÆTA, Ehr.—A genus of Rotatoria, of the family Hydatinæa.

Char. Eye single, cervical, rotatory organ furnished with styles; foot forked.

Jaws each with a single tooth.

Some of the species are furnished with one or more so-called crests, which in some appear to correspond to the calcar.

S. baltica (Pl. 35. fig. 26). Body ovate; rotatory lobes four; styles four; a single median sessile crest. Marine; length 1-108″. Phosphorescent.

Three other species.

BIBL. Ehrenberg, *Infus.* p. 436.

SYNCRYPTA, Ehr.—A doubtful genus of Volvocineæ (Confervoid Algæ), composed of organisms consisting of a hyaline spherical membrane ("gelatinous envelope," Ehr.) enclosing a number of ovate green bodies placed at the periphery and sending out a pair of free vibratile cilia (only *one*, Ehr.) from the surface of the envelope. Green bodies not attenuated at the posterior extremity; "no eye-spot." *S. Volvox* (Pl. 3. fig. 14 *b*), globe 1-576″ in diameter, green "animalcules" 1-2880″ long; aquatic, not marine. This object, which we have observed in company with those represented in figs. 14 *a*, 31 and 32 of the same plate, is most probably a young specimen of either VOLVOX or PANDORINA.

BIBL. Ehrenberg, *Infus.* p. 60.

SYNCYCLIA, Ehr.—A genus of Diatomaceæ.

Char. Frustules cymbelliform, united in circular bands, immersed in an amorphous gelatinous substance. Marine.

The nodules appear to be the same as those of *Cymbella*.

1. *S. salpa* (Pl. 14. fig. 14). Frustules semi-ovate, unstriated (ord. illum.), commonly six together, united into a ring; endochrome bright green.

2. *S. quaternaria.* Frustules two or four together; endochrome yellow or reddish; length 1-860″.

BIBL. Ehrenberg, *Infus.* p. 233; *Ber. d. Berl. Akad.* 1840. 32: Kützing, *Sp. Alg.* 61.

SYNDENDRIUM, Ehr.—A genus of Diatomaceæ.

Char. Frustules single, subquadrangular, destitute of a median umbilicus; valves unequal, slightly turgid,—one smooth, the other with numerous spines or little horns branched at the ends, situated upon the median flat portion, the margins being free from them.

S. diadema (Pl. 43. fig. 59). Frustules lanceolate; spines five or six, bifurcate or tufted at the end, as long as the frustules are broad. Breadth 1-1150″. Found in Peruvian guano.

BIBL. Ehrenberg, *Ber. d. Berl. Akad.* 1845. p. 155; Kützing, *Sp. Alg.* p. 141.

SYNEDRA, Ehr.—A genus of Diatomaceæ.

Char. Frustules prismatic, rectangular, or curved; at first attached to a gelatinous sometimes lobed cushion, subsequently often becoming free; valves linear or lanceolate.

The valves usually exhibit a longitudinal line, with a dilated median and two terminal nodules; they are also generally covered with transverse striæ; in some species the median line and appearance of a median nodule correspond to a clear space, free from the transverse striæ.

Kützing describes seventy species; Smith twenty-four as British.

1. *S. splendens*, K. (*S. radians*, Sm.) (Pl. 13. fig. 23 *a, b, c*). Frustules elongated, in front view dilated and truncate at the ends; valves gradually attenuated from the middle to the obtuse ends. Aquatic; common; length 1-70″.

Frustules radiate upon the cushion.

2. *S. fulgens* (*Licmophora fulg.* K.) (Pl. 13. fig. 24). Frustules linear; valves slightly dilated in the middle and at the rounded ends, arranged in a fan-shaped manner upon the branched cushion. Marine; length 1-120″.

3. *S. capitata* (Pl. 13. fig. 25). Frustules linear, truncate, ends slightly dilated; valves linear, ends dilated into a triangular head. Aquatic; length 1-60″.

BIBL. Smith, *Brit. Diat.* i. p. 69; Kützing, *Sp. Alg.* p. 40.

SYNOVIAL MEMBRANES.—In minute structure these resemble serous membranes.

They are sometimes furnished with appendages, some of which contain fatty tis-

2 x

sue, others abound in capillaries and are met with forming fringes where the synovial membrane is attached to the articular cartilages. The latter consist of a basis of indistinctly fibrous areolar tissue, covered by the synovial epithelium, with a few fat-cells, sometimes isolated cartilage-cells, and the capillaries. Attached to their margins are flattened, conical, stalked, smaller appendages (fig. 715), seldom containing blood-vessels, and composed of indistinctly fibrous areolar tissue, with scattered cartilage-cells, and a thick epithelial layer; while some of the smaller ones consist almost entirely of epithelial cells or of areolar tissue.

Fig. 715.

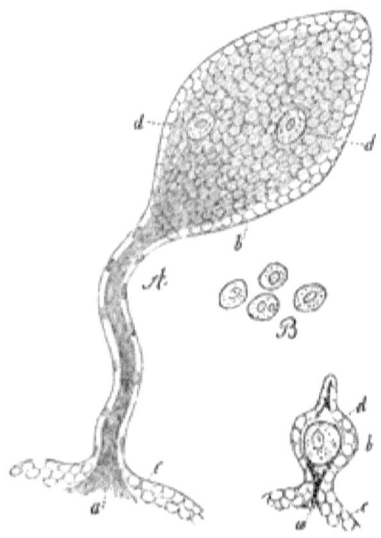

From the synovial membrane of a finger-joint.

A. Two appendages of the synovial processes. *a,* areolar tissue in its axis; *b,* epithelium of the free margin; *c,* that continuous with the epithelium of the processes; *d,* cartilage-cells.

Magnified 250 diameters.

B. Four epithelial cells from the synovial membrane of the knee-joint, one of them with two nuclei.

Magnified 350 diameters.

BIBL. Kölliker, *Mikrosk. Anat.* i. p. 322.

SYNTETHYS, Forbes. — A genus of Tunicate Mollusca, of the family Botryllidæ.

Char. Mass sessile, gelatinous, forming a single system; animal sessile, having simple orifices, without rays. One species:

S. Hebridicus.

BIBL. Gosse, *Mar. Zool.* ii. p. 34.

SYNURA, Ehr. — A doubtful genus of Volvocineæ (Confervoid Algæ), described as consisting of a number of oblong corpuscles attached together by their prolonged filiform posterior extremities in the form of a globe, the whole enclosed in a gelatinous sphere (or a membrane?); the corpuscles are said to have only one "flagelliform filament" (cilium), and no "eye-spot." In *S. Uvella* the corpuscles are yellowish, the "tails" three times as long as the bodies. Diameter of globes 1-200 to 1-190″. See VOLVOX.

BIBL. Ehrenberg, *Infus.* p. 6.

SYRINGIDIUM, Ehr. — A genus of Diatomaceæ.

Char. Frustules single, terete; valves acuminate at one end, two-horned at the other. Marine.

S. bicorne (Pl. 43. figs. 32). Frustules oblong, smooth, not striated, turgid in the middle, one end attenuate, with two slight constrictions, and acuminate, the other subglobose, turgid, and with two horns. Length 1-370″. Coast of Africa.

S. palemon (Pl. 43. fig. 33).

BIBL. Ehrenberg, *Ber. d. Berl. Akad.* 1845. p. 365; Kützing, *Sp. Alg.* p. 32.

SYSTEPHANIA, Ehr. — A genus of Diatomaceæ.

Char. Frustules circular; valves alike, neither radiate nor septate, with a crown of spines or an erect membrane on the outer surface of each valve (not on the margin). Fossil.

S. corona (Pl. 43. fig. 57); *S. diadema* (fig. 58).

One other species; found in Bermuda.

BIBL. Ehrenberg, *Ber. d. Berl. Akad.* 1844. p. 264; Kützing, *Sp. Alg.* p. 126.

SYZYGITES, Ehrenberg. — A genus of Mucorini (Physomycetous Fungi), containing one species, a kind of mould growing over decaying Agarics, remarkable among all the class to which it belongs for the occurrence of the phænomenon of conjugation of its branches as a preliminary to the formation of the spores. The only species is *S. megalocarpus,* in which the conjugation was discovered by Ehrenberg many years ago. The young filaments are simple, slender, rather rigid, pellucid and straight,—soon becoming forked, thickish, whitish yellow (somewhat olive when dry). The rudiments of the peridioles spring out as papillæ from the branches, becoming pear-shaped; and when two come in contact, they cohere, and become confluent into a fusiform body. The contents of the filaments next ascend and accumulate in the peridiole, at length

Fig. 716.

Sytygites megalocarpus.
A branched filament, exhibiting the conjugation in various stages.
Magnified 200 diameters.

forming a black globule (sporange?). While this is ripening, the apices grow out into long simple filaments.

BIBL. Ehrenb. *Verhandl. Naturf. Freund.* Berlin, i. p. 91; Fries, *Syst. Myc.* iii. p. 329; Berkeley, *Ann. Nat. Hist.* i. p. 257.

T.

TABELLARIA, Ehr.—A genus of Diatomaceæ.

Char. Frustules tabular, attached, at first united into a filament, subsequently cohering only by the angles, with longitudinal vittæ interrupted in the middle; valves inflated in the middle and at each end, striated. Aquatic.

1. *T. flocculosa* (Pl. 13. fig. 27 *a, b*). Septa 3–5 on each margin. Length 1-900 to 1-840".

2. *T. fenestrata.* Frustules oblong; vittæ opposite. Length 1-600 to 1-200".

Five fossil species.

BIBL. Kützing, *Sp. Alg.* p. 118; Smith, *Brit. Diat.* ii. p. 44.

TABLE.—A table for the conversion of foreign into English measures, is given under MEASUREMENT (p. 450).

TADPOLE. See FROG (p. 295).

TÆNIA (Tape-worm).—A genus of Entozoa, order Sterelmintha, family Cestoidea.

Char. Body elongate, compressed, jointed.

Head mostly broader than the narrowed neck, with four suctorial depressions; and usually a median, imperforate, retractile rostellum, very frequently armed with one or two circles of minute recurved hooks, especially in the young state. Genital orifices situated at the margins of the joints, either on one side only, or on both margins and on alternate joints.

The *Tæniæ*, of which the common tapeworm may be taken as the type, are found in vertebrate animals alone, and in these only in the alimentary canal. They are most common in birds, next in mammalia, then in fishes, and lastly in reptiles.

The species are very numerous; Rudolphi enumerates 146, of which 53 were considered doubtful. Dujardin admits 135 species.

Tænia solium, the common human English species, varies in breadth from 1-50 to 1-40" at the anterior part, to about 1-3" at the middle and posterior part. At the anterior extremity is situated a central rostellum, which is surrounded by a crown of small recurved hooks, as in Pl. 16. figs. 1 *f* & 10. Behind these are four suctorial depressions, which are not pervious at the bottom. The digestive system, according to Blanchard, is represented by two tubes or lateral canals (Pl. 16. fig. 14 *a*), having between them a transverse canal at the summit of each joint. These extend from the anterior to the posterior end of the body. In the cephalic portion, directly behind the suckers, there is a kind of lacuna or furrow communicating directly with these intestinal tubes; and it appears that the nutritive matters respired by means of the suckers penetrate into this lacuna, and thence into the digestive canals. These tubes have distinct walls, and are best seen when the animal has been macerated in water, and is examined by transmitted light, or after having been injected.

The vascular system, according to the above author, consists of four longitudinal vessels (Pl. 16. fig. 14 *b*) situated a little above the intestinal tubes, and infinitely more slender than these. They traverse the whole length of the body, and between them are numerous transverse vessels (Pl. 16. fig. 14).

The male generative organ consists of a slender coiled tube, extending to near the principal ovigerous canal, where it is preceded by some very small testicular capsules (Pl. 16. fig. 14 *c*). The slender tube terminates in a duct (Pl. 16. fig. 14 *d*), which opens into the lateral orifice, or sometimes it projects externally in the form of a spiculum. The ovary consists of a principal median canal, presenting slight flexuosities, and extending nearly from one end to the other of each joint. It presents cæcal branches on both sides, and opens by a slender oviduct (Pl. 16. fig. 14 e) just within the genital orifice.

The ova are innumerable; one is figured in Pl. 16. fig. 15. They consist of an outer delicate membrane enclosing a gelatinous substance containing numerous highly refractive globules. Within this is another very delicate and transparent membrane, closely applied upon a brittle, dark-looking (by transmitted light, but white by reflected light), thick envelope, within which is the yolk or embryo, according to the state of development of the ovum. Very frequently the hooks of the young tænia are seen imbedded in its centre, as shown in the figure. The thick brittle coat of the ovum exhibits an appearance of radiating fibres (canals?), and when broken, the fractures are radiant. When the middle of the outer surface of the brittle envelope is brought into focus, it presents a tolerably regular appearance, as if composed of cells; this arises, however, from the extremities of the fibres being brought into focus.

The spermatozoa are readily found, simply by picking any joint containing ova to pieces with needles.

The old genera *Cœnurus*, *Cysticercus*, and *Echinococcus* represent the larval or nurse-forms of *Tænia*.

The young animal, consisting of head and neck only, was formerly considered as distinct, and placed in a genus—*Scolex*.

See ENTOZOA.

Tænia lata=*Bothriocephalus latus*.

BIBL. That of ENTOZOA and BOTHRIOCEPHALUS; Weinland *on Tape-worms*.

TÆNIOPTERIS, Hook. — A genus of Tænitideæ (Polypodioid Ferns). Exotic.

TÆNITIDEÆ.—A tribe of Polypodioid Ferns, without an indusium.

Illustrative Genera.

1. *Pleurogramma*. Sori contiguous on each side of the rib, parallel, linear, and continuous. Veins simple.

2. *Tænitis*. Sori submarginal in the middle of the disk of the leaf, linear, elongated and continuous. Veins anastomosing more or less regularly into meshes.

3. *Notholœna*. Sori marginal, linear, continuous. Veins pinnate.

TÆNITIS, Sw.—The typical genus of Tænitideæ (Polypodioid Ferns). Exotic.

TALC. See MICA.

TAONIA, J. Ag.—A genus of Dictyotaceæ (Fucoid Algæ), containing one rare British species, *T. atomaria*, which has a flat, membranous, fan-shaped, deeply cleft frond, 3 to 12" high, of brownish olive colour; marked on both faces, at intervals of 1-4 to 1-2", with concentric wavy lines, formed by rather crowded dark-brown "spores," the interspaces being dotted over with scattered spores. The disk of attachment is covered with woolly filaments.

Thuret has recently shown that the Dictyotaceæ should be separated from the Fucoideæ, and stand between them and the Florideæ, since he has found not only that their spores are analogous to the conceptacular spores of the latter, and do not produce ciliated zoospores, but also that they produce *tetraspores*, and what appear to be *antheridia* (DICTYOTA) in different individuals.

BIBL. Harvey, *Brit. Mar. Alg.* p. 38, pl. 7 A; Thuret, *Ann. des Sc. Nat.* 4 sér. iii. p. 7.

TAPHROCAMPA, Gosse.—A genus of Rotatoria, of the family Hydatinæa.

Char. Rotatory organs absent; body fusiform, annulose, tail forked, gizzard oval.

T. annulosa. Aquatic; length 1-110".

BIBL. Gosse, *Ann. Nat. Hist.* 1851. viii. p. 199.

TAPIOCA.—A very pure fecula prepared from the finer particles of the starch of the Mandioc or Cassava plant (Pl. 36. fig. 14). The starch-granules of tapioca of the shops appear to have undergone the action of heat, which disguises the characters. See STARCH.

TARDIGRADA (Water-bears). — An order of Arachnida.

Char. See ARACHNIDA, p. 62.

These microscopic animals are found in stagnant fresh water, amongst water-plants, in patches of wet moss, in the gutters of houses, &c.

Body soft, cylindrical or elongate-oval in outline, with four transverse furrows or indistinct segments, and a fifth anterior, corresponding to a head, short, conical, retractile and with indications of two or three segments; sometimes dilated at the end to form a sucker, or furnished with unequal, short, palp-like processes. Eyes two.

The oral organs are represented by a tubular rostrum, through the sides of which, from without inwards, two calcareous styles or mandibles pass, and serve to wound the animals forming their prey. At the base of the rostrum is a gizzard with radiating muscular fibres, in *Macrobiotus* enclosing a kind of framework consisting of six parallel jointed cylinders.

The alimentary canal is straight, and furnished with lateral cæcal appendages. The ovary is a simple sac, behind which is situated a seminal vesicle containing spermatozoa, both opening into a cloaca. But few eggs are produced at a time; they are either smooth, rugous, or studded with points, and are usually deposited during the ecdysis, the exuviæ serving as a protection to them during the process of hatching. The young resemble the parents.

The Tardigrada resemble some of the Rotatoria in reviving after having been kept dried for years.

Genera: *Emydium, Macrobiotus, Milnesium (Arctiscon,* doubtful).

BIBL. Doyère, *Ann. des Sc. Nat.* 2 sér. xiv. 269, xvii. 193, xviii. 1; Dujardin, x. 185; Vogt, *Zoolog. Briefe,* i. 496'; Kaufmann, *Siebold und Kölliker's Zeitschr.* iii. 220.

TARGIONIA, Mich.—A genus of Pel-

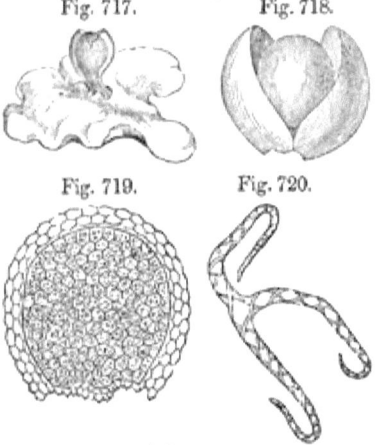

Targionia hypophylla.

Fig. 717. Lobe of a frond with fruit. Magnified 5 diameters.

Fig. 718. Perichæte opened, showing the globular sporange. Magnified 20 diameters.

Fig. 719. Vertical section of a very young sporange. Magnified 200 diameters.

Fig. 720. A branched elater. Magnified 200 diameters.

lieæ (Hepaticæ), characterized by the almost

sessile globose capsule arising from the end of the midrib of the under face of the frond, which is somewhat fleshy, smooth, deepgreen, purplish at the edges, and forms large patches on rather moist but exposed banks. The frond has an epidermis on both faces, with stomata and intermediate parenchyma; the midrib is only apparent beneath, and has radical hairs, with purple scales. The perichæte originates from this rib, on the under surface, rising to the upper side (fig. 717). When mature, it is globose, of dark purplish colour and firm texture, and marked with a vertical prominent line or keel; at this line it ultimately splits into two valves (fig. 718). Hofmeister's recent observa-

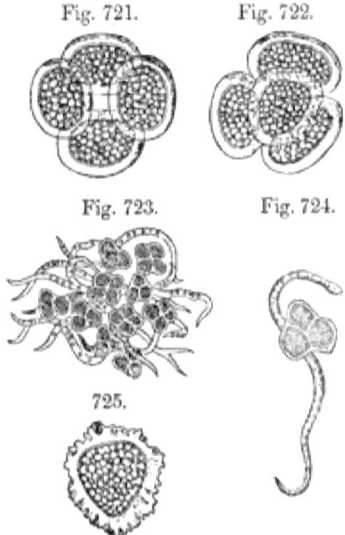

Figs. 721 & 722. Groups of four spores, not quite mature. Magnified 400 diameters.

Fig. 723. Parent cells of spores and imperfect elaters, from a more advanced fruit. Magnified 100 diameters.

Fig. 724. The same. Magnified 200 diameters.

Fig. 725. A single ripe spore. Magnified 400 diameters.

tions, however, show that this envelope grows up after the fertilization of the archegone, which is originally naked in its upper half; hence it would seem to be a *perigone.* Several archegones are found half-immersed in the end of the midrib, and one of these is converted into a fruit; the lower part becomes spherical, and the neck forms for a long time a filiform point or style. This epigone bursts irregularly and vertically. The spherical capsule emerges from it, but is not protruded beyond the perichæte. The globular capsule bursts irregularly at the summit, and discharges spores and elaters resembling those of *Marchantia* (figs. 723 to 725). The antheridia are imbedded in the midrib, opening on papillæ on the lower face.

BIBL. Hook. *Brit. Flor.* ii. pt. 2. p. 105; Corda, *Sturm's Deutschl. Fl. Jungerm.* pl. 36; Nees, *Lebermoose*, iv.

TARTARIC ACID. — The crystals of this substance, which belong to the oblique-prismatic system, exhibit beautiful colours under the polariscope.

TAXUS, L.— *Taxus baccata* is the Yew-tree, belonging to the Coniferæ. Its wood (Pl. 39. fig. 4), as also that of *T. canadensis*, shows the remarkable combination of spiral fibres with the coniferous pits. Its embryology is also interesting. See CONIFERÆ and OVULE.

TAYLORIA, Hook.—A genus of Splachnaceæ (Acrocarpous operculate Mosses), containing some *Splachna* of authors.

Tayloria serrata, Br. and Sch. γ *tenuis* = *Splachnum tenue*, Dicks.

TEA (the prepared leaves of *Thea viridis* and *T. Bohea* (Nat. Ord. Ternstrœmiaceæ). —This important article of commerce has afforded some of the most remarkable examples of systematic fraud, practised not merely by the vendors in this country, but by the Chinese manufacturers. The principal adulterations of tea consist of re-manufactured exhausted tea-leaves, spurious tea made up of the dust of tea and other leaves, together with earthy matter, by the aid of gum, and of spurious tea made of leaves of other plants,—the whole of these being prepared either for black or green tea by 'facing,' or imparting a colour or bloom with black-lead, indigo, prussian blue, mica, turmeric, &c.

The leaves of tea may be distinguished when moistened and spread out, and still more decidedly, even in fragments, by the aid of the microscope, which shows the peculiarities of the epidermis of the upper or lower faces. Other leaves fraudulently introduced may be thus separated, and often identified by careful comparison with known kinds likely to have been employed. The spurious tea made up of agglutinated rubbish falls to pieces instead of unrolling when infused with hot water. The 'facing' of the various kinds is mostly distinguishable with a common lens, and when the tea is infused forms a sediment, the characters of which may be determined by the microscope and by chemical analysis.

BIBL. Hassall, *Food and its Adulterations*, p. 268; Warington, *Trans. of Chemical Society of London*, 1851.

TEETH.—The teeth of the Mammalia are inserted in sockets or alveolar cavities of the jaws.

The teeth consist of a crown, or that portion which projects beyond the alveolar cavity and the gum; the fangs, or the portions which are inserted into the bony structures; and a neck, or narrower intermediate portion. The crown of the tooth contains the pulp-cavity, which is closed above, but prolonged below through the fangs.

Fig. 726.

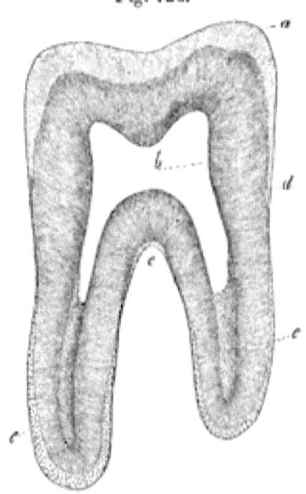

Molar tooth, human; longitudinal section.
a, enamel; *b*, pulp-cavity; *c*, cement; *d*, ivory, with the ivory-tubes. Magnified 5 diameters.

In regard to their structure, teeth are in part identical with bone, in part closely allied to it; but in respect to their development, they must be regarded as formations of the mucous membrane, as modified papillæ.

The substance of human teeth consists of three parts: the ivory or dentine (fig. 726 *d*), which constitutes the greater portion of their mass, and to which their form is mainly owing; the cement, or bony portion (fig. 726 *c*), which forms an external cover-

ing, principally of the fangs; and the enamel (fig. 726 a), which covers the crown.

The *ivory* or *dentine* (figs. 726 d, 727 d) is
whitish and of a silky lustre, and, excepting

Fig. 727.

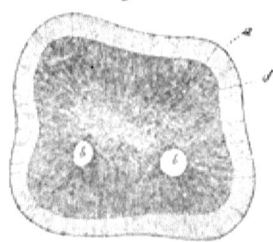

Transverse section of the same; the references as above.
Magnified 5 diameters.

a small portion at the base of the fangs,
forms the entire boundary of the cavity of
the teeth. It consists of a homogeneous
basis enveloping numerous tubes or canaliculi, called the 'ivory-tubes' (fig. 729 a, b).
These are very fine, and pursue an undulating course, at first curving, then bifurcating, throughout giving off numerous fine
lateral communicating branches, which are
best seen in a horizontal section (fig. 728),
and ultimately ramifying and anastomosing
freely. They commence at the surface of
the pulp-cavity, in the crown following a
somewhat radiating direction from its centre

Fig. 728.

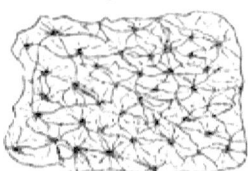

Transverse section of the ivory-tubes of the fang (a,
fig. 729), showing their numerous anastomoses.
Magnified 450 diameters.

(fig. 726), whilst in the fangs their course is
more horizontal. They have distinct walls,
about equal in thickness to their calibre,
although in transverse sections (fig. 730),
this thickness is generally exaggerated, on
account of their being obliquely divided.
They contain air in the dry state, which
may be displaced by liquids. By removing
the inorganic salts from a tooth with dilute

muriatic acid, and macerating the remaining
cartilage with acids or caustic alkalies until

Fig. 729.

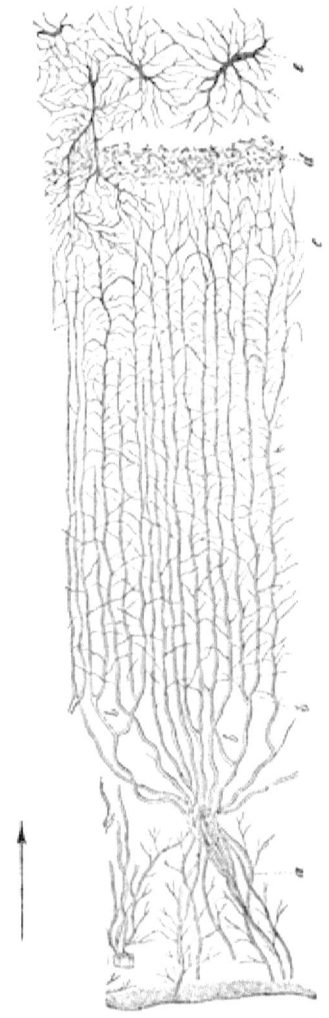

Ivory-tubes of a fang of a human tooth. a, inner
surface of the ivory, with few tubes; b, their branches;
c, their terminations in loops; d, granular layer, consisting of small ivory globules at the boundary of the
ivory; e, lacunæ of bone, one anastomosing with an
ivory-tube. Magnified 350 diameters.

it forms a pasty mass, the tubes may be isolated from the basis.

Fig. 730.

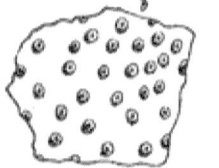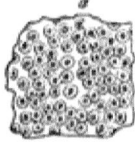

Transverse section of the ivory tubes. *a*, closely aggregated; *b*, wider apart. Magnified 450 diameters.

The ivory not unfrequently exhibits indications of a laminated structure, forming, in longitudinal sections, curved lines more or less parallel to the outline of the crown

Fig. 731.

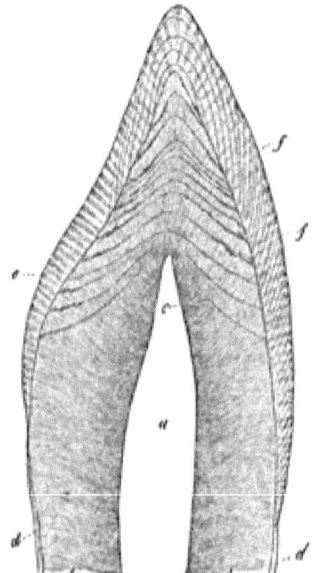

Perpendicular section of the apex of a human incisor tooth. *a*, pulp-cavity; *b*, ivory; *c*, curved contour lines with interglobular spaces; *d*, cement; *e*, enamel, with indications of the course of the fibres in various directions; *f*, coloured stripes of the enamel.

Magnified 7 diameters.

(fig. 731), appearing as rings in transverse sections, and called the *contour-lines.*

Near the enamel (fig. 731) and the cement (fig. 729 *d*) also, the ivory presents one or more irregular dark patches or bands, often continuous with the ends of the contour

Fig. 732.

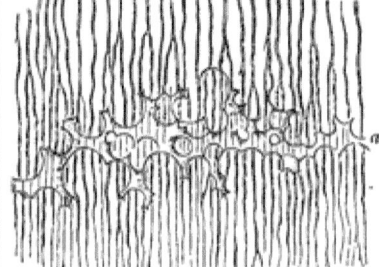

Portion of the ivory, with ivory globules and interglobular spaces filled with air. Magnified 350 diameters.

lines, and exhibiting a coarsely cellular appearance. On careful examination, the dark appearance is seen to result from a number of irregular spaces filled with air

Fig. 733.

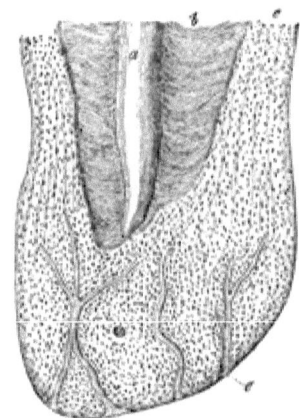

Cement and ivory of the fang of a tooth of an old person. *a*, cavity; *b*, ivory; *c*, cement with lacunæ; *c*, Haversian canal. Magnified 30 diameters.

(fig. 732 *a*) intervening between certain globules, called *ivory-globules,* the spaces being termed the *interglobular spaces.* In the recent tooth, these spaces are filled with the organic basis of the ivory, containing tubes like the rest of that substance, in which, however, the inorganic matter has not been deposited; hence this structure arises from imperfect development.

Other, ill-defined iridescent stripes, running parallel to the pulp-cavity, are sometimes seen; these correspond to the primary curves of the ivory-tubes.

The *cement* or bone of teeth forms the outer, coating of the fangs (c, figs. 726 & 733), sometimes cementing them together. It commences as a very thin layer at the part where the enamel ceases, increasing in thickness towards the ends of the fangs. The cement does not differ from bone in structure, except in rarely containing Haversian canals. In the molar teeth of old persons, these are, however, met with (fig. 733 c). The lacunæ are frequently absent from the thinner portion of the cement; and it sometimes contains tubes like those of the ivory. The interlacunar substance is sometimes striated, and exhibits a laminated structure.

The *enamel* (fig. 726 a) covers the ivory of the crown of the teeth. It is thickest at the opposing surface, decreasing towards the neck, where it terminates. It is covered by a very thin membrane, separable

after the action of muriatic acid, and containing calcareous matter; this has been regarded as a continuation of the cement.

Fig. 734.

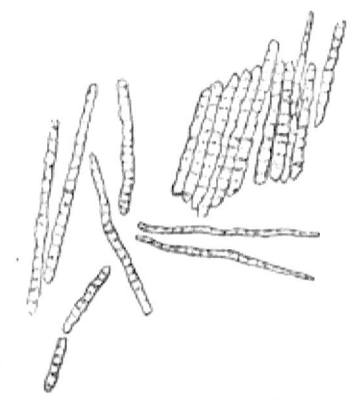

Enamel-fibres, isolated by the very slight action of muriatic acid; human. Magnified 350 diameters.

The enamel has a fibrous aspect, and appears of a bluish-white colour by reflected light, and of a greyish brown by transmitted

Fig. 735.   Fig. 736.

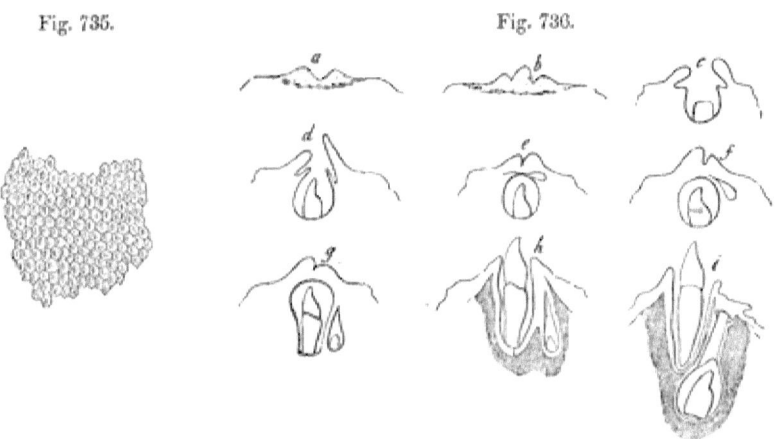

Fig. 735. Surface of the enamel, with the ends of the enamel-fibres, from the tooth of a calf. Magnified 350 diameters.

Fig. 736. Diagram showing the development of a milk-tooth, and the corresponding permanent tooth. *a*, furrow; *b*, the same with the papilla; *c*, the same closing, with the commencement of the reserve cavity; *d*, the same, further closing; *e*, follicle completely formed, with the reserve cavity; *f*, the reserve cavity receding; *g*, the same, with a tooth-germ; *h*, the alveoli of both capsules formed, the milk-tooth being through the gum; *i*, the same, further advanced, the neck of the capsule forming a solid cord.

light. It is very brittle, and so hard as to strike fire with steel. It consists of numerous solid fibres or prisms (fig. 734), about 1-6000 to 1-5000″ in breadth, mostly six-sided, more or less wavy, slightly varicose, and transversely striped. These usually extend throughout the thickness of the enamel, and are placed in a direction generally perpendicular to the surface of the portions of the ivory which they cover (figs. 720, 731). The form of the fibres is best seen by viewing their ends or a transverse section (fig. 735). The prisms do not run exactly parallel with each other, but are arranged in groups or zones, the fibres of which cross each other. The fibres are readily isolated before they have become so developed as to be hard, and when very slightly acted upon by muriatic acid. Sometimes the ivory-tubes extend into the enamel.

Two kinds of dark bands or stripes are seen traversing the enamel (fig. 731). The direction of one of these coincides pretty nearly with that of the fibres, and it arises from the crossing of the zones of fibres, allowing more or less light to pass through, the bands being light and dark. The other set (fig. 731 ff) consists of arched, brownish stripes, indicating the laminated structure of the enamel. Under the polariscope, a third set becomes visible, arising from the variable inclination of the axes of the fibres to the plane of polarization.

The enamel is often traversed by cracks, mostly running parallel with the fibres, and containing air in dry teeth.

Chemically, teeth consist of an organic, cartilaginous basis, agreeing in composition with that of bone, and inorganic matter, consisting principally of phosphate of lime with a small quantity of the carbonate.

Development.—The rudiments or germs of the first (milk) teeth are met with in the sixth week of foetal life, and consist of small papillæ, one for each tooth, which become visible in grooves of the mouth, afterwards forming the alveolar processes. Processes from the sides of these dental grooves are then formed, and, approaching each other, enclose the papillæ in distinct follicles, the margins of which gradually grow over the papillæ, and uniting, convert them into closed sacs or capsules. The pulps then become moulded into the form of the future teeth ; the bases of the pulps dividing into as many portions as the teeth have fangs ; and as the capsules increase at this stage

faster than the pulps, a space is left between them, in which a gelatinous-looking substance is deposited from the wall of the capsule forming the enamel organ.

Fig. 737.

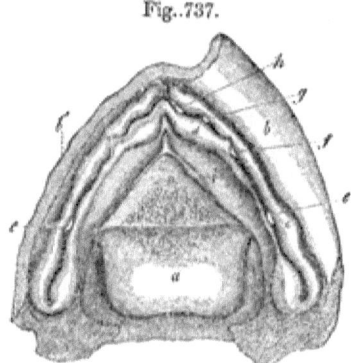

Lower jaw of a human nine weeks' fœtus. *a*, tongue, turned back ; *b*, right half of the lower lip turned aside ; *b′*, left half of the lip cut off ; *c*, outer wall of the gum ; *d*, inner wall of the gum ; *e, f, g, h*, papillæ of the teeth ; *i*, fold where the sublingual duct subsequently opens.

Magnified 9 diameters.

Fig. 738.

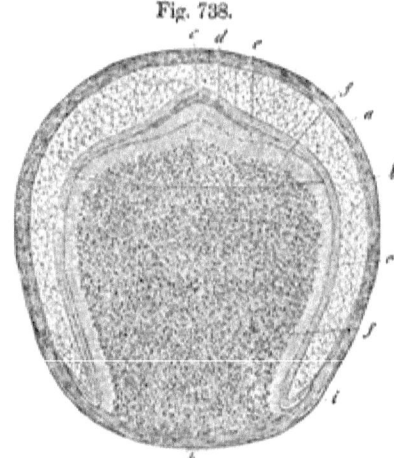

Capsule of the second incisor tooth of an eight months' human fœtus. *a*, capsule ; *b*, enamel-pulp ; *c*, enamel-membrane ; *d*, enamel ; *f*, ivory cells ; *h*, papilla of tooth or pulp ; *i*, free margin of enamel-organ.

Magnified 30 diameters.

The capsule (fig. 738 *a*) possesses an areolar coat with vessels and nerves ; and from its base arises the tooth-germ or pulp (fig. 738 *h*). The pulp consists of an outer non-vascular layer of elongated nucleated cells, with filiform processes, in close apposition (fig. 739 *a*), covering the surface of

Fig. 730.

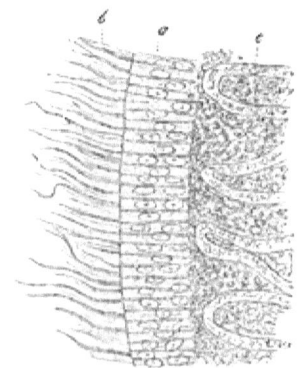

Surface of the pulp of a newly-born infant. *a*, ivory-cells; *b*, their appendages; *c*, vascular part of the pulp.

Magnified 300 diameters.

the pulp—the ivory-membrane (fig. 738 *f*), not distinctly defined internally, but gradually passing into the vascular parenchyma of the pulp. The inner part of the pulp consists of indistinctly fibrous areolar tissue with nuclei, the vessels terminating in loops beneath the enamel membrane (fig. 739 *c*).

The enamel organ (fig. 738 *b*) covers by its inner concave surface the pulp, its outside being in apposition with the capsule. It forms a spongy tissue, composed of anastomosing stellate cells or reticular areolar tissue; in its inside is the enamel membrane, consisting of cylindrical epithelium (fig. 738 *c*).

Ossification commences by the deposition of calcareous matter in the cells of the ivory membrane at the summit of the pulp; this is soon followed by similar deposition in the cells of the enamel membrane. By the further formation of new cells and fresh deposition, the structure of the teeth becomes more and more consolidated, the spongy tissue of the enamel gradually being absorbed.

When the entire enamel and a considerable portion of the ivory have been formed in the capsules, these become too small to contain the teeth, which then rupture them, and continue to grow at the root, until the crown projects above the margin of the jaw. The remainder of the capsule then forms the periosteum of the alveoli, and by deposition from the side next the tooth, produces the cement.

The permanent teeth are formed upon the same plan:—the three last molars in the remains of the primitive dental groove; the others in distinct sacs, called reserve sacs, and formed in the wall of the follicles of the milk-teeth.

The teeth of animals present numerous interesting varieties, to which we can but briefly refer. Thus, in the Mammalia the enamel is often absent, the cement frequently extends over the crown, the three component structures are folded, the teeth are compound, the ivory contains Haversian canals, and the ivory-tubes enter the enamel. In Reptiles the teeth are often anchylosed to the jaws. In Fishes the teeth are often solid; the ivory is furnished with Haversian canals, sometimes isolated, and each surrounded by a layer of ivory and cement, so that the teeth appear to consist of aggregations of little teeth; the vessels often branch and anastomose freely; the ivory tubes are often very large or absent, the ivory then consisting of a finely granular base with numerous vascular canals, true enamel appearing to be absent.

The method of making sections of teeth is described under PREPARATION. They should be very thin, and preserved in the dry state.

BIBL. Kölliker, *Mikroskop. Anat.* ii. p. 54; Owen, *Odontography*, and *Todd's Cycl. Anat. &c.* iv. 864; Goodsir, *Edinb. Med. and Surg. Journ.* 1839. i.; Tomes, *Lectures on Dental Surgery, &c.*, and *Phil. Trans.* 1849, 1850; Nasmyth, *Researches on the Teeth*; Retzius, *Müller's Archiv,* 1837. p. 486; Heusinger, *Histologie*; Hanover, *Verh. d. Leopold. Carol. Akad.* xxv. p. 2 (*Micr. Journ.* 1857. v. p. 166).

TEMORA, Baird.—A genus of Entomostraca, of the order Copepoda, and family Diaptomidæ.

Char. Thorax composed of five, abdomen of three joints; lesser antennæ two-branched; first four pairs of legs each giving off a two-jointed branch.

T. finmarchica. Found on the coast of Ireland.

BIBL. Baird, *Brit. Entomostr.* p. 227.

TENDON. See LIGAMENTS.

TENTHREDO, Leach.—A genus of Hy-

menopterous Insects, of the order Tenthre-
dinidæ (Saw-flies).

The species of *Tenthredo* and of the other
genera belonging to the family, both of
which are very numerous, are interesting on
account of the remarkable structure of the
ovipositor, which consists of two flattened
and curved saw-like plates. These are used
to saw the leaves of plants, for the deposition of the eggs.

The insects are found upon gooseberry-
bushes, rose-bushes, the white thorn, the
willow, alder, poplar, the plum, and other
fruit-trees, cabbage, turnip, bramble, &c.
The larvæ are very destructive to agricul-
tural crops.

T. nassata is represented in figure 363
(p. 301).

Bibl. Westwood, *Introduction, &c.* ii.
p. 90, and the *Bibl.* therein.

TERPSINOE, Ehr.—A genus of Diatomaceæ.

Char. Frustules tabular, obsoletely
stalked, subsequently connected by isthmi,
and with transverse, short, interrupted,
capitate vittæ; valves in side view with
lateral inflations.

T. musica (Pl. 14. fig. 33, side view; Pl. 19.
fig. 10, front view). Frustules very faintly
punctate, in front view rectangular oblong;
side view equally inflated in the middle and
at the ends, in older specimens constricted
in the middle, inflated beyond the middle
towards both ends, the apices produced and
obtuse, the nodules separated by septa.
Length 1-180″.

T. indica (*Anaulus ind.*, E.).

Bibl. Ehrenberg, *Abhand. d. Berl. Akad.*
1841. p. 402; Kützing, *Bacill.* p. 128; *Sp.
Alg.* p. 119.

TESSELLA, Ehr.—A genus of Diatomaceæ.

Char. Frustules broadly tabular, not concatenate, with crowded, longitudinal, alternate vittæ, interrupted in the middle; stipes
absent (?). Marine.

T. interrupta (Pl. 14. fig. 35). Length of
frustules 1-580; breadth 1-560 to 1-120″.
Found with *Striatella*.

Bibl. Ehrenberg, *Infus.* p. 202; Kützing,
Bacill. p. 125; *Sp. Alg.* p. 114.

TEST-BOX. Introduction, p. xxiii.

TEST-OBJECTS.—Test-objects are microscopic objects used to determine the
value of object-glasses.

We must presume that the reader has
perused the remarks upon object-glasses in
the Introduction (p. xiv), also the article

Angular Aperture; otherwise the observations made here will be unintelligible.

The main points in which object-glasses
differ from each other are four: viz. 1. their
magnifying power; 2. their defining power;
3. their penetrating power; and 4. their
corrective adaptations.

1. The magnifying or separating power
scarcely requires notice; it must be adapted
to the size of the objects likely to come
under examination. Usually, several object-
glasses are kept, of different powers; at all
events, if scientific investigations are to be
pursued, a power of 400 diameters must be
accessible, and this without the use of the
highest eyepiece. The magnifying power
should be ascertained by Measurement,
and not by judging from the focal length.

2. Good defining power is the most important character of an object-glass; and if
good in respect to this, the dark boundary
lines of the test-objects will appear clear,
black, sharp, as if engraved, and quite free
from colour. If this is ascertained to be
the case, the higher eyepieces should be
put on; and it must be observed that
although the sharpness of the outline is
somewhat diminished, all the parts are
clearly distinguishable as before. In this
examination the light should be as direct
as possible.

3. The power of displaying the minute
structural peculiarities of objects, or the
penetrating power, as it is called, depends
upon two distinct circumstances—the good-
ness of the defining power, and the magni-
tude of the angular aperture of the object-
glass: the degree of obliquity of the light
is also of great importance in connexion
with the latter.

Thus, in examining the scale of a *Podura*
(Pl. 1. fig. 12 *a, b, c*), the magnifying power
being sufficiently high, if the defining power
be good, the wedge-shaped bodies will be
clearly and sharply displayed by direct light,
and whether the angular aperture be large
or small. Now, if we examine a valve of
Gyrosigma (Pl. 1. figs. 17 & 18) by direct
light, the minute structure will be invisible,
however small or large the angular aperture
may be, or however perfect the defining
power; but if the light be thrown obliquely,
and the aperture be sufficient, the striæ will
at once become evident. Hence there are
two distinct kinds of penetrating power,
one of which is the same as the defining
power, the other depending upon a different cause; and hence the term penetration

or penetrating power should be laid aside, as tending to cause confusion, the properties of object-glasses being reducible simply to their defining power and their angular aperture.

The defining power should be tested upon the different objects mentioned below in connexion with each object-glass, and the angular aperture should be determined by measurement (ANGULAR APERTURE); for judgment founded upon the examination of the valves of the Diatomaceæ may be very fallacious to an unpractised observer, on account of the influence of the obliquity of the light, and of the correcting adjustment. If, however, an opinion is to be formed in this way, the valves should be examined by oblique light thrown from all sides, as with the central stop in the condenser, so that the dots may be viewed; for an object-glass may show the lines very fairly, but the dots very badly.

4. The correcting adjustment is of importance in examining very delicate objects or structures with the high powers; it should therefore always be present.

We subjoin, in connexion with each object-glass, the magnitudes of the angle of aperture which they usually have in this country, and which may be regarded as standards for comparison; also those objects which will be found most suitable for the purpose of testing an object-glass.

$1\frac{1}{2}$ *or 2-inch object-glass.* Magnifying power 20 diameters; angular aperture 12 to 20°.

Test-objects: the pygidium of the flea (Pl. 1. fig. 13 a), in which the general outline and the hairs should be distinct; the hair of the mouse (Pl. 1. fig. 3). Also, as an opake object, a piece of an injected preparation (Pl. 31. figs. 33–35).

1-inch or $\frac{2}{3}$rds object-glass. Magnifying power 60 diameters; angular aperture 22 to 35°.

Tests: hair of *Dermestes* (Pl. 1. fig. 1); of the bat (Pl. 1. fig. 2); of the mouse (Pl. 1. fig. 3); the pygidium of the flea, the outline of the areolæ being distinguishable under the high eyepiece (120 to 200 diameters), but not the rays. Also an injection, as a piece of lung.

$\frac{1}{2}$*-inch or $\frac{4}{10}$ths-inch object-glass.* Magnifying power 100 to 120 diameters; angular aperture 65°.

Tests: hairs (Pl. 1. figs. 1, 2, 3); the disks on deal (Pl. 1. fig. 4); the coarser scales of *Lepisma* (Pl. 1. fig. 6 a); the pygidium of

the flea (Pl. 1. fig. 13 a, b), the entire structure visible under the high eyepiece; a dark scale of *Podura* (Pl. 1. fig. 12 b).

$\frac{1}{4}$*-inch object-glass.* Magnifying power 220 diameters; angular aperture 75 to 140°.

Tests: hair of *Dermestes*; the disks of deal; the salivary corpuscles (Pl. 1. fig. 5), the moving molecules being clearly distinguishable; the smaller scales of *Lepisma* (Pl. 1. fig. 6 a, b); the scales of *Podura*; the filaments of *Didymohelix* (Pl. 1. fig. 10 a); the pygidium of the flea, and the scales of *Pontia brassicæ* (Pl. 27. fig. 24).

$\frac{1}{8}$*th object-glass.* Magnifying power 420 to 450 diameters; angular aperture 110 to 150°.

Tests: the paler scales of *Podura*; the pygidium of the flea; the scales of *Pontia brassicæ*; the filaments of *Didymohelix*, showing the component fibres; the salivary corpuscles.

$\frac{1}{12}$*th or $\frac{1}{16}$th-inch object-glass.* Magnifying power 600 to 650 diameters; angular aperture 80 to 170°.

Tests: the paler scales of *Podura*; the filaments of *Didymohelix* mounted in balsam; and the primitive fibrillæ of muscular fibre (Pl. 17. fig. 36 b, d).

It will be observed that we have omitted the tests for angular aperture, which many of our microscopists look upon as the true tests of the value of an object-glass. Our reasons for this are given in the INTRODUCTION (p. xv). Those, however, who wish for an interesting series of difficult objects in this respect, will find one in the valves of *Gyrosigma*, *Grammatophora*, *Fragilaria*, *Rhipidophora*, *Amphipleura*, some species of *Nitzschia*, as *N. tænia*, and *Berkeleya* (see those articles). We regard large angular aperture in an object-glass as of little importance; because it is only of service for showing the markings upon the valves of the Diatomaceæ, and the time is probably near at hand when the presence and size of these will be shown to possess neither generic nor specific importance; moreover, object-glasses of large aperture and high power approach so nearly to the object, that they are inapplicable to important physiological investigations. This defect is, however, considerably obviated in the new high powers.

We shall now offer a few

General remarks on the application of test-objects to the choice of an object-glass. A great difficulty presents itself in this question in the case of persons commencing the use of the microscope; for on viewing almost any object, they will see so much that was invisible before, that they are naturally led to regard an object-glass as good which may simply possess tolerable magnifying power.

There is also some difficulty to an unpractised eye in discriminating between a well-defined margin of an object, and one which is ill-defined. This may be overcome by purchasing one or two test-objects from those who mount objects for sale, and first viewing them under their microscopes; or by examining some of the objects exhibited at the evening meetings of the learned societies.

The objects themselves are also variable, some being much more delicate than others even of the same kind. The best plan in regard to this point is to select an object, as the scale of an insect or whatever it may be, in which the test-structure is not distinguishable under the next highest power, and then to examine the same object under the power to be tested.

The manner in which objects are mounted is also of importance; for if they are immersed in too much balsam or covered by too thick a cover, no object-glass will show them well, however good it may be. Hence the necessity of purchasing the test-objects, in the case of an inexperienced observer. They may be obtained from Mr. Norman, Fountain Place, City Road; Mr. Topping, New Winchester Street, Pentonville; or of Messrs. Smith and Beck, Ross, or Powell.

A few notes upon the test-objects themselves may not be out of place here.

Hairs of animals (Pl. 1. figs. 1–3). These should be mounted in Canada balsam. Many of those represented in Pl. 22 might be used with equal advantage.

Disks of deal (Pl. 1. fig. 4). Form a good test-object on account of their freedom from colour, whence the colours from uncorrected chromatic aberration are easily seen with a bad object-glass.

Salivary globules (Pl. 1. fig. 5 a, b, c). Obtained from the saliva. A good test-object for those engaged in physiological investigations; the marginal granules and the moving molecules should be very distinct.

Scales of insects (Pl. 1. figs. 6 a, b, c, 12 a, b, c; Pl. 27. fig. 24). These should be mounted dry. The scales of *Tinea* and many others have nothing to recommend them. Nor do we advise the use of those scales which exhibit the transverse striæ by oblique

light, as those of *Morpho* (Pl. 1. fig. 7), of *Hipparchia* (Pl. 1. fig. 9), &c.; as they are easy tests even to inferior English objectglasses of the present day. The long scales of *Pontia brassicæ*, however, are good.

Didymohelix (Pl. 1. fig. 10 a, b, c, d). The filaments should be mounted in solution of chloride of calcium, or in Canada balsam. It is very difficult to display the component fibres of this beautiful object when in balsam. It also forms a good test of magnifying power.

Didymoprium (Pl. 1. fig. 11). The longitudinal lines upon the cells require considerable magnifying power.

The pygidium of Pulex. An excellent test-object, mounted in as small a quantity of balsam as possible. Dujardin represents the rays upon the disks as round, like so many beads, whereas they are wedge-shaped with the bases outwards.

The valves of the Diatomaceæ. It is a difficult matter to show the lines upon *Grammatophora marina* with an object-glass of 110° of angular aperture, requiring extremely oblique light.

The ultimate fibrillæ of muscular fibre. Mounted in liquid. Kölliker represents them as beaded (Pl. 17. fig. 36 c); they have also been represented as in a: probably both these inaccuracies arise from imperfect adjustment, and from their immersion in too much liquid. Their true structure is figured in b, d, f.

Nobert's test-lines. These consist of from ten to fifteen parallel bands or groups of parallel lines scratched upon a slide with a diamond. The bands are of equal breadth, and the lines in each successive band are more numerous and consequently closer than those of the preceding. The breadth of the intervals between the lines in the two end bands is from 1-11,000 to 1-60,000″. The resolution of these lines forms a test for angular aperture and oblique light; but it can be effected by a moderately good English 1-8th, and is much easier than that of the markings upon the valves of many Diatomaceæ.

We have omitted to notice several testobjects, as the scales of some insects, a minute globule of mercury, &c.; and this advisedly, because the former have been so obscurely described that we are unable to comprehend in what the test-structure consists; and the test-appearances presented by the latter viewed as an opaque object are inappreciable to one unaccustomed to the use of the microscope, by whom mainly are remarks upon test-objects required.

Amici's test-object is *Navicula gracilis*, the display of the lines forming the test; it is a test for angular aperture.

Chevalier's test-object consists of the scales of *Pontia brassicæ* (Pl. 27. fig. 24), the granules being rendered distinct; this is a test for definition.

Mohl recommends the scales of *Hipparchia janira* for testing "penetrating" power; pollen-grains, the scaly elytra of the diamond beetle or bat's hair, for "definition."

Schacht's test-object consists of the scales of *Hipparchia janira* (Pl. 1. fig. 9 c) (a test for moderate angular aperture and oblique light).

BIBL. That of the INTRODUCTION (p. xl), and of ANGULAR APERTURE, and especially the "Microscopic Cabinet" of Goring and Pritchard.

TETHEA, Lam.—A genus of marine Sponges.

Char. Solid and compact, rounded, covered with a skin; without sensible pores; interior fleshy, with acicular and globulo-subulate spines (Pl. 37. fig. ε).

Two species: *T. cranium* and *lyncurium.*

BIBL. Johnston, *Brit. Spong.* p. 81; Gosse, *Mar. Zool.* i.; Huxley, *Ann. Nat. Hist.* 1851. vii. p. 370.

TETMEMORUS, Ralfs. — A genus of Desmidiaceæ.

Char. Cells single, simple, elongated, straight, cylindrical or fusiform, constricted in the middle; segments emarginate at the ends.

Sporangia square or round.

1. *T. granulatus* (Pl. 10. figs. 33, 34). Cells fusiform both in front and side view, ends colourless and lip-like; dots irregular. Length 1-130′′.

2. *T. lævis* (Pl. 10. fig. 35, in conjugation). Cells in front view somewhat tapering, ends truncate; side view fusiform; dots none, or very indistinct (under ord. illum.). Length 1-350′′.

3. *T. Brebissonii.* Dots in longitudinal rows.

BIBL. Ralfs, *Brit. Desmid.* p. 145.

TETRABÆNA, Duj.—Spores of an Alga, undergoing division?

BIBL. Dujardin, *Infus.* p. 330.

TETRACYCLUS, Ralfs.—A genus of Diatomaceæ.

Char. Frustules compound, aggregated into a filament, in front view broadly tabular,

with longitudinal interrupted vittæ; valves inflated on each side in the middle.

Valves with coarse transverse striæ.

T. Thienemanni, Ehr. (*lacustris*, Ralfs) (Pl. 13. fig. 28). Valves rounded or subacute at ends; inflations rounded.

T. emarginatus. As the last, but valves constricted towards the rounded and subapiculate ends, and the inflations emarginate.

BIBL. Ralfs, *Ann. Nat. Hist.* 1843. xii. p. 105; Kützing, *Sp. Alg.* p. 118; Smith, *Brit. Diat.* ii. p. 37.

TETRAGRAMMA, Ehr. = *Terpsinoe.*

TETRANYCHUS, Duf.—A genus of Arachnida, of the order Acarina, and family Trombidina.

Char. Palpi incumbent upon the rostrum, stout, short, and conical; mandibles and labium as in *Raphignathus*; coxæ inserted in two groups on each side, one for the two anterior, the other for the two posterior; anterior legs longest, third joint (femur) largest; claws short and greatly curved.

Several species.

1. *T. glaber* (Pl. 2. fig. 32). Very minute; eyes two, whitish, upon the anterior prominence. Under stones in damp places.

2. *T. lapidum* (*cristatus*) Dugès (Pl. 2. fig. 35). Legs slender, anterior very long; eyes three on each side; several rows of white points upon the back and margins of the body. Found under stones and upon plants.

3. *T. telarius.* Abdomen produced in front in the form of a cone; yellowish; a dark yellow spot on each side of the back. On ill-conditioned greenhouse plants; forms a kind of web.

BIBL. Dugès, *Ann. des Sc. Nat.* 2 sér. i. 24, & ii. 55; Gervais, *Walckenaer's Aptères*, iii. 165; Dufour, *Ann. des Sc. Nat.* 1 sér. xxv. 279; Koch, *Deutschl. Crustac.*

TETRAPHIS, Hedwig.—A genus of Mosses. See GEORGIA.

TETRAPLOA, Berk. and Br.—A genus of Torulacei (Coniomycetous Fungi), comprising at present a single species, *T. aristata*, a curious little fungus growing upon leaves of grass, forming an olive-coloured stratum composed of bodies consisting of four connate quadri-articulate spores, each terminated by a bristle.

BIBL. Berk. & Br. *Ann. Nat. Hist.* ser. 2. v. p. 450, pl. 11. fig. 6.

TETRAPLODON, Br. and Sch.—A genus of Splachnaceæ (Acrocarpous operculate Mosses), containing some of the *Splachna* of authors.

Tetraplodon angustatum, Br. and Sch.= *Splachnum angustatum*, Linn. fil.

T. mnioides, Br. and Sch. = *Spl. mnioides*, Linn. fil.

TETRASPORA, Link.—A genus of Palmellaceæ (Confervoid Algæ), nearly related to the Ulvaceæ; indeed it is very difficult to draw any very distinct line of demarcation between *Tetraspora* and MONOSTROMA, the fronds of both of which are membranous strata formed of a single layer of cells; the latter, however, has its constituent cells crowded, while in *Tetraspora* the green 'cell-contents' lie scattered, mostly in groups of two or four, in the gelatinous frond. Thuret states that the primordial utricles of the cells possess long cilia in the stage when they are imbedded in a continuous frond (Pl.3.fig.10). The history of development of this genus is imperfectly known at present; the ciliated cell-contents break out as swarming zoospores, but their next following changes have not been observed. Two recorded British species appear to be distinct, growing in stagnant pools (see MONOSTROMA, MERISMOPÆDIA, and SARCINA).

1. *T. gelatinosa* (Pl. 3. fig. 10). Frond gelatinous, soft, of irregular shape and division, pale green; cells 1-10800 to 1-4200″ in diameter (Kützing, *Tab. Phyc.* i. p. 28).

2. *T. lubrica*. Frond green, elongated, mesentery-shaped, lobed and sinuated, lobes often anastomosing; cells angulo-globose, 1-3600″ in diameter (Kützing, *l. c.* p. 30).

BIBL. Hassall, *Brit. Fr. Alg.* p. 300, pl. 78; Kützing, *Sp. Alg.* p. 225; *Tab. Phyc.* i.; Thuret, *Ann. des Sc. Nat.* 3 sér. xiv. p. 248, pl. 21; Nägeli, *Einzell. Alg.* p. 71, pl. 2.

TEXTULARIA, Defrance (TEXTILARIA, Ehr.).—A genus of Foraminifera, of the order Enallostegia, and family Textularidæ.

Char. Shell regular, equilateral, conical, oblong or cuneiform; *chambers* globular or cuneiform, regularly alternating at all ages, partly embracing or simply superposed upon two regular alternate lines; *orifice* semilunar, transverse, lateral, on the inner side of each chamber.

Differs from *Bigenerina* in observing the same kind of growth at all ages; from *Bolivina* in the transverse orifice; from *Sagrina* and *Vulculina* in the position of the orifice, which is lateral (not superior) and on the inner side of the chambers.

The shells are often covered with foreign bodies, or particles of sand agglutinated during the growth. Two recent British species:

1. *T. cuneiformis* (Pl. 18. fig. 34), *a. conica*. Shell cylindrical. Length 1-20″.

2. *T. variabilis*, with three varieties.

Several fossil species, some found in chalk.

BIBL. That of the order.

THAMNOMYCES, Ehr.—A genus of Sphæriacei (Ascomycetous Fungi). *T. hippotrichoides* is referred by Fries to *Rhizomorpha*. It appears to require further examination.

BIBL. Berk. *Brit. Flor.* ii. pt. 2. p. 284; Fries, *Summa Veg.* p. 382.

THECA.—A term used very loosely in the descriptions of Cryptogamic plants. In the case of the Lichens and Fungi it is synonymous with ASCUS, a sac in which free spores are developed; these are called *theca-spores* or ascospores, in contrast with BASIDIOSPORES or stylospores. In the higher Cryptogamia, as Ferns, &c., it is used in the sense of *sporangium*.

THECAMONADINA, Duj.—A family of Infusoria (=Cryptomonadina and some Astasiæa, E.).

Char. Usually coloured; covered with a non-contractile tegument, which is either hard and brittle, or membranous; no other locomotive organs present than one or more flagelliform filaments.

The organisms probably consist of Algæ, or their spores. They are minute, usually green, but some are red; and they often colour stagnant water from existing in vast numbers. They are mostly recognizable by their rigidity and the uniformity of their motion.

It is thus subdivided:—

A single flagelliform filament.	Body ovoid or globular .... { Tegument hard and brittle................		1. *Trachelomonas*.
	{ Tegument membranous....................		2. *Cryptomonas*.
	Body depressed or foliaceous....... { with a tail-like prolongation		3. *Phacus* (*Euglena*, pt. E.).
	{ without a prolongation		4. *Crumenula*.
Two filaments.	Two similar filaments		5. *Diselmis* (*Chlamidomonas*, E.).
	One flagelliform filament, and one trailing retractile filament { Body prismatic or boat-shaped		6. *Plaotia*.
	{ Body ovoid or pip-shaped....		7. *Antxonema*.
	Several filaments............ { Body prolonged into a point in front		8. *Oxyrrhis*.

BIBL. Dujardin, *Infus.* p. 323.

THELACTIS, Mart.—A doubtful genus

of Mucorini (Physomycetous Fungi), consisting apparently of a Mucor with one or more whorls of barren branches near the lower part of the erect fertile filaments.

BIBL. Fries, *Summa Veg.* p. 487.

THELOTREMA, Ach.—A genus of Endocarpeæ (Angiocarpous Lichens), containing two British species.

BIBL. Leighton, *Brit. Angioc. Lichens,* p. 31.

THEORUS, Ehr.—A genus of Rotatoria, of the family Hydatinæa.

Char. Eyes colourless, more than three, cervical, in two groups; foot forked; jaws each with a single tooth.

1. *T. vernalis* (Pl. 35. fig. 32). Toes small, frontal hook absent. Aquatic; length 1-140 to 1-120".

2. *T. uncinatus.* Toes long, frontal (or rather cervical) region with hooks. Aquatic; length 1-240".

BIBL. Ehrenberg, *Infus.* p. 454.

THOREA, Bory.—A genus of Batrachospermeæ (Confervoid Algæ), of which one species (*T. ramosissima*) occurs in Britain; its fronds are branched filaments, a foot or more long, about as thick as a crowquill, with a villous surface, of olive-black

Fig. 740.

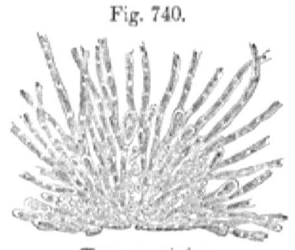

Thorea ramosissima.

Horizontal section of a filament (halved). The semicircular denser portion represents the axis, the loose spreading branches the villi. Magnified 25 diameters.

colour. The filaments are composed of radiating branched cells, closely compacted into a kind of solid axis, from which proceed lax, radiating ramuli (forming the villous surface). The spores (or sporangial cells) arise from these ramules (fig. 740).

BIBL. Kützing, *Phyc. generalis,* pl. 16, *Sp. Alg.* p. 534; *Eng. Bot.* Supp. No. 2948; Hassall, *Brit. Fr. Alg.* p. 64.

THUIARIA, Flem.—A genus of Polypi, of the order Hydroida, and family Sertulariadæ.

Char. Those of *Sertularia,* but the cells closely pressed to or imbedded in the stem or branches. Two species :

1. *T. thuia.* Cells ovate - elliptical,

acutish; vesicles pear-shaped. On shells from deep water.

2. *T. articulata.* Cells ovate, obtuse or truncate, vesicles elliptical ; rare.

BIBL. Johnston, *Brit. Zooph.* p. 83; Gosse, *Mar. Zool.* ii. p. 23.

THUJA, L.—A genus of Coniferæ (Gymnospermous Plants), to which belongs the *arbor vitæ* of gardens, *Thuja occidentalis*; *T. orientalis* is placed by some authors under another genus, *Biota.* The characters of Coniferous wood, Gymnospermous ovules, &c., may be observed in these plants (see CONIFERÆ and OVULE).

THYMELEACEÆ.—An order of Dicotyledons to which the Spurge-Laurels (*Daphne*) belong. In *D. Lagetto* (= *Lagetta lintearia*) the fibres of the liber are separated into lozenge-shaped meshes, arranged in such beautiful and easily-separable layers, as to have acquired for the plant the name of the LACE-BARK TREE.

See LIBER.

THYRSOPTERIS, Kunze.—A genus of Dicksonieæ (Polypodioid Ferns), with a curious structure of the fertile fronds. Exotic (figs. 741-4).

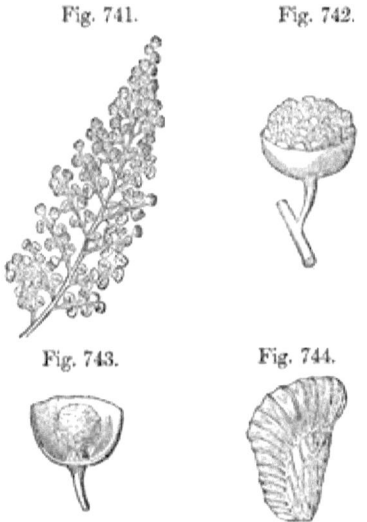

Fig. 741.　　　　　Fig. 742.

Fig. 743.　　　　Fig. 744.

Thyrsopteris elegans.

Fig. 741. A fertile pinna.

Fig. 742. A pinnule converted into a cup-like sorus. Magnified 20 diameters.

Fig. 743. Vertical section of the same, with the sporanges removed from the columella.

Fig. 744. Side view of a sporange.　Magn. 100 diams.

2 Y

THYROID GLAND.—The thyroid gland is one of the vascular glands, or glands without ducts.

It consists of rounded, closed, glandular vesicles (fig. 745), surrounded by or imbedded

Fig. 745.

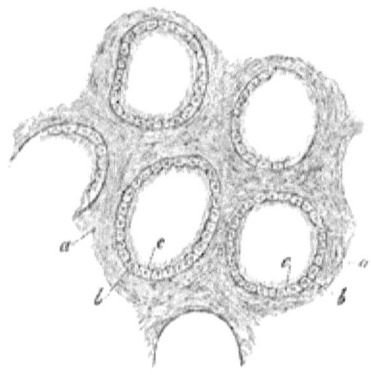

Glandular vesicles from the thyroid gland of a child. *a*, intervening areolar tissue ; *b*, basement membrane ; *c*, epithelium.

Magnified 250 diameters.

in a fibrous stroma (*a*), and aggregated into roundish, elongate, or somewhat polygonal

Fig. 746.

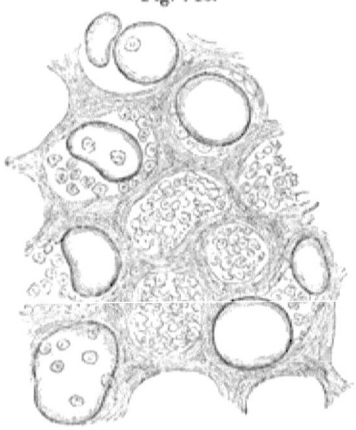

Glandular vesicles with colloid matter. Magnified 50 diameters.

acini or minute lobules, these being grouped in secondary lobules, which unite to form lobes. The vesicles are from 1-600 to 1-240″

in diameter, the acini from 1-50 to 1-24″. The stroma is condensed around the lobules, to form a fibrous coat.

The stroma consists of ordinary interlacing bundles of areolar tissue, with fine elastic fibres ; at its outer surface containing fat-cells.

The vesicles consist of a basement-membrane (fig. 745 *b*), lined by a single layer of polygonal epithelial cells (*c*), and containing a yellowish, tenacious, albuminous liquid.

The capillaries form plexuses surrounding the vesicles.

In *goitre*, the vesicles become greatly enlarged, and confluent, so as to form cysts containing colloid matter, with fat-globules and crystals of cholesterine. The same conditions, in a minor degree, are so frequently met with, that they can scarcely be regarded as abnormal. The epithelium is also often found loose in the vesicles (fig. 746). The minute arteries and capillaries are often found varicose.

BIBL. Kölliker, *Mikrosk. Anat.* ii. 327 ; Förster, *Pathol. Anat.* ii. 233.

THYSANURA.—An order of Insects, to which *Lepisma* and *Podura* belong.

See INSECTS (p. 391).

TILLETIA, Tulasne.—A genus of Ustilaginei (Coniomycetous Fungi), forming the *Bunt*, a kind of blight of various corn grains, in which the ears are attacked, and the internal substance of the grains is replaced by a fœtid, black powder, consisting of the spores of the fungus. *T. Caries* (*Uredo Caries*, D.C.) attacks wheat and other grain. The interior of the ovaries of the corn is at first occupied by an interwoven mycelium, from which the globular spores arise on short stalks ; as the latter grow, the ears become more or less deformed, the mycelium disappears, and the spores are set free as a pulverulent mass ; the spores have a reticulated surface, and their pedicel is often found attached. (See USTILAGINEI.)

BIBL. Berk. *Brit. Flor.* ii. pt. 2. p. 375 ; Tulasne, *Ann. des Sc. Nat.* 3 sér. vii. p. 112, pl. 5, 4 sér. ii. p. 161.

TIMMIA, Hedw.—A genus of Mniaceous mosses, containing one British species, *Timmia austriaca*, Hedw. (*megapolitana*, Hook. and Tayl.).

TINEA, Fabr.—A genus of Lepidopterous Insects, of the family Tineidæ.

The small scales from the under side of the wings of *T. pellionella*, the common clothes' moth, have been proposed as test-objects ; but they can hardly be regarded as such for object-glasses of the present day. The longitudinal lines form the test-structure.

BIBL. Westwood, *Introduction, &c.*; Stainton, *Manual of Butterflies, &c.* p. 292.

TINTINNUS, Schrank. — A genus of Infusoria, of the family Ophrydina.

Char. Single; body contained in a cylindrical, sessile, bell-shaped carapace, to the bottom of which it is attached by a stalk.

Five species. In one, the carapace is covered with dots, and its orifice toothed.

T. inquilinus (Pl. 25. fig. 4). Body hyaline or yellowish; carapace cylindrical, hyaline. Marine; length 1-240″.

Dujardin unites this genus with *Vaginicola*, where it properly belongs.

BIBL. Ehrenberg, *Infus.* p. 294; id. *Ber. d. Berl. Akad.* 1840; Dujardin, *Infus.* p. 561.

TISSUE, FIBRO-PLASTIC. — A term applied by Lebert to imperfectly developed abnormal areolar tissue. The separate elements are often found diffused through those of normal tissues, or products of inflammatory exudation. They consist of rounded or oblong cells, from 1-2300 to 1-1600″ in diameter; in a more advanced stage becoming fusiform or angular, and finally forming distinct fibres; hence resembling the elements of embryonic areolar tissue (Pl. 40. fig. 43). In some instances the development is arrested at one of the early phases, so that the tissue consists almost exclusively of the rounded or the fusiform cells; and in others, the cells enlarge and produce a number of nuclei or secondary cells (Pl. 30. fig. 10 c).

Fibro-plastic tissue or its elements are met with in inflammatory effusions upon the serous and synovial membranes, but rarely; in the interstitial effusions of pneumonia, especially when chronic; in cirrhosis of the liver; in the products of suppurating surfaces; on the surface of chronic ulcers, and non-malignant fungoid vegetations; in the soft yellow vascular tissue occupying the cancelli of ulcerated bones; in certain tumours, &c. See TUMOURS.

BIBL. Lebert, *Physiol. patholog.*; Wedl, *Patholog. Histolog.*; Förster, *Patholog. Anat.* i.

TISSUES, ANIMAL. — The following synoptical arrangement of the principal animal tissues is intended to facilitate reference to the various articles scattered through the work.

A. Simple.

1. *Blastemic or protoplastic* .. Sarcode.
2. *Membranous* .... Basement membrane.
3. *Cellular* .... { Fatty tissue; nerve-cells; simple cartilage; unstriated muscular fibre.
4. *Blastemic and cellular* .. { Without secondary deposit. True cartilage. With secondary deposit. Bone.
5. *Fibrous* .... { Areolar (cellular) tissue; tendon; ligament; elastic tissue; muscle.
6. *Fibrous and cellular* .... Fibro-cartilage.
7. *Tubular* .... { Without secondary deposit. Vessels. With secondary deposit. Nerve-tubes.

B. Compound. Glands; mucous and serous membranes; skin; synovial membrane; teeth.

TISSUES, VEGETABLE. — The tissues composing the substance of vegetables are all comparatively slight modifications of one type, being composed of cellulose sacs, or "cells" *par excellence*, varying only in form and consistence and in their mode of union. The tissues may be divided into groups on different principles; but for our purpose a very simple arrangement will suffice, based chiefly on the character of the compound tissues, leaving the secondary divisions to be determined by the nature of the component cells.

1. *Cambium tissue*, occurring in the growing regions of all plants having stems, is composed of minute cells of variable form, densely filled with protoplasm, and without intercellular passages. It is a transitional structure, forming the first stage of all the rest.

2. *Parenchyma*, or "cellular tissue," is composed of cells in which the diameter is not excessive in any one direction, and the walls are comparatively thin. This is divided by authors into many sections, according to the form of the cells, the laxity of their coherence, &c. The only distinctions worth note are between —

a. *Parenchyma proper*, where the cells have polygonal forms.

b. *Merenchyma*, where the cells are round, oval, &c.

c. *Collenchyma*, which is a form of cellular tissue where the walls are greatly thickened with softish secondary deposits; it occurs beneath the epidermis of many herbaceous plants, in the fronds of the larger Algæ, of Lichens, &c.

d. *Sterenchyma*. A name which might be used to distinguish the bony cellular tissue of shells, stones of fruits, &c.

3. *Prosenchyma*. Cellular tissue, usually forming the mass of wood and various fibrous structures, where the cells are attenuated to a point at each end, the cells, "fibres," being intercalated and applied side to side.

4. *Tela contexta*. This name is used to

indicate the interwoven tissue formed by the ramified jointed filaments of the mycelium of Fungi, and the cottony substance in the interior of the thallus of many Lichens.

5. *Fibro-vascular tissue* is composed of vessels, ducts, and prosenchymatous cells or "fibres" associated in various ways, forming fibrous or fibro-vascular bundles, which either remain distinct or cohere to form masses of wood.

a. *Fibrous bundles*, occurring in liber, in the outer part of many Monocotyledonous stems, and in the stems of Mosses, consist of cords formed of prosenchymatous cells, which are often of great length.

b. *Fibro-vascular bundles*, composed of vessels and ducts together with prosenchyma, form the "woody fibres" of every part (except the bark) of all plants above the Mosses.

c. *Clathrate tissue*, found in the bark of Dicotyledons and in the vascular bundles of Monocotyledons (see LIBER).

6. *Laticiferous tissue* and *Reservoirs for Secretion*, composed either of intercellular passages lined by a proper coat, or of lines of cells fused at their ends, so as to form continuous branched canals; they occur in the bark, wood, and pith of the Flowering Plants.

7. *Epidermal tissue*. Composed of cellular tissue, forming a continuous firm layer over the external surface of the higher plants. It is composed usually of a single layer of cells, and presents very varied appendages, such as HAIRS, GLANDS, &c., and is perforated by STOMATA. Its outer surface is rendered dense by the deposit of CUTICLE. The epidermis is replaced, on stems, by the CORK or suberous layer of BARK.

For further particulars see the various heads above-named.

BIBL. General Works on Botany.

TMESIPTERIS.—A genus of Psiloteæ (Lycopodiaceæ) (fig. 747), remarkable for

Fig. 747.

Tmesipteris tannensis.

its peculiar habit and bivalved sporanges bursting by a vertical crack.

BIBL. See LYCOPODIACEÆ.

TOBACCO.—The leaves of Tobacco, *Nicotiana Tabacum* and other species, may be distinguished from the leaves of the plants commonly used for adulteration by the peculiar structure of the EPIDERMIS with its hairs, and the form of the section of its FIBRO-VASCULAR BUNDLES. Paper, which has been sometimes used, is still more readily detected. As in other similar cases, the nature of a foreign ingredient can only be determined by careful comparative investigations.

BIBL. Hassall, *Food and its Adulterations*, p. 538; Prescott, *Tobacco and its Adulterations*, London, 1858.

TODEA, Willdenow.—A genus of Osmundæous Ferns (fig. 748–50). Exotic.

Fig. 748. Fig. 749. Fig. 750.

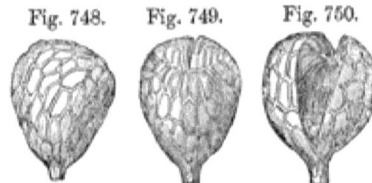

Todea africana.
Sporanges closed and bursting.
Magnified 40 diameters.

TOLYPOTHRIX, Kütz.—A genus of Oscillatoriaceæ (Confervoid Algæ), apparently not very satisfactorily defined. Hassall describes six species as British, of which *T. distorta* (Pl. 4. fig. 14) is said to be common, adhering to sticks, stems, &c. in stagnant water, forming tufts from 1-2 to 1" in height, dark green when fresh, verdigris or blue-green when dry; primary filaments 1-1800 to 1-1440" in diameter; joints about as long as broad. *Tolypothrix Dillwynii* = *Desmonema*, Eng. Bot. Supp. no. 2958.

BIBL. Kütz. *Sp. Alg.* p. 312; *Tab. Phyc.* ii. pls. 31–33; Hassall, *Brit. Freshw. Alg.* p. 240, pls. 68 & 69.

TONGUE.—We have only space here to notice the structure of the beautiful papillæ of the human tongue.

The filiform or conical papillæ (fig. 755) are whitish, very numerous, and occupy the intervals between the fungiform papillæ. The papillæ of the mucous membrane at their bases (*p, p*) are conical, and covered either at the end only, or all over the surface with a number of smaller or secondary papillæ; the whole being coated by an epithelial investment (e), terminating in a tuft of free filiform processes (f). The inner layers of the epithelium agree in structure with that of the mouth, whilst the outer layers, and especially the epithelium of the processes, resemble rather the scales of the epidermis, in their hardness, small size, and considerable resistance to the action of alkalies and acids. The papillæ themselves consist of areolar tissue, with a large number of undulating nuclear fibres, each containing a small artery (a) and vein (b), with an intermediate plexus of looped capillaries, and numerous nerve-tubes.

The fungiform or clavate papillæ (fig. 751)

Fig. 751.

Fig. 753.

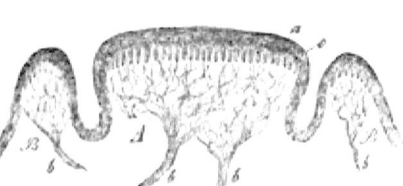

Fig. 754.

Fig. 752.

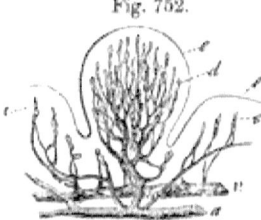

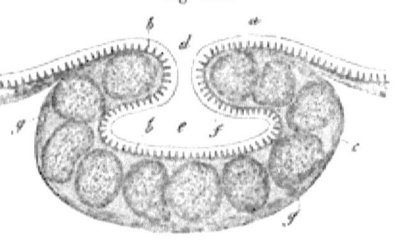

Fig. 751. Fungiform papilla covered by the epithelium e on one side, and with the secondary or simple papillæ p. Magnified 35 diameters.
Fig. 752. The same, with the vessels; the epithelium e represented in outline. a, artery; b, vein; d, capillary loops of the simple papilla; e, capillaries in the simple papillæ of the mucous membrane at the base of the fungiform papilla. Magnified 18 diameters.
Fig. 753. Perpendicular section of a human circumvallate papilla. A, proper papilla; B, wall; a, epithelium; b b, nerves of the papilla and wall; c, secondary papillæ. Magnified 10 diameters.
Fig. 754. Follicular gland from the root of the human tongue. a, epithelium; b, papillæ of the mucous membrane; c, areolar coat; e, cavity; f, epithelium lining it; g g, follicles in the thick capsule. Magnified 30 diameters.

are reddish, distributed over the entire surface of the tongue, and are very numerous at its point. Each has at its base a club-shaped mucous papilla, and is covered all over with simple or secondary conical papillæ (p p), and a simple epithelial layer (e), without filiform processes. The vessels (fig. 752) are more numerous, but otherwise resemble those in the filiform papillæ.

The circumvallate or lenticular papillæ (fig. 753) consist of a flattened central papilla (A), surrounded by an elevated wall or ridge (B). The flat surface is furnished with crowded conical secondary papillæ (c), the whole being covered with epithelium (a) free from processes. The wall appears as a simple fold of the mucous membrane, and also exhibits beneath its smooth epithelial coat numerous rows of simple, conical, secondary papillæ. In other respects these papillæ do not differ essentially in structure from the fungiform.

In some of the papillæ of the tongue, axial bodies are found resembling those in the papillæ of the skin.

The epithelial processes of the filiform papillæ are often covered by a fungus (Leptothrix), the mycelium closely surrounding them, whilst some of the filaments project from the surface.

The glands of the tongue consist of mucous and follicular glands.

The mucous glands resemble those of the mouth (MOUTH).

The follicular glands are most numerous between the epiglottis and the circumvallate papillæ, and are so superficially situated as to form projections of the mucous membrane. They form lenticular or globular masses, from 1-24 to 1-6″ in diameter, imbedded in the submucous tissue, and in the middle of the free surface is the orifice (755 d) of a conical cavity (e), formed by a depression of the mucous membrane. Each gland forms a thick-walled capsule, surrounded by a fibrous coat (c) continuous with the deeper portion of the mucous

Fig. 755.

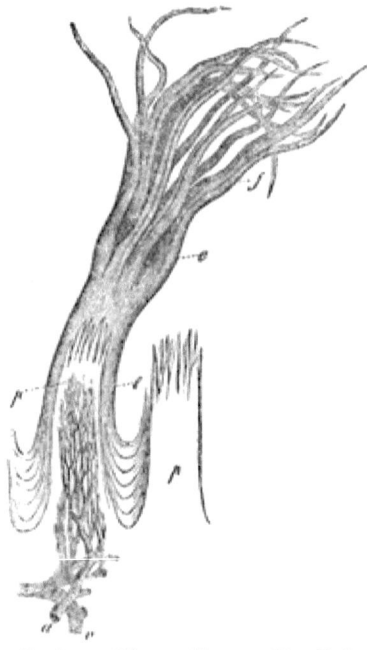

Two human filiform papillæ, one with epithelium. *p, p,* papillæ; *a, v,* artery and vein, with the capillary loops; *e,* epithelial covering; *f,* its processes.

Magnified 35 diameters.

membrane, and lined internally by a prolongation of the mucous membrane with papillæ and epithelium (*b, a*); and between

the two are closed capsules or follicles (*g*), imbedded in a fibrous and vascular basis. The follicles are from 1-120 to 1-48″ in diameter, rounded or somewhat elongate, whitish, composed of a coat of areolar tissue without elastic fibres, and with greyish-white contents consisting of cells 1-6000 to 1-4000″ in diameter and free nuclei.

The tongues of the Mollusca have long formed interesting microscopic objects, on account of the elegant horny (or chitinous?) teeth placed upon them in numerous rows, and in various patterns; the number and arrangement of which are also of importance in characterizing the families, genera, &c. They may be easily examined in the limpet (*Patella*), the whelk (*Buccinum*), or in the freshwater snails, *Lymnæus, Planorbis,* &c.

BIBL. Kölliker, *Mikrosk. Anat.* ii.; Todd and Bowman, *Physiol. Anat.* &c.; Mollusca: Woodward, *On Shells*; Gray, *Mic. Journal,* 1853. p. 170; Siebold, *Vergleich. Anat.*; Semper, *Siebold und Kölliker's Zeitschrift,* 1858. ix. p. 270; Troschel, *das Gebiss der Schnecken,* 1857.

TONSILS.—These organs may be regarded as consisting of from ten to twenty follicular glands, resembling those found at the root of the tongue, surrounded by a common fibrous coat or capsule.

The blood-vessels are numerous, forming elegant networks around the follicles.

BIBL. Kölliker, *Mikroskop. Anat.* ii.

TOPAZ.—The crystals of this mineral belong to the rhombic or right-rhombic prismatic system. They consist principally of silicate of alumina, with the fluorides of aluminium and silicium.

Sections of topaz exhibit remarkable microscopic cavities, often of most singular and elegant forms, frequently containing crystals and one or two non-miscible liquids; the latter sometimes including bubbles of gas, vapour or vacuities.

Sir David Brewster recommends the spherical cavities as the best objects for examining the aberrations of lenses, and as infinitely preferable to the globules of mercury.

BIBL. Brewster, *Edinb. Phil. Trans.* x. & xvi.; *Treat. on the Microscope,* p. 186.

TORTOISE-SHELL. See SHELL (p. 621).

TORTULA, Hedw. A genus of Mosses. See BARBULA.

TORULA, Pers.—A genus of Torulacei (Coniomycetous Fungi). The plants ordinarily referred here appear to be somewhat heterogeneous in their nature. In what may be considered as the true species, the chains of spores form the principal bulk of the plants, little or no filamentous mycelium existing. Other forms very generally included under this head agree in their characters with OIDIUM, which itself is a doubtful genus, probably founded on the conidiiferous states of more perfect kinds. But in *T. sacchari* (or *cerevisiæ*), the Yeast fungus, usually referred here, we find both forms presented; for when actively vegetating in fermenting liquids, it presents the characters shown in fig. 23. Pl. 20, while, when the liquid becomes exhausted, portions of the fungus float to the top, and produce a filamentous structure, terminating in chains of "spores," such as are represented in fig. 24 (Pl. 20), and in fig. 756. The simply beaded form is taken as the type of a genus *Cryptococcus* by some authors, of whom a part consider it a Fungus,

Fig. 756.

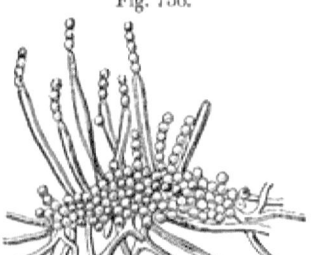

Torula sacchari (aerial form).
Magnified 200 diameters.

another part (Kützing especially) an Alga. The same varieties of form occur in the Vinegar plant; and in both cases *Penicillium glaucum* seems invariably to succeed to the preceding when kept at a moderate temperature. Thus between all these various forms, together with *Oidium lactis*, there appears to be a relation, not yet quite clearly made out, indicating that they probably represent different states of the same plant growing under different conditions of nutrition and temperature. Further remarks on this head are made under YEAST and VINEGAR PLANT. A growth similar to *T. sacchari* presents itself sometimes in decomposing urine (Pl. 20. fig. 7), from healthy subjects; and indeed scarcely any decomposing animal or vegetable fluid, in which

there exist fermentable elements, remain long free from *Torula*-like growths, if left exposed to the air (see FERMENTATION).

We find it impossible to give definite characters for the species that have been enumerated. *T. herbarum* may be named as a common form growing on decaying stems of plants; it forms at first erect greenish tufts, which afterward become blackish, ramify and form a black crust, the spores readily separating. *T. Sporendonema*, a form growing on decaying cheese, represents the *Sporendonema casei* of Desmazières. *T. Fumago* is now separated with other forms under the genus CAPNODIUM. *T. alternata* also is the type of the genus ALTERNARIA.

BIBL. Berk. *Brit. Flor.* ii. pt 2. p. 359; *Ann. Nat. Hist.* i. p. 263, vi. p. 439; 2 ser. v. p. 460, xiii. p. 460; Fries, *Syst. Myc.* iii. p. 499; *Summa Veget.* p. 505; Fresenius, *Beitr. z. Myc.* Heft. ii. p. 58, pl. 6. fig. 55; Corda, *Icones Fungorum.*

TORULACEI.—A family of Coniomycetous Fungi, forming moulds and mildews on decaying vegetable substances, or acting as ferments in decomposing vegetable and animal fluids. They are compound microscopic

Fig. 757.   Fig. 759.

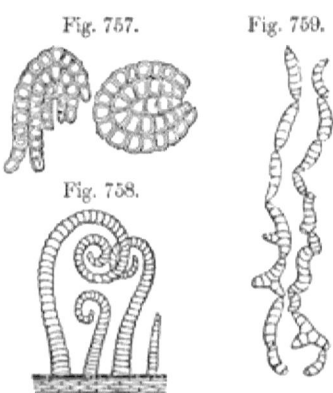

Fig. 758.

Fig. 757. Speira toruloides. Magnified 200 diameters.
Fig. 758. Gyrocerus ammonis. Magnified 200 diams.
Fig. 759. Trimmatostroma salicis. Magn. 200 diams.

cylindrical or beaded filaments, simple or ramified, the joints of which (all or part) separate from each other to form the "spores." There is no definite receptacle here, the mycelium grows as a cottony web over or in the infected body, or forms clouds or flocks in liquids. Much obscurity prevails respecting most of the genera included below, and it is indeed doubtful whether most of them are independent productions. Some species of *Torula*, such as *T. cerevisiæ* (the Yeast fungus), appear intimately connected with certain Hyphomycetous genera, perhaps merely representing their conidiiferous forms (see TORULA). ACHORION again seems to be merely the spermogonous form of a *Puccinia*. *Sporendonema* is founded apparently on imperfect observation; *S. muscæ*, the true characters of which are given under that head, has been re-named *Empusa*; and its proper position is as yet obscure, but it would appear to be referable to the Mucorini. *Dictyosporium* (fig. 172, page 229), *Speira* (fig. 757) and *Trimmatostroma* (fig. 759) appear to consist merely of the spores of some other genera; *Gyrocerus* (fig. 758) cannot be regarded as a perfect form; and indeed all the genera require a thorough examination in a fresh state.

Synopsis of Genera.

1. *Torula*. Spores in beaded chains, simple, readily separating, placed on a short continuous or septate pedicel (fig. 756; Pl. 20. figs. 7 & 23).

2. *Bispora*. Resembling the last, but the spores uniseptate (fig. 60, page 87).

3. *Septonema*. Resembling the preceding, but having several transverse septa in the spores (fig. 640, page 620).

4. *Alternaria*. Resembling the preceding, but with cellular spores connected by a filiform isthmus (fig. 9, page 29).

5. *Sporidesmium*. Spores in tufts, straight, subclavate or fusiform, shortly stalked or sessile, transversely septate or cellular (fig. 690, page 655).

6. *Tetraploa*. Spores sessile, quadriseptate, coherent in bundles of four, each spore crowned with a bristle.

7. *Sporochisma*. "Filaments erect, simple, external membrane inarticulate, cell-contents at length separating into spores, articulated in fours, emerging."

8. *Coniothecium*. Spores without septa, collected in heaps, finally separating more or less into a powder.

9. *Echinobotryum*. Spores rounded-apiculate, collected in fascicles, attached on simple, erect, annulated filaments.

10. *Spilocæa*. Spores globose, simple, adhering firmly together and to the matrix, forming spots laid bare by the separation of the epidermis of the subject infected.

11. *Sporendonema*. Described as com-

posed of erect filaments, containing single rows of spores in the interior. *S. muscæ* (*Empusa*, Cohn) really consists of short, tufted, erect, simple filaments, terminating in a bell-shaped cell (spore or sporange?), thrown off with elasticity when mature.

12. *Achorion*. Mycelium somewhat ramose, articulated, joints terminating in round, oval, or irregular spores (conidia?).

13. *Speira*. Spores connate into concentric filaments, forming laminæ resembling a horseshoe, finally separating.

14. *Trimmatostroma*. Spores more or less curved, multiseptate, chained in beaded rows, finally separating.

15. *Gyrocerus*. Spores connate into spirally coiled filaments, finally separating.

16. *Dictyosporium*. Spores tongue-shaped, reticularly cellular (fig. 172, page 229).

TOURMALINE.—Sections of the crystals of this mineral, cut parallel to the axis, were formerly used as polarizers or analysers. They are now mostly replaced by Nicol's prisms (INTR. p. xviii). Crystals of the quinine-salt (QUININE) form cheap substitutes for either. The crystals of tourmaline belong to the rhombohedric system. They consist principally of silica with alumina, also containing boracic acid, magnesia, iron, &c.; but their composition is not constant.

Good tourmalines are transparent, brownish or pinkish: the colourless ones do not polarize.

BIBL. Pereira, *Lectures on Polarized Light* ; Naumann, *Mineralogie*, p. 319.

TOUS-LES-MOIS. — A kind of fecula consisting of the starch of species of *Canna*, remarkable for the large size, great transparency and numerous striæ of the granules (Pl. 36. fig. 25). The mixture of any of the common kinds of starch with *Tous-les-mois* is readily detected by microscopic examination. The granules are excellent subjects for studying the physical characters of starch, in particular the appearance with polarized light (Pl. 31. fig. 40), &c. See STARCH.

TOXONIDEA, Donkin. — A proposed new genus of Diatomaceæ, the frustules of which resemble those of *Gyrosigma*, except that the longitudinal line is curved on each side of the median nodule in the same direction, so as to resemble a bow. Two species.

T. Gregoriana (Pl. 42. fig. 42).

BIBL. Donkin, *Micr. Journ.* 1858. vi. p. 12.

TRACHEA. See LUNGS (p. 433).

TRACHEÆ OF INSECTS, &c. The respiratory tubes of Insects and Arachnida (ARACHNIDA).

Tracheæ (Pl. 27. fig. 17 ; Pl. 28. fig. 2 h) are cylindrical tubes containing air. They are broadest at their origin from the spiracles, afterwards branching freely, the minute branches being distributed to all parts of the body and anastomosing freely. By reflected light they appear white, with a metallic lustre, or slightly iridescent ; by transmitted light the smaller ones are black, the larger usually of a violet tint.

The tracheæ consist of two coats, between which lies a spiral fibre (Pl. 27. fig. 17) ; in the larger trunks a second external envelope exists. The fibre becomes more slender and indistinct in the smaller tracheal branches, until it finally disappears. The outer membrane appears to arise from the confluence of cells ; for in the tracheæ of caterpillars and other larvæ of insects, the remaining nuclei are visible (Pl. 28. fig. 17). The inner coat forms a pavement epithelium. The spiral fibre arises from the splitting up of a homogeneous membrane deposited in the space bounded by the confluent cells of the outer membrane.

In many insects the tracheæ are furnished with dilatations forming air-sacs, in which the spiral fibre is absent.

An unsettled point in regard to the tracheæ is the presence of a peritracheal circulation. When larvæ are fed with indigo or carmine, or when the dorsal vessel is injected with colouring matter, the tracheæ become coloured, which some authors believe to arise from the nutritive liquid circulating between the membranes of the tracheæ ; whilst by others this circulation, or the existence of a space between the tracheal membranes, is denied.

BIBL. That of INSECTS ; Newport, *Phil. Trans.* 1836. p. 529 ; Platner, *Müller's Archiv*, 1844. xxxviii. ; Stein, *Vergleich. Anat. d. Insekten* ; Agassiz, *Ann. des Sc. Nat.* 3 sér. xv. ; Bassy, *ibid.* ; Joly, *ibid.* xii. ; Blanchard, *Comptes Rendus*, 1851, or *Ann. Nat. Hist.* 1852. ix. 74 ; Dufour, *Comptes Rendus*, 1851, or *Ann. Nat. Hist.* 1852. ix. 435 ; Meyer, *Siebold und Kölliker's Zeitschr.* i. 175.

TRACHEÆ OF PLANTS. — This name was formerly applied to the unrollable SPIRAL Vessels of Plants, from their resemblance to the tracheæ of Insects.

TRACHELINA, Ehr.—A family of Infusoria.

Char. Carapace absent ; alimentary canal with two distinct orifices, the anal only terminal.

Locomotive organs consisting of cilia covering the body in longitudinal rows, but absent in *Phialina* ; those around the mouth longer. In two genera teeth are present. Mouth situated on the under surface of the body.

Eight genera : *Bursaria, Chilodon, Glaucoma, Loxodes, Nassula, Phialina, Spirostoma, Trachelius.*

BIBL. Ehrenberg, *Infus.* p. 319.

TRACHELIUS, Schrank, Ehr.—A genus of Infusoria, of the family Trachelina.

Char. Body covered with cilia : mouth not spiral, without teeth ; upper lip much elongated in the form of a proboscis.

In three species the cilia have not been detected !

T. lamella (Pl. 25. fig. 5). Body depressed, lamellar, linear-lanceolate, often truncate in front, rounded behind. Aquatic ; length 1-430 to 1-290″.

Eight other species (Ehr.). — Dujardin places some of the species in the genera *Loxophyllum* and *Amphileptus*, and adds three new ones.

BIBL. Ehrenberg, *Infus.* p. 320, and *Ber. d. Berl. Ak.* 1840. p. 202 ; Dujardin, *Infus.* 398.

TRACHELOCERCA, Ehr.—A genus of Infusoria, of the family Ophryocercina.

Char. Those of the family (=caudate *Lachrymariæ*).

Four species.

1. *T. olor* (*Lachrymaria olor*, D.). Body fusiform, white ; neck very long, simple, very moveable, and the dilated end containing the ciliated mouth. Aquatic ; length 1-36″.

2. *T. viridis* (Pl. 24. fig. 33). Body green ; neck as in the last. Aquatic ; length 1-120″.

3. *T. biceps.* Neck bifid at the end.

BIBL. Ehrenberg, *Infus.* p. 341, and *Ber. d. Berl. Akad.* 1840. p. 202.

TRACHELOMONAS, Ehr.—A genus of Infusoria, of the family Cryptomonadina.

Char. Body enclosed in a spherical or ovoid hard and brittle envelope, having a small aperture, from which a long flagelliform filament projects, but no neck (?) ; eyespot present.

1. *T. volvocina* (Pl. 23. fig. 24 d, empty envelope). Spherical, green, brownish, or red ; eye-spot red. Aquatic ; length 1-865″.

2. *T. nigricans.* Ovate-globose, green, blackish brown or reddish ; eye-spot brownish. Aquatic ; length 1-1730″.

3. *T. cylindrica.* Oblong-subcylindrical ;

bright green; eye-spot red. Aquatic; length 1-1000″.

The bodies represented in Pl. 23. fig. 24 (*b* to *g*), and which are commonly found in bog-water, probably belong here, with the genera *Chætoglena* (*a*), *Chætotyphla* (fig. 26), and *Doxococcus* (fig. 47). The margins of the red envelope appear as a bright-red ring, on account of the greater thickness traversed by the light. They are probably spores of Algæ.

BIBL. Ehrenberg, *Infus.* p. 47.

TRADESCANTIA, L. — A genus of Commelynaceæ (Monocotyledons), commonly cultivated in gardens under the name of 'Spider-worts.' These plants are celebrated for having served as material for some of the most remarkable observations on the physiological processes of vegetables — as the ROTATION of the cell-contents, and the multiplication of the cells, so well seen in the hairs of the stamens when young (Pl. 38. figs. 8 & 9). The stems, petioles, &c., afford beautiful spiral, annular, and reticulated vessels, &c.

TRAGACANTH.—A gum derived from various species of *Astragalus*, not consisting of a formless exudation, but of partly disorganized collenchymatous tissue which is extruded from the medullary rays.

BIBL. Von Mohl, *Ann. Nat. Hist.* 2 ser. xix.

TREBIUS, Krøyer.—A genus of Crustacea, of the order Siphonostoma, and family Caligidæ.

Char. Head in the form of a large buckler, with the large frontal plates destitute of sucking disks; thorax three-jointed, segments uncovered; legs four pairs, with long plumose hairs, fourth pair slender, and two-branched; antennæ small, flat, and two-jointed; second pair of foot-jaws two-jointed, and not in the form of a sucking disk.

T. caudatus. Found upon the body of the skate. Male much smaller than the female.

BIBL. Baird, *Brit. Entomostraca*, p. 280; Thompson, *Ann. Nat. Hist.* 1847. xx. 248.

TREMELLA. See TREMELLINI.

TREMELLINI.—A family of Hymenomycetous Fungi, consisting of polymorphous, often convoluted or lobed, more or less gelatinous masses, growing upon branches or stumps of trees, in crevices of the bark, or on the dead wood. The hymenium extends over the whole of the upper exposed surface, and, from the recent researches of Tulasne, appears to present remarkable characters. The gelatinous substance of these Fungi is composed of ramified filaments, with more or less effused mucilage between them. In *Tremella* a portion of the filaments terminate at the surface at first in expanded globular cells, which become divided by vertical septa into four somewhat pyriform cells (*basidia*); from each of these arises a slender filament (*sterigma*), which terminates in a slender point tipped with a globular spore (*stylospore* or *basidiospore*). Other filaments coming to the surface in like manner ramify extensively, with short divergent branches, finally bearing numerous minute globular bodies (*spermatia*), solitary or in groups of four, which, like the basidiospores, fall off and rest on the hymenial surface, involved in jelly, but, unlike these, do not germinate. The basidiospores are about 1-3000″ in diameter, the spermatia about 1-12000″. In *Tremella mesenterica* the surface covered with basidiospores assumes a whitish colour, the layers of spermatia and the jelly are orange.

In *Exidia* the production of the basidiospores is similar; but the spores are reniform and unilocular, about 1-2500″ long and 1-5000″ in diameter. Spermatia have not been detected.

In *Dacrymyces* the basidia are represented by simple clavate or bifurcated branches at the hymenial surface, these terminating in points bearing single reniform spores exhibiting three septa (quadrilocular). In germination some of these spores produce a long filament from each loculus; others behave differently, producing the *spermatia* of the plant, each loculus sending out a short pointed process bearing a globular cellule exactly resembling the spermatia of *Tremella*. Other examples of *Dacrymyces* bear a different kind of reproductive body, apparently representing *conidia*. In these the peripheral filaments terminate in a mass of many-jointed *Torula*-like processes, which ultimately break up into the separate joints. (See DACRYMYCES and EXIDIA.)

BIBL. Berk. *Brit. Flor.* ii. pt 2. p. 215; *Ann. Nat. Hist.* 2 ser. xiii. p. 406, pl. 15. fig. 4; Tulasne, *Ann. des Sc. Nat.* 3 sér. xix. p. 193, pls. 10–12.

TREPOMONAS, Duj.—A genus of Infusoria, of the family Monadina.

Char. Body compressed, thicker and rounded behind, twisted in front into two narrowed lobes, which are inflexed laterally, and each terminated by a flagelliform filament, which produces a very lively rotatory and jerking motion.

T. agilis (Pl. 25. fig. 6). Body granular, unequal. Length 1-1100″. Found in decomposing marsh-water.

BIBL. Dujardin, *Infus.* p. 294.

TRIARTHRA, Ehr.—A genus of Rotatoria, of the family Hydatinæa.

Char. Eyes two, frontal; foot simply styliform; body with lateral cirrhi or fins.

Movement jerking. Jaws two; each bidentate.

1. *T. longiseta* (Pl. 35. fig. 30). Eyes distant, cirrhi and foot nearly three times as long as the body. Aquatic; length 1-216″.

2. *T. mystacina.* Eyes approximate; cirrhi and foot scarcely twice as long as the body.

3. *T. breviseta* (Gosse). Cirrhi much shorter than the body.

BIBL. Ehrenberg, *Infus.* p. 446; Gosse, *Ann. Nat. Hist.* 1851. viii. p. 200.

TRICERATIUM, Ehr.—A genus of Diatomaceæ.

Char. Frustules free; valves triangular, areolar, each angle mostly with a minute tooth or short horn.

Kützing describes fourteen species; Smith admits three British.

1. *T. favus* (Pl. 13. fig. 29). Valves plane or convex, angles obtuse, with horn-like processes; areolæ hexagonal. Marine; diameter 1-240″.

2. *T. alternans.* Angles of valves slightly elevated; areolæ circular. Marine.

3. *T. striolatum* (?). Angles subacute; areolation faint. Brackish water.

BIBL. Ehrenberg, *Ber. der Berl. Akad.* 1840; Smith, *Brit. Diatomaceæ*, i. p. 26; Kützing, *Bacill.* p. 138, and *Sp. Alg.* p. 139; Brightwell, *Micr. Journ.* 1858. p. 153.

TRICHIA, Hall.—A genus of Myxogastres (Gasteromycetous Fungi) growing upon rotten wood, &c., characterized by a stalked or sessile, simple, membranous peridium, which bursts at the summit, whence the densely interwoven free capillitium expands elastically, carrying with it the spores. The capillitium is composed of tubular filaments (*elaters*), containing spiral-fibrous secondary deposits, like the elaters of Marchantia (Pl. 32. fig. 39). In some species the elaters bear numerous little spinulose processes. The genus is divisible into two groups. In the first (*Hemiarcyria*) the dehiscence of the peridium is obscurely circumscissile (fig. 700), the capillitium dense; these are always stalked, usually of reddish colour when young. Some species have the peridia fasciculate on a compound peduncle (fig. 700), others separate. In the other division (*Goniospora*), the dehiscence of the peridium is irregular, the capillitium lax, the peduncle short or

Fig. 700.

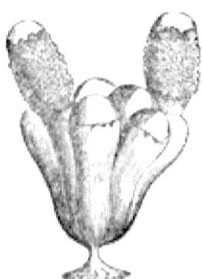

Trichia rubiformis.

Magnified 25 diameters.

absent, the colour at first whitish, changing to yellow, and the spores rather angular. In *T. serpula* and *reticulata* the sessile peridia are irregular, flexuous, serpentine or annular bodies; in most of the other species the peridia are pyriform, turbinate, or of some analogous form. The elaters (Pl. 32. figs. 39 & 40) are interesting objects, and form good tests for the defining power of the microscope under very high powers. They must be mounted in a very thin stratum of liquid.

BIBL. Berk. *Brit. Flor.* ii. pt. 2. p. 319; *Ann. Nat. Hist.* vi. p. 432, 2 ser. v. p. 367; Fries, *Syst. Myc.* iii. p. 182; *Summa Veg.* 457; Greville, *Sc. Crypt. Fl.* pls. 266, 281; Henfrey, *Linnean Trans.* xxi. p. 221; Currey, *Microsc. Journ.* iii. p. 15, v. p. 127.

TRICHINA, Owen.—A genus of Entozoa, of the order Cœlelmintha and family Nematoidea.

T. spiralis (Pl. 16. figs. 16, 17, 18) inhabits the human body, forming opaque white specks, visible to the naked eye, in the voluntary muscles. The worms usually exist singly within a cyst situated between the muscular bundles (fig. 16). At each end of the cyst is a group of fat-cells resembling those of ordinary fatty tissues. The cysts are about 1-50″ in length, elliptical or oval, usually narrowed and slightly produced at the obtuse ends, and consist of numerous structureless laminæ, in which are frequently imbedded minute granules consisting of fatty or calcareous matter. The worm is cylindrical, narrowed towards the anterior end, the posterior end being obtuse and rounded. The integument is transversely striated or annular, and exhibits an anterior and a posterior longitudinal muscular band. The mouth (fig. 17 a) is situated at the anterior extremity, from which a small papilla is sometimes protruded. The first part of the alimentary canal is very narrow, and leads to a broader sacculated portion ; this behind the commencement of the posterior half of the body terminates in a funnel-shaped expansion (fig. 18 c), the remainder of the canal being narrow and lined with pavement-epithelium (fig. 18 d). The manner in which the posterior end of the alimentary canal terminates is doubtful—whether directly continuous with the anal orifice, or free in the abdominal cavity. M. Luschka describes three valves as existing at the posterior end of the body. At the commencement of the funnel-shaped portion of the alimentary canal (fig. 16 b) are two rounded glandular sacs. The reproductive organs are not well known. Just below the funnel-shaped portion of the alimentary canal is the cæcal origin of a tubular sac (figs. 17 & 18 c), containing a dark granular-looking body (fig. 17 d ; fig. 18 e) near its commencement ; this extends to the posterior end of the worm, where it either terminates in the anus or in the abdominal cavity. Luschka regards this as the male organ, and the dark-looking body as the testis ; but no spermatozoa have been detected.

Some of the cysts and worms are found in a state of fatty degeneration, with granules or globules of fat, and calcareous matter.

It appears that the *Trichina* is derived from the food ; for M. Herbst found the muscles of two dogs, which had been fed upon parts of a badger containing the worms, to be loaded with them.

Three or four other doubtful species have been described.

BIBL. Owen, *Trans. of Zool. Soc.* i. p. 315; Luschka, *Siebold & Kölliker's Zeitschr.* iii. 09; Bristowe and Rainey, *Trans. Path. Soc.* v. 274; Dujardin, *Hist. nat. d. Helminthes*, p. 203; Herbst, *Ann. des Sc. Nat.* 3 sér. xvii. ; Kobelt, *Valentin's Repertorium*, 1841.

TRICHOCEPHALUS, Goeze.—A genus of Entozoa, of the order Cœlelmintha, and family Nematoidea.

Char. Body elongate, composed of two parts, the anterior longer and capillary, the posterior becoming suddenly broader ; spi-

culum of male simple, long, and surrounded by a sheath.

The (ten) species occur in the large intestine, principally the cæcum of man and the mammalia.

T. dispar (Pl. 16. fig. 19, the male ; fig. 21, the female, in which the narrowed portion is too short).

Anterior portion of the body spiral in the male, containing the œsophagus only, or the first moniliform portion of the intestine ; posterior portion containing the rest of the intestine and the reproductive organs. Anus situated at the posterior obtuse end of the body. Integument transversely striated, and with a longitudinal band studded with papillæ (Pl. 16. fig. 20). Oviduct terminating at the point of junction of the two portions of the body ; ova (fig. 21 a) oblong, covered by a resistant shell, with a short neck at each end.

BIBL. Dujardin, *Helminthes*, p. 30 ; Owen, *Todd's Cycl. Anat & Phys.* art. *Entozoa* ; Wedl, *Pathol. Histolog.* p. 787.

TRICHOCOLEA, Nees. — A genus of Jungermanniew (Hepaticæ), containing one British species, *T. (Jung.) tomentella*, growing in moist places in the west and north of England, Scotland, and Ireland. It is remarkable for the character of the leaves, which are cut up into compound capillary segments, giving the plant a spongy texture. Colour pale.

BIBL. Hook. *Brit. Flor.* ii. pt. 1. p. 127 ; *Brit. Jung.* pl. 36; Eckart, *Synops. Jung.* pl. 6. fig. 49 ; Endlicher, *Gen. Plant.* Supp. 1. no. 472, p. 15.

TRICHODA, Müll., Ehr.—A genus of Infusoria, of the family Enchelia.

Char. Body free from hairs or cilia ; teeth absent ; mouth obliquely truncated, ciliated, with a lip, but neck absent.

The six species are colourless.

1. *T. pura.* Body oblong, clavate, attenuate in front. Aquatic ; length 1-720″. A species of Dujardin's genus *Acomia*.

The other species have been very imperfectly examined and illustrated.

Dujardin's genus, which is placed in the family Trichodina, D., differs entirely from that of Ehrenberg. The characters are :— Body ovoid-oblong or pyriform, slightly flexible in front, with a row of cilia directed backwards, and appearing to indicate the presence of a mouth.

2. *T. angulata* (Pl. 25. fig. 7). Body oblong, obliquely and irregularly folded or angular, frequently with one or more

superficial vacuoles.   Aquatic; length 1-000".

3. *T. pyrum*, D. = *Leucophrys carnium*, E.

BIBL. Ehrenberg, *Infus.* p. 306; Dujardin, *Infus.* p. 395.

TRICHODACTYLUS, Dufour.—A genus of Arachnida, of the order Acarina, and family Acarea.

Char. Rostrum short, with minute setæ; fourth pair of legs shorter than the rest, without claws, and terminated by a very long seta.

T. osmiæ. Glabrous, with two marginal setæ on each side; pale red; legs and posterior part of the body darker.   Length 1-50".

Found upon the thorax of an *Osmia* (a kind of mason-bee).

BIBL. Dufour, *Ann. des Sc. Nat.* 2 sér. xi. p. 276; Gervais, *Walckenaer's Aptères*, iii. p. 206.

TRICHODECTES, Nitzsch. — A genus of Anoplurous Insects, of the family Philopteridæ.

Char. Antennæ filiform, three-jointed; maxillary palpi none or inconspicuous; mandibles two-toothed; tarsi with one claw.

Ten species, parasitic upon quadrupeds, viz. the dog, cat, fox, weasel and stoat, ox, horse, sheep, the red and the fallow deer.

T. latus (Pl. 28. fig. 6).   Abdomen pale fulvous; head and thorax ferruginous yellow; head subquadrate, with two black spots in front, and a black lateral band on each side; abdomen oval.

Common upon dogs, especially puppies.

BIBL. Denny, *Anoplur. Monograph*, p. 186.

TRICHODERMA, Pers.—A genus of Fungi placed by Fries among the Gasteromycetes, but apparently of doubtful place. The plants are characterized by a roundish peridium composed of interwoven, ramified, septate filaments, evanescent at the summit; the spores minute, heaped together, at first conglobated.   *T. viride*, growing on fallen trees, has a white villous peridium, and dusky-green globose spores.   The peridia appear as scattered spots 1-20 to 1-8" or more in diameter.

BIBL. Berk. *Brit. Flor.* ii. pt. 2. p. 323; Greville, *Sc. Crypt. Fl.* pl. 271; Fries, *Summa Veg.* p. 417.

TRICHODESMIUM, Ehrenb.—A genus of microscopic Algæ, apparently belonging to the Nostochaceæ, discovered by Ehrenberg to produce the red colour over large tracts in the Red Sea, and found also in the Atlantic and Pacific Oceans by Darwin and Hinds, and in the Chinese Sea.   No vesicular cells or spermatic cells have been detected; hence the characters are as yet imperfect.   Montagne has separated the plant of Hinds from Ehrenberg's; and Kützing characterizes the two species in his *Sp. Algarum*, and figures them in his *Tabulæ Phycologicæ*, but neither the figures nor the descriptions indicate any very marked differences.

1. *T. Ehrenbergii*, Montagne.   Blood-red (at length becoming green); bundles widish, confluent; filaments 1-3000" in diameter, joints about twice as wide as long.   Montagne, *Ann. des Sc. Nat.* 3 sér. vol. ii. p. 360, pl. 10; Kützing, *Tab. Phyc.* i. pl. 9. fig. 3. *Tr. erythræum*, Ehr., *Pogg. Annalen*, 1830. p. 506.   *Oscillaria erythræa*, Kütz. *Phyc. generalis*, p. 188.   Found floating in vast strata in the Red Sea by Ehrenberg and Dupont, and in the Yellow Sea (China) by Mollien, Bellot, and others.

2. *T. Hindsii*, Montagne.   Blood - red, with a strong odour; bundles longish, slenderish; filaments 1-3600 to 1-2760" in diameter, joints twice or thrice as broad as long, transversely granulated.   Montagne, *Ann. des Sc. Nat.* 3 sér. ii. p. 360, pl. 10; Kützing, *Tab. Phyc.* i. pl. 91, iv.

For further information on these species, and on the red coloration of the sea by plants, see Montagne's papers in the *Annales des Sc. Naturelles*, 3 sér. ii. p. 332, vi. p. 262; 4 sér. i. p. 81; *Ann. Nat. Hist.* 2 ser. xix. p. 431.

TRICHODINA, Duj.—A family of Infusoria.

Char. Body soft, flexible, more or less variable in form, ciliated; mouth either visible or simply indicated by a row or fringe of larger cilia; no cirrhi (styles or hooks).

Genera : *Acineria*; *Dileptus*; *Pelecida*; *Trachelius*; *Trichoda*, D. (not E.).

BIBL. Dujardin, *Infus.* 392.

TRICHODINA, Ehr.—A genus of Infusoria, of the family Vorticellina.

Char. No tail, nor pedicle; cilia absent from the surface of the conical or discoidal body, but forming a frontal crown or a tuft; oral orifice not spiral.

1. *T. pediculus* (*Urceolaria stellina*, D.) (Pl. 24. fig. 16).   Body discoidal, the under and upper surfaces each with a crown of cilia.

Parasitic upon *Hydra vulgaris* and *viridis*. Breadth 1-575 to 1-290".   On the under surface is an annular undulatory membrane; and within and at the base of this is a horny ring, with an outer and inner row of teeth, forming an organ of adhesion.

2. *T. mitra.* Parasitic upon *Planaria torva.*

3. *T. grandinella* and *T. vorax* are swarm-germs or free gemmæ of Vorticellina.

4. *T. tentaculata.* Body discoidal, cilia large, forming a tuft; a styliform, tentacle-like process present. Aquatic; diameter 1-290".

Bibl. Ehrenberg, *Infus.* p. 265; Dujardin, *Infus.* p. 527; Siebold, *Vergl. Anat.* p. 12; *Siebold und Kölliker's Zeitschr.* ii. p. 361; Stein, *Infus.* p. 174.

TRICHODISCUS, Ehr.—A genus of In-fusoria, of the family Acinetina, E. (Actino-phryina, D.).

Char. Body depressed, stalkless; seta-ceous tentacles forming a simple row at the margin of the body.

T. sol (Pl. 25. fig. 8). Body suborbicular, hyaline or yellowish, tentacles variable. Aquatic; diameter 1-432 to 1-216".

Bibl. Ehrenberg, *Infus.* p. 304.

TRICHOGASTRES (*Puff-balls*).—A fa-mily of Gasteromycetous Fungi, character-ized by the contents of the leathery peridium breaking up when mature into a pulverulent mass of spores and filaments, without a central column, the whole being expelled by the bursting of the case (see Gasteromy-cetes).

Bibl. Berkeley, *Ann. Nat. Hist.* iv. p. 155; Tulasne, L. R. and C., *Ann. des Sc. Nat.* 2 sér. xvii. p. 1.

TRICHOMANES, Linn.—A genus of

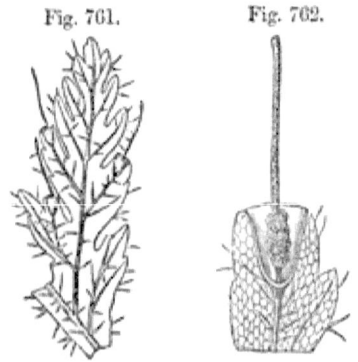

Fig. 761.　　Fig. 762.

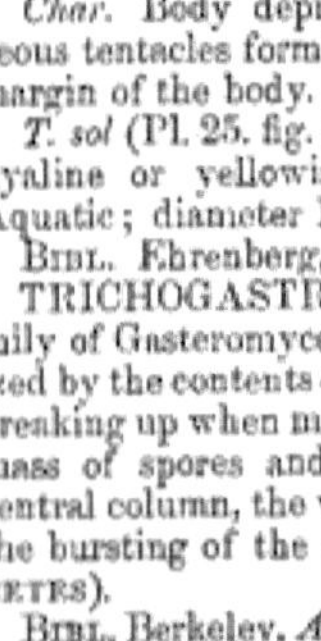

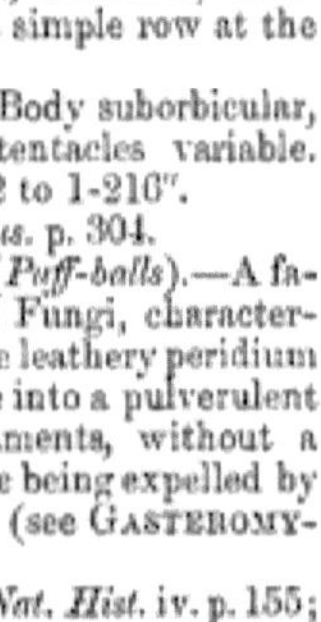

Trichomanes alatum.

Fig. 761. A pinnule. Magnified 5 diameters.
Fig. 762. Section through a sorus, showing the vein prolonged as columella, and continued out beyond the border. Magnified 25 diameters.

Hymenophyllaceous Ferns, of elegant and delicate habit.

Fig. 763.

A sporange, with horizontal annulus. Magnified 100 diameters.

TRICHOMONAS, Duj.—A genus of In-fusoria, of the family Monadina.

Char. Body ovoid or globular, becoming drawn out when adherent to the slide, hence sometimes exhibiting a tail-like prolonga-tion; an anterior flagelliform filament pre-sent, with a group or row of vibratile cilia.

1. *T. vaginalis* (Pl. 25. fig. 9). Body glutinous, nodular, unequal, frequently be-coming agglutinated to other objects; move-ment vacillating. Length 1-2500". Found in morbid vaginal mucus.

2. *T. limacis* (Pl. 25. fig. 10). Body ovoid, smooth, pointed at each end; movement forwards, by revolution upon its axis. Length 1-1000". Found in the intestine of *Limax agrestis.*

Bibl. Dujardin, *Infus.* p. 290.

TRICHOPHYTON. See Parasites.

TRICHOPTERIS, Presl.—A genus of Cyatheous Ferns. Exotic.

TRICHORMUS (*Anabaina*, Bory, Bré-bisson, Kützing, Montagne, &c.).—A genus of Nostochaceæ (Confervoid Algæ), grow-ing on wet earth, or rising to the surface of lakes, brackish ditches, &c., forming an in-determinate stratum, at first nearly colour-less and transparent, with the filaments sparingly scattered through the mass; the filaments afterwards increasing rapidly in number, causing the mass to become opake, deep bluish green, and occasionally mottled with brown, especially beneath. The fila-ments are mostly short, moniliform, and frequently as much curved as in *Nostoc.* The cells are more or less globular, and the spermatic cells resemble the ordinary cells more in this than in the allied genera. The filaments closely resemble those of *Nostoc;* and some of the floating aquatic species can only be distinguished from that genus by the absence of definite form or size, and of the hardened peridium. It differs from *Dolichospermum* in the globular shape of its sporangia, and from *Sphærozyga* and *Cylindrospermum* in the arrangement of its vesicular and spermatic cells, which are iere always separated by ordinary cells. Mr. Ralfs enumerates five British species. In Pl. 4. fig. 2, we have represented what appears to be a new species.

1. *T. flos-aquæ* (Lyngbye). Filaments flexuose or curved, moniliform; cells orbicular, vesicular ones larger, terminal, and interstitial. Ralfs, *Ann. Nat. Hist.* 2 ser. vol. v. pl. 8. fig. 2. *Anabaina flos-aquæ*, Kützing, *Spec. Algarum*; *Trichormus incurvatus*, Allman, *Ann. Nat. Hist.* xi. 163. t. 5 (1843); Hassall, *Brit. Freshw. Alga*, t. 75. fig. 1. Rising to the surface of stagnant pools or other still waters in gelatinous masses of considerable size, generally of a rich bluish-green colour.

2. *T.* (?) *spiralis* (Thompson). Filaments coiled or spiral; ordinary cells subquadrate or orbicular; vesicular and spermatic cells orbicular.—Ralfs, *l. c.* pl. 8. fig. 3. (?) *Anabaina spiralis*, Thompson, *Ann. Nat. Hist.* vol. v. p. 81; *Spirillum Thompsonii*, Hassall, *Br. Fr. Algæ*, lxxv. p. 7. (See SPIRULINA.)

3. *T. Thwaitesii* (Harvey). Filaments moniliform, slightly flexuose; ordinary cells globular or nearly so; vesicular cells larger, globular when interstitial, ovate when terminal, ciliated; sporangia oval, catenate.—Ralfs, *l. c.* pl. 8. fig. 4. *Sphærozyga Thwaitesii*, Harvey, *Phyc. Britannica*, t. 113 B. Salt-marshes, forming thin, gelatinous, dark-green patches, either on damp soil, covered at spring-tides, or at the bottom of brackish ditches or pools, afterwards floating in large gelatinous masses, and then abounding in spermatic cells.

4. *T. oscillarioides* (Bory). Filaments elongated, flexuose; ordinary joints subquadrate, distinct; vesicular cells barrel-shaped or elliptic, naked; spermatic cells oval, catenate.—Ralfs, *l. c.* pl. 8. fig. 5. *Anabaina oscillarioides*, Bory, *Dict. d'Hist. natur.*; *Sphærozyga oscillarioides*, Kützing, *Tabulæ Phycologicæ*, pl. 96. fig. 5. In brackish ditches, bluish green.

5. *T. rectus* (Thwaites). Filaments bright green, straight, short, slightly tapering towards the extremities; ordinary cells subspherical, rather shorter than wide; vesicular cells oblong, smooth, scarcely wider than the ordinary cells, and never terminating the filament; spermatic cells spherical or oblong, numerous.—Ralfs, *l. c.* pl. 8. fig. 6. Pools (near Bristol, Thwaites); of a beautiful green colour.

BIBL. The works cited above.

TRICHOSPORIUM, Fr.—A genus of Mucedines (Hyphomycetous Fungi), nearly allied to BOTRYTIS, characterized by a cæspitose mycelium, whence arise fertile, continuous filaments, bearing solitary, simple, acrogenous spores. *T. nigrum* = *Sporotrichum nigrum*, Fries (*Syst. Myc.*), *Botrytis nigra*, Link.

BIBL. Fries, *Summa Veg.* p. 492; Grev. *Sc. Crypt. Fl.* pl. 274.

TRICHOSTOMUM, Hedw.—A genus of Pottiaceous Mosses, so called from the hair-like peristome, resembling closely that of BARBULA (*Tortula*), but with the teeth straight instead of twisted; in *T. rigidulum*, however (fig. 764), there exists a slight curling even in this genus. Mr. Wilson combines LEPTOTRICHUM with this. The *Trichostoma* grow on the ground and on stones.

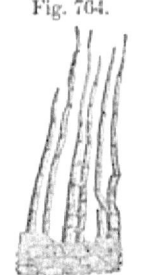

Fig. 764.

Trichostomum rigidulum. Fragment of the peristome with filiform teeth. Magnified 100 diameters.

TRICHOTHECIUM, Link. (*Diplosporium*, ejusd.).—A genus of Mucedines (Hyphomycetous Fungi), growing upon dead sticks, herbaceous parts of plants, &c., forming a cæspitose entangled mycelium, from which arise erect fertile filaments, bearing at the summit a few acrogenous, free, didymous spores. These plants are nearly allied to DACTYLIUM, under which Mr. Berkeley includes them; but apparently they may be separated by the uniseptate, not multiseptate spores. From some observations recently published by Hoffmann, and confirmed by Bail, the spores of *T. roseum*, when they germinate, produce a mycelium whence arise fertile filaments of *Verticillium ruberrimum*, the 'spores' of which they consequently consider as the *spermatia* of this plant. Several species are British, as *T. roseum*, *obovatum* (*Dactylium*, Berk.).

BIBL. Berk. *Brit. Flor.* ii. pt. 2. p. 348; *Ann. Nat. Hist.* vi. p. 437, pl. 14; Greville, *Sc. Crypt. Fl.* pl. 172; Fries, *Summa Veg.* p. 492; Hoffmann, *Botan. Zeit.* xii. p. 240 (1854); Bail, *ibid.* xiii. p. 673 (1855).

TRILOCULINA, D'Orb.—A genus of Foraminifera, of the order Agathistegia, and family Multiloculida.

Char. Shell inequilateral, globular or compressed, of the same form at all ages; chambers aggregated on three opposite faces, embracing, three only apparent, their cavity simple; *orifice* single, rounded or oval alternately at each end, and with a tooth.

Williamson unites this genus with his *Miliolina*.

Some British species, both recent and fossil.

M. trigonula (Pl. 42. fig. 6).

BIBL. That of the order.

TRIMMATOSTROMA, Corda (fig. 759, page 695).—An obscure genus of Torulacei (Coniomycetous Fungi), perhaps founded on the spores of a species of PHRAGMOTRICHUM.

BIBL. Corda, *Icon. Fung.*; Fries, *Summa Veg.* p. 475.

TRINEMA, Duj.—A genus of Infusoria, of the family Rhizopoda.

Char. Carapace membranous, diaphanous, elongate-ovoid, narrower in front, with a large oblique lateral orifice; expansions two or three, filiform, very slender, as long as the carapace.

T. acinus = *Difflugia enchelys*, E. (Pl. 25. fig. 11, after Ehr. In Dujardin's figure the expansions are represented as much more slender). Aquatic.

BIBL. Dujardin, *Infus.* p. 249.

TRIOPHTHALMUS, Ehr.—A genus of Rotatoria, of the family Hydatinæa.

Char. Eyes three, red, cervical, in a transverse row; foot forked.

Jaws single-toothed.

T. dorsualis (Pl. 35. fig. 31). Body crystalline, turgid, suddenly attenuated at the foot, which is half the length of the body. Aquatic; length 1-48 to 1-36".

BIBL. Ehrenberg, *Infus.* p. 450.

TRIPHRAGMIUM, Link.—A genus of Uredinei (Coniomycetous Fungi), distinguished by their trilocular spores (fig. 765). *T. ulmariæ* (*Uredo ulmariæ, Brit. Fl.*), grows upon the leaves of *Spiræa ulmaria*, forming orange, subsequently blackish, effused patches, bursting from beneath the epidermis. Tulasne has shown that it possesses all three forms of reproductive structure of the Uredinei, viz. 1. spermogonia with *spermatia*; 2. *Uredo*-fruits, with ellipsoid or globose *stylospores*; and 3. perfect fruits, arising either among the stylospores or in special sori containing stipitate, three-lobed spores (fig. 765), each lobe of which is unilocular and exhibits a single pore in its black tubercular outer coat. The last germinate in the spring, and pro-

Fig. 765.

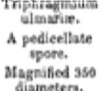

Triphragmium ulmariæ.
A pedicellate spore.
Magnified 350 diameters.

duce from each pore a tubular filament which becomes divided into four or five chambers, from three or four of which arise single styliform processes (*sterigmata*), each bearing a small smooth spherical "sporidium." The globular stylospores also germinate (in the first summer), but produce only a long filiform process, probably the rudiment of a new mycelium. (See URE-DINEI.)

BIBL. Berk. *Brit. Fl.* ii. pt. 2. p. 368; Tulasne, *Ann. des Sc. Nat.* 4 sér. ii. p. 181, pl. 10; Fries, *Summa Veg.* p. 513; Currey, *Micr. Journal*, v. p. 126.

TRIPOSPORIUM, Corda.—A genus of Dematiei (Hyphomycetous Fungi), characterized by the three-lobed septate spores. *T.*

Fig. 766.

Triposporium elegans.
Magnified 200 diameters.

elegans (fig. 766) has been found in this country on bare oak trunks. Another species, *T. Gardneri*, forms a blight in the coffee plantations of Ceylon.

BIBL. Berk. *Ann. Nat. Hist.* 2 ser. vii. p. 98; *Hortic. Journal*, iv. p. 8.

TRITON, Laur. (water-newts).—A genus of Reptiles.

If a male and female *T. cristatus* (fig. 767),

Fig. 767.

one of the common water-newts, be kept in a glass jar with healthy water-plants, they

Cotton.

Magnified 500 diam.

Gossypium herbaceum, L.
(cotton plant). A hair from
the seed (the cotton of commerce)
taken from a piece of cotton
wool.

Some cells of the hair examined were simply split open
lengthways, but most of them
were split and feathered out
like the one in the figure.
This splitting occurs in the process of manufacture.

Easily distinguished from
other substances.

, Dec. 12 1878.

X 500

will lay their eggs upon them. The larvæ are very beautiful microscopic objects for showing the circulation in the gills and tail, the chorda dorsalis and the embryonic tissues; they should be kept in a vessel separate from the parents, otherwise these will devour them.

The injected skin of *T. palustris*, the large warty newt, forms a beautiful opake object, showing the loose capillary network, which contrasts well with the brilliantly mottled skin.

BIBL. Bell, *British Reptiles.*

TROCHILIA, Duj.—A genus of Infusoria, of the family Ervilina.

Char. Body irregularly oval, narrower in front, where there are some vibratile cilia; carapace obliquely furrowed, slightly twisted, and terminated behind by a moveable pedicle; no distinct mouth.

T. sigmoides (Pl. 25. figs. 12 & 13). Body narrowed and sinuous in front; carapace with five or six rounded oblique ribs; pedicle capable of adhering to the slide. Marine; length 1-630″.

Fig. 12 represents the animal undergoing transverse division.

TROMBIDINA.—A family of Arachnida, of the order Acarina.

Char. Palpi with the last joint obtuse, the last but one unguiculate, and the second very large; legs for walking, with two claws; eyes usually latero-anterior.

Gen. ANYSTIS, CHEYLETUS, MEGAMERUS, PACHYGNATHUS, RAPHIGNATHUS, RHYNCHOLOPHUS, SMARIS, TETRANYCHUS, TROMBIDIUM.

TROMBIDIUM, Latr. — A genus of Arachnida, of the family Trombidina.

Char. Palpi large, free; mandibles unguiculate; body turgid, bearing the four posterior legs, and an anterior narrow moveable prominence, upon which the eyes, the four anterior legs and the mouth are situated; anterior legs longest.

The species are numerous and not well characterized.

1. *T. phalangii* (Pl. 2. fig. 37). Body subtriangular, angles obtuse; of a velvety appearance, from the presence of numerous plumose hairs; eyes two, placed upon auricular appendages.

An external parasite of *Phalangium* (the harvest-spider) and insects, at least in its early hexapodous stage.

2. *T. elongatum.* Crimson; eyes approximate. Found under stones.

3. *T. cinereum* (Pl. 2. fig. 40) (*Rhyncho-*

lophus ciner., Dug.). Body with brown and greyish-white spots; hairs spathulate; eyes two on each side. Length 1-12″. Found in ditches amongst plants and stones.

4. *T. autumnale* (Pl. 2. fig. 38) (*Leptus autumn.*). The harvest-bug. This well-known but imperfectly examined arachnidan insinuates itself into the human skin in autumn, causing troublesome irritation. It is found on plants and the stubble of cornfields, and may easily be caught by tying a white pocket-handkerchief around the legs, and walking through stubble-fields. The young form with six legs is most frequently met with.

BIBL. Dugès, *Ann. des Sc. Nat.* 2 sér. i. p. 36; Gervais, *Walckenaer's Aptères*, iii. p. 178; Johnston, *Transact. of Berwickshire Naturalists' Club,* 1847. p. 221; Koch, *Deutschl. Crustac. Myriap. &c.*

TRUNCATULINA, D'Orb.—A genus of Foraminifera, of the order Helicostegia, and family Turbinoidæ.

Char. Shell fixed; spire discoidal, coiled in the same plane, apparent on the fixed side, embracing and convex on the other; *chambers* convex above, flat beneath; *orifice* slit-like, slightly apparent above and continued beneath, along the line of suture, as far as the second or third chambers.

One recent British, and many fossil species.

T. lobatula (Pl. 18. fig. 38). Attached to sea-weeds.

BIBL. That of the order.

TRYBLIONELLA, Smith.—A genus of Diatomaceæ.

Char. Frustules free, linear or elliptical in front view; valves plane, with parallel transverse (tubular?) striæ, and submarginal or obsolete alæ.

In some a median line is present, in others not. The alæ are not marginal, as in *Surirella*, but arise from the surface of the valves, as shown by the diagram of a transverse section in Pl. 13. fig. 32.

1. *T. scutellum* (Pl. 13. fig. 30). Valves elliptical, with a median longitudinal line; alæ very short; striæ faint. Marine; length 1-140″.

2. *T. gracilis* (Pl. 13. fig. 31). Frustules linear, narrowed at the ends; valves linear, acuminate, striæ coarse; alæ distinct. Fresh and brackish water; length 1-200″.

Four other species.

BIBL. Smith, *Brit. Diatom.* i. p. 35.

TRYPETHELIEÆ.—A family of Angiocarpous Lichens.

2 z

Illustrative Genera.

1. *Sphæromphale.* Nucleus solid, subglobose, gelatinously diffluent, in a simple excipulum formed from the medullary stratum of the thallus, papilliform (coloured), papillate-ostiolate.

2. *Astrothelium.* Nucleus gelatinous, perithecia confluent, multilocular, within a prominent heterogeneous papilla, ostioles confluent in a common pore.

3. *Trypethelium.* Nucleus gelatinous, perithecia distinct, within a prominent heterogeneous papilla, ostiole simple.

TUBER, Mich.—A genus of Tuberacei (Ascomycetous Fungi), to which belongs the common truffle (see TUBERACEI).

TUBERACEI.—A family of Ascomycetous Fungi, growing underground or upon the surface, of more or less round form, and solid, fleshy texture, excavated with sinuous cavities lined by *asci* containing usually four or eight spores, elegantly reticulated or spinulose (figs. 768-770). The internal

Fig. 768.

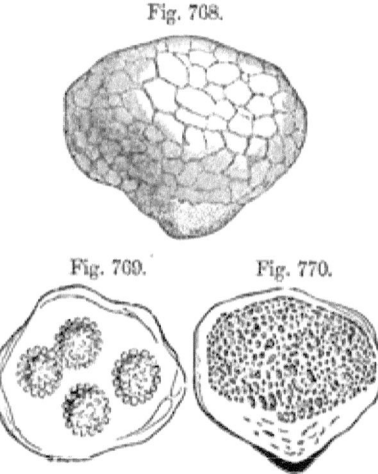

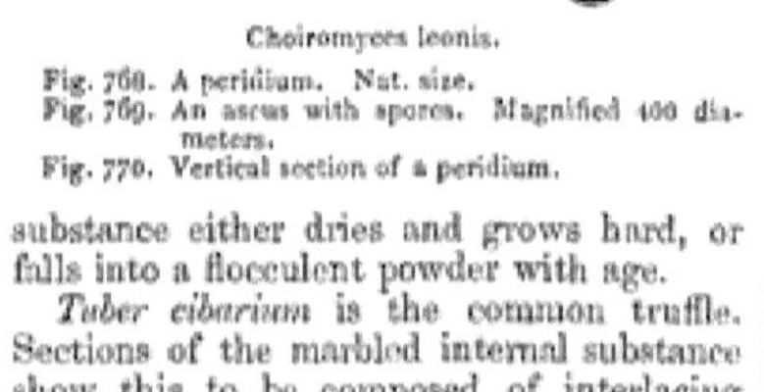

Choiromyces leonis.

Fig. 768. A peridium. Nat. size.
Fig. 769. An ascus with spores. Magnified 400 diameters.
Fig. 770. Vertical section of a peridium.

substance either dries and grows hard, or falls into a flocculent powder with age.

Tuber cibarium is the common truffle. Sections of the marbled internal substance show this to be composed of interlacing branched filaments, forming fleshy convo-

lutions, between which serpentine cavities are alternately excavated; branches of the filaments free at the surface of the lacunæ bear spherical sacs (*asci*), each containing four globular spores of yellow-brown colour, having an elegantly reticulated outer coat. When the spores germinate, they produce a subterranean cottony mycelium, which after a time presents villous nodules, in the interior of which the peridia are developed; as these advance, the villous coats gradually vanish, together with the mycelial structure, and the mature peridia appear free, either a little beneath (*Tuber cibarium*) or upon the surface (*T. album*) of the soil (see also ELAPHOMYCES).

BIBL. Berk. *Brit. Flor.* ii. pt. 2. p. 227; Tulasne, *Ann. des Sc. Nat.* 2 sér. xvi. p. 5, 3 sér. p. 348; *Monog. Fungi Hypogæi,* Paris 1851; *Ann. Nat. Hist.* 2 ser. viii. p. 19; Lespiault, *Ann. des Sc. Nat.* 3 sér. ii. p. 316; Vittadini, *Monog. Tuberacearum; Monog. Lycopod., Mém. Turin Acad.* 2nd ser. v. p. 145.

TUBERCLE or TUBERCULAR MATTER.—This morbid deposit consists of three parts, the relative proportions of which are variable: viz., 1. an amorphous transparent basis, rendered pale by, and finally soluble in acetic acid; 2. minute granules and molecules, some of them consisting of proteine-compounds, others of fatty matter; and 3. a number of nuclei, or so-called tubercle-corpuscles (Pl. 30. fig. 9 *a*), about 1-5000 to 1-4000" in size, of an oblong angular form, containing irregular granules, and unaffected, or simply rendered paler, by acetic acid (Pl. 30. fig. 9 *b*).

Tubercular matter is deposited in the substance of the tissues or in the cavities of organs (Pl. 30. fig. 8). The corpuscles have been supposed to be peculiar to and characteristic of tubercle; but late researches tend to the conclusion that they are the nuclei of normal cells, the development of which has been arrested.

When softening occurs, the tuberculous matter usually undergoes fatty degeneration; the number of free fatty granules is much increased, and the tubercle becomes yellowish.

It sometimes becomes a question as to whether a morbid deposit consists of tubercle or not. The diagnosis must be founded mainly upon negative characters—the absence of the elements of other abnormal products, as those of inflammation, cancer, &c.

In cretaceous tubercle, carbonate and phosphate of lime, usually in the amorphous state, are met with.

BIBL. Works on Medicine; Lebert, *Phys. Pathol.*; Hasse, *Patholog. Anatomy* (Sydenham Soc. Vol.); Vogel, *Pathol. Anat.* (by Day); Wedl, *Path. Anat.* p. 365; Förster, *Path. Anat.* i. 312, & ii. 156; Rokitansky, *Path. Anat.* i. & iii.

TUBERCULARIA, Tode.—A supposed genus of Stilbacei (Hyphomycetous Fungi), but apparently only preparatory forms of Sphæriaceous Fungi. *T. vulgaris* is a state of *Nectria* (*Sphæria*) *cinnabarina*; it is extremely common in autumn and winter, on dead sticks, damp wooden palings, stumps, &c., forming scarlet-orange rounded nodules or irregular masses of fleshy consistence, sometimes more or less stipitate, composed of parenchymatous tissue, the surface at a certain stage exhibiting the ends of the filaments terminating in chains of cellules breaking up into a pulverulent substance. These cellules are probably the *conidia* of the *Nectria*.

TUBIFEX, Lamk.—A genus of Annulata, of the order Setigera, and family Lumbricini.

Char. Body filiform, attenuated at the ends, pellucid, with four rows of setæ—two dorsal and two ventral.

The worms live and burrow in the mud of stagnant pools or the still parts of rivers, giving it a red appearance. When the water or mud is disturbed, the red patches instantly disappear, from the retraction of the animals. Length from 1-5 to 3-4″ or more.

They are transparent, and show well the alimentary canal, with its peristaltic actions, and the cilia lining it; the blood-vessels and their movements, with the loops bathed in the chylaqueous liquid, and the coiled water- (respiratory or renal) vessels with their cilia.

BIBL. Schmidt, *Müller's Arch.* 1846. p. 406; Dugès, *Ann. des Sc. Nat.* 2 sér. xv. p. 319; Johnston, *Ann. Nat. Hist.* 1845. xvi. p. 443.

TUBULARIA, Linn.—A genus of marine Polypes, of the order Hydroida, and family Tubulariadæ.

Five British species.

BIBL. That of the family.

TUBULARIADÆ.—A family of Polypes, of the order Hydroida. Genera:

1. *Clava.* Naked, fleshy; tentacles scattered, filiform; mouth terminal, naked.

2. *Hydractinia.* Naked, fleshy, gregarious; tentacles in one circle, filiform; egg-germs sessile, clustered on untentacled individuals.

3. *Myriothela.* Naked, solitary, club-shaped, extensile, crowded with short wart-like tentacles; egg-germs globose, on branched footstalks, clustered around the base.

4. *Coryne.* Simple or branched, naked or enclosed in a rudimentary tube; tentacles with globular ends; mouth terminal, expansile, and capable of being used as a sucker; egg-germs simple, on short stalks.

5. *Eudendrium.* Enclosed; polypidom fibrous-rooted, erect, branching; polypes protruding from ends of branches, not retractile, with a single ring of filiform tentacles.

6. *Tubularia.* Enclosed; polypidom unbranched; tentacles filiform in two rows; egg-germs on short footstalks, clustered at the bases of the lower tentacles.

7. *Corymorpha.* Partly enclosed; polypidom short, thin, membranous, swollen at the base, which is immersed in the sand; polype single, head club-shaped, encircled at the base by long filiform tentacles, and a circle of short ones around the tip.

8. *Cordylophora.* The only fresh-water genus.

BIBL. Johnston, *Brit. Zooph.* p. 53; Gosse, *Mar. Zool.* i. p. 19.

TUBULI URINIFERI. See KIDNEY (p. 403).

TUBULIPORA, Lam.—A genus of Infundibulate Cyclostomatous Polyzoa, of the family Tubuliporidæ.

Nine British species. Some of them are common upon shells, sea-weeds, &c.

Pl. 33. fig. 30 represents a species (not British).

BIBL. Johnston, *British Zoophytes*, p. 266.

TUBULIPORIDÆ.—A family of Infundibulate Cyclostomatous Polyzoa.

Char. Polypidom calcareous, massive, circular, lobed or divided dichotomously; cells long, tubular, with a round, prominent, unconstricted orifice. Genera:

1. *Tubulipora.* Wart-like, with a defined base; cells suberect, aggregated or in imperfect rows, more or less free at the end.

2. *Diastopora.* Encrusting, undefined; cells alternate, tubular, horizontal, immersed, with a raised circular orifice.

3. *Idmonea.* Divided dichotomously, erect; cells on one side, tubular, in transverse rows, divided into two sets by a median longitudinal line.

4. *Pustulipora.* Erect, cylindrical; cells semi-immersed, on all sides, orifices prominent.

5. *Alecto.* Creeping, adherent, irregularly branched; cells horizontal, in one or more rows, their ends free.

BIBL. Johnston, *British Zooph.* p. 264; Gosse, *Mar. Zool.* ii. p. 7.

TUBURCINIA, Fries.—An obscure genus of microscopic Fungi, referred by Fries to the Sepedonei (Hyphomycetous Fungi), growing in roots and tubers, or on leaves, forming 'scabs.' The evanescent mycelium creeps through the tissue of the infected organ, and produces solitary globular spores, of cellular texture (hollow), ultimately becoming free. *T. Scabies* forms one kind of scab on potatoes (not that in the ordinary disease).

BIBL. Berk. *Hort. Journal,* i. p. 33, pl. 4. figs. 30, 31; *Ann. Nat. Hist.* 2nd ser. v. p. 464; Fries, *Summa Veg.* p. 497.

TUMORS.—Under this head we shall make a few brief remarks upon some of the more interesting elements of certain tumors and other morbid growths.

Cancer. — The most constantly present elements of a cancerous growth are—1. organic molecules and granules, with globules of fat; 2. fibres; and 3. cells in all stages of development. As occasional or accidental elements, are found—4. fibroplastic cells; 5. granule-cells; 6. pigment; 7. inorganic matters, in the form of molecules, granules, and crystals; and 8. the products of inflammation.

The cells only require distinct notice, the other elements resembling those usually met with in other healthy or morbid products. They are comparatively large, varying considerably in diameter, of a rounded oblong or ovate form, usually arranged in no definite order, in the intervals of the fibres (Pl. 30. figs. 11 & 12), although sometimes in the meshes formed by the aggregation of the fibres into loose bundles (fig. 17). Their most important feature is the indication of endogenous growth, shown by their usually containing numerous nuclei and nucleoli, or secondary and tertiary cells. In some of them a tendency to the formation of fibres is evidenced by the elongation of their ends (fig. 21). When acted upon by acetic acid, the primary cell becomes pale and transparent, the nuclei or inner cells remaining distinct.

The interspaces of the cells and fibres are occupied by a pale-yellowish or colourless liquid; and the cells are so loosely imbedded in the fibrous basis, that on scraping the surface of a section of a cancer, numerous cells are found in the juice thus obtained.

The number of fibres present varies according to the form or stage of development of the cancer. In hard or schirrous cancer, they preponderate, the cells being few; whilst in soft or medullary cancer they are scanty, the cells being very abundant; globules of fat usually also abound in the latter form.

Other varieties of cancer have received special names. Thus, when the capillaries are very numerous and distended, extravasated blood being also frequently present, we have hæmatoid cancer, or fungus hæmatodes; when the fibres are grouped into bundles, forming marked areolæ, we have areolar, colloid or gelatiniform cancer (Pl. 30. fig. 18); again, when the cancercells abound in pigment, we have melanotic cancer, &c.

The diagnosis of a cancerous growth is of great importance, and cannot in general be regarded as a matter of difficulty. It cannot, as was formerly supposed, be based simply upon the characters of the cells; for cells exhibiting a marked endogenous reproduction, which is the most striking feature of cancer-cells, are also met with in normal tissues; but when these cells exhibit no tendency to the formation of a definite tissue, but retain their cell-form, and contain or are mixed with numerous fatglobules, the whole being loosely imbedded in a serous liquid, the cancerous nature of the morbid product may be considered as certain.

In regard to cells generally, an insuperable difficulty is met with in discovering the exponent of their power, as it might be termed; thus the embryonic cells or corpuscles in an early stage are undistinguishable from each other; and yet some grow into areolar fibres, others into nerve-tubes, &c. Chemistry lends no aid here, and the difficulty will probably ever remain.

Cancroid growths.—This term has been applied to certain kinds of tumors or growths which somewhat resemble cancerous growths in their course and tendency to recur, yet differ from them in the nature of their morphological elements. They consist generally of epithelial formations, or of some kind of fibrous development. As instances, may be mentioned socalled epithelial cancer, as of the lip, and certain forms of fibroid, fibro-plastic, or sarcomatous tumors.

In epithelial cancer, the general arrangement of the elements is not strikingly altered, but the papillæ of the skin are hypertrophied, the epithelial cells more numerous than natural, sometimes containing many nuclei or secondary cells, and the intercellular juice is more abundant. The flattened epithelial cells are often also arranged around the papillæ in the form of concentric rings, resembling fibres; but the cell-structure is at once rendered evident by the addition of solution of potash.

In the fibroid or fibro-plastic tumors, the arrest of development at the cell-stage is often well shown by the presence of numerous nuclei or secondary cells within the primary ones (Pl. 30. fig. 10). These brood-cells are also met with in obstinate fungous granulations and vegetations.

Enchondroma, cartilaginous growth or tumor.—In some kinds of this, the cartilage is undistinguishable from normal true cartilage; in others it exhibits the formation of secondary deposits in the cells, as in imperfectly-formed bone· (Pl. 30. fig. 19), the cavities of the cartilage-cells being filled up with the exception of the irregularly stellate median portions.

In the examination of tumors and other morbid growths, sections should be made with a Valentin's knife, the elements being first observed in water, and then in the natural fluid. The sections and elements are best preserved in water.

BIBL. Paget, *Lectures on Tumors* (1851), and *Surgical Pathology*; the *Bibl.* of TUBERCLE; Bennett, *on Cancer*, and *Edinb. Monthly Journ.* vii. & viii.; Redfern, *ibid.* xi.; and the *Trans. of Pathol. Soc.*, *passim.*

TUNICATA.—A class of animals, of the subkingdom Mollusca.

Char. Marine; often microscopic; bodies single or aggregate; acephalous; enclosed in an elastic tunic with two orifices, one anterior (oral and branchial), the other posterior (anal or cloacal); mouth concealed in the body, at some distance from the anterior orifice; respiration branchial, branchiæ internal, generally perforated by fissures; nervous system a dorsal ganglion; circulation effected by a tubular heart, with vessels, the current of blood varying in direction; hermaphrodite; evolution accompanied by metamorphosis, or following the law of alternation of generations (Pl. 43. figs. 10, 20).

The smaller Tunicata are commonly found aggregate, and investing rocks, stones, and shells; some are adherent to sea-weeds, &c., a few are free; many are common on the sea-shore.

The body is sac-shaped or elongate, sometimes slightly constricted so as to exhibit a thorax, abdomen, and a posterior portion or post-abdomen. The outer coat, test or tunic, is cartilaginous, leathery, gelatinous, or membranous; and consists partly of cellulose, often containing calcareous spicula. Within this is another coat, the mantle, usually adhering to the former at the orifices only, and containing numerous muscular fibres. Below the wide anterior orifice is the usually dilated pharynx or branchial cavity, within which is placed the branchial apparatus (Pl. 43. fig. 10, *b*). At the base of this cavity is the mouth (*m*), which is slit-like, and leads into a narrow œsophagus (*e*); to this succeeds an expanded stomach (*s*), which terminates in a longish intestine (*i*) curved upwards near its origin, and terminating at the base of the cloaca (*i**), which opens externally at the posterior orifice (*c**). Within the anterior orifice, at the commencement of the branchial cavity, is a ring of rudimentary tentacles.

The branchial apparatus (fig. 10, *b*) consists of numerous cross-bars, with slit-like openings between them; these are cilated, and copiously supplied with networks of blood-vessels. The current excited by the cilia draws the water through the anterior orifice into the pharynx, where it traverses the openings, flowing outwards to collect in the cloaca, from which it is expelled through the posterior orifice. In some of the larger Tunicata, the branchial apparatus is strap-shaped, and traverses the body obliquely.

The heart (*h*) is a spindle-shaped sac, enclosed in a pericardium (*p*), and situated near the base of the body; the principal vessels running on the dorsal and ventral surface of the branchial apparatus. The current of blood varies in direction, being at one time expelled from one end of the heart, in others from the other. In those Tunicata which are connected by a common tube, the blood passes freely from one to the other.

The nervous system consists of a single ganglion (fig. 10, *g*), situated between the two orifices, and giving off its principal branches to the branchial sac and the alimentary canal. In some an eye is present, resembling the compound eye of the Articulata, and with a reddish pigment.

The liver (*l*) consists either of a dark glandular layer lining the alimentary canal, or of distinct glandular cæca.

The Tunicata are reproduced by gemmation, by sexual organs, and by intermediate generations.

The testis (*t*) and ovary (*o*) are usually strap-shaped organs, either adherent to the alimentary canal, or situated in the posterior part of the body; the former has a long spermatic duct (*d*), which opens into the cloaca, into which also the ova or larvæ are discharged, to escape by the posterior orifice. The larvæ often resemble at first tadpoles with three anterior sucker-like organs, by means of which they adhere to foreign bodies to complete their development, the tail gradually disappearing.

In the large free Tunicata, the intermediate generations are united into long chains, the final product being a sexual individual; but into the further structure of these curious beings we have no space to enter.

Synopsis of the Families.

* *Attached; mantle and test united only at the orifices.*

1. BOTRYLLIDÆ. Bodies united into systems.
2. CLAVELINIDÆ. Bodies distinct, but connected by a common root-thread.
3. ASCIDIADÆ. Bodies unconnected.

** *Free; mantle and test united throughout.*

4. PELONÆADÆ. Orifices near together.
5. SALPADÆ. Orifices at opposite ends.

BIBL. M.-Edwards, *Mém. s. les Ascid. Comp.*, and *Mém. de l'Institut*, 1842; V. d. Hoeven, *Zool.* i. p. 577; Leuckart, *Supplement to the same*, p. 126, and *Zool. Untersuch.* Heft 2; Gosse, *Mar. Zool.* ii. p. 24; Forbes and Hanley, *Brit. Moll.* i. p. 1; Vogt, *Zool. Briefe*, i. p. 258; Siebold, *Vergleich. Anat.* p. 234; Lister, *Phil. Trans.* 1834; Huxley, *ibid.* 1851, and *Todd's Cyclopædia*, Art. *Tunicata*; Carpenter, *on the Microscope*, p. 581; Krohn, *Archiv f. Naturgesch.* 1852. i. p. 53; id. *Müller's Archiv*, 1852. p. 312.

TURBINOLINA, D'Orb.—Consolidated with ROSALINA.

TURMERIC. See CURCUMA.

TYMPANIS, Fr.—A genus of Phacidiacei (Ascomycetous Fungi), consisting of horny bodies growing on branches of trees, breaking out through the bark. *T. conspersa* (fig. 771) grows upon Rosaceous

Fig. 771.

Tympanis conspersa.

A collection of perithecia, more or less mature, bursting through the bark. Magn. 10 diam.

trees, *T. saligna* on the privet. In the former the perithecia are collected in tufts; they are first closed, afterwards opening into cups, the disk of which is occupied by the hymenium, bearing long and broad asci containing numerous spores and, as has been recently shown by Messrs. Berkeley and Broome, sometimes also septate stylospores simultaneously. In *T. saligna* the perithecia occur only two to four together. Tulasne has shown, in addition, that the plants have *spermogonia* (which are oblong or conical bodies) intermixed with the perithecia, perforated by a terminal pore (resembling perithecia of *Sphæria*); these are lined with delicate branched filaments bearing minute corpuscles (*spermatia*), which when mature escape from the pore in a tendril (as in *Cytispora*) if moistened or pressed (see also CENANGIUM).

Fig. 772.

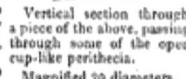

Vertical section through a piece of the above, passing through some of the open cup-like perithecia.

Magnified 20 diameters.

BIBL. Berk. *Brit. Flor.* ii. pt. 2. p. 210; *Ann. Nat. Hist.* 2 ser. vii. p. 185; *Hook. Journ. of Botany*, iii. p. 322 (1851); Tulasne, *Ann. des Sc. Nat.* 3 sér. xx. p. 143, pl. 16. figs. 15, 16; Fries, *Summa Veg.* p. 399; Greville, *&c. Crypt. Fl.* pl. 335.

TYNDARIDEA, Bory. See ZYGNEMA.

TYPHLINA, Ehr.—An imperfectly-examined genus of Rotatoria, of the family Philodinæa.

T. viridis (Pl. 35. fig. 33). Found in Egypt.

BIBL. Ehrenberg, *Infus.* p. 483.

U.

ULOTHRIX.—A genus of Confervoid Algæ, probably referable to the Confervaceæ, allied to *Draparnaldia* and *Stigeoclo-mium*. They consist of unbranched filaments adhering loosely together to form a mucous stratum, growing upon stones, &c. in fresh water. The filaments are composed of short hyaline cells (Pl. 5. fig. 6), the green contents of which are at first granular, adhering to the walls (*a*), then contracted into transverse bands (*b*), and finally converted into two, four, or more zoospores, with four cilia (*c*). Hassall appears to have confused these plants with the Oscillatoriaceous genus *Lyngbya*: his *L. muralis* is apparently the true plant, his *L. copulata* perhaps a *Schizogonium*; the rest of his species belong here, since, according to Kützing, Berkeley's *Sphæroplea crispa* and *punctalis* belong to this genus. There appear to be several British species; but we give them with some doubt.

1. *U. zonata*. Filaments 1-900″ in diameter, joints about as long (*Lyngbya zonata*, Hass. pl. 59. figs. 2, 3, 6).

2. *U. pectinalis*. Filaments 1-1800, 1-1200, 1-900″ in diameter, joints one-half or one-fourth the length; fertile cells swollen (*L. zonata*, Hass. pl. 60. figs. 1, 4, 5).

3. *U. crispa*. Filaments very long, 1-600″ in diameter, joints one-half or one-third as long (*Conferva bicolor*, Eng. Bot. p. 2288).

4. *U. floccosa*. Filaments 1-2100 to 1-1800″ in diameter, joints about as long (*Lyngb. floccosa*, Hass. pl. 60. figs. 1 & 2).

5. *U. punctalis*. Filaments 1-3000 to 1-2500″ in diameter, regularly torulose; joints two and a half times as long as broad (*Lyngb. punctalis*, Hass. pl. 60. fig. 4; *L. virescens*, fig. 3, and *L. vermicularis*, Hass. fig. 5, are scarcely distinct from this).

6. *U. speciosa*. Filaments 1-780 to 1-420″ in diameter, curled; sterile joints one-half or one-third as long.

BIBL. Kützing, *Sp. Alg.* p. 345; *Tab. Phyc.* ii.; Hassall, *Brit. Fr. Alg.* p. 219; Thuret, *Ann. des Sc. Nat.* 3 sér. xiv. p. 222, pl. 18.

ULVA, Linn. — A genus of Ulvaceæ (Confervoid Algæ), here taken in the sense of Thuret. The plants are all marine, consisting of broad, green, simple or lobed, membranous fronds, growing upon rocks and stones. They are distinguished from *Monostroma* by being composed of a double plate of cellular tissue, and from *Entero-morpha* by the two plates being permanently adherent, and not separating so as to convert the flat plate into a sac. The cells are rounded-angular (Pl. 5. figs. 2 & 3), and are at first filled with amorphous green colouring matter, which subsequently becomes collected into masses (*a*), ultimately converted into numerous zoospores. Under the influence of light, these soon "swarm" and break out from the cells by a pore in the outer wall (fig. 3 *b*). The emptied cells give a pale colour to the parts of the frond where they are situated. The zoospores appear in two forms, some large and bearing four cilia (fig. 3 *c*), others much smaller, and possessed of only two cilia (fig. 2 *b*). The fronds in which the latter occur are generally of a yellower colour. Thuret has seen both kinds germinate. As defined by that author, the British species stand as follows:—

1. *U. Lactuca*, L. Frond broadly ovate or oblong, 6 to 18″ long, and several inches wide (*Engl. Bot.* pl. 1551; *U. latissima*, Harvey and Greville; *Phycoseris gigantea*, Kütz.).

β. *latissima*. Frond 3′ or more long, 18″ or more wide; found in the muddy water at the entrance of harbours (*Phycoseris My-riotrema*, Kütz. *Sp. Alg.*).

2. *U. Linza*, L. Frond linear-lanceolate, 6 to 24″ long, ½ to 1¼″ wide. (*U. Lactuca*, Greville, *Sc. Crypt. Fl.* pl. 313; Harvey, *Phyc. Brit.* pl. 243=*Enteromorpha Grevillei*, Thuret, *olim*.)

BIBL. Harvey, *Brit. Mar. Alg.* p. 216, pl. 25 B; Thuret, *Mém. de la Soc. de Cherbourg*, ii. (1854); *Ann. des Sc. Nat.* 3 sér. xiv. p. 224, pl. 20; Greville, Harvey, Kützing, *l. cit. supra*.

ULVACEÆ.—A family of Confervoid Algæ. Marine or freshwater Algæ, consisting of membranous, expanded, saccate or tubular, sometimes filiform fronds, composed of spherical or polygonal cells, united together firmly into layers, either single or double. Reproduced by roundish spores formed from the whole contents of cells, or by ciliated zoospores formed in twos, fours, or many in each cell. British genera:

1. *Ulva*. Frond plane, simple, or lobed, formed of a double layer of cells closely packed, producing zoospores.

2. *Enteromorpha*. Frond hollow, simple, or branched, of a single layer of cells closely packed, forming a sac or tube; with zoospores.

3. *Monostroma*. Frond flat or saccate, simple or lacerate-lobed, forming a single layer of cells, which are scattered in a homogeneous membrane; with zoospores.

4. *Prasiola*. Fronds membranous, lace-

rate-lobed, formed of a single layer of cells arranged in simple or compound lines, or in groups multiple of four. Spores formed from the whole contents of the cells, motionless.

5. *Schizogonium.* Fronds filiform, dilated here and there into flat ribands containing two or four rows of cells. Spores formed from the whole contents, motionless.

ULVINA, Kütz.—A supposed genus of Algæ, founded on the "mother" of Vinegar. (See VINEGAR PLANT).

BIBL. Kütz. *Sp. Alg.* p. 147.

UMBILICARIA, Fée (*Gyrophora*, Ach.). —A genus of Pyxineæ (Gymnocarpous Lichens). *U. pustulata* grows on rocks in various parts of Britain. It is remarkable for the tubercles or hollow papillæ occurring on its surface. The apothecia are flat, and at first black, at length tuberculate. Spermogonia also occur, in the form of little tubercles containing a nucleus of densely packed sterigmata, enclosed by a thin black rind. The species in which the disk of the apothecia is concentrically plicate form the proper *Gyrophoræ* of Ach.; they occur on mountain-rocks.

BIBL. Hook. *Brit. Flor.* ii. pl. 1, p. 223; Tulasne, *Ann. des Sc. Nat.* 3 sér. xvii. p. 207, pl. 5. figs. 5–12; Schærer, *Enum. crit.* p. 25.

UNICELLULAR ALGÆ. See PALMELLACEÆ.

UNILOCULINA, D'Orbigny.—A genus of Foraminifera, of the order Agathistegia, and family Miliolida.

Char. Shell regular, equilateral, globular; *chambers* completely embracing, regularly wound round the axis, one only apparent, this making a complete revolution around the preceding; cavity simple; *orifice* single, with a tooth.

In the other genera of the family, each chamber occupies only half the circumference, whilst here it forms a complete circle. No British species.

U. indica (Pl. 42. fig. 3).

BIBL. That of the order.

URATES. See URIC ACID and URATES.

URCEOLARIA, Ach.—A genus of Parmeliaceæ (Gymnocarpous Lichens), included under *Parmelia* by Fries, but agreeing in almost every particular with LECANORA. *U. scruposa,* the commonest species, grows on heaths, walls, and rocks. The disk of the apothecia is black, and the border crenated. The spores are cellular or multilocular (Pl. 29. fig. 17). The spermogonia are scattered over the thallus, sometimes in the outer wall of the (thallodal) border of the apothecia; they are very inconspicuous, on account of the light colour of their ostiole.

BIBL. Hook. *Brit. Flor.* ii. pt. 1. p. 175; Tulasne, *Ann. des Sc. Nat.* 3 sér. xvii. p. 172, pl. 4. figs. 5–14; Schærer, *Enum. crit.* p. 85.

URCEOLARIA, Duj.—A genus of Infusoria, consisting of *U. stellina,* D. (= *Trichodina pediculus,* E.), and three doubtful species described by Müller.

BIBL. Dujardin, *Infus.* p. 525.

URCEOLARINA, Duj.—A family of Infusoria.

Char. Body variable in form, alternately top-shaped or hemispherical, or globular, sometimes ciliated all over, furnished at the upper and anterior end with a marginal row of very large cilia, spirally arranged, and leading to the marginal mouth; sometimes swimming, sometimes temporarily fixed by means of the cilia of the posterior end.

This family includes the genera *Ophrydia, Stentor, Urceolaria,* and *Urocentrum.*

BIBL. Dujardin, *Infus.* p. 518.

UREA.—This substance occurs normally in the urine of man and the carnivora, in small quantity in that of the herbivora; also in the amniotic liquid, and the vitreous and aqueous humours of the eye. Pathologically, it is found in the blood, dropsical effusions, vomited liquids, and doubtfully in the saliva, the bile, and perspiration.

When pure, it forms colourless four-sided prisms, sometimes longitudinally striated, and with one or two oblique terminal facets. The crystals are readily soluble in water and alcohol, but not in pure æther.

When nitric or oxalic acid is added to a solution of urea, the nitrate or oxalate separates in the crystalline form.

The nitrate of urea, when rapidly formed, consists of irregularly aggregated scaly crystals (Pl. 9. fig. 18 *c*); when more slowly formed, rhombic or hexagonal plates, or distinct prisms (Pl. 9. fig. 18 *a, b*). The crystals of the nitrate of soda (Pl. 6. fig. 19) bear some resemblance to those of the urea salt.

The crystals of the oxalate of urea somewhat resemble those of the nitrate, the rhombic form being evident.

BIBL. That of CHEMISTRY, *Animal.*

UREDINEI.—The genus *Uredo* is shown by Tulasne to have no satisfactory claim to a distinct existence, since the structures which have represented it appear to be merely a form of the reproductive organs common to a number of plants, which, in their most perfect state, represent the genera *Puccinia*, *Phragmidium*, *Uromyces*, &c. These constitute the genera of the family Uredinei.

Of the genus *Phragmidium*, *P. bulbosum* (*Puccinia rubi*, Schær.) is a species commonly occurring on the leaves of brambles, forming reddish, then orange, and finally blackish rusty spots (fig. 773). The first signs of reproductive organs appear in the middle of the spots on the upper face of the leaf, consisting of a few minute unilocular cavities (*spermogonia*) excavated in the leaf, with a little flat ostiole; in these occur ovate *spermatia* (see ÆCIDIUM), which are accompanied by a yellowish mucous liquid, and are ex-

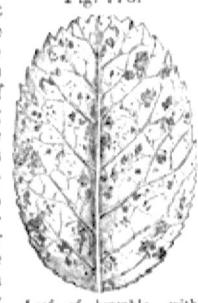

Fig. 773.

Leaf of bramble, with "Uredo ruberum." Half the nat. size.

pelled with this in the form of drops. Subsequently to this, the *Uredo*-fruits are developed, mostly on the lower face of the leaf, at the back of the spermogonia, or more rarely on the upper face, in a circle around them. They are pulverulent patches (fig. 773), solitary or a few together; and a vertical section (fig. 774) shows them to consist of paraphyses (fig. 775), and simple or branched short filaments bearing globose *stylospores* (fig. 776), which soon become detached, and in ripening acquire an echinate outer coat with numerous pores. When

Fig. 774.

Vertical section of the same Uredo-fruit, with paraphyses and imperfect stylospores. Magnified 400 diams.

these germinate, they produce merely a long slightly branched filament. Finally the perfect fruits (*spores*) appear on the same, or in distinct sori (on the lower face of the leaf), in the form represented in fig. 565

(p. 542). The loculi of these have each three or four pores in the upper part of the side-walls, whence emerge in germination (in spring) short tubular filaments, which

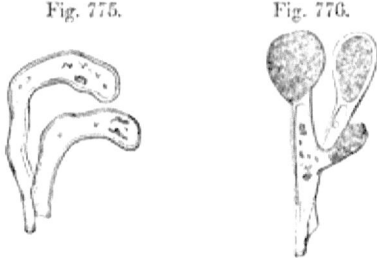

Fig. 775.   Fig. 776.

Fig. 775. Separate paraphyses.
Fig. 776. Detached pedicels with stylospores.
Magnified 400 diameters.

soon divide into four cells, from each of

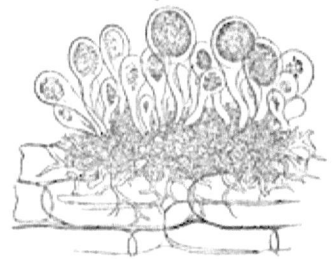

Fig. 777.

Vertical section of the sorus of "Uredo suaveolens," with immature stylospores. Magnified 400 diameters.

Fig. 778.

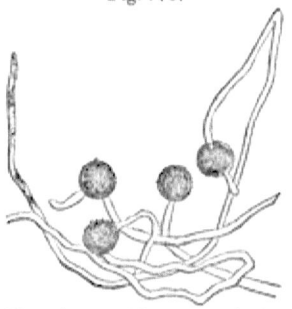

Ripe stylospores of the same, germinating.
Magnified 400 diameters.

which arises a minute "sporidium" borne on a pointed sterigmatous process.

Puccinia compositarum exhibits very similar phænomena; its *Uredo*-fruit has been described as *Uredo suaveolens.* Fig. 777 represents a vertical section through an immature sorus of this; fig. 778 some of the *stylospores* detached and germinating; the outer spinulose coat is here fully developed,

Fig. 779.   Fig. 780.

Deformed stylospores, with the spinulose coat developed. Magnified 460 diameters.

and the tubular filaments are seen emerging from the pores. The spores of the perfect fruits of this genus differ from those of *Phragmidium* in being only bilocular, or, by abortion, unilocular (see Puccinia).

In Æcidium, Cystopus, and some other genera, only *spermogonia* and *stylosporous* fruits (*Uredo-fruits,* Tulasne) have been observed. In *Cronartium,* spermogonia are unknown, but the *Uredo*-fruit exists. In *Podisoma* both *spermogonia* and *Uredo*-fruits are unknown; in both of these genera the *perfect* fruits are placed on a fleshy *columella* or *ligula.*

We subjoin Tulasne's synopsis of the family; but as his generic characters are far too long to transcribe, we can only cite the typical species.

I. *Albuginei* (white or pale yellow, heterosporous).

1. *Cystopus,* Lév. (Type, *Uredo candida,* Pers.).

II. *Æcidinei* (with a peridium, homœosporous).

2. *Cæoma,* Tul. (Type, *Uredo euonymi,* Mart.; *U. pinguis,* Duby).

3. *Æcidium,* Lk. (Type, *Æc. cichoracearum,* D.C.; *Æ. tussilaginis,* Pers.; *Æ. riolarum,* D.C.).

4. *Ræstelia,* Rebent, Fr. (Type, *Æc. cancellatum,* Pers.).

5. *Peridermium,* Lk. (Type, *Per. pini,* Fries).

III. *Melampsorei* (solid, pulvinate, biform).

6. *Melampsora,* Cast. (Type, *Uredo populina,* Pers.; *U. capræarum,* D.C.).

7. *Coleosporium,* Lév. (Type, *Uredo rhinanthacearum,* D.C.; *U. campanulæ,* Pers.).

IV. *Phragmidiacei* (pulverulent, biform, infuscate; centre of the family).

8. *Phragmidium,* Lk. (Types, *Phragm.*

incrassatum, bulbosum, with *Uredo ruborum,* D.C.; *Puccinia potentillæ,* Pers., with *U. potentillarum,* D.C.).

9. *Triphragmium,* Lk. (Type, *T. ulmariæ,* Lk.).

10. *Puccinia,* Lk. (Type, *Pucc. compositarum,* Schl. with *Ur. suaveolens,* Pers.; *P. graminis,* Pers., with *Ur. linearis,* Pers.).

11. *Uromyces,* Lk. (Type, *Uredo ficariæ,* Alb. and Schw.).

12. *Pileolaria,* Cast. = *Uromyces ?,* which itself may consist of species of *Puccinia* with spores unilocular by abortion.

V. *Pucciniei* (fleshy, ligulate, or tremelliform, naked, and uniform in the fruits; the largest plants of the family).

13. *Podisoma,* Lk., Fr. (Type, *P. juniperi communis*).

14. *Gymnosporangium,* Lk., Nees, Fr. (Type, *G. juniperinum,* Fr.).

VI. *Cronartiei* (peridiate, biform, ligulate; perhaps the most highly organized of all the genera).

15. *Cronartium* (Type, *Cr. asclepiadeum,* Fr., with *Uredo vincetoxici; Cr. pæoniæ,* with *Ur. pæoniæ,* Cast.).

Genera cancelled by Tulasne:— *Uredo, Epitea, Podocystis, Trichobasis, Lecythea, Physonema, Solenodonta.*

Genera referred to Ustilaginei: *Ustilago, Tilletia, Thecaphora.* Doubtful Ustilaginei: *Protomyces, Polycystis, Testicularia.*

Bibl. Berk. *Brit. Flor.* ii. pt. 2. arts. *Æcid., Pucc., Uredo, &c.; Ann. Nat. Hist.* i. p. 264, 2 ser. v. p. 463; Tulasne, *Ann. des Sc. Nat.* 3 sér. vii. p. 12, 4 sér. ii. p. 77; Léveillé, *ibid.* 3 sér. viii. p. 309; De Bary, *Brandpilze,* Berlin, 1853; Fries, *Summa Veg.* p. 500; Unger, *Exanthem. Plant.*; and the works cited under the Genera.

UREDO, Pers. See Uredinei.

URIC ACID and URATES, or lithic acid and lithates.—Uric acid may easily be procured in small quantity from human urine, by adding a few drops of dilute muriatic acid, and setting the liquid aside for some hours, when it subsides in crystals. In larger quantity it may be obtained by heating the excrement of serpents with excess of dilute solution of potash, until the odour of ammonia has disappeared, and filtering the solution whilst hot into dilute muriatic acid, when it falls in a colourless state. Or the excrement may be digested, without heat, with excess of strong sulphuric acid, the mixture set aside that the impurities may subside, and subsequently poured gradually into a large quantity of distilled water.

It exists also in the excrement of birds, in the urine of Mollusca and insects, and of all the Mammalia, excepting those which are herbivorous; it has also been found in the human blood, of which it is probably a normal constituent in minute quantity, although mostly secreted with the urine as soon as formed.

In the natural state of solution in the urine, uric acid exists combined with soda and ammonia; but it is frequently found as an abnormal deposit in the human urine, and is often precipitated after the secretion has been evacuated, from the occurrence of an acid fermentation. The crystals of the free acid are sometimes also met with in the urine or excrement of the lower animals, as Insects, &c.

Uric acid is but little affected by water, alcohol, acetic or muriatic acid; slowly soluble in solution of ammonia, but readily in solution of potash, from which it is re-precipitated by a dilute acid.

The crystals belong to the right-rhombic prismatic system.

Their various forms are represented in Pl. 8. figs. 1-10, and fig. 15. Those in fig. 1 are frequently met with as natural deposits from human urine, although most of the same forms, with those in fig. 15, are also found in the artificially precipitated acid. The most common and characteristic form is the rhomb (a), the side view being linear or rectangular. When the urine is strongly acid, the crystals often appear striated from the presence of linear fissures (c, d). Sometimes they are narrower and more elongate, with a prismatic form (e). They are frequently aggregated, and either fused into twin crystals (f, g), or form aigrettes or tufts (k, l, m, n, o). The other forms are noticed in the description of the plate.

The crystals forming a natural deposit are almost invariably coloured, from combining with the colouring matter of the urine; sometimes their colour is very brilliant (fig. 4); they may also be coloured artificially by precipitation from a solution of purpurate of ammonia (fig. 3), madder, &c.

The test for uric acid is the production of the colour of purpurate of ammonia or murexide, which may be effected by dissolving the crystals or suspected substance in a small quantity of dilute nitric acid, gently evaporating the solution to dryness, and

adding a little ammonia to the residue, or exposing it to the vapour of ammonia, when the red colour becomes visible. But the rhombic form, when present, with the action of potash and dilute acid, would be sufficient to distinguish uric acid from most substances.

The formation of the crystals of uric acid presents an interesting object for examination. A drop or two of solution of uric acid in potash is first placed upon a slide and covered with thin glass; a little dilute muriatic acid is then applied to the edge of the liquid, or a drop of strong acetic acid placed near its edge, so that the vapour may be absorbed by the liquid. The latter soon becomes turbid, from the formation of a precipitate of numerous molecules and granules. If the turbid liquid be watched under the microscope, a minute crystal will presently be seen to form suddenly in some part of the field. The molecules and granules then slowly dissolve immediately around the crystal, leaving this in the middle of a clear space. The crystal now enlarges, and the surrounding molecules gradually disappear, until they at last entirely vanish from the field. By careful inspection, it may easily be seen that the crystal is not formed by the conflux of the precipitated molecules, but is deposited from a state of solution.

Some crystals of uric acid polarize light splendidly, and some of the feathery crystals (Pl. 8. fig. 8 e) possess considerable analytic power.

The forms of the crystals and crystalline groups of the urates are represented in Pl. 8. figs. 11-14; they are not very characteristic, and the aid of chemistry is required for determining with certainty the composition of the respective crystals.

The urate of ammonia may be prepared artificially by adding ammonia to a boiling mixture of uric acid and water; the urate of lime by mixing urate of potash with chloride of calcium; the urate of soda by dissolving uric acid in solution of soda; and the urate of magnesia by mixing solutions of sulphate of magnesia and urate of potash.

See URINARY DEPOSITS.

BIBL. That of CHEMISTRY, *Animal.*

URINARY DEPOSITS.—We shall give here a list of the deposits most commonly occurring in the human urine, with the references to the plates in which they are represented, and the articles in which they are described.

Since the publication of the important

paper, by Vigla (*L'Expérience*, 1839), in which most of these deposits were first illustrated, the use of the microscope has constantly been called in to aid in their detection. In regard to the pathological indications afforded by their presence, upon which we cannot enter, it may be remarked that most of the deposits are formed after the evacuation of the urine.

Uric acid. Pl. 8. figs. 1, 2; and *Urates*, Pl. 8. figs. 11 *c*, *d*, *e*, 13 *a*, 14 *a* (URIC ACID and URATES).

Oxalate of lime. Pl. 9. figs. 9, 10, 11, 12 (LIME, Salts of). The concretionary forms of this salt (figs. 10, 11, 12) are more slowly acted upon by reagents than simple crystals.

Ammonio-phosphate of magnesia. Pl. 9. figs. 1, 2, 3, 4 (MAGNESIA, Salts of).

Carbonate of lime. Pl. 9. fig. 8 (LIME, Salts of).

Cystic oxide. Pl. 9. fig. 5 (CYSTIC OXIDE).

Blood-corpuscles. Pl. 40. fig. 21, especially the form fig. 21 *e* (BLOOD).

Mucous corpuscles. (Pl. 1. fig. 5 (MOUTH, p. 472).

Pus-corpuscles. Pl. 30. figs. 4, 5 (PUS).

Spermatozoa. Pl. 41. fig. 25 (SPERMATOZOA). These are found in the urine of the female for several days after intercourse; and we have detected them in the uterus more than a fortnight after the same.

Sarcina. Pl. 3. fig. 5 (SARCINA).

Fungi. *Penicillium* (fig. 557, page 533; Pl. 20. fig. 15) and *Torula* (Pl. 20. fig. 7). The spores of *Penicillium* form the so-called small organic globules.

Casts of the tubuli uriniferi. The extreme diameter of these is rather less than that of the tubules; but they are often much more slender. They are cylindrical, generally wavy, sometimes hollow, at others solid. Some are very transparent, finely granular, and are composed of fibrine; others consist entirely of, or contain imbedded in them, renal epithelial cells, with or without globules of fat either free or within the cells; they sometimes also contain mucous and pus-corpuscles, with blood-globules; some of the epithelial cells occasionally contain lithates. The epithelium of the bladder agrees essentially in structure with that of the pelvis of the kidney (KIDNEY, p. 405).

BIBL. That of CHEMISTRY, *Animal*; Lehmann, *Phys. Chem.*; Bird, *Urinary Deposits*; Schmidt, *Versuch. &c.*; Griffith, *Urinary Deposits*, and *Med. Gaz.* 1843.

URNATELLA, Leidy. — A genus of freshwater Polyzoa.

Not yet found in Britain.

BIBL. Leidy, *Proc. Acad. Nat. Sc. Philadelphia*, v. & vii.; and Allman, *Freshwater Polyzoa*, 117.

UROCENTRUM, Nitzsch, Ehr.—A genus of Infusoria, of the family Vorticellina.

Char. Free, no pedicle; tail awl-shaped; cilia absent from the body, but forming an anterior crown; mouth not spiral.

U. turbo (Pl. 25. fig. 14). Body hyaline, ovate, trilateral, tail one-third the length of the body. Aquatic; length 1-430 to 1-200″.

BIBL. Ehrenberg, *Infus.* p. 268.

UROCOCCUS, Hassall. — A genus of Palmellaceæ (Confervoid Algæ), remarkable for the peduncular processes formed by the gelatinous coats of the cells. The cells are invested by a gelatinous coat or "membrane" (like that of GLŒOCAPSA), which is originally simple; but new gelatinous layers are successively produced on the immediate surface of the cell-contents, and as each new one is formed, the preceding layer is ruptured on one side and partially thrown off, the cell with its new layer lying in the preceding layer as in a cup; by the repetition of this process the cup-like exuviæ accumulate, packed one within another so as to form a peduncle the structure of which may be roughly compared to a pile of wooden washing-bowls or tea-cups standing one in another. When the cell-contents divide into two portions, the peduncles bifurcate (Pl. 3. fig. 7). The striæ indicating the successively shed coats are more or less distinct in different species, and probably in different conditions of the same. Several species are named by Hassall, but no satisfactory distinctive characters are given. The cell-contents of four are blood-red. *U. Hookerianus* is represented in Pl. 3. fig. 7; *U. insignis* is very much larger; *U. Allmanni* and *U. cryptophila* are much alike, and neither present the striæ. A green species is also described with the synonym (erroneous?) of *Chlorococcum murale*, Grev.

The mode of reproduction is unknown.

BIBL. Hassall, *Brit. Mar. Alg.* p. 322, pl. 80; A. Braun, *Verjüngung, &c.* (*Ray Soc. Vol.* 1853, p. 178).

UROGLAUCINE. — This substance, which was first detected by Heller, may be obtained by evaporating human urine with concentrated nitric acid (Pl. 9. fig. 20). Its true nature is unknown, but it is probably a product of the decomposition of the colouring matter of the urine; it has perhaps some relation with indigo.

BIBL. Heller, *Archiv f. phys. Chemie und Mikrosk.*; Lehmann, *Physiolog. Chem.*; Funke, *Atlas*, &c.

UROGLENA, Ehr.—A supposed genus of Volvocineæ (Confervoid Algæ), consisting of a family of zoospore-like individuals arranged at the periphery of a membranous sphere, as in *Volvox*, but said to differ from that genus in having only one cilium, and also a basal prolongation or tail running toward the centre of the sphere. *U. Volvox* is described as a sphere, 1·05″ in diameter, with yellowish corpuscles 1·1728″ long, exclusive of the tail, which is three or four times as long. Inhabiting bog-pools. We very much doubt whether it is distinct from VOLVOX.

BIBL. Ehrenb. *Infus.* p. 61.

UROLEPTUS, Ehr.—A genus of Infusoria, of the family Colpodea.

Char. Eye-spot absent; no tongue-like process, nor proboscis; a tail present.

1. *U. piscis* (Pl. 25. fig. 15 *a*) = *Oxytricha caudata*, Duj. Body terete, subturbinate, gradually narrowed behind into a tail; internal granules green. Aquatic; length 1·288 to 1·144″.

2. *U. lamella* (Pl. 25. fig. 15 *b*). Body depressed, hyaline, linear-lanceolate, flat and very slender. Aquatic; length 1·216″.

Three other species.

BIBL. Ehrenberg, *Infus.* p. 358.

UROMYCES, Lk.—A supposed genus of Uredinei (Coniomycetous Fungi), perhaps not properly separated from *Puccinia*, but distinguished from the ordinary state of that genus by the unilocular spores of the perfect fruit (see UREDINEI and PUCCINIA). The genus *Pileolaria*, Cast., does not appear to differ from *Uromyces* in any essential particular. The *Uromycetes* are rusts occurring upon leaves, presenting at least two forms of fructification (spermogonia have not yet been observed), viz., 1. *Uredo-fruits*, consisting of stylospores unaccompanied by paraphyses, which have been described as species of *Trichobasis*, Lév., and 2. the perfect fruit, resembling that of PUCCINIA, but with unilocular spores, unaccompanied by paraphyses. *Ur. ficariæ*, Lév. (*Uredo ficariæ*, Alb. and Schw.) is not uncommon on Ranunculaceæ, *U. appendiculatus*, Lk. (*Uredo appendiculosa*, Berk.) on various Leguminosæ.

BIBL. Berk. *Brit. Flor.* ii. pt. 2. pp. 380, 382; Tulasne, *Ann. des Sc. Nat.* 4 sér. ii. pp. 145 & 185; Léveillé, *ibid.* 3 sér. viii. p. 370; De Bary, *Brandpilze*, p. 33.

URONEMA, Duj.—A genus of Infusoria, of the family Euchelia.

Char. Body elongate, narrowed in front, slightly curved, surrounded with radiating cilia, and with a long, straight cilium behind.

U. marina (Pl. 25. fig. 16). Body colourless, semitransparent, nodular, and with four or five faint longitudinal ribs. Marine; length 1·570″.

BIBL. Dujardin, *Infus.* p. 392.

UROPODA, Latr.—A genus of Arachnida, of the order Acarina and family Gamasea.

Char. Palpi and rostrum inferior; dorsal shield consisting of a single, broad, circular or oval piece; legs nearly equal; body frequently with a caducous anal peduncle.

U. vegetans (Pl. 2. fig. 25). Sixth joint of legs longest. The peduncle forms a horny filament, secreted from the anus, and serving to attach the body to Coleopterous insects, of which this animal is the parasite, although it is sometimes found under stones.

Four other species, most of them doubtful.

BIBL. Dugès, *Ann. d. Sc. Nat.* 2 sér. ii. 29; Gervais, *Walckenaer's Arachniden*, iii. 220.

UROSTYLA, Ehr.—A genus of Infusoria, of the family Oxytrichina.

Char. Body ciliated; styles present, but no hooks.

On the under surface of the posterior part of the body is a small cleft, with styles.

U. grandis (Pl. 25. fig. 17). Semicylindrical, subclavate, rounded at the ends, anterior portion slightly thickened. Aquatic; length 1·144 to 1·96″.

BIBL. Ehrenberg, *Infus.* p. 309.

URTICA, L.—The botanical name of the genus to which the stinging-nettle belongs (see STINGS). The plants yielding the fibre of Chinese grass-cloth, and *Puya*, are placed by some authors under *Urtica*, by others under BOEHMERIA.

USNEA, Ach.—A genus of Parmeliaceæ (Gymnocarpous Lichens), with a somewhat crustaceous branched thallus, bearing peltate apothecia, which often have a ciliated margin. *U. barbata* is common on parkpales and old trees, *U. florida* and *plicata* in similar situations, mostly in mountainous regions; it is possible they are all forms of one species. The pendulous fibrillous thallus and ciliated apothecia of *U. barbata* are very characteristic.

BIBL. Hook. *Brit. Flor.* ii. pt. 1. p. 230; Schærer, *Enum. Crit.* p. 3.

USTILAGINEI.—A family of Coniomycetous (?) Fungi related to the Uredinei, generally distinguished by their growing in the interior of the organs (especially the ovaries and anthers) of Flowering Plants, causing deformity, absorption of the internal tissue, and its replacement by a pulverulent substance consisting of the spores of the Fungi. In the earlier stages, the infected organ exhibits either a grumous mass, or an interwoven filamentous mycelium, from which acrogenous spores arise; finally the mycelium disappears, and a dark-coloured (often fœtid) powder remains, composed entirely of the spores, which are simple, or

Fig. 781.   Fig. 782.    Fig. 783.

Fig. 784. 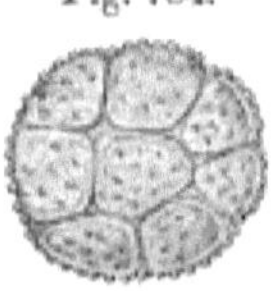   Fig. 785.

Theeaphora deformans.
Compound spores, entire and broken up.
Magnified 450 diameters.

more rarely compound (figs. 784, 785), *i. e.* several coherent within a common coat, at length free (figs. 781–783), smooth or unequally echinate or reticulated.

They are thus divided by Tulasne:—

I. *Ustilaginei veri*:

Stroma at first mucilaginous or grumous-mucous, entire, or soon broken up into variously-conglomerated masses, afterwards divided into unappendaged spores; few or no filaments persistent.

1. *Ustilago.* Spores simple.
2. *Thecaphora.* Spores compound.

II. *Tilletiei.* Stroma composed of interwoven fragile filaments; spores acrogenous on their ramules, hence often appendaged when free.

3. *Tilletia.*

Polycystis, Lév. and *Testicularia*, Klotsch, are doubtful. PROTOMYCES, Unger, is apparently allied to *Tilletia*.

The species of *Ustilago* are very numerous (see USTILAGO). The *Thecaphoræ* are fewer

and more rare; *T. deformans* is an Algerian plant, infesting *Medicago tribuloides*. *Tilletia* infests corn-grains and other grasses, *T. Caries* being the *Uredo Caries*, D.C., and *U. fœtida*, Bauer, forming the fœtid blight called *Bunt*, or *pepper-brand*, of corn (see TILLETIA).

Tulasne has observed the germination of the spores in some *Ustilagines* and in *Tilletia*; they produce filamentous processes, from which arise pedicels (*basidia*) bearing minute 'sporidia,' as in the Uredinei.

BIBL. Berk. *Brit. Fl.* (art. *Uredo*); Tulasne, *Ann. des Sc. Nat.* 3 sér. vii. p. 5, 4 sér. ii. p. 157; DeBary, *Brandpilze*; Bauer and Banks in *Curtis's Pract. Obs. on Brit. Grasses*, London, 1805; Unger, *Exanthem. Plant.*

USTILAGO, Fries.—A genus of Ustilaginei (Coniomycetous Fungi), forming *smuts*, infesting the ears of corn and other grasses, the ovaries and anthers of other Flowering Plants, and in some cases the leaves and stems of plants. The interior of the organ

Fig. 786.   Fig. 787.

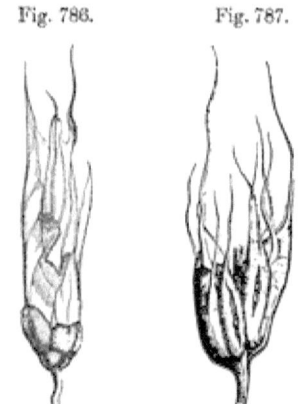

Fig. 786 Ustilago Carbo, on oats. Nat. size.
Fig. 787. Ustilago Carbo, on barley. Nat. size.

infested by them presents at first a grumous-mucous whitish mass, which grows at the expense of the tissue and juice of the infested organ, and is finally converted into a pulverulent mass of simple spores, mostly of deep colour, and with a smooth, spiny or reticulated surface.

The species growing upon leaves and stems occur on grasses, *e. g.* U. *longissima* (*Uredo longissima*, Sow.), U. *hypodytes* (*Ur.*

hypodytes) and *U. grandis* (or *typhoides*); they form linear patches, ultimately containing smooth black spores.

The greater number, however, occur in the parts of flowers, especially of grasses; of *Ust. Carbo* (*Uredo segetum*, Pers.), forming the blight called smut of corn, commonly infesting wheat, oats (fig. 786), barley (fig. 787) and other grasses, filling the ears with a black powder of smooth spores, about 1-5000″ in diameter in corn, sometimes about twice as large in the varieties attacking species of *Bromus.* The smut of maize (*U. maidis*, fig. 788) has minutely echinate spores, 1-2500″ in diameter.

Fig. 788.

Portion of a spike of Maize infested with *Ustilago maidis*. Some of the lower grains perfect and mature : above these, female flowers with abortive ovaries. The projecting bodies are grains which have become deformed by the *Ustilago* developed within them.

Sedges are infested by *Ust. urceolarum* with dark brown, and *Ust. olivacea* with olive-coloured spores (*Uredines*, Brit. Flor.). *Ust. antherarum*, growing in the anthers of Caryophylleæ, has violet-coloured spores. Many other species are described by Tulasne, several of which have occurred in Britain.

BIBL. Tulasne, *Ann. des Sc. Nat.* 3 sér. vii. p. 73, 4 sér. ii. p. 157; *Berk. Brit. Flor.* art. *Uredo*; *Ann. Nat. Hist.* 2 ser. v. p. 463.

UTERUS.—The substance of the uterus consists of longitudinal, transverse, and oblique unstriated muscular fibres, interwoven with imperfectly-developed areolar tissue resembling that in the stroma of the ovary.

Three layers of the muscular fibres are described, but they are intimately connected. Those in the cervix are principally transverse or circular; and immediately beneath the mucous membrane at the mouth of the uterus, the transverse fibres form a sphincter.

The muscular fibres are from 1-600 to 1-400″ in length, fusiform, with elongate-oval nuclei, and very difficultly separable on account of the large amount of areolar tissue intermingled with them.

Fig. 789.

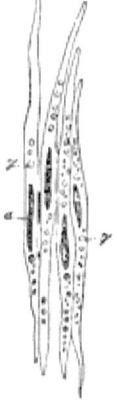

The epithelium is simple and ciliated. The mucous membrane of the body has no papillæ, but here and there some folds, and contains numerous tubular or uterine glands resembling the Lieberkuhn's glands of the intestines, their cæcal ends being simple, bifurcate, or spiral, and consisting of a basement - membrane with cylinder-epithelium.

Uterine muscular fibres, three weeks after parturition, treated with acetic acid. *a*, nuclei; *y*, globules of fat.

Magnified 350 diameters.

In the cervix are situated glandular depressions of the mucous membrane, which secrete a transparent tenacious mucus; some of these are closed, and form the ovules of Naboth.

The lower third or half of the canal of the cervix contains papillæ covered with ciliated epithelium.

During pregnancy, the uterine elements, especially the muscular fibres, as also the vessels and probably the nerves, become enlarged and more numerous, from new formation (fig. 790).

All three of the coats of the veins of the pregnant uterus contain muscular fibres. After parturition, many of the muscular fibres undergo fatty degeneration, and become absorbed (fig. 789).

Fig. 790.

Muscular elements from a uterus at five months' gestation. *a*, formative cells; *b*, young, *c*, fully developed muscular fibres. Magnified 350 diameters.

BIBL. Kölliker, *Mikr. Anat.* ii.

UVELLA, Bory, Ehr.—A genus of Infusoria (Algæ?), of the family Monadina.

Char. Corpuscles tailless, without an eye-spot, moving by means of one or two flagelliform filaments, or an anterior circle of cilia, and aggregated into spherical revolving clusters.

U. virescens (Pl. 25. fig. 18). Corpuscles ovate, rounded at each end, bright green. Aquatic; diameter of clusters 1-288″, length of corpuscles 1-2016″.

Five other species—one green, the rest colourless.

Dujardin regards the presence of the flagelliform filament as a character of the genus.

BIBL. Ehrenberg, *Infus.* p. 19; Dujardin, *Infus.* p. 300.

UVIGERINA, D'Orb.—A genus of Foraminifera, of the order Helicostegia, and family Turbinoidæ.

Char. Shell free, spiral, turriculate; spire elongate; *chambers* very prominent, globular, the last with a tubular prolongation, pierced with the *orifice*, which is round and central. Two recent British species, none fossil.

U. pygmæa (Pl. 18. fig. 8).
BIBL. That of the order.

V.

VAGINICOLA, Lamarck, Ehr.—A genus of Infusoria, of the family Ophrydina.

Char. Solitary; body ovoid or campanulate, sessile, in a membranous, urceolate, sessile sheath.

Cilia forming an anterior circle.

V. crystallina (Pl. 25. fig. 19). Sheath crystalline, urceolate, straight, internal granules green. Aquatic; length 1-216″.

Stein has observed the *Acineta*-form (*Acineta mystacina*) of this animal, and the subsequent development of swarm-germs within it.

Several other species.

BIBL. Ehrenb. *Infus.* p. 295; Dujardin, *Infus.* p. 560; Stein, *Infusoria*, passim.

VAGINULINA, D'Orb. — A genus of Foraminifera, of the order Stichostegia, and family Æquilateralidæ.

Char. Shell free, elongate, equilateral, conical, depressed or angular; *chambers* not embracing, oblique, the last truncate and not prolonged; *orifice* round, marginal, always situated in one of the projecting angles of the shell.

Williamson unites the genus with *Dentalina*.

V. badenensis, D'Orb. (Pl. 18. fig. 41) = *Dentalina legumen*, one form, Willn.

Two fossil species.

BIBL. That of the order.

VALKERIA, Flem.—A genus of Infundibulate Ctenostomatous Polyzoa, of the family Vesiculariadæ.

Char. Variously branched; cells oval, irregularly clustered; eight tentacles, but no gizzard. Three species:

1. *V. cuscuta.* Stem with subverticillate branches; cells in clusters or opposite pairs.

2. *V. uva.* Stem creeping, irregularly branched; cells scattered.

3. *V. pustulosa.* Dichotomous or alternately branched; cells clustered, unilateral.

BIBL. Johnston, *British Zooph.* p. 373; Gosse, *Mar. Zool.* ii. p. 20.

VALLISNERIA, Mich.—An aquatic genus of Angiospermous Flowering Plants, belonging to the family Hydrocharidaceæ.

V. spiralis, a native of the South of Europe,

occurring wild also in North America, India, &c., is commonly grown in jars for the sake of observing the ROTATION in the leaves. This plant is diœcious, and the specimens ordinarily found in cultivation are the pistillate forms, which often produce flowers, but the seeds, remaining unfertilized, never ripen; the plant increases rapidly, however, by runners, if in a healthy condition. We find it thrive well in any situation indoors near a window and not exposed to frost, but it attains a far larger size in water kept at a high temperature, as in *Victoria*-tanks in Botanic Gardens. It is necessary, when growing it in jars, not to keep too many or too large "snails" in the water, as they destroy the leaves. See ROTATION.

VALVULINA, D'Orb.—A genus of Foraminifera, of the order Helicostegia, and family Turbinoidæ.

Char. Shell free, spiral, conical, turriculate or depressed, rugose, formed of an elongate, trochoid or depressed spire; *chambers* few, somewhat prominent, placed in a regular spiral axis; *orifice* crosier-like, transverse to the axis, placed near the umbilical angle, and partly covered by a projecting convex layer or valvular operculum, occupying the umbilicus.

United with *Rotalina* by Williamson.

No British species (?).

V. austriaca (Pl. 18. fig. 42).

BIBL. That of the order.

VARIOLARIA, Pers.—A spurious genus of Lichens, founded upon imperfect forms of PERTUSARIA, &c.

BIBL. Hook. *Brit. Flor.* ii. pt. 1. p. 172; Schærer, *Enum. Crit.* p. 229.

VASCULAR BUNDLES.—This title is applied to the fibrous cords which form the ribs, veins, &c., of the leaves, petioles and other appendicular organs of all plants ranking above the Mosses, and which by their confluence and more considerable development constitute the wood of stems and trunks. The vascular bundles of petioles (fig. 600, page 639), &c., running into leaves to form their ribs, and lying imbedded in parenchyma, resemble the bundles which form the rudiments of wood of the stem itself. The bundles remain isolated as fibrous cords in the stems of the herbaceous Monocotyledons, or are only combined into a wood, in the Palms, &c., by the lignification of the cells of the parenchyma in which they are imbedded (fig. 461, p. 463). In the Dicotyledons, the rudimentary bundles are developed in a circle surrounding the pith (fig.

455, p. 450), and soon unite to form a tube of wood, with an external cambium layer and a true bark; and the cambium layer is the seat of renewed development of the vascular bundle in each successive year. On such characters of growth, Schleiden founded a division of the vascular bundles into classes, which are convenient in reference to microscopical investigations, and affixed tolerably perfect systematic characters to them.

In the higher Flowerless Plants, viz. Ferns, Equisetaceæ, &c., the vascular bundles are composed chiefly of ducts, surrounded by elongated tubular cells, almost devoid of secondary deposits, the whole enclosed by a layer of tolerably firm prosenchymatous wood-cells, especially developed

Fig. 791.

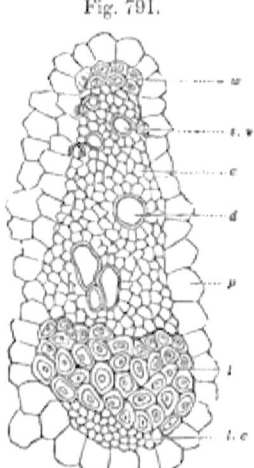

Monocotyledon.

Transverse section of a fibro-vascular bundle of a Palm; the upper end is directed towards the centre of the stem. *w*, woody fibres resembling liber in structure; *s. v*, spiral vessels; *c*, cambium (*casu propria*); *d*, ducts; *p*, parenchyma; *l*, liber; *l. c*, laticiferous canals. Magnified 150 diameters.

in the Ferns. In the Ferns, the ducts are mostly of the kind called *scalariform* (fig. 664, page 640; Pl. 39. fig. 10), in the Equisetaceæ *annular* (fig. 661, page 639), in the Lycopodiaceæ *spiral* (fig. 659, page 639; Pl. 39. figs. 11 & 12). They are variously arranged in the different orders, but agree in the mode of development, namely in growing only at the end next the *punctum regetationis*, in proportion to the elongation of

3 A

the stem and the evolution of leaves. Hence Schleiden calls them *simultaneous bundles*, their various elements—ducts, tubular and prosenchymatous cells—being formed simultaneously.

In the Monocotyledons, where the vascular bundles occur isolated, they originate in the *punctum vegetationis*, and are developed with the growth of the stem, outwards and upwards into the leaves, and outwards and downwards towards the permanent circumference of the stem, old and new bundles crossing each other in a more or less complicated manner (fig. 461, page 463). Here (fig. 791) the first trace of the vascular bundle consists of spiral vessels, followed on the outer side by spiral, annular, or reticulated ducts; next comes a collection of elongated tubular cells of delicate structure (*vasa propria*), and in the outer part, at first, a *cambium* region, which is gradually converted into prosenchymatous woody structure having the character of LIBER-cells. In this case, the development is not only gradual from the *punctum vegetationis* outward, but the inner side of each bundle is perfected first, and the conversion of the outer part into wood occupies a whole season of growth. Hence these are entitled *progressive bundles*; but as no new development occurs in these in successive seasons, they are further distinguished from those of the Dicotyledons as *definite* bundles. The structure of the vascular bundles of Monocotyledons is very well seen, in different characteristic conditions, in vertical and horizontal sections of the stems of the white lily, of the large grasses, rhizomes of sedges and rushes; affording well-developed examples in herbaceous structures; of the bamboo (an arborescent grass), of the common cane or the "partridge cane" (both species of Palms), where the bundles are connected by lignified parenchyma. In leaves of bulbous Monocotyledons, &c., the bundles consist chiefly of spiral vessels; in the palms, bananas, &c., the woody fibre extends also into the ribs of the foliaceous organs.

In the Dicotyledons, the bundles of the stem appear first as a circle of cords composed of spiral vessels, around the pith, outside which larger vessels and ducts, and subsequently woody fibre or wood-cells are developed, passing into the elongated prosenchymatous liber (fig. 792). The development of the successive regions is *progressive* during the first season; but here the *cambium* layer remains capable of renewed

activity, and a new layer of wood (and of liber) is added on the outside of the bundle in each successive season; hence these bundles are distinguished as *indefinite*. These

Fig. 792.

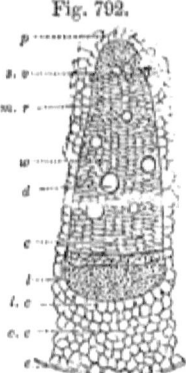

Dicotyledon.

Transverse section of a fibro-vascular bundle of a Melon stem; the upper end next the centre of the stem. *p*, pith; *s. v*, spiral vessels; *m. r*, medullary rays; *w*, wood; *d*, pitted ducts; *c*, cambium; *l*, liber; *l. c*, laticiferous canals; *c, c*, cellular envelope of the bark; *e*, epidermis. Magnified 50 diameters.

may be observed in sections and young shoots of any common tree (figs. 455 & 457, pages 450 & 451).

Infinite variety of modification occurs in the character and arrangement of the vascular bundles within the limits above laid down, or very slightly overstepping them. A few remarkable cases may be mentioned here; in the Orobanchaceæ (parasites) no spiral vessels occur in the vascular bundles forming the wood; in *Victoria regia* the isolated bundles are composed of spiral vessels without any prosenchymatous wood-cells; other peculiarities, influencing more especially the characters of WOOD, are given under that article. (See also CAMBIUM and MEDULLA.)

BIBL. Works on Structural Botany.

VAUCHERIA, D.C.—A genus of Siphonaceæ (Confervoid Algæ), consisting of green filamentous plants growing in fresh and salt water, and on damp ground, characterized by the continuity of the cavity throughout the branched tubular filament (sometimes several inches long) of which each plant is composed, and by the modes of reproduction, both by gonidia and by spores. *Vaucheriæ* may be gathered on damp borders in every garden, or by the sides of ditches, where they form fine silky green tufts; they are very variable in form and size, so that the specific distinctions heretofore laid down appear to be worth little. The ordinarily occurring species presents itself as a tubular cell of comparatively gigantic dimensions, containing more or less protoplasm, coloured by chlorophyll in the form of minute granules applied upon the wall or occupying more or less of the cavity. The green granules may be seen to lie imbedded in a colourless protoplasm at the inner surface of the cellulose wall; and it is curious to observe, when the filament is accidentally or intentionally ruptured, that the green granules which may escape are contained in a mucous investment, which soon rounds itself into a globular body, of size proportionate to the quantity of green granules extruded; these globules sometimes even exhibit a slight rolling movement, but they appear ultimately to decay. Such globules sometimes occur inside the filaments, when the growth is unhealthy; and Itzigsohn calls them *spermatospheres*, stating that they produce spermatozoids. This, like all this author's observations, requires confirmation.

If the *Vaucheria*-filaments are gathered at a favourable epoch, or if they are cultivated in a vessel of water well exposed to light, the blind ends of the filaments (or rather of the ramifications of the filament) are found very densely filled with green contents, appearing almost black; and if these ends are watched early in the morning, a remarkable series of phænomena is observed in them. The ends of the filaments about to produce gonidia are found swollen into a slightly clavate form, the green contents of the "club" part from the general contents of the filament, leaving a transparent space (fig. 793); then, having as it were acquired a definite independence, the isolated mass returns so as to fill up the transverse light space, but does not again coalesce with the lower mass of contents. Next, a light space is observed between the surface of the terminal body of contents and the cellulose wall surrounding it; and the latter soon gives away at the apex, forming a passage for the escape of the contents. This mass of contents is now clearly recognizable as the *gonidium* or zoospore; it gradually extricates itself from the tube, with a rotatory motion around its own axis, and it exhibits a remarkable elasticity of structure, giving way and altering its form (fig. 794) to squeeze through the narrow orifice of es-

cape; sometimes it becomes "pinched" in this process into two independent gonidia of half the usual size. As soon as it has perfectly emerged, it assumes an elliptical form, increases much in size, and is seen to be covered with innumerable vibratile cilia (fig. 796)), arising from its gelatinous (protoplasmic) coat (these are rendered much more distinct by applying tincture of

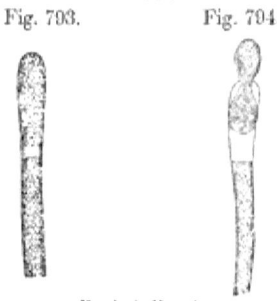

Fig. 793. Fig. 794.

Vaucheria Ungeri.
Fig. 793. End of a filament in which a gonidium is being developed.
Fig. 794. Gonidium escaping from the filament. Magnified 30 diameters.

iodine): no cellulose membrane exists at this time, and the gonidium swims about actively in the water, revolving on its long axis. The large number of cilia existing on

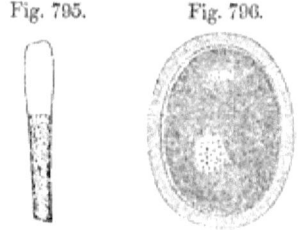

Fig. 795. Fig. 796.

Vaucheria Ungeri.
Fig. 795. End of the filament from which the gonidium has escaped. Magnified 30 diameters.
Fig. 796. Gonidium which has been treated with iodine and dried between two slips of glass, showing the cilia very clearly. Magnified 110 diameters.

this gonidium distinguish it remarkably from all others; but we are inclined to believe that there is a nearer relationship than appears at first sight. The green substance at the surface of the gonidium presents a peculiar granular or globular appearance; and it appears not far-fetched to regard this body as composed of a densely combined family of ordinary two- or four-ciliated zoospores, such as would be formed by the

3 A 2

swarming-spores of *Hydrodictyon* if they remained in their primitive crowded condition. This, however, is a point requiring further examination. The end of the tube from which the gonidium has escaped appears as a hyaline sac (fig. 795), which soon decays down to the point where the contents parted, where a septum, now closing the tube, is developed.

After swimming about for some time, from one to several hours (usually about two), the gonidium falls to the bottom of the vessel, its cilia disappear, and it assumes a spherical form, acquiring very soon a distinct cellulose coat; after this it soon germinates by pushing out one or more tubular processes (fig. 797), which grow up into

Fig. 797.   Fig. 798.

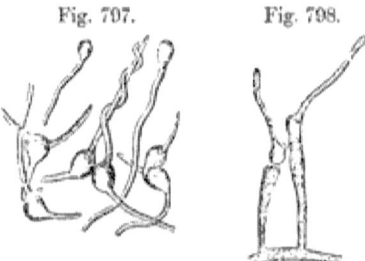

Vaucheria Ungeri.

Fig. 797. Gonidia germinating. Magnified about 15 diameters.

Fig. 798. Filament with gonidia germinating in the parent tube; the left-hand figure, half a divided gonidium. Magnified 25 diameters.

filaments like the parent. Sometimes the gonidium cannot make its escape; sometimes half of it escapes and becomes pinched off, the other half being left behind: in these cases, the arrested body, or the remaining portion of the divided one, germinates *in situ* (fig. 798).

It should be mentioned that the contents of the vegetative filaments have a remarkable tenacity of life; for if the tube is slightly injured at any point, the primordial utricle commonly retracts from the wound, and secretes a cellulose layer on its surface, shutting off the injured part. Filaments are sometimes met with having several living regions of this kind, shooting out into branches, separated from each other by dead, empty lengths of the filament.

Besides the vegetative reproduction above described, the *Vaucheriæ* are reproduced by spores formed by the concurrence of two distinct kinds of reproductive organs. Fila-

ments growing on damp ground ordinarily exhibit lateral organs of two kinds, associated together, but variously grouped and collected in varying numbers at particular points, apparently according to external conditions. The larger kind of organ appears first as a pouch-like process, which expands into a squat, flask-shaped body, stalked or sessile, the neck of which is gradually turned over in the development, until it projects at one side, the form then somewhat resembling that of a bird's head (or a chemist's glass retort cut off short at the neck) (Pl. 45. fig. 12 A, B, s). Near this, on the main filament, or on a common pediced with one or more of the bird's-head organs, is developed another organ, at first straight and tubular, but soon curving over into the form of a hook or scroll, without, however, expanding (Pl. 45. fig. 12 A, B, a). The expanded part of the bird's-head organ (or *sporangium*) becomes filled with dense green granular matter, and cut off by a septum from the main filament. The upper part of the "hook" is likewise cut off by a septum; and the contents of the apical cell thus formed are of a light colour, and soon lose most of the chlorophyll. From the association of these two kinds of organ, and the production of spores in the sporanges, it was supposed, as long ago as in Vaucher's time, that they represented sexual organs. Vaucher thought the "hooks" discharged a kind of pollen to fertilize the sporanges. Other algologists, especially Nägeli, supposed or asserted that a conjugation took place between them (like that in *Spirogyra*), —a view more or less favourably received until a few years since, when Karsten asserted that he had actually observed it in all its details. But Pringsheim has lately published a very complete and certainly more trustworthy account of the development of these structures, in which he denies the conjugation, but asserts that the "hook" is an *antheridium*, and that when mature it bursts at the apex and discharges bicilinted spermatozoids resembling those of *Fucus*, which enter the simultaneously opened neck of the sporange and fertilize its granular contents. The contents become isolated from the wall, secrete a proper coat, and form a free cell (spore) lying in the sporange, its granular matter gradually losing the green colour and becoming brown (Pl. 45. fig. 12 C). Two coats, at least, are developed; and the spore ultimately escapes by the decay of the parent filament and sporange. According to Pringsheim, about three months elapse before germination, in which process the outer spore-coat splits, and the inner grows out into a tube, forming the basis of a new ramification of the *Vaucheria*-filament.

In the systematic works on Algology, numerous species of aquatic and land *Vaucheria* are described; but we agree with Thuret in believing that the characters by which most of the forms are distinguished are unessential, therefore we omit any synopsis of them. Even *V. racemosa*, Decaisne, appears merely an extreme of the kind of development producing *V. geminata*. Thuret proposes the name *V. Ungeri*, to include all but *V. racemosa*; Hassall suppresses the name *V. clavata*, as indicating a form common to all the species, of which he describes a large number. We do not find anything sufficiently distinctive in the characters of the marine species cited by Harvey.

The admirable essay of Unger should be consulted by those studying the gonidial reproduction.

Bibl. Vaucher, *Conferves d'eau douce* (Ectosperma); Hassall, *Brit. Fr. Alg.*; Harvey, *Brit. Mar. Alg.* p. 195; Unger, *Nova Acta*, xiii. p. 11, *Die Pflanze im Mom. der Thierwerdung*, Vienna, 1843; Decaisne, *Ann. des Sc. Nat.* 2 sér. xvii. p. 430; Thuret, *ibid.* xix. p. 266; Karsten, *Bot. Zeitung*, x. p.85 (1852), xv. p. 1; Pringsheim, *Ber. Berlin. Akad.* March 1855; *Ann. Nat. Hist.* 2 ser. xv. p. 346; Alex. Braun, *Verjüngung* (*Ray Soc. Vol.* 1853, *passim*), *Alg. unicell.* (1855), pp. 8, 105; Nägeli, *Neues Algensyst.* p. 175, pl. 4; Itzigsohn, *Bot. Zeit.* xi. p. 225 (1853); Dippel, *Flora*, 1856. p. 481.

VEGETABLE IVORY.—This substance consists of the seeds of the Palm called *Phytelephas macrocarpa*, composed of a large round mass of bony Albumen, in which a small embryo is imbedded. Slices of this ivory-like albumen, placed under the microscope, afford very beautiful examples of vegetable cells with the cavities almost obliterated by Secondary deposits (Pl. 38. fig. 23).

VEGETABLE KINGDOM.—The large number of natural orders of Angiospermous Flowering Plants and the subordinate character of their diversities in microscopic structure, lead us to depart from the plan on which the synopsis of the Animal Kingdom is given, and carry it into effect here only in reference to the Cryptogamous plants. For the microscopic phænomena in the Phanerogamia described in this work, reference should be made to the articles Tissues, Wood, Ovule, Embryo, &c.

Kingdom. VEGETABILIA.

Subkingdom 1. Axophyta or Cormophyta.

Div. 1. **Phanerogamia.** Flowering Plants.

　Subdiv. 1. *Angiospermia.*
　　Class I. Dicotyledones.
　　　Most common trees and herbs.
　　Class II. Monocotyledones.
　　　Grasses, rushes, most bulbous plants, palms, &c.

　Subdiv. 2. *Gymnospermia.*
　　Class III. Coniferæ.
　　　Firs, pines, yew.
　　Class IV. Cycadaceæ.
　　　Cycas, Zamia.

Div. 2. **Cryptogamia.** Flowerless plants with stems and leaves.

　　Class I. Lycopodiales.
　　　Order 1. Marsileaceæ.
　　　　Pilularia, Pill-wort.
　　　Order 2. Lycopodiaceæ.
　　　　Club-mosses.
　　Class II. Filicales.
　　　Order 1. Filicaceæ.
　　　　Ferns.
　　　Order 2. Equisetaceæ.
　　　　Horse-tails.
　　Class III. Muscales.
　　　Order 1. Muscaceæ.
　　　　Mosses.
　　　Order 2. Hepaticæ.
　　　　Liverworts and Scale-mosses.
　　(Order of uncertain place, Characeæ.)

Subkingdom 2. Thallophyta.

　　Class I. Algæ.
　　　Order 1. Florideæ.
　　　　Red sea-weeds.
　　　Order 2. Fucoideæ.
　　　　Olive sea-weeds.
　　　Order 3. Confervoideæ.
　　　　Green silk-weeds, slime-weeds and brittle-weeds (Diatomaceæ).
　　Class II. Lichenes.
　　　Order 1. Gymnocarpi.
　　　Order 2. Angiocarpi.
　　Class III. Fungi.
　　　Order 1. Hymenomycetes.
　　　　Mushrooms, toadstools, dry-rots.

Order 2. GASTEROMYCETES.
   Puff-balls.
Order 3. CONIOMYCETES.
   Blights, rusts.
Order 4. HYPHOMYCETES.
   Mildews, moulds and blights.
Order 5. ASCOMYCETES.
   Truffles, toadstools, rusts.
Order 6. PHYSOMYCETES.
   Moulds and mildews.

BIBL. Lindley, *Vegetable Kingdom*; Endlicher, *Gen. Plant.*; Fries, *Summ. Veget. Scan.*; Henfrey, *Elementary Course of Botany*; and other General Works on Botany.

VEINS, OF ANIMALS.—The walls of the veins are thinner than those of the arteries, which depends principally upon the less development of the contractile and elastic elements. The inner coat is less developed, but otherwise agrees with that of the arteries in structure. The middle coat is not yellow,

Fig. 799.

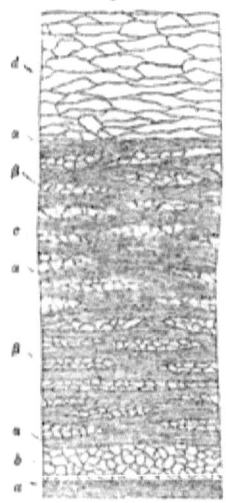

Longitudinal section of the vena cava inferior, near the liver. *a*, inner coat ; *b*, middle coat without muscular fibres ; *c*, inner layer of the outer coat—*a*, its longitudinal muscles ; *β*, its transverse areolar elements ; *d*, outer portion of the outer coat, without muscles. Magnified 30 diameters.

but greyish red, containing more areolar tissue and fewer elastic fibres and muscles ; in addition to the transverse, it has longitudinal layers. The outer coat is usually the thickest, agreeing in structure with that of the arteries, except that in many veins,

especially those of the abdominal cavity, it contains well-developed longitudinal muscular fibres.

The veins of the brain and some other parts contain no muscular fibres.

BIBL. Kölliker, *Mikrosk. Anat.* ii.

VEINS OF PLANTS.—The name commonly applied to the ramifications of the VASCULAR BUNDLES, forming the ribs of leaves and similar organs.

VERMICULARIA, Fr.—A genus of Sphæronemei (Coniomycetous Fungi), but seemingly stylosporous states of Sphæriacei, most of the species being included under *Sphæria* in the British Flora. They grow on decaying stalks, leaves, or wood. *S. relicina, Dematium, culmifraga, trichella* and others of the Br. Fl. belong here. Another species, *V. atramentaria*, is common on decaying potato-stems, forming black velvety patches. This is distinguished from *V. Dematium* by its straight spores. The erect black hairs of the perithecia are characteristic.

BIBL. Berk. *Brit. Flor.* ii. pt. 2. p. 274, &c., *Ann. Nat. Hist.* 2 ser. v. p. 378; Fries, *Summa Veg.* p. 419.

VERMILION, or bisulphuret of mercury, is used as a pigment for injecting. It should be in a finely-divided state, in which it is best obtained by levigation ; and should not exhibit any white crystalline particles when examined as an opake object.

See INJECTION (p. 379).

VERNEUILINA, D'Orb.—A genus of Foraminifera, of the order Helicostegia, and family Turbinoidæ.

Char. Shell free, spiral, elongate, rugose, spire conical ; *chambers* depressed, arranged in three distinct rows, each keeled, around the longitudinal axis ; *orifice* a transverse fissure, on the inner part of the last chamber, and without an opercular valve.

Two fossil British species.

BIBL. That of the order.

VERRUCARIA, Pers.—A genus of Verrucarieæ (Angiocarpous Lichens), containing numerous species having a crustaceous or cartilagineo - membranous thallus growing upon and adherent to the bark of trees or stones ; named from the wart-like processes corresponding to the perithecia, which open by a pore at the surface. The perithecia have a black rind, enclosing either the whole or the upper half of the nucleus. The spermogonia much resemble the perithecia, only they are much smaller ; they occur either scattered among the perithecia, or collected towards the margins of the thallus.

BIBL. Hook. *Brit. Flor.* ii. pt. 1. p. 152; Leighton, *Brit. Angioc. Lich.* p. 35; Schærer, *Enum. crit.* p. 213; Tulasne, *Ann. des Sc. Nat.* 3 sér. xvii. p. 215, pl. 3.

VERRUCARIEÆ.—A family of Angiocarpous or closed-fruited Lichens, characterized by rounded apothecia, closed by a special *perithecium*, perforated by a contiguous pore, and containing a somewhat hyaline, gelatinous, dissolving nucleus.

Synopsis of British Genera.

1. *Sagedia.* *Thallus* crustaceous, apothecia solitary; excipulum waxy-membranous (coloured); ostiole simple, somewhat papillate; nucleus gelatinous, somewhat hyaline.

2. *Verrucaria.* *Thallus* crustaceous or cartilagineo-membranous, spreading, adnate, uniform. Apothecia hemispherical or subglobose, innate and immersed or sessile, excipulum horny, mostly black, with a simple, papillary or perforated ostiole; nucleus gelatinous, fluid or deliquescent, subhyaline.

VERTEBRALINA, D'Orb.—A genus of Foraminifera, of the order Helicostegia, and family Nautiloidæ.

Char. *Shell* free, regular, greatly compressed, mostly inequilateral, more convex on one side than on the other, suborbicular or elongate, of a compact unforaminated texture; spire embracing in the young state only, afterwards straight; *chambers* in the spire, two or three; *orifice* single, terminal, occupying the entire upper surface.

One recent British species:

V. striata (Pl. 18. fig. 14).

BIBL. That of the order.

VERTICILLIUM, Nees.—A genus of Mucedines (Hyphomycetous Fungi), distinguished from *Botrytis* (under which it is included, with *Acrostalagmus*, by Fries) chiefly by the verticillate arrangement of the sporiferous branches. A number of species are described; but from the observations of Hoffmann and Bail on the germination of *Trichothecium*, this genus represents only one form of the plants belonging to other genera,—*V. ruberrimum*, Bonorden (*Botrytis verticilloides*, Corda, which Hoffmann regards as identical with *Acrostalagmus parasitans* and *cinnabarinus*), having been raised from the spores of *Tri-*

Fig. 800.

Verticillium cylindrosporum. Magnified 200 diameters.

chothecium roseum, and its "spores" being barren (see TRICHOTHECIUM). Berkeley and Broome describe and figure several new species.

BIBL. *Ann. Nat. Hist.* 2 ser. vii. p. 101, pl. 7. figs. 15–18; Fries, *Summa Veg.* (*Botrytis*), p. 491.

See also TRICHOTHECIUM.

VESICULARIA, Thomps.—A genus of Infundibulate Ctenostomatous Polyzoa, of the family Vesiculariadæ.

V. spinosa, the only species; general on the sea-shore.

BIBL. Thompson, *Zool. Illustr.* p. 98; Johnston, *Brit. Zooph.* p. 370.

VESICULARIADÆ.—A family of Infundibulate Ctenostomatous Polyzoa.

Char. Polypidom plant-like, horny, tubular; cells free, deciduous, the ends flexible and invertile. Genera:

1. *Serialaria* (*Amathia*). Shoots slender, filiform, erect, branched; cells tubular, adherent, uniserial and unilateral, rows interrupted by blank intervals; tentacles eight.

2. *Vesicularia.* Shoots branched, jointed; cells oval, distinct, uniserial and unilateral; eight tentacles and a gizzard.

3. *Valkeria.* Variously branched; cells oval, irregularly clustered; eight tentacles, no gizzard.

4. *Mimosella.* Variously branched; cells ovate, in two rows, opposite, jointed at the base; eight tentacles and a gizzard.

5. *Arenella.* Filiform, creeping, nearly simple; cells large, solitary, scattered, in one row, slightly contracted at the top, curved; twenty to twenty-four tentacles, and a small gizzard.

6. *Nolella.* Cells erect, subcylindrical, crowded on tubes which form an undefined encrusting mat; tentacles eighteen.

7. *Bowerbankia* (Pl. 43. fig. 19). Matted and creeping, or erect and irregularly branched; cells tubular, densely clustered; tentacles eight to ten, and a strong gizzard.

8. *Farrella.* As *Bowerbankia*, but tentacles twelve to thirty, and no gizzard.

9. *Anguinella.* Branched palmately, one tube springing from another, largely composed of mud; animals with twelve tentacles and no gizzard.

BIBL. Johnston, *Brit. Zooph.* p. 367; Gosse, *Mar. Zool.* ii. p. 19.

VESPA, Linn.—*Vespa vulgaris*, the wasp, and *V. crabro*, the hornet, are readily accessible insects for the examination of the sting (STING).

VESSELS OF PLANTS.—This name was

applied by the earlier observers to various elongated tubular structures of vegetable tissues, from an idea that they corresponded with the vessels of animals; and the name is still retained. The *spiral, annular,* &c. vessels are described under SPIRAL STRUCTURES. The term *vessel* is now generally contrasted with DUCT, to indicate a single long tubular cell, or row of confluent elongated cells, with *spiral* secondary deposits upon their walls, in contradistinction to a canal formed of a row of cells with *pitted* secondary deposits, applied end to end and confluent. The LATICIFEROUS tubes are sometimes called laticiferous or milk vessels.

VIBRIO, Müll.—A genus forming the type of the family VIBRIONIA, Infusoria of authors, but part of which we have provisionally placed in the Oscillatoriaceæ (Confervoid Algæ).

Char. Filiform, more or less distinctly jointed from imperfect division; movement undulatory, like that of a serpent.

These filamentous bodies are extremely minute; their simple structure is best seen when they are dried.

1. *V. subtilis* (Pl. 3. fig. 18). Filaments colourless, elongate, hyaline, straight, distinctly jointed, motile vibrations very slight and not perceptibly altering their form. Aquatic, in pools; length reaching 1-430''; breadth 1-24000''. Probably an *Oscillatoria.*

2. *V. rugula* (Pl. 3. fig. 19). Filaments hyaline, distinctly jointed, very tortuous when in motion. In decomposing infusions; breadth 1-12000''.

3. *V. prolifer* (Pl. 3. fig. 20). Filaments short, hyaline, distinctly jointed, tortuous in their slow motion. In decomposing infusions; length 1-9200 to 1-1150''; breadth 1-9200''.

4. *V. bacillus* (Pl. 3. fig. 21). Filaments elongate, hyaline, joints sometimes distinct only after drying, flexuous in their slow motion; length 1-288''; breadth 1-1700''

Two or three other species; one of them, *V. ambiguus,* is branched: these are still more evidently algæ.

BIBL. Ehrenberg, *Infus.* p. 77; Dujardin, *Infus.* p. 216.

VIBRIONIA.—A family of Infusoria, according to the classifications of Ehrenberg and Dujardin, but which appear, at all events in part, to be Algæ (OSCILLATORIACEÆ).

Char. Active, filiform, extremely minute, colourless, jointed bodies, of obscure organization, and without visible locomotive organs (except *Bacterium?*); straight, or spirally coiled, multiplied by division at the joints.

These organisms form some of the most minute which the microscopist is called upon to examine; and it is with the greatest difficulty that their structure can be made out. But although, in the ordinary method of examination, structure is invisible, yet by allowing them to dry spontaneously on a slide, or adding solution of iodine to them in the wet state or when dried, it can be distinctly seen that they are composed of minute joints, resembling very minute, colourless, Oscillatoriaceous Confervæ. When treated with potash, they are unacted upon, although the minute monads with which they are invariably accompanied are burst and dissolved. Nor have we succeeded in colouring them by Millon's or Pettenkofer's test, although their minute size is such that the magnifying power used to render them visible would so dilute the colour, by diffusing it over a large surface, that it is difficult to speak positively upon this point. They are propagated by the formation of new joints, and subsequent separation at one of the articulations. They are almost invariably the first organisms found in decaying and putrefying organic matters, especially animal. When treated with iodine and then sulphuric acid, their jointed structure is rendered very distinct; and it appears that they are composed of two parts, an outer portion which seems pale or but slightly coloured, and an inner which becomes very dark; but the tints cannot be distinguished with certainty: they appear purplish or reddish-purple brown, quite different from the surrounding infusoria when thus treated.

M. Pineau believes that animal matter is directly transformed into Infusoria and Algæ; but when tests are used in the proper manner, this view is rendered altogether improbable.

Probably some of the *Vibriones* are but the earlier stages of other algæ, but what these algæ are is unknown.

The motion of these minute bodies would seem to indicate that some are furnished with cilia; but in others it is evidently produced by general contractility. M. Dujardin thinks, however, that he has sometimes seen a flagelliform filament analogous to that of the Monadina, or rather undulating helically ; and Ehrenberg describes a cilium or flagelliform filament in one *Bacterium.* Our own repeated observations, made in such a manner (see CILIA) as will detect cilia with ease when present, or at least in any part where they have hitherto been found certainly, have failed to detect them in the Vibrionia (excluding *Bacterium,* which is doubtfully referred to this family).

We have included the genera *Bacterium* and *Vibrio* among the OSCILLATORIACEÆ, but the relations are still somewhat obscure, and this is even more the case with *Spirillum* and the rest, which are excluded there. We think it advisable, therefore, to add here a table of the genera according to the views of those who regard them as Infusoria, or at all events as a distinct family. More details are given under the respective heads.

Filament { Inflexible.................1. *Bacterium.*
straight. { Flexible like a serpent.......2. *Vibrio.*

Filament { Spiral helical.............3. *Spirillum*
spiral. { 　　　　　　　　　　(*Spirochæta*).
{ Spiral flat, like a watch-spring 4. *Spirodiscus.*

They are best preserved by allowing them to dry spontaneously on the slide.

For *Vibrio tritici* see ANGUILLULA *tritici.*

BIBL. Ehrenberg, *Infus.* p. 73 ; Dujardin, *Infus.* p. 209.

VILLI.—These are minute folds or prolongations of the mucous membrane of the small intestines. They are most numerous in the jejunum and ilium ; in the former conical and flattened, sometimes plate-like, cylindrical, club-shaped or filiform ; whilst in the latter they are broader and flattened.

The villi form solid processes of the mucous membrane, consisting of areolar tissue without elastic elements, but abounding in roundish nuclei ; containing also bloodvessels, lacteals, and unstriated muscular fibres.

Their surface is covered with a basement membrane, and a single layer of cylindrical epithelial cells.

The villi are exceedingly vascular, and form beautiful microscopic objects when injected ; exhibiting a network of capillaries with rounded or elongate meshes.

Fig. 801.　　　　　　　　Fig. 802.

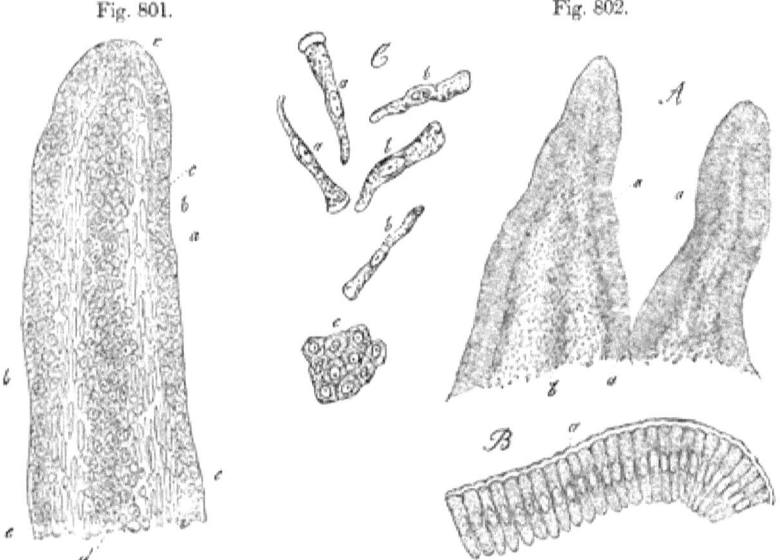

Fig. 801. Intestinal villus of a kitten, free from epithelium, and after treatment with acetic acid : *a,* boundary of villus ; *b,* subjacent nuclei ; *c,* nuclei of the muscular fibres ; *d,* roundish nuclei in the middle of the villus. Magnified 350 diameters.

Fig. 802. *A,* magnified 75 diameters. Two villi with their epithelium, from a rabbit : *a,* epithelium ; *b,* parenchyma. *B,* magnified 300 diameters. A row of detached epithelial cells. *a,* membrane separated by water. *C,* magnified 350 diameters. Detached epithelial cells. *a* with, *b* without the separated membrane ; *c,* surface view of some epithelial cells.

Fig. 803.

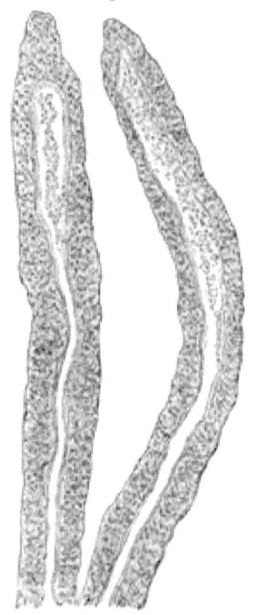

Fig. 804.

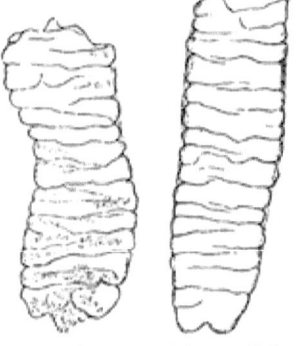

Fig. 803. Two villi from a calf without epithelium, and containing each a lacteal vessel; after treatment with dilute solution of soda. Magnified 350 diameters.

Fig. 804. Two contracted villi, from a cat. Magnified 60 diameters.

Each villus contains a lacteal, the origin of which commences either in a single cœcal dilatation, or in a network of branches.

The muscular fibres form a thin layer, not very distinct in man, surrounding the lacteals, and capable of greatly contracting or shortening the villi.

The epithelial cells are intimately connected with each other, but easily detached from the villi, often in groups or rows. When acted upon by water, the cell-membrane at the surface is separated, leaving a clear space between the granular cell-contents and the former.

BIBL. Kölliker, *Mikrosk. Anat.* ii.

VINCA, L.—The generic name of the garden plants called *Periwinkles*; interesting to microscopists on account of the striated liber-fibres (Pl. 39. fig. 30). (See SPIRAL STRUCTURES, p. 641.)

VINE-FUNGUS. — The vine-mildew, *Oidium Tuckeri*, Berk., which has in recent years caused such extensive destruction, has formed a subject of investigation for most of the principal mycologists; and, notwithstanding that its natural history is not yet wholly cleared up, many interesting points have been discovered. As it ordinarily appears, it forms a white and very delicate cottony layer upon the leaves, young shoots, and fruit of the vine, soon causing a production of brown spots upon the green structures, and subsequently a hardening and a destruction of the vitality of the surface. Under the microscope, the white substance is seen to be composed of delicate ramified filaments, creeping horizontally over the surface, and, when the plant is much developed, forming a dense interlacement. The horizontal filaments exhibit few septa, these occurring at the points of branching, and they do not penetrate into the interior of the epidermal layer; here and there, however, they are found fixed to the epidermis by a more or less developed organ of attachment, consisting of a disk or lobed expansion (comparable roughly to the so-called "root" of some of the Fucoid Algæ), which adheres firmly to the cuticle, and, when removed, leaves a brownish scar behind. The destructive effect of the Fungus seems to arise from its arresting the development of the epidermis, by binding its structures together, and excluding the surface from the influence of the air, since when young berries are invaded, the internal development proceeds, and, the sphacelated epidermis preventing the natural expansion, the grapes burst and rot. [In this case, species of *Botrytis*, &c. appear upon the decomposing pulp, as on all similar substances; and these must be distingui-hed from the proper mildew.] When full-grown leaves are affected to a moderate extent, the vitality is often only partially affected, causing a laxity of the tissue, and more or less fading of the green colour, without inevitable decay.

When the mildew is observed with a low magnifier, its surface exhibits a mealy appearance, arising from minute bead-like or pearly shining bodies of oval form; and the application of sufficient power shows that the horizontal filaments bear numerous erect branches or pedicels, consisting of short-jointed filaments (Pl. 20. fig. 8), the terminal cells of which (or the two last) are elliptical and expanded. These terminal cells are soon matured and then fall off; vast numbers of them are produced, and are found lying upon the surface among the creeping filaments, where they quickly germinate (Pl. 20. fig. 9), and produce new ramifications of mycelium. The fungus, as thus described, constitutes the *Oidium* proper, and the deciduous terminal cells form the so-called *spores*. But the history of the development of the mildew does not cease here.

In the first place, the detached 'spores' do not always produce a filament as represented in fig. 9; some of them present, while still attached, a kind of segmentation of the protoplasmic contents (fig. 10), and detached examples are found filled with minute 'sporules' of elongated-elliptical form. These minute 'sporules' are either discharged by a dehiscence of the 'spore' (fig. 11), and then germinate, or sometimes they germinate *in situ*, and send out slender filaments through the walls of the spore. We have found also that the large filaments produced by the simple large 'spore' (fig. 9), do not always at once form a regular mycelium, but sometimes give rise to slender pedicels, terminating in a point bearing minute solitary corpuscles of about the size and form of the 'sporules' above described, and resembling the *spermatia* of many of the higher Fungi.

In addition to this, we have sometimes observed those 'spores' which produce the 'sporules' in their interior, with their outer membrane finely punctate; and in very rare cases this form of fruit was not composed of a single terminal cell, but presented indications of cross septa, as if two or more cells of the summit of the pedicel were confluent into one sac; here the

punctation of the surface was very strongly marked.

Thus far we depend upon our own observations, but Mohl, Tulasne, and others describe a still more highly-developed fruit than that last noticed: they have found the terminal body, producing 'sporules,' with a distinct cellular coat (Pl. 20. fig. 12), from which the sporules are discharged by a terminal dehiscence. Mohl found this body, very rarely, of spherical form. We have never seen this cellular coat; in the cases we have met with, the coat was certainly only punctate or tubercular; probably the structure was not mature, nevertheless the 'sporules' were distinctly evident.

These phænomena, exhibited by the Vine-fungus, clearly agree with those exhibited by the *Oidia* always accompanying certain ERYSIPHÆ, as described under that article; and therefore most of the authors who have written on this subject conclude that the Vine-fungus is really an *Erysiphe*, of which the perfect, ascophorous fruit has not yet been discovered. A comparison of the figures marked 12 (Pl. 20), from the Vine-, copied from Mohl, with those of the Hop-*Erysiphe*, fig. 14, will show the agreement of structure between the two plants.

It remains only to add a few remarks as to the interpretation or nomenclature of the different organs. Mohl, Tulasne, &c. have denominated the simple 'spores' above described (figs. 8, 9) *conidia*; but as we have stated, the cells are convertible into what may be called *sporanges*, producing 'sporules' (or true spores) without alteration of structure. When their walls become cellular (fig. 12), the sporangial character is more decided; but as the *Erysiphæ* produce a more perfect *sporange*, in which *asci* are developed, the name of *pycnidia* is applied to them. This fruit it was which gave rise to the establishment of a supposed distinct genus, by Cesati, under the name of *Ampelomyces*; while Ehrenberg, also regarding it as a distinct plant, made it the type of a genus called *Cicinobolus*, on account of the peculiar tendril-like extrusion of the 'sporules' (fig. 12 s). Mohl distinguishes it as the *Cicinobolus*-fruit, which he, like Tulasne, finds constantly associated with other (undoubted) *Erysiphæ* (fig. 14), in very slightly different and equally irregular forms.

There can be no doubt whatever, in the minds of those who have watched the development and progress of the Vine-fungus, that it is the cause and not a consequence of the 'murrain;' still there are various curious circumstances connected with it not at all understood. It is probable that peculiar atmospheric conditions induce predisposing states of the plants; but the phænomena are enigmatical: we have had it completely covering a vine in a small greenhouse, destroying all the fruit one year; and although no precautions were taken (as it was desired to study the disease), no sign of mildew appeared there the next year; while on an out-door trellis, a few yards off, the disease reappeared in a slight form in the second season. The application of sulphur appears to arrest the growth.

BIBL. Berkeley, *Gardener's Chron.* 1847, no. 48, &c.; *Journ. Hort. Soc.* vi. p. 284, ix. p. 61; Mohl, *Botan. Zeit.* x. p. 9, xi. p. 585, xii. p. 137 (translated, *Journ. Hort. Soc.* vii. p. 132, ix. pp. 1 & 64), and *Bibl.* therein; Montagne, *Bull. Soc. Centr. Agric.* 2 sér. v.; *Journ. Hort. Soc.* ix. p. 112; Amici, *Atti dell' Accad. de' Georgofili,* xxx. (transl. *Journ. Hort. Soc.* viii. p. 231; Savi, *ibid.* 241); Tulasne, *Bot. Zeit.* xi. p. 257 (1853); *Comptes Rendus,* xxxvii. (Oct. 1853); Visiani and Zanardini, *Atti Instit. Veneto, &c.* 2 ser. iv.; Ehrenberg, *Bot. Zeit.* xi. p. 16; Cesati, Klotzsch.*Herb. Viv. Myc. Cent.*xvii.no.1609 b; *Bot. Zeit.* x. p. 301 (1852); Leveillé, *Revue horticole* (June 1851).

VINEGAR, EELS IN. See ANGUILLULA.

VINEGAR-PLANT.—Under this name is known a remarkable vegetable production formed in fluids rich in sugar, when undergoing fermentation at ordinary temperatures and conversion into vinegar. As ordinarily met with, it forms a tough gelatinous mass floating on the surface of the liquid, its shape (superficially) defined by that of the vessel in which it is contained, extending itself so as to occupy the whole surface even in very large pans,—its depth or thickness depending on its age and the amount of nutriment contained in the liquid. The gelatinous substance decreases in density from above downwards, the lower part being very lax and flocculent, the inferior surface being in a state of continuous development. The general mass, however, displays remarkable tenacity, which, together with its lubricity, renders it difficult to tear; but if the lower surface is examined, it is found possible to strip off layer after layer, each a few lines thick, to an extent depending on conditions of growth, the lower, less dense portion being thus distinctly stratified.

When portions are placed beneath the microscope very varied forms of structure are discovered in the interior. The general mass of jelly appears structureless, as if formed by some exudation, or solution of the organized portion; but the mode of origin of this jelly is not yet ascertained. Imbedded in the jelly are cellular structures, polymorphous indeed, but exhibiting transitions which render it impossible to regard them as of distinct origin. In the middle portion often occur innumerable isolated masses of short rows of cells, resembling the cells of YEAST when coherent, except that they are generally elliptical; some of them have short cylindrical joints; others short cylindrical portions arising from long tubular filaments, and terminating in elliptical cells, so as to resemble exactly OIDIUM. The diameter of all these structures is most variable, from 1-4000 to 1-8000″. In the upper part, the elongated branched filaments more abound, the length of the internodes and the diameter of the tubes still varying extremely. At the lower, laxer surface, the cellular structures are accompanied by less of the tough gelatinous matrix. The lamination of the lower growing surface is very curious, but perhaps may be accounted for by supposing that the inferior growing surface of the mass, which is certainly the mycelium of a fungus, periodically produces a crop of *conidia*, which become detached and fall into the body of the liquid on which the mass floats; there quickly germinating, they form a new entangled mass of filaments and chaplets of cells, which then acquires its gelatinous consistence, and, buoyed up by the liquid, applies itself against the lower surface of the parent-mass, with which it adheres, more or less, on account of the gelatinous condition. In the upper part of old and thick masses, the layers become inseparable—probably in some measure from the pressure of the floating force from below, together with the condensation arising from the evaporation of the liquid of the jelly at the upper surface.

When a vinegar-plant is left upon the solution after the saccharine matter is exhausted, we find it always display, after a certain time, patches of the ordinary fructification of PENICILLIUM *glaucum* (fig. 805), as stated by Turpin and others, forming green, blue, and yellow "mould" upon the surface, and imbedded in the upper strata, in which also heaps of the spores occur; the vinegar sometimes ultimately suffers more or less decomposition, so that the common "mother" of vinegar, which by its growth destroys the acidity, appears to be another condition of this same organism. In some cases where we kept an exhausted liquid in the dark for some months, the acidity of the vinegar disappeared, the gelatinous layer became greatly condensed, and assumed a bright crimson tint, and remained as a dull-red membranous film, somewhat like a smear of blood when dried upon paper.

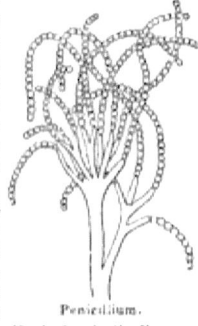

Fig. 805.

Penicillium.

Head of a fertile filament bearing strings of spores.

Magnified 250 diameters.

From the above observations it would appear that the vinegar-plant consists of the mycelium of *Penicillium glaucum*, vegetating actively and increasing also by crops of *conidia* or *gemmæ*. This opinion is entertained by Turpin, Berkeley, and other observers; and the various genera and species founded on the different forms of structure occurring in it cannot be entertained : among these are *Ulvina*, Kütz., and species of *Hygrocrocis*, *Leptomitus*, &c. But the moniliform growth is at the same time scarcely distinguishable from the Yeast plant by any satisfactory characters; and repeated observations strongly impress us with the idea, that these objects are all referable to one species,—the vinegar-plant being the form of vegetative growth taking place at low or ordinary temperatures in highly saccharine liquids, while the true Yeast plant or *Torula* is formed in the more rapid fermentation taking place at more elevated temperatures. Another circumstance, mentioned under PENICILLIUM, is that we have found stale beer-grounds, kept at a rather low temperature, always ultimately acquire a gelatinous crust, on which *Penicillium*-fruit becomes developed.

In connexion with this subject may be mentioned the objects called *Cryptococcus glutinis*, Fres., and the "blood on bread," which appear nearly related to the red-coloured condition of the vinegar-plant above mentioned. These are possibly merely forms of the same plant; indeed we have observed, on some flour paste partially covered with *Penicillium glaucum*, small circular patches of a crimson tint, which under the microscope were found to consist wholly of minute elliptical bodies, generally exhibiting two internal granules or "nuclei," and exactly resembling the articulations of some of the moniliform structures of the vinegarplant, which readily separate into their component cells. All these phænomena require further investigation, to which long-continued and constant observation must be applied in order to ascertain with certainty the relation the different objects bear to each other. It is a kind of research occupying much time, and demanding great care and patience, but calculated to repay the trouble far better than the amassing of isolated characters of forms seen at different periods and under special conditions. Further particulars concerning various points treated in this article will be found under the heads FERMENTATION, OIDIUM, PENICILLIUM, TORULA, and YEAST.

BIBL. Turpin, *Mém. de l'Institut*, xvii. p. 135; Berkeley, *Journ. Hort. Soc.* iii. p. 91; Lindley's *Medic. & Econ. Bot.* p. 17 ; Fresenius, *Beitr. z. Mycol.* Heft ii. p. 77.

VIRGULINA, D'Orb.—A genus of Foraminifera, of the order Enallostegia, and family Polymorphinidæ.

Char. Shell free, inequilateral, vitreous, elongate, compressed; *chambers* few, slightly embracing, more on one side than the other, alternate in two nearly regular rows; *orifice* comma-like and decurrent, at the upper part of the last chamber.

No British species.

BIBL. That of the order.

VISCUM, Linn.—A genus of Loranthaceæ (Dicotyledons).

V. album is the misletoe, alluded to under EMBRYO-SAC, LIBER, and OVULE.

VITREOUS HUMOUR or body. See EYE (p. 278).

VITTÆ of the valves of the Diatomaceæ.—These are internal projections or inflections of the valves, forming imperfect septa; they appear as dark lines, visible under ordinary illumination.

VITTÆ OF FRUITS. See SECRETING ORGANS of Plants.

VITTARIEÆ.—A subfamily of Polypodioid Ferns in which the sori are naked and immersed in the margin of the leaf, which resembles an indusium. The capsules are pedunculate. Exotic.

VOLUTELLA, Fr.—A genus of Stilbacei (Hyphomycetous Fungi), comprising several species of parasites which have been variously distributed. The plants consist of minute fleshy papillæ (*stromata*) of cellular structure, the surface of which is clothed with elliptic, oblong, or fusiform stylospores, from between which project long jointed hairs (fig. 806) traversing the

Fig. 806.

Volutella buxi.
Magnified 20 diameters.

stroma. It may be desirable to give the synonymy of these plants according to Berkeley and Broome.

1. *V. ciliata*, Fr. (*Psilonia rosea*, Br. Fl.). Whitish or rosy; on potatoes.

2. *V. buxi*, Berk. and Br. (*Fusisporium buxi*, Br. Fl., and *Chætostroma buxi*, Corda). White; on dry box leaves (fig. 806).

3. *V. setosa*, B. and Br. (*Psilonia setosa*, Br. Fl., *Ægerita setosa*, Greville). White, on wood and herbaceous stems.

4. *V. hyacinthorum*, B. and Br. (*Psil. hyacinthorum*, Br. Fl.). White, stipitate; on hyacinths grown in water.

5. *V. melaloma*, B. and Br. Orange, with black hairs; on sedges.

Bibl. Berk. *Brit. Flor.* ii. pt. 2. p. 352–3; *Ann. Nat. Hist.* 2 ser. v. p. 466, pl. 11. fig. 3; Greville, *Crypt. Fl.* pls. 102, & 268. fig. 2; Corda, *Icon. Fung.* ii. pl. 13. fig. 107; Fries, *Syst. Myc.* iii. p. 447.

VOLVOCINEÆ.—A family of microscopic organisms which, in agreement with the majority of recent writers on Algology, we have included among the Confervoid Algæ, although they have been included until lately among the Infusorial animalcules, among which they form one of Ehrenberg's families. The most striking general character of these objects, is their composition of individual elements which exhibit in their mature and most perfect stage of existence the characters of the transitory zoospores of the other Confervoids. The Volvocineæ may be characterized as plants composed of a number of permanently-active zoospore-like bodies associated together into families of definite form (a kind of "polypidom"), in which the members, connected or held together in various ways by cell-membranes, retain their distinct individuality for all physiological purposes of nutrition, growth, reproduction, &c., but represent only one being in relation to the surrounding objects. *Protococcus*, however, consists of only a single cell. The best-known and most beautiful example of this family is the genus *Volvox* (Pl. 3. fig. 24), consisting when mature of a spherical membranous sac, at the periphery of which, within the membrane, are arranged a large number of zoospore-like bodies (*gonidia*), each provided with a pair of cilia, which pass out through the enveloping membrane, collectively forming a coating all over the external surface, and by their vibration causing a rotatory motion of the entire globe. The foreign genus STEPHANOSPHÆRA, Cohn, differs principally from *Volvox* in the fact that the ciliated gonidia are only eight in number, and are placed in a circle at the equator of the spherical sac; while PANDORINA, which appears to be identical with *Eudorina*, has an ellipsoidal sac, with either sixteen or thirty-two gonidia, arranged in parallel equatorial rows at the periphery. GONIUM is very distinct in form, and resembles *Volvox* only in the essential character of the family above laid down. It is composed of a group of usually sixteen gonidia, which are not enclosed in a common sac, but each possesses a thick gelatinous coat or membrane (appearing like a transparent limb or border to the green body, as in *Glæocapsa*, *Coccochloris*, &c.), and the individuals cohere together by a few points of the surface of this special coat or "cell-membrane" (Pl. 3. fig. 11). Ehrenberg's representation of a plate-like continuous coat is erroneous; our drawing from nature exactly agrees with the older figures, and Cohn's (see GONIUM). The relations of the doubtful genera *Syncrypta*, *Uroglena*, and *Sphærosira* are treated under the article VOLVOX. It may be observed here that there is certainly a close resemblance between the objects termed *Chlamidomonas* and *Gyges*, and the constituent individuals of the "family-stocks" of *Volvox*, &c., and the nature of the latter is best comprehended by considering them as representatives of the former. Hence PROTOCOCCUS (including *Hæmatococcus*), to which these solitary forms appear to be referable, is now referred by most authors to Volvocineæ, of which it constitutes the simplest form.

The modes of reproduction of the Volvocineæ, both vegetative and by spores, are fully described under PANDORINA, VOLVOX, and GONIUM; hence it is unnecessary to dwell on these points here.

It might be useful to observers to give the characters of all the above genera as laid down in Ehrenberg's work, in spite of our disbelief in their validity; but in so doing it would be necessary to describe them from his drawings, as his written characters are altogether useless, from being founded on false analogies. The red eye-spot is certainly found in *Gonium*, and probably in all; we doubt the statements about a *single* "proboscis" (vibratile cilium); and the so-called tail, a posterior prolongation of the body, is an obscure character. The tabular analysis which Ehrenberg gives would not enable any one to distinguish the forms without the assistance of plates. We have therefore prepared a new table, founded on his characters and drawings, marking those genera which appear to us really distinct.

Char. Permanently active zoospore-like bodies, ciliated (except *Gyges*), surrounded by a gelatinous coat (like COCCOCHLORIS), solitary, or combined in definite groups, with or without a common enveloping membrane. Individuals pyriform, or with the body prolonged posteriorly.

Solitary.
Without cilia............... *Gyges.*
With a pair of cilia .... { PROTOCOCCUS (*Chlamidomonas*).
Grouped.
Forming a square layer, goni- } GONIUM.
dia with two cilia ....
Forming a spherical body.
  Cilium solitary.
    With a "tail" .... *Uroglena**.
    Without a "tail."
      Without an eye-spot.
        With special coats.... *Syncrypta**.
      With an eye-spot.
        Gonidia dividing into } *Sphærosira**.
        clusters ....
  Cilia two.
    Without an eye-spot ... *Synura**.
    With an eye-spot.
  Common envelope spherical.
    Gonidia numerous, all } VOLVOX.
    over the periphery....
    Gonidia eight, in a circle } STEPHANOSPHÆRA.
    at the equator ......
  Common envelope ellipsoidal. Gonidia sixteen or thirty-two.

* Probably stages of development of VOLVOX or PANDORINA.

The names in small capitals are well-established genera.

BIBL. See the genera.

VOLVOX, L.—A genus of Volvocineæ (Confervoid Algæ), of which only one spe-cies, *V. globator* (Pl. 3. fig. 24), seems satis-factorily established. This organism, occur-ring not uncommonly and often in great abundance in clear pools on open commons, &c., appears to the naked eye as a minute pale-green globule gently moving about in the water; its dimensions variable, but gene-rally about 1·50″ when full-grown. When placed under a low magnifying power, it is found to be a spherical membranous sac, studded all over with green points, the en-tire body rolling over in the water with a motion which is readily discerned to be caused by innumerable cilia arranged upon the surface of the globe. In the interior of the sac are generally seen dense globes, in summer mostly of a green colour (Pl. 3. fig. 24): sometimes the cavity is wholly filled up by a number of membranous sacs exactly resembling the parent, but de-formed by mutual pressure (Pl. 3. fig. 25); and inside these are seen smaller green bodies, as in the former case. The parent envelope is also flexible, yielding to pressure and recovering its form, and in full-grown specimens is generally ruptured at one point, where the internal bodies escape, so that the number varies; usually, however, the original number is eight.

The application of higher powers is requi-site to discover the intimate structure of *Volvox*, which, by the researches of Wil-liamson and Busk, most of whose observa-tions we have verified, has been pretty clearly made out. The outer envelope con-sists of a layer of cell-membrane, in all probability composed of a modification of cellulose, although we have never succeeded in producing more than a faint purple tinge with sulphuric acid and iodine. By the application of a sufficient magnifying power, the green corpuscles at the periphery are found to consist of zoospore-like bodies (*go-nidia*) (Pl. 3. fig. 28), which are seated inside the membranous envelope, each sending out its pair of vibratile cilia (figs. 24–30) through separate orifices in the external coat. The same investigation will reveal that the green gonidia have radiating processes ex-tending from their sides, and running from the different centres to meet each other in the light interspace, forming thus a kind of delicate network beneath the membrane. The gonidia are pyriform, have a transpa-rent anterior end bearing a pair of cilia, and contain a reddish-brown eye-spot and a contractile vacuole, thus exactly resembling those of *Gonium*, and indeed the zoospores of Confervoids generally. The radiating processes resemble those found in particular stages of Protococcus *pluvialis*, running through the gelatinous coat, and probably may be compared with the radiating filaments proceeding from the nucleus of Spirogyra (Pl. 5. fig. 26). There is somewhat more difficulty in determining the nature of the structure in which the gonidia are enclosed. There is a layer of soft consistence of some thickness within the external membrane; the green gonidia are wholly imbedded in this, and their radiating processes and cilia traverse the substance of it. We are inclined to believe that this presents a firm membranous layer again at the internal surface, looking toward the general cavity of the sphere. The nature of the soft layer has been the subject of discussion; we believe Busk's view to be correct, that it is not formed by the collocation of distinct membranous cells, like those of ordinary parenchymatous structures, but by the close juxtaposition of gelatinous envelopes of the individual green bodies, resembling those of *Coccochloris, Glæocapsa*, &c. We could never detect a true line of demarcation halfway between neighbouring gonidia: an appearance is indeed sometimes presented in preparations kept in chloride of calcium, which might lead to an error on this point; for the outer membrane is then sometimes swollen into papillæ opposite each corpuscle (Pl. 3. fig. 30), the furrows between which, in certain foci, give the appearance of a septum running round each corpuscle (Pl. 3. fig. 29). Similar preparations also often show the gonidium contracted and leaving an empty ring round it, separating it from the gelatinous coat, which runs undistinguishably into those of the neighbouring gonidia. But the strongest fact we have observed, is that by the application of solution of potash, the substance surrounding the gonidia is so entirely dissolved, that the oily substance extracted from the green bodies will run freely about beneath the external membrane (apparently confined internally by another film), in sheets extending over considerable segments of the sphere, yet leaving the gonidia and their radiating processes intact, or at least only shrunk and discoloured. If a true cell-membrane existed around each gonidium, forming septa dividing them, the above phænomenon could not display itself, since the potash would not so dissolve the structures.

The modes of reproduction of *Volvox* have recently been entirely elucidated. In certain conditions, some of the gonidia appear larger than the rest, and as if undergoing division (Pl. 3. fig. 28); it is possible that some of the gonidia, or of such grouped gonidia, escape into the cavity, and there become developed into the large green bodies (Pl. 3. fig. 24), which are rudimentary globes; but Williamson believes these are detached in an earlier stage: perhaps both modes of development take place. Forms with the grouped gonidia (Pl. 3. fig. 29) would appear to represent Ehrenberg's *Sphærosira*. Ehrenberg's genus *Uroglena* again would seem to be a *Volvox* either imperfectly developed or decaying.

The deep-green bodies (Pl. 3. fig. 24) seen in the cavity of the spheres, are young *Volvoces*, and in an early stage they appear as spherical cells filled with granular green substance; the green substance divides by segmentation (Pl. 3. figs. 31, 32) until it forms a group of gonidia, on each of which a pair of cilia appears; the enclosing membrane expands, and they follow it and remove apart, until they form a perfect *Volvox*-sphere, studded with the gonidia. As above mentioned, a second generation is sometimes met with in the parent-sphere (Pl. 3. fig. 25). We are uncertain whether to regard the objects represented in Pl. 3. fig. 14, as the young of *Volvox*; they would seemingly equally represent the genus *Pandorina, Syncrypta*, or *Eudorina*, Ehr.

Volvox, examined in autumn and early winter, often exhibits either the green bodies with a thick coat (Pl. 3. fig. 33), or the inner globes are of an orange colour (Pl. 3. figs. 26 & 34), which appear to be successive stages of development of a *resting-spore*. When mature, this possesses at least two coats, one immediately surrounding the granular contents, another at some distance outside the former, transparent, colourless, and as it were glassy and brittle, breaking with sharp-angled cracks when pressed (Pl. 3. figs. 34 & 35). We cannot detect any intermediate substance or layer, which would be required to complete the analogy with the resting-spore of Spirogyra, as described by Pringsheim (Pl. 5. fig. 21); perhaps it does not exist in either case. Sometimes the outer coat of the enclosed yellow globes is tuberculated or covered with conical elevations (Pl. 3. fig. 36). The form with the smooth yellow resting-spores (Pl. 3. figs. 26 & 34) represents Ehrenberg's *Volvox aureus*, and the form with the spines (Pl. 3, fig. 36) his *V. stellatus*. The development of the resting-spores of *Volvox* has been fully described by Cohn, and presents an essential resemblance to the process in PANDORINA and STEPHANOSPHÆRA. A portion of the gonidia become enclosed in special cyst-like coats; and their contents are then converted into spermatozoids, which break out and move actively in the interior of the spherical common envelope. These bodies fertilize other gonidia, which take on the function of spore-cells; and after their impregnation the latter acquire the firm coats and yellow contents characteristic of the resting-spores. They are set free at first into the common cavity of the spherical envelope.

A doubt remains as to the nature of the object described as *Synura Urella*; it may belong here, or, not improbably, to the genus *Urella* (Pl. 25. fig. 18), which itself may be no more than a complex form of the PROTOCOCCUS or *Chlamidomonas* (Pl. 3. fig. 2; Pl. 23. fig. 30), which doubtless includes also *Chlorogonium* (Pl. 23. fig. 31), *Cryptoglena* (Pl. 23. fig. 35), and *Gyges* (Pl. 41. fig. 14), if not more supposed Infusorial animalcules.

When a pool contains *Volvox*, the individuals are generally abundant, and may be readily seen by the naked eye, as pale-green globules, in a phial of water held up to the light; but they are kept with difficulty, being devoured by ROTATORIA, &c. The cilia are best seen by drying them and wetting again, or by applying iodine. The gonidia are a good deal altered by chloride of calcium.

BIBL. Ehrenberg, *Infus.*; Pritchard, *Infus.*; Williamson, *Trans. Phil. Soc. Manchester*, vol. ix.; *Trans. Micr. Soc.* 2 ser. i. p. 45 (1853); Busk, *ibid.* p. 31; Cohn, *Ann. des Sc. Nat.* 4 sér. v. p. 323; *Ann. Nat. Hist.* 2 ser. xix. p. 187.

VORTICELLA, Linn.—A genus of Infusoria, of the family *Vorticellina*.

Char. Body campanulate, with an anterior ring of cilia, stalked; stalk simple, spirally contractile.

These interesting Infusoria are very commonly met with in decomposing vegetable infusions, as of hay, portions of dead flowers, &c. Their curious metamorphoses and modes of reproduction are noticed under INFUSORIA.

Ehrenberg describes nine species.

1. *V. nebulifera* (Pl. 25. fig. 21). Body conico-campanulate, colourless; anterior margin dilated; body without rings when contracted. Length of body without the stalk 1-576 to 1-288".

2. *V. microstoma* (Pl. 25. fig. 26, body with gemmæ). Body ovate, narrowed at the ends, greenish white; anterior margin not dilated, nor body ringed when contracted. Length of body 1-2000 to 1-250".

3. *V. convallaria*. Body ovato-conical, whitish hyaline, annulate; expanded anterior margin slightly prominent. Length of body 1-430 to 1-240".

Dujardin unites the genera *Carchesium* and *Zoothamnium* to his genus *Vorticella*.

BIBL. Ehrenberg, *Infus.* p. 269; Dujardin *Infus.* p. 546; Stein, *Infus.*, *passim*; Lachmann, *Ann. Nat. Hist.* 1857. xix.

VORTICELLINA.—A family of Infusoria.

Char. Isolated and free, or fixed and aggregate; alimentary canal with two orifices, separate, but in the same groove carapace none.

The characters are very vague, and the family an unnatural one. The genera *Stentor*, *Trichodina* and *Urocentrum* have little affinity with the others. In the true genera, the bodies are stalked, the stalk usually branched, and the cilia form a ring at the anterior end of the body.

Genera:

```
Stalk absent.
  Tail none.
    Body ciliated .... .......... 1. Stentor.
    Body smooth, cilia anterior.... 2. Trichodina.
  Tail present ................. 3. Urocentrum.
Stalk present.
  Bodies all uniform.
    Stalk spirally flexible.
      Stalk simple ............ 4 Vorticella.
      Stalk branched .......... 5. Carchesium.
    Stalk inflexible ............ 6. Epistylis.
  Bodies of two shapes.
    Stalk inflexible ............ 7. Opercularia.
    Stalk spirally flexible ...... 8. Zoothamnium.
```

BIBL. Ehrenberg, *Infusoria*, p. 259.

VULVULINA, D'Orb.—A genus of Foraminifera, of the order Enallostegia, and family Textularidæ.

Char. Shell free, regular, equilateral, somewhat rugose, oval, compressed; *chambers* compressed, regularly alternate at all ages, on each side of the longitudinal axis, partly embracing, and forming two regular alternate lines; *orifice* single, at the upper part of the last chamber, a fissure parallel to the compression.

V. gramen (Pl. 18. fig. 39).

BIBL. That of the order.

3 B

W.

WASP. See VESPA.

WATER.—Under this head we might form a kind of index referring to a large proportion of the articles of which this volume is composed, since water, existing under different circumstances, forms one of the most fertile sources of microscopic objects; but as our space and plan do not admit of such an enumeration, we must be content to dwell shortly upon two of the most important questions in which the microscope is applied to the examination of the contents of water.

Ordinary examination of water.—Here it appears merely necessary to point out that the mode of examining the contents of samples of water, for the purpose of ascertaining the extent to which organic beings are contained in them, should be very different from that pursued by the microscopist who is engaged in collecting specimens. We make this remark in consequence of the gross misrepresentations which are sometimes made respecting the "animalcules" in water, carried to their most absurd extreme in the so-called "drop" of water shown by oxy-hydrogen microscopes, where we often see the field covered with larvæ of dragon-flies, of beetles, of gnats, &c., Entomostraca, and worms of different kinds, not only perceptible without a microscope, but in the case of the larvæ, perhaps really more than an inch long. Less violent exaggerations occur when water which appears cloudy is selected, allowed to stand for some time, and the *sediment* examined. Very false results must also be obtained when water is exposed to the air for any length of time before examination, since Infusoria and microscopic Algæ always appear in a short time, even in distilled water, when exposed to the atmosphere; and a rain-water butt will generally be found a very fertile source of microscopic objects. We regard the presence of most of those organisms which do not sufficiently affect the water to render its impurity discernible by the naked eye, as a matter of little consequence. Large quantities of Entomostraca, certain Rotatoria and Infusoria, and Oscillatoriaceous Algæ, generally very perceptibly clouding or colouring the water, of course indicate the presence of much decomposing organic matter in the water, which, however, reveals itself very clearly in a short time, when the water is kept, by a fœtid odour. The presence of green Confervoid Algæ is by no means a sure sign of impurity (properly so called) in water; for some will only grow in very clear and pure water, while many of them may be regarded as agents of purification. The presence of Zygnemaceæ, however, and Diatomaceæ is particularly objectionable, as they become very fœtid in decomposition, which generally takes place very soon when they are disturbed and injured. When large quantities of the minute Algæ appear in water, discolouring it over extensive surfaces, the microscope will enable us to detect the nature of the object producing the appearance, but will scarcely be requisite to prove the impurity of the water.

Coloration of Water.—Under this head we shall refer to those plants and animals which most commonly produce such appearances, premising that the commonest cases of coloration depend upon suspended mineral substances (mud), of different colours according to the soils washed by the water.

1. Producing a general *green* colour, or a thick film on the surface.—PROTOCOCCUS (*Chlamidomonas*, Ehr., *Diselmis*, Duj.), very common in the spring; and various Nostochaceous Algæ, as TRICHORMUS, CONIOPHYTUM, &c. (see NOSTOCHACEÆ; many with a bluish tinge); CLATHROCYSTIS (forming a granular verdigris-green layer), MICROHALOA, and various other PALMELLACEÆ; EUGLENA *viridis*, &c. The DESMIDIACEÆ form greenish patches at the bottom of water or on plants, as do certain OSCILLATORIACEÆ.

2. Producing a *red* colour in fresh water.—ASTASIA *hæmatodes*, Ehr., species of DAPHNIA. TUBIFEX produces a red colour on the mud in shallow water. Red forms of species of PROTOCOCCUS (see also RED SNOW).—In salt water, DISELMIS *Dunalii*, Duj.; TRICHODESMIUM.

3. A brown cloudy appearance often appears in masses near the source of small springs of water flowing out of blue clay, or in pools on peat-bogs. This mostly consists of peroxide of iron; but sometimes a similar brown appearance is produced in pools by collections of amorphous granular decaying organic matter, in which occur great abundance of certain OSCILLATORIÆ, DIATOMACEÆ, INFUSORIA, and ROTATORIA. The obscure mycelioid structure called by Kützing LEPTOTHRIX *ochracea* produces a yellowish-brown tint. Diatomaceæ often

form a yellowish-brown coat on mud at the bottom of water. Many Rotatoria and larger Infusoria (PARAMECIA, &c.), when abundant, give water a slightly milky appearance.

The above list is undoubtedly very imperfect, but may afford some useful hints. Microscopists who meet with such colorations will naturally examine them carefully; they will find further information under the heads of the articles cited.

WATER-BEARS. See TARDIGRADA.

WEBBINA, D'Orb.—A genus of Foraminifera, of the order Stichostegia, and family Inæquilateralidæ.

Char. Shell fixed, irregular, inequilateral, rugose, elongate, arched, convex above, plane beneath ; *chambers* depressed, convex above, concave beneath, oval, embracing at the ends only ; *orifice* single, round, placed at the end and upper part of the last chamber, or lateral to the longitudinal axis.

One fossil British species :

W. rugosa (Pl. 18. fig. 47).

BIBL. That of the order.

WEISSIA, Hedwig.—A genus of Pottiaceous Mosses, variously defined by different authors, related to *Gymnostomum*. *W. controversa*, Hedw. (*W. viridula*, C. Müll.) is common. Wilson includes *Blindia* here, and separates *Rhabdoweissia* (*W. fugax* and *denticulata*).

WELLS, DARK. See INTRODUCTION, p. xvi.

WHALEBONE.—In whales the teeth are rudimentary ; and arising from a depression in the upper jaw on each side are a number of parallel horny plates, many feet in length, which project downwards : these plates, which are technically known as fins or blades, constitute whalebone; and through them the water containing the animals upon which the whale lives is strained, and the food thus obtained. These plates are situated upon a vascular membrane, folds of which enter a cavity at their base, which is the portion connected with the jaw.

Whalebone may be pretty easily divided into longitudinal laminæ and fibres ; but these are only secondary forms resulting from the aggregation of a number of cells, of which whalebone wholly consists.

On examining a transverse section of a blade or plate of whalebone with the naked eye, or a lens, two structures are readily distinguishable—an inner porous-looking medullary portion, surrounded by an outer compact or cortical substance. A longitu-

dinal section through the plate exhibits a number of dark lines or stripes, from about 1-100 to 1-150" in diameter, parallel to each other and to the axis of the plate, and corresponding to the pores seen in the transverse section. These stripes, which have been called whalebone-canals, but which we shall denominate medullary lines, are seen to be surrounded by a paler substance.

With a higher power ($\frac{1}{2}$ inch), the transverse section exhibits in the centre a number of rounded apertures or circles corresponding to the pores (Pl. 17. fig. 31), surrounded by very fine, concentric, interrupted dark lines ; whilst towards the circumference these lines run parallel to the surface of the plate. In the longitudinal section, viewed with this power, the medullary lines are seen to consist of a number of cells (Pl. 17. fig. 30), mostly arranged in single longitudinal series, and in dried whalebone, having a very dark appearance by transmitted light, from the presence within them of a large quantity of pigment and air. These are the medullary cells. The substance between the lines of medullary cells exhibits very fine longitudinal striæ, and in parts, the ends of divided laminæ.

On macerating whalebone for twenty-four hours in solution of caustic potash, it becomes soft ; and on afterwards digesting it in water, the cortical portion resolves itself into numerous large transparent cells, from 1-230 to 1-310" in length, and from 1-500 to 1-330" in breadth (Pl. 17. fig. 33). These contain a variable number of granules of pigment, of a deep brown colour, also some small globules of fat, which are especially numerous in those portions nearest the base of the plate. These cells in the natural whalebone are laterally compressed or flattened ; and the transverse axes of those surrounding the medullary lines are arranged tangentially to the latter, whilst in the cortical portions these axes are parallel to the surface of the plate. The concentric lines seen in a transverse section arise principally from the pigment-granules within those cells which surround the medullary cells becoming arranged in a linear series, by the flattening of the cells enclosing them. This may be shown by treating a transverse section of whalebone with caustic potash, and then adding water and watching its resolution into cells. As these expand, the interrupted lines are seen also to expand as it were, and to become resolved into a number of distinct pigment-

3 B 2

granules existing within each cell. The lines seen in a longitudinal section arise from the unequal refraction of light by the laminæ of compressed cells surrounding the medullary lines.

The medullary cells contain a large quantity of pigment, as do also those compressed cells which immediately surround them; in the former, these granules are frequently aggregated. In the common dry whalebone of commerce the medullary cells also contain air, which has been mistaken for fat—and hence the cells denominated fat-cells. The air is readily displaced by liquids. Between the compressed cells minute cavities containing air, sometimes assuming a linear form, at others representing mere dots, are seen both in the transverse and longitudinal sections; these are distinguished by the displacement of their contents. Hence ordinary whalebone closely resembles hair or horn in its structure; and the fibres which are seen projecting from the margin of the blades as found in commerce have a remarkable similarity to hair (Pl. 17. fig. 32). Chemically, it consists of a proteine compound, and is therefore coloured by Millon's and Pettenkofer's test-liquids.

Whalebone polarizes light like horn.

BIBL. Donders, *Mulder's Physiol. Chemie*; Lehmann, *Phys. Chem.*; Hunter, *Phil. Trans.* 1787.

WHEAT.—The STARCH of the grain of wheat (*Triticum vulgare* and other species and varieties) presents itself in the form of delicate little flattish lenticular bodies, very characteristic (Pl. 36. fig. 8). Wheat is subject to various BLIGHTS, which are referred to under that head, depending on the growth of parasitic Fungi, especially TILLETIA, attacking the ear, PUCCINIA attacking the straw, &c. In other cases the ear is found infested with a minute worm (ANGUILLULA *tritici*) remarkable for its tenacity of life.

WINGS OF INSECTS.—The arrangement of the veins or nerves of the anterior wings of the Hymenoptera is sometimes used to form the basis of systematic arrangement; and the several veins and interspaces have received distinct names, which may be illustrated by means of Pl. 27. fig. 11, representing the anterior wing of the humble-bee (*Bombus terrestris*) (it must be remarked, however, that in our figure the nerves, *a, d, e*, are not sufficiently distinguished): *a*, costal nerve; *b*, cubital nerve; *c*, posterior margin

of wing, with the fold (*n*) for the attachment of the hooks; *d*, post-costal nerve; *e*, externo-medial; *f*, anal; the nerve between 3 and 10, the transverso-medial; *h*, the radial nerve; *k*, the discoidal; *l*, the subdiscoidal; *m, m, m*, transverso-cubital nerves; *s*, stigma; 1, costal cell; 2, medial cell; 3, interno-medial; 4, anal; 5, marginal; 10, first discoidal cell; 11, second ditto; 12, third ditto; 13, first apical cell.

See INSECTS, *wings*.

BIBL. That of INSECTS; Jurine, *Nouvelle Méthode*, &c.; Shuckard, *Trans. Entom. Soc.* i.

WINTEREÆ.—A section of the Dicotyledonous family Magnoliaceæ (DRIMYS, *Tasmannia*), remarkable for the character of the elementary structure of the wood, approaching closely to that of the Coniferæ. It consists, as in that family, wholly of pitted prosenchymatous cells without ducts, the cells having two or three rows of bordered pits, as in ARAUCARIA. A distinction exists, however, in the character of the medullary rays, which are very numerous in Wintereæ, occurring both large and small, six or seven in the breadth of 1-12″ in a vertical section at right angles to the rays; some of them being thin, composed of one or two parallel layers of cells, extending to a vertical extent of about ten cells; others much larger, ten or twelve cells thick (or broad), and of a vertical extent of eighty or a hundred cells; the latter are very evident on the surface of the wood, when the bark is removed. The medullary rays here traverse all the annual layers of wood, which is not the case in the Coniferæ.

BIBL. Goeppert, *Linnæa*, xvi. p. 135 (1842); *Ann. des Sc. Nat.* 2 sér. xviii. p. 317.

WOOD.—The mode of origin of wood is explained in the articles CAMBIUM, MEDULLA, MEDULLARY RAYS, and VASCULAR BUNDLES, while the characters of the elementary organs of which wood is composed are described under the heads of CELL; FIBROUS, PITTED, and SPIRAL STRUCTURES; and SECONDARY DEPOSITS. Peculiar composition of the wood in certain classes, families, or genera of plants is also noticed under their especial heads, which will be referred to presently. In this article the principal kinds of modification of the wood (taken as a whole) occurring in these said cases, and in certain others, are to some extent classified, in order to indicate their relations, and to furnish a guide to microscopists seeking to observe the most remarkable varieties of structure occurring in this substance.

The elements entering into the composition of wood are :—1. FIBRO-VASCULAR BUNDLES, which in their most complete form contain SPIRAL and other VESSELS, PITTED DUCTS, PROSENCHYMATOUS cellular tissue with thickened walls (*woody fibre*); and in the Monocotyledons, *vasa propria*, as they are called by Mohl, viz. elongated tubular cells of membranous structure occurring in the centre of the bundles. 2. MEDULLARY RAYS in the Dicotyledons, or a generally diffused medullary parenchyma in the Monocotyledons. 3. Woody PARENCHYMA, which is found under different conditions and in different quantities in different cases.

The GYMNOSPERMS may be considered in the above enumeration as agreeing with the Dicotyledons. The less-generally diffused structures connected with Secretion are here left out of view.

In classifying the kinds of wood, we may commence with the less perfect forms.

Monocotyledons.—In our native plants of this class the stem is mostly herbaceous, and the woody structure then occurs simply in the form of "fibres" (*fibro-vascular bundles*) (fig. 456, p. 451), the structure of which has been described elsewhere (fig. 791, p. 721). The same kinds of elements are arranged in nearly the same way in most of the arborescent plants of this class, such as Palms : for example, in the Cocoa-nut Palm, in the common Cane (*Calamus*), or the various striped solid canes (all Palms) used for walking-sticks, &c. The solid woody texture depends in these upon the interspace between the fibro-vascular bundles being filled up with *woody parenchyma, i. e.* the general medullary substance, which in such stems as that of the White Lily is soft and spongy, in the Palms, &c. become solidified by the great deposition of secondary layers upon the walls of the cells ; thus the bundles, at first "fibres," are bound together into a solid *wood*. The thick woody walls of the hollow Bamboo cane are constructed on the same plan, being highly-developed and lignified forms of the structure which is exhibited in a soft and herbaceous condition in our common Grasses.

Certain Monocotyledons present a structure which differs from the above in the appearance presented by transverse sections. In the Smilaceæ, and some of the

Dioscoreaceæ, the fibro-vascular bundles are arranged in more definite order in one or two circles ; but there is no distinction of pith, medullary rays, and bark here ; the bundles are bound together by *woody parenchyma*, and there is no cambium region beneath the rind. The anomalous growth exhibited by the stems of other Monocotyledons, such as *Dracæna, Yucca,* &c., cannot be regarded as depending on the formation of *wood* in the proper sense ; in them, layers of fibrous structure are formed between the central region of the stem (containing the original vascular bundles) and the rind, which take their origin from the ends of the vascular bundles at the periphery of the stem beneath the rind, and extend down in a kind of false cambium-layer beneath the rind.

Interesting objects illustrating the above structures are furnished by longitudinal and transverse sections of the trunks of large Palms and of the large woody leaf-stalks of these, of canes of different kind, of Bamboo-canes, the rhizome of Sarsaparilla-plants (*Smilax*), *Ruscus,* the harder parts of the stem often found attached to imported Pine-apples, &c. Sections of silicified fossil Palm-stems, prepared by the lapidary, can also be obtained from the dealers in objects.

Dicotyledons.—In this class we meet with a remarkable diversity in the character of the wood, which moreover here exhibits, from the indefinite power of growth of the FIBRO-VASCULAR BUNDLES, a much more extensive and perfect development than in the Monocotyledons. In the articles MEDULLA (fig. 455, p. 450), MEDULLARY RAYS (fig. 457, p. 451), and VASCULAR BUNDLES (fig. 792, p. 722) are described the conditions of ordinary Dicotyledonous stems in the first year of their growth ; it is stated in the account of the vascular bundles, that a new layer of wood is developed in the cambium-layer in each succeeding season (fig. 457, p. 451). The nature of the elementary structures in such cases is illustrated by the accompanying figures from the Maple (*Acer campestre*) (figs. 807 & 808), of which the former represents sections of a shoot at the beginning of its second year, when the cambium layer (c) is swelling, the latter a shoot of three years' growth, the portions belonging to each year being indicated by the figures. The only difference between the structure developed in each succeeding season is the absence of a layer of spiral vessels (*medullary sheath*, in the first year) at the point where each year's growth commences. Here, as is seen, the body of the wood is composed chiefly of

Fig. 807.

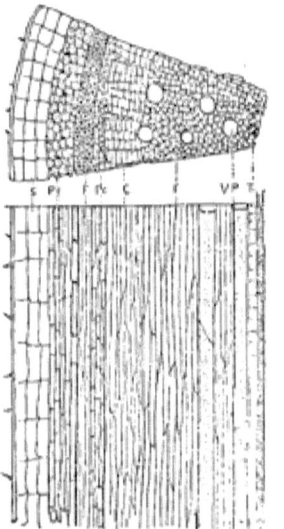

Transverse and vertical section of a segment of a shoot of the Maple in the early part of the second year of its age. T, spiral vessels; V P, pitted ducts; F, woody fibre; C, cambium; Pc, cortical parenchyma; P, liber fibres; Pr, cellular envelope of the bark; S, corky layer of ditto. Magnified 60 diameters.

Fig. 808.

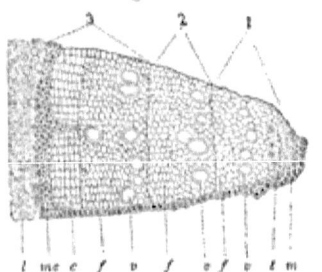

Transverse section of Maple-wood three years old. The figures 1, 2, 3 indicate the annual rings of wood, the rest is bark. m, medulla; t, spiral vessels; v, ducts; f, woody fibre; c, cambium; me, medullary parenchyma; l, liber. Magnified 40 diameters.

prosenchymatous cells (wood-cells or woody libre) (f), with a few pitted ducts (v) near

the commencement of each annual layer; the medullary rays are narrow in this wood. In the Hornbeam (*Carpinus Betulus*) the wood is of very similar composition; the wood-cells, however, are more thickened, and the ducts exhibit a spiral marking; the annual layers are not very clearly defined in sections under the microscope. This is the case, again, with the excessively hard wood of the *box* (*Buxus sempervirens*), which is of analogous composition. The Birch (*Betula alba*) has the same structure. Other common timber trees exhibit an additional structure in their wood, namely masses of *woody parenchyma* interspersed in various ways among the ordinary prosenchymatous structure of the wood. A very small quantity of this occurs in scattered groups in the common oak (*Quercus pedunculata*); here also the ducts are very large, appearing as open holes to the naked eye in cross sections; the larger medullary rays are likewise very evident. In the beech (*Fagus sylvatica*) there is a small quantity of woody parenchyma, but greatly thickened prosenchyma prevails; the ducts are rather small, but the broader medullary rays are very evident, appearing to the naked eye as brown streaks in longitudinal sections. The Chestnut (*Castanea vesca*) differs from this chiefly in wanting the broader medullary rays. In the Elm (*Ulmus campestris*) the prosenchyma is interposed between bands of woody parenchyma and wide ducts, which renders the distinction of the annual layers obscure. The Walnut tree has no woody parenchyma; the Apple and Pear trees have alternate bands of prosenchyma and woody parenchyma; these exist, but are narrower in the Plum and Cherry. In the wood of most of the Leguminosæ (*Robinia, Ulex, Genista, Gleditschia*, &c.) the woody parenchyma appears in bands of considerable size; but the walls of its cells are less thickened than those of the prosenchymatous cells. Woody parenchyma occurs extensively in Mahogany and Rose-wood, producing a peculiar variation of colour in the wood; the large holes are the orifices of the very wide ducts.

The wood of the Poplars (*Populus*) and Willows (*Salix*) has the prosenchymatous cells little thickened. The Hazel (*Corylus Avellana*) and the Alder (*Alnus glutinosa*) present a peculiarity: the wood appears to the naked eye to have broad medullary rays, but under the microscope these rays are found to be portions of the wood devoid of ducts, intervening between segments with closely-pitted ducts placed at particular points in the annual rings. The Lime (*Tilia*) and the Horse-chestnut (*Æsculus*) have wood of soft texture, the prosenchymatous cells being only slightly thickened; while the ducts are large and numerous (these exhibit a spiral band, very evident in the Lime). The wood of the Plane (*Platanus occidentalis*) has strongly marked medullary rays; the prosenchymatous cells are greatly thickened, and mingled with them are very numerous ducts, and a small quantity of woody parenchyma. The stem of the Vine (*Vitis vinifera*) has likewise long and broad medullary rays: the wood is composed of prosenchymatous cells, with a spiral-fibrous deposit on their walls, while the cells of the woody parenchyma are devoid of this; the ducts are very long, and exhibit every gradation of form, from spiral, reticulated, and scalariform to pitted ducts. The various species of *Clematis* have strongly marked medullary rays, and wood chiefly composed of pitted ducts, as is the case also in the common Rose.

Hartig and Sanio have recently published some elaborate and interesting researches on the peculiar intimate structure of wood in particular trees; but we have not space to analyse these long papers here.

In many of the above trees the wood acquires a special peculiarity when it attains a certain age; the prosenchymatous cells generally become more solid, year by year, through the filling-up of their cavities by the increasing thickness of the secondary deposits on their walls: in the lighter-coloured and softer woods, such as the Lime, there is no distinct line of demarcation between the older and younger part of the trunk—the *alburnum* or *sap-wood* and the *duramen* or *heart-wood*; but in many cases, as in the Ebony (*Diospyros*), Lignum-vitæ (*Guaiacum*), to a less extent in the Elm, Oak, &c., the *duramen* assumes a remarkable solidity and a deeper colour, so that after a certain time the colours of the *duramen* and *alburnum* are very different. This appears to arise from a chemical alteration of the substance of the secondary deposits of the prosenchymatous cells.

A great degree of regularity and agreement of structure exists between the woods of the Dicotyledons above mentioned. It remains to direct attention to various kinds which depart more or less from the type thus selected.

In the various parasitical Dicotyledons, such as *Lathræa*, *Melampyrum*, *Cuscuta*, &c., there is no layer of spiral vessels corresponding with the medullary sheath; and in the Misletoe (*Viscum*) only annular ducts occur in this situation; the wood in the latter is largely composed of woody parenchyma, the cells of which are punctated, or possess spiral-fibrous layers (figs. 665, 666, page 640). The stem of *Myzodendron* also exhibits some remarkable anomalies.

In the Bombaceæ (*Bombax*, *Carolinea*, &c.) the mass of structure corresponding to the wood is chiefly composed of membranous parenchymatous cells, with scattered isolated prosenchymatous cells, and large pitted ducts. The wood of *Avicennia* is principally composed of large pitted ducts, with narrow interspaces filled up with small pitted parenchymatous cells.

The wood of the Cactaceæ, *Mammillaria*, *Melocactus*, is composed of dotted ducts, together with a kind of cell, apparently referable to parenchyma, the walls of which have a remarkably broad spiral-fibrous band (Pl. 39. fig. 7). The wood of the *Casuarina* exhibits a curious structure: it is composed of long prosenchymatous cells, the walls of which, together with those of the numerous large ducts, have bordered pits (Pl. 39. fig. 2); while concentric lines of cellular tissue appear at intervals in the cross section, consisting of plates of parenchyma extending from one medullary ray to the next, and connecting them. The stems of some of the Menispermaceæ have likewise concentric processes of parenchymatous tissue. In the WINTEREÆ, a section of the Magnoliaceæ, the wood is wholly composed (with the exception of the medullary sheath) of pitted prosenchymatous cells resembling those of *Araucaria* (Pl. 39. fig. 5), without any ducts.

In certain families of Dicotyledons a remarkable appearance arises from the arrangement of the bundles in several circles, almost as in the Monocotyledons; but this results in a very different kind of structure, on account of the unlimited growth of the cambium in Dicotyledons. Examples of this kind of wood occur in the Chenopodiaceæ, Nyctaginaceæ, Piperaceæ, &c. In *Pisonia*, which has been supposed to grow in the same way, the result is a solid mass of wood, composed of prosenchymatous cells and ducts, with isolated perpendicular cords of parenchyma (exactly the reverse of what occurs in the Monocotyledonous stems.

The woods of *Phytocrene* and *Nepenthes* may be further cited as offering remarkable peculiarities.

It would exceed the space which we can allow to this article to enter into a description of the anomalous Dicotyledonous stems of the tropical *lianes* or climbing trees, of the families *Bignoniaceæ*, *Menispermaceæ*, *Malpighiaceæ*, &c., the irregularities of the wood of which depend upon deviations from the normal type arising in the course of the growth of the stems, which, from the observations of Treviranus, Crüger, and others, appear to be mostly regular when quite young. Isolation of one or more fibro-vascular bundles from the central cylinder of wood, producing distinct centres of development, is the most common cause of irregularity.

The wood of Dicotyledons must be examined by transverse sections and perpendicular sections parallel with and at right angles to the medullary rays. The same applies to the wood of Gymnosperms. The mode of cutting these sections is stated elsewhere.

Sections of recent woods are best preserved wet in chloride of calcium. Fossil wood, if silicified, is cut (in similar directions) by the lapidary's wheel; wood in the state of coal in like manner, or in the way stated under Coal (see PREPARATION, FOSSIL WOOD, and COAL).

Gymnosperms.—In this division of the Flowering Plants we also meet with two types of structure:

Coniferæ. — Here the character of the wood agrees in general with that of the typical Dicotyledons, with certain distinctions; namely, although the medullary sheath of spiral vessels exists, no ducts or vessels occur in the mass of wood external to this, which is wholly composed of prosenchymatous cells with bordered pits, in single (Pl. 39. fig. 4) (usually), double, or treble (*Araucaria*) rows (Pl. 39. fig. 5); in *Taxus* accompanied in part by a spiral-fibrous band (Pl. 39. fig. 4). The particulars of these forms are given under CONIFERÆ. It may be mentioned that the 'woody parenchyma' of Dicotyledons seems to be represented here by the cords of parenchymatous cells in some cases traversing the prosenchyma, ultimately filled with resinous deposits ("cords of secretion cells").

Cycadaceæ. — The earliest condition of the stems here appears to resemble that in Coniferæ; but no annular rings are formed.

Concentric layers are produced at intervals, however, separated by parenchymatous layers. The true mode of origin of these does not appear to be clearly made out. The wood is composed of pitted prosenchymatous cells (Pl. 39. fig. 20), without vessels or ducts, excepting in the medullary sheath of spiral vessels.

For further details on the markings of the ducts, &c., see PITTED and SPIRAL STRUCTURES.

The subject of the development of the wood of stems has been more discussed perhaps than any other point in structural botany. We cannot enter upon it here, beyond the statement that the key to its comprehension lies in the thorough appreciation of Schleiden's characters of the *fibro-vascular bundles* in the different classes, and of the fact that the *cambium* region exists at the growing points and all over the outer surface of the wood in Dicotyledons; in a conical mass at the summit alone, of Monocotyledons; and in a still more limited region at the summit of the stems of the Flowerless plants. The researches of Trécul have furnished the completion of the evidence against the doctrines of Gaudichaud and others, and the earlier views of the nature of cambium entertained by Mirbel.

BIBL. Lindley, *Introd. to Botany*, 4th ed. i. p. 198; Link, *Elem. Phys. Bot.* i. p. 257, *Ann. des Sc. Nat.* 2 sér. v. p. 20; DeCandolle, *Organographie*, i. p. 161; Meyen, *Pflanzenphys.* i. p. 331; Schleiden, *Grundz.* 3rd ed. i. p. 253 (*Principles*, p. 56), *Wiegmann's Archiv*, 1830. i. p. 220, *Beitr. z. Bot.* p. 29, *Mém. Acad. St. Pétersb.* 6 sér. iv. (1842); Treviranus, *Bot. Zeit.* v. p. 377 (1842), *Ann. Nat. Hist.* 2 ser. i. p. 124; Mohl, *Verm. Schrift. passim*; Miquel, *Linnæa*, xvii. p. 405, xviii. p. 125, *Ann. des Sc. Nat.* 2 sér. xix. p. 164, 3 sér. v. p. 11; Goeppert, *De Struct. Conifer.* Vratislav. 1841, *Linnæa*, xvi. p. 747, xvii. p. 135, *Ann. des Sc. Nat.* 2 sér. xviii. pp. 1 & 317; Brongniart, *Végét. Fossiles*, Paris, 1828, *et seq.*, *Ann. des Sc. Nat.* 1 sér. xvi. p. 580; Jussieu, *Ann. des Sc. Nat.* 2 sér. xv. p. 234; Decaisne, *ibid.* xii. p. 92, 3 sér. v. p. 247; Hooker, J. D., *Flor. Antarc.*, *Ann. des Sc. Nat.* 3 sér. v. 193; Gaudichaud, *Recherches Anatom., &c.* Paris, and *Ann. des Sc. Nat.* 3 sér. *passim*; Meneghini, *Ricerche sulla Struttura Monoc.*; Schacht, *Pflanzenzelle*, p. 193, *Das Baum*, p. 94; Crüger, *Bot. Zeit.* viii. p. 90, x. p. 465; Trécul, *Ann. des Sc. Nat.* 3 sér. xviii. xix. xx., 4 sér. i. ii. iii.; Milde, *Beitr. z.*

Bot. Heidelb. 1850 ; Hanstein, Pringsheim's *Jahrb. f. wiss. Bot.* i. p. 232 ; Sanio, *Linnæa,* 1858 ; Hartig, *Bot. Zeitung,* xvii.

WOODSIA, R. Brown.—A genus of Cyatheous Ferns, represented by two rare indigenous species. The indusia are of an open

Fig. 809.

Woodsia hyperborea.
A sorus and indusium with a hair-like fringe.
Magnified 50 diameters.

cup-shape, and bear long hairs on the margin (fig. 809).

WOODWARDIA, Smith.—A genus of Asplenieæ (Polypodioid Ferns). Exotic. (fig. 810).

Fig. 810.

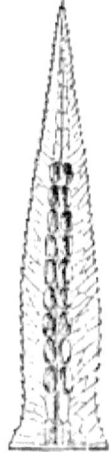

Woodwardia.
A fertile pinnule. Magnified 5 diameters.

WOOL of ANIMALS. See HAIR (p. 335). The fibres of wool are coloured by the testliquids of Millon and Schultze.

WRANGELIA, Ag.—A genus of Ceramiaceæ (Florideous Algæ), differing from *Griffithsia* chiefly in the scattered tetraspores. *W. multifida,* the only British species, has rose-red feathery fronds, an inch high, consisting of a main filament, about as thick as a bristle, composed of a single row of cells, bearing long, pinnately-arranged, patent branches, mostly branching in the same way again. At the articulations occur two opposite (or more rarely a whorl of) pinnatomultifid or sub-dichotomous ramelli 1-12 to 1-6″ long. The fructification consists of —1. *favellæ,* borne on stalks at the joints, and surrounded by a whorl of ramelli ; and 2. elliptical *tetraspores,* opposite, secund or tufted, on the lower part of the ramelli. In some foreign species *antheridia* have been observed in similar situations to the tetraspores.

BIBL. Harvey, *Brit. Mar. Alg.* p. 160, pl. 24 D ; *Phyc. Brit.* pl. 27 ; Derbès and Solier, *Ann. des Sc. Nat.* 3 sér. xiv. p. 273, pl. 35 ; Thuret, *ibid.* 4 sér. iii. p. 38.

X.

XANTHIDIA.—The bodies found in flint, and thus called, are sporangia of Desmidiaceæ (Pl. 19. figs. 22-28). They have been distributed in genera and species, the description of the characters of which would be useless.

It is a curious circumstance that these sporangia should be found in flint, which is supposed to be of marine origin, considering that the Desmidiaceæ are none of them marine.

XANTHIDIUM, Ehr.—A genus of Desmidiaceæ.

Char. Cells single, constricted in the middle ; segments compressed, entire, spinous, with a circular, usually tuberculated projection near the centre. Spines more than two to each segment.

1. *X. armatum* (Pl. 10. fig. 23 ; fig. 24, empty cell, showing the projections). Segments broadest at the base ; spines short, stout, tri- or multi-fid. Length 1-180″.

2. *X. fasciculatum* (Pl. 10. fig. 25). Segments with from four to six pairs of subulate marginal spines ; central projections minute, conical, and not beaded. Common. Length 1-400″.

Four other British species.

BIBL. Ralfs, *Brit. Desmid.* p. 111.

XANTHIOPYXIS, Ehr.—A genus of fossil Diatomaceæ, consolidated with PYXI-

DICULA. It consisted of those species the margins of the valves of which are furnished with a dentate membrane, or the surface covered with setæ or hair-like processes. From Bermuda.

BIBL. Ehrenberg, *Ber. d. Berl. Akad.* 1844. p. 264; Kützing, *Sp. Alg.* p. 23.

XENODOCHUS, Schlecht.—A genus of Uredinei (Coniomycetous Fungi), consisting of black tufts, found on the leaves of *Poterium*, containing microscopic, short, curved, usually shortly stipitate filaments, attenuated at each end, composed of a moniliform row of (five to fifteen) globose cells filled with black granules.

These bodies occur associated with *Uredo miniata*, of which *X. carbonarius* appears to be the perfect form. *Xenodochus* is only distinguished from PHRAGMIDIUM by the greater number of joints of the stylospores.

BIBL. Schlechtendahl, *Linnæa*, i. p. 237, pl. 3. fig. 3; Fries, *Summa Veg.* p. 505; Berkeley, *Ann. Nat. Hist.* i. p. 263.

XYLARIA, Schrank.—A genus of Sphæriacei (Ascomycetous Fungi), several of which are common on rotten wood, stumps of trees, &c. They are branched, horny or fleshy bodies, with often clavate lobes, whitish and mealy when young, afterwards brown or black, with black, horny, immersed perithecia all over the branches, or with the tips barren; the perithecia have a black centre composed of asci, each containing eight (usually uniseptate) spores.

BIBL. Berk. *Brit. Flor.* ii. pt. 2. p. 234 (Nos. 8 to 11); Fries, *Summa Veget.* p. 381.

Y.

YEAST(-PLANT). — This well-known substance, which possesses the remarkable property of resolving sugar in solution into alcohol and carbonic acid, consists of a minute fungus, or rather of a particular condition of development of a certain fungus.

When yeast from an actively fermenting liquid is examined with the microscope, it is seen to consist of myriads of minute cells or vesicles, of about 1-3000 to 1-2400″ (Pl. 20. fig. 23) in diameter, containing a nucleus and some granules. During the progress of the fermentation, these cells increase in number, by budding, until either the sugar or the nitrogenous matter of the fermenting liquid is exhausted, when the cells, especially those nearest the surface, become elongated, remaining connected end to end, until they reach the surface, where they produce their fructification.

The growth of the yeast-plant has been carefully studied by several observers. We may describe some observations of our own, which confirm those of Mitscherlich and others. Some fresh wort, in which fermentation had commenced, was obtained from a brewery, and a drop of the liquid, containing yeast-globules, placed upon a slide, and covered with a piece of thin glass. After the removal of the extraneous liquid, the upper glass plate was cemented to the lower one; the slide was then placed under the microscope, with the 1-4th object-glass and the micrometer eyepiece, in such a manner that several well-formed globules were visible; and these were drawn on ruled paper.

At first the globules or cells enlarged until they had attained a certain size; then there elapsed a short interval, during which no change was observable. Next there took place a projection of some point of the cell-wall, which first appeared as a little point-like bud, afterwards becoming larger and larger, until at last a new cell, of the size of the parent-cell, was formed. Within three hours, a cell was so far developed that a new one was formed from it, and thus an independent individual perfectly developed. The rapidity of growth probably varies with the temperature and the nature of the process: in twenty-four hours, when the thermometer was at about 78° in the day, sixteen cells were developed from one; after a time the growth slackened; finally no further increase took place, undoubtedly because all was removed from the liquid which could serve for their growth. Growing globules from this experiment are figured in Pl. 20. fig. 23.

By the observations of numerous competent investigators, it seems certain that the fermentation of beer, of wine, and in fact all vinous fermentation, is effected by the growth of this plant; and after the evidence brought forward in the articles FERMENTATION, TORULA, and VINEGAR-PLANT, there is little doubt that the Vinegar-plant, the *Oidium lactis*, and other supposed distinct plants are but forms of the Yeast-plant. Fig. 24 (Pl. 20) exhibits the condition of the Yeast-plant on the surface of exhausted wort of malt, before the Vinegar-fungus appears; fig. 756, page 695, the *Torula*-form at the margins of the surface of liquids.

We cannot clearly make out any difference between the 'top-yeast' and 'bottom-yeast'

(*Ober-hefe* and *Unter-hefe* of the Germans), beyond the difference resulting from more or less active development; when the growth is rapid the cells are more spherical and become quickly detached, and the evolution of gas comes up more to the surface. When the yeast vegetates quietly at the bottom of the liquid, its cells are more elongated. We do not believe the yeast-cells ever burst to discharge reproductive granules. The globular form is known by various names, as *Mycoderma cerevisiæ*, Desm., which agrees with *Cryptococcus glutinis*, Kutz.; the globular form in the Vinegar-plant is Kutzing's *Ulvina aceti*; the filamentous form with simple moniliform fruit (fig. 756) is *Torula cerevisiæ*, Turpin; without fruit, species of *Hygrocrocis* or *Leptomitus*; the final form being apparently *Penicillium glaucum*.

It is needless to repeat here the details given under FERMENTATION; but it may be added that Turpin imagined that yeast was formed by metamorphosis of the starch-granules or similar bodies of vegetable cells; and Schleiden seems to believe still (what Kutzing, Reissek, and others decidedly assert) that the globular cells, the earliest condition of yeast, quickly appearing in all saccharine vegetable juices, or solutions containing sugar and albuminous matters, are 'autochthonous,' or rather pseudo-organisms, formed by the abnormal and extraordinary development of organic matters separated from their natural position, and capable of advancing only to a certain degree of this false or diseased organization, when they perish. These views are scarcely worth notice after the numerous experiments which have proved that no such phænomena occur when the germs of these certainly definitely organized species of plants are carefully excluded. The Yeast-plant is truly most ubiquitous, but so are the conditions for its growth, while its reproductive power is enormous, and its small size renders it liable to be scattered by imperceptible movements of the air. *Aspergillus glaucus* is almost as constant in its favourite nidus, cheese; *Mucor mucedo* on paste, &c.; *Botrytis vulgaris* on dead leaves and stems in damp places, &c.; and all these are certainly no pseudo-morphic productions; and if, as we believe really to be the case, yeast is but the *conidial* form of *Penicillium glaucum*, there has been no lack of the spores of the latter in the air, in any situation where we have ever exposed vegetable substances

for any length of time to a damp atmosphere.

BIBL. Turpin, *Mém. de l'Institut*, xvii. p. 93 (1840); Lowe, *Trans. Edinb. Bot. Society*, 1857; Bail, *Flora*, 1857. p. 417; Berkeley, *Crypt. Botany*, pp. 242, 299; Schleiden, *Grundzüge der Botanik*, 3rd ed. i. p. 235 (*Principles*, p. 32); and the *Bibl.* of FERMENTATION.

YEW. See TAXUS.

Z.

ZAMIA, Lindl. See CYCADACEÆ.

ZASMIDIUM, Fr. See ANTENNARIA.

ZETES, Koch.—A genus of Arachnida, of the order Acarina, and family Oribatea. It is consolidated with *Galumna*.

ZINC.—The crystals of the *lactate*, as deposited from an aqueous solution, are represented in Pl. 7. fig. 20; they belong to the right-rhombic prismatic system.

The *chloride of zinc* is useful as a preservative of animal tissues. (See PRESERVATION, p. 578).

Chloriodide of zinc. See SCHULZE'S TEST, p. 613.

BIBL. That of CHEMISTRY.

ZONARIA, Harvey (*Aglaozonia*, Zanard, Kutz.).—A genus of Dictyotaceæ (Fucoid Algæ), of which the British species, *Z. parvula*, forms olive-green, membranous, fan-shaped fronds, 1″ or more in diameter, growing over stones or corallines, to which it attaches itself by whitish fibres on the lower surface. It is scarcely marked with concentric lines like PADINA. The fructification occurs in scattered sori on both surfaces, and is apparently analogous to that of PADINA, but requires further examination, since Thuret has shown that the true Dictyotaceæ have peculiar reproductive organs, spores, tetraspores, and antheridia, so that they stand between the Fucaceæ and the Florideæ.

BIBL. Harvey, *Brit. Mar. Alg.* p. 38, pl. 6 D; Thuret, *Ann. des Sc. Nat.* 4 sér. iii. p. 25.

ZOOGLŒA, Cohn. See BACTERIUM.

ZOOPHYTES. See POLYPI.

ZOOSPORES.—The name given to the ciliated active gemmæ or GONIDIA produced either singly or more frequently, after segmentation, in numbers, out of the contents of ordinary or special cells of the Algæ, without any previous process of fertilization. These bodies are generally discharged from the parent cell in the state of PRIMORDIAL

UTRICLES, and acquire a cellulose coat subsequently, when they cease to move, and settle down to germinate and produce a structure resembling the parent. In some cases (in HYDRODICTYON normally, in many other Confervoids abnormally) they become encysted within the parent-cell; and it appears most probable that the small cysts with dense (and often spinulose) coats, such as occur in *Spirogyra* (Pl. 5. figs. 24, 25) and other genera under certain circumstances, are of similar origin. In the VOLVOCINEÆ, zoospore-like bodies form the permanently-active individuals of the families.

True zoospores occur pretty generally throughout the Confervoid Algæ (with the exception of Oscillatoriaceæ, Nostochaceæ, and perhaps Diatomaceæ), and are described under the heads of the families or genera. A brief review may be permitted here. The largest form is that produced in the apices of the filaments of VAUCHERIA (fig. 790); it is ciliated all over, and very unlike that of any other genus. In *Œdogonium* (Pl. 5. fig. 7 *c*, & fig. 811) the zoospores are formed out of the whole contents of a cell, and have a crown of cilia around the transparent 'beak.' In other Confervaceæ, as *Cladophora* (Pl. 5. fig. 13 *c*, *d*), *Conferva* (Pl. 5. figs. 10 *b*, 11 *c*); in Chætophoraceæ, as in *Chætophora* (Pl. 5. fig. 9), *Draparnaldia* (fig. 180, page 238), *Stigeoclonium* (Pl. 5. fig. 5 *c c*); in Ulvaceæ, *Ulva* (Pl. 5. figs. 2 *b*, 3 *c*, *d*), *Enteromorpha* (Pl. 5. fig. 4 *b*); in *Protococcus* (Pl. 3. fig. 2 *b*), in ACHLYA, in

Fig. 811.

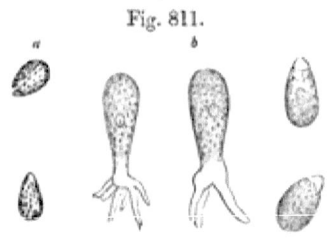

a　　　　　*b*

Zoospores of Œdogonium. *a* have lost their cilia; and in *b* germination is more or less advanced. Magnified 200 diameters.

Desmidiaceæ (Pl. 6. fig. 11), &c., as in all other cases, they are formed either singly from the entire contents, or in small or large number by the segmentation of the entire contents, and mostly break out in various ways, as pyriform bodies with two or four cilia on the transparent beak, moving actively for a time, and then germinating to

produce new plants. They appear usually to be surrounded at the moment of discharge by a delicate common sac, composed of cellulose, which expands and quickly disappears, apparently by solution, setting them free; in PEDIASTRUM, however, this envelope appears to be permanent and to hold the gonidia together in the characteristic group or family (Pl. 6. fig. 11). In HYDRODICTYON, as described under that article, their history is different, though the earlier conditions are analogous. It has been found that zoospores of two very different sizes are produced in many Confervoids: these are called *macrogonidia* and *microgonidia* by A. Braun (see HYDRODICTYON); and a different function is supposed to be exercised by the latter by some authors, who believe they are fertilizing bodies (like SPERMATOZOIDS).

Zoospores exist in a large proportion of the Algæ usually included under the FUCOIDEÆ, but which Thuret separates under the name of Phæosporæ, including all the families except the FUCACEÆ, DICTYOTACEÆ and Tilopterideæ, which are (for the present?) distinguished by possessing antheridia and spores proper. The Phæosporous families bear organs called SPORANGES (usually described in Algological works as " spores "), from which are discharged *zoospores*, agreeing in all essential respects with those of the Confervoids, except that the two cilia are often arranged fore and aft, instead of being both in front. Examples of these are described under ECTOCARPUS, MYRIONEMA, CUTLERIA, LAMINARIA, &c.

It remains to direct attention to the distinction between ZOOSPORES and SPERMATOZOIDS, which are sometimes confused together. This confusion is rendered more imminent by the manner in which the *forms* pass one into another. The essential character of a *zoospore* is, that when separated from the parent, it becomes encysted and at once developed into a new individual resembling the parent. An exception to this occurs in some of the zoospores of ŒDOGONIUM, which, as the *androspores*, produce special structures in which are developed spermatozoids.

Spermatozoids are transitory structures; when discharged from the parent-cell, they either make their way to a germ-cell of a spore, fertilize it and disappear; or if debarred from this, at once perish, without germination. As stated under SPERMATOZOIDS, these bodies vary much in form. In the higher Cryptogamia they are spiral filaments (Pl. 32. figs. 31–4). In the Fucaceæ they are minute globular bodies with two cilia (fore and aft) closely resembling some zoospores; in the Florideæ they appear to be globules without cilia; and those recently described as existing in VAUCHERIA, among the Confervoids, are also biciliated globules with the cilia fore and aft, while those in SPHÆROPLEÆ resemble the *microgonidia* of this family, having their pair of cilia on the beak; in ŒDOGONIUM they resemble the zoospores, but are smaller. The latter observation is in favour of the microgonidia of *Hydrodictyon*, &c. being spermatozoids.

BIBL. Thuret, *Ann. des Sc. Nat.* 3 sér. xiv. p. 214, xvi. p. 5, 4 sér. ii. p. 197, iii. p. 5; A. Braun, *Verjüngung, &c., Ray Soc. Vol.* 1853, and under the articles above-cited.

ZOOTHAMNIUM, Bory.—A genus of Infusoria, of the family Vorticellina.

Char. Those of *Carchesium*, the stalked bodies being of two different kinds.

According to Stein, the remarks made under OPERCULARIA, in regard to the two kinds of bodies, apply equally here, so that the genus is untenable.

Ehrenberg describes two species, Stein adds two more.

Z. arbuscula (Pl. 25. fig. 22). Branches of polypidom racemose-umbellate, bodies white, stalks very thick. Aquatic; length of polypidom, 1-4″; of bodies, 1-430″.

BIBL. Ehrenberg, *Infus.* p. 288; Stein, *Infus. passim.*

ZOSTERA, L.—A genus of Monocotyledonous Flowering Plants (Nat. Ord. Zosteraceæ), growing in sea-water; remarkable for the POLLEN, of which the grains are represented by tubular filaments destitute of an outer coat and exhibiting ROTATION when fresh.

ZYGNEMA, Agardh, in part (*Tyndaridea,* Bory, Hassall).—A genus of Zygnemaceæ (Confervoid Algæ), consisting of filamentous plants, with the green contents of the cells arranged in twin, stellate or lobed masses in each joint (fig. 137, page 181). This stellate appearance arises from the presence of radiating threads, like those from the nucleus of SPIROGYRA; hence it cannot be well observed in dried specimens. Cell-division with previous division of the stellate masses may be well studied in this genus. Kützing separates from this genus all the forms in which the spore is formed in the cross branch produced in conjugation, associating them with *Zygogonium.* We prefer to follow Hassall's distribution of the forms, seeing

that *Zygogonium ericetorum* is a plant of very different appearance. If the said character is constant, this genus might be divided into two.

Spores in one of the parent-cells.

1. *Z. cruciata* (fig. 137, p. 181). Filaments 1-600″ in diameter; joints equal or twice as long; spores globose (Hassall, *l. c. infra,* pl. 38. fig. 1; Kütz. *l. c. infra,* v. pl. 17. fig. 4). *Z. Dilwynii* and *stellina* of Kützing appear to be only smaller states of this; as also *Tynd. lutescens,* Hassall, and *T. anomala,* Ralfs.

2. *Z. stagnalis.* Filaments 1-2040″ in diameter, joints three or four times as long; spores globose or oblong (Hassall, *l. c.* pl. 38. figs. 9, 10). *Tynd. ovalis,* Hass., is pehaps a larger form of this.

3. *Z. insignis.* Filaments 1-1800 to 1-1500″ in diameter, joints twice as long; spores globose (Hass. *l. c.* pl. 38. figs. 6, 7; Kütz. *l. c.* v. pl. 17. fig. 1).

4. *Z. bicornis.* Filaments 1-440 to 1-200″ in diameter, joints twice as long; spores globose (Hass. *l. c.* pl. 38. fig. 5; Kütz. *l. c.* v. pl. 16. fig. 3).

Spores in the cross branches.

5. *Z. immersa.* Filaments 1-1200″ in diameter, joints about half as long again; transverse processes very thick, filled by the large and globose spore (Hass. *l. c.* pl. 39. fig. 3; Kütz. *l. c.* v. pl. 12. fig. 5).

6. *Z. conspicua.* Filaments 1-1440 to 1-1080″ in diameter, joints equal or twice as long; transverse processes long, ventricose in the middle, where they enclose the ovate-globose spore (Hass. *l. c.* pl. 39. figs. 1, 2; Kütz. *l. c.* v. pl. 12. fig. 2).

7. *Z. decussata.* Filaments 1-1440″ in diameter, joints three times (more rarely five times) as long; transverse processes short and filled by the globose spore (Hass. *l. c.* pl. 39. fig. 6; Kütz. *l. c.* v. pl. 11. fig. 4).

8. *Z. Ralfsii.* Filaments 1-1920 to 1-1440″ in diameter, joints three or four times as long; transverse processes very much dilated in the middle, containing an elliptical spore, with the long axis at right angles (Hass. *l. c.* pl. 39. figs. 4, 5; Kütz. *l. c.* v. pl. 11. fig. 2).

9. *Z. pectinata.* Filaments 1-600″ in diameter, joints equal or a little shorter; cell-contents transversely bipartite, more frequently radiato-dentate, pectinate, dull green (Kütz. *l. c.* v. pl. 14. fig. 4; *Eng. Bot.* pl. 1611?). Possibly this is only a state of

Z. *cruciata* with the spores in the transverse processes; if so, the subdivision above indicated cannot stand.

Probably other species exist in Britain; but we cannot satisfactorily ascertain them. BIBL. Hassall, *Br. Fr. Algæ*, p. 160, pls. 38, 39 (*Tyndaridea*); Kützing (*Zygnema* and *Zygogonium*, in part), *Tab. Phyc.* v. pls. 11–17, *Spec. Alg.* pp. 444, 445.

ZYGNEMACEÆ (Pl. 5. figs. 16–28).—A family of Confervoid Algæ, consisting of plants composed of articulated cylindrical filaments, the cells of which often have the green contents arranged in elegant patterns. The principal mode of reproduction, whence the family takes its name, is by CONJUGATION, followed by a mixture of the entire contents of the united cells, and their conversion into a spore. Other phænomena occur in some instances, such as the production of ciliated zoospores, and small spore-like bodies with a dense spinulose coat (*asteridia*); but these appearances are not yet thoroughly understood (see SPIROGYRA and MOUGEOTIA).

Synopsis of British Genera.

1. *Spirogyra.* Filaments simple, with the green contents arranged in one or more spiral bands upon the cell-wall. Conjugation normally by transverse tubular processes; spores formed in one of the parent-cells (or occasionally in both).

2. *Zygnema.* Filaments simple, with the green contents arranged in two globular or stellate masses in each cell. Conjugation by transverse processes; spores formed in one of the parent-cells, or in the cross branch.

3. *Zygogonium.* Filaments simple, or slightly branched, with the contents diffused or arranged in two transverse bands. Conjugation by transverse processes; spores globose, formed in the cross branches, or in blind lateral pouches without conjugation.

4. *Mesocarpus.* Filaments simple, with the contents diffused. Conjugation by transverse processes, from which the filaments become recurved; spores in the dilated cross branches.

5. *Staurocarpus.* Filaments simple, with the contents diffused (or rarely in moniliform lines). Conjugation by transverse processes, from which the filaments become recurved; spores (or sporanges) square or cruciate, in the dilated cross branches.

6. *Mougeotia.* Filaments simple, soon bent at intervals, contents mostly diffused, sometimes in several serpentine lines. Conjugation by the inosculation of the filaments at the convexity of the angles; spores not satisfactorily known.

Thwaitesia, Montagne, resembles *Zygnema* in its stellate cell-contents; but the spore (?) formed in one of the parent-cells divides into four portions (perhaps not distinct from *Zygnema*).

A. Braun has lately described two new genera, viz. *Craterospermum*, nearly resembling *Staurocarpus* and *Mougeotia*, but with the spore and the short tube in which it is contained subconstricted in the middle.

Pleurocarpus. Simple filaments, with diffused contents, the conjugation taking place between adjacent cells of the same filaments, by means of a short arcuate tube; spore globose, in the tube.

Rhynconema, Kützing, has spiral cell-contents like *Spirogyra*, but conjugates like *Pleurocarpus*, by an arched tube connecting adjacent cells of the same tube.

BIBL. Kützing, *Spec. Alg., Tabulæ Phycolog.*; A. Braun, *Alg. Unicell.* p. 60.

See also the genera.

ZYGOCEROS, Ehr.—A genus of Diatomaceæ. Detached frustules of BIDDULPHIA. BIBL. Ehrenberg, *Abhandl. d. Berl. Akad.* 1839. p. 131; Kützing, *Bacill.* p. 138, and *Sp. Alg.* p. 139.

ZYGODESMUS, Corda. —A genus of Sepedoniei (Hyphomycetous Fungi). *Z. fuscus* occurs upon bark of fallen branches. Mr. Berkeley thinks it possibly may be a form of some Thelephoroid Fungus. Mr. Currey has shown that Corda's figure (fig. 812) is

Fig. 812.

Zygodesmus fuscus.
Magnified 400 diameters.

not completely accurate, since he finds the points at the apex of the fertile pedicels each crowned by a spore; and the normal number of sterigmata is probably four, so that the structure would resemble a basidium of Hymenomycetes.

BIBL. Berk. *Crypt. Bot.* p. 298; Currey, *Micr. Journal*, v. p. 126.

ZYGODON, Hook. and Taylor.—A genus of Orthotrichaceous Mosses, deriving its name from the yoking of the teeth in pairs; the species are mostly found in mountainous districts and rarely in fruit.

ZYGOGONIUM, Kütz.—A genus of Zygnemaceæ (Confervoid Algæ), consisting of filamentous plants, growing on damp ground or in water, green or yellowish when fresh, purple or brownish when dry. Kützing includes here all Hassall's species of *Tyndaridea* (ZYGNEMA) which produce the spore in the cross branch.

Z. ericetorum, Kütz. Filaments 1-2160 to 1-1440″ in diameter, joints as long or half as long again; cylindrical or torulose (filaments sometimes slightly branched). Conjugation rare, apparently mostly 'chain-like,' from one cell to the next in the same filament. Contents green when growing in water, purple when growing on wet heaths (Hass. pl. 41; Greville, *Sc. Crypt. Fl.* pl. 261. fig. 1). *Conferva ericetorum*, Dillw.

See ZYGNEMA.

BIBL. Hassall, *l. c.*; Greville, *l. c.*; Kützing, *Sp. Alg.* p. 445, *Tab. Phyc.* v. pl. 10, &c.; *Eng. Bot.* pl. 1553.

ZYGOSELMIS, Duj.—A genus of Infusoria, of the family Euglenia.

Char. Form variable; movement effected by two similar flagelliform filaments, incessantly in action.

Z. nebulosa (Pl. 25. fig. 23). Body colourless, sometimes globular, at others variously expanded so as to become pyriform or topshaped, turbid from the presence of numerous granules. Aquatic; length 1-1100″.

BIBL. Dujardin, *Infus.* p. 369.

The following articles have been accidentally omitted to be inserted in their proper places:—

ENALLOSTEGIA.—An order of Foraminifera.

  Char. Chambers alternate in two or three rows, not spiral.

  Fam. I. POLYMORPHINIDÆ. Sides of the shell dissimilar, and unsymmetrical.

    * *Chambers alternate on three faces.*

    Gen. 1. *Dimorphina.* Chambers at first on three faces, afterwards in a straight line.

    2. *Guttulina.* Chambers on three faces at all ages.

    ** *Chambers alternate on two faces.*

    3. *Polymorphina* (Pl. 42. fig. 27). Orifice round, terminal.

    4. *Virgulina.* Orifice latero-terminal, comma-shaped.

  Fam. II. TEXTULARIDÆ. Sides of shell alike, the parts symmetrical.

  * *Chambers at first alternate, subsequently rectilinear.*

    5. *Bigenerina* (Pl. 42. fig. 12). Orifice central.

    6. *Gemnulina.* Orifice lateral.

    ** *Chambers alternate at all ages.*

      † *Orifice single.*

    7. *Textularia* (Pl. 18. fig. 34). Orifice transverse, on the inner side of the chambers.

    8. *Vulvulina* (Pl. 18. fig. 39). Orifice longitudinal, on the middle of the chambers.

    9. *Bolivina.* Orifice longitudinal, on the side of the chambers.

    10. *Sagrina.* Orifice round, on the upper part of the chambers, at the end of a prolongation.

      †† *Orifices numerous.*

    11. *Cuneolina.*

ENTOMOSTEGIA.—An order of Foraminifera.

  Char. Chambers in two rows, alternate, coiled into a spiral.

  Fam. I. ASTERIGERINIDÆ. Sides of the shell dissimilar, the alternation of the chambers on the two sides being different.

  * *Spire oblique, apparent on one side only.*

    Gen. 1. *Robertina.* Shell turriculate.

    2. *Asterigerina* (Pl. 42. fig. 11). Shell depressed.

  ** *Spire alike on both sides.*

    3. *Amphistegina* (Pl. 42. fig. 7). Chambers divided longitudinally.

    4. *Heterostegina.* Chambers divided transversely.

  Fam. II. CASSIDULINIDÆ. Sides alike, the alternation of the chambers being alike on the two sides.

    5. *Cassidulina* (Pl. 42. fig. 16).

SERIALARIA. See VESICULARIDÆ; and add, *S. lendigera*, the only British species, is not uncommon on Fuci, near low-water mark.

DIRECTIONS TO BINDER.

For the convenience of those who may wish to have the Plates bound as a separate Volume, two Titles have been printed ; in which case the Frontispiece should face the description of Plate I. in the Second Volume.

The Introduction (pages ix *et seq.*) may precede the Plates in the second volume.

PRINTED BY TAYLOR AND FRANCIS,
RED LION COURT, FLEET STREET.

THE

MICROGRAPHIC DICTIONARY;

A GUIDE TO THE EXAMINATION AND INVESTIGATION

OF THE

STRUCTURE AND NATURE

OF

MICROSCOPIC OBJECTS.

BY

J. W. GRIFFITH, M.D., F.L.S. &c.,

MEMBER OF THE ROYAL COLLEGE OF PHYSICIANS;

AND

ARTHUR HENFREY, F.R.S., F.L.S. &c.,

PROFESSOR OF BOTANY IN KING'S COLLEGE, LONDON.

SECOND EDITION.

ILLUSTRATED BY FORTY-FIVE PLATES AND EIGHT HUNDRED AND TWELVE WOODCUTS.

VOL. II.—PLATES.

LONDON:

JOHN VAN VOORST, PATERNOSTER ROW.

MDCCCLX.

PRINTED BY TAYLOR AND FRANCIS,
RED LION COURT, FLEET-STREET.

ALERE FLAMMAM.

DESCRIPTION OF PLATES.

The number of diameters which each object is magnified, is expressed in the Plates by small figures placed beneath the objects.

PLATE 1.—Test-Objects.

Frontispiece

Figure

1. Hairs of the larva of *Dermestes lardarius*, viewed in balsam.

2. Hairs of the common bat (*Vespertilio pipistrellus*), in balsam. *a b*, coloured hairs; *c*, a white hair.

3. Hairs of mouse (*Mus domesticus*), in balsam.

4. Pits of coniferous wood, common deal (*Abies excelsa*), viewed dry.

5. Mucus- (or salivary) corpuscles, seen under different powers.

6. Scales of *Lepisma saccharina*, dry.

7. Scale from the wing of *Morpho menelaus*, dry.

8. Scale from under side of wing of common clothes-moth (*Tinea pellionella*), dry.

9. Scales of *Hipparchia janira*. *a*, dry, and by oblique light; *b*, in balsam, by direct light; *c*, dry, after Schacht.

10. *Didymohelix ferruginea*, under different powers; *b*, with imperfect correction or adjustment, *c* with perfect correction and adjustment; *d*, separate fibres.

11. *Didymoprium Grevillii*, empty cells.

12. Scales of *Podura plumbea*, under different powers, dry; *a*, 220 diameters.

13. Pygidium of flea.

14. Frustule of *Grammatophora marina* (diagram). *a*, front view; *b*, side view.

15. Frustule of *Grammatophora subtilissima* (diagram). *a*, front view; *b*, side view.

16. *Gyrosigma angulatum*; dry valve showing the dots.

17. *Gyrosigma attenuatum*; dry valve showing the lines.

18. *Gyrosigma elongatum*; dry valve showing the lines.

PLATE 2.—Arachnida.

Figure

1. *Acarus domesticus* (cheese-mite). *a*, labium and mandibles; *b*, hair; *g*, labium; *i*, end of leg.
2. *Acarus longior.*
3. *Anystis ruricola.* *a*, palp; *b*, mandible of. (See Pl. 41. fig. 4.)
4. Epidermis of *Epeira diadema.*   5. Epidermis of a *Dermanyssus.*
6. Mandibles of *Epeira.*
7. Mandibles, &c. of male *Tegenaria.* *a, b*, mandibles; *c*, palpi; *d*, maxillæ; *e*, labium.
8. End of leg of *Epeira.* *a, b*, hairs of the same.
9. Lung-plates of *Epeira*; 9 *b*, piece more magnified.
10. Spinneret of *Tegenaria domestica.* *a*, two separate spinning-tubes, the right-hand one from *Epeira*, the left-hand one from *Tegenaria.*
11. Portion of cobweb of *Epeira.*   12. Epidermis of *Arrenurus.*
13. *Arrenurus viridis*, female, dorsal view. *a*, palp; *c*, under view of male, showing round mouth with hood and two first joints of palpi, the coxæ, two stigmata and two granular plates, anal orifice and penis.
14. *Atax histrionicus.* *a*, mandible; *b*, palp; *c*, under view, with labium, coxæ, and genital plates.
15. *Hypopus muscarum.*   16. *Sarcoptes hominis*, under view, female.
18. *Psoroptes equi*, under view.   19. *Ixodes Dugesii*, from above.
20. *Ixodes Dugesii*, anterior portion, from above. *a*, dorsal plate; *b*, basilar piece of support of rostrum; *c*, palpi, between which part of mandibles is visible.
21. *Ixodes Dugesii*, side view of palp.
22. *Ixodes Dugesii*, basilar piece from above. *a*, dotted lines indicating first joint of mandibles (*b*) seen through support; *c*, moveable toothed claw.
23. *Ixodes Dugesii*, sixth and seventh joints of leg, with claws and caruncle.
24. *Dermanyssus avium*, from beneath. *a*, labium of male, compressed, with palp (*) and mandible (†); *b*, mandible of female; *c*, leg.
25. *Uropoda vegetans.* *a*, mandible; *b*, its end more magnified; *c*, sixth and seventh joint of leg in side view.
26. *Gamasus coleoptratorum*, from above. *a*, end of leg; *b*, body from beneath; *c*, mandible.
27. *Limnochares aquatica.* *a*, under view of labium and palpi; *b*, side view of labium; *c*, tarsus; *d*, scaly plate supporting eyes; *e*, two posterior coxæ of one side only; *f*, rostrum protruded, with palpi and anterior coxæ, trochanters and femora of one side only.
28. *Eylais extendens.* *a*, mouth with its hood, and first joint of palps; *b*, palp; *c*, end of mandible, with hook; *d*, under view of body, showing mouth, hood, and one palp, two groups of anterior coxæ with intervening genital orifice and two stigmata, posterior coxæ, anal orifice, and two other stigmata.
29. *Hydrachna globula.* *a*, under view, showing rostrum and palps, coxæ, heart-shaped genital plate and anus; *b*, mandible; *c*, rostrum or labium, with a palp; *d*, palp of larva; *e*, end of leg; *f*, nymphs adherent to *Nepa.*
30. *Diplodontus scapularis.* *a*, labium with palp seen from beneath; *b*, mandible.
31. *Bdella longicornis.* *b*, mandible; *a*, end more magnified; *c*, mandible of *Bd. cærulipes.*
32. *Tetranychus glaber.* *a*, end of leg, front view, *b*, side view; *c*, palp; *d*, mandible.
33. *Megamerus celer.* *a*, labium; *b*, palp; *c*, mandible of *Megamerus roseus.*
34. *Pachygnathus velutinus.* *a*, palp; *b*, end of leg; *c*, mandible.
35. *Tetranychus cristatus*, vel *lapidum.* *a*, labium of *Raphignathus ruberrimus* with palp and mandibles *in situ*; *b*, mandible of same.
36. *Smaris papillosa*, from above. *a*, mandible.
37. *Trombidium phalangii.* *a*, palpi; *b*, mandible.
38. *Trombidium (Leptus) autumnale*, from above. 39. *Pteroptus respertilionis*, from above.
40. *Trombidium cinereum.* *a*, labium with a palp; *b*, tarsus; *c*, plume of the labium more magnified; *d*, a mandible.
41. *Scirus (Bdella) elaphus*, side view. *a*, end of mandible.
42. *Demodex folliculorum*, from beneath.
43. *Demodex folliculorum*, anterior portion from above. *a*, palps; *b*, maxillæ; *c*, labrum; *d*, tubercles.

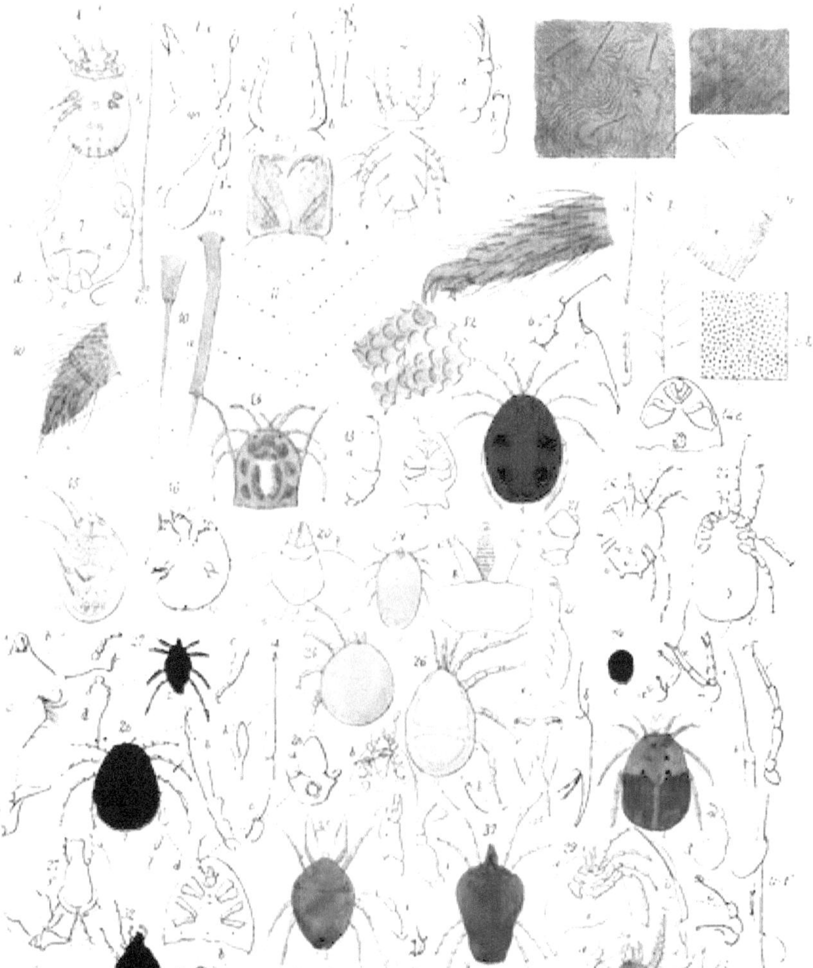

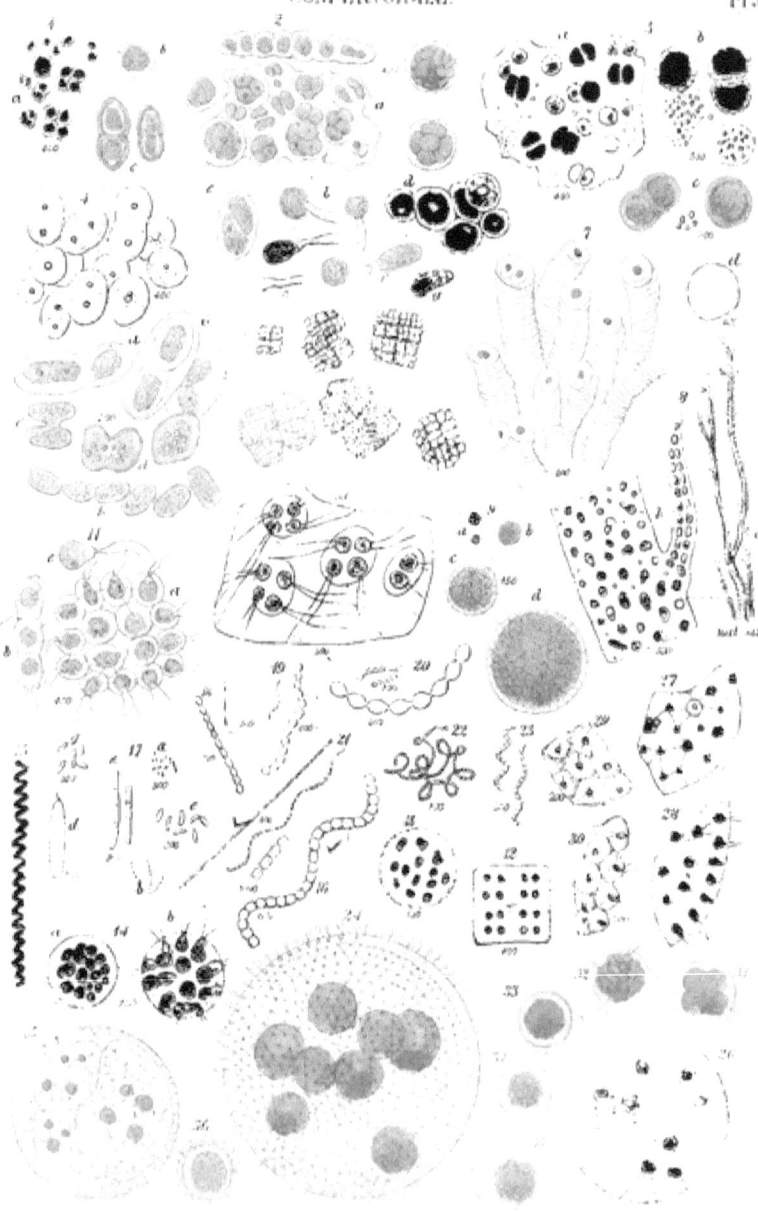

PLATE 3.—Confervoideæ.

PLATE 4.—Confervoideæ.

PLATE 5.—Confervoideæ.

Figure

1. *Monostroma bullosa*, Thuret. *a*, fragment of frond, with some cells empty; *b*, ciliated zoospores from the cells; *c*, zoospore germinating.
2. *Ulva lactuca*, L. *a*, fragment of frond; *b*, small ciliated zoospores from ditto.
3. Ditto. *a*, fragment of frond; *b*, ditto, with the cells nearly empty, showing the orifices by which the zoospores escape; *c*, large zoospore; *d*, zoospores germinating.
4. *Enteromorpha clathrata*, Grev. *a*, fragment of frond; *b*, zoospores from ditto; *c*, the same in germination.
5. *Stigeoclonium protensum*, Kütz. *a* and *b*, fragments of branched filaments, *b* emitting zoospores, *c*, *c*; *d*, germinating zoospores.
6. *Ulothrix mucosa*, Thur. *a*, *b*, fragments of filaments; *c*, zoospores; *d*, *e*, ditto germinating.
7. *Œdogonium vesicatum*, Link. *a*, fragment of a filament; *b*, ditto, breaking up and emitting a zoospore; *c*, zoospore with a crown of cilia; *d*, *e*, germinating zoospores; *f*, membrane of a zoospore which has burst by a lid and discharged small zoospores immediately after germination; *g*, fragment of a filament with one cell containing a resting-spore; *h*, fragment of a filament in an abnormal state, containing globular bodies; *i*, germinated zoospore containing similar globular bodies.
8. *Chætophora elegans*, Ag.
9. A fragment of the same, emitting zoospores.
10. *Conferva ærea*, Dillw. *a*, fragment of filament, one cell of which has discharged its contents in the form of zoospores, *b*.
11. *Conferva floccosa*, Thur. *a*, filament breaking up; *b*, fragment of growing filament; *c*, zoospores.
12. *Rhizoclonium obtusangulum*, Kütz.
13. *Cladophora glomerata*, Kütz. *a*, filament with one fertile branch; *b*, apex of a fertile branch discharging zoospores, *c*.
14. *Sphæroplea annulina*, Kütz. *a*, growing filament; *b*, filament with the contents converted into spores.
15. *Codium tomentosum*, Ag. *a*, apex of clavate branch, with fertile cell; *b*, zoospores.
16. *Staurocarpus gracilis*, Hass.; conjugating filaments.
17–23. *Spirogyra quinina*, Kütz; 17, growing filament.
18. Conjugating filaments, with spores.
19. Ditto, with the spores germinating.
20. Half-decomposed cell, with the contents converted into almost colourless bi-ciliated zoospores.
21. Spore formed after conjugation.
22. The same shortly before germination.
23. A similar spore, with the contents converted into globular bodies.
24. *a* and *b*, portions of a *Spirogyra*? with the contents converted into spiny globular bodies.
25. *Spirogyra quinina*, Kütz.; imperfectly conjugated cells, with the contents converted into globular bodies.
26. *Spirogyra nitida*; cell with nucleus, *n*.
27. *Spirogyra pellucida*, Kütz.; cell with nucleus, *n*, and gelatinous outer coat, *s*.
28. *Spirogyra nitida*, Kütz., half-decayed, the contents partly changed into globular masses.

PLATE 6.—Confervoideæ.—Crystals.

Figure

1. *Cosmarium margaritiferum*, Turp.; conjugating pair with imperfect sporange.

2. *Cosmarium botrytis*, Bory; conjugating pair with sporange, enveloped in jelly.

3. A. *Closterium acerosum*, Schrank. *a, b, c*, different stages of conjugation; *d*, frustules apparently produced from a sporange.

3. B. *Closterium lunula*, Müll.; the contents converted into globular bodies.

4. *Fragilaria penicillata*, Lyngb. *a* and *b*, successive stages of conjugation.

5. A. *Surirella bifrons*, Ehr.; conjugating pair, with intermediate large sporangial frustule.

5. B. *Surirella bifrons*, Ehr., with the contents converted into globular bodies.

6. *Eunotia turgida*, Ehr. *a, b, c, d, e*, successive stages of conjugation producing pairs of sporangial frustules.

7. *Melosira (Aulacosira) crenulata*, Thw. *a*, filament with two conjugating pairs of cells and perfect sporangial frustules; *b* and *c*, large filaments produced by sporangial frustules.

8. *Melosira varians*, Ag. *a*, small filament producing sporangial frustules by conjugation; *b*, large filament developed from sporangial frustules.

9. *Orthosira Dickiei*, Thw. Successive stages of production of sporangial frustules after conjugation.

10. *Pinnularia viridis*, Sm., with the contents converted into globular bodies.

11. *Pediastrum granulatum*, Ktz. *a*, a frond with most of the cells empty, three full, and the contents of another swarming out as zoospores; *b, c, d*, swarm of zoospores producing a new frond.

12. Crystals of sugar of milk.

13.   ,,   diabetic sugar.

14.   ,,   indigo, sublimed.

15.   ,,   oxalate of soda.

16.   ,,   sulphate of lime.

17.   ,,   phosphate of lime.

18.   ,,   sulphate of strontia.

19.   ,,   nitrate of soda.

1*.   ,,   allantoin.

2*.   ,,   antimoniate of soda.

3*.   ,,   protoxide of antimony.

4*.   ,,   butyrate of baryta. *a*, rapidly, *b*, slowly formed.

5*.   ,,   hydrofluosilicate of baryta.

6*.   ,,   sulphate of baryta. *a*, precipitated from concentrated, *b*, from very dilute solution.

7*.   ,,   carbonate of potash.

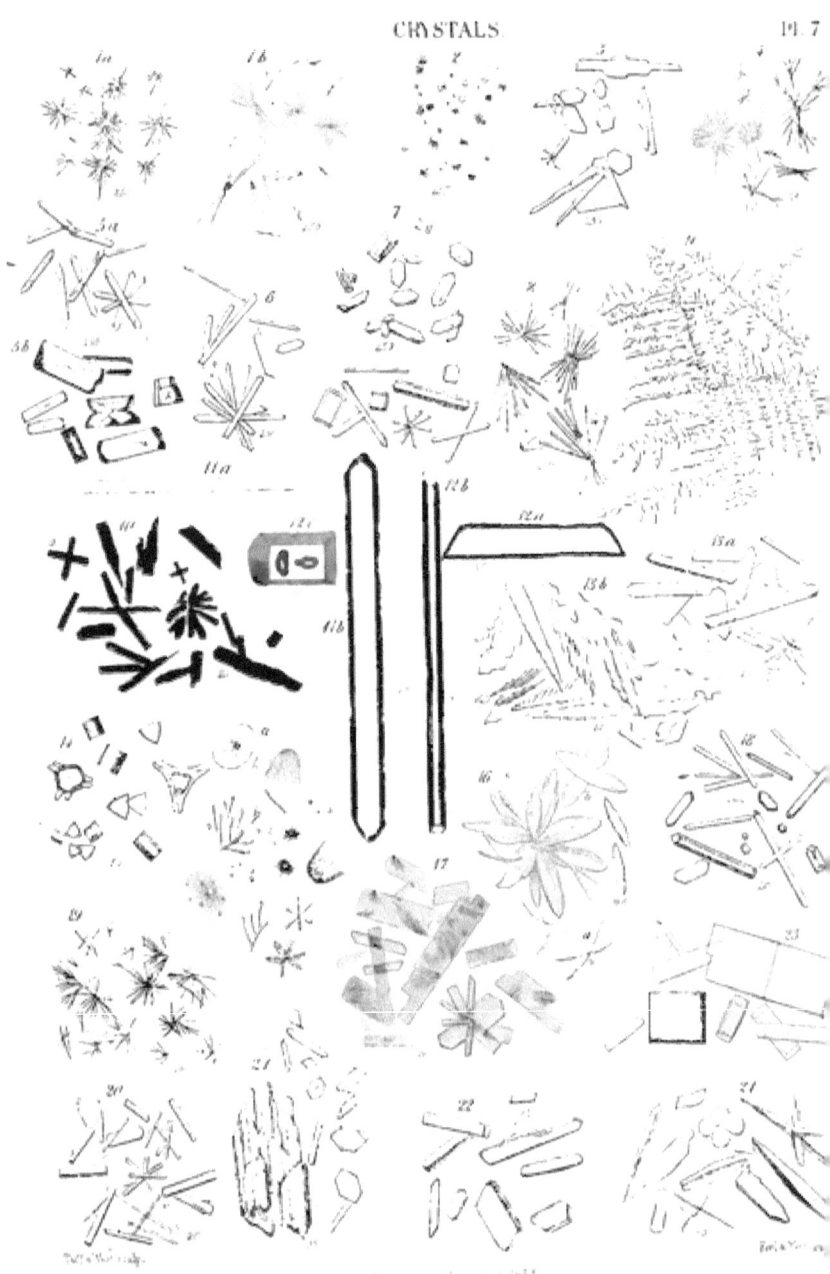

PLATE 7.—Crystals.

Figure

1. *a*, brucia ; *b*, sulphocyanide of brucia.
2. Cinchonine.
3. Sulphocyanide of cinchonine.
4. Narcotine.
5. *a*, *b*, Strychnine.
6. Sulphocyanide of strychnine.
7. Morphia.
8. Sulphocyanide of quinine.
9. Muriate of ammonia.
10. Purpurate of ammonia (murexide).
11. ⎫
    ⎬ Nitrate of potash (ANALYTIC CRYSTALS).
12. ⎭
13. Benzoic acid.   *a*, crystallized from water ; *b*, sublimed.
14. Lithofellinic acid.
15. Margarine.
16. *a*, Margaric acid ; *b*, stearic acid.
17. Iodo-disulphate of quinine.
18. Hippuric acid.
19. Lactate of lime.
20. Lactate of zinc.
21. Succinic acid crystallized from water.
22. Creatine.
23. Creatinine.
24. Compound of creatinine and chloride of zinc.

PLATE 8.—Crystals from Animal Secretions.

Figure

1. Uric acid; human, natural. *a*, rhombs, front view, *b*, side view; *c*, *d*, striated; *e*, rhombs with obtuse angles truncated; *f*, twin crystals; *g*, ditto; *h*, hourglass crystals; *i*, nucleated ditto; *k*, *l*, *m*, *n*, *o* (and lower *h*), aigrettes; *p*, large dumb-bell forms.

2. Uric acid; human, natural. *a*, front, *b*, side view.

3. Uric acid, coloured artificially by murexide.

4. Uric acid, natural. *a*, front, *b*, side view; *c*, aigrette.

5. Uric acid, precipitated from solution in sulphuric acid by water.

6. Uric acid, rhombs, slightly acted upon with potash, showing spurious nuclei.

7. Uric acid, precipitated from gout-stones.

8. Uric acid of *Boa*, artificially precipitated. *a*—*d*, from solution in sulphuric acid by water; *e*—*h*, from solution in potash by muriatic acid.

9. Uric acid, precipitated from the excrement of the tortoise.

10. Uric acid, precipitated:—*a*, from the excrement of the clothes-moth; *b*, from stag-beetle (*Lucanus cervus*).

11. Urate of soda and ammonia. *a*, spheres with nuclei and concentric rings, artificial; *b*, surface covered with radiating needles; *c*, *d*, *e*, natural forms; *f*, *g*, artificial.

12. Urates of soda and ammonia. *a*, artificial urate of ammonia, deposited on cooling of an aqueous solution; *b*, natural urate of soda, as composing the chalky matter around gouty joints.

13. *a*, *b*, Urate of lime.

14. *a*, *b*, Urate of magnesia.

15. Uric acid, precipitated by an acid from human urine.

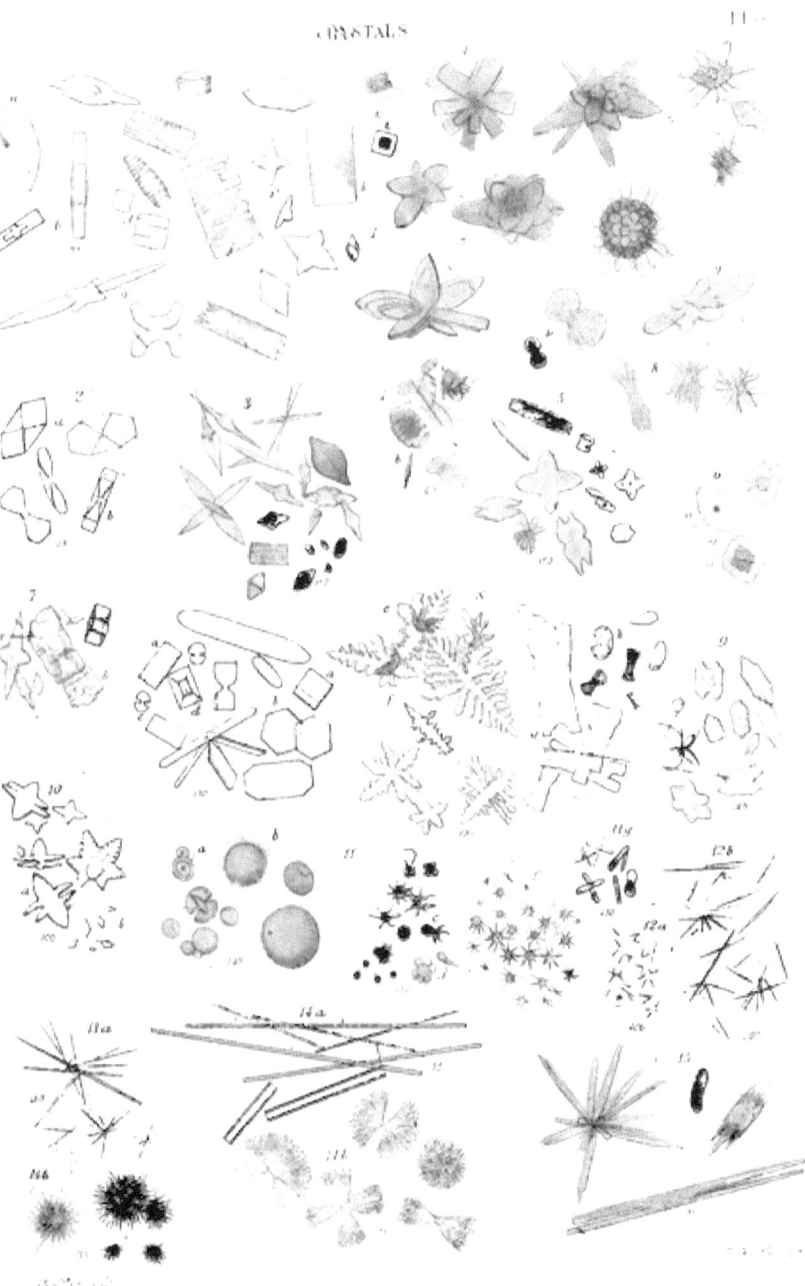

Pl 3

PLATE 9.—Crystals from Animal Secretions.

Figure

1. Various prismatic forms of the ammonio-phosphate of magnesia (triple phosphate), naturally formed in human secretions.
2. Feathery or penniform crystals of the same salt.
3. Stellate form of the same salt.
4. Minute imperfectly formed prisms of the same.
5. Cystic oxide.
6. Carbonate of lime deposited from water by standing.
7. Carbonate of lime from the urine of the horse ; natural.
8. Carbonate of lime from the urine of man ; natural.
9. Octohedra of oxalate of lime, as seen in water.
10. Octohedra of oxalate of lime, as seen when dried.
11. Ellipsoidal forms of oxalate of lime ; natural.
12. Ellipsoidal constricted, or dumb-bell forms of the same ; natural.
13. Crystals of oxalate of lime, prepared with acid.
14. Modified octohedra of the same salt, formed by double decomposition.
15. Crystals of bilifulvine ; natural, human.
16. Crystals of hæmatoidine.
17. Crystals of urea.
18. Nitrate of urea. *a*, *b*, slowly, *c*, rapidly formed.
19. Oxalate of urea.
20. Uroglaucine.
21. Cholesterine.

PLATE 10.—Desmidiaceæ.

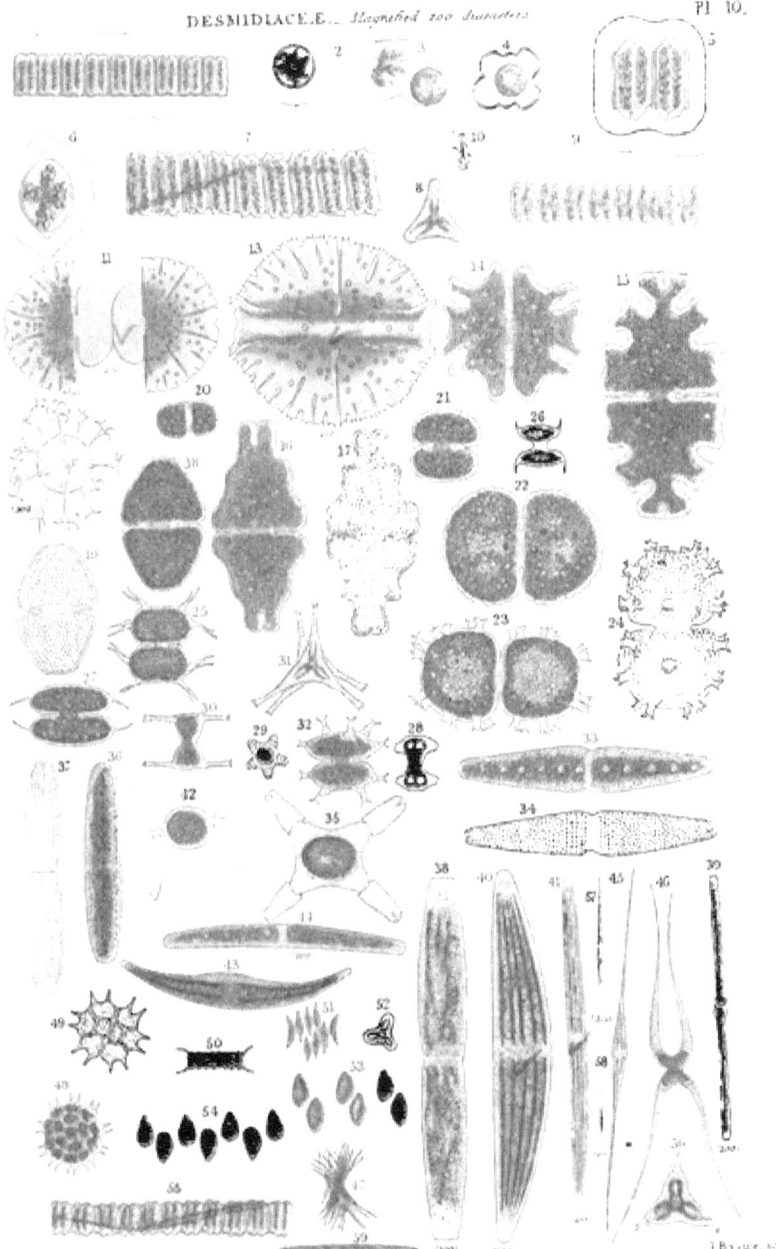

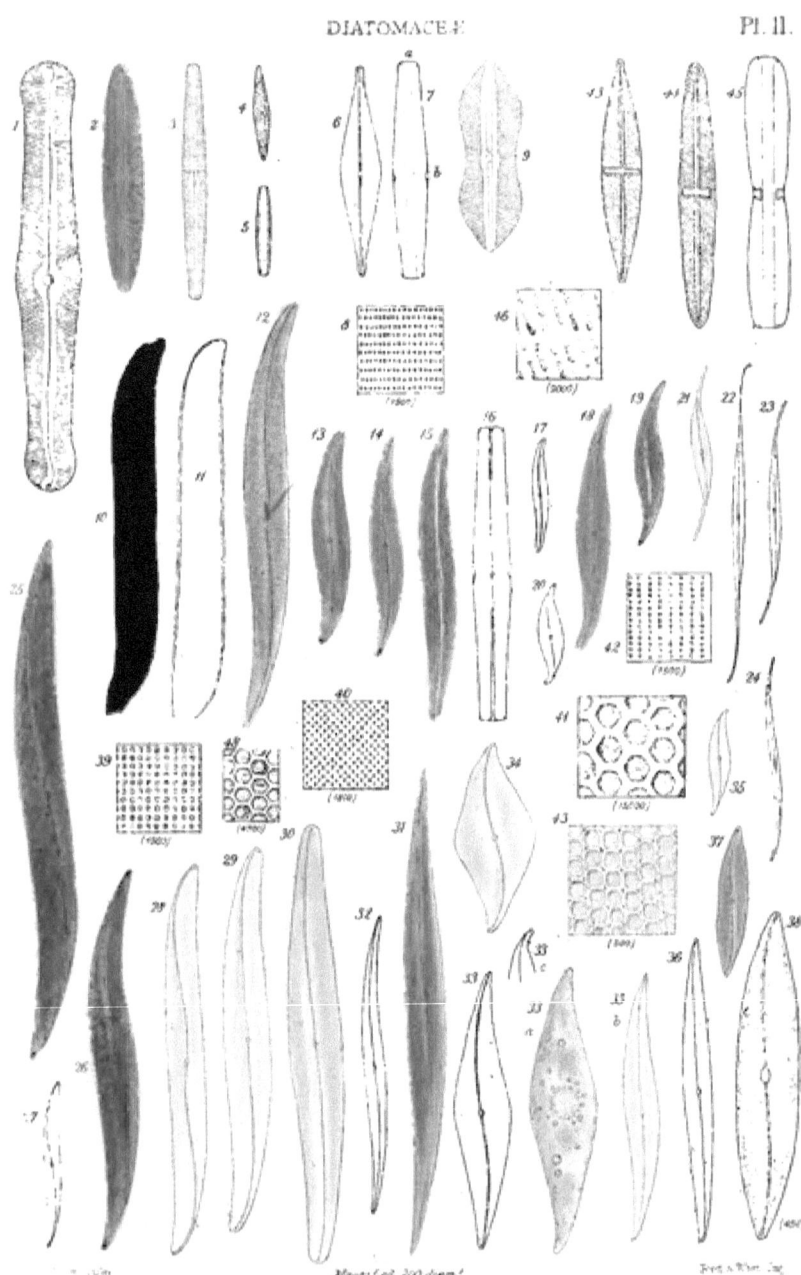

PLATE 11.—Diatomaceæ.

The figures represent the prepared frustules or valves, except when otherwise stated.

Figure
1. *Pinnularia nobilis*, side view.
2. *Pinnularia viridis*, side view, with endochrome.
3. *Pinnularia oblonga*, side view.
4. *Pinnularia radiosa*, side view.
5. *Pinnularia radiosa*, front view.
6. *Navicula cuspidata*, side view.
7. *Navicula cuspidata*, front view.
8. Portion of the valve of a *Navicula*, showing the transverse rows of dots.
9. *Navicula didyma*, side view.
10. *Gyrosigma balticum*, side view.
11. Hoop of the same, side view.
12. *Gyrosigma strigilis*, side view.
13. *Gyrosigma hippocampus*, side view.
14. *Gyrosigma acuminatum*, side view.
15. *Gyrosigma attenuatum*, side view.
16. *Gyrosigma attenuatum*, front view.
17. *Gyrosigma Spencerii*, side view.
18. *Gyrosigma lacustre*, side view.
19. *Gyrosigma littorale*, side view.
20. *Gyrosigma distortum*, side view.
21. *Gyrosigma fasciola*, side view.
22. *Gyrosigma macrum*, side view.
23. *Gyrosigma prolongatum*, side view.
24. *Gyrosigma tenuissimum*, side view.
25. *Gyrosigma formosum*, side view.
26. *Gyrosigma decorum*, side view.
27. *Gyrosigma obscurum*, side view.
28. *Gyrosigma speciosum*, side view.
29. *Gyrosigma strigosum*, side view.
30. *Gyrosigma rigidum*, side view.
31. *Gyrosigma elongatum*, side view.
32. *Gyrosigma delicatulum*, side view.
33. *Gyrosigma angulatum*, side view. *a*, with endochrome; *b*, variety β; *c*, variety γ, end of.
34. *Gyrosigma quadratum*.
35. *Gyrosigma æstuarii*.
36. *Gyrosigma intermedium*.
37. *Gyrosigma transversale*.
38. *Gyrosigma transversale*.
39. Portion of valve of *G. balticum*.
40. Portion of valve of *G. strigosum*.
41. Portion of valve of *G. angulatum*.
42. Portion of valve of *G. littorale*.
43. *Stauroneis phœnicenteron*, side view.
44. *Stauroneis pulchella*, side view.
45. *Stauroneis pulchella*, front view.
46. *Stauroneis pulchella*, portion of valve.
47. Portion of *Isthmia enervis*.
48. Portion of valve of *Gyrosigma strigosum*.

PLATE 12.—Diatomaceæ.

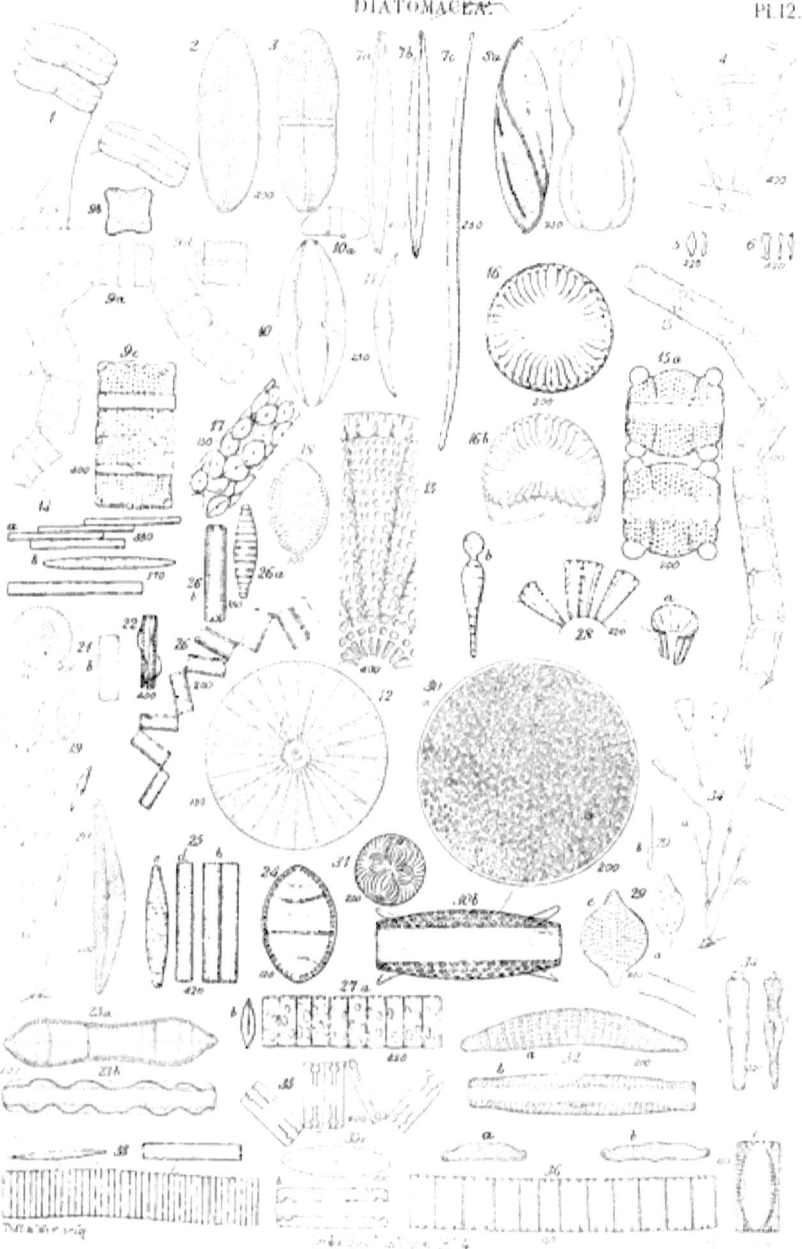

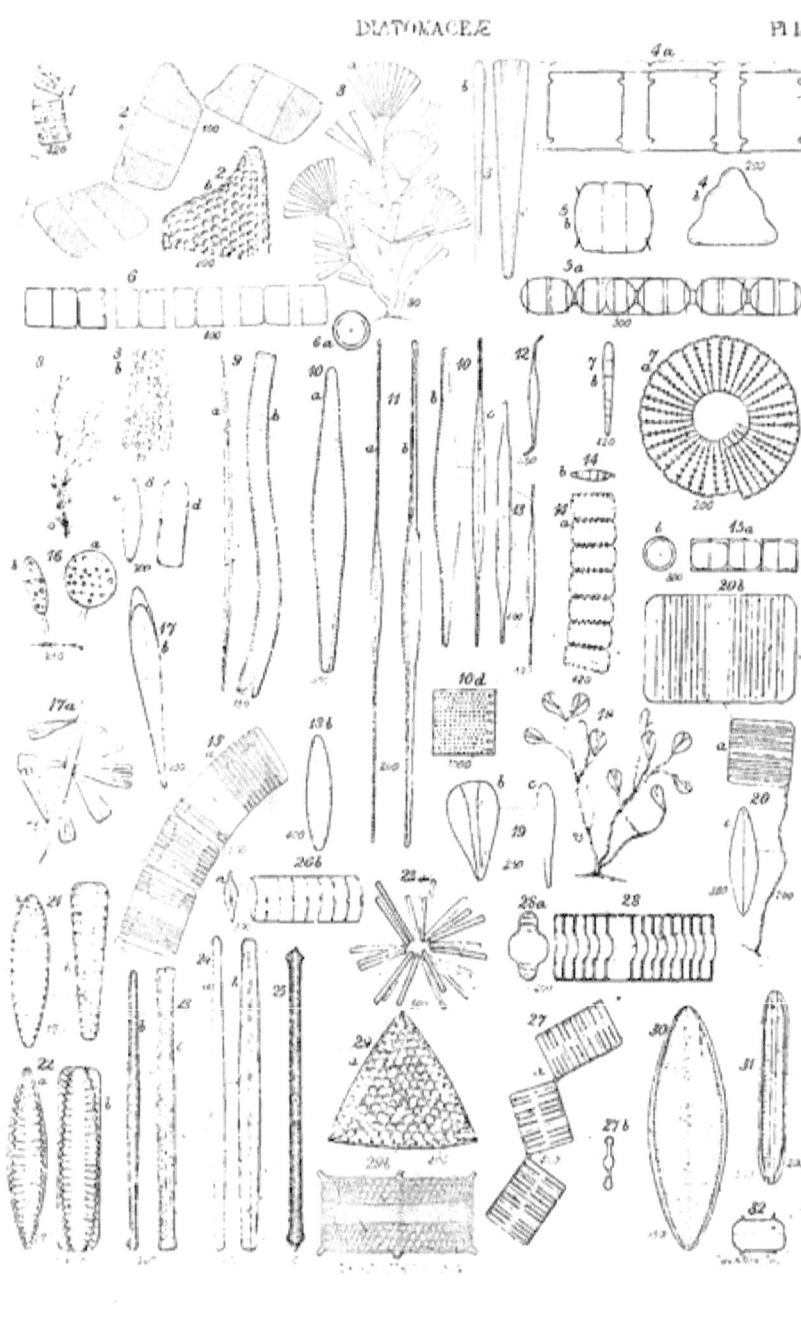

PLATE 13.—Diatomaceæ.

Figure

1. *Hyalosira rectangula*, front view of connected frustules.
2. *Isthmia enervis*, front view.
3. *Licmophora splendida.* *b*, side view ; *c*, front view of single frustule.
4. *Lithodesmium undulatum,* *a*, front view ; *b*, side view.
5. *Melosira nummuloides*, front view.
6. *Melosira varians*, front view. *a*, side view.
7. *Meridion circulare.* *a*, frustules united into a coil, front view ; *b*, side view of single frustule.
8. *Micromega parasitica*, natural size. *b*, portion of a filament containing the frustules ; *c*, side view, *d*, front view of a frustule.
9. *Nitzschia sigmoidea.* *a*, side view ; *b*, front view.
10. *Nitzschia lanceolata.* *a*, front view ; *b*, separate valve ; *c*, side view of the same.
11. *Nitzschia longissima.* *a*, side view ; *b*, front view.
12. *Nitzschia reversa*, front view of single valve.
13. *Nitzschia.* *a*, *tænia* ; *b*, *acicularis*.
14. *Odontidium turgidulum.* *a*, frustules united, front view ; *b*, single valve, side view.
15. *Orthosira Dickieii.* *a*, front view ; *b*, side view.
16. *Pododiscus jamaicensis.* *a*, side view ; *b*, front view.
17. *Podosphenia Ehrenbergii.* *a*, front view ; *b*, side view of single frustule.
18. *Rhabdonema arcuatum.* *a*, united frustules, front view ; *b*, side view of single frustule. (See also Pl. 43. fig. 69.)
19. *Rhipidophora paradoxa.* *b*, front view of single frustule ; *c*, side view of the same.
20. *Striatella unipunctata.* *a*, front view ; *b*, the same ; *c*, side view.
21. *Surirella gemma.* *a*, side view ; *b*, front view.
22. *Surirella bifrons.* *a*, front view ; *b*, side view.
23. *Synedra splendens.* *a*, attached frustules ; *b*, side view of prepared frustule ; *c*, front view of the same.
24. *Synedra fulgens.* *a*, side view ; *b*, front view of a prepared frustule.
25. *Synedra capitata*, side view.
26. *Sphenosira catena.* *a*, united frustules, front view ; *b*, side view of single frustule.
27. *Tabellaria flocculosa.* *a*, united frustules, front view ; *b*, side view of single frustule.
28. *Tetracyclus lacustris*, united frustules, front view. *a*, side view.
29. *Triceratium favus.* *a*, side view ; *b*, front view.
30. *Tryblionella scutellum*, side view.
31. *Tryblionella gracilis*, front view.
32. *Tryblionella gracilis*, diagram of transverse section.

PLATE 14.—Diatomaceæ and Entomostraca.

Figure

1. *Acroperus nanus.*   2. *Acroperus harpæ.*

3. *Alteutha depressa.*   *a*, first pair of legs.

4. *Alona reticulata.*   5. *Alona quadrangularis.*

6. *Anomalocera Patersonii*, male.

7. *Anchorella uncinata.*   *a*, arms ; *b*, abdomen ; *c*, ovarian tubes.

8. *Berkeleya fragilis.*   *a*, natural size ; *b*, portion of a branch containing frustules ; *c*, side view, *d*, front view of a single frustule.

9. *Biddulphia aurita.*   Frustules undergoing division : *a*, hoop of original frustule, to which two new halves (*c*) have been formed ; the hoop of the new frustules is seen at *b* ; the hoop of the parent has separated from the two frustules *d d*, which are perfectly formed, each with its new hoop.

10. *Encyonema paradoxum.*   *a*, frustules contained in a gelatinous tube, side view ; *b*, front view ; *c*, separate frustules, side view.

11. *Raphidoglœa micans.*   *a*, natural size ; *b*, group of frustules ; *c*, single frustule, front view.

12. *Schizonema Dillwynnii.*   *a*, natural size ; *b*, filaments containing frustules ; *c*, front view, *d*, side view of frustule.

13. *Zygoceros rhombus.*   *a*, front view ; *b*, side view.

14. *Syncyclia salpa* ; frustules immersed in a gelatinous mass.

15. *Homœocladia anglica.*   *a*, portion of the natural size ; *b*, part of a filament containing two frustules ; *c*, front view, *d*, side view of a prepared frustule.

16. *Dickieia ulvoides.*   *a*, natural size ; *b*, portion of frond containing frustules ; *c*, *d*, *f*, prepared frustules, front view ; *e*, side view.

17. *Frustulia saxonica* ; frustules immersed in a gelatinous mass.

18. *Cymbosira Agardhii.*   *a*, united frustules ; *b*, front view, *c*, side view of prepared frustules.

19. *Sphenella vulgaris.*   *a*, front view ; *b*, side view.

20. Spermatozoa of a *Cypris.*

21. *Cetochilus septentrionalis*, dorsal view.

22. *Notodelphys ascidicola*, female.   23. *Lepeophtheirus pectoralis*, female.

24. *Lerneonema spratta*, female.   25. *Macrothrix laticornis*, female.

26. *Moina rectirostris*, female.   27. *Sida crystallina.*

28. *Nebalia bipes.*   29. *Polyphemus pediculus.*

30. *Evadne Nordmanni.*

31. *Peracantha truncata.*   *a*, superior antenna.

32. *Pleuroxus trigonellus.*

33. *Terpsinoe musica* (front view, Pl. 19. fig. 10).

34. *Podosira hormoides*, front view.   35. *Tessella interrupta*, front view.

36. *Nicothoe astaci.*   *a*, ovaries.

37. *Grammatophora marina*, as seen by ordinary illumination.   *a*, front view ; *b*, side view.

38. *Grammatophora subtilissima*, as seen by ordinary illumination.   *a*, front view ; *b*, side view.

PLATE 15.—Entomostraca.

PLATE 16.—Entozoa.

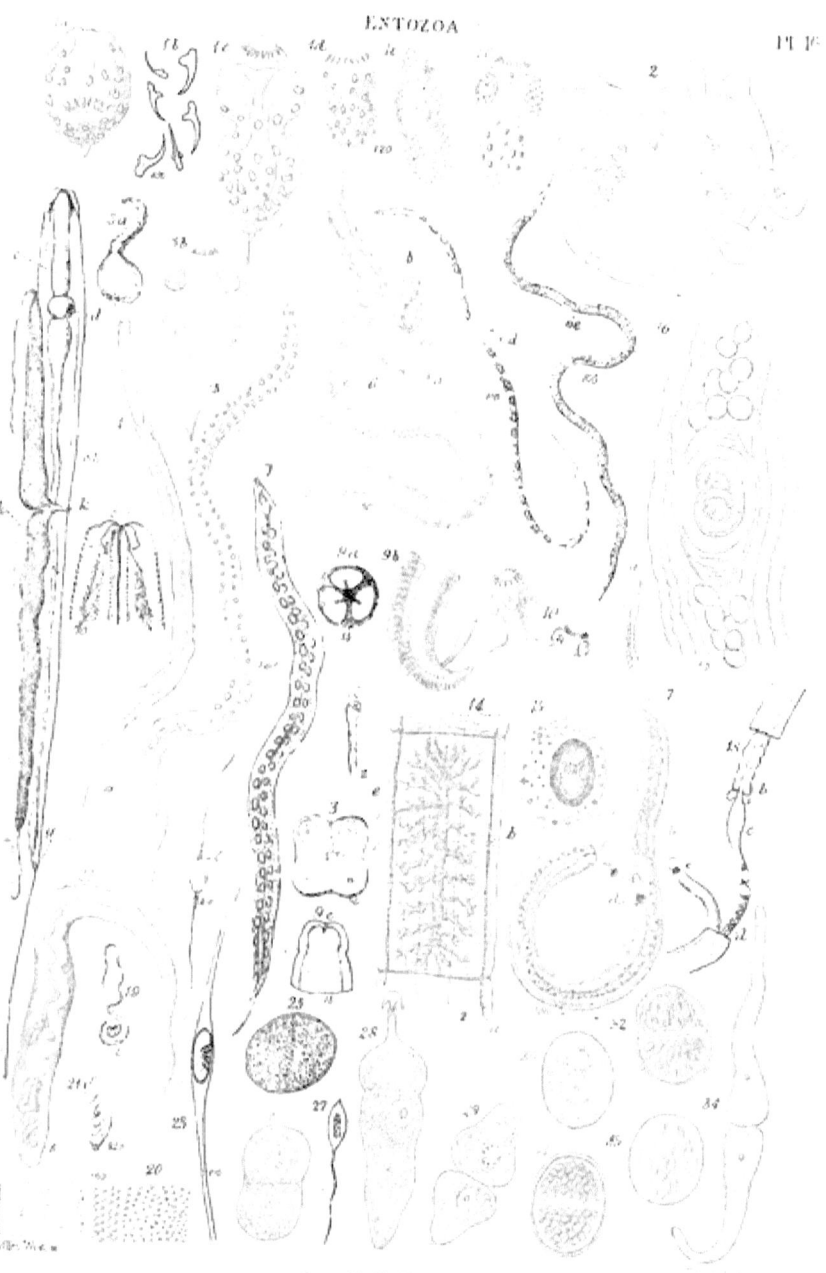

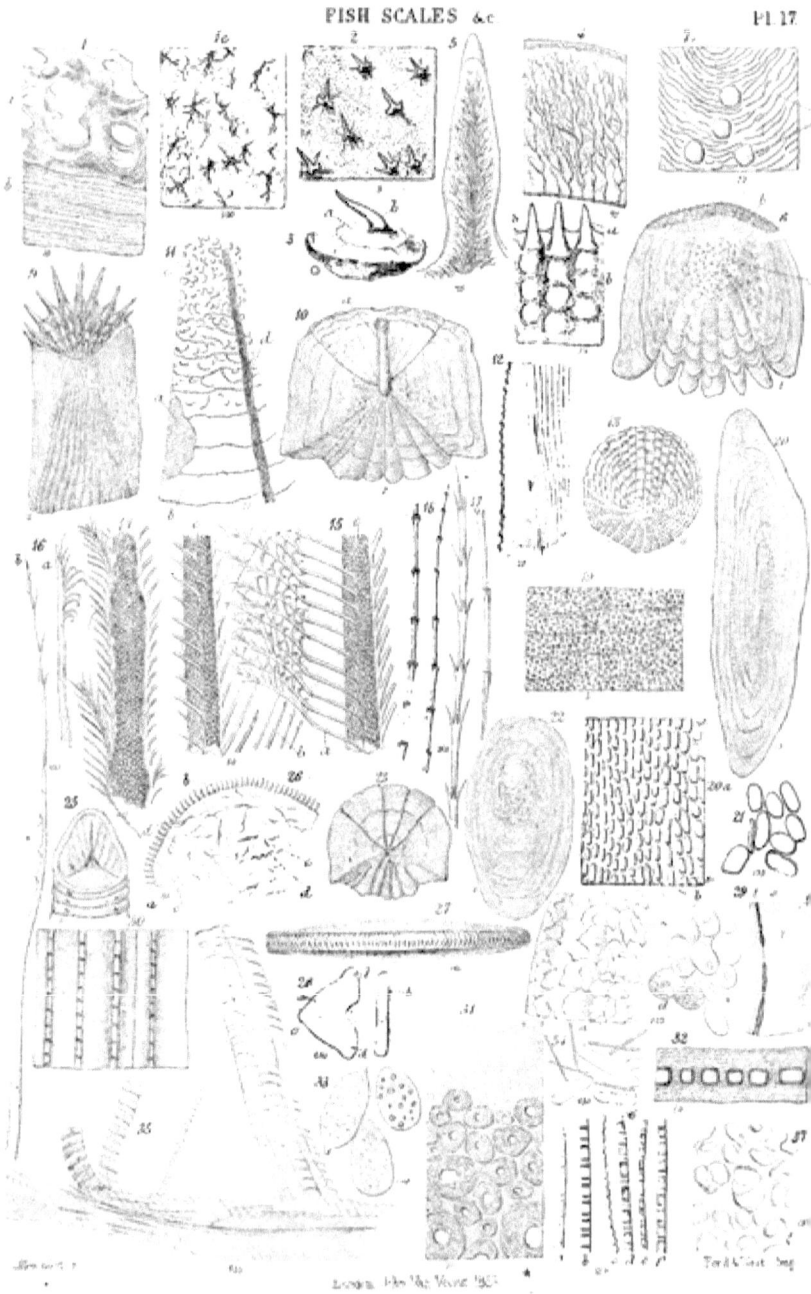

PLATE 17.—Fish-scales, etc.

Figure

1. Scale of sturgeon, perpendicular section. *a*, outer spongy portion ; *b*, inner laminated portion ; 1 *c*, transverse section of outer portion.
2. Skin of thornback-skate (*Raia clavata*), viewed from above.
3. Large spine of skate, side view.
4. Portion of transverse section of large spine of skate (fig. 3 *b*).
5. Longitudinal section of tooth of a small spine of skate (fig. 2).
6. Scale of perch (*Perca fluviatilis*).
7. Perch-scale, portion of (fig. 6 *a*), more magnified.
8. Perch-scale, portion of (fig. 6 *b*), more magnified.
9. Scale of sole (*Solea vulgaris*).
10. Scale of roach (*Leuciscus rutilus*).
11. Scale of roach (*Leuciscus rutilus*), portion of surface more highly magnified.
12. Scale of roach (*Leuciscus rutilus*), perpendicular section.
13. Scale of minnow (*Leuciscus phoxinus*).
14. Feather of finch ; shaft with medullary cells.
15. Feather of goose (*Anser cinereus*). *a*, pinnæ with hooks ; *b*, pinnæ with teeth ; *c*, barbs.
16. Separate pinnæ. *a*, with hooks ; *b*, with teeth.
17.
18. } Feather (downy), free barbs of.
19. Skin of eel (*Anguilla vulgaris*), with stellate pigment-cells, and indications of subjacent scales.
20. Scale of eel (*Anguilla vulgaris*). 20 *a*, portion more magnified.
21. Calcareous corpuscles from the same, left after red heat.
22. Scale of jack or pike (*Esox lucius*).
23. Scale of dace (*Leuciscus vulgaris*).
25. Leech (*Hirudo medicinalis*), anterior sucker of.
26. Leech, jaw of, side view. *a b*, teeth ; *c*, fibro-cartilaginous substance of jaw ; *d*, pigment-cells.
27. Leech, jaw of, the free margin turned towards the observer.
28. Leech, teeth of. *a*, side view ; *b*, front view.
29. Horn of cow. *a*, section parallel to surface ; *b*, cells softened by potash, *d*, containing pigment ; *e*, perpendicular section ; *f*, cracks between laminæ ; *g*, edges of divided laminæ.
30. Whalebone, longitudinal section.
31. Whalebone, transverse section.
32. Whalebone, longitudinal section of hair of.
33. Whalebone, cells of, resolved by potash.
34. Fish, crystals from scales of.
35. Muscular fibres of lobster (*Astacus marinus*).
36. Muscular fibrillæ, various appearances presented by.
37. Large spine of skate, outer portion of.

PLATE 18.—Foraminifera, etc.

Figure

1. *Rosalina beccarii*, shell of, from sea-sand.
2. *Globigerina*, the cells filled with air.
3. *Nodosaria radicula.*
4. *Nonionina crassula.*
5. *Rosalina beccarii*, body freed from the shell.
6. *Orthocerina quadrilatera.*
7. *Globulina gibba.*
8. *Uvigerina pygmæa*
9. *Marginulina pedum.*
10. *Marginulina raphanus*, shell, longitudinal section.
11. *Orbulina universa.*
12. *Nummulina planulata.*
13. *Hauerina compressa.*
14. *Vertebralina striata.*
15. *Spirolina austriaca.*
16. *Sorites orbiculus*, shells, nat. size, side- and edge-views.
17. *Sorites orbiculus*, shell, side view; two of the cells are broken open, others are shown partly closed by dendritic calcareous particles.
18. *Orbiculina rotella.*
19. *Polystomella crispa.*
20. *Polystomella umbilicatula.*
21. *Rotalina Haidingerii.*
22. *Operculina arabica*, shell, side view, nat. size.
23. *Operculina arabica*, shell, surface view. *a*, small, *b*, large papillæ.
24. *Operculina arabica*, spicula.
25. *Operculina arabica*, vertical section of shell over the chambers. *a*, large, *b*, small papillæ; *c*, lines of growth; *d*, vertical tubes.
26. *Operculina arabica*; vertical section of septum, showing—*a*, intraseptal vessel; *b*, septum; *c*, grand channel of intercameral communication; *d*, part of spicular cord.
27. *Operculina arabica*; horizontal section of three large chambers, showing—*a*, chambers; *b*, septa; *c*, intraseptal vessels; *d*, branches to surfaces of septa; *e*, branches to wall of shell, &c.; *f*, marginal plexus; *g*, terminal branches on the surface; *h*, spicular cord; *i*, half-formed septum.
28. *Operculina arabica*, perpendicular section. *a*, spicular cord; *b*, papillary tubes; *c*, truncated vessels of marginal plexus; *d*, small channels of intercameral communication; *e*, grand channel of the same; *f*, septum.
29. *Nummulites acuta*, vertical section. *a*, spicular cord, *b*, truncated vessels of marginal plexus; *c*, chambers of central plane; *d*, vertical intraseptal vessels; *e*, horizontal intraseptal vessels; *f*, chambers on each side of central plane; *g*, vertical tubes.
30. *Eunotia tetraodon*. *a*, side view; *b*, front view.
31. *Cymbella Ehrenbergii*. *a*, side view; *b*, front view.
32. *Coscinodiscus radiatus*. *a*, side view; *b*, front view.
33. *Globigerina bulloides.*
34. *Textularia cuneiformis.*
35. *Guttulina communis.*
36. *Rosalina beccarii.*
37. *Robulina cultrata.*
38. *Truncatulina lobulata.*
39. *Vulvulina gramen.*
40. *Faujasina carinata.*
41. *Vaginulina badensis.*
42. *Valvulina austriaca.*
43. *Actinocyclus undulatus*. *a*, side view; *b*, front view.
44. *Campylodiscus clypeus*, side view.
45. *Actinoptychus senarius*. *a*, side view; *b*, front view.
46. *Dictyocha gracilis*. *a*, oblique view; *b*, side view; *c*, front view.
47. *Webbina rugosa.*

Pl. 18

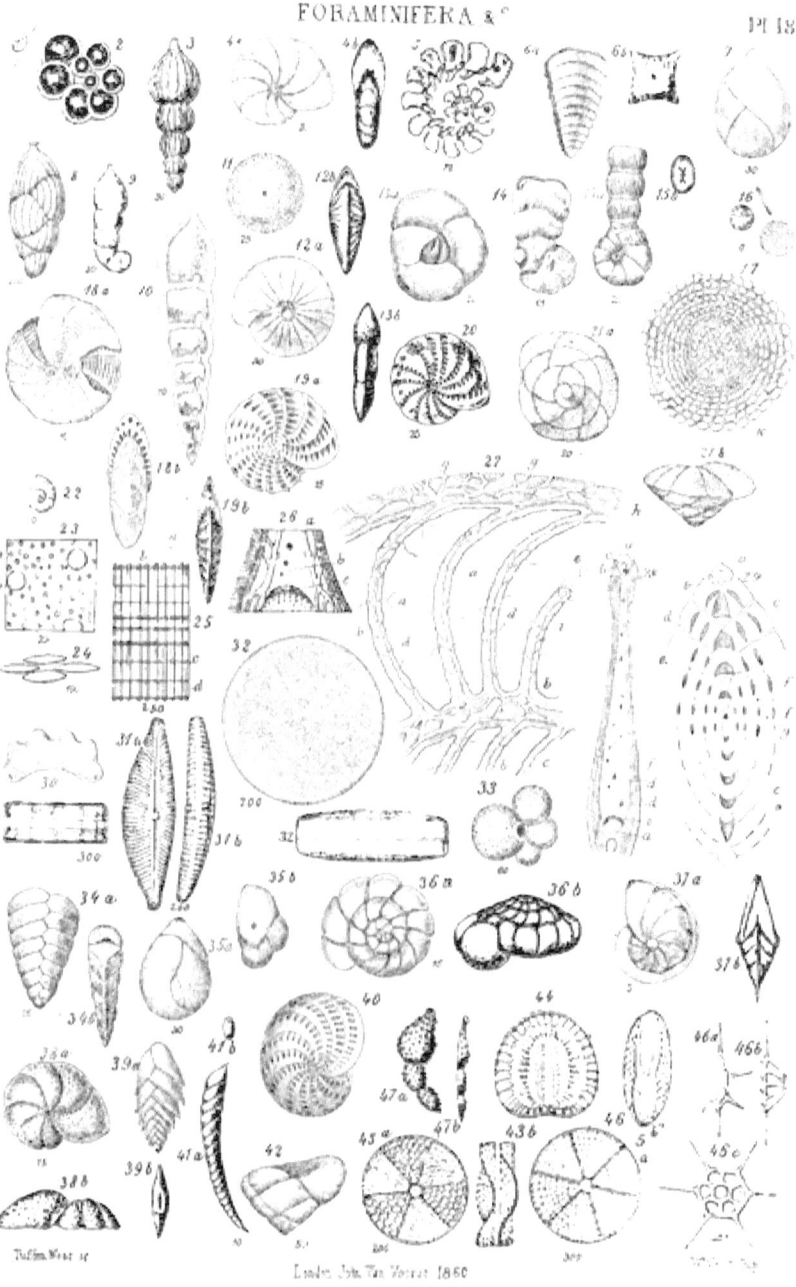

Pl. 19.

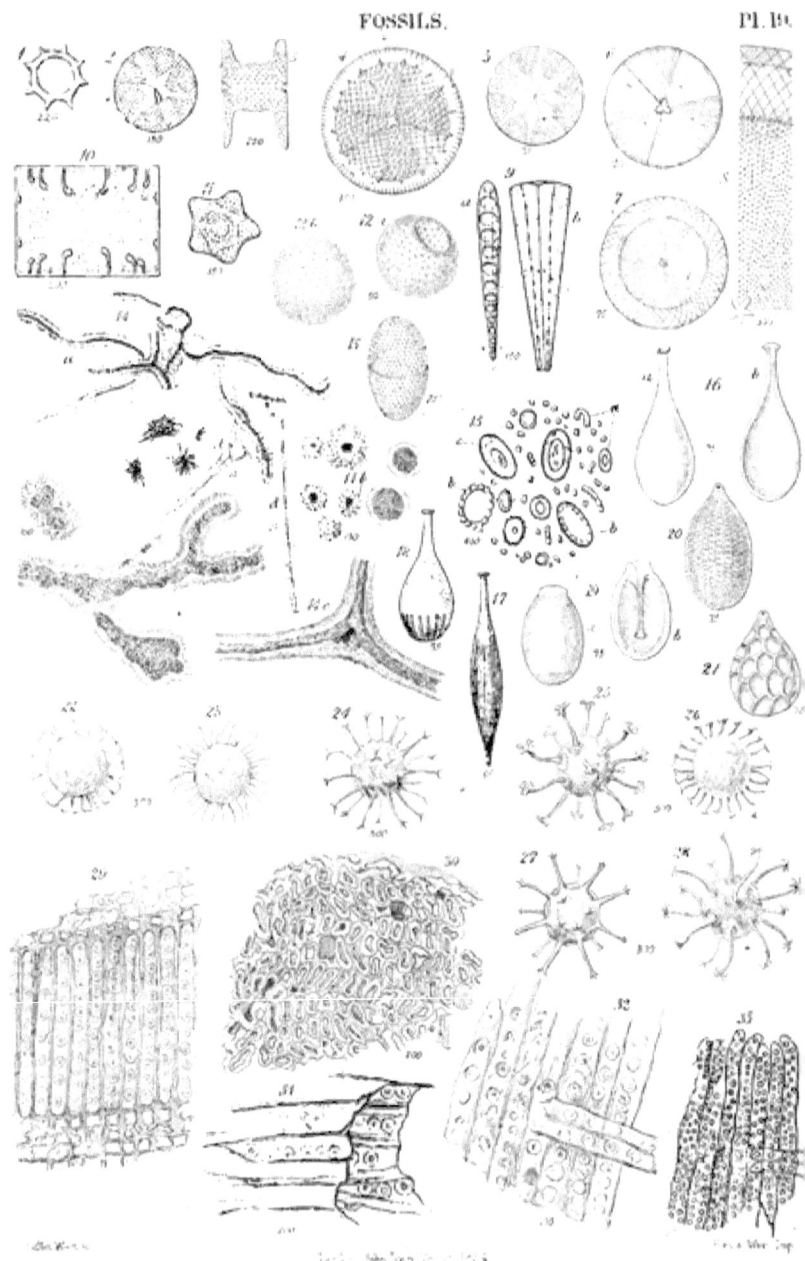

PLATE 20.—Fungi.

Figure

1. Vertical section of a leaf of black currant, infested with *Æcidium grossulariæ*. *sp*, spermogonia ; *p*, perithecia.

2. Sterigmata (*st*) and spermatia (*sp*) from the spermogonia of *Æcidium euphorbiæ*.

3. Ditto, from *Æcidium berberidis*.

4. Vertical section of a spermogonium of *Æcidium berberidis*.

5. *Botrytis infestans*, young plants growing out from the stomate of a potato.

6. Full-grown plants of the same.   6 *a*, spore of ditto.

7. *Torula* ——?, growing in urine (not diabetic).

8. Grape fungus, conidial form (*Oidium Tuckeri*) as commonly found on the leaves and fruits.

9–11. Conidia of the same, germinating.

12. Sporiferous form (*Circinobolus*).

13. Spores from the same.

14. Hop-mildew, *Erysiphe* (*Sphærotheca*) *Castagnei*.   *a*, Oidial form ; *b, b*, form resembling *Circinobolus* ; *c, d*, Erysiphal form ; *e*, spores.

15. Fragment from the summit of a fertile filament of *Penicillium glaucum*.

16. Spores of ditto.   *a*, two still united ; *b*, one detached.

17. Section of a conceptacle of *Cenangium fraxini*, containing *st*, stylospores, and *s*, spermatia.

18. Ergot of rye, *Cordyceps purpurea*, Tulasne ; fruits sprouting from the ergot.

19. Vertical section of the head of one of the fruits, bearing conceptacles in its periphery.

20. Vertical section of a conceptacle containing asci.

21. Asci removed from the same.

22. Spores from the interior of the asci.

23. Yeast-fungus (*Torula cerevisiæ*), large form at the bottom of liquid.

24. Ditto, minute form, appearing as a white mealy substance on the surface of stale beer.

25. *Sphæria inquinans* (*a*) with *Stilbospora macrosperma* (*b*) in the bark of an elm-tree.

26. A portion of the common matrix separating the two, with the stylospores of *Stilbospora* (*b*) above, and the asci of *Sphæria* (*a*) below.

27. Spore of *Stilbospora macrosperma*.

28. Spore of *Sphæria inquinans*.

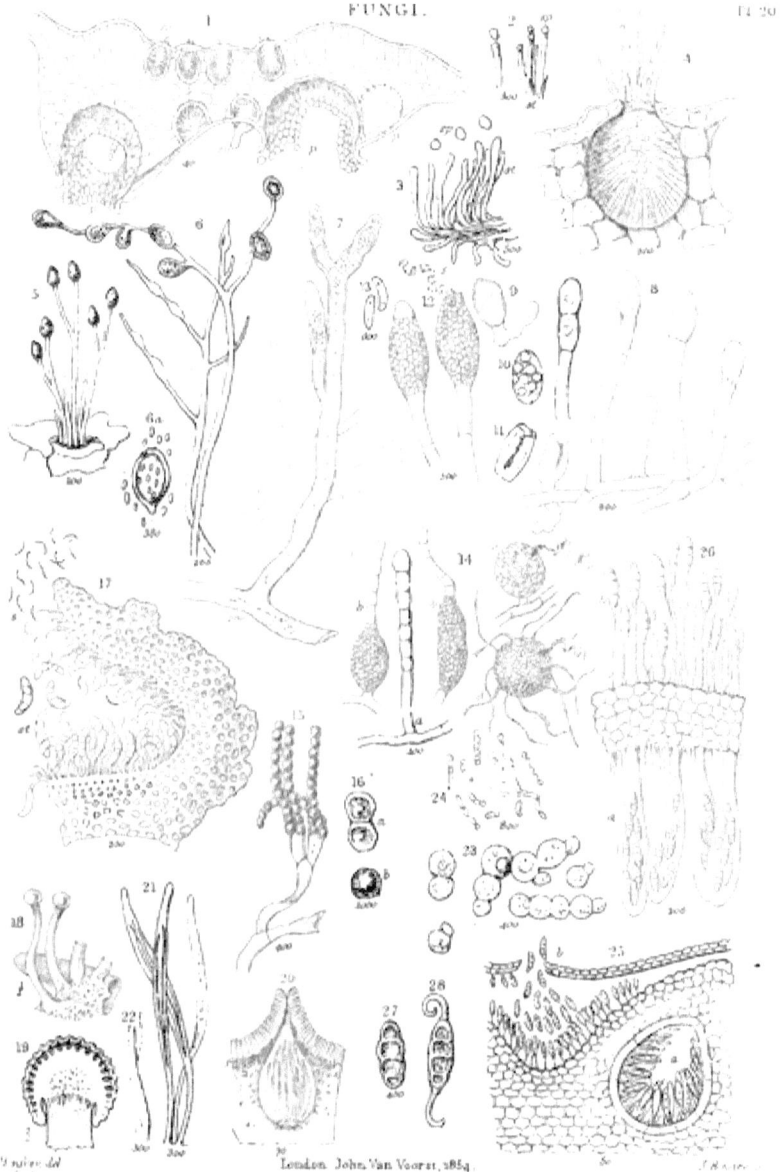

PLATE 21.—Hairs, Fibres, Glands, &c. of Plants.

Figure

1. Cotton. *a*, normal condition ; *b*, portion treated with sulphuric acid and iodine ; *c*, a fragment of gun-cotton.
2. Flax. *a*, normal fibre ; *b*, portion boiled with nitric acid ; *c*, treated with nitric acid, and afterwards with sulphuric acid and iodine.
3. Jute. *a*, normal fibre ; *b*, *c*, portions boiled with nitric acid.
4. Coir (Cocoa-nut fibre), bundle of fibres.
5. Ditto. *a*, *b*, portions of fibres boiled with nitric acid.
6. Hemp. *a*, normal fibre ; *b*, portions boiled with nitric acid.
7. Manilla hemp. *a*, normal fibres ; *b*, fragment boiled with nitric acid.
8. Sting of *Urtica urens*.
9. Surface of the cuticle of *Helleborus fœtidus*.
10. Ditto of *Cakile americana*.
11. Imbedded gland of *Ruta graveolens*, vertical section.
12. Glands of *Magnolia*, seen from above.
13. Hair of *Siphocampylus bicolor*, the cuticle detached by sulphuric acid.
14. Glands of hop. *a*, side view ; *b*, from above.
15. Stellate body from the air-spaces in the leaf of *Nuphar lutea*.
16. Hair of *Delphinium pinnatifidum*. 17. Hair of *Anchusa crispa*.
18. Hair of *Pelargonium*. 19. Branched hair of *Verbascum Thapsus*.
20. Scale-like hairs from the seed of *Cobaa scandens*.
21. Annulated hairs from the seed of *Ruellia formosa*, in water; *b*, detached cell-wall.
22. Spiral-fibrous hairs from the seed of *Collomia grandiflora*, in water. *b*, *c*, fragments showing the cell-wall and free fibre.
23. Hair from the seed of a *Salvia*.
24. Hair from the seed of *Acanthodium spicatum*. *b*, a fragment of a branch.
25. Chinese grass-cloth fibre. *a*, normal fibre ; *b*, fragments boiled with nitric acid ; *c*, afterwards treated with sulphuric acid and iodine.
26. Puya fibre. *a*, normal fibre ; *b*, fragments boiled with nitric acid ; *c*, afterwards treated with sulphuric acid and iodine.
26*.Stellate hairs from the epidermis of *Deutzia scabra*.
27. Stellate hair of ivy-leaf. 28. Stellate hair of *Alyssum*.
29. Horizontal stalked hair of *Grevillea lithidophylla*.
30. T-shaped hair of garden *Chrysanthemum*.
31. Ramentum or scale from a germinating fern.
32. Hair from the bulbil of *Achimenes*.
33. Hair from the corolla of *Digitalis purpurea*.
34. Hair from the corolla of *Antirrhinum majus*.
35. Branched hair from the epidermis of *Sisymbrium sophia*.
36. Forked hair from *Capsella bursa-pastoris*.
37. Branched hair of *Alternanthera axillaris*.
38. Gland of *Dictamnus fraxinella*.
39. Epidermis of *Dictamnus fraxinella*. *a*, *b*, hairs ; *c*, gland vertically divided.
40. Glandular hair of *Lysimachia vulgaris*.
41. Glandular hair of *Scrophularia nodosa*.
42. Glandular hair of *Bryonia alba*.
43. Scale of *Begonia platanifolia*.
44. Glandular hair of *Gilia tricolor*.
45. Vertical section of papilla of *Mesembryanthemum crystallinum*.
46. Seta of a rose.
47. Tufted hairs of *Marrubium creticum*.

PLATE 22.—Hairs of Animals.

Figure

1. Human whisker, white ; air partly displaced from medulla.
2. Human hair, transverse sections.
3. Human hair, foetal, with imbricated scales.
4. Monkey, Indian (*Semnopithecus*).
5. *Lemur.*
6. Bat, Indian.
7. Bat, Australian.
8. Mole (*Talpa europæa*).
9. Lion (*Felis leo*); left-hand figure by transmitted, right by reflected light.
10. Bear (*Ursus arctos*).
11. Wolf (*Canis lupus*).
12. Coati mondi (*Nasua*).
13. Seal, Falkland Island (*Phocæna falklandica*).
14. Horse (*Equus caballus*).
15. Elephant (*Elephas indicus*), segment of a transverse section.
16. Pig (*Sus scrofa*).
17. *Cheiropotamus.*
18. Camel (*Camelus bactrianus*).
19. Dromedary (*Camelus dromedarius*).
20. Deer, moose- (*Cervus alces*).
21. Deer, musk- (*Moschus moschiferus*).
22. Wool, sheep (*Ovis aries*).
23. Sloth (*Bradypus didactylus*).
24. Armadillo (*Dasypus sexcinctus*).
25. Beaver (*Castor fiber*).
26. Shrew (*Amphisorex rusticus*).
27. Mouse (*Mus musculus*).
28. Ditto, treated with potash.
29. Guinea-pig (*Cavia cobaya*).
30. Squirrel (*Sciurus vulgaris*).
31. Rabbit (*Lepus cuniculus*).
32. Sable (*Mustela zibellina*).
33. Mink-sable (*Mustela lutreola*).
34. Badger (*Meles taxus*).
35. Chinchilla (*Chinchilla lanigera*).
36. Kangaroo (*Macropus*).
37. Opossum (*Didelphis virginiana*).
38. *Ornithorhynchus paradoxus.* *a*, entire hair ; *b*, *c*, *d* and 38*, portions more magnified.
39. Crab (*Cancer mænas*), from antenna of.
40. Spider (*Lycosa saccata*).
41. Spider (*Mygale*).
42. Spider (—— ?), from South America.

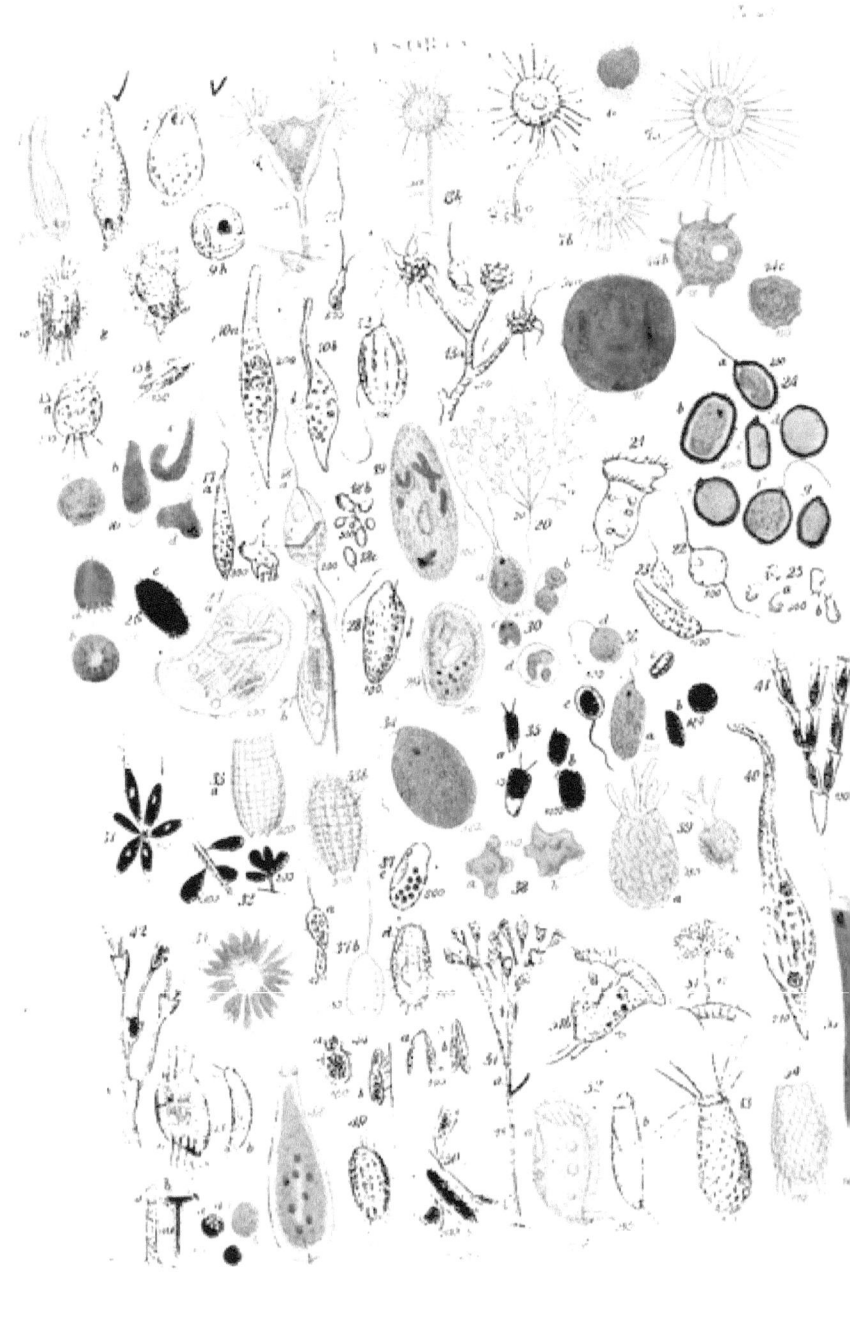

PLATE 23.—Infusoria.

Figure

1. *Acineria incurcata*, Duj.
2. *Acineria acuta*, D.
3. *Acomia vitrea*, D.
4. *Acineta tuberosa*, Ehr.
5a. *Podophrya fixa*, E.; 5 *b*, the same, or the *Podophrya*-stage of *Vorticella* ?
6. *Actinophrys viridis*, E.
7a. *Actinophrys Eichornii*, E.; 7 *b*, *Actinophrys sol*, E.
8. *Alyscum saltans*, D.
9. *Amaba diffluens*, E. 9 *a*, expanded; 9 *b*, contracted.
10. *Amphileptus fasciola*, E. 10 *a*, dorsal view; 10 *b*, side view.
11. *Amphimonas dispar*, D.
12. *Anisonema sulcata*, D.
13. *Anthophysa Mülleri*, Bory, Duj. (*Epistylis vegetans*, E.); 13 *a*, entire organism; *b*, single body.
14a. *Arcella vulgaris*, E., dorsal view; 14 *b*, *Arcella aculeata*, E., under view; 14 *c*, *Arcella dentata*, E., under view.
15a. *Aspidisca lynceus*, E., under view; 15 *b*, *Asp. denticulata*, E., side view.
16. *Astasia hæmatodes*, E. *a*, contracted; *b*, *c*, *d*, in different states of expansion.
17. *Astasia limpida*, D. (*A. pusilla*, E.). *a*, expanded; *b*, altered in shape.
18a. *Bodo grandis*, E.; 18 *b*, *c*, *Bodo socialis*, E.
19. *Bursaria vernalis*, E., under surface.
20. *Carchesium polypinum*, E.
21. *Carchesium polypinum*, E., separate body.
22. *Cercomonas acuminata*, D.
23. *Cercomonas crassicauda*, D.
24. Various forms of *Trachelomonas*, arranged by Ehrenberg in the genera *Trachelomonas*, *Chætoglena* and *Doxococcus*. See TRACHELOMONAS.
25a. *Chætomonas globulus*, E.; 25 *b*, *Ch. constrictus*, E.
26. *a*, *b*, *Chætotyphla armata*, E.; *c*, *Ch. aspera*, E.
27. *Chilodon cucullulus*, E. *a*, under view; *b*, side view.
28. *Chilomonas granulosa*, D.
29. *Chlamidodon mnemosyne*, E., ventral surface.
30. *Chlamidomonas pulvisculus*, E. (*Diselmis viridis*, D.), in various stages of development.
31. *Chlorogonium euchlorum*, E. (upper and lower figure), in different stages of development.
32. *Colacium vesiculosum*, left-hand figure; *C. stentorium*, right-hand figure.
33. *Coleps hirtus*, E. (*a*, after Ehr., *b*, after Duj.).
34. *Crumenula texta*, D.
35a. *Cryptoglena conica*, E.; 35 *b*, *Cr. pigra*, E.
36a. *Cryptomonas ovata*, E.; *b*, *C. lenticularis*, E.; *c*, *C. fusca*, E; *d*, *C. globulus*, D.; *e*, *C. inæqualis*, D.
37a. *Cyclidium distortum*, D.; *b*, *C. abscissum*, D.; *c* and *d*, *C. glaucoma*, E.; *c*, side view; *d*, dorsal view.
38. *Cyphidium aureolum*, E. *a*, dorsal view; in *b*, the expansion is seen.
39. *Difflugia proteiformis*, E., *a* and *b*.
40. *Dileptus folium*, D.
41. *Dinobryon sertularia*, E. 42. *Dinobryon petiolatum*, D.
43. *Diophrys marina*, D. *a*, under view; *b*, side view.
44. *Discocephalus rotatorius*, E. *a*, dorsal view; *b*, side view.
45. *Disoma vacillans*, E.
46. *a*, *Distigma proteus*, E.; *b*, *D. viride*, E.
47. *a*, *Doxococcus ruber*, E.; *b*, *D. pulvisculus*, E.
48. *Enchelys pupa*, E. 49. *Enchelys nodulosa*, D.
50. *Epipyxis utriculus*, E.
51. *a*, *Epistylis anastatica*; *b*, single body of *E. grandis*.
52. *Errilia legumen*, D. (*Exoplotes monostylus*, E.). *a*, under view; *b*, side view.
53. *Euglypha tuberculata*, D. 54. *Euglypha alveolata*, D.
55. *Amblyophis viridis*, E.

PLATE 24.—Infusoria.

Figure
1. *Euglena pyrum*, E.
2. *Euglena viridis*, E.   *a, b,* in different states of contraction and extension.
3. *Euglena longicauda*, E. (*Phacus longicauda*, D.), with the body twisted. (Fig. 63, the same, after Duj.; the body flat.)
4. *Euglena acus*, E., undergoing longitudinal division.
5. *Euplotes patella*, D.   *a,* under view; *b,* lateral view.
6. *Euplotes vannus*, E., under view.   7. *Gastrochæta fissa*, D.
8. *Glaucoma scintillans*, E.   9. *Peridinium cinctum*, E.
10 *a, b. Glenodinium cinctum*, E.; 10 *c* (between figs. 49 & 50), *Glenodinium apiculatum*, E.
11. *Peridinium fuscum*, E.   12. *Peridinium tripos*, E.
13. *Peridinium fusus*, E.   14. *Glenomorum tingens*, E.
15. *Gromia fluviatilis*, D., with its expansions extended.
16. *Trichodina pediculus*, E.   *a,* side view; *b,* under view.
17. *Heteronema marina*, D.   18. *Himantophorus charon*, E., under view.
19. *Himantophorus charon*, E., side view.   20. *Hexannita nodulosa*, D.
21. *Holophrya brunnea*, D.   22. *Holophrya orum*, E.
23. *Ichthydium podura*, E.   24. *Chætonotus larus*, E.
25. *Colpoda cucullus*, E.   26. *Kerona pustulata*, D. (*Stylonichia p.*, E.)
27. *Kerona mytilus*, D. (*Stylonichia m.*, E.), under view.
28. *Kerona mytilus*, D. (*Stylonichia m.*, E.), side view.
29. *Stylonichia histrio*, E., under view.
30. *Stylonichia lanceolata*, E.   *a,* under view; *b,* side view.
31. *Kondylostoma patens*, D., under view.
32. *Kondylostoma patens*, D., half side view.
33. *Trachelocerca viridis*, E.   34. *Amphileptus papillosus*, E.
35. *Lagenella euchlora*, E.   36. *Cryptomonas* (*Lagenella*, E.) *inflata*, D.
37. *Leucophrys striata*, D.
38. *Leucophrys patula*, E.   *a,* dorsal, *b,* ventral surface.
39. *Loxodes rostrum*, E. (*Pelecida rostrum*, D.)
40. *Loxodes dentatus*, D.   41. *Loxodes bursaria*, E., under view.
42. *Loxophyllum* (*Amphileptus*, E.) *meleagris*, D.   *a,* dorsal view; *b,* anterior portion twisted.
43. *a, Microglena punctifera*, E.; *b, M. monadina*, E.
44. *a, Monas lens*, D.; *b,* the same (?) with two anterior cilia; *c, M. attenuata*, D.
45. *Nassula elegans*, E.; *b,* teeth.   46. *Nassula aurea*, E.
47. *Opalina* (*Bursaria*, E.) *ranarum*, Purk. and Val.
48. *Ophrydium versatile*, E.; portion expanded by compression.
49. *Ophrydium versatile*, E.; marginal portion, in the natural state.
50. *Ophrydium versatile*, E.; isolated body.
51. *Ophryoglena atra*, E.   52. *Oxytricha pellionella*, D.
53. *Oxytricha gibba*, E., side view.   54. *Oxyrhis marina*, D.
55. *Panophrys chrysalis*, D.   56. *Paramecium aurelia*, E., dorsal view.
57. *Paramecium aurelia*, E., side view.   58. *Pantotrichum lagenula*, E.
59. *Peranema globulosa*, D.   60. *Phialina vermicularis*, E.
61. *Phialina viridis*, E.   62. *Phacus* (*Euglena*, E.) *pleuronectes*, D.
63. *Phacus* (*Euglena*, E.) *longicauda*, D.   64. *Plagiotoma lumbrici*, D.
65. *Planariola rubra*, D.   66. *Pleuronema chrysalis*, D.
67. *Plœotia vitrea*, D.   68. *Polyselmis viridis*, D.
69. *Polytoma uvella*, E.   70. *Prorocentrum micans*, E.
71. *Prorocentrum micans*, E., side view.   72. *Prorodon teres*, E.
73. *Prorodon teres*, E., teeth.   74. *Scyphidia rugosa*, E.
75. *Spathidium hyalinum*, D. (*Leucophrys spathula*, E.)
76. *Spathidium hyalinum*, D.; anterior part twisted.
77. *Spirostomum ambiguum*, E.
78. *Spirostomum ambiguum*, E.; posterior end more magnified.

Pl 24

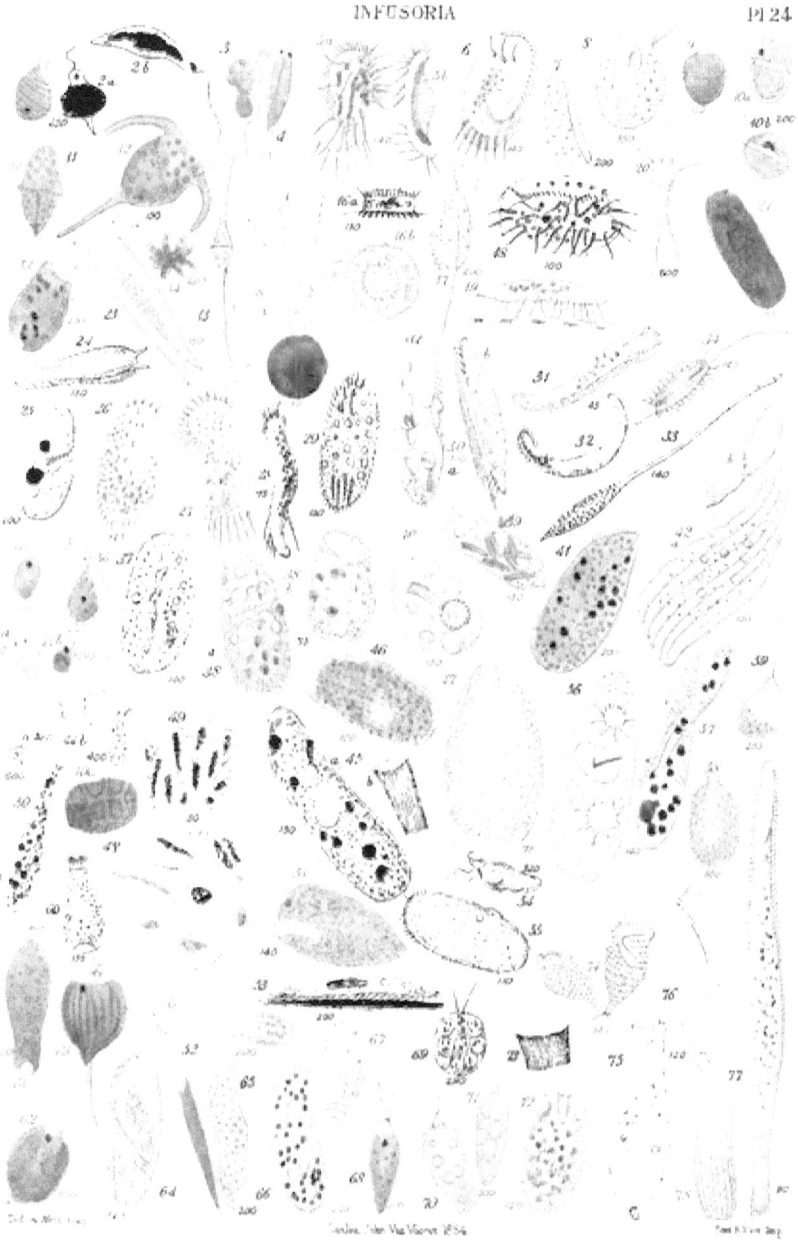

Pl. 25.

PLATE 25.—Infusoria.

Figure
1. Tegument of *Paramecium aurelia*, dried, showing the depressions at different foci, &c. (Intr. p. xxxii.)
2*a*.*Paramecium aurelia*, with globules of sarcode; 2 *b*, free globule of sarcode, with numerous vacuoles.
3. *Stentor Mülleri*, E.
4. *Tintinnus inquilinus*, E.
5. *Trachelius lamella*, D., *a* and *b*.
6. *Trepomonas agilis*, D.
7. *Trichoda angulata*, D.
8. *Trichodiscus sol*, E.
9. *Trichomonas vaginalis*, D.
10. *Trichomonas limacis*, D.
11. *Trinema acinus*, D.
12. *Trochilia sigmoides*, D., ventral view.
13. *Trochilia sigmoides*, D., dorsal view.
14. *Urocentrum turbo*, E.
15. *a*, *Uroleptus piscis*, E.; *b*, *U. lamella*, E.
16. *Uronema marina*, D.
17. *Urostyla grandis*, **E.**
18. *Uvella virescens*, E., *a* and *b*.
19. *Vaginicola crystallina*, E.
20. *Cothurnia imberbis*, E.
21*a*.*Vorticella nebulifera*, E.; 21 *b*, body separated by division; 21 *c*, separate body. *a*, mouth; *b*, nucleus (auct. testis, E.); *c*, contractile vesicle (vesic. seminal., E.).
22*a*.*Zoothamnium arbuscula*, E.; 22 *b*, separate body.
23. *Zygoselmis nebulosa*, D. *a*, *b*, in different states of contraction.
24. *Arcella vulgaris*, E., half side view of young, with expansions extended.
25. *Acineta*-stage of *Opercularia articulata*, E. *a*, dendritic nucleus; *b*, envelope; *c*, tentacles; *d*, vacuoles; *e*, group of fat-granules; *f*, enlarged stalk.
26. *Vorticella microstoma*, E., full-grown. *a*, œsophagus; *b*, peristome; *c*, contractile vesicle; *d*, nucleus; *e*, gemma or bud; *f*, mature bud.
27. *Vorticella microstoma*, E. (old), encysted upon its extended stalk, with its nucleus, contractile vesicle, and retracted cilia.
28. *Vorticella microstoma*, E. (young), encysted upon its contracted stalk.
29. *Vorticella microstoma*, E., encysted and stalkless. *a*, cyst; *c*, contractile vesicle; *d*, nucleus.
30. Isolated nucleus of an old *Vorticella microstoma*.
31. *Actinophrys*-stage of *Vorticella microstoma*. The cyst is partly separated from its contents; the nucleus and contractile vesicle are visible.
32. Two of the above in conjugation.
33. Two *Podophrya*-stages of *Vorticella microstoma* in conjugation.
34. Cyst of *Vorticella microstoma* discharging its brood of germs. *a*, gelatinous substance, containing *b*, the germs; *c*, neck-like orifice of parent-vesicle; *d*, cyst; *e*, parent-vesicle.
35. *Spirochona gemmipara*, Stein. *a*, peristome with its funnel-shaped process; *b*, nucleus; *c*, gemma or bud.
36. *Acineta*-stage of the same. *a*, tentacles; *b*, nucleus; *c*, mature swarm-germ.
37. *Paramecium chrysalis*, E., undergoing longitudinal division.
38. *Glaucoma scintillans*, E., undergoing transverse division.

PLATE 26.—Insects.

Figure

1. Head of *Blatta orientalis*, from before. *a*, antennæ, cut off; *b*, epicranium; *c*, eyes; *d*, clypeus; *e*, labrum; *g*, maxillæ; *h*, maxillary palpi; *k*, labial palpi.

2. Head of *Blatta orientalis*, under portion. *g*, stipes, *h*, palp of maxilla; *i*, palpiger, *k*, palp, *l*, mentum, * paraglossa of labium; *m*, submentum and gula; × occiput.

3. Head of *Hydröus piceus*, under view. *a*, antennæ; *c*, eye; *e*, labrum; *f*, mandible; *g*, maxilla; *h*, maxillary palp; *i*, ligula; *k*, labial palp; *l*, mentum; *m*, submentum; *n*, gula; × occiput.

4. Ocelli of *Agrion fulvipes*.

5. Portions of cornea of eye of *Acheta domestica*. *a*, with hexagonal, *b*, with quadrangular facets.

6. Perpendicular section of part of eye of *Libellula*. *c*, cornea; *b*, anterior convex margin; *d*, anterior chamber; *f*, crystalline lens; *g*, choroid.

7. Antenna, setaceous (Achetidæ, &c.).

8. Antenna, ensiform (Locustidæ).

9. Antenna, filiform (Carabidæ).

10. Antenna, moniliform (Tenebrionidæ, &c.). *a*, scapus; *b*, pedicella; *c*, clavola.

11. Antenna, serrated (Elateridæ).   12. Antenna, imbricated (Prionidæ).

13. Antenna, pectinated (Lampyridæ).   14. Antenna, bipectinated (Bombycidæ).

15. Antenna, flabellate (Elateridæ).

16. Antenna, clavate (Coleoptera).

17. Antenna, capitate (Coleoptera).

18. Antenna, lamellate and perfoliate (*Melolontha*). *a*, scapus; *b*, pedicella; *c*, clavola; *d*, lamellæ.

19. Antenna of *Globaria*. *a*, scapus; *b*, pedicella; *c*, clavola; *d*, capitulum.

20. Antenna, plumose (Muscidæ).

21. Antenna, plumose (*Culex pipiens*, male).

22. Trophi of *Blatta orientalis*. *a*, labrum; *b b*, mandibles; *c*, maxillæ († lacinia, * galea); *d*, internal tongue; *e*, labium.

23. Tongue of cricket (*Acheta domestica*). *a*, *b*, *c*, parts of a fibre more magnified.

24. Head of mason-bee (*Anthophora retusa*), front view. *a*, antenna; *b*, ocelli; *c*, eye; *d*, clypeus; *e*, labrum; *f*, mandible; *g*, maxilla; *h*, its palp; *i*, palpiger or part of the ligula; *k*, labial palp; * ligula, commonly called the tongue; *x*, paraglossæ.

25. Maxillæ and labium of honey-bee (*Apis mellifica*); *g*, maxilla; *h*, its palp; *k*, labial palp; *l*, mentum; * ligula, commonly called the tongue.

26. Trophi of water-scorpion (*Nepa cinerea*). * lingua; *f*, mandibles; *g*, maxilla; *i*, labium.

27. Trophi of bug (*Cimex lectularius*). *a*, mandibles united; *b*, maxillæ; the median organ is the labium.

28. Antlia of red admirable butterfly (*Vanessa atalanta*). *a*, separate papilla; *b*, end of antlia extended; *c*, transverse section of antlia near its root; * ‡ tracheæ, † tube; *d*, entire organ with two maxillæ slightly separated at the end; *e*, tooth; *f*, section near the end, showing the position of the papillæ *, and the canal ×.

29. Proboscis of the blow-fly (*Musca vomitoria*). *a*, maxillary palpi; *c*, lobes of labium; 29 *a*, portion of margin more magnified.

30. Trophi of female gnat (*Culex pipiens*). *a*, antennæ; *e*, labrum; *f f*, mandibles; *g g*, maxillæ; *d*, tongue; *i*, labium.

31. Setæ of the same, more magnified. *d*, tongue; *e*, labrum; *f*, mandible; *g*, maxilla.

32. Trophi of flea (*Pulex irritans*). *d*, labrum; *f*, mandibles or lancets; *g*, maxilla; *h*, maxillary palpi; *k*, sheaths corresponding to labial palpi.

33. Trophi of flea more magnified. *d*, labrum; *f*, end of mandible; *k*, sheath; *l*, labium; *m*, mentum.

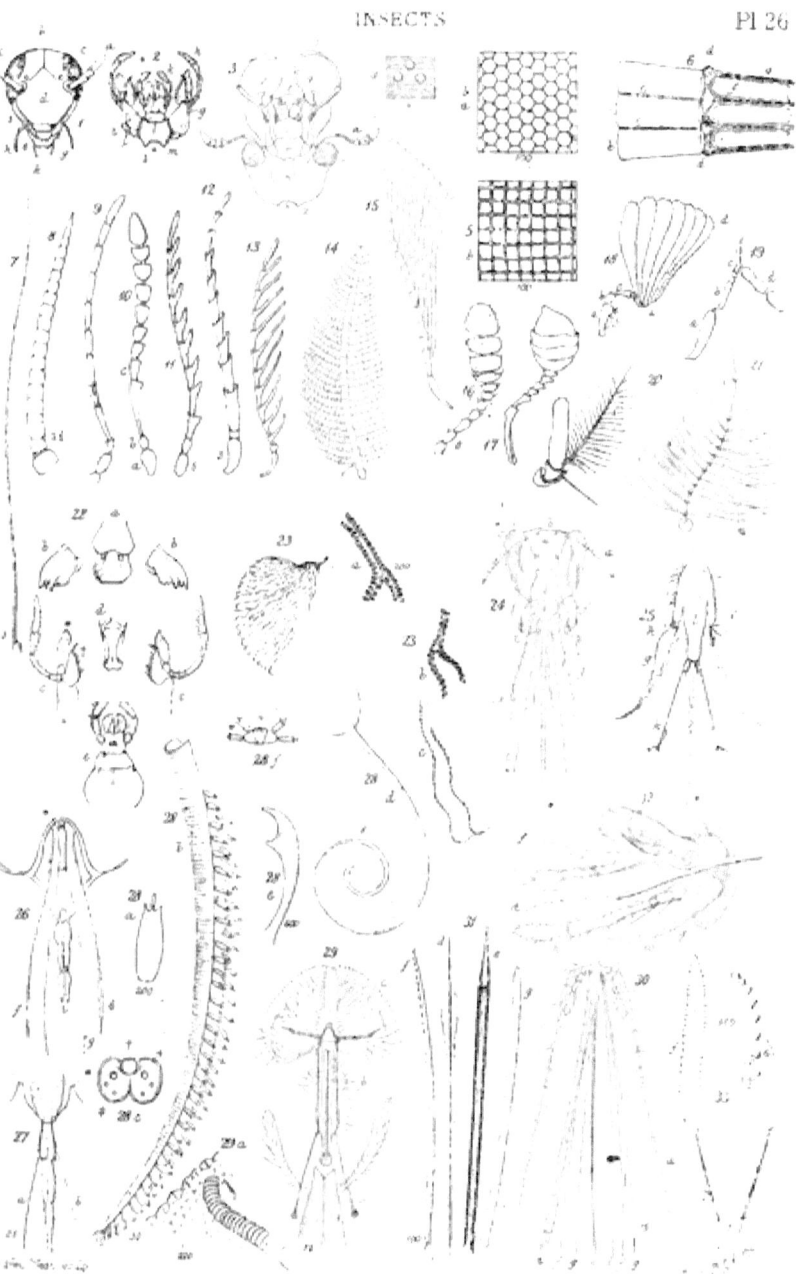

PLATE 27.—Insects.

PLATE 28.—Insects.

Figure

1. Larva of gnat (*Culex pipiens*).

2. Organs of larva of *Agrion puella*. *a*, ocelli; *b*, œsophagus; *c*, gizzard; *d*, stomach; *e*, Malpighian vessels truncated; *f*, intestine and rectum; *g*, caudal branchiæ; *h*, tracheæ.

3. Clothes-louse (*Pediculus vestimenti*).

4. *Hæmatopinus suis*; 4*, leg more magnified.
5. *Philopterus* (*Docophorus*) *communis*.
6. *Trichodectes latus*; 6*, labium and labial palpi. ⎱ ANOPLURA.
7. *Liotheum* (*Menopon*) *pallidum*.
8. *Gyropus ovalis*.

9. *Pulex felis* (flea of cat), female. *a*, spiracles; *b*, head; *c*, thorax; *d*, maxillary palpi; *e*, setæ; *f*, epimera; *g*, coxæ; *h*, trochanter; *i*, femur; *k*, tibia; *l*, tarsus; ×pygidium; 9 *a*, separate antenna.

10. Part of *Pulex canis* (dog's flea). *a*, prothoracic setæ; *b*, cephalic setæ.

11. Head of flea from common bat (PULEX).

12. Antenna of flea from pigeon (PULEX).

13. Posterior end of abdomen of pigeon's flea; male (PULEX).

14. Head of larva of *Dytiscus marginalis*. *a*, eyes; *b*, antennæ; *c*, mandibles; *d*, maxillæ; *e*, maxillary palpi; *f*, labial palpi.

15. Pupa of *Ephemera vulgata*. *a*, abdominal branchiæ.

16. Larva of *Acilius sulcatus* (formerly *Dytiscus sulc.*).

17. Pupa of *Agrion puella*; the ocelli are omitted (LIBELLULIDÆ); 17*, caudal branchial plate.

18. *Lepisma saccharina*.

19. Larva of *Gyrinus natator*.

20. Rectum of *Æshna grandis*; 20*, portion more magnified (LIBELLULIDÆ).

21. Pupa of *Calepteryx virgo*.

22. End of abdomen of *Libellula ferruginea*.

23. Sheep-tick (*Melophagus ovinus*).

24. Flea from the mole (PULEX).

25. Head of a *Scolopendra* (one of the MYRIAPODA).

26. Head of a *Lithobius* (one of the MYRIAPODA).

27. Fibres of silk-worm's silk.

28. Three lobes of the fatty body of the larva (caterpillar) of *Saturnia carpini*.

29. End of abdomen of *Æshna grandis*.

30. (between 2 and 3), Epidermis of cricket (*Acheta domestica*).

31. Fat-body of *Ichneumon*-larva, developing from cells.

32. Egg of an aquatic insect (?) common in bog-water.

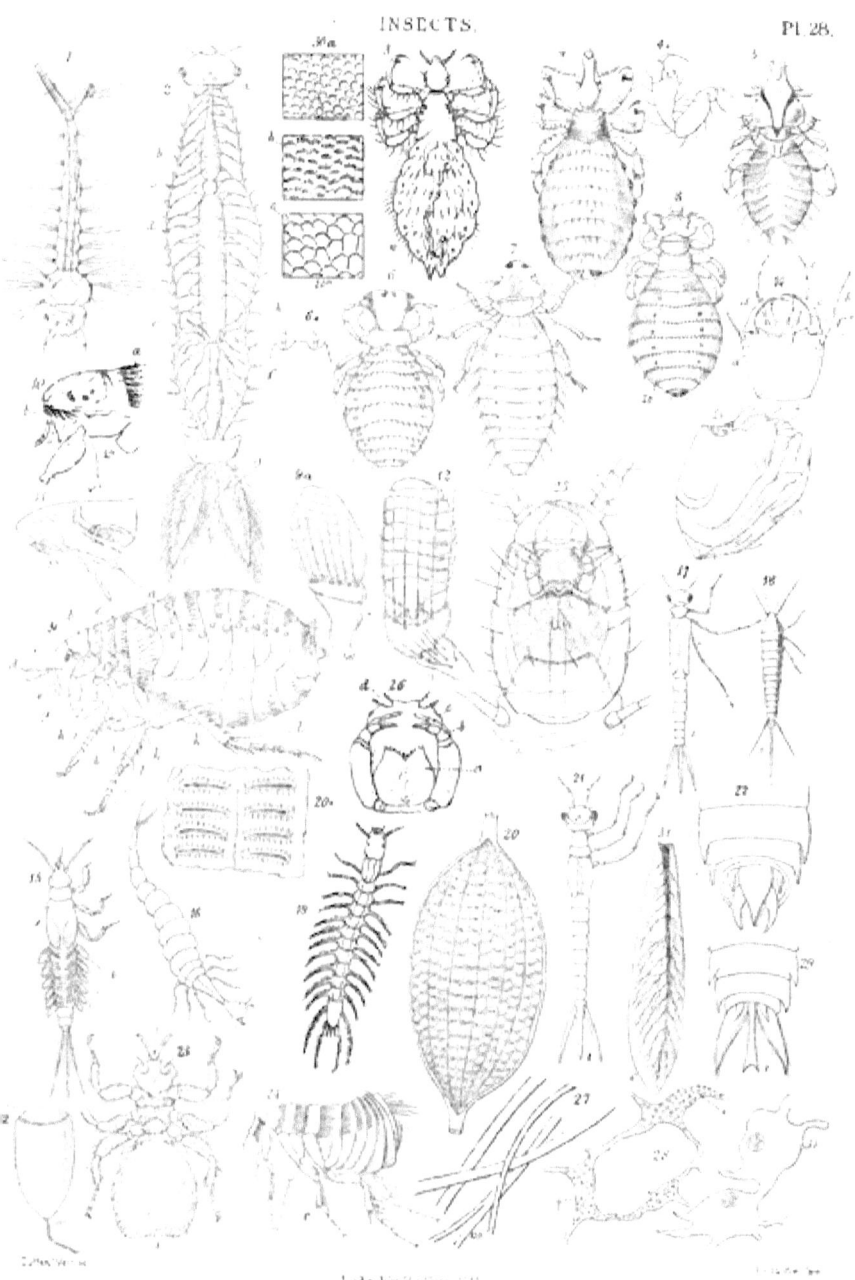

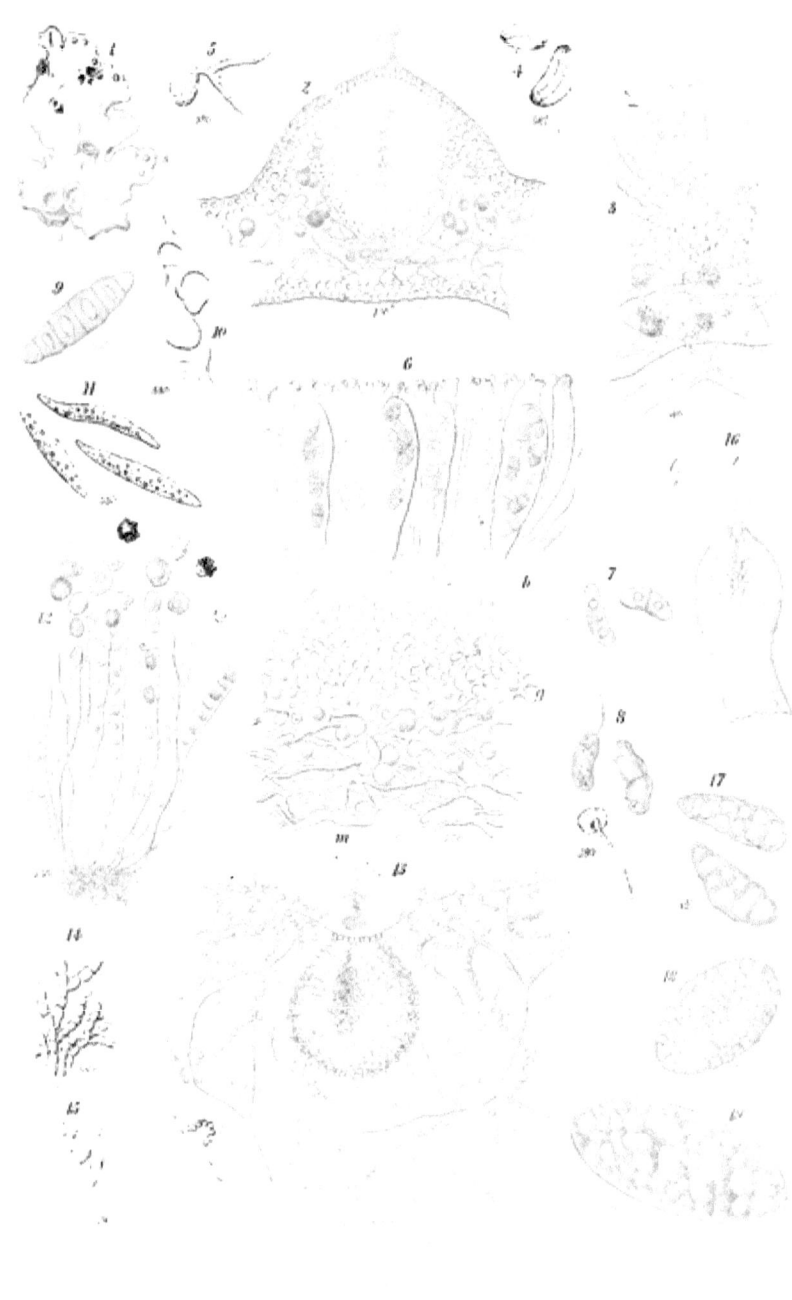

PLATE 29.—Lichens.

PLATE 30.—Morbid products, human.

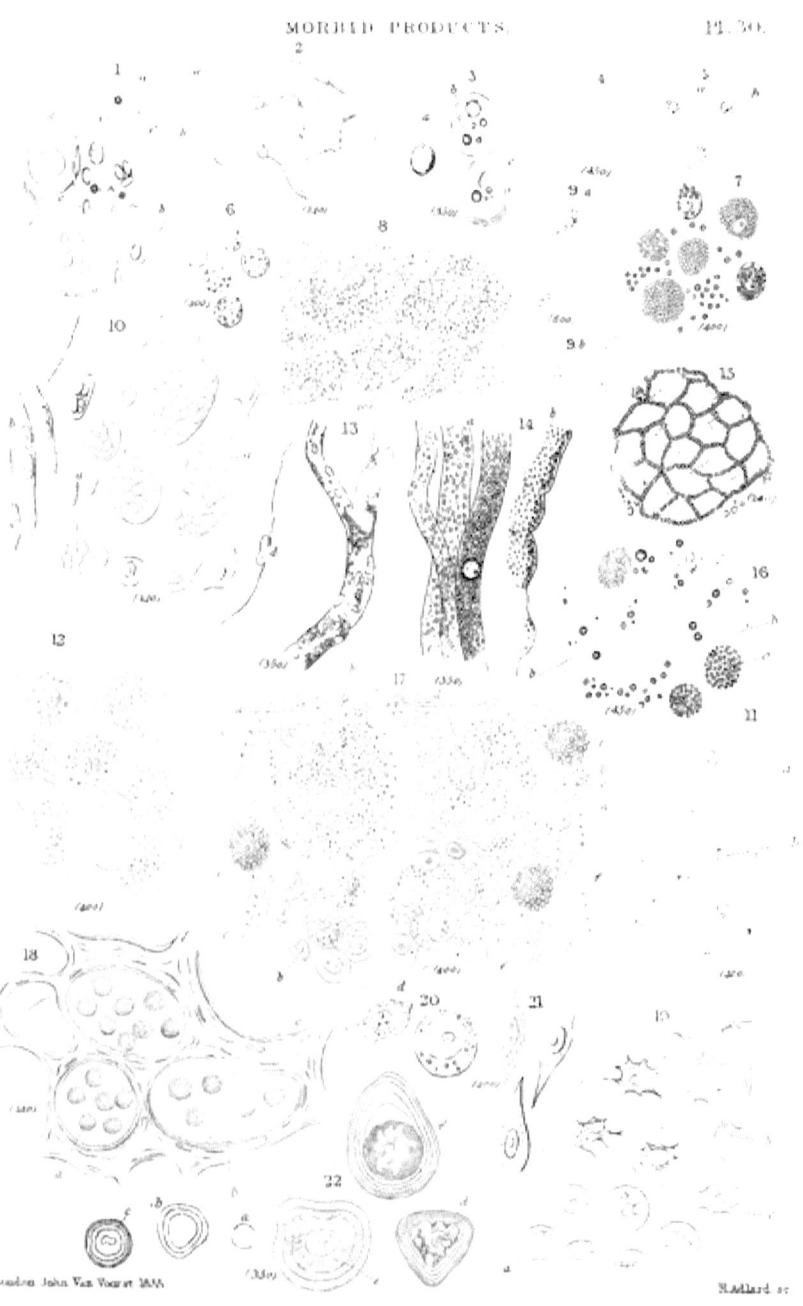

London John Van Voorst 1858

N.Adlard sc

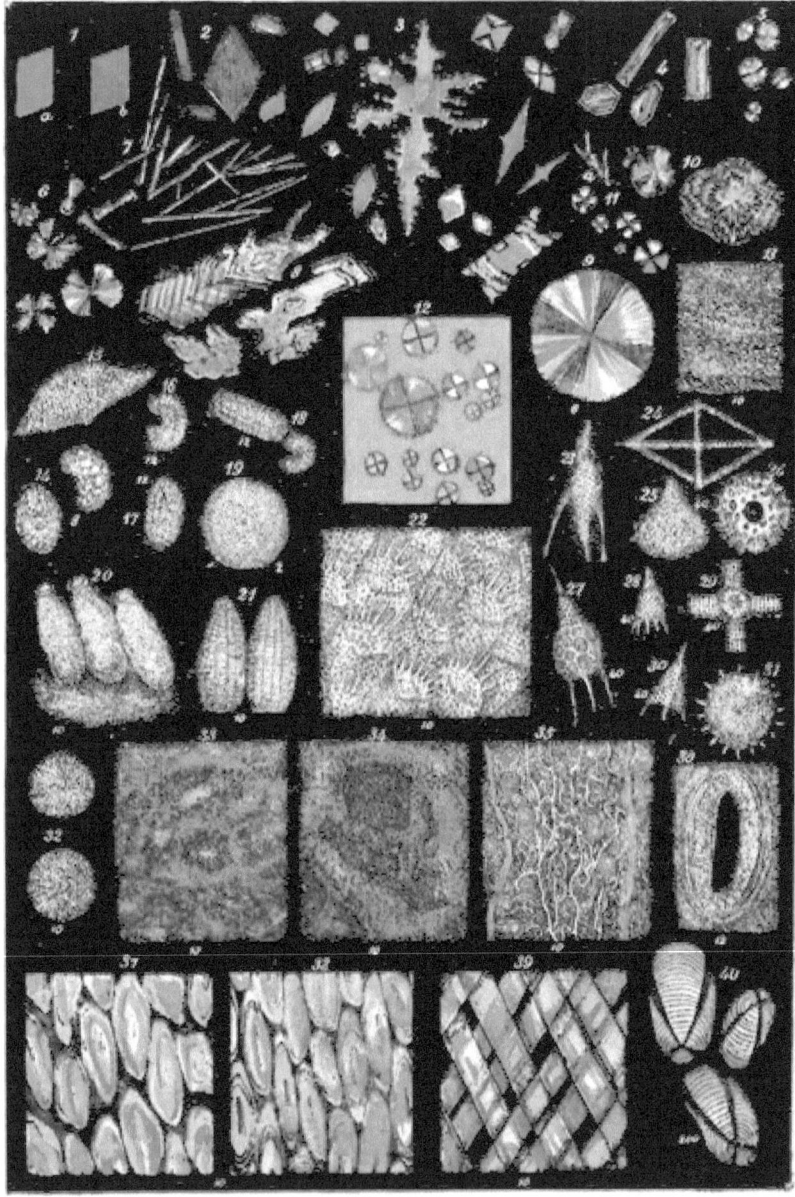

PLATE 32.—Pollen, etc.

Figure

1. *a* and *b*, spiral tissue of lining of anther from wallflower (*Cheiranthus cheiri*).
2. Ditto, from London Pride (*Saxifraga umbrosa*).
3. Ditto, from *Lupinus nanus*.
4. Ditto, from a cactus (*Cereus speciosus*). *a*, side view; *b*, from above.
5. Ditto, from daisy (*Bellis perennis*).
6. Pollen of *Viola odorata*. *a*, side view; *b*, end view; *c*, in water.
7. Pollen of *Apocynum venetum*.
8. Pollen of daisy (*Bellis perennis*).
9. Pollen of *Mesembryanthemum*.
10. Pollen of *Alisma plantago*.
11. Pollen of *Lupinus nanus*.
12. Pollen of garden geranium (*Pelargonium speciosum*). *a*, front view; *b*, side view.
13. Pollen of passion-flower (*Passiflora cærulea*). *a*, perfect grain; *b*, grain with the lid of a pore opening.
14. Pollen of *Epilobium montanum*.
15. Pollen of *Periploca græca*.
16. Pollen of *Scorzonera hispanica*.
17. Pollen of *Erica multiflora*.
18. Pollen of *Sherardia arvensis*. *a*, side view; *b*, end view; *c*, ditto in water.
19. Pollen of *Basella alba*.
20. Pollen of *Passiflora aquilegiæfolia*. *a*, side view; *b*, end view; *c*, ditto in water.
21. Pollen of *Impatiens noli-me-tangere*.
22. Pollen of *Cucurbita pepo*, in water.
23. Pollen of *Ruellia formosa*.
24. Pollen of musk-plant (*Mimulus moschatus*).
25. Compound pollen of *Acacia laxa*.
26. Pollen of *Hibiscus trionum*.
27. Pollen of chicory (*Cichorium intybus*).
28. Pollen of *Sonchus palustris*, side and end view.
29. Pollen of *Statice linifolia*, end and side views.
30. Pollen-grain with tube upon the stigmatic papillæ, from *Lathræa squamaria*.
31. Spermatozoid from the globule of *Chara fragilis*.
32. Spermatozoids from the antheridium of *Marchantia polymorpha*.
33. Spermatozoids from the antheridium of *Polytrichum commune*.
34. Spermatozoids from the antheridium of a Fern (*Gymnogramma*).
35. Spiral fibrous cells of the sporange of *Marchantia polymorpha*.
36. Elater of *Marchantia polymorpha*.
37. Fragments of ditto. *a*, from the middle; *b*, one end.
38. Elater of *Frullania dilatata*.
39. Elaters (*a*) and spores (*b*) of *Trichia*.
40. Fragment of the same elater showing the three internal spiral fibres.

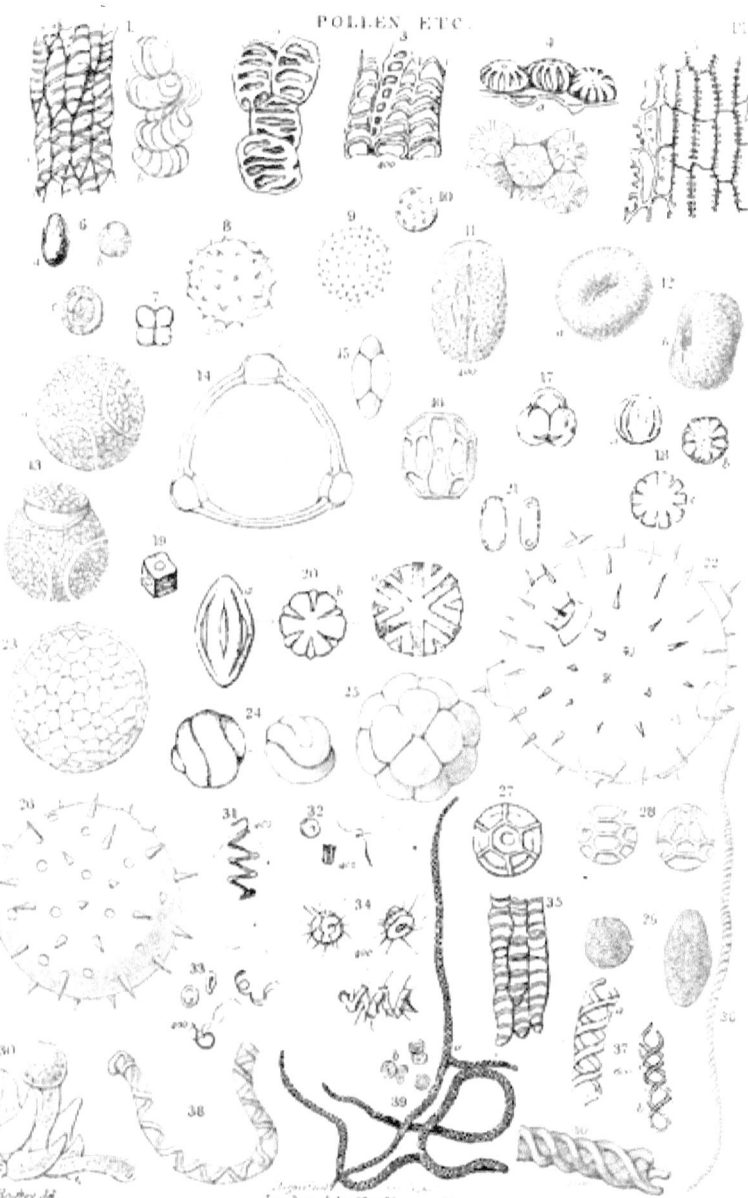

PLATE 34.—Rotatoria.

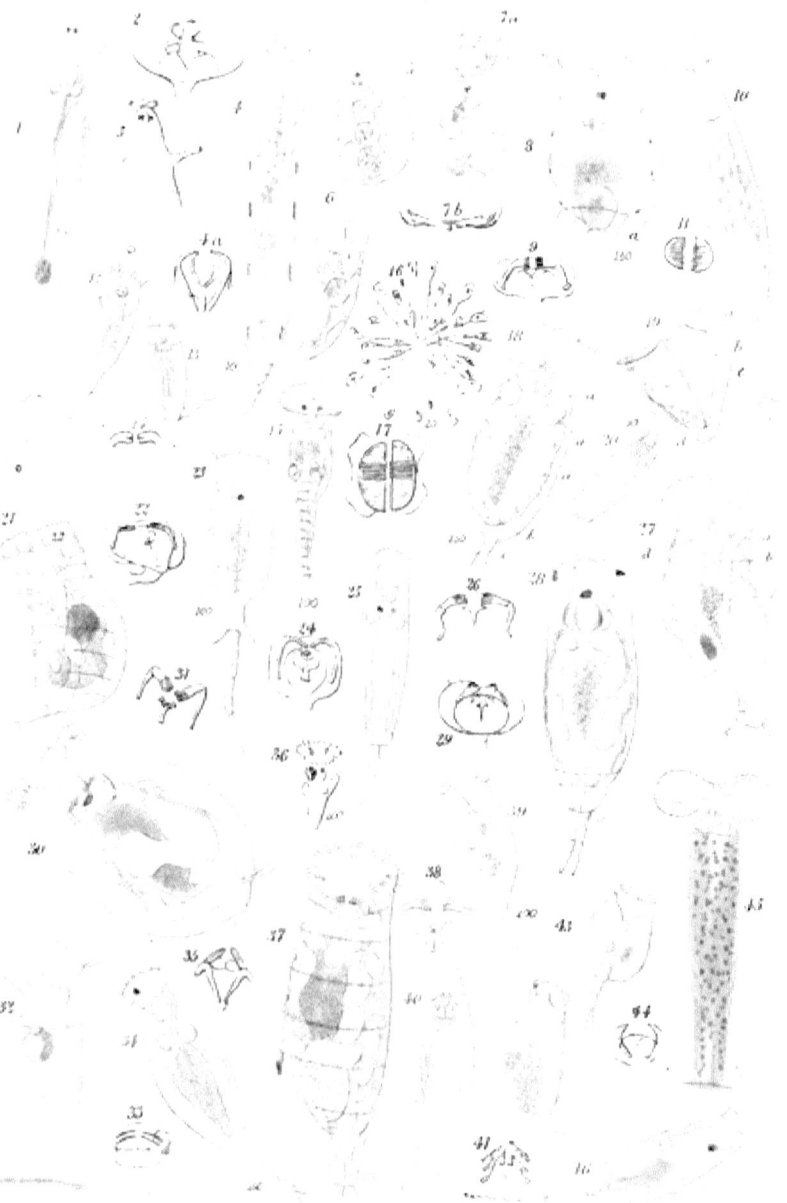

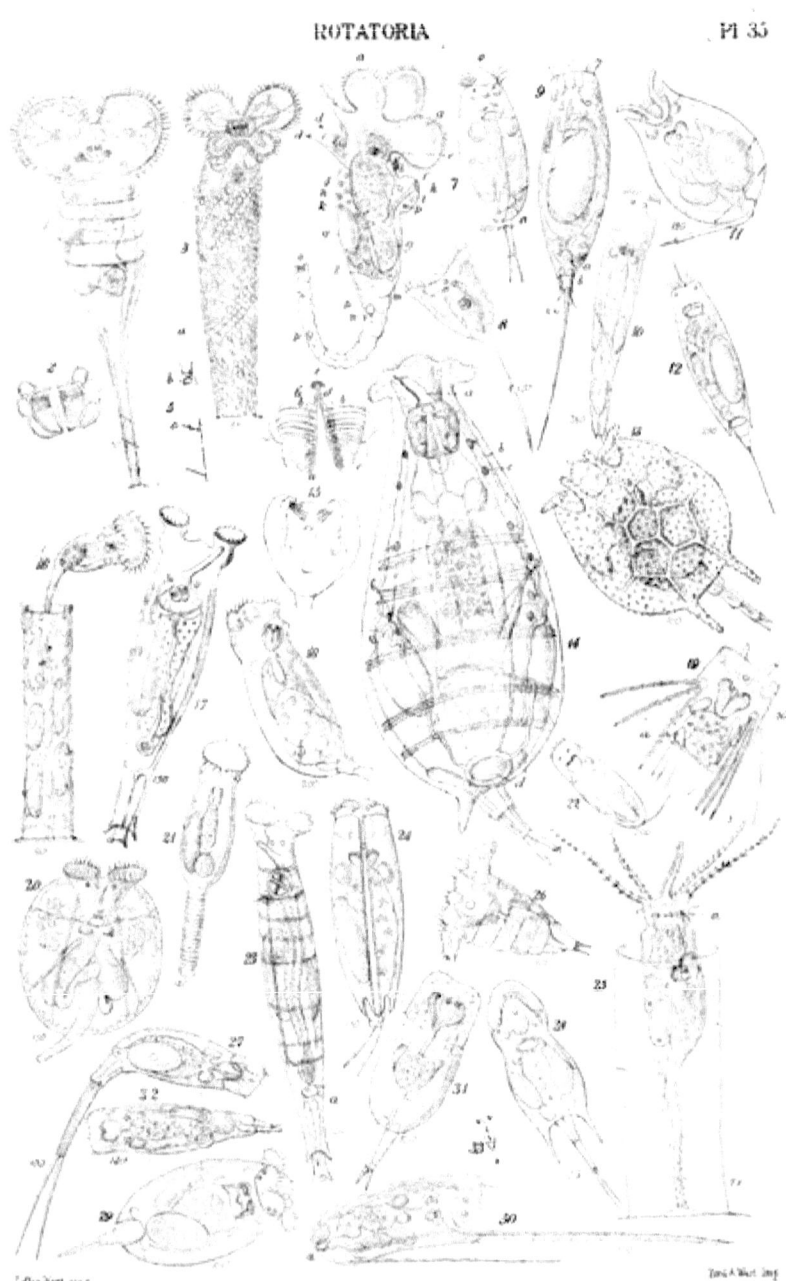

PLATE 35.—Rotatoria.

PLATE 36.—Starch.

Figure

1. Section of a cell of the albumen of a young maize seed, showing the nascent starch-grains imbedded in protoplasm.
2. The same, somewhat older; most of the starch-grains exhibit a central point or "hilum."
3. Section of a cell from the outer horny part of the albumen of maize; the starch-grains completely fill the cell, and by their crowded condition have compressed each other into polygonal forms.
4. Part of a similar section treated with iodine. *a*, starch-grain cut across (with a central cavity); *b*, intervening protoplasm.
5. Free starch-grains of maize from the cells of the centre of the seed.
6. Young starch-grains of ditto.
7. Compound starch-grains and separated granules, from the corm of the crocus.
8. Lenticular starch-grains of wheat. *a*, seen in face; *b*, seen edgewise.
9. Discoid starch-grains of barley. *a a*, front view; *b*, edgewise.
10. Compound starch-grains and separated granules of oats.
11. Compound grains and separated granules of Portland arrow-root (*Arum maculatum*).
12. Part of a section of a cell of the grain of rice, exhibiting very minute starch-grains, firmly compacted as in maize.
13. A portion of the same, more magnified.
14. Starch-grains of Cassava (*Jatropha Manihot*)*. Tapioca.
15. Young starch-grains from the cells of the *prothallium* of a fern (*Gymnogramma*).
16. Compound starch-grains and separated granules of the bread-fruit (*Artocarpus incisa*)*.
17. Starch-grains of *Cycas circinalis**.
18. Starch-grains of arrow-root from Singapore*.
19. Starch-grains of an East Indian arrow-root obtained from a species of *Curcuma**.
20. Cell of a potato, showing the loosely-packed starch-grains.
21. Isolated starch-grains of the potato.
22. Starch-grains of *Tacca pinnatifida*, from Tahiti*.
23. Starch-grains of sago (from a *Sagus*?)*.
24. Starch from plantain-meal (*Musa*). *a*, front view; *b*, edgewise*.
25. Starch of Tous-les-mois (*Canna*). *a*, front view; *b*, edgewise*.
26. Starch-grains of true West Indian arrow-root (*Maranta arundinacea*).
27. Isolated starch-grains from the cotyledon of a haricot-bean.
28. Part of a cell of the stem of the white lily (*Lilium candidum*), showing nascent starch-grains: *a*, forming in cavities of the protoplasm *c*; *b*, nucleus.

* The figures to which this asterisk is appended, were taken from specimens with which we were favoured from the Museum of Economic Botany at Kew.

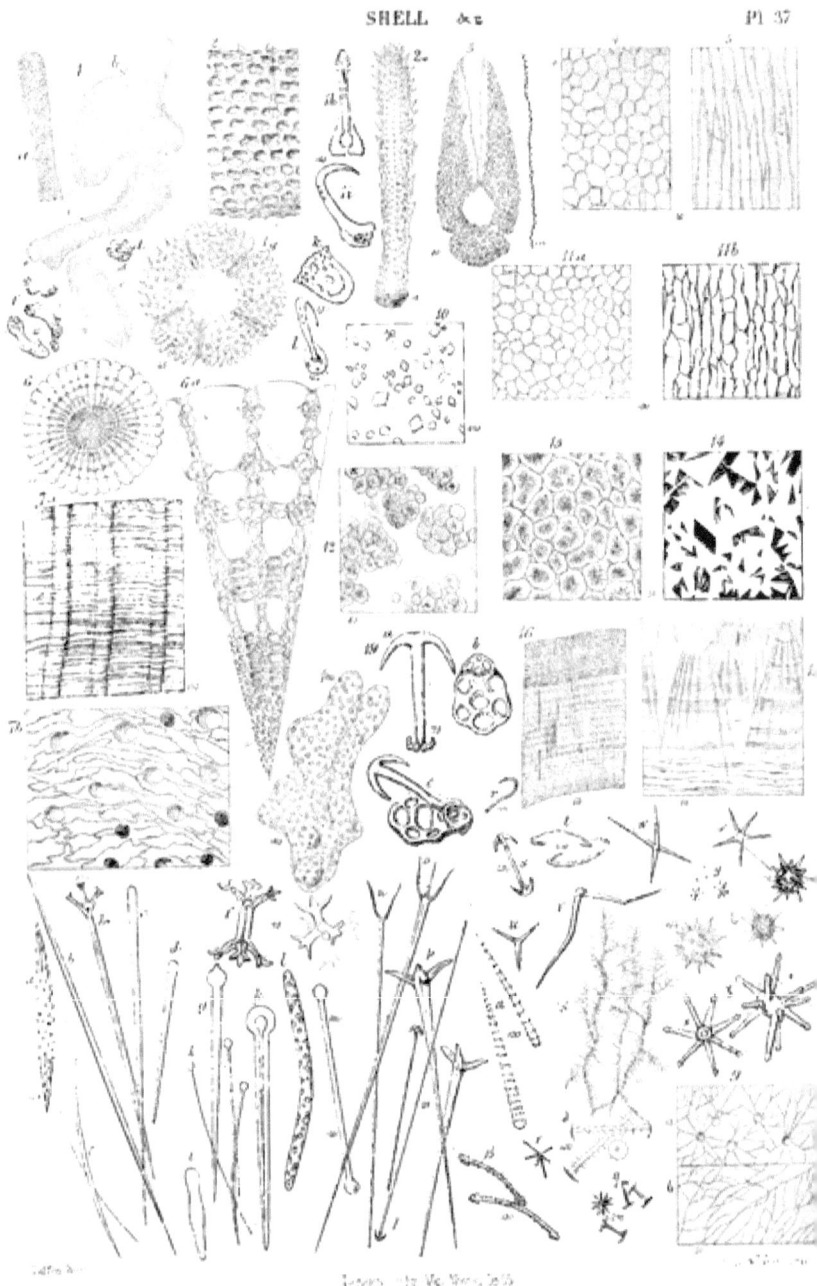

PLATE 37.—Shell, etc.

Figure

1. Calcareous corpuscles of common star-fish (*Asterias* (*Uraster*) *rubens*), a, b, c, d, e; f, the same from an *Ophiura*; g, calcareous disk from an *Echinus*; h, i, k, l, m, from an *Ophiura* (ECHINODERMATA).

2*.Spine of an *Ophiura*; 2, portion of the same more magnified.

3. A pedicellaria of the common star-fish (*Asterias rubens*); on the right hand is a portion of the margin more magnified to show the teeth.

4. Shell of *Pinna*, section parallel to the surface.

5. Shell of *Pinna*, section perpendicular to the surface.

6. Spine of an *Echinus*, transverse section. 6 a, segment of the same, more magnified.

7. Sections of shell of a *Terebratula*; a, perpendicular to, b, parallel with the surface.

8. Portion of a sponge, with the spicula projecting from its surface.

9. Shell of oyster.   a, b, sections parallel to surface.

10. Shell of oyster, showing the rhomboidal crystals of carbonate of lime.

11. Shell of oyster, showing the cellular appearance; a, parallel with, b, perpendicular to the surface.

12. Shell of hen's egg; from a "soft" egg.

13. Shell of hen's egg, perfectly formed.

14. Shell of egg of ostrich; section parallel to surface.

15. Shell of egg of ostrich; section perpendicular to surface.

16. Shell of lobster; section perpendicular to surface.

19. Anchor-shaped spicular hooks of *Synapta* (ECHINODERMATA).

   The remaining figures represent the spicula of sponges.

a. Elongato-fusiform, tubercular.

b. Acicular, acute at both ends.

b*. Subulato-acicular, base trifid, rays shortly bifid.

c. Subulato-acicular.

d. Subulato-acicular, base swollen.

e. Arcuato-acicular, acute at both ends.

f. Shortly cylindrical, ends doubly trifid.

g. Subulato-acicular, base turbinate.

h. Subulato-acicular, base capitate.

i. Subulato-fusiform.

k. Elongato-subulate, base capitate.

l. Terete, geniculate.

m. Filiform, ends capitate.

n. Acicular, ends bifurcate.

o. Acicular, ends trifurcate.

p. Subulato-acicular, base triradiate.

q. Acicular, base tri-retro-cuspid.   r. Uncinato-filiform.

s. Bacilliform, ends tri-retro-cuspid.

t. Arcuate, ends uncinate.   u. Stellato-triradiate.

v. Geminate, arms subulato-filiform, geniculate.

w. Stellato-quadriradiate.   x. Stellato-quinquiradiate.

y. Stellato-multiradiate, ends capitate.

α. Subulate, tuberculate.   β. Arcuate, spinulose, ends clavate.

γ. Stellate, inæquiradiate.

δ. Bacilliform, spinulose, with dentate, discoid, rotate ends.

ε. Globular, with subulate spines.

ζ. Oblong, with irregularly stellate ends, the rays capitate; *side view, ✕ end view.

η. Bacilliform, with stellate rotate ends.

PLATE 38.—Vegetable Tissues.

Pl 35

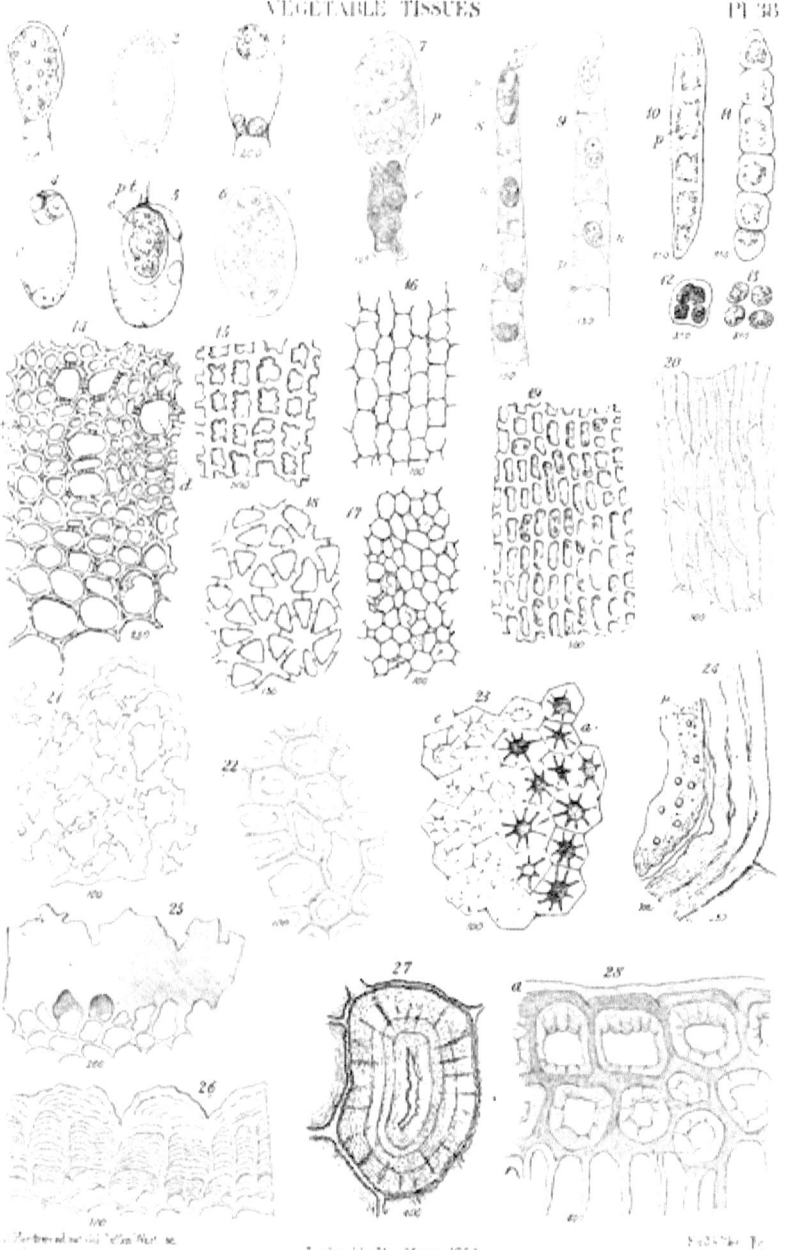

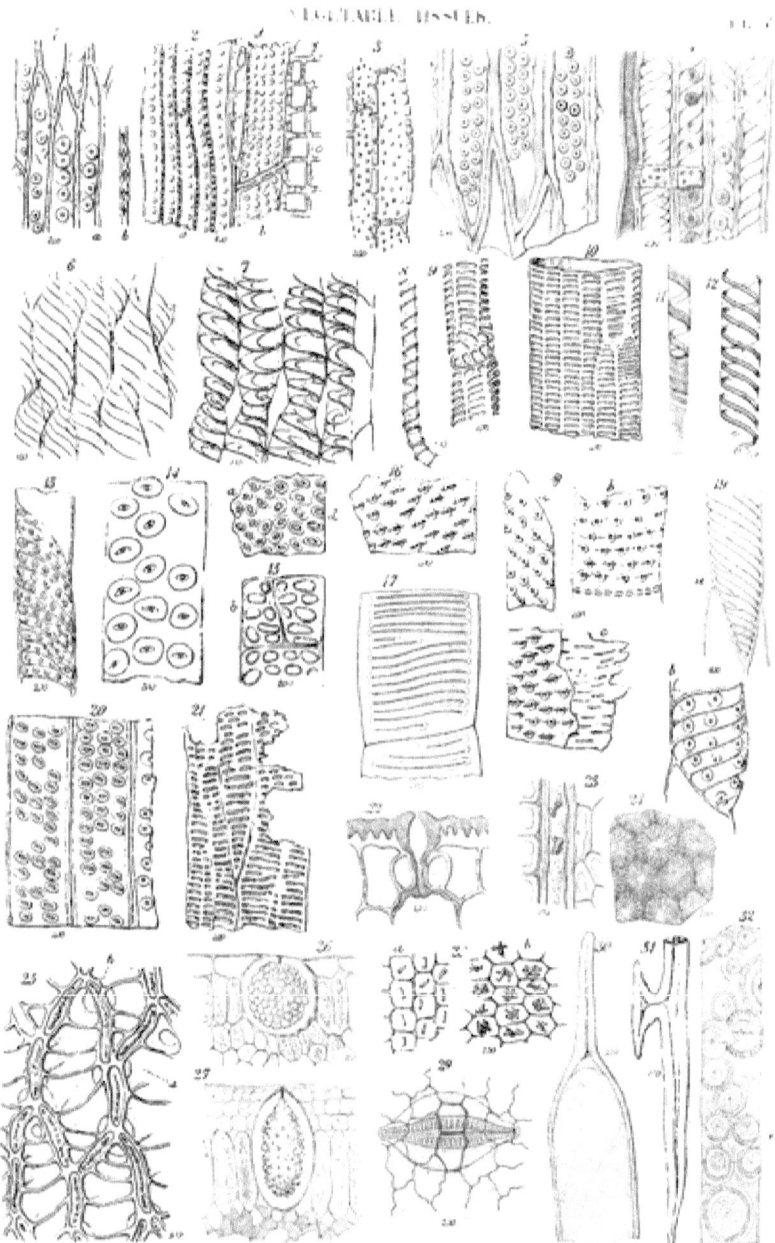

PLATE 39.—Vegetable Tissues.

Figure

1. Wood of *Pinus sylvestris*. *a*, radial vertical section ; *b*, tangental section of the walls of two contiguous pitted wood-cells.

2. Tangental section of the wood of *Casuarina equisetifolia*. *a*, pitted wood-cells ; *b*, duct ; *c*, cells of a true medullary ray ; *d*, cells of one of the concentric medullary layers.

3. Vertical section of wood-cells of box.

4. Vertical (radial) section of wood-cells of the yew.

5. Vertical (radial) section of wood-cells of *Araucaria imbricata*.

6. Spiral-fibrous cells from the roots of *Dendrobium alatum*.

7. Wood-cells of *Mammillaria*, with broad spiral bands.

8. Spiral and annular vessel of Rhubarb.

9. Reticulated duct from the same.

10. Scalariform duct of a tree-fern.

11. End of a spiral vessel of the white lily.

12. Fragment of a larger and looser one.

13. Pitted duct of the lime (*Tilia parvifolia*).

14. Wall of a pitted duct of *Cassyta glabella*.

15. Wall of pitted ducts of *Bombax pentandra*. *a*, next another duct ; *b*, next cells.

16. Wall of a pitted duct of *Laurus Sassafras*.

17. Wall of a pitted duct of *Chilianthus arboreus*.

18. Wall of pitted ducts of Clematis (*Clematis Vitalba*).

19. End of a spiral-fibrous duct of *Daphne Mezereon*.

20. Walls of pitted wood-cells of *Cycas*.

21. Fragment of the wall of a large pitted duct of *Eryngium maritimum*.

22. Vertical section through the stomate of *Aloe ferox*. The darkly shaded part represents the cuticular layer.

23. Fragment of a latex-duct of *Euphorbia antiquorum* ; the latex containing starch-grains of peculiar shape.

24. Epidermis of the petal of the daffodil, from above.

25. Fragment of the leaf of *Sphagnum cymbiforme*. *a*, empty cells with spiral fibre ; *b*, interstitial cells with chlorophyll.

26. Vertical section of the upper face of the leaf of *Parietaria officinalis*, with a cystolithe. Magnified 100 diameters.

27. A similar section from the leaf of *Ficus elastica*. Magnified 100 diameters.

28. *a* and *b*, Sections of the cellular tissue of an onion-bulb, containing raphides.

29. Stomate and epidermis of *Equisetum* ; the siliceous coat remaining after the destruction of the organic matter.

30. End of a liber-fibre of the periwinkle (*Vinca major*), with fine spiral striæ.

31. Branched liber-cell of the radicle of *Rhizophora Mangle*.

32. Siliceous cast of the inside of a duct of unknown fossil wood ; the peculiar concentric concretions of the silica imitate to a certain extent the so-called glandular markings of Coniferæ.

PLATE 40.—Various Objects.

Figure

1. Mixtures of oil and water (INTR. p. xxxii). *a*, water in oil ; *b*, *c*, oil in water.
2. *Oceania cruciata* (ACALEPHÆ), epidermis of.
3. *Oceania cruciata.* *a*, *b*, stinging capsules with filament included ; *c*, *d*, with filament expelled.
4. *Diphyes Kochii* (ACALEPHÆ) ; organs of adhesion upon tentacles.
5. *Oceania cruciata*, portion of margin of disk slightly magnified. *a*, ovary ; *b*, muscular bundles ; *c*, transverse vessel coming from the stomach ; *d*, marginal vessel ; *e*, *f*, tentacular filaments ; *g*, auditory organs. Fig. 5* spermatozoa.
6. Infusorial embryos of ACALEPHÆ.
7, 8, 9, 10. The same, further developed.
11. Epidermis of *Triton cristatus* (water-newt).
12. Ciliated epithelium from frog's throat.
13. —— apiculosa ⎫ Alder's animalcules, considerably magnified (ALDERIA).
14. —— ovata ⎬ This generic name being already in use, cannot be re-
15. —— pyriformis ⎭ tained.
16. *Hæmocharis*, epidermis of. ⎫
17. *Hæmocharis* ; transverse section of muscular fibres. ⎪
18. *Hæmocharis* ; muscular fibre, showing the sarcolemma. ⎬ (ANNULATA.)
19. *Hæmocharis* ; margin of cephalic disk, with branching muscular fibres *c* ; and *a*, *b*, *d*, glands and ducts. ⎭
20. *Aphrodita aculeata*, hair of, treated with potash.
21. Blood-corpuscles, human. *a*, *d*, surface view at different foci ; *c*, side or edge view ; *b*, colourless or lymph-corpuscle ; *e*, coloured corpuscles altered, either spontaneously or by mixture with foreign matters, as urine, &c.
22. Blood-corpuscles of the goat (*Capra hircus*).
23.   ,,   ,,   whale (*Balæna*).
24.   ,,   ,,   ostrich (*Struthio*).
25.   ,,   ,,   pigeon (*Columba*).
26.   ,,   ,,   stickleback (*Gasterosteus aculeatus*).
27.   ,,   ,,   loach (*Cobitis fossilis*) ; *b*, colourless corpuscle.
28.   ,,   ,,   frog (*Rana temporaria*) ; *b*, colourless corpuscle ; *c*, *d*, the same altered by water.
29.   ,,   ,,   triton (*Triton cristatus*) ; *b*, colourless corpuscle ; *c*, *d*, *e*, *f*, altered coloured corpuscles.
30.   ,,   ,,   *Siren* ; *b*, colourless corpuscle.
31.   ,,   ,,   crab (*Carcinus*).
32.   ,,   ,,   spider (*Tegenaria domestica*).
33.   ,,   ,,   cockroach (*Blatta orientalis*).
34.   ,,   ,,   worm (*Lumbricus terrestris*). *a*, corpuscle partly drawn out, as occurs with the bodies of some Infusoria.
35.   ,,   ,,   garden-snail (*Helix aspersa*).
36.   ,,   ,, human, coloured, undergoing division.
37. Blood, human, in coagulation ; *b*, colourless corpuscle.
38. Cartilage of the ear of a mouse ; the fat is partly removed from the cells.
39. Cartilage of human rib.
40. Cartilage of human epiglottis.
41. Areolar tissue, human, with fat-cells.
43. Formation of areolar tissue from cells.

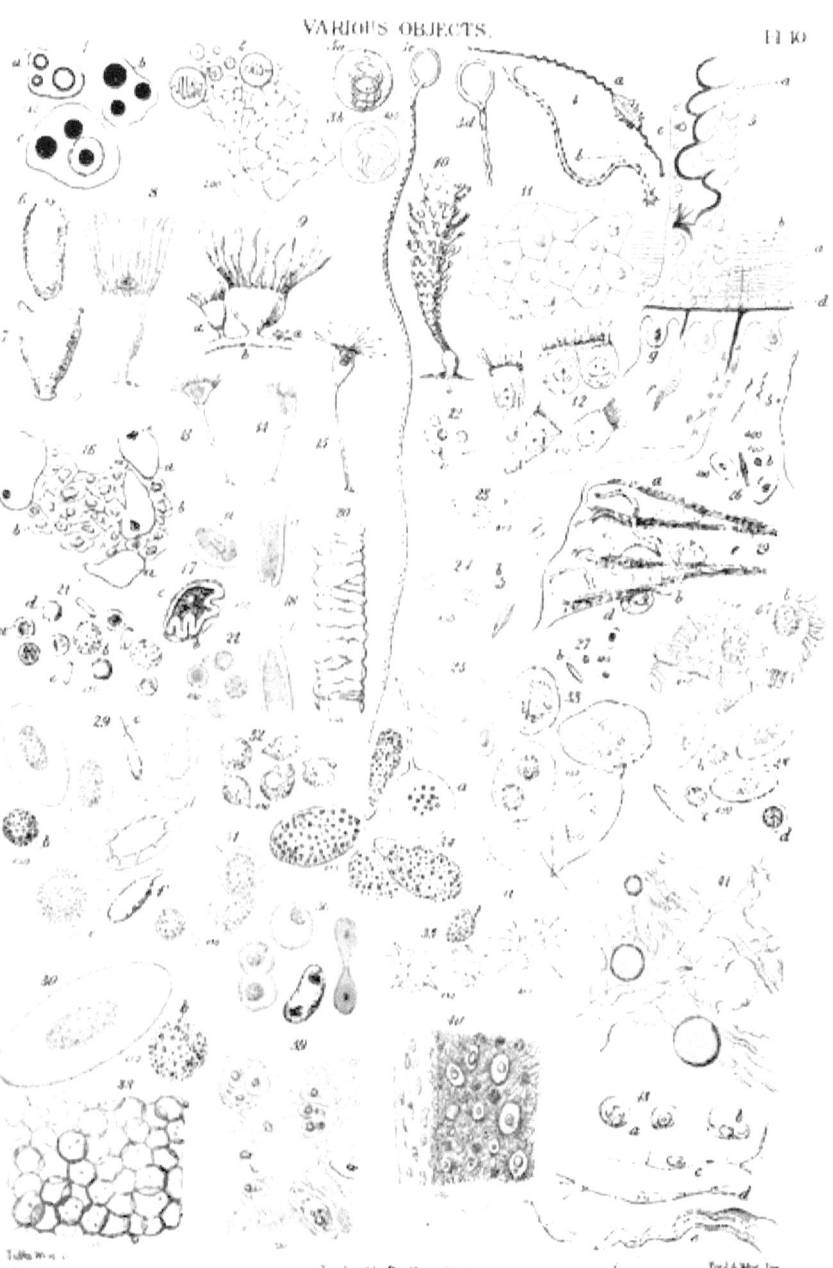

PLATE 41.—Various Objects.

Figure

1. *Chlorogonium euchlorum*, E., undergoing oblique division.
2. Elements of the chyle. *a*, molecules; *b*, free nuclei; *c*, chyle-corpuscles; *d*, one of the same with processes.
3. *Coccudina costata*, D.
4. *Anystis ruricola*.
5. Bacilli and cones of the retina of animals. *a*, *β*, from the pigeon. *a*, bacillus; *a*, proper bacillus; *b*, its pale inner extremity; *c*, line of demarcation at the boundary of the bacillar layer; *d*, corpuscle of the outer granular layer. *β*, cone; *e*, as above; *e*, bacillus of cone; *f*, proper cone; *g*, globule of fat in the same; *h*, expansion of cone. *γ*, from the frog, letters as above. *δ*, from the perch, letters as above; *i*, part at which the cone usually breaks off; *k*, radial fibre; *l*, expansion of inner granular layer. *ε*, twin cones.
6. *Frustulia membranacea*. *a*, valve; *b*, front view of frustule.
7. *Emydium testudo*. 7 *a*, isolated style; 7 *b*, claw of leg.
8. *Macrobiotus Hufelandii*. † ovary; 8 *a*, œsophageal bulb; × its framework.
9. *Milnesium tardigrada*. 9 *a*, pharynx, with + internal buccal lobes, and † styles; 9 *b*, right posterior leg, seen from beneath.
10. *Eucampia zodiaca*.
11. *Halteria grandinella*, D., seen from above.
12. *Halteria grandinella*, D., side view.
13. *Kerona polyporum*, E.
14. *Gyges granulum*, E.
15. *Lacinularia socialis*, E.; 15 *a*, the same more magnified.
16. Mask (labium) of *Æshna* (LIBELLULIDÆ).
17. Spermatozoa of *Triton cristatus*.
18. Sarcolemma of muscle, twisted.
19–24. *Navicula amphirhynchus* in conjugation. Fig. 19, side view of valve of parent-frustule; 20, frustules in an early state of conjugation; 21, sporangial sheath; 22, sporangial sheath, with parent-frustules attached; 23, sporangial frustule (front view), with sheath and one parent-frustule; 24, side view of sporangial frustule.
25. Spermatozoon, human.
26. Spermatozoa of rat (*Mus rattus*).
27. Spermatozoa of field-mouse (*Arvicola* (*Hypudœus*) *arvalis*).
28. Spermatozoa of rabbit (*Lepus cuniculus*).
29. Spermatozoa of goldfinch (*Fringilla* (*Carduelis*) *elegans*).
30. Spermatozoa of blackbird (*Turdus merula*).
31. Spermatozoa of wood-shrike (*Lanius rufus*).
32. Spermatozoa of a Coleopterous Insect.
33. Spermatozoa of frog (*Rana temporaria*).
34. Spermatozoa of perch (*Perca fluviatilis*).
35. Spermatic cyst of rabbit, with five globules. *a*, separate globule.
36. Spermatic cyst of rabbit, the globules containing each a spermatozoon. *a*, separate globule.
37. Spermatic cyst of the common creeper (bird) (*Certhia familiaris*), containing a bundle of spermatozoa.
38. *a*, *b*, *c*, *Staurosira construens*, E.
39. *Biblarium crux* (*leptostauron*), E.
40. *Goniothecium gastridium*, E.
41. *Periptera chlamidophora*, E.
42. *Periptera chlamidophora*, E.
43. *Aulacodiscus crux*, E.
44. *Goniothecium odontella*, E.
45. *Actiniscus sirius*, E.
46. *Rhizoselenia americana*, E.
47. *Chætoceros didymus*, F.

PLATE 42.—Foraminifera, etc.

Figure
1. *Adelosina bicornis.*
2. *Alveolina fusiformis.*
3. *Uniloculina Indica.*
4. *Biloculina ringens.*
5. *Spiroloculina depressa.*
6. *Triloculina trigonula.*
7. *Amphistegina Hauerina.*
8. *Articulina gibbosula.*
9. *Sphæroidina Austriaca.*
10. *Quinqueloculina seminulum.*
11. *Asterigerina planorbis.*
12. *Bigenerina agglutinans.*
13. *Arachnoidiscus Indicus.*
14. *Arachnoidiscus Nicobaricus.*
15. *Bulimina pupoides.*
16. *Cassidulina lævigata.*
17. *Cristellaria simplex.*
18. *Dentalina subarcuata.*
19. *Dictyocha fibula.*
20. *Epithemia gibba.*
21. *Podocystis Americana.*
22. *Mastogloia lanceolata.*
23. *Arthrogyra Guatemalensis.*
24. *Cladogramma Californica.*
25. *Coscinophæna discoplæa.*
26. *Disiphonia australis.*
27. *Polymorphina lactea.*
28. *Flabellina rugosa.*
29. *Frondicularia spathulata.*
30. *Fusulina cylindrica.*
31. *Gaudryna pupoides.*
32. *Liostephania Rotula.*
33. *Vaginula legumen.*
34. *Goniothecium anaulus.*
35. *Goniothecium barbatum.*
36. *Goniothecium didymum.*
37. *Goniothecium monodon.*
38. *Goniothecium navicula.*
39. *Goniothecium Rogersii.*
40. *Glandulina lævigata.*
41. *Nonionina crassula* (see Pl. 18. fig. 4).
42. *Toxonidea Gregoriana.*
43. *Rhizoselenia alata.*

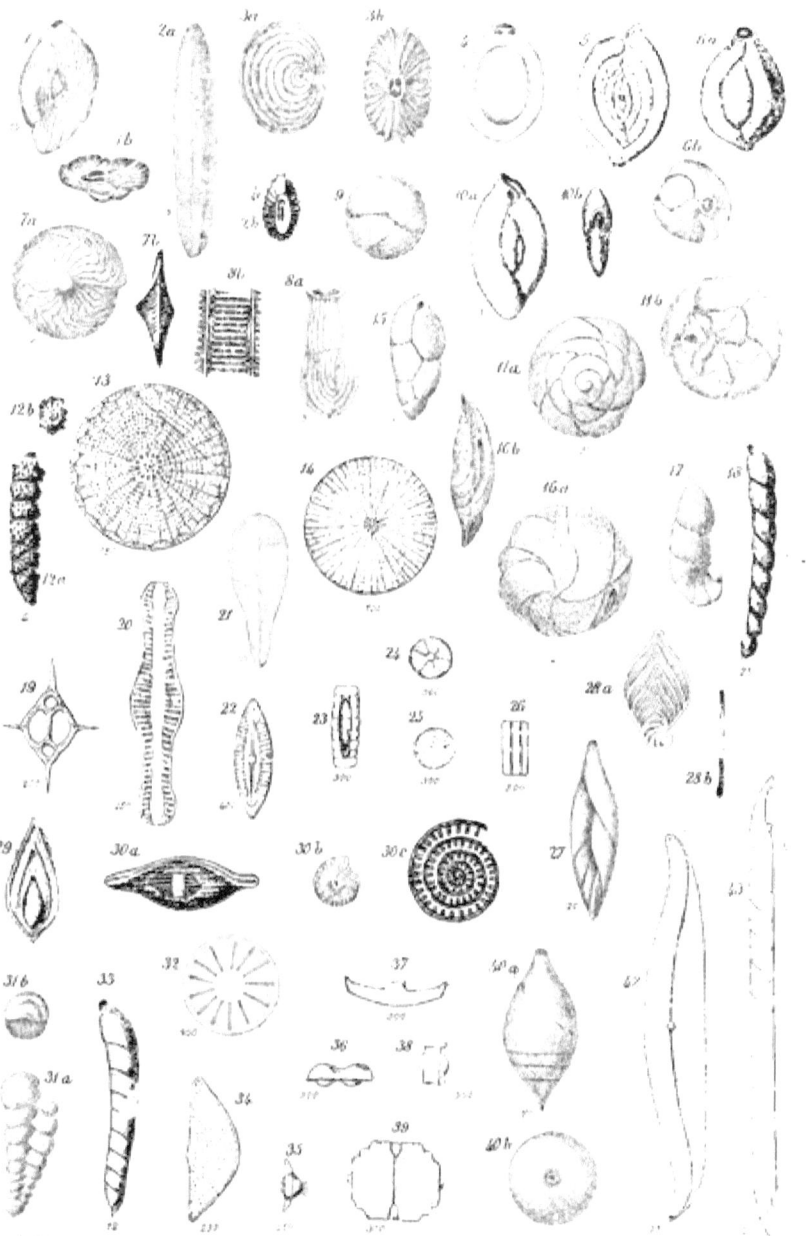

PLATE 43.—Diatomaceæ, etc.

See page 65

Figure

1. *Actiniscus tetrasterias.*
2. *Actiniscus pentasterius.*
3. *Actiniscus quinarius.*
4. *Actiniscus discus.*
5. *Actiniscus rota.*
7. *Anaulus scalaris.*
8. *Actinogonium septenarium.*
9. *Arthrodesmus minutus.*
10. *Amaroucium proliferum*: *a,* nat. size ; *b,* individual body magnified.
11. *Amphicampa eruca.*
12. *Amphicampa mirabilis.*
13. *Asellus vulgaris.*
14. *Asterionella formosa.*
15. *Asteromphalos Beaumontii.*
16. *Biddulphia rhombus.*
17. *Bacillaria paradoxa* (compare pl. 12. fig. 14).
18. *Bacteriastrum curvatum.*
19. *Bowerbankia imbricata*: *a,* nat. size ; *b,* portion magnified ; *c,* single body
20. *Botryllus polycyclus*: *a,* nat. size ; *b,* separate body.
21. *Coscinodiscus (Craspedodiscus) pyxidicula.*
22. *Gammarus pulex.*
23. *Mastogonia*: *a, crux* ; *b, actinoptychus.*
24. *Mastogonia prætexta.*
25. *Mastogonia sexangula.*
26. *Stephanodiscus Niagaræ.*
27. *Stephanodiscus lineatus.*
28. *Stephanodiscus sinensis.*
29. *Stephanodiscus Ægyptiacus.*
29*. *Stephanodiscus Bramaputræ.*
30. *Stephanogonia polygona.*
31. *Hercotheca mammillaris.*
32. *Syringidium bicorne.*
33. *Syringidium palæmon.*
34. *Biblarium castellum.*
35. *Biblarium compressum.*
36. *Biblarium compressum.*
37. *Biblarium elegans.*
38. *Biblarium ellipticum.*
39. *Biblarium emarginatum.*
40. *Biblarium emarginatum.*
41. *Biblarium strumosum.*
42. *Biblarium stella.*
43. *Biblarium speciosum.*
44. *Biblarium rhombus.*
45. *Biblarium lineare.*
46. *Biblarium lancea.*
47. *Biblarium glans.*
48. *Biblarium follis.*
49. *Stylobiblium clypeus.*
50. *Stylobiblium*: *a, b, clypeus* ; *c, divisum* ; *d, eccentricum.*
51. *Halionyx undenarius.*
52. *Odontodiscus eccentricus.*
53. *Omphalopelta areolata.*
54. *Symbolophora acuta.*
55. *Symbolophora micrasterias.*
56. *Symbolophora pentas.*
57. *Systephania corona.*
58. *Systephania diadema.*
59. *Syndendrium diadema.*
60. *Auliscus pruinosus.*
61. *Dicladia antennata.*
62. *Dicladia bulbosa.*
63. *Dicladia capreolus.*
64. *Dicladia capreolus.*
65. *Dicladia clathrata.*
66. *Periptera tetraclodia.*
67. *Periptera capra.*
68. *Dictyolampra stella.*
69. *Rhabdonema arcuatum* ; compound frustule.

PLATE 44.—Various Objects.

Figure
1. Head of *Lachnus*, from below (APHIDÆ).
2. Head of *Aphis*, from above (APHIDÆ).
3. *Aphis brassicæ* (APHIDÆ).
4. *Tetraneura ulmi* (APHIDÆ).
5. *Pemphigus bursarius* (APHIDÆ).
6. *Trama radicis* (APHIDÆ).
7. *Forda formicaria* (APHIDÆ).
8. *Chalcidite*, head of (CHALCIDIDÆ).
9. *Chalcidite*: a, under surface of abdomen of female (CHALCIDIDÆ); b, separate ovipositor.
10. *Eulophus nemati*, larva of (CHALCIDIDÆ).
11. *Eulophus nemati*, pupa of (CHALCIDIDÆ).
12. *Encyrtus atricollis* (CHALCIDIDÆ).
13. *Eulophus pectinicornis* (CHALCIDIDÆ).
14. *Callimome cynipedis* (CHALCIDIDÆ).
15. *Cynips*, section of abdomen of female (CYNIPIDÆ).
16. *Rhodites rosæ* (CYNIPIDÆ).
17. *Cynips folii* (CYNIPIDÆ).
18. *Teras terminalis* (CYNIPIDÆ).
19. *Neuroterus longipennis* (CYNIPIDÆ).
20. *Ibalia cultellata* (CYNIPIDÆ).
21. *Notamia bursaria*.
22. *Monachinus duodenarius*.
23. *Distoma rubrum*: a, portion of common mass; b, individual body.
24. *Eucratea* (*Scruparia*) *chelata*.
25. *Salpingia Hassallii*.
26. *Gemellaria loricata*.
27. *Limnoria terebrans*.
28. *Patellina corrugata*.
29. *Planorbulina mediterranensis*.
30. *Spirorbis nautiloides*.

London, John Van Voorst 1859

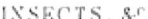

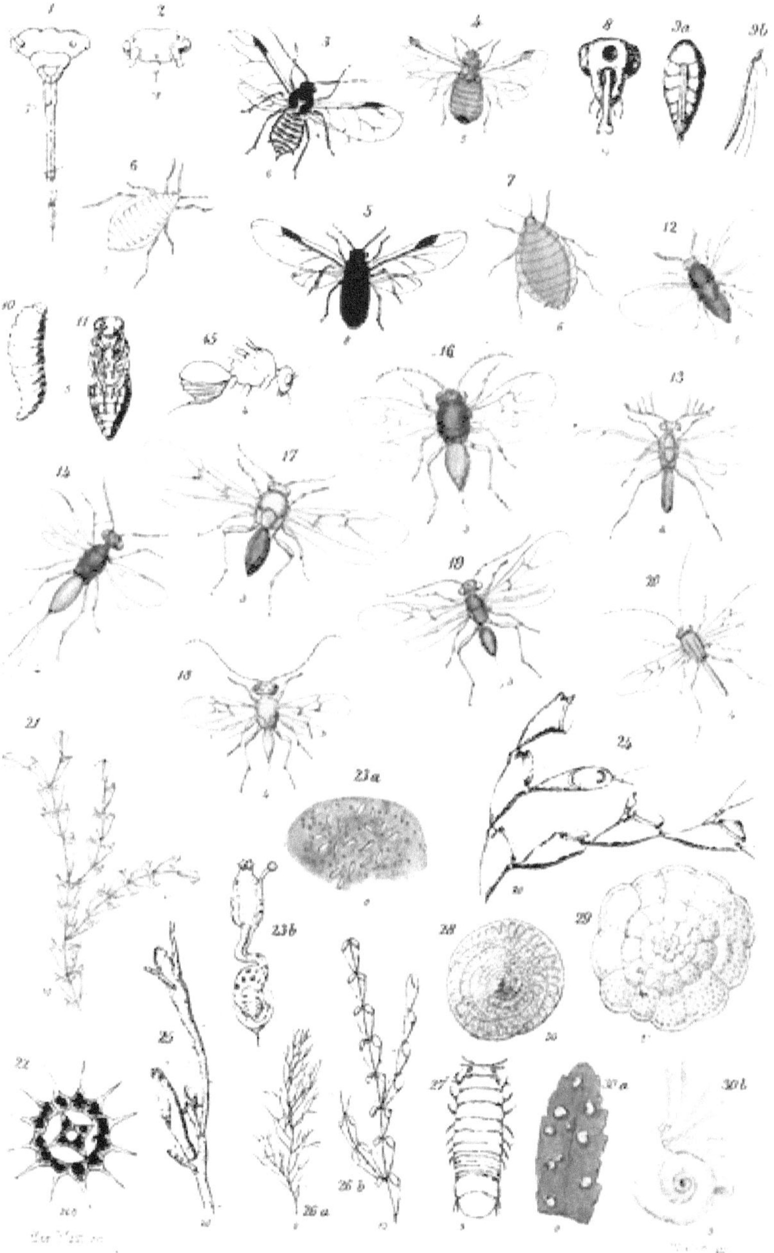

PLATE 45.—Unicellular Algæ, etc.

Figure

1. *Hydrocytium acuminatum.* *a*, young plant; *b*, more advanced; *c*, older stage, with the gonidia divided; *d*, cell about to burst; *e*, cell burst and discharging zoospores.

2. *Characium Sieboldii.* *a*, *b*, *c*, successive stages of young plant; *d*, mature cell discharging its zoospores.

3. *Sciadium arbuscula.* *a*, young plants, the right hand one setting free the gonidia of the second generation; *b*, an older plant with an umbel of secondary cells, some discharging their gonidia of the third generation; *c*, part of an umbel of cells from the last generation of a family, the gonidia being discharged as free zoospores.

4. *Chlorosphæra Oliveri.* *a*, perfect plant; *b*, a plant dividing into two; *c*, the same with the two new cells discharged from the parent.

5. *Apiocystis Brauniana.* *a*, perfect plant; *b*, zoospore; *c*, germinating plant from a zoospore.

6. *Codiolum gregarium.* *a*, young plant; *b*, nearly mature.

7. *Chytridium Olla* upon an *Œdogonium.* *a*, *a*, *Chytridia* burst and discharging their zoospores; *b*, a cell not yet open.

8. *Pythium entophytum* on *Chlorosphæra.* *a*, group, partly mature; *b*, side view of a single cell perforating the cell-wall of the *Chlorosphæra*, and with its neck opened, discharging the contents.

9. *Clathrocystis æruginosa.* *a*, *b*, *c*, fronds in successive stages of growth, the natural colour; *d*, a frond dried; *e*, highly magnified fragment, showing the minute cells imbedded in the gelatinous frond.

10. *Pandorina Morum.* *a*, side view of active form with sixteen gonidia; *b*, side view of larger form with thirty-two gonidia; *c*, end view of *a*; *d*, form with crowded gonidia after fertilization, the cilia lost; *e*, the same more advanced, having lost the gelatinous common envelope, and the cell-contents red; *f*, a single encysted gonidium (resting-spore) from *e* more magnified; *g*, side view of a gonidium with the contents becoming converted into spermatozoids; *h*, a single spermatozoid.

11. *Ophiocytium majus*, in different stages of development.

12. Spore-formation of *Vaucheria sessilis.* A, the sporange *s*, and the antheridium *a*, not yet open; B, both open, the epoch of fertilization; C, decaying filament with ripe spore.

13. Fragment of a filament of *Œdogonium tumidulum*, consisting of antheridial cells, one discharging a spermatozoid.

14. Fragment of *Œ. ciliatum*, consisting of parent-cells of androspores, one of which is escaping.

15. Fragment of *Œ. gemelliparum*, male plant, consisting of antheridial cells, some bursting to discharge their twin spermatozoids.

16. Sporange with sessile dwarf male plant of *Œ. ciliatum.*

17. The same older, the dwarf male plant *a* having burst and discharged the spermatozoid which has entered the sporangial cell.

18. Spermatozoids of *Œ. ciliatum.*

19. A dwarf male plant of *Œ. ciliatum*, discharging an androspore from its large basal cell.

20. Filament of *Œ. Braunii.* *a*, *a*, dwarf male plants, sessile on the filament; *b*, *b*, fertilized spores in the sporangial cells.

21. Ripe spore of *Œ. ciliatum.*

22. Gemmation of the resting-spore of *Bulbochæte intermedia.* *a*, ripe spore; *b*, the same enlarged; *c*, the contents dividing; *d*, the contents converted into four ciliated zoospores.